Charity

KU-215-752

When Charity asked later where the children were, they told her that all three had been taken to foster parents who lived on Clapham Common and she would be going there too once the doctor decided she was well enough. She wasn't badly hurt, she discovered: minor burns on her arms, hands and legs and the cut on her head.

Between sleeping and waking, nurses kept telling her how brave she was, reassuring her that none of the children was hurt and she'd soon be seeing them.

As the misty, sleepy feeling gradually faded and the bright ward full of children became clearer, a sense of jubilation filled her. She'd been rescued! She would never again have to submit to her father's will, never step into that dark, cold house again. No more sermons, no more wondering why their mother never stood up for them or showed any love. It was a new beginning, a brand new start for all of them.

Lesley Pearse's first novel, *Georgia* was based loosely on some of her own experiences in the 1960s music scene. Her second novel, *Tara* was also set in that turbulent decade. Lesley Pearse has three daughters and lives in Bristol. She now works as a writer full-time.

*Also by Lesley Pearse
and available in Mandarin*

**Georgia
Tara**

LESLEY PEARSE
Charity

Mandarin

'Girl', words and music by John Lennon
and Paul McCartney. Used by permission
of Music Sales Limited. © Copyright
1965 Northern Songs. All Rights Reserved.
International Copyright Secured.

A Mandarin Paperback
CHARITY

First published in Great Britain 1995
by William Heinemann Ltd
and Mandarin Paperbacks
imprints of Reed Consumer Books Ltd
Michelin House, 81 Fulham Road, London sw3 6RB
and Auckland, Melbourne, Singapore and Toronto

Copyright © Lesley Pearse 1995
The author has asserted her moral rights

A CIP catalogue record for this title
is available from the British Library
ISBN 0 7493 1813 9

Printed and bound in Great Britain by
BPC Paperbacks Ltd

This book is sold subject to the condition
that it shall not, by way of trade or otherwise,
be lent, resold, hired out, or otherwise circulated
without the publisher's prior consent in any form
of binding or cover other than that in which
it is published and without a similar condition
including this condition being imposed
on the subsequent purchaser.

For every adopted child, especially those born in the Fifties and Sixties. It is my hope that some of the events in this book will give them a clearer understanding of the climate for unmarried mothers at the time, and perhaps give them the comfort of knowing they were never given up easily, or ever forgotten by their natural birth mother.

Acknowledgements

Louise Moore, Katie Green and Rebecca Salt at Mandarin for their unfailing enthusiasm and hard work on my behalf; John Potter for his support and wisdom and Darley Anderson, my agent, for just being there whenever I needed him.

Special thanks too for all those people who helped in my research, Sig. Capineri of the Hotel Berchielli in Florence, the staff of Studley Priory near Oxford, Dr Jane Fornear in Bristol and Peter Marsh.

Chapter One

Greenwich, London 1960

'Make sure you get carrots from the front of the counter,' Gwen Stratton glanced up from writing a shopping list. 'There were several bad ones last week. And don't go hanging around in Woolworth's, Prudence, you know how Father feels about that!'

To an outsider stepping in from the frosty streets, the Saturday morning scene in the kitchen of number 14 Easton Street had a look of almost Victorian cosy domesticity. Mother sitting at the scrubbed wood table juggling a list of requirements against the meagre pile of coins in front of her; the four children dutifully engaged in various tasks around her.

An Aladdin paraffin stove, a pan of boiling handkerchiefs and meat being browned in a frying pan added diverse smells to the warm, steamy fug. The clatter of dishes, the polishing of brass and little James chattering to himself as he sat on his potty, almost concealed the resentment which emanated from all but the youngest member of the family.

All four children were remarkably alike and small for their ages. Four white-blond heads, pale, thin faces, big blue eyes. Charity and Prudence, fifteen and ten respectively, dressed alike in quaintly old-fashioned navy blue serge smock dresses and long grey socks, both with their hair neatly plaited. Tobias was nine, his shirt, long shorts and pullover all grey,

1

his face streaked with black from the Brasso he was rubbing into candlesticks and an embossed wall plaque of a boat.

Young James, aged two, was shuffling around on his pot. Chuckling with delight at a rag book, he was wearing only a yellowing wool vest, his baby hair still fluffy and as yet unbrushed.

Everyone in Greenwich thought the Strattons were odd, but despite their eccentricity and poverty they were accepted, even admired.

Bertram Stratton was a preacher. Not an ordinary vicar like Reverend Soames at St Michael's but an Evangelical preacher at Babylon Hall. He took his fiery sermons out into the streets, shouted out hell and damnation to anyone that would listen. His flock weren't the people with smart clothes and nice houses but the poor and the downtrodden.

Their neighbours in Easton Street were ordinary people – bricklayers, plumbers and bus drivers – but they had a grudging admiration for a man who could stand out in all winds and weathers shouting out his godly messages with such ferocious certitude. They respected his life of piety, the lack of comfort or luxury in his home and nudged each other when they saw the four blond children who looked like frail angels going with him to his church.

Extreme orderliness masked the poverty and lack of modern appliances in the somewhat gloomy kitchen. Jars of bottled fruit sat in lines on bare wood shelves. Scoured saucepans hung with military precision on hooks above the old gas cooker. Even the few items of clothes hanging on the overhead airing rail were ironed and folded. There was nothing unnecessary, no letters poked behind cups on the dresser, odd buttons, books or toys left carelessly.

The only word which summed up Easton Street accurately was 'mean'. Built in 1890 of plain red brick, this terrace close to the River Thames was intended to house the poorest workers in the community. Even the amount of land used was frugal. The houses squashed and stretched up to squeeze in more rooms, rather than give their inhabitants comfort or space.

The Strattons' neighbours had made the best of their homes. They painted and papered, knocked down walls, built bathrooms and modernised their kitchens. But number 14 remained just as it was built; even the old gas mantles on the walls were still in place, despite the addition of electric light.

A dark, draughty house, almost impossible to heat. Damp crept in each winter, peeling off paint and paper, leaving a musty smell that nothing could disguise.

No one could accuse Reverend Stratton of the sin of pride or even of laying up treasures on this earth. Although it was kept scrupulously clean and tidy, every stick of furniture had been given to them. The only adornments were framed biblical quotations on the walls; the one in the kitchen read 'Honour thy Father and Mother'.

'Are you listening?' Gwen Stratton scowled round towards Prudence washing up just inside the scullery. 'If you bring back mouldy carrots again I shall just send you back!'

'Yes mother,' Prudence sighed. She was dreaming of a pale blue velvet dress in the window of the haberdashery shop. She knew of course she'd never own it, any more than she'd ever be allowed to have her hair curled in rags or have patent leather bar shoes. But then, even her parents couldn't stop her dreaming.

'That's enough Brasso.' Gwen Stratton rapped her pencil over the back of Tobias's hand. He was sulking because he wasn't allowed out to play football in the street like the neighbours' children. 'Polish it off and put some elbow grease into it.'

3

Charity cut carrots and onions into slices at the end of the table.

'What is the matter with you?' Gwen Stratton looked up at her eldest daughter, irritated by her slow progress. 'There's more to do this morning than chopping carrots. Get a move on!'

Charity couldn't meet her mother's eyes.

'I'm just tired.' She glanced up at that biblical text on the wall. 'I didn't sleep much last night.'

The glass on the text acted as a mirror, revealing all her shortcomings so clearly. The childish plaits, pale face and stick-thin legs showed exactly how she got the nickname of Weed.

She was tidy enough – many people pointed out what a credit all four children were to their mother – but no one else at school had such awful old-fashioned clothes and clumpy shoes.

'Pass the iron tonic here,' her mother snapped. 'You're always tired these days. As if I haven't got enough to worry about without you dripping around the place complaining all the time.'

Charity handed the bottle and spoon over silently.

Had a stranger observed Gwen Stratton pouring two large tablespoons of tonic into her eldest daughter's mouth, they might very well have wondered why she didn't take the medicine herself. For although the obedience of the children, the cleanliness and order in the house suggested she was a good wife and mother, something clearly ailed her.

Everything about Gwen Stratton was drab, from her weary voice, her clothes and her stooped narrow shoulders to the plain brown dress and shapeless cardigan she wore every day except Sundays. Thick lisle stockings, feet in worn carpet slippers suggested she was far older than her forty years. Bitterness wafted out of her like a sour odour.

Charity gulped down the tonic, quickly following

4

it with a glass of water, then turned to the stove to flip over the browning meat. She had no need to ask what chores she had to do today. As the eldest, five years older than Prudence, she was responsible for the washing.

She added flour, stirred it well in, adding a jug of stock, then deftly transferred the bubbling mixture to a large saucepan, scraping in the vegetables. Nausea welled up again as a thick brown scum rose to the surface. She spooned it off, wishing she could do the same for her teeth, which seemed to be coated with the iron tonic.

'Turn that down and leave it,' Mother barked. 'James has finished!'

Charity dutifully turned to her little brother, and lifted him from the pot to wipe his bottom.

'Pooh!' She smiled lovingly at James. 'Hang on while I empty this, then I'll get you dressed.'

She took the pot out through the scullery to the outside lavatory, emptied it and sluiced it round. She paused for a moment in the frosty air, fighting back the desire to burst into tears.

A burning soreness down below, hatred for her father seething in her heart and a feeling of utter dejection were enough to make her run down the back alley to the river and let herself sink into the glutinous brown mud. Yet as always she knew she had to stay here and bear it, for the sake of her brothers and sister.

Charity hadn't even known there was a name for it until just recently. She'd heard the rude ones in the school playground, but not the real one.

She was looking up the word 'incessant' in the dictionary when she stumbled upon it: 'incest'. Sexual intercourse between persons related within prohibited degrees.

Being able to put a name to it didn't really help. It just made her dark secret even more shameful. She

5

was certain her mother knew, or at least suspected. If Mother let it happen, how could Charity expect anyone else to help, or even believe her?

It tainted everything, like an incurable disease. Father had come to her the first time just after baby Jacob died four years ago. It had hurt so terribly she'd cried for days, but everyone assumed she was just upset about Jacob dying. It had stopped for a while until James was born but then started again soon after. Now she was sure nothing would stop it.

She could bear the funny handmade dresses mother insisted on her and Prudence wearing. She accepted the endless prayers, church and chores and even lack of freedom, but Father made her feel so dirty inside, nothing could wash it away.

In a few weeks' time, at Easter, she was due to leave school. To any other girl this might mean a chance to escape. But Charity was more than just the eldest child. She was nursemaid, cook, cleaner and house-keeper. She could turn her back easily on her parents, but not on Prudence, Tobias and James. If she left who would love them? Would her father turn his attentions to Prudence?

'Come on!' A sharp tap on the window from her mother brought her back to reality. There was no escape, not from Father, nor Mother, or the chores.

Back in the kitchen Charity sat down and took James on to her lap, smiling at his round pink and white baby face, despite her misery.

'Me come wif you?' he said, holding her face between his two plump starfish hands.

'Can he, Mother?' Charity asked, pulling on his pants and threading his legs into knitted trousers.

'If you put his snow-suit on,' Gwen snapped. She was stuffing towels and sheets into a pillowcase with the kind of speed which suggested she was anxious

6

to get all the children out of the house. 'Mind you take Father's surplices out of the dryer when they're still damp. And don't go losing any socks.'

Almost the moment Charity bumped the pram down the two front steps into the street, her spirits rose slightly. For a couple of hours she was free of her mother's carping, weak March sunshine was melting the thick frost and although there was nothing beautiful to look at on the way to the public baths down by the Blackwall tunnel, she had James to give her some comfort.

'Me walk,' James said in a high-pitched squeak of excitement, stretching up to hold the handle of the pram. 'We go see boats?'

'Not now.' Charity smiled down at her little brother, feeling a surge of love for him. 'Maybe after dinner, if you're a good boy.'

For all the bad things in her life, Charity loved her brothers and sister with a consuming passion. She hadn't been allowed to have a childhood herself. At five, when Prudence was born, she was expected to fetch and carry; when Tobias arrived a year later she was already an accomplished nursemaid.

She had never owned a doll – never needed one as these children had been living, breathing ones. Each one of them had been born in the house, put into her arms just minutes after their deliveries. It was she who tucked them into bed and told them stories; she had spoon-fed them, changed their nappies, walked them in the pram. Father had never encouraged outside friendships, so she had turned in on her family and as shame isolated her further from girls of her own age, her devotion to the children had grown.

It was a long walk to the baths, skirting through dismal back streets much like her own and and James was tired of walking long before they got there.

7

Charity sat him between the two bags of washing, smiling as he attempted to sing baby songs for her entertainment. As they crossed the road to enter the old soot-ingrained building, Mrs Bayliss and her daughter Jenny stopped by the steps to wait for them.

'Hullo ducks.' Mrs Bayliss beamed a welcome. 'Let's take one of them pillers. 'Ow's yer ma?'

'About the same.' Charity smiled shyly. She liked Mrs Bayliss, she was fat, fifty and what her mother called 'common' with peroxided hair set on curlers under a headscarf, but she was kindly.

'Your dad ought to try and move you. That Easton Street's too near the river. Enough to make anyone's chest bad.' Mrs Bayliss clucked in sympathy. 'And all you kids to look after too!'

Charity didn't comment. There was nothing wrong with her mother's chest, but this and 'nerves' were the common diagnosis of Gwen Stratton's problems.

She put the brake on the pram, passed one pillow-case to the woman, then grabbing James under one arm, hoisted out the other bag.

'How are you two?'

'Fine, ducks.' Mrs Bayliss caught the heavy door opened by her daughter with her ample rump, making room for Charity to sweep through. 'Be better still once we've got this lot clean and 'eard a bit of gossip.'

The damp heat hit them like walking into a steam room.

'Grab those three machines,' Mrs Bayliss ordered her daughter. She turned to Charity and tickled James's chin affectionately. 'We'll share one for our whites, ducks. Give us yer money and I'll pay.'

Charity felt a flush of unaccustomed pride. It showed your status at the baths if someone offered to share a machine. Of all the things Charity could charge her parents with, lack of hygiene wasn't one

8

of them. Their sheets and towels might be threadbare, but they were snowy white. Father's shirts and surplices wouldn't have shamed an archbishop.

Twenty huge washing machines with stainless steel lids took up the central position. On the far wall were as many vast dryers, filling the air with roaring, sloshing and tumbling sounds, belching out heat and steam. To the right was a row of sinks where women scrubbed collars or washed woollens; on the left an area for ironing, with boards, and roller machines for sheets.

The steamy air was enough to flatten a 'beehive' or turn straight hair like Charity's kinky in seconds. Winter-white arms bared, faces glistening with sweat from the intense heat and the rich sound of raucous laughter gave the room a party atmosphere.

A place where fifty or so women displayed their dirty washing openly was bound to make them more gregarious. Stains were discussed in detail, and the events that had led up to them. Nothing was too personal. Whether it was blood from a fight, soiled linen from an incontinent parent or child, or even the aftermath of childbirth, it was aired in public.

'He thinks I'm bloody stupid.' One woman waved a shirt with a bright red lipstick mark on the collar. 'He tried to tell me I done that! I tell you next time 'e goes down that club I'll follow 'im and if I catches 'im with that cow, I'll split 'her 'ead right open.'

Charity had learned a great deal about the rich tapestry of women's lives just by listening to conversations in here. She learned about unfaithful husbands, domestic violence, miscarriages, childbirth and sex. Though the conflicting items she heard about the latter often puzzled her.

Were women supposed to like it, or hate it? It was hard to tell. One moment they spoke tenderly, at other times it was with spite and anger. Stories ranged from

9

funny to crude, but now and again were poignantly romantic.

But of all the things that caused her fright and alarm, that expression 'up the spout' was the one which played on her mind. She learned that the first symptom of pregnancy was 'being late'. As Charity hadn't even started her periods perhaps she didn't need to be anxious about this. But it niggled at her like a sore tooth.

Her lack of breasts worried her too. Jenny Bayliss was only a year older and she'd had big ones since she was thirteen. Was she a freak? Was her thin, flat, boyish shape somehow connected to what her father did? Suppose even now she had a baby growing inside her, some hideously deformed creature that would one day pop out and prove to the world how badly she had sinned?

Once the machines were filled, the soap powder added, Charity took off James's snow-suit and sat down with him on her lap. Muriel Jenkins was in today and she watched as the slender blonde ironed miles of net can-can petticoats.

Like most of the women Muriel had her hair in curlers, a chiffon scarf over them, but she didn't subscribe to the common uniform of crossover pinny and down-at-heel shoes. She took part in ballroom dancing competitions and even when she came in here to wash, she was always dressed to kill. Today she wore a red wool sheath dress and matching stilettos, and her eyebrows were a thin pencilled line of astonishment. She did her ironing with a cigarette dangling from the corner of her mouth, yet could carry on a conversation at the same time.

Muriel fascinated Charity more than any of the other women. She was glamorous, outspoken and very funny. Although she was married to a man called Brian, she went dancing with other men. Today she was telling a tale about a partner whose zip broke as they were doing the quickstep.

' "Hold me tighter," he says to me,' she mimicked the man, moving back from her ironing board to show the stance with an invisible partner. 'He says, "Me zip's gone Mew. Press closer or someone will see." I says "If I press closer there'll be more things going up than the score".'

Charity never knew quite how to react to these adult conversations. Should she laugh knowingly as the other women did? Or pretend not to understand?

She had been coming here with the washing since she was nine. It was the only place she felt comfortable in, because she was accepted. The women admired her blonde hair and told her that one day she'd be a beauty. They teased her because she spoke 'proper'; but they showed admiration for the way she cared for her little brothers and sister.

'Get yourself a job in an office,' Muriel had said once. 'Work hard and save your money and you'll soon be able to move into a flat of your own. Stop worrying about them kids, that's yer ma's job. Before you can say Jack Robinson some chap will be asking you to marry him.'

Muriel's words were kindly meant, but Charity knew she had no skills to get an office job. Neither would she be able to save her pay, as Mother would take it all. As for the hope that a man might ask to marry her, the very thought made her feel quite sick.

It was just before one when Charity loaded up the pram to go home. James made no protest now about riding between the bags of warm, dry washing and the afternoon ahead was something to look forward to. On wet Saturdays Charity often took the children into the Maritime Museum. Prudence liked to see Nelson's uniform, Tobias, the model boats. But as it was dry and sunny, today she might be able to take them up to Greenwich Park.

As Charity bumped the pram backwards up the steps into the hall, almost immediately she sensed something was wrong.

Tobias and Prudence were sitting glumly at the already laid table, Mother stirring the stew at the stove.

'Mrs Bayliss shared a machine with me.' Charity put the two shillings down on the table, looking enquiringly at the two younger children.

Her mother merely turned and scooped up the change. No look of appreciation, not even a glimmer of a smile.

'Call Father, dinner's ready,' she said tartly. 'And I hope you left his shirts damp?'

Tobias rolled his eyes fearfully at Charity as Father strode into the kitchen.

Bertram Stratton was a big man, but in the small and crowded room he looked huge, his dominant personality overshadowing them all.

A broad nose, fleshy lips and square, strong chin made him miss being handsome by a hair's breadth, but the effect was spoilt by an overlarge forehead and small blue eyes under thick eyebrows. Darker blond hair than his children, weatherbeaten skin from hours spent out in the streets and the width of his shoulders sat uneasily with his dog collar.

Father beckoned for the children to stand for grace. He stretched out his arms, bringing his hands together slowly, fingertips just touching.

'We thank you God for these gifts you have set at our table. Amen.'

Chairs scraped on the lino as they were pulled out again to sit. Charity noted the way Prudence and Tobias were squirming nervously and wondered what they'd done.

Mother ladled out the stew into bowls, Charity hurriedly tied a bib round James's neck, sitting him on a cushion on the chair next to her.

Father lifted his spoon to his mouth, sipped and smiled. 'This is excellent, Mother,' he pronounced sanctimoniously.

Mother lifted her eyes from her own plate.

'I suspect Prudence and Tobias have stolen from me this morning,' she said, her tone almost malicious. 'There has been an alteration on the shopping list.'

Charity's heart sank. She began eating fast, guessing she would be drawn into this before long and she wanted to finish her dinner before that happened.

'Explain!' Father looked hard at Tobias and Prudence sitting side by side, then back to his wife.

'Eightpence has been added to the final sum,' she said, her mouth pursing as if sucking lemons.

Charity kept her eyes down. Sweets were forbidden in the Stratton household. It was an odd coincidence that eightpence would buy each child a quarter!

'Prudence! Your explanation please.' Father rapped her over the knuckles with his knife.

'Mrs Moore must've made a mistake.' Prudence's voice shook and Charity knew immediately she was lying.

Charity glanced at Tobias through her lashes. Her brother had a very sneaky streak and she was certain this was his idea. But however wrong it was, she felt a great deal of sympathy. None of them ever had pocket money like other children.

'Charity will go down to Mrs Moore to find out the truth.' Father glared first at her, as if daring her to cover up for them, then at Prudence and Tobias. 'If I find you have been dishonest, you know what will happen, don't you?'

Charity dawdled at the chemist's window. The display of home permanent waves attracted her attention. Some of the girls at school used Toni and she wished she could too.

Greenwich High Street was packed with shoppers – girls of Charity's age flocking into Woolworth's to look at lipsticks and to listen to the top twenty pop records; boys hanging around on street corners watching the giggling girls. Women with bulging string bags gossiped in groups. The Clipper and the Nelson were both packed to capacity with men swilling down beer.

Father had gone out while the children washed up. He was probably down by the *Cutty Sark*, his usual spot on Saturday afternoon for giving one of his open-air sermons. Charity had no wish to see him being heckled by crowds of drunks as they turned out the pubs; she got ribbed enough at school for having such a strange father.

Reluctantly she moved on towards the greengrocer's, dreading the further embarrassment of being forced to explain to Mrs Moore what her mother suspected.

The shop was as busy as always on Saturday afternoons so Charity lingered outside by a display of fruit arranged on fake grass, waiting for a lull when she could speak to Mrs Moore.

Something slimy on the ground made Charity look down, and as she moved her foot from the old cabbage leaf, she saw a shilling lying there. For a moment she was transfixed, blinking disbelievingly at the silver coin. To anyone else it might have seemed like luck; to Charity it was surely a gift from heaven!

Under cover of tying her shoelace, she bent down and retrieved it, offering up a quick prayer of thanks, then ran straight to the sweet shop to get it changed.

There was just a tiny stab of guilt as she bought a quarter of dolly mixtures for fourpence, but the jing-

14

ling of the eightpence in her pocket, and knowing she'd saved Tobias and Prudence a caning, more than made up for it.

'Mrs Moore added it up wrong,' she lied breathlessly as she entered the kitchen. Mother was ironing Father's surplice on a blanket on the table, Tobias and Prudence sitting close to her, faces drawn with anxiety. 'She said she was sorry, but she was rushed off her feet when the children came in. Can I take them to the park now?'

Mother looked at the offered eightpence, eyes narrowing with suspicion. Charity seemed far too pleased with herself and her face was flushed with more than just running home.

'You may,' she replied. 'But make sure you're back before it gets dark.'

After the children had gone, Gwen sat down at the table, resting her head on folded arms. She was tired, so tired, and deep down she knew she needed help. She had long since stopped questioning why she felt no happiness at anything. She went through the days, the weeks and months like a robot programmed not to think. Craving solitude, but when it came, like now, she felt desperately lonely.

'You made your bed,' she murmured, too weary even to voice the rest of the expression. Charity flitted into her mind, but she blanked out the dark suspicion by mentally recalling the ingredients she needed for a cake.

'I'll go to the doctor on Monday,' she murmured as she got up to finish the ironing. 'Perhaps he can give me something.'

'How did you do it?' Tobias asked once they'd crossed the main road by the Maritime Museum. James was in the pushchair, tucked in with a blanket. Tobias and Prudence either side of Charity were holding the handles.

Charity looked down at him. Admiration shone out of his big blue eyes, but she saw no real guilt, which worried her. Prudence had the grace to look ashamed, biting her lip as if she was on the point of confession.

The bag of dolly mixtures in her pocket was a reminder of her own guilt. She couldn't share them out without seeming to condone their wrongdoing, and neither would she enjoy them alone.

'Never you mind how I managed it,' she said sternly. 'The point is you did steal that money and it was very wrong. Mother has little enough spare cash as it is. The only reason I covered up for you was because I didn't want you to be caned.'

'It was Tobias's idea,' Prudence whined. 'I said it was wrong.'

Charity looked from one to the other, seeing faults in both children. Prudence could be an insufferable little prig, sucking up to adults and showing no real loyalty. Tobias was deceitful and wilful despite endless punishments, but then he was just a child.

'You are both equally to blame,' she said firmly. 'Stealing is a sin. You must promise me you'll never do such a thing again.'

'I hate Father.' Tobias stuck out his lip belligerently. 'He's mean to us. I'm going to run away to sea as soon as I'm old enough.'

Charity felt duty bound to admonish him, but her words were softened by deep sympathy. Tobias was a real boy: he loved football, climbing trees and wide open spaces. She and Prudence could accept the constraints of their life more easily because they'd already discovered this was how it was for females, but Tobias had only other boys at school as examples and they had all the freedom they wanted.

'I'll be leaving school soon,' Charity said gently as

16

they walked in through the big park gates. 'I'll find myself a flat somewhere, then maybe you can come and visit me.'

'Couldn't we come to live with you too?' Tobias looked up at her imploringly. 'It'll be awful once you've gone!'

Charity sighed deeply. 'You and Prudence have to work hard at school,' she said, taking one hand from the pushchair to ruffle his hair affectionately. 'That's the way out, so you can get a good job.'

She let James out of the pushchair then, smiling as he ran forward over the grass shrieking with delight as Prudence and Tobias chased him.

Here in the park Charity felt a sense of peace that she found nowhere else. She'd learned at school how the meridian line passed through here, giving time to the rest of the world, so if Greenwich was important, perhaps she was too? All these huge old trees planted centuries ago, all the vast expanse of grass and the view over the river and London when they climbed up to the observatory gave her a sense of belonging to a greater scheme of things.

Charity seldom went out of Greenwich. Her knowledge of the world and the rest of London was only from books and hearsay, but here in the park she felt God's hand as she never did in Father's church. If he could look out for each squirrel and deer, work all those miracles of changing seasons, then surely he saw too that she needed just a minor one to make her and her family happy?

They played a brisk game of hide and seek, humouring James by pretending they couldn't see him when all he did to hide himself was cover his face with his hands. Tobias climbed trees, flattening himself on bare branches then jumping down to frighten them.

Dusk crept up on them suddenly. Charity put the now tired James back into his pushchair and they hurried back down the hill chattering to each other, each small face rosy from the cold, fresh air, earlier events in the day forgotten.

But as Charity opened the door and hauled in the pushchair, she knew something more had happened in their absence. The fire was lit in the parlour, the cosy flickering through the open door offering a warm welcome, yet a pall of something unpleasant hung in the air.

'Come in here!' Father's voice boomed out from the kitchen. 'All of you!'

Mother sat at the table, arms folded in front of her. Father stood with his back to the paraffin stove, warming his backside, and his eyes were colder than a January morning.

'What is it?' Charity ventured, bending to take off James's snow-suit.

'Leave that,' Father pointed an accusing finger at her. 'Stand there the three of you and let me ·look at three liars and thieves.'

When Charity saw the shopping list on the table alongside the sixpence and two pennies she had brought home earlier, her insides churned and she had a strong desire to visit the lavatory.

Father prolonged the torture by merely staring hard at each of them in turn as they stood in a row quaking.

'Explain to me how you came by this money,' he said at last, fixing Charity with a look of intense hatred.

There was nothing for it but to admit what had happened. Clearly Father had checked up.

'I found some money,' she whispered.

'Liars and thieves,' he hissed, crossing the room and slapping Charity hard round the face. 'But I blame you most of all, daughter, for you have covered up one crime with another.'

Charity reeled against the wall from the force of his

18

blow. Prudence covered her head with her arms and Tobias backed towards the door.

'Upstairs, all of you!' Father roared. 'I'll be up the minute I've eaten my tea to deal with each of you.'

James let out a howl of fear, ran to Charity and clutched at her legs. Mother got up from the table snatched him back from her and dumped him on a chair.

'I'm ashamed of you,' she shot at the terrified children. 'Get out of my sight.'

'I feel sick,' Prudence sobbed. 'I'm so scared.'

For once Tobias had nothing to say. His face was ashen, shaking like a leaf.

'Keep quiet or he'll be worse,' Charity implored them. 'Get undressed and into bed. I daren't stay here with you.'

Alone in her own room Charity forced herself to hate rather than allow fear to overcome her. She undressed, put her nightdress on and sat down on her bed.

It was an icy, bare room, the ceiling sloping down sharply to a small window overlooking backyards. An iron bed, a Windsor chair and a chest of drawers were the only furniture.

She heard the kitchen door open some ten minutes later, a bad sign, as it meant her father hadn't mellowed by eating his tea. There was no creeping up the stairs this time, the way he did on Friday nights. His steps were heavy and measured, his breathing laboured.

As she expected, he went past the children's room and came straight to her. She stood up, holding the end of the bed for support.

'What have you got to say for yourself?' he bellowed, even before he came into the small room, the cane twitching in his hand.

'I'm sorry, Father,' she whispered. 'Please don't cane Prudence and Tobias, they're only little.'

She moved back towards the window. His head was almost touching the sloping ceiling; if he followed her here he would need to stoop. But even as that thought shot across her mind she remembered how practised he was at negotiating this room, even in the dark.

'You dare now to try and tell me what to do?' he roared in astonishment.

Everything about him was repulsive: his high shiny forehead, thick wet lips, the faint smell of stale sweat and even that brown cardigan knitted by one of his doting parishioners.

'Lay one finger on them and I'll tell everyone what you do to me,' Charity blurted out without considering the consequences.

He lifted the cane threateningly, bushy brows knitting together.

'Cane me if you must – ' she cringed further away from him, scared by her own daring but unable to back down now – 'but if you touch them I swear I'll tell the world what you do.'

He lunged forward, the cane raised, but the fact that he knocked his head on the ceiling proved he wasn't as controlled as he'd been earlier.

'They did wrong,' she went on, letting anger take her along with it. 'But what you do to me is a real sin. It's called incest.'

The word she'd never dared say openly before floored him. She saw fear in his pale blue eyes and his tongue flickered across his lips like a big slug.

'Get into bed!' he roared out. 'Tomorrow I'll find a job for you, well away from this house so you cannot influence those innocent children further. Another word from you and I'll strip the skin from your back. I have nursed a viper in the bosom of my family.'

He turned and stamped down the stairs. The only

satisfaction Charity had was hearing him pass the children's room with an order for them to say prayers for God's forgiveness.

It was over an hour before she could even cry. She didn't dare creep down to see Prudence and Tobias and reassure them they could sleep easily because Father wouldn't punish them further. She had done all she set out to do; she had protected her brother and sister. But the triumph was hollow.

Charity knew exactly what sort of job he would find for her. A skivvy for one of his parishioners. Not quality people who would treat her fairly, but cranks like himself who would show suspicion from the outset.

Desolation engulfed her as she lay sobbing in her narrow bed. Her mother had abandoned her years before. Now she was to lose the children she loved.

Prudence was so quick and clever, top of her class at school, but how long would it be before she was as dull as her older sister? What would happen to Tobias without someone to sympathise when he fought against his fetters? Would Father suck him into his church, or would he rebel against everything in defiance and end up in serious trouble?

As for James, what would become of him? Kept in the house all day with a mother who barely looked at him. Slapped and scolded continually. Charity might be able to explain to Prudence and Tobias why she had to go. But how could anyone make a child of two understand why the only person who had shown him love was suddenly gone?

A foghorn rasped out a warning to other boats down on the river, and it sounded to Charity like an omen of worse things yet to come.

'Help me, God!' she whispered in the darkness. 'Do something to help all of us.'

Chapter Two

'Get up!'

The curt order woke Charity instantly.

She sat up and rubbed her eyes. Her mother stood over her wrapped in her camel wool dressing-gown, her hair loose on her shoulders. Under the dim overhead light her face was grey and haggard and her mouth twisted with spite.

'Is it morning?' she said sleepily, glancing towards the window. The curtains were open just enough to see that it was still dark and there was no sound of traffic.

'Satan finds work for idle hands,' her mother snapped viciously, pulling the bedclothes from her. 'So you can clean the kitchen and the lavatory and prepare the vegetables for dinner now, before you get any breakfast.'

She was gone before Charity could speak, clonking down the stairs on shoes with broken backs.

Charity sighed wearily, got out of bed, hauled on her everyday dress and tied back her hair. Sundays were always interminable.

It was freezing in the kitchen, with ice on the inside of the window. Her mother had gone back to bed and it was just six o'clock. Aside from two unwashed cocoa cups in the sink, there was nothing to warrant a demand for it to be cleaned.

The wooden rail hoisted to the ceiling was clear of

airing clothes, the plain wood table was scrubbed almost white; even the chairs were tucked under it. But she knew exactly what was expected of her. She must spring-clean it. Every pan must be scoured, every shelf washed and the contents replaced, the cooker stripped down and the floor washed.

Two hours later Charity had finished. She took some pleasure in the fact that she'd discovered dirt her mother had missed and found mice droppings behind the stove. The room didn't look much different, but her red hands and the clean smell of polish on the old dresser proved she'd completed her task.

The potatoes were peeled and placed in a scoured saucepan, cabbage washed and cut up, carrots scrubbed and sliced and now she was laying the table for breakfast.

'Haven't you lit the stove?' Her mother came in as Charity filled the kettle, intending to take her parents tea. 'Get the others up,' Mother snapped. 'Then get yourself washed and changed for church.'

It was clear there would be no respite today. Charity obeyed silently.

James was soaked right through. It was only recently that he had stopped having a nappy on at night. Charity normally lifted him late at night to use the potty, and no one else had bothered. She stripped off his pyjamas and the sheets and made them into a bundle, then lifting him up into her arms she carried him downstairs to wash him.

'Dirty boy!' Mother slapped him on the leg as Charity carried him in.

James howled indignantly, wrapping his arms round Charity's neck and burying his small face in her shoulder. She took James and the sheets into the scullery, filled the sink with warm water and plonked him into it.

Although the temperature was well below freezing,

he reached out for a cup and spoon on the draining board, the smack forgotten.

'No time for playing today,' Charity said gently, standing him up so she could wash him. 'Smelly boy!'

'Not smelly.' He sat down, making the water splash over the sink.

She lifted him out and wrapped him in a towel, then took him back into the kitchen to dry and dress him. Mother handed her his clothes without a word.

'Smart boy,' Charity said as she pulled on his navy blue knitted trousers and matching jumper with a sailor collar. 'Now mind you don't get in a mess before church!'

Mother was cutting the bread, banging the knife down on the breadboard hard to show her displeasure. Charity reached out for a bib and put it round James's neck, then sat him on a chair.

'Now behave,' she warned him, filling his bottle with weak tea. 'I've got to get washed too.'

She hated taking all her clothes off when someone, particularly her father, might walk in at any minute, but this was the routine every morning and had been since she was thirteen when he had accused her of smelling like a polecat.

She shivered, goosepimples all over her thin body as she soaped herself from head to foot. Standing on a cork board, she wondered if there was anything she could do today that would be right.

The children sat at the table, subdued and white-faced as they heard Father coming downstairs. Mother had ignored them so far, turning her back on them while she boiled eggs. She banged a fresh pot of tea down on the table just as he came through the door, looking up at him enquiringly.

'Stand for grace,' he said.

His voice was calm and measured. He was always

more amenable on Sundays, perhaps because he knew it was the one day of the week when he could preach to people who actually wanted to hear him.

He smiled benignly round at his children, all in their Sunday clothes and with well-scrubbed faces and brushed hair.

'Today in church you must pray for God's forgiveness. Yesterday you broke one of his Commandments. After dinner today I want all three of you to write all ten of them out, a hundred times. Now Tobias, what is the first one?'

It struck Charity that her parents' attitudes were opposing. Why, if Father had decided to forgive them all, was Mother still smarting with anger? But then Mother was always a mystery. She wouldn't speak of the past, even though she sometimes hinted she'd been used to better; neither did she ever speak of the future. Was it Father who made her so unhappy? Or her children?

By half-past nine Father was washed and shaved, dressed in his Sunday suit with a clean white collar. Charity stood awkwardly as Mother put the mutton with the potatoes round it into the oven. She spooned some rice into an earthenware dish, added sugar and milk and grated a nutmeg over the surface.

'Don't stand there staring at me,' she snapped at Charity as she put the dish on the bottom shelf of the oven. 'Go upstairs and make the beds, or we'll all be late for church!'

Charity stood for a moment in her parents' room, just looking. Like all the rooms it was devoid of colour or real comfort. A plain wooden bed, a dressing-table holding nothing but a hairbrush, comb and glass receptacle for hairpins, and a battered wardrobe with a full-length mirror. But it was the bed which held her attention, and the clear indentations made by her parents' bodies.

All of them had been born in that bed and there was a time when she had considered it a magical place. But now as she bent over to pull the bottom sheet tight and smelt that smell of her father, it was just another shameful reminder of what men, marriage and having babies entailed.

Once the bed was made and the quilt smoothed over, Charity paused in front of the mirror to look at herself. Her grey Sunday dress was identical to every other dress her mother had made her since she was a small child: a loose smock gathered on to a wide yoke, only this one had a white lace collar and pearl buttons on the cuffs.

She was probably the only girl at Maze Hill Secondary Modern who preferred wearing her uniform. At least in a navy gym-slip and blazer she looked like everyone else. There was no point in fantasising about buying a full skirt with a can-can petticoat beneath it, pretty pointed shoes, and having her hair permed in a bubble cut when she started work. By Easter she would be in an overall, cleaning up after people she'd like even less than her parents and still with no money.

In church Charity held James still with one hand and her prayer book with the other, but her mind wasn't on the prayers.

Babylon Hall was a grubby little place with a corrugated iron roof and many of the windows boarded up. Father's religious convictions didn't allow adornments or comfort, so the chairs were rickety and the hassocks threadbare. Even the altar was covered in a simple white cloth with a plain brass cross.

Prudence, on the other side of James, was dressed just like Charity, except that her coat, dress and hat with an upturned brim were brown instead of grey. The colour gave a peachy glow to her cheeks and she was putting on that goody-goody face that fooled

26

everyone. Prudence had never had it as hard as Charity. Because she was clever and five years younger, she managed to get out of chores. Sometimes she treated her older sister like a maid and she had precious little loyalty to anyone.

Toby was fidgeting, his mouth set in a surly expression of boredom. His hands were in his blazer pockets and his long grey socks had fallen down round his ankles. If Father was to notice he would get more punishment than writing out the Ten Commandments. Charity worried a great deal about Tobias. He was cunning, greedy and untruthful. Although some of this was only because he was kept on such a close rein at home, sometimes she saw a ruthless streak in him that she couldn't find an excuse for.

There were a great many new faces in church today, but all of them looked remarkably like the regulars: poor, feeble-minded and lost.

Tobias called the lady in the red hat in the front row 'Mrs Amen' because every time Father paused for breath she would shout out 'Amen' and wave her arms. There was Mr Beavis who belched continually and went straight from church into the Stag's Head on the corner, and frail little Miss Wilkes who had paper flowers tucked into her hat-band, along with a dozen more equally sad people.

Why was it that her father's rousing sermons only moved people like this? There was not one rich or beautiful person in his entire congregation. Was it just that people further up the social scale didn't need the support of religion in their lives?

Father was positively bouncing with good humour at dinner. Not only had the collection brought in nine pounds, twelve shillings and tuppence, but three new followers had all spoken up about their changed lives since they found Christ and Preacher Stratton.

'It's never too late to turn from wickedness.' His voice filled the kitchen as he carved the mutton. 'A man can be in the gutter, even in a prison cell awaiting hanging, but if he offers his heart and life to the Lord, even at that late hour, he will be saved.'

Charity kept her eyes on her dinner plate. She knew he would move on to the bit about how not a sparrow falling from his nest was missed by the Lord, and she wondered if God had been looking the other way when Father came to her room at night.

'I spoke well today, didn't I, Mother? Some days my words fall on stony ground, but not today I think.'

'You were very eloquent and rousing,' Mother replied. 'Let's hope the new followers manage to keep your light inside them and resist temptation.'

Charity found the interchanges between her parents interesting. Their conversations were always so stilted, like two strangers on a bus speaking out of politeness, rather than interest. Charity looked from one to the other, through her lashes.

Mother wore her Sunday brown wool dress with a cream lace collar. The drab colour made her skin even duller; the shapeless style would have been more suitable to an older fatter woman. Charity had vague recollections that she hadn't always looked like this. Was this something that happened to most women as they grew older? Or was it a manifestation of her inner unhappiness, just like her imagined illnesses?

The clock in the parlour struck eight and Charity sighed with relief. It had been an endless day. Sundays always were.

The wind grew stronger and stronger as Charity lay in bed. It was coming straight from the river with fierce gusts that made Mrs Rumbelow's washing line next door slap against their yard wall like a whip.

28

Someone further down the street had a tin bath hanging on a nail and it banged like a bass drum.

Father came home soon after Charity had gone to bed and he seemed in high spirits about something. His greeting to his wife was jovial and he laughed loudly. Perhaps he'd called into the Nelson or the Clipper on his way back from church; maybe tonight they'd put money in his collection box, instead of heckling him. The rumble of his voice lulled her into a comfortable dreamlike state, not sleep exactly as she could still hear the wind, but for once her mind was free of anxiety. When he intended to visit her he always slipped upstairs for a drink first. Maybe the scene last night had frightened him off for good?

The wind woke her later. Something fell down into the yard at the back with a sharp crack. Charity knelt up on her bed and peered out, but it was too dark to see anything but the big poplar tree at the end of the terrace.

It was being thrown from side to side, so violently it would surely come crashing down soon. In the house across the backyard there was a light in an upstairs room. Were they listening to the wind too and feeling frightened?

Then she smelt it. Something acrid and smoky. She pressed her face up against the glass trying to see if it was a chimneypot on fire, but could make out nothing other than the dark outline of roofs against the sky.

She sniffed again.

It seemed to be coming from downstairs. Could Mother have forgotten to turn out the paraffin stove in the kitchen and now it was burning the wick?

Pulling her cardigan on over her nightdress she made her way down to the next landing by the children's room. The smell was far stronger here and to her horror she saw smoke wafting up the stairs.

29

It was pure instinct to run into their room first. The kitchen was underneath it and just those seconds on the landing were making her choke.

'Quick, get up!' she screamed. 'There's a fire!'

Tobias was out of bed in a trice. Prudence sat up sleepily.

'Come on,' Charity called again, shaking her sister's shoulder. 'Just slip your feet in your shoes and put your cardigan on.'

She reached into the cot and lifted the still sleeping baby out, wrapped a blanket round him, then looked again at the other two.

Tobias had a pullover on and was fumbling under his bed for shoes, but still Prudence was sitting in a trance.

'Prudence! Hurry,' Charity screamed at her. 'We've got to get out!'

Only then did the girl move, hastily stuffing her arms into her cardigan, blue eyes wide with fear.

'Come on.' Charity opened the door, clutching James to her shoulder, but as she turned to go down the few steps to where their parents slept she could see flames licking round the corner of the hall below.

'Mother, Father!' she yelled. 'Fire!'

For a split second she was uncertain what to do. Reason said she must rouse her parents now, but another voice was urging her to concentrate on getting the children out.

'Cor! A real fire!' Tobias said almost gleefully, pushing round to look closer. Prudence's wail of fear made her reach out to cuff Tobias's ear.

'Back to the bedroom,' she ordered them. 'We'll have to get out the window.'

Nails had been hammered in so the sash would only open a few inches, a precaution against the children falling out. Tobias struggled with it, Prudence began to cry and James was now coughing hard with the smoke coming in.

'Hold James.' Charity shoved the baby into Prudence's arms, picked up a cricket bat of Tobias's, and whacked the glass.

'Let me do it.' Tobias stepped forward when Charity failed to break it. He took a few steps back, ran at the window and crashed the bat hard into the middle. The glass was shattered, but still holding together. Using the bat like a battering ram, Tobias thumped again until there was a hole big enough to climb through.

Charity could hear the fire now, even over the wind and the tinkling, falling glass. It was a roaring, whooshing sound that seemed to be coming closer with every second.

'You first, Tobias.' Charity quickly scooped up an eiderdown and draped it over the spiky shards left in the window frame. 'On to the kitchen roof and I'll pass James down to you. Once you're down shout to Mrs and Mrs Rumbelow for help.'

He wriggled through the hole and jumped the eight feet to the roof below effortlessly, as Prudence let out a howl of terror.

'Is the fire in the kitchen?' Charity shouted down, ignoring her sister for a moment. Tobias showed up clearly in the darkness in his striped pyjamas, his blond hair ruffled by the wind.

'I don't think so, it's OK out here,' he called back, tottering down to the edge of the roof, peering over and shouting loudly.

For a moment Charity hesitated, staring down into the darkness. She realised to her horror that she couldn't reach far enough down to place James into Toby's arms and if she dropped him he could roll off the roof and be killed.

'Prue! Shut up and help me make a sling for James.'

She snatched up one of the bedspreads and put it down on the floor.

'I'm scared, I want to get out,' Prudence wailed, backing away from Charity towards the window, her eyes on the smoke billowing under the door.

'Don't wriggle, James.' Charity sat James down in the centre of the bedspread and pulled up each of the four corners above his head. He immediately stood up, poking his head through one corner.

'Sit down and stay down.' Charity pushed him firmly on the head. 'Please be a good boy.' Her heart was thumping, her mouth dry and she coughed with the smoke. Surely Mother and Father had smelt it by now? Why didn't they come?

Her fingers wouldn't work properly, the bedspread was too thick to tie securely and Prudence was no help at all.

She had the quivering bundle on the windowsill now. Charity couldn't trust Prue to hold anything, so she thrust her aside with her hip and leaned out.

'Ready, Toby?' she yelled, unable to see him now. 'I'll lower him bit by bit until I feel your hands grab him. Don't drop him, whatever you do!'

Her arms were almost pulled from their sockets as she lowered the bundle, slowly feeding it through her hands. Wind bit into her bare arms, pieces of glass were pricking through the eiderdown beneath her belly, but still she talked to James.

'I've got you and Toby's waiting. Hold on to my waist, Prue!' she called out.

Prue screamed.

'Hold on to me!' Charity yelled back, letting her hands slowly slip back up the bedspread. 'I'll get you out too in a minute.'

James was screaming now, the bundle swinging from side to side as he struggled to get free, but at last Charity felt the weight supported.

'That's it! I've got him,' Toby called back. 'You can let go!'

A piece of glass hit Charity on the head as she pulled herself back in. Prudence was coughing, leaning towards the window doubled over.

'You now.' Charity lifted her sister up on to the eiderdown and gently pushed her on to the windowsill. 'Jump, Prue, it's not far.'

Prudence was frozen on the sill, too scared to jump. Charity leaned out behind her, taking her sister's hands in hers. 'Don't be scared,' she said. 'Just let yourself dangle, then I'll drop you the rest of the way.'

Charity couldn't hold her any longer anyway. She let her sister's fingers slip through hers and heard her fall with a thump.

She was jumping up on to the windowsill when she paused and looked back towards the door. A flickering light beneath it showed that flames were close, but she had to make certain her parents had got out.

'Prue, hold James and stay there for a moment,' she called down. 'Toby, try and get down to next door over the wall and get help. I'm going to get Mother and Father.'

Both James and Prudence were screaming now. Lights were coming on in the houses at the back.

As Charity opened the door to the landing, the smoke and heat nearly drove her back. She could hear crackling. The wall at the bottom of the few steps was lit with reflected light from flames further down. Clamping the bottom of her nightdress over her mouth she inched her way down towards it.

But as she turned the corner on to the narrow landing opposite the study, tongues of fire were licking over the sisal mat towards her. Another second or two and she'd be caught in it.

'Jump out the window!' she yelled, unable to get to their door.

33

For just one second she stood there, staring in horrified fascination. The fire was like a monster, lapping up everything in its path. The heat was so intense it scorched her bare legs and arms and she knew she could do nothing more to save them from here.

'Mother, Father,' she yelled one more time. 'Get out. Get out!'

A blast of flames knocked her back, catching the hem of her nightdress. She turned and fled into the dark room, shouting in terror. In one desperate leap she got to the window. Clinging to the eiderdown she flung herself through mindlessly and only the sudden chill and the crash as her body hit the roof told her she was safe.

Dimly she heard Prudence crying as she lay there coughing her lungs up. Then a man's voice urging her sister to help.

'Put the cover over her first,' she heard. 'Then pass me the babby. It's all right, sweetheart, we'll soon have you safe.'

It was a strange, disjointed nightmare. Screams, shouting, sirens and gruff male voices. Suddenly it was so bright and hot she thought it was summer. But then someone lifted her. She could feel rough serge against her skin, hear a man's voice telling her she was safe and she was carried away into darkness.

Chapter Three

The events between Charity being lifted down from the kitchen roof and ending up in the children's ward in Lewisham hospital were hazy.

A fleeting glimpse of a crowd of neighbours watching the fire consuming the house as she was carried to the ambulance on a stretcher. Firemen wrestling with hoses, dark shapes against the glow of the fire. Prudence crying and Tobias's white, scared face. Then bright lights and many faces looming over her and a doctor telling her she needed just a couple of stitches in the cut on her head, but he was giving her some medicine so all the pain would go away.

When she woke up, for a moment she thought she had dreamt it all, but her dry mouth, the bandages on her hands and a dull ache all over her made sense of the flowered curtains pulled round the bed. A nurse came to give her a drink: a big woman with copper-coloured hair and gentle brown eyes who sat on the bed and told her both her parents were dead. Charity listened while the nurse explained how a hot coal had fallen from the fire in the parlour and smoke had found its way up into the bedroom above long before the fire got a grip on the house. She tried to soften it by telling Charity that her parents didn't even wake, that they had died peacefully long before flames reached them, but somehow it meant nothing.

Charity felt she ought to cry, but she couldn't. It was as if she was in a cocoon, able to see and hear, but she felt nothing more than the cut on her head and the sting of the burns.

When Charity asked later where the children were, they told her that all three had been taken to foster parents who lived on Clapham Common and she would be going there too once the doctor decided she was well enough. She wasn't badly hurt, she discovered: minor burns on her arms, hands and legs and the cut on her head.

Between sleeping and waking, nurses kept telling her how brave she was, reassuring her that none of the children was hurt and she'd soon be seeing them.

As the misty, sleepy feeling gradually faded and the bright ward full of children became clearer, a sense of jubilation filled her. She'd been rescued! She would never again have to submit to her father's will, never step into that dark, cold house again. No more sermons, no more wondering why their mother never stood up for them or showed any love. It was a new beginning, a brand new start for all of them.

The next morning a social worker called Miss Downes came to collect her, bringing brand new clothes. Even as she slipped on the pretty white underwear, a navy pleated skirt and a pale blue twinset, Charity's delight was tinged with deep remorse. Her injuries were slight and she couldn't brush her hair properly because of the cut on her head, but when more nurses came and offered sympathy about her parents and complimented her on her bravery she felt like a fraud.

She felt she ought to be crying; to be feeling a real sense of loss. But all she felt now was guilt, not grief.

'Well don't you look nice.' Miss Downes looked her up and down as Charity emerged bashfully from behind the screens not knowing whether to smile or cry. 'Now put on this coat. It's too big, I know, but we'll get you one that fits in the next day or two.'

Miss Downes intimidated Charity. Perhaps it was only because she said they would stay with foster parents until they were 'assessed', but her manner and appearance didn't inspire trust.

She was tall and thin, a middle-aged spinster who blinked continually behind thick gold-rimmed spectacles, made a humming sound and nodded her head. At first this seemed to mean agreement to everything, but in fact it was a daunting habit which meant nothing. She didn't seem to be able to manage to smile at all.

Miss Downes explained that Mr and Mrs Charles were temporary foster parents who took children in until relatives were found, or other arrangements could be made. During the car ride to Clapham she fired terse questions at Charity, not about the little ones, but about her school, what she planned to do as a career and if she knew if her father had any insurance?

Charity did what she always did when she was uncertain about anything: merely shook her head and looked at her lap. She didn't know if she was expected to cry all the time, or try to be grown-up, but the same desolate feeling she'd had before the fire came back with a vengeance.

She remembered her father urging social workers to keep a family together when the parents were killed in a train crash a couple of years earlier. Later they heard that the youngest was adopted and the other four split up between children's homes miles away from one another. What if that happened to them?

The Charleses' house was welcoming. Not only did it overlook a common that reminded her very much of Blackheath, but all three children were standing at the upstairs window waving as they pulled up, only to disappear and run to open the door.

A big, double-fronted house, its front garden bright with crocus and daffodils. Better still, Miss Downes left after only the briefest word with Mrs Charles and Charity was drawn in by the children to a home she could only gaze at in wonder. That first impression was of colour, space and light, and a sense of having arrived in paradise.

Mr and Mrs Charles, or Auntie Lou and Uncle Geoff as they told the children to call them, were the kind her father called 'Bohemians'. Auntie Lou wore trousers and a kind of artist's smock and she had long curly red hair tied up in a ponytail. Uncle Geoff was thin, with a big black bushy beard and hardly any hair and he said he was a writer.

Lou and Geoff Charles had no children of their own, but over the years they had taken in countless children in similar emergencies to that of the Stratton family. They operated what they called 'a halfway house', a place of safety where they could monitor and assess the needs of the often emotionally disturbed and traumatised children until a permanent home could be found for them. Deeply committed and caring, they were often appalled at the local authorities' insensitivity and lack of appropriate training. They had learned too that many of the children who passed through their hands would not end up in ideal homes. But however short a time children were to stay, they endeavoured to make it a happy time.

The first two days Charity was at Clapham was a whirl of new experience. A real bathroom, carpets on all the floors, no chores to do – and television. The food was different too. Strange, wonderful things like spaghetti and grapefruit, and hot chocolate to drink. The house was bright and colourful, there were toys, books and puzzles and the Charleses opened their arms and hearts to all of them without reservation.

Uncle Geoff said he wrote books on germs. Charity didn't really believe anyone could write a whole book on such a subject, but he certainly knew a whole lot about everything and he made things so interesting she found herself wishing she could overcome her fear of him. Auntie Lou was just as fascinating: she could cook a meal, hold a conversation, do a bit of ironing, all without looking as if she was doing anything. The house was clean, but she never worried if it was untidy. They had hundreds of books, paintings, ornaments and artefacts from all over the world. On top of all the other strange and wonderful new experiences, Lou and Geoff didn't believe in standing on ceremony about anything.

It was they who shortened Tobias and Prudence to Toby and Prue, something that had always made the children's parents smart with anger. They complimented the children on their good table manners, but didn't turn a hair when they occasionally forgot themselves and grabbed food, or turned their forks to scoop up tricky morsels. They turned bathtime into play, let the girls wear their hair loose and allowed Toby to kick a football around the common whenever he liked.

'It's good here, ain't it?' Toby said gleefully, just a few days after their arrival.

'Isn't it.' Charity corrected his speech out of force of habit, but her thoughts were miles away.

They were standing at the window of Toby's room. Across the road was Clapham Common, grass and trees stretching almost as far as they could see.

A man and a small boy were flying a kite in the distance. They had been watching for some time as the man ran with it trying to get it into the air. At last the wind caught the kite and up it went, the little boy waving his hands in glee.

'I shouldn't feel quite so happy though, should I?' He moved his head back from her shoulder and she saw tears glinting in his clear blue eyes.

'You aren't happy because they're dead,' Charity reproved him. 'It's just because Auntie Lou and Uncle Geoff are so kind and this house is so wonderful. Don't feel bad about anything, Toby. Mother and Father have gone to heaven and they wouldn't want you to be sad.'

'But you're sad.' He buried his face in her thin bony chest and hugged her fiercely.

She wished she could tell him her sadness wasn't grief so much as anxiety about their future. But he was just a little boy and she couldn't lay her burdens on him.

When Toby said it was lovely here that was an understatement. It was heaven. The kind of wonderland Charity had never even imagined in her dreams. But a voice of reason kept telling her that it was only temporary.

Downstairs a radio was playing and she could hear Prue laughing as she rolled out pastry with Auntie Lou. Uncle Geoff had taken James along to the shops and soon it would be dinnertime. The fire was such a short time ago, ahead was the funeral and she didn't dare look beyond that point.

But Charity kept thinking of that word Miss Downes had used. 'Assessing.'

For one thing Auntie Lou made notes about things they said and did. Her questions came out so naturally, with such interest that Toby and Prue fell over themselves to inform her about every aspect of their former life, about their school and how they felt. But Charity was more wary.

It was good to have smart new clothes. To see Prudence's eyes light up with pleasure at a short grey pleated skirt, patent leather strap shoes and a pale blue jumper with a matching ribbon for her hair. It made her happy to see Toby making friends with other children as naturally as if he'd always lived here. But not so good to have James snatched away from her.

Auntie Lou said she was too young for so much responsibility and insisted on washing and dressing James herself. She wouldn't even let him sleep in the same room as the girls. Was this preparing Charity for the time when she would be pushed out the door, not only to work, but to find lodgings of her own?

'But I've always looked after James,' Charity said on her second day there, when Auntie Lou took James off to bed. 'It was my job.'

Auntie Lou let her come up to the big bathroom while she bathed James, but in her gentle way she spelt things out.

'You're only fifteen, Charity and I know you've shouldered a great deal of responsibility for your brothers and sister all your life.' She sat back on her heels beside the bath as James splashed vigorously, her red hair loose and attractively tousled round her thin, expressive face. 'But soon you'll be going to work and they have to learn to lean on someone else. Now's a golden opportunity for you to sit back and let them get used to new people. Because you *aren't* their mother, only a loving sister, and you deserve a life of your own.'

Deep down she knew what Auntie Lou said was right but her feelings were so mixed up. On one hand she wanted an adult to take over, she wanted to be a little girl, to cry and be comforted the way Prue was. But she was angry and jealous, cut off from everything that was familiar, with a sense of betrayal that her

41

brothers and sister were accepting this new woman as a mother.

'Lunchtime!' Auntie Lou bellowed up the stairs, startling Charity and Toby. 'Wash your hands before you come down. Don't be long now!'

Toby moved away from his sister, turning at the door of his room with a wide grin lighting up his pale face.

'Don't worry. All we have to do is make them like us so much they keep us for ever.'

'They already like you, you little scamp.' Charity forced herself to smile reassuringly. 'Just be a good boy, that's all.'

There were four rooms downstairs. A very grand one the Charleses called the drawing room. A dining room and a huge kitchen right along the back of the house, then the one they referred to as 'the den'. It overlooked the Common, and had big bay windows and a settee big enough for five people all at once. There was a table to do jigsaws on, hundreds of books on shelves, games, paints and the television.

It was quite the jolliest room Charity had ever seen. Auntie Lou had a way of flinging herself down on the settee or carpet which encouraged them all to feel relaxed in here. She never told them to put things away, she watched the children's programmes with as much enthusiasm as they did and let James curl up on her lap whenever he felt like it.

Charity waited until both younger children had gone up to bed. Uncle Geoff was working in his study and Auntie Lou had sat down with some sewing.

The den was very warm and cosy with a stove kind of fire that never went out. Two big lamps either side of the fireplace shed soft, golden pools of light and the bright print curtains were drawn tightly.

42

Auntie Lou was on the settee. Charity sat opposite in an armchair, one eye on the television, the other weighing up the older woman.

Everything was remarkable about these people. They believed even children were entitled to an opinion. They never brought up God or church. They used the word 'fun' a great deal, a word that just hadn't been in her parents' vocabulary. They laughed uproariously at jokes, sometimes cuddled like sweethearts, and they argued quite heatedly at times. Their world felt so good, yet alien to everything Charity had been taught. Part of Charity's mind still clung to her parents' values, and it confused her.

'Can we stay here for ever if we behave?'

She regretted the rash question the moment the words had left her lips and, worse still, she saw a flicker of uncertainty in the woman's green eyes.

'Come and sit beside me.' Lou patted the settee. 'Come on! I like to be close when I talk to people about important things.'

Lou was very anxious about Charity. She was concerned with the future of all four of them, but could sense that this child was deeply troubled.

Such a sad little girl. Of course she looked forlorn because of her bandages and sticking plaster, but it went deeper than that. In many ways she seemed younger than Prue, even though she was very maternal and protective. She was so thin and under-developed for a girl of fifteen.

Lou had already had a glimpse into the Stratton household from things Toby and Prue had said and she shuddered. A chronically depressed mother, a bible-thumping father, a home that was ruled by fear. She'd planned to wait until after the funeral to discuss their future, when she herself knew what would happen, but she wasn't going to tell lies now, not even to soothe.

'I can't say what will happen for certain.' Lou's thin, vivacious face took on a slightly tense look. 'You see right now Miss Downes, your social worker, is trying to discover if your parents had any close relations. If they did, one of them might become your legal guardian. But at the moment we have to take each day as it comes. I wish I could promise you that you'll all stay here for ever. But I can't, Charity.'

'I don't think we have any relations,' Charity said quickly. 'I've never heard of any.'

'What do you know about your mother and father?' Lou raised one fair eyebrow. 'Where did they grow up?'

Charity thought hard, then shrugged. 'I don't know. I've often wondered about it. How she came to meet Father and why she was always so sad.'

'Tell me what your mother was like.' Lou changed tack. 'Describe her to me.' She had already been given a description by Miss Downes, of both parents.

'She looked older than she was,' Charity said.

Lou was surprised by this sparse description. Children usually listed the things their mothers were noted for: their cooking, sewing or reading stories.

'Was she blonde, like you? Did she like reading, or music?'

Charity shrugged again.

'I think she liked birds, she used to put the breadcrumbs out in the yard. She was good at sewing.'

Lou could tell by the children's speech and their manners that Mrs Stratton hadn't been from a working-class background.

'Did you talk together much?'

Charity looked baffled at the question.

'I don't mean about everyday things. But feelings, what you wanted to do when you were grown up.'

Charity shook her head.

44

'Well what about other things? Did she ever explain about getting married and having babies?'

Lou expected a blush, even an embarrassed giggle, but she didn't expect the fearful look that came into the girl's eyes, or the way her fingers nervously picked at the hem of her skirt.

'No! I mean, I knew about babies because I was there when James was born.'

'Well that's good,' Lou smiled warmly. 'No wonder you're so close to him. Lots of girls of your age find all that a complete mystery. I know I did. Can you believe, I never even knew about periods? I was terrified when it happened. I thought I was dying.'

Charity had a blank look on her face.

'You have started them, haven't you?' Lou asked.

Charity felt herself growing very hot and uncomfortable.

'No,' she whispered.

Lou wasn't surprised. Charity showed no sign of any kind of development, but she felt the girl's anxiety.

'Well perhaps I should explain the whole thing.' Lou smiled, putting down her sewing and picking up a pad and pencil. 'It's bound to happen soon and when it does you'll be prepared.'

She drew a sketch of a woman, putting in the Fallopian tubes and the womb, then proceeded to go through what would happen.

'We all pick up some funny ideas,' Lou grinned. 'I always thought our tummy buttons had some vital purpose, but of course they don't. We just go along having a period once a month until such time as we get married.' She paused at that point to make sure Charity was taking it in.

'When a couple marry they make love to have babies. The man puts his penis in here and his sperm travels all the way up here – ' she pointed to the

45

womb on her sketch. 'Then the female egg comes down and joins it, and snuggles down in this nice cosy place and grows into a baby. I've got a good book about all this, would you like to read it?'

'No,' Charity snapped. Just the mention of the word 'penis' made her feel sick. She wanted Lou to shut up, to tear up that sketch and leave her in peace.

'Oh dear, I've embarrassed you.' Lou put one hand on Charity's face and tried to draw it round to hers. 'I didn't mean to. I'm sorry, but girls have to know these things.'

Charity was mortified, sure she'd given herself away, but she didn't know how to put it right.

'I knew all that,' she said, twisting her hands together, the sick feeling growing stronger. In fact she didn't know properly, even though technically she was no longer a virgin.

'Well that's good.' Lou refused to be frozen out. 'But I think I should take you along to my doctor and get him to check you out.'

'I'm not going to a doctor,' Charity panicked and jumped up. 'I don't want a man looking at me!'

'Charity!' Lou caught hold of Charity's arms and held her. She knew such a violent reaction had to mean something more than plain embarrassment, and she knew she couldn't ignore it. 'It doesn't have to be a man. I know a lady doctor too and it's only a blood sample, nothing more.'

The moment passed. Lou made a cup of tea, dropped the subject and they watched *Wagon Train* together.

That night Charity dreamed of splashing through a pool of water and woke suddenly to find she had wet the bed. In the dark she lay there sobbing, not knowing what to do. It turned cold and she got out of bed, stripped off her nightdress and shoved it down the back of the radiator. She put her clothes on, then lay on the floor wrapped in the eiderdown till morning.

She didn't sleep again. Terror gnawed at her. If Auntie Lou was to find out she'd surely throw them all out. Should she run away now? Leave a note begging Lou to look after the others?

Charity felt like a five-year-old as she lay on the floor. She had no money, nowhere to go. This was God's way of paying her back for all the bad things she'd done. No one would ever like her; she was tainted.

Geoff was surprised to find Charity down in the kitchen fully dressed when he came down at seven to make some tea.

'Couldn't sleep?' He rubbed his eyes, then wrapped himself tighter into his plaid dressing-gown. He noted that the table was laid for breakfast and also, more importantly, the dark circles under Charity's eyes.

'I had a bad dream.' She tried to smile but her lips refused to co-operate. 'I think it was just the burns prickling.'

'Well let's have some tea then,' he said, glancing down at Charity's legs. He noticed she'd removed the bandages. 'Lou will look at them later. I expect a touch of ointment will soothe them.'

Charity was in the den looking at a book when Lou called her into the kitchen. Toby and Prue were sitting at the table, drawing. James was pushing around a woolly dog on wheels. It was eleven o'clock, no one had remarked on anything unusual over breakfast and the fear inside her was gradually subsiding.

She saw Auntie Lou bundling sheets and her night-dress into the washing machine. The blood froze in her veins, and panic overwhelmed her.

'Why didn't you tell me?' Lou turned towards

Charity and opened her arms. 'Did you think I'd be cross?'

Charity avoided her arms and just hung her head in silence. She was sure Auntie Lou would find out the truth. The temptation to spill it all out was so strong, she felt as if she was being drawn into a wind tunnel. But in the back of her mind was that embroidered text on the parlour wall: 'Honour thy Father and Mother'.

Father couldn't hurt her again. Prudence was safe. What good would it do bringing something so shameful out into the open? It wouldn't make her forget, she couldn't go back to being as innocent as Prue. All a confession would do was bring shame to the family name.

'Life's been hard,' she whispered. 'Sometimes I wished I could just leave home. But I never wanted anything like this to happen.'

'You'll feel better soon,' Lou murmured, enveloping Charity in an aroma of Blue Grass perfume and newly shampooed hair. 'It's nature's way of healing, don't try to hold it back.'

The funeral service would have pleased Father. The sun shone and Babylon Hall was full to capacity with all his reformed drunks, the sad and the lonely people who thought so much of him. There in the one place Charity had felt proud of her father she was able to mourn. Silently she promised her parents she would take care of her brothers and sister and vowed to keep her secrets to herself. Auntie Lou had said no more about seeing a doctor. Everything was over.

Easter came with the suggestion that happy times were here to stay. Uncle Geoff led an Easter egg hunt in the garden after church. Prudence was beside herself with happiness because Auntie Lou had bought her the pale blue dress with a smocked yoke she'd admired for so long. Charity got a full circular skirt, a wonderful emerald green one with a separate can-can petticoat and a white 'Goosegirl' blouse with a ruffle round the scoop neck.

On Easter Monday Uncle Geoff took them over to the fair on the Common and they went on every single ride. It was magical. The big wheel whizzing round with its load of screaming passengers, all lit up like a huge Catherine wheel. 'Jailhouse Rock' was blasting out, vying with the noise from the rifle range, the carousel and the waltzer.

It was dark when they went home, Uncle Geoff carrying the sleeping James up on his shoulder. People were still flocking to the fair. Young men in smart suits with girls on their arms. Teddy boys on motor-bikes and teenage girls in great giggling gangs. Toby and Prue had candyfloss stuck to their faces and a pink glow on their cheeks.

'What's going to happen now?' Charity asked Uncle Geoff. 'I was supposed to start work after Easter,' she said, glancing back over her shoulder to take one last look at the fairground.

'Lou suggested that you stay at home till the summer,' Uncle Geoff said and grabbed sleeping James more securely. 'We could give you a bit of private coaching. How does that sound?'

'Nice,' Charity said cautiously. She meant it sounded wonderful, but she was always cautious. 'What about Prue and Toby?'

'We've got them moved into the local school.' Uncle Geoff smiled down at her. 'A new start, eh!'

Charity had grown fond of Uncle Geoff, despite her nervousness of men in general. He laughed a great deal, great guffaws that shook his bushy beard and made his eyes wrinkle up. She liked his lean, unthreatening frame, the careless way he dressed and his gentle voice.

'There's things we should talk about in the next day or two.' His dark brown eyes looked down at her with kindness and understanding. 'Not now with little ears pinned back,' he said, nodding his head towards Prue and Toby in front.

It was at the end of the week that Miss Downes called. She wasn't alone this time, but with a younger woman called Miss Brady. When it was suggested that Miss Brady take the younger children out for ice-cream while Miss Downes stayed behind 'for a chat', Charity felt very apprehensive.

'Now let's sit down and have a drink together.' Auntie Lou handed Charity a glass of milk and the adults had coffee.

They made small talk for a while, discussing James's new words, Prue's desire to learn dancing and Toby's passion for football. Miss Downes kept blinking and humming as if in agreement with everything.

'Let's get right to the point,' Auntie Lou said eventually. 'Miss Downes has found some relatives, Charity.'

Just the way everyone had been trying to delay this news gave Charity a feeling of impending disaster and all she could do was stare at Aunt Lou.

'You have an uncle and a grandmother,' Miss Downes spoke at last. 'We discovered both grandparents on your father's side are dead, and he had no brothers or sisters. But your mother's mother is still alive and your mother's older brother, Stephen.'

'Are they nice?' Charity asked. 'Do they want to see us?'

The adults exchanged glances that seemed ominous.

Charity looked from one to the other desperately. 'Tell me the truth. I want to know.'

Uncle Geoff cleared his throat.

'It's not that they aren't "nice",' he said carefully, his brown eyes gentle. 'It's just a bit awkward.'

Geoffrey Charles had learned about these relatives several days earlier, but was still stunned by the news.

'You see your grandmother is very old, Charity,' Geoff said carefully. 'Your uncle is crippled. They didn't even know about you four, they lost touch with your mother before any of you were born.'

Charity immediately imagined these relatives as much like the kind of people who lived in Greenwich.

'Well that's that, then.' She shrugged philosophically. 'So what happens now?'

She saw the three adults look at one another and knew there was more. It was very odd that Miss Downes was saying nothing. She just sat, hands clasped in her lap, still wearing her black cloche hat.

'What is it?' she asked, looking hard at Lou. 'Have we got to go somewhere else now?'

Lou ran her fingers through her hair.

'Oh Charity,' she sighed. 'Where do I begin? You see your mother's family are rather grand. They don't live in a house like this one, but a mansion in Oxfordshire.'

Charity's eyes nearly popped out of her head.

'Let me start at the beginning,' Lou went on. 'Your mother's maiden name was Pennycuick. Brigadier Pennycuick, her father, came from a long line of military men, but he died some years ago. Your uncle was a colonel in the same regiment, but he was wounded during the war and he still lives with your grandmother in Studley Priory.'

'Studley Priory?' Charity questioned.

'That's the name of their house,' Lou explained.

51

'From what we can gather, your grandparents fell out with your mother when she married your father.'

'Why?' Charity asked.

'We don't know. It was during the war and odd things happened to lots of people then. Maybe they even had someone else in mind for their daughter; she was born twenty years after Stephen, so perhaps they over-protected her.'

'Does that mean they don't even want to see us?' Charity felt a certain pride that she had an interesting lineage, though judging by Lou and Geoff's expressions they weren't so happy about it.

'They haven't made a date yet,' Auntie Lou said softly. 'But your uncle is prepared to become your legal guardian, and indeed to provide for you.'

Charity mulled this over for a moment. She knew enough about foster parents to know they got paid for looking after children.

'So does that mean he'll pay for us to stay here?'

Geoff Charles half smiled. He was surprised by Charity's grasp of the situation. He just wished he could assure her that it was only a question of money.

'He hasn't had time to think that through yet,' he said gently. 'But for the present, at least, this is your home.'

Charity had a sinking feeling about that phrase 'at present'.

'He won't split us up or anything?' she asked fearfully. 'You will tell him we all need to be together?'

'We already have,' Miss Downes chipped in. 'Mr Charles has outlined that you need a little coaching and that the younger children are about to start at the local school. Of course little James needs stability right now too. I did suggest to your uncle that maybe the first point of contact could be that you spend a short holiday with him and his mother during the summer holidays.'

52

Charity nodded. The summer holidays were ages away and any threat seemed to have vanished. No one was even speaking about her getting a job! Maybe they *would* get to stay here for ever.

'Why don't you run down to the ice-cream shop and catch up with Miss Brady?' Miss Downes held out a half-crown to her and smiled with unusual warmth. 'Don't say anything about our little chat just yet to Toby and Prue, though.'

'I think she took that very well,' Miss Downes said, turning in her seat to watch Charity running down the road, her can-can petticoat bouncing beneath her green skirt showing rainbow colours. 'A nice, sensible girl!'

Lou looked sharply at Miss Downes, colour rising in her cheeks.

'You haven't any idea, have you?' she exploded. 'That "sensible" girl has been through hell. She might be fifteen and old enough to work, but she's still a child. Now you plan to let some old codger who hasn't a clue about children put her through more!'

'Now that's unfair.' Miss Downes's thin lips quivered with indignation. 'He's their uncle and it is only right and proper that he should decide their future.'

'His words on the phone were, "Send the girl here, we could do with another pair of hands." ' Lou's green eyes blazed. 'Don't you think she's had enough of being a skivvy?'

'She could fare worse,' Miss Downes said, pushing her glasses back on to her nose with one finger. 'She has no aptitude for anything other than domestic work.'

'That's not fair,' Geoff spoke. He sat forward in his chair, putting a warning hand on his wife's to calm her. He knew Lou was on the point of blurting out that Miss Downes had no 'aptitude' for working with

53

children, but that wouldn't help Charity. 'Charity hasn't had a chance to shine at anything else, but she's intelligent and a great deal quicker than you give her credit for. Can you possibly imagine what it would do to her if she was sent away from the children to look after some grumpy old cripple in the middle of nowhere?'

'Well it's not ideal,' Miss Downes agreed with a shrug of her shoulders.

Geoffrey Charles had never considered himself anything but fortunate. He had married the woman he loved, pursued a career in biology that excited him. His grandmother had left him this house and with his writing they had enough money to live comfortably. Having no children of their own was a disappointment, but they'd compensated by helping children in need.

When the Strattons arrived they'd had no thought of holding on to them for more than a few weeks. But that was then – before he'd taken Prue and Toby sailing boats on the pond, before he'd bounced James up and down on his knee and felt the deep need in Charity.

She loved her brothers and sister passionately and could care for them almost singlehandedly; take them away, and she had nothing.

Barely able to read, her spelling was appalling and she could manage no more than the simplest of sums. But she had a quick mind. With tuition she could get a decent job, with love she could flourish . . .

'I am backing my wife in this,' he said, turning to Miss Downes, his gentle face for once hard and unyielding. 'Maybe the ideas Colonel Pennycuick has for Toby and Prue might be feasible and even desirable. But you must do everything in your power to make sure James stays with us and that Charity is allowed to choose her own job.'

Miss Downes wilted under his stern gaze.

'I'll do what I can,' she said and blinked furiously. 'But as I'm sure you've realised, Colonel Pennycuick is a very difficult man.'

Chapter Four

'Read it again, Charity,' Uncle Geoff leaned back in his deckchair, tucking his hands behind his head. 'This time think about the beautiful words and put some passion into it.'

'I can't,' Charity giggled. 'I feel silly.'

They were alone in the garden, reading the poems of Elizabeth Barrett Browning. It was three months since the fire and Charity was settled and happy.

A glorious June day, the sky a canopy of blue velvet. Leaves on bushes and climbing shrubs glossy with newness. Brilliant purple, blue and yellow pansies fronted clumps of lupins, with towering delphiniums taking up the rear, hiding the fence in a wall of colour.

'Why should you feel silly?' Geoff lifted one eyebrow enquiringly. 'It's just you and me! Is it right to read it like a shopping list when you feel your heart touched by the words?'

Charity picked up the book again.

She loved her lessons with him. He brought books and poetry alive, she was always hungry for more. Until she came to live with the Charleses it had even been a struggle to read Enid Blyton, but now she had her nose in a book almost continually.

'I wish I could learn maths as fast,' she sighed. 'I don't think I'm ever going to grasp that!'

'You've achieved a great deal there too,' he said encouragingly. 'Not all of us are born with mathematical minds. You've mastered the basics, you can add up a row of figures, multiply and divide, that's enough to get by with.'

'Cup of tea?' Lou called out.

James came out into the garden wearing only a pair of pants, his bucket and spade in his hands. His first proper haircut had changed him from a baby into a little boy. He appeared to have grown a couple of inches in as many months, but his face was as endearingly cheeky as ever.

'That's enough learning for one day.' Geoff gathered up the books, put them in a pile and got up to stretch. 'Hullo James, where are you off to, the seaside?'

'Make a castle,' he said, running across the lawn to the sandpit they'd made for him at the bottom of the garden.

Charity lowered the back of her chair, sat down again and leaned back.

In Greenwich the house had been stuffy and gloomy, with smells coming up from the drains and the river, and even the air made her feel tired. Here she woke early to look out at the garden, excitement rising inside her at the prospect of the day ahead.

After Prue and Toby had gone to school her lessons started: English, maths and science with Uncle Geoff; history and geography with Auntie Lou. Usually after lunch she took James out for a walk so the Charleses could get on with their own work, or sometimes she wrote an essay for the following morning. But even when she wasn't having formal lessons, she was learning. Watching and listening to Lou and Geoff, reading and discussing the news in the papers. It was as if her brain had been expanded, making so much more room she could cram with fascinating information.

She thought less and less of the past now. Sometimes it seemed like a story she'd read, nothing to do with her at all. She'd refused to see a doctor and Auntie Lou had forgotten all about it.

Charity glanced down at her bust. It was beginning to grow at last and after a course of iron tablets her periods had started, which finally stopped her vague fear that she might be pregnant. Since then she had discovered new confidence in almost every direction, particularly where Geoff was concerned. She could kiss him goodnight now, she didn't back away if he slung an arm round her shoulder. Once or twice she'd even let him cuddle her.

'So how is our little Elizabeth Browning?' Lou came out with a tray of tea and put it down on the grass.

It gave her immense pleasure to see the new colour in Charity's cheeks, the sparkle in her eyes and the extra pounds she'd put on. She would always be slender, but she was growing prettier every day now the haunted look had gone. She had all the energy and enthusiasm of a puppy; given another year, she'd be a beauty.

Geoff came back and sat down on the grass by their feet. He wore faded baggy khaki shorts and an equally old shirt open over his bare chest. His bushy beard was rather at odds with his almost bald head.

'Are you going to be mother?' he grinned up at his wife. 'Or has the morning sweating over a hot stove earned you the privilege of indolence?'

'You do it.' Lou lay back in her deckchair and pushed her hair back from her face.

The sun had brought out a crop of freckles all over her face, arms and shoulders. She wore a faded sundress with thin straps and her legs were bare.

Charity was in turn appalled, delighted and curious at her foster parents' lack of style. They had no interest in material things. Lou spent money on flowers for the house, Geoff collected books, but they never bought new clothes for themselves.

'Shabby is comfortable,' Lou had said more than

58

once and she would make Charity laugh with her version of a quotation from the Bible, 'Consider the Charleses of Clapham. They write books that nobody reads, they know things no one cares to share and King Solomon in all his glory had better clothes than they.'

'We had a letter from your Uncle Stephen today,' Auntie Lou said as her husband passed her tea. 'He's invited you for a holiday. How about it?'

Charity had noticed that Lou always fired out things that were troubling her. No hedging or dressing them up.

'Do I have a choice?' Charity asked.

'Not really.' Lou sighed and looked to her husband for support. 'He's your guardian, and I'm sure you are as curious about him as he must be about you.'

Charity *was* curious. She liked the thought of having rather grand relatives and she wanted to know more about her mother. But she was scared of them too.

'I don't have to stay if I don't like it, do I?' Her voice shook.

'No of course not.' Geoff reached out and patted her hand. 'If you hate it, just phone us and we'll make the excuses for you. But try to stick with it, sweetheart, think of it as a bit of family research.'

'When do I go?' Charity was torn now between fright and excitement.

'He suggested this Friday.' Lou was leaning down pouring herself another cup of tea to avoid looking at Charity directly. 'Geoff will put you on the train and they'll pick you up at Oxford.'

'I hope they like me,' Charity blurted out in a moment of pure panic.

'There's something wrong with them if they don't,' Uncle Geoff retorted. 'Mind you, we'd better gloss up on some Kipling before you leave. Old soldiers usually go more for him than Elizabeth Browning.'

Lou and Geoff weren't happy about Colonel Penny-cuick becoming the children's guardian, but there was nothing they could do about it. Their first impressions of him as a crusty, bombastic man hadn't changed. If anything they were even more wary of him. He spoke of the children like men under his command. There was no compassion for what they'd been through, or even real interest in their personalities.

Geoff had written a long impassioned letter explaining not only the need for stability in their future lives but the Charleses' own desire to act as parents, even if it was decided that Prue and Toby should go away to school.

The Colonel's reply had daunted them. His curious statement 'as their legal guardian he had a duty to safeguard their future in the most cost-effective manner', left them wondering if he thought his nieces and nephews were like furniture which had to be stored at the cheapest price.

Now he was demanding that Charity should visit him, and although Charity's health and appearance had improved since her stay with the Charleses, neither of them felt she was ready to cope with further upset.

Charity's heart was fluttering so wildly she thought she might faint.

At first it had been fun to be on a train alone. She had a magazine, a cake and some fruit. Every now and then she would look in the new handbag Auntie Lou had bought her, just the way grown-up women did. She had a pale pink lipstick in there, a comb, a clean handkerchief, her ticket and a purse full of money. There was even a small mirror in a felt pouch tucked in with photographs of the children.

But now she was almost there she was so scared she felt sick.

'Next stop, love.' The cheery guard opened the sliding door and reached up to swing her small case down from the luggage rack. 'Have a good holiday!'

A rosy-faced woman smiled up at Charity as she made her way into the corridor.

'Don't look so scared,' she said soothingly. 'I bet they're every bit as nervous as you.'

This lady had offered her tea from her flask and Charity had explained where she was going but the conversation had been halted when the lady dropped off to sleep.

Charity managed a tight smile and, case in hand, went to wait by the door.

She paused as she stepped down from the train into bright afternoon sunshine. Oxford station was tiny after the London ones, but there were dozens of people waiting to get on or meeting people. Uncle Geoff had sent a photograph of her to the Pennycuicks, but she had no idea who would be meeting her.

Moving out of the way of the train seemed the best idea. She pushed through the crowd and went over to a mail trolley to wait.

There was a woman in a red hat who seemed to be looking for someone, but she was too young to be grandmother. There was an old lady with blue rinsed hair, but somehow she didn't look right. There was an entire family meeting a man: his children were hugging his legs, clamouring over each other to get close while his wife kissed him passionately on the lips. They made her think of Geoff and Lou and already she was homesick.

Grit from the open train window seemed to be stuck in her eyes, her hands felt sticky and dirty and her hair had gone all limp since this morning. She wished she dared slip into the toilets to wash and brush up, but she was afraid to move.

'Miss Charity?'

An elderly male voice made her wheel round sharply.

'Hullo,' she replied, startled by the rather formal 'Miss' being put before her name. 'Are you Uncle Stephen?'

The man was old, perhaps seventy, with stooped shoulders and a long, thin, weatherbeaten face. It seemed odd that he was wearing a navy blue suit and a peaked cap.

'Me!' He laughed, showing crooked yellow teeth. 'No, I'm Jackson.'

Charity looked puzzled, but Jackson picked up her case in one hand. 'I'm the general dogsbody: today I'm your chauffeur, tomorrow gardener or handyman. I'd have known you, Miss Charity, even without getting a look-see at your picture. You're the image of Miss Gwen when she was young.'

'You knew my mother?' Charity tried to stay by his side, but the crush of people kept separating them. Considering his age, bowed legs and stooped shoulders, he moved nimbly.

'Right from a little tot. I was with the brigadier, your grandfather, as his batman. Through the first war, right up to when he retired. Then I stayed on at Studley to help with the colonel when he lost his legs.'

Charity gulped. When they'd said her uncle was crippled in the war, she'd imagined nothing more than a limping man on sticks.

'It makes him a bit grumpy sometimes, but his bark's worse than his bite, if you know what I mean. Don't you get upset now if he's a bit sharp.'

That sounded ominously like a warning and she felt he'd moved on from her mother a bit fast too. She wasn't sure whether to question him further in case she appeared too nosy.

Jackson led Charity to the old Daimler, smiling at

the way her eyes widened in delight at the gleaming car.

'It's like my baby,' he admitted, running his hand over the highly polished bonnet. 'My wife thinks I care more about it than I do about her.'

Charity felt very small, sitting in the back of the car, sliding around on the leather seat. It made her think of her parents' funeral and she clutched her handbag tight to her stomach for comfort.

This morning she'd thought she looked really smart in her circular skirt, goosegirl blouse and short navy blue jacket, but now her skirt was crumpled, there was an orange juice stain on her blouse and her jacket was shedding balls of blue fluff. To her further horror there was a ladder in her new nylons. Whatever would her grandmother and uncle think of her?

'These are all part of the university.' Jackson half turned his head towards her, pointing towards majestic buildings on either side of a wide road.

Charity forgot her appearance and her anxiety for a moment.

'It's very beautiful,' she said, awed now as she remembered Uncle Geoff speaking of punting on the river, splendid gardens and the halls being so different from one another. 'Is my uncle's house nearby?'

'It's right out in the country, love. But there's a bus comes in, or maybe your grandmother will bring you in again to look around.'

Charity was distracted for a moment as they drove over a narrow humpbacked bridge. Weeping willows hung right over the river and at last she saw the punts Geoff had mentioned.

'I never got the hang of that meself,' Jackson chuckled. 'Years ago I took a young lady out in one to impress her and I fell in. Made a real fool of meself.'

'What's my grandmother like?' Charity asked,

wriggling forward on the seat to get closer to Jackson. His friendly admission made her feel a little braver.

He didn't answer for a moment and Charity found his need to think out a reply disconcerting.

'She's a real lady,' he said eventually. 'A game old girl. Since the brigadier died she seems to have aged quickly, but she's still very active.'

They were out of the town now and driving down narrow country lanes. They passed through several tiny villages with pretty stone cottages, but Jackson remained stubbornly silent until they came to a brow of a hill.

'That's Studley Priory,' he said, slowing down and pointing over to Charity's right.

Her mouth fell open in astonishment. She had expected a big house, and knew too that it was very old, but she hadn't imagined anything so awe-inspiring.

Studley Priory was at least a mile away, set on a small hill as if surveying the surrounding open countryside. A mellow grey stone mansion with pointed gables, it was flanked by tall trees.

'I can't go there,' she whispered, suddenly terribly afraid.

Jackson heard her whisper and his heart went out to her. He could remember his feelings of awe when he accompanied the brigadier there the first time back in 1919.

He stopped the car and turned to her. All colour had gone from her face.

'It's just a house,' he said gently, 'even if it is big. Nothing to be scared of, and it's your family home, remember.'

'But . . .' Her lips quivered and she couldn't voice the thoughts in her head. She belonged in a city, in an ordinary house, with ordinary people.

'Know what I thought when I first went in there?'

Jackson said comfortingly, inwardly cursing Mrs Pennycuick for not coming to the station to meet her grandchild the way any normal grandmother would. 'I thought I was having a dream where everything was giant-sized and I was the size of an ant. I was older than you are now, and I'd already been to France and seen all sorts. But I had me first cup of tea in the kitchen and I looked around me and then I said "Well Jackson, they are only people that live here, just like you. They all blow their noses, they use the lav and wipe their backsides. The only difference between them and me is they've got money and I ain't." It worked, y'know! After that I weren't scared no more.'

Charity smiled weakly at his irreverence.

'That's better,' he grinned, showing his yellow teeth. 'A couple of days and you'll be right as rain. Just keep reminding yourself about what I said.'

Charity sat on the edge of the seat as the car turned off the road on to a drive overhung by trees. Her stomach was in knots with fear and she clung to the leather strap as the car hit a rut.

'Years ago this was as smooth as a pavement,' Jackson said. 'But things have slid a bit since then, half the house is shut up now. It takes me all me time just to keep the grass cut.'

All at once they were out of the trees, and there, beyond a circular lawn, was the house.

The view from back up the road had given her the scale of the place. Now as she saw it close up, bathed in sunlight, an unexpected lump came to her throat.

She had sometimes seen pictures in glossy magazines at the dentist's, of houses as big and as old, but a black and white photograph couldn't show the serenity, the softness of the colours or the sheer beauty of such a place, with its warm grey stone walls, dozens of twinkling mullioned windows, tall chimneypots and a terracotta coloured roof. The turret-like

65

porch with an arched front door and a coat of arms evoked castles in history books; the small belltower on the north wing and the stained glass in a bay window an image of a church. With the clear blue sky above, the lawn in front and the ancient cypresses grouped protectively round it, no one, least of all a girl from the back streets of Greenwich, could fail to be moved by its magnificence.

Jackson stopped the car and got out to open her door. Charity stepped out hesitantly, looking up at the inscription above the front door.

FEARE HIS GLORIOUS AND FEAREFUL NAME. THE LORD THY GOD. HONOUR THE KING.

It brought back an image of her father and made her shiver.

'Remember what I said.' Jackson took her case from the boot and, holding her elbow, led her towards the door. 'They're only people, just like you and me!'

Charity's first impression of the interior of the house was of walking into an old church. The hall was stone, the floor made uneven by feet over the centuries and chillingly gloomy with a strong smell of mildew. But before she had a chance to catch her breath, an old lady came out of a door to her left.

'Charity,' she said. 'How good to see you at last.'

Her voice rang out like a melodious bell, echoing round the hall. Although she was small and slender and her hair a fluffy white cloud round a lined face, there was no sign of infirmity. Her back was straight, the hands that reached out to clutch Charity's arms in greeting, unwavering.

'Hallo.' Charity wasn't sure whether she should kiss her grandmother or not. Although her words were welcoming enough, she gave only a tight, cool smile and there was no inclination of her cheek towards Charity. 'It's kind of you to invite me.'

She'd pictured her grandmother as an older version of her mother, but in fact there was no similarity. Grandmother's face might be heavily lined, but it had a healthy glow and a sweetness that Gwen's had lacked. Her eyes were faded blue, her mouth slack and puckered with tiny lines, but she was still undeniably pretty.

'Take Charity's case up, Jackson,' her grandmother said, and caught Charity's elbow in exactly the same way that Jackson had done, waving her hand dismissively towards the man hovering in the background.

As Jackson disappeared, Grandmother opened the door she'd come through earlier, nudging Charity before her.

'Stephen!' she said. 'Charity.'

Charity stopped short as she saw her uncle. She was aware of the vast room which seemed to dwarf her, but the man in the wheelchair moving himself towards her intimidated her still more.

Despite his sitting position, he was huge. He had a bloated, purple-tinged face and a shock of white hair that hung over the neck of a navy blue sweater. His trouser legs were pinned up, just two short flaps where his knees should have been.

'Hallo, Uncle Stephen.' Charity took a deep breath and stepped forward to shake his hand, trying to remember the polite greetings Uncle Geoff had suggested. 'I've been looking forward to meeting you.'

He shook her hand with surprising strength. 'You're even smaller and thinner than the picture,' he said, his voice hoarse, as if he'd spent a lifetime shouting.

She knew instantly she would never like this man. He was fat, so very fat it made her stomach churn. He didn't have one chin, but four or five, almost like a pelican, and his blue eyes were small and bright as a bird's. Even his mouth was nasty, with loose, shiny

67

lips that suggested he would dribble, and the hand that held hers was covered in engorged veins.

'I'll go and see how dinner's progressing,' Grandmother said, 'and leave you to get acquainted.'

To be left alone with this monster of a man brought Charity out in a cold sweat. Her heart thumped alarmingly and the last of her courage left her.

'Don't stand there gawping like an idiot.' Stephen wheeled his chair round and pointed to an armchair. 'Sit down and tell me all about yourself. You look very like your mother.'

Charity had assumed when Jackson had said the same thing that it was out of politeness; she'd never seen any similarity between them. But then she couldn't imagine this man being her mother's brother either, he was far too big.

'Well speak up, girl!' he bellowed. 'Gwen didn't inform me she'd four children. If she had we might not be strangers now.'

His ferocity and insensitivity reminded her of her father, and all the confidence Geoff and Lou had built up in her vanished. What did he expect her to tell him? About the fire? About her father's preaching? Or about her brothers and sisters?

'Mother never told me she had a brother,' she ventured in a shaky voice. Her eyes were straying from his face to her surroundings and that was enough to rob her of speech entirely.

'Why should she mention me? I wasn't much use to her, too far apart in age,' he barked. 'I was off at Sandhurst when she was a baby. You've left school, I hear? Why's that?'

'It was arranged before Mother and Father died.' Charity wished he wouldn't bellow; it made her shake. 'Uncle Geoff is coaching me and I've learned such a lot since I went to live with them.'

She wanted to phone home now and beg to go back.

Her uncle was staring at her so intently she wanted to hide behind a chair. Was he already disappointed by her appearance?

'Are your foster parents vegetarians?'

Charity was startled by this odd question.

'Do they eat meat, girl?'

'Well yes,' she replied, wondering if that was a crime.

He snorted.

'Huh. Thought they were plant eaters, browsers, they sound like it. Full of all that weak claptrap.'

Charity didn't understand the remark.

'Uncle Geoff's a writer,' she said in his defence. 'He's very clever and kind.'

'What service was he in during the war?'

'The air force.' Uncle Geoff had told her he hated service life more than anything, but he'd advised her not to mention that.

'Damn Brylcreem boy.' He snorted again. 'Still, I half expected him to be a conchie. Do you know what that is?'

Charity shook her head.

'Conscientious objector, the yellow-bellied cowards who refused to fight. If I'd had my way I would have lined them all up and shot 'em.'

This seemed a very odd thing to spurt out and it crossed Charity's mind that her uncle might be mad.

'Uncle Geoff went back to Germany to help the refugees,' she said stoutly. 'And Auntie Lou. They weren't cowards.'

'Does your brother Tobias want to join the army?' He shot the question at her and took her by surprise. 'Every man in our family for eight generations has been in the Rifle Brigade. If we get his name down now he could go to Sandhurst.'

Uncle Geoff was a pacifist, but even he had agreed that Toby would be an ideal candidate for the army, with his fascination with guns, tanks and just about everything overtly masculine. But she wasn't going to say anything that might make Toby attractive to this bully of a man.

'He likes sport,' she said, playing it safe.

'Plenty of chance for sport in the army,' he said. 'A real man's life. Boys should be made into men at the earliest opportunity with plenty of discipline.'

Panic rose up within her, robbing her of speech. Toby resented discipline more than any of them and suppose her uncle was also including little James in this toughening-up process?

'Prudence is clever,' she volunteered. 'She should pass her eleven-plus.'

'Girls don't need education,' he said airily. 'It's wasted on them. Boys are different.'

Charity could imagine Lou's hair standing on end at that remark. She had got a first-class degree at university and even now she taught classes in history at evening schools.

'Times are changing though, Uncle Stephen.' Charity would have loved to come out with one of Lou's fiery speeches but she wasn't that articulate or brave. 'Girls have a right to a career too.'

'Secretaries, nurses maybe.' He snorted again. 'They have their place in society of course. But higher education is a waste and they take places which should go to men.'

Fortunately Grandmother came in at that point with a cup of tea for Charity. She must have heard her son's last remark, and half smiled at Charity.

'Don't take too much notice of him,' she said. 'If a woman doctor could give him back his legs he'd be straight off to see her. Now Stephen! Would you like a whisky? And will you need the fire?'

'Just the one in my room,' he said. 'Doubtless the

girl is tired after her journey and it's warm enough for the time being.'

'Can I do anything to help?' Charity asked. She couldn't imagine why they would even be discussing fires in June; the room was hot from the sun.

'Not tonight,' Grandmother said, and went over to one of the big cabinets. It looked Chinese: shiny black with glistening patterns of mother of pearl set in it. She opened a door to reveal dozens of bottles with glasses on a lower shelf, and poured her son a large tumbler full of whisky. 'Tomorrow will be soon enough. Dinner's at six, I hope you like fish?'

'Yes, thank you.' In fact Charity wasn't keen, not unless it was the kind from the fish and chip shop, but it had been drilled into her at an early age to eat whatever was put in front of her.

'Shall I show Charity her room now?' Grandmother gave the drink to Stephen.

'You might as well.' He gave Charity a withering look which seemed to imply he had nothing further to say to her. 'And bring me the paper.'

'Don't mind Stephen too much,' her grandmother said once they'd left the room. 'He's always been a grumpy devil, but he gets more amenable once he's had a drink or two.'

Charity had no idea how to respond to this so she smiled weakly.

'Who looks after all this?' she asked instead as they turned a corner past a grandfather clock and walked towards a big wide oak staircase. There were doors everywhere and she couldn't get a fix on exactly where she was in relation to the the drawing room. Even a glance out the window on the staircase didn't help. A large tree blocked any view.

'We have help,' her grandmother said vaguely. 'But

it's much too large now there's just Stephen and myself.'

Grandmother drew Charity along a narrow, dark passage, in which there were many more closed heavy oak doors.

'I've given you this one because it's well aired,' she said as she opened a door right at the end. 'It's above the kitchen, you see. An old house like this gets very damp.'

There were high, twin single beds with carved headboards, a matching dressing-table with dozens of tiny drawers and a wardrobe big enough for ten people. Beneath a window stood an old-fashioned tiled washstand equipped with china basin and jug.

'This is nice,' Charity lied, hoping her grandmother might unbend with flattery. The room had the same kind of austerity as her parents' bedroom back in Greenwich and although the view was of garden and rolling fields beyond, the decoration was dingy as if it hadn't been touched since Victorian times.

'It needs decorating,' her grandmother said tartly, but she sat down on the edge of the closest bed as if suddenly realising Charity expected more of her. 'I'm sorry my dear, you must be feeling very strange to be suddenly landed here without knowing anything about us. The house has become a terrible burden since my husband died. We find it hard to get reliable staff and there's so much that needs attention. If you could only have seen it as it used to be when Gwen was a girl!'

Charity had an inkling. Everything she'd seen so far created an image of decaying grandeur. In its heyday Studley Priory must have housed droves of servants to keep it all in order; now it was silent and empty, her grandmother and crippled uncle rattling around in it like two peas in a dusty shoebox.

'Maybe I can help?' Charity wanted the old lady to

like her. 'I can cook and clean. I used to do nearly everything at home when Mother was ill.'

'Gwen was ill?' Consternation flitted across Grandmother's lined face.

'It was her nerves.' Charity fell back on the excuse everyone had used for Gwen Stratton. 'She got much worse after baby Jacob died and I did everything for James when he was born.'

If she expected this to bring forth an explanation of why Gwen never contacted her family or even spoke of her, Charity was disappointed. Grandmother stood up, smoothed down her dress and made for the door.

'I'll leave you to unpack,' she said, and once more her face registered nothing other than polite deference to a passing stranger. 'The bathroom's the last door on the left by the stairs. Come down again when you're ready. Put something tidier on for dinner, please.'

It took only a couple of minutes for Charity to unpack her few belongings. She hung up her best blue dress in the wardrobe, put her underwear, shorts, jumper and skirt in the chest of drawers and shook the creases out of a pink dress with a white Peter Pan collar to change into.

She was close to tears. The house was so big and silent and she hadn't the least idea what was expected of her.

In her pink dress, with clean white ankle socks to replace her laddered nylons, and with her hair brushed, she looked closer to twelve than fifteen. She paused outside her room, looking along the narrow winding corridor with its many heavy doors, tempted to open some of them and peep inside.

The silence made her skin prickle and the gloom conjured up pictures of ghosts, even though it was still hot and sunny outside. But as she placed her hand on the latch of the first door, a loud booming sound made her jump back in fright.

For a second or two she thought it was some device to warn her uncle she was intending to snoop. But as the sound reverberated around the house, it dawned on Charity that it was nothing more than a gong, to call her for dinner.

It was quite an ordeal. Charity had never seen a formally laid dining room, much less eaten in one. Aside from the formidable sight of all the heavy silver plate and a long table big enough to seat at least sixteen, the atmosphere in the room made her jumpy.

She was put opposite her grandmother, with Uncle Stephen in his wheelchair at the head of the table and a big, sour-faced woman, to whom she was offered no introduction, dished out the meal in sullen silence.

First came soup and her uncle glared at her as she picked up the dessert spoon. But although the soup was red, it wasn't tomato as she expected, but something fiery which almost blew her head off.

The fish was flat. Grandmother said it was plaice and tutted when Charity couldn't get the bones out. With it came a strange green vegetable called kale, and new potatoes.

'No wonder you're so thin,' Uncle Stephen said, looking disapprovingly at her plate. She had eaten all the potatoes and some of the fish, but no more than a mouthful of the kale.

Charity privately thought he was incredibly greedy. He gobbled vast quantities of everything, covering it in a nasty-looking sauce that had green things in it. Aside from pouring his mother one small glass of wine, he drank the rest of the bottle himself and each time he downed another glass he belched loudly without even excusing himself.

Grandmother, in contrast, ate hardly anything, but she listened intently as her son fired questions at

74

Charity. There was nothing subtle or gentle in the way he phrased them, and if his mother was appalled at his lack of tact as he broached the subjects of the fire and the funeral, she showed no sign of it.

'I'll leave you two now.' Stephen wiped his lips on his napkin and wheeled himself away from the table once the baked apples and custard had been eaten. 'Tell Jackson to come in about ten to help me into bed.'

As the door slammed behind him, Charity looked to her grandmother hopefully.

'I'm sorry, Charity,' Grandmother said softly. She got up from the table and stacked the dirty dishes on to a trolley. 'My son isn't the easiest man to live with at any time, but I hadn't expected him to be quite so terse with you.'

'He doesn't like me, does he?' Charity's lips trembled, wishing she dared ask if she could phone Aunt Lou.

The old lady pushed the trolley towards the door that led to the kitchen, rolled it through, then closed the door firmly behind her. She came back and put her hand on Charity's shoulder.

'It isn't a question of likes or dislikes,' she said in a low tone.

Charity heard the trolley being wheeled away and it crossed her mind that it was no wonder the big woman who prepared the meal looked so sullen if no one ever thanked her or even spoke to her.

'Quite honestly, Charity, it might've been better if he'd remained in ignorance of you all. It's upset him a great deal.'

'We don't have to be a burden to him,' Charity said timidly. 'Uncle Geoff is happy to have us.'

Grandmother sat down next to Charity and looked right into her eyes.

'That isn't this family's way.' She sighed, her faded

75

blue eyes tinged with sympathy. 'We are strong on duty. To my son that means he must see you all get a good education and start in life. Unfortunately Stephen has decided that Mr Charles is what he calls a "lefty". He feels you will all be indoctrinated by his ideals.'

Charity didn't understand what 'lefty' meant. She assumed it meant Uncle Geoff's gentleness, his aversion to corporal punishment, to public schools and indeed the armed forces.

'Don't let him take the little ones away,' she begged her grandmother. 'Mr and Mrs Charles are kind, and all three of them are so happy and settled there. I can get a job and when I'm big enough I'll look after them.'

'Charity, my dear – ' Isobel Pennycuick was torn now between loyalty to her son and a surge of unexpected tenderness for her motherless grandchildren – 'you are only fifteen. If you were twenty-one things might be different.'

She wished she could explain how confused she had felt when she heard of her daughter's death. Grief and guilt had been tormenting her ever since she'd received the news of the fire.

'Is he thinking of bringing them here?' Charity was aghast.

'Now don't be silly.' Grandmother laughed lightly. 'You've seen how things are. We couldn't possibly look after small children. No, he's more keen to find homes where each one of them would get a chance in life.'

'Split them up?' The room seemed to spin. Charity could hardly believe she was hearing this.

'My dear.' Her grandmother put one cool hand on Charity's chin and lifted her face up to hers. 'I can't promise anything just now. Ideally we'd like them to stay together. But it's like finding good homes for

76

puppies. How many people could care for three bois-
terous dogs and train them all?'

'But they aren't puppies, they're children who love
one another. We're a family, Grandmother, and we
must stay together. Can't you make him see that?'

'I doubt I could ever make him see anything my
way,' she said tartly. 'My husband brought Stephen
up to believe women were put on this earth to serve,
not to have opinions. He feels it is his duty to give all
four of you the advantages he had as a boy.'

Charity lay in the high narrow bed too upset to sleep.
It was quiet in Clapham, but here the absolute silence
was eerie. Back there a small light was always left on
out on the landing, she could hear Prue's breathing
and the comforting sound of passing cars. It was so
dark here she felt crushed by it. She needed to go to
the lavatory but she was too scared to get out of the
safety of her bed.

Moving away from Greenwich and learning from
books had made her far more aware of a bigger world
and all the opportunities out there waiting for them
all. But she still couldn't understand why Uncle
Stephen thought more disruption in the children's
lives would benefit them.

Uncle Geoff would see all three of them got a good
education. Auntie Lou would see they had good manners and bring them up to be truthful and honest.
What was it that Uncle Stephen was suggesting about
these nice people anyway?

Anxiety deepened as the days went slowly past.
Exploring the house and grounds, both alone and
with her grandmother, brought some measure of
excitement to alleviate the feeling of oppression, but
Charity felt as if she was under close scrutiny, being
tested for something.

77

Studley Priory was a house so steeped in history, so far removed from anything in her experience that she couldn't fail to be enthralled. Aside from the lawns being cut, the grounds had been sadly neglected. Bushes grew out through the stable roof, a walled garden was choked with weeds, yet there were signs everywhere of how gracious it had once been. Rotting saddles still hung in the stables and there was a whiff of gleaming hunters and a ghostly ring of hooves on the mud-covered cobbled floor.

Winding corridors, dusty rooms packed with treasures from all corners of the globe . . . On her first morning she saw the old library beyond the drawing room that Uncle Stephen had as his room and marvelled at the wall-to-wall old leatherbound books, his collection of guns, knives and a huge mock battleground where he manoeuvred a vast collection of lead soldiers to re-enact famous battle scenes. Beyond this room there was the shut-up north wing. She saw the octagonal chapel, still with a small altar and pews and looked at the immense family bible. Here she traced her ancestors, some of whom had as many as eight children, until the last entry, which was her mother's birth and subsequent christening back in 1921.

A picture formed in her head when she saw how far the nursery suite was from her grandparents' rooms in the main wing, of a child shut away with nursemaids and governesses, perhaps only presented to her mother and father for a few minutes a day. Was this why Charity had been relegated to nursemaid almost as soon as her brothers and sister were born?

Charity learned from her grandmother that the only staff now left were Ellen who cooked their meals, Jackson who should by rights be retired, one gardener and a couple of women who came in from the village to clean. There was also a nurse who came in from time to time to bath Stephen. No scurrying maids in those attic rooms, no grooms or butler; not even a live-in housekeeper.

But though Charity was happy to clean silver, to sweep down the cobwebs in the shut-up rooms and help Jackson with some weeding, she couldn't like her uncle.

Grandmother was changeable. Sometimes she was warm, sometimes frosty, but Charity felt that with time they might become closer. But Uncle Stephen treated her with scorn, belittling every attempt she made to please him. He rapped her knuckles for picking up the wrong cutlery, sneered at her few questions and his piggy eyes followed her every movement with suspicion.

Charity was aware he couldn't do much for himself. Getting him in and out of bed or to and from his chair involved a great deal of huffing and puffing and shouting at both Jackson and her grandmother. But she'd seen him wheel himself into the bathroom adjoining his room, so she assumed he used the toilet too. When Grandmother told her the district nurse couldn't make it that day and Uncle Stephen had to have an enema, it meant nothing to Charity. She assumed this meant some kind of injection, or even medicine.

'I know this is going to be difficult for you,' Grandmother said as she took a length of rubber tubing from a cabinet in his bathroom. 'But I need another pair of hands.'

She mixed up a soap solution and poured it into an enamel can, then attached the rubber tube to a nozzle.

Even then Charity didn't catch on, and Grandmother didn't attempt to explain.

Stephen was lying in bed like a great whale, wearing what seemed to be an old-fashioned nightshirt. The bed was similar to hospital beds that could be raised or lowered with a crank. It had canvas straps dangling at the sides which she'd heard were for strapping him in at night in case he fell out.

'We have to get him on to his side.' Grandmother approached Stephen, who gripped his mattress. 'Now when I get to three, roll him.'

Charity took her place by her uncle's shoulder and at the count of three heaved and pushed until she was presented with his broad back.

'Now just slide this under him.' Grandmother had a stiff rubber mat thing and as she pushed it against him, Uncle Stephen managed to lift himself a little with his elbow.

The horror started as Grandmother pulled back his nightshirt to reveal his bottom and what was left of his legs.

His bottom was huge, white and flabby, covered in wiry hair. In contrast, his thighs were wasted away, little thicker than Charity's own and the stumps were an angry red, hideously puckered, resembling crudely made sausages.

Grandmother sat on the bed beside him and moved his thighs up into a crouching position. Charity got a glimpse of a red anus and hairy testicles. Suddenly she understood where the tube was going.

'Hurry up, woman,' he grunted churlishly, thankfully unable to see the disgust on Charity's face. 'It's bad enough without you taking all day about it.'

'Hold the can,' Grandmother said sharply, indicating that Charity should pick it up from the small trolley. 'Come closer, it won't stretch that far. When I tell you, turn on that little tap.'

Charity had to stare, even though she wanted to vomit, as Grandmother pushed the hard nozzle on the end of the tube into her son. 'Turn the tap on now,' she ordered.

Uncle Stephen was making the most horrible noises,

a cross between grunting and heavy breathing, and the mountain of flesh in front of her was quivering.

It seemed like hours that she stood there holding the can aloft. She wanted to cry, she was so embarrassed and disgusted.

'Look inside the can. Tell me when the water's gone right down.' Grandmother's slender fingers held the nozzle in his anus.

'There's about an inch left,' Charity told her in a shaking voice.

'Turn the tap off, then.'

She did as she was told, averting her eyes as the tube was pulled out of his bottom and excess liquid dabbed up with a towel. Alone, Grandmother pulled her son on to his back again, quickly covering his nakedness.

'Right, dear.' She patted Stephen's fat stomach. 'Up now!'

Charity thought for a moment her task was finished. Her uncle gripped the mattress either side of him and with his mother pushing at him, he hoisted himself to a sitting position. But to her horror it didn't end there. Stephen was pushing hard on his hands either side of the bed, looking expectantly at her.

'The bedpan,' Grandmother barked, nodding towards the china receptacle on the bottom of a trolley beside the bed. 'As I help lift him, you slide it under him.'

Charity did as she was told, too shocked to refuse, and as Grandmother put her arms round her son's middle and strained to lift him, she slid it across the bed. A glimpse of her uncle's flaccid penis hanging beneath him made Charity gasp.

'Not that way,' Grandmother snapped. 'Can't you see the way it's pointed at one end? That goes to the front.'

81

'Hurry up, for God's sake, if you don't want shit all over the place,' her uncle bellowed.

Charity pushed it under him, closing her eyes in nausea. But the nightmare was by no means over. As they moved back, the most hideous, farting, squelching noise came from him, bringing with it an evil smell.

'We'll leave him now till he's finished,' Grandmother said quite calmly as if they were discussing a child on his pot, not a grown man spewing out two pints of noxious fluid into a bedpan and grunting with obvious satisfaction. 'Ring when you want me,' she added to her son.

Charity couldn't get out fast enough. She rushed to the open back door by the still room and took great gasps of clean air.

'Not very nice, is it?' Grandmother said grimly behind her. 'Sometimes I think it would've been better if he'd died of his injuries.'

Charity looked round and saw bitterness on the old lady's face.

'I used to give him opening medicine,' she continued, her mouth a thin line of disgust. 'But he messed his bed and trousers so often that I resorted to this. Well, what else can I do?'

Charity said nothing. She wouldn't want to clear that sort of mess either, especially for someone who showed no affection or even appreciation of all his mother did for him, but just the same she couldn't help feeling there had to be a less disgusting way of dealing with a necessary bodily function.

Charity picked up the duster she'd left when Grandmother had asked her to help and continued polishing the Chinese drinks cabinet. Grandmother sat on the settee, staring into space.

'What was he like before he was wounded?' Charity wanted something attractive or romantic in her mind rather than that vision of his huge flabby belly hanging over his stumps.

'Very handsome.' Grandmother turned her head towards Charity, half smiling as if glad of a diversion. 'Everything you'd expect of an officer – dashing, athletic, with lovely blond hair like yours. He was always a little pompous, mark you. Of course as his mother I didn't notice that so much then. Would you like to see a photograph?'

A disgusting smell wafted out from the direction of Stephen's room. Grandmother wrinkled her small nose distastefully, closed the door tightly and moved over to open one of the windows.

'I keep these tucked away,' she said, taking a leatherbound album out of a drawer in the desk. 'After he was wounded and Barbara left him, he couldn't bear to see them.'

'Barbara?' Charity asked.

'His wife,' Grandmother frowned. 'She skipped off the moment she knew he wasn't going to die. Always was a flibbertigibbet – no sense of duty. But there, wasn't he handsome?'

There was no resemblance to the monster in the study. This man was slender with the perfect features she associated with swashbuckling heroes of the screen. His hair was indeed as blond as her own and parted on one side. His eyes looked huge and a thin moustache gave him a dashing air. He was in full dress uniform, a silver chain with a whistle attached across his chest, shiny peaked cap tucked under one arm, a sword at his side.

'The jacket was green with black buttons.' Grandmother touched the faded photograph with obvious nostalgia. 'I try to remember him like this, but it isn't easy now.'

It was the first time Charity had felt a need to touch

83

her grandmother. She wanted to comfort her, yet felt that any physical contact would be rebuffed.

The bell rang loudly before she could study the picture further, or even comment. Grandmother hastily shoved the album back in the drawer, and patted Charity's shoulder in a gesture that indicated her understanding of how the girl felt.

'Don't worry. I'll get them out again,' she whispered. 'But now we have to finish off in there.'

It was even worse. Charity had to draw out the bedpan from beneath him and he was partially stuck to it. The smell was overpowering and she had to hold her breath and look away.

'Go and empty it, girl,' Uncle Stephen bellowed at her. 'I don't want you peering up my arse while she wipes it.'

It was almost full to the brim, and slopped as she walked. This time she couldn't hold back the nausea and as she emptied the pan into the lavatory she brought up her breakfast too.

'No Scrabble tonight, Charity, it's time we discussed the future.' Uncle Stephen moved his wheelchair till he was facing her. His face seemed even more bloated tonight, a sly look in his small, sharp eyes. 'We thought the beginning of September would be a good time for you to come back permanently.'

As his words growled out, Charity felt as if someone had pulled a trapdoor open under her feet and she was falling into a pit.

She looked to her grandmother, hoping for some support, but Grandmother bent her head, afraid to meet her eyes.

'Permanently!' Charity looked at him in horror.

Stephen Pennycuick had no interest in female children and Charity had turned out to be much as

84

he'd expected, frail, skinny and timid. She did, however, have two unexpected attributes: his mother liked her and the girl wasn't afraid of hard work.

'Yes of course permanently.' He waved his hands in a gesture that said she had no choice in the matter. 'Your grandmother needs help, and there's nothing else for you.'

In that instant Charity knew this was what he'd always intended, this week hadn't been a holiday but a trial period and she had played right into his hands.

'I want to work with children,' she said in a small voice. 'It's kind of you to offer me a home, Uncle Stephen, but I'd be lonely here.'

'Bosh.' Stephen's fat face grew an even darker shade of purple. 'You'll have too much to do to feel lonely. Besides the village is only down the road, you can visit Oxford.'

Charity had already discovered that the village of Studley-cum-Norton had nothing more than a post office. Even the bus into Oxford only ran once a day.

'But the children?' she blurted out. 'It's so far away from them!'

'They'll be away at boarding-schools soon,' he snapped. 'They don't need a nursemaid at their age.'

Charity sensed she was edging towards a trap, the kind with steep sides she'd never get out of. She needed advice from Lou and Charles before she said another word.

'You won't mind if I think it over first?' she said more boldly than she felt. 'I didn't expect this.'

Stephen Pennycuick had never considered that females had minds of their own. They were there to be decorative, useful and to provide comfort for men. Two or three times in the week he'd been brought up sharply when he discovered this girl was actually quite bright.

'I suggest you think of your brothers and sister.'

His tone was oily, his words carefully chosen to frighten her. 'As their guardian I have the right to provide for them as I see fit. Any awkwardness from you and I might very well feel less amenable to them.'

The threat hung in the air. Charity looked across the room to her grandmother for support, but she was studying a book as if she couldn't hear or see anything. She was old and growing frail and although she wasn't cruel like her son, she was selfish.

Charity had learned from Ellen that staff, with the exception of Jackson, never stayed long. Grandmother wanted Charity as a companion, a nurse and a housekeeper, someone to take over when she was too old to cope.

As her son wheeled his chair round and made for the door, she allowed herself to look at Charity for the first time. 'Stephen has suffered greatly since he was wounded. He lost his legs and his wife and it's hardly surprising he's so bitter sometimes. Until his father died a few years ago, he didn't consider the future of Studley very much. But once he inherited it, all at once he realised what it stood for.'

Charity frowned, not understanding what she meant.

'His family were all brave, strong men,' Grandmother went on. 'For eight generations they've fought for their King and country and this house signifies their courage, fortitude and patriotism. Stephen saw himself and this house crumbling and he didn't know where to turn. All at once he can see fresh troops: the line isn't dead. All he has to do is make sure your oldest brother receives the right upbringing and education and Studley Priory can stay in the family for another few generations.'

'You mean Toby would own it one day?' Charity asked, hardly able to believe what she was hearing.

'Well provided he lives up to Stephen's expectations.'

'And Prue? What's he got in mind for her?'

'From what we understand she is very bright. Stephen intends her to go to a good school, to turn her into a lady of quality.'

'But if I say no, what then?' Charity couldn't bring herself to admit she considered Stephen spiteful enough to do something disastrous to all of them if she refused. 'Will it spoil it for Toby? And James is only a baby. What about him?'

'Stephen is a little hot-headed. He hasn't thought all this through yet. My suggestion is that he leaves all three of them with the Charleses for the time being, then once you're settled here and their schools are sorted out, they spend the holidays with us.'

That last evening, as she sat with her grandmother, Charity learned what had happened to her mother. Grandmother stated the facts in a cold, detached way, almost as if were talking about someone else's daughter, but Charity could see that dredging up the past cost her dear.

Though Stephen went away to Eton, followed by Sandhurst, Gwen's education had consisted of scratchy lessons with a governess. The summer of 1939 she was eighteen and left to her own devices because of the threatened war.

'All the male staff enlisted,' Grandmother explained. 'Jackson joined the brigadier as his batman. Even Miss Cody the governess left to offer herself as a nurse. When Rory Calhoun came by one day and offered his services I was delighted. The house and grounds were becoming terribly neglected and able-bodied men were much in demand.'

Charity sat very still on the bed. She wanted to

picture the scene and find the missing piece in what she knew of her mother.

'The man was an Irish gypsy,' Grandmother said. 'He had been turned down for active service because of an old injury to his leg, though aside from a slight limp I could see nothing wrong with him. At the time I saw him as a godsend: groom, gardener, plumber, carpenter and chauffeur, he handled it all. Henry held him in very high regard, even gave him a room above the stables. It never occurred to him that the man would seduce his daughter.'

'Mother fell in love with him?' Charity had read enough romantic books to identify with a happy black-haired Irishman, even if she was too young to understand about first love.

'But why wouldn't you let Mother marry him if he was nice?'

'Oh Charity! Your grandfather was an officer and a gentleman. It just wasn't done. Gwen was an innocent trusting girl who was taken in by a charming wastrel.'

'But poor Mother – was she very upset?'

'She ran off! We sent her to some relatives in Sussex once we'd dismissed Calhoun, but she never arrived. Henry refused even to try and find her. As he pointed out, there was a war going on and he didn't want her shaming the family further.'

'When did you see Mother again, then?' Charity asked. She had a strong feeling her grandmother was only telling her part of the story.

'Not until '44. It was chaos here. Bitterly cold. What with rationing and no help in the house it wasn't very welcoming. On top of that the house had been requisitioned by the military, so there were strange men coming and going at all hours. I was in bed with influenza when Gwen just arrived out of the blue with your father, Bertram, in tow and informed me they were getting married.'

88

'Did you like my father?'

Isobel Pennycuick gave her granddaughter an odd look, as if she wondered what had prompted the question.

'I was impressed by him,' she said. 'He was a handsome man, big and strong with a beautiful speaking voice. But he made me nervous. He was too forceful, too opinionated.'

She couldn't bring herself to tell Charity the whole truth; not now, not ever. Gwen had become a different person in her long absence. The old Gwen had been vibrant and confident, could ride as well as any man, dance, sing and charm anyone. But that pretty daredevil was gone. In her place was a clean but shabbily dressed woman, her hair scraped back in a tight bun, looking much older than a twenty-three-year-old. The old Gwen had gone for ever.

'Why did she have to marry Father? Couldn't she have got a job somewhere?'

The old lady hesitated. It was a golden opportunity to warn her granddaughter against the dangers of tasting the sweetness of first love without the security of marriage. Something worse than losing Rory Calhoun had robbed her daughter of her looks and youth.

Charity picked up the picture of her mother that had been taken at her uncle's wedding. She felt unbearably saddened by the fact that such a happy, pretty girl should grow up to become the defeated, bitter woman she remembered. 'I wish she'd told me about all this. I shan't ever keep secrets from my children.'

'You might.' Isobel Pennycuick caught hold of her granddaughter's hand tightly. 'You'll understand that one day. None of us goes through life without being ashamed of something.'

It was the first time she'd touched Charity since the girl had arrived.

Chapter Five

'How could that old bastard make her help give him an enema?' Lou ranted to Geoff. 'I suspected he was a pervert!'

Charity had told Geoff most of the tale about her stay with her uncle during the ride home from the station but it was heavily censored for the benefit of the children. Later she spilled out the whole story.

It was raining heavily, as it had been all day, but in the den it was cosy, the curtains drawn and a large jigsaw Lou had been doing with the children left out on the table.

'I hate the man without even meeting him.' Geoff moved from a seat at the table and flung himself down beside his wife on the settee. 'I don't like any of his ideas, but most of all I despise his plans for Charity.'

Lou had a really bad feeling about Stephen Penny-cuick. It seemed to her this man was seeing the children as lumps of clay he could mould as he chose, without any thought to their needs, personalities or talents. Although at the moment Charity was their prime concern, Toby was another problem area.

As the months had passed it had become clear that Toby was a little disturbed. He was sneaky, told lies and on several occasions Lou had suspected he stole pennies from her purse. Worse still in her eyes was his tendency to bully other children. He seemed to look for weakness and then prey on it.

Yet however much they felt for all four children, they had no choice but to comply with the colonel's wishes. He was their legal guardian and to go against him would only jeopardise the future of the entire family.

'We'll have to move fast,' she said. 'Find Charity a job he can't argue about.'

'But what?'

'It would have to be a live-in one.'

'A school?' Geoff raised one eyebrow. 'Under-housekeeper, assistant matron or something? We could suggest it was good training for her.'

'If we side with Charity, he might take the others away,' she said in a weak voice. 'What do we do, Geoff?'

Geoff pondered the question for a moment, stroking his wife's neck comfortingly.

'There's no guarantee he'll let us keep them anyway,' he said at length. 'But if we didn't try to protect Charity's interests, we'd never forgive ourselves.'

'I'm not so worried about Prue,' Lou said. 'A good school and an upper-class environment wouldn't do her any harm.'

Geoff smiled. Neither of them had any doubt that Prue would pass her eleven-plus with flying colours. She liked order and nice things, gravitated to those children at school who came from good homes. She was anxious to have ballet and piano lessons and expressed a strong dislike for all things 'common'. The truth was, she was a little snob and at heart she was very much a Pennycuick. If she knew her uncle was intending to turn her into 'a lady', she would heartily approve.

'It might turn out all right for Toby too,' Geoff said reluctantly. 'You know my views on public schools,

91

but he'd probably relish it – all that sport and plenty of male company.'

'But the holidays?' Lou pulled a face. 'I bet that stupid man hasn't even thought of that! Toby's a little rascal and he needs love and stability. A bully of an uncle is hardly a good role model!'

Geoff patted her hand.

'Let's concentrate on Charity first,' he suggested. 'Who knows, he might lose interest in the others when he's had a chance to think about it.'

'Pigs might fly!' Lou said darkly.

'It looks a nice place!' Charity studied the Bowes Court school prospectus intently. It was in Heathfield, Sussex, a part of England she'd been told was very lovely. The photographs showed a splendid mansion set in acres of playing fields and it had a reputation for being a fine, if lesser-known, public school for boys. 'But what would I do there?'

'They are looking for a kitchen maid.' Geoff smiled reassuringly. 'That doesn't sound very thrilling, but the vicar's niece worked there for a year and she loved it. You'd be helping the cook, laying tables, all the things you help us with here, only on a bigger scale. There's other staff for company, you'll have a nice room and long holidays you can spend with us. If you continue to study, in a year or two's time you'll be able to move on to something better.'

Charity was nervous about working anywhere and the thought of having to leave the Charleses' home was terrifying. But this was a better prospect than working for Uncle Stephen, and she trusted Geoff's judgement.

'When can I go for an interview?' she said in a tremulous voice.

'I'll ring now.' Geoff smiled encouragingly. 'Don't

worry, I'll take you down there. We aren't just going to abandon you.'

Geoff went off to this study to telephone the school, but his heart was still heavy. Charity had been back from her uncle's for two weeks now and he knew she was still brooding about it.

Miss Downes, whom they thought they could count on, had taken the colonel's side. In fact she described Charity's reluctance to live with her uncle as 'ingratitude' and stated quite bluntly that she believed the girl was being malicious towards him.

In another child Geoff might have suspected this too, but Charity was very honest and the kind of detail she'd given them was too clear to be anything but the truth. Evidently Colonel Pennycuick had charmed the social workers, and suggested she was incapable of earning her own living. Now Charity had to prove she was.

'I didn't expect it to be as lovely as this,' Charity said breathlessly as Geoff drove in through huge wrought-iron gates and up the long gravel drive. 'It looks like a palace, not a school.'

Lush green playing fields surrounded the I-shaped house, with a tower at each end. Mullioned windows twinkled in the bright sunshine and brightly coloured flowers cascaded over two huge urns on either side of steps up to a vast studded front door.

'Well it was a home to the Bowes family for three hundred years before it became a school,' Geoff told her. Charity's mood on the drive from London had swung between sheer terror and excitement and he wished he could find the right words to soothe her anxiety. 'Now all you have to remember is that it is a school. They are used to young people and they won't be cruel to you. It may seem huge and scary, but it's run just like any other household.'

93

He glanced round at Charity as he drove past the front of the school towards the side door Mr Alderton the head had directed him to. She looked so small and vulnerable in the navy blue suit Lou had bought her for this interview. Her knees sticking out from the straight skirt were thin and childlike and her white blouse too severe for one so young; even her hair tied back with a ribbon at the nape of her neck merely accentuated her tender years.

'It must need dozens of people to look after it,' she whispered in awe. 'It's even bigger than Studley!'

'You'll find it's better run. Most of the domestic staff come in from the village,' Geoff said. 'I shouldn't fancy the job as groundsman, though. Imagine if Lou sent me out to cut all that grass!'

Charity laughed. Auntie Lou was always badgering him to cut their lawn, and compared to this it was nothing.

'Imagine me cooking bacon and eggs for two hundred boys,' she retorted. 'I hope I don't have to peel all the spuds on my own!'

A slender grey-haired lady in a dark blue uniform and stiffly starched cap came out of a semi-basement door and up a few steps to greet them as Geoff stopped the car. She had a severe face, with a chin that disappeared into her neck, and the kind of bright, dark eyes that suggested she missed nothing.

'You must be Miss Stratton,' she smiled as she came forward. 'I'm Miss Hawkins, the school housekeeper. Do come in, I trust you had a pleasant drive down?'

Uncle Geoff thrust out his hand. 'Geoffrey Charles,' he said, shaking the housekeeper's firmly. 'Would you prefer to speak to Miss Stratton alone? I could wait out here.'

'That won't be necessary.' Miss Hawkins held out her hand to Charity. 'I'm sure you'd prefer your uncle to stay, wouldn't you? May I call you Charity?'

She ushered them back down the steps and through a huge deserted kitchen. 'It's not usually like this.' She smiled. 'This is the hub of the whole school during term time. Sheer bedlam.'

Charity noticed the grease-free pale blue walls, the spotless tiled floor, vast cooker and two big sinks in an adjoining room. Afternoon sunshine came in at the windows, and despite its size the kitchen had a homely look.

Miss Hawkins led them through an arched door into a stone-flagged lobby.

'I'll show you round a bit later, but for now I think tea in my office will suffice while we have a little chat.'

Charity lost her bearings almost immediately as they were led up a narrow plain wooden staircase, and down a corridor past umpteen doors. There was complete silence everywhere and although Miss Hawkins explained that a skeleton staff was still here cleaning up now the boys had gone home, they neither saw nor heard anyone.

'It's like a rabbit warren,' Miss Hawkins said cheerfully. 'Staircases and doors all over the place. I was enchanted with it from my first day here over twenty years ago.'

The office was a bright sunny room at the back, overlooking the quadrangle with steps down on to the playing fields. In the distance Charity could see a wall; beyond that were woods and farmland. The office was furnished with only a desk and a few chairs, yet the walls were covered in shelves holding everything from cans of cleaning materials to recipe books, and even a few sad-looking soft toys.

Miss Hawkins followed Charity's glance.

'Left behind by boys that outgrew them,' she smiled. 'I can't bring myself to throw them out. Now do sit down, Carol our other maid will bring up the tea shortly.'

She outlined the duties expected of Charity: helping prepare meals, cleaning the refectory between meals, washing up, laying tables and generally helping with anything that needed doing.

'We work it on a rota system,' she explained. 'Some days you will start work early and go right through till after lunch, with the rest of the day off. Others you will start at noon and work through the afternoon until supper. You will have a regular day off once a week, but these can be arranged sometimes so you have two together; then you can go home if you so wish. I have a curfew for my younger staff of ten. If for any reason you wish this to be extended, or you wish to have a night away, you must ask my permission.'

They were interrupted by the girl Carol coming in with the tea. Aged around eighteen, she was a buxom, fresh-faced girl with a mop of red curly hair, wearing a blue and white striped overall. She put the tray of tea down on the desk and smiled at Charity with obvious interest.

'This is Carol Lomas,' Miss Hawkins introduced them. 'Should you decide to come, she will show you the ropes and I hope you will become friends. How long have you been with us, Carol?'

'Two years, ma'am, come this September.' She had an engaging accent that Charity didn't recognise, and sparkling brown eyes.

'Carol, like most of the domestic staff, is cleaning up now after the boys. Next week she will be going home for the rest of the holidays. Where is home, Carol? It's slipped my memory.'

'Newton Abbot, ma'am.'

'Thank you Carol.' Miss Hawkins dismissed her. 'I

may call you later to show Charity the staff rooms if I don't have time for the full tour.'

Charity realised that Uncle Geoff had told Miss Hawkins a great deal about her, for she asked few personal questions. Instead she asked her about what books she liked, and her ambitions.

'Nursing or looking after children,' Miss Hawkins said thoughtfully. 'Well being here might change your mind about the latter. But at seventeen you can apply to a hospital or even a nursery nursing college. Now, how do you feel about the position? Have you any questions?'

'I'd like to work here, please,' Charity replied quickly. 'Do I have to wear a uniform?'

'An overall, cap and apron.' Miss Hawkins smiled at her eagerness. 'I'll kit you out on arrival. Sensible, flat shoes and your hair tied back at all times when you are working. Your salary will start at four pounds ten shillings a week for a trial period of one term. That of course includes your room and board. If you are considered suitable, this will be raised then.'

'It's wonderful, Uncle Geoff,' Charity trilled as they drove back out of the gates. She'd seen her little room up on the top floor, with Carol right next to her. She'd seen the classrooms, the refectory, the kitchens and staff-rooms and although her head was swimming with it all she was so excited she couldn't wait to start in September.

'It sounds like quite hard work,' Geoff reminded her. 'Those huge pans and trays of food looked pretty heavy to me.'

'I'm sure no one will be like Uncle Stephen,' Charity giggled. 'I've had plenty of training with grumpy, difficult people.'

She really liked Carol. She said she was glad Charity was young because they could spend their spare time together. She also said the cook Mrs Cod was a witch, but Miss Hawkins was 'fair enough', but as long as she did her job properly it was quite a 'cushy number'.

'I don't want you to go away,' Prudence whined as Charity folded her clothes into her case. 'I'll miss you so much.'

Charity looked round at her sister and smiled affectionately. Prue's moods were mercurial: only yesterday she had said she couldn't wait to have the room to herself.

'Now Prue,' Charity reproved her. 'With all the homework you'll get at the grammar school you won't have time to miss me.'

'But it won't be the same without you here,' Prue sniffed. 'Who will I tell about school and things?'

Charity half smiled. Prue was entirely self-centred. Since hearing she'd passed her eleven-plus her conversation had rarely moved away from herself. She had taken to reading boarding-school books and peppered her speech with words like 'super' and 'frightfully'. Not once had she shown any real interest in Charity's job at Bowes Court. When she wasn't sniping at Toby for being untidy or noisy, she was continually admiring herself in the mirror. Toby had attempted to cut off her plaits as an act of revenge, and although Auntie Lou had scolded him she privately admitted to Charity that it would have served Prue right for being so insufferable.

'You can write and tell me everything.' Charity sat on the bed beside her sister and drew her into her arms. 'I shan't forget you. I'll write back and I'll be home at Christmas. I'll have money of my own then. I'll be able to take you shopping and to the pictures and we'll have so much to talk about.'

Charity was anxious to get going. Each time she looked at the children she wanted to cry, she loved them so much. The thought of not being able to kiss them goodnight, to tuck them in and read them stories filled her with dread. They were too young to understand what work meant. They couldn't possibly imagine how scared she was, or how lonely it would be without them around. But to tell them would only put sad thoughts in their heads.

'Just think, Prue, in a few years I could come back to London and find a flat where we can all live together. You make sure you work hard at school now and make me proud of you.'

She had no doubt Prue would do well; she was too bright, too determined, to do anything else. But Charity had a sinking feeling that once Prue mixed with girls from wealthier homes she wouldn't want to admit her sister was a kitchen maid.

Toby slunk round the door. His gloomy face showed he too was worrying. He had grown tall during the summer, had a spray of freckles across his nose from being outside all the time, and his knees were scabby from the many tumbles he took.

Charity reached out for him too and sat on the bed with one arm round each of them.

Subtle changes in all three of them made them less alike now. The white-blond hair and bright blue eyes were the only common denominator. Prue had put on weight and the extra flesh made her face seem flatter and rather bland. Toby showed a remarkable similarity to the pictures of Uncle Stephen as a young man now; a less severe haircut and a golden glow suggested he would become a very handsome man. But of all three, Charity's transformation was most marked. Her slender body had gentle curves where once had been straight lines, and her anxious look was replaced by wide-eyed interest. Her hair shone like a bolt of white satin; sunshine, fresh air and good food had filled the hollows in her face, turning her into a very pretty girl.

'Remember I love you,' she whispered, fighting back tears. 'You'll be in my thoughts all the time. Try to be nice to one another and look out for James. If you feel sad, remember what it was like back in Greenwich and how lucky we've been.'

She knew they would perk up when she'd gone. Toby would go out and play football, Prue would play with her dolls and pester Auntie Lou to join her in a play tea party. In September they would be back at school and other things and people would fill up the hole she'd left.

'Will you think about us?' Toby whispered. He wasn't usually soppy, going through each day without a backward glance and considering nothing deeper than the next meal.

'All the time,' she assured him. 'Each time I see a little blond boy or girl I'll wish I could cuddle you. I'll look at your pictures each night and kiss you. I promise faithfully I'll write every week and every chance I get I'll be back to see you.'

'Are you taking that with you?' Toby pointed to an empty toffee tin shaped like a London bus.

'No, I haven't got room for it,' she replied.

'Can I have it then?' he asked, suddenly brightening up. 'I could keep my enamel paints in it.'

The quick change of mood was typical of Toby and very reassuring.

'OK.' Charity handed it to him. She wanted to remind him that just because she was leaving, that didn't mean she wouldn't care whether he was naughty or not. But warnings about telling lies and being sneaky might make him think she didn't trust him.

'Anything you want, Prue?' she asked.

'Could I have that charm bracelet?'

Charity didn't hesitate: she undid the clasp and handed the bracelet to her sister. It wasn't real silver and it had only come from Woolworth's, but it had taken three weeks of pocket money to buy it and it made her feel grown-up.

'Fancy asking for that,' Toby said indignantly. 'Charity loves it!'

'Not as much as I love Prue.' Charity fastened it round her sister's wrist. 'Just don't lose it.'

They were off then, racing down the stairs, all thought of her forgotten. Charity went back to her packing.

Auntie Lou had bought her so many new clothes. The smart navy suit for the interview, then a raincoat with a furry lining. There was a whole pile of pretty underwear, including three teen bras. Even now they were hardly necessary, but Charity had been touched that Lou considered an emotional need more important than a physical one. She had a pencil skirt, three new sweaters and the sensible shoes Miss Hawkins had insisted on. She buried those at the bottom of the case because she didn't like them. They were very comfortable brown ones but she'd really wanted a pair of winklepickers.

But then, she could buy what she liked with her wages. She could have four-inch heels, her hair done at the hairdresser's in a beehive, and she could wear makeup all the time if she wanted to.

She put the new diary into her case. This was Uncle Geoff's gift to her. It would last for five years and he said she must write down her thoughts every day so she could look back on it when she was an old lady.

'Imagine all those first times to record,' he'd said with a twinkle in his eye. 'Your first wages and what you spent them on. The first kiss, the first alcoholic drink. Five years from now you might be married with a child on the way. You'll have spurned dozens of suitors, broken as many hearts. But if you write down your feelings, all your little worries, joys and moments of sadness, it will end up like a glorious tapestry for you to look back on with pleasure.'

Auntie Lou bought her a little travelling alarm clock, as always the more practical of the pair.

There was a small bible from the vicar, a manicure set from Auntie Lou's friend Josie, and a sewing kit from Mrs Howard who lived next door.

Uncle Stephen had replied to her letter telling him about her job with just the kind of vindictive sneering she'd expected.

> You've made your choice, though to me it appears a remarkably shortsighted and selfish one. I hope when you are washing floors and scraping plates you think now and then of the gracious life I offered you at Studley Priory. Under the circumstances I feel unable to offer you any further support and I have informed Mr and Mrs Charles that they are to relinquish any further responsibility for you.

Charity had felt very scared when she read the letter, but both Lou and Geoff reassured her that it only meant he wouldn't be sending them any money for her keep in future. They insisted that as far as they were concerned, this would still be her home. But Charity couldn't get rid of the dark thoughts in her head. She had overheard Geoff talking to her uncle on the phone and from what she'd picked up, he was very angry with her. Would he retaliate by taking the children away from here? If he stopped her seeing them altogether she couldn't bear it.

'All packed?' Lou put her head round the bedroom door.

'Just about.' Charity lifted the case to the floor. 'I've got a great deal more than I came with, haven't I?'

'None of that's important.' Lou came closer and put an arm round Charity's shoulder. She tapped her on the head. 'It's what we've put in here and in your heart that counts. No one can take that away.'

Charity moved round to lean her head against Lou's shoulder. She wound her arms round Lou's slender waist. 'I love you both,' she said.

She had always told the children she loved them, but this was the first time she felt able to say it to an adult.

Lou was feeling unreasonably emotional. She had said goodbye to so many children over the years, and most she knew she'd never see again. It didn't help to know that Charity would be home for the holidays.

Charity looked up and was stunned to see tears on the older woman's cheeks.

'Silly, isn't it?' Lou brushed them away quickly. 'I never cry and anyone would think you were going to the other side of the world. But then it never hurts to show your true feelings.'

Charity buried her face closer into Lou's bony, flat chest. 'Don't let the children forget me, will you?'

'They won't ever forget you, silly goose.' She forced herself to smile. 'You've stamped yourself in their hearts my darling. Nothing can ever erase that.'

'Well this is it.' Uncle Geoff lifted her case into the luggage rack. 'Now one last hug before I have to get off.'

Victoria Station was frantically busy. The first of September, and most of the people seemed to be returning from holidays with bulging suitcases. Strange crackling voices over a Tannoy which seemed to be in a foreign language, newspaper men shouting, the sound of trains chugging in and out. Children

103

yelling, babies crying, businessmen and women shoppers all pushing and shoving their way through the crowds of people who just stood watching the arrival and departure boards crank over.

The train was filling up rapidly. The empty compartment Uncle Geoff had found for her would soon be as full as the rest.

'Don't be too hard on yourself,' Geoff said with forced jollity. 'Spend your wages recklessly, have fun in your spare time and don't take yourself too seriously. I want to hear some good descriptions of everyone. If I get a letter that says, "Nothing to tell you much" I won't write back. I expect a warts-and-all rundown on everything.'

'You'll have to get off.' Charity lifted her face and kissed his cheek just above his beard. 'Thank you for everything, Uncle Geoff!'

'It's me who should be thanking you,' he replied, and his gaze faltered. 'You and your family have given Lou and me such a lot. You'll be constantly in our thoughts.'

Chapter Six

'Haven't you finished those pans yet?' Mrs Cod barked at Charity through the scullery door.

Charity was exhausted: not just tired but dead on her swollen feet. It was almost two in the afternoon but she still had a huge pile of cutlery to dry and put away before she could climb up the stairs and lie down on her bed.

Her back ached from leaning over the sink, her head throbbed and her hands were so sore it was agony to keep them in hot water.

It had seemed a perfect job at first – polishing floors, making beds and cleaning windows, in preparation for the boys' arrival back at school for the new year. But the honeymoon period had been brief. The real job wasn't chatting and laughing with Carol as she found her way around an empty school. It wasn't about doing tasks she found rewarding; it was a nightmare of endless drudgery.

Before the first of the flashy cars came rolling into the drive, bringing two hundred boys to fill those rows of empty beds, Charity discovered the meaning of real work.

All the bread was made at the school and though there was a machine for mixing and kneading, the dough had to be put into tins. Huge slabs of cake needed fruit to be picked over and washed. Then there were the mountains of vegetables every day.

Potatoes were peeled in a machine, but all the other vegetables had to be done by hand.

It seemed as if no sooner was one meal over than another began, day in day out relentlessly.

Charity, in her junior position, didn't actually cook anything; she was just the chopper, mixer, washer-up, collector of ingredients from the store rooms and the one who cleared and wiped down the long tables after the boys had finished eating.

She didn't have time even to glance out of the window. The boys in their blue blazers, grey flannel shorts and striped ties were nothing but an incessant noise in the background.

She heard their feet on the big oak staircase beyond the staff wing, but her world was the scullery, where she stood at the big stainless-steel sinks, scouring huge pots, baking trays, mountains of dinner plates and cutlery. The window in front of her looked out on to the dustbins and a brick wall. Through the door, Mrs Cod presided over the kitchen. A sometimes terrifying place, shrouded in steam, hot with the many gas burners going all at once and blasts of extra fierce heat each time the ovens were opened to haul out huge meat pies, apple crumble and treacle tarts.

Charity had the greatest respect for Mrs Cod. Anyone who could roll out enough pastry for two hundred hungry boys, yet glaze the pies and decorate them with fancy leaves to make them look nice, deserved a medal. She ran the kitchen with military precision, judging quantities with her eagle eye, bellowing out orders to her minions so that everything was ready to split-second timing.

A barrage of conversation came from the kitchen as the staff chopped, rolled and mixed: peals of laughter above the noise of the machines, jokes she was never included in. Salacious gossip, which halted whenever she appeared through the door, was the only way Charity knew she wasn't invisible.

The other women had their tea breaks together, often lounging on the steps outside the kitchen door, sharing cigarettes and more gossip, while she was excluded by the huge piles of washing-up dumped on the surface next to the sinks. The smell of cooking took away her appetite, the dirty plates strewn with leftovers made her feel nauseous.

'Charity, where are the rest of the knives? Haven't you washed those plates yet? I need those big saucepans. Do you call that clean?' were the sorts of comment that were flung at her. Up at six, ready to serve breakfast at half-past seven. At nine she got ten minutes sit down to eat her own breakfast, providing the scullery and kitchen were clear of dishes.

Scraping out burnt porridge with her fingernails from the bottom of pans. Two hundred eggcups and spoons which she didn't dare let one trace of egg stay on. No sooner had she eaten than it was time to haul in the vegetables from the store and start peeling.

Her blue nylon overall stuck to her body with sweat, her white cap slid down her forehead and, because of her slender shape, the huge white apron almost drowned her. Sometimes when she caught sight of her reflection she was reminded of Uncle Geoff discussing the plight of girls in service in Victorian times and wondered if he knew that things hadn't changed much.

At two-thirty, with her day's work done, she was always too tired to do anything but stagger up the stairs and lie down on her bed. When her shift changed to afternoons and evenings she'd foolishly thought this would be easier, but once again she was wrong. Maybe there weren't the vegetables to peel or the porridge pots to scour, but the workload was just as daunting. Huge piles of bread to be buttered, heavy teapots to be carried, cleaning the kitchen, scrubbing the floor, more washing-up from tea, then polishing and laying the tables in the refectory for breakfast the next day. Late at night found her crying with exhaustion and homesickness, wondering how she'd find the strength to face another day.

'Come on, girl, get those pots back in here!' Mrs Cod called out again. 'I'm going off now. Make sure you clean up before you go today. Yesterday you left an inch of scum round the sink.'

Charity picked up the pots and took them into the kitchen, reaching up to hang them on the hooks above the stove.

Mrs Cod already had her coat on, ready to go home to her cottage in the grounds. She was standing by the back steps with Pat, one of the part-time helpers from the village, both smoking, heads bent together as if chewing over some meaty bit of gossip.

Charity had found private names for each of the kitchen staff; planning letters about them to Lou and Geoff helped to ease the misery of the work. Mrs Cod she called the Fire-Eating Dragon. Dragon she certainly was, never satisfied with anything, and when she'd gone out to have a quick cigarette she came in with smoke billowing out through her nostrils. Pat she called the Viper, mainly because of her narrow face and stinging remarks. But Charity had discovered little about these two, or any of the other women, since term started, because she was always working alone and against the clock.

'What's that miserable look for?' Pat yelled in through the open door. 'It's enough to turn the milk sour!'

Charity turned away, blinded by sudden tears. They were all so horrid. Even Carol hadn't been near her since the boys came back, and no one had noticed how sore her hands were. How could she keep on writing cheerful letters to the children and Lou and Geoff? It was all very well people saying she would get used to hard work, but surely they had no conception of just how much she was supposed to do?

Carol was in the refectory laying the tables for tea as Charity limped by. Only occasionally did she have to take food to the refectory. The first time she had been so scared she had barely lifted her eyes off the floor.

It was a huge, oak-panelled room with low, small mullioned windows overlooking the drive. The boys sat at narrow refectory tables on forms in four long rows, with a member of staff at each who kept them under control.

A sea of faces, all seemingly staring at her, and when they moved to form a line to get their lunch, their vivid royal blue sweaters and grey trousers appeared like some huge centipede, bearing down on her.

Charity hesitated at the door, tempted to go and ask Carol's advice, but the lack of communication between them in the last couple of weeks daunted her. Carol was so outgoing, so full of fun and laughter . . . maybe she thought Charity was a drip?

Peeling off her overall, Charity lay down on her bed and closed her eyes. Her room was on the top floor of the tower, looking out across the quadrangle. She could hear the boys playing rugby and their shouting reminded her painfully of Toby.

Her hands throbbed and she lifted them up wearily. They were identical to those of the woman who used to run the baths at Greenwich: swollen and red with her fingernails broken. There were small lacerations on each of her fingertips and one on her thumb was oozing a mixture of blood and pus.

She missed the children so much she felt like a part of her had been torn off. For as long as she could remember they had been everything to her and without them she was empty. She missed Lou and Geoff too. For the six months in their house she'd felt secure. She missed all those discussions with them, the joy of just being like any other teenager, their warmth and laughter. Now there was only work, no one to care if she was tired. No one interested in her. Letters were the only link, read and reread, but only to find she was guilty of jealousy. Sometimes it smarted like her sore hands as she imagined Prue bounding home from school to tell Lou about her day, or Toby playing with friends on the Common. Who had ever cared how *she* did at school? She had never played like other children.

Was this how it would be for ever? Too tired to do anything but lie on a bed once she'd finished work. Just a kitchen maid at everyone's beck and call, with no life outside the scullery.

She had thought this room nice when she arrived. Now it looked like a prison cell with its iron bed and plain green walls. She had intended to explore Tunbridge Wells on her day off, buy some posters, but the room was just as impersonal now as it was when she moved in.

She must have fallen asleep, but woke later to find herself even more unhappy. She turned her face into the pillow and wept bitterly.

A tap on the door startled her, but before she could compose herself, it was opening.

'Coo-ee!' Carol called out. 'Fancy a cup of tea and a slice of cake?'

She was in the room too quickly for Charity to do more than try to dab at her face. Carol stopped short in the middle of the room, the tea and cake on a small tray in her hands.

'What on earth's the matter?' she said, her brown

eyes wide with astonishment. 'How long have you been like this?'

The sympathetic tone was enough to make the tears run even faster.

'I can't bear it here,' Charity sobbed. 'The work's so hard, I'm tired all the time and I miss home.'

'Is that all?' Carol laughed, but not unkindly. 'It's the commonest cry in this place. What you've got to learn is how to cope with it.'

'I can't. No one likes me. The women shout at me all the time.'

'They shout because the kitchen's noisy.' Carol sounded exasperated. 'They all think you're a nice little thing. The trouble is you take it so seriously.'

'I have to, Mrs Cod's on my back all day.'

'She isn't. She says you're the best maid she's ever had. But the more you do, Charity, the more they'll put on you, that's human nature.'

The bit of praise from the indomitable Mrs Cod was like a shaft of light coming into a dark tunnel, but still Charity couldn't stop crying.

'But all those pots, all those vegetables. If I didn't do them who would?'

A look of puzzlement and concern swept across Carol's pink and white face and her smile vanished.

'Are you trying to say you do it all alone?'

'Yes.' Charity raised a tear-stained face. She and Carol were on opposite shifts; the only time they saw one another was at a distance, when Carol went into the refectory to serve. 'I wash everything, don't you?'

'Not on my own, someone always helps me. Don't you ask?'

'No, I thought that was my job.'

'You silly pudding,' Carol laughed, her brown eyes twinkling. 'They must think they've died and gone to heaven since you came here. Are you stuck in the scullery all the time?'

'Mostly, except for getting the stores and cleaning the tables.'

'You do that too?' Carol's voice rose to a squeak of indignation. 'No wonder you're always asleep when I've finished work. I've looked round the door loads of times and you're always spark out.'

Carol had welcomed Charity's arrival. The last girl had been sullen and unfriendly and everyone had been glad when she left. In the first few days after the long holiday she had seen the small blonde girl as a potential friend and ally and had been baffled when Charity seemed to withdraw into her shell once the new term started.

Now she understood. This kid needed help and support and she felt a pang of remorse that she hadn't made sure the other women were being fair.

'The other staff are supposed to share that work with you,' she said, flushing with shame. 'If Miss Hawkins found out she'd be livid. But don't worry, I'll sort it out for you, Charity. Mrs Cod is a dragon, but she's fair and she likes you. Those cows from the village are taking advantage and it's got to stop. Let me look at your hands.'

Charity held them out.

'Good God!' Carol exhaled noisily. 'Don't you wear gloves for the washing-up?'

Charity shook her head. 'They're all too big, I'd drop the plates.'

'But they've got small ones in the store. Oh Charity, fancy getting yourself into this state and saying nothing.'

Carol got up and went into her room. She came back with a pot of handcream, opened the top and scooped out a dollop.

'Is that soothing?' she asked, rubbing it in with her big, capable hands. 'You must stand up for yourself, silly. This is the big adult world, we've got no mummies here to tell us what to do.'

Carol had a bright, perky nature. The middle one of six children she was as used to hard work as Charity had once been. The difference was that Carol wasn't afraid to speak out about anything and she was much stronger.

She was a big girl, at least five foot seven, with a sturdy body honed by farm work from an early age. Her curly hair couldn't be contained by her cap, her overall gaped in the front as if her bosom was trying to escape too and her wide hips had a seductive wiggle as she carried the trays of food from the kitchen to the refectory.

Now as she spoke with such warmth and understanding, Charity felt a real desire to become her friend.

The next day at twelve when Charity walked into the kitchen, there was a marked change in the atmosphere.

'Hallo, love!' Pat from the village yelled out. 'How's yer poor little hands today?'

There was no sarcasm in the question, just concern. Clearly Carol had spoken to them all. Mrs Cod asked to see Charity's hands and said she was just to help dish up the food into serving trays.

'People always take advantage if you let them,' she said, her plump shiny face bent over Charity. 'I'm sorry I didn't notice it was getting too much for you. I thought you was one of them as likes being on your own.'

'I didn't dare say anything,' Charity admitted. 'I thought that was the job.'

It was still hard work lifting heavy trays of food and stacking them on a heated trolley, but suddenly

113

she was part of what was going on in the kitchen and the women began to include her in their conversation.

In the days that followed Charity even felt a little guilty about describing Mrs Cod's body as a sack of blancmange to Geoff and Lou. Pat might have stringy greasy hair, a long nose and a sharp tongue, but she wasn't a viper. Poor Jill with the wide body and long arms shouldn't be nicknamed Orang-utan. After all, she couldn't help being simple.

Now Charity found out that Mrs Cod had been widowed at the start of the war, and had come here to work with her baby son, doing the very same job Charity was doing now. Her whole life was the school, and even now that her boy had gone on to university she still had no life of her own. For twenty years she'd worked from six to three, for much of that time with a small child in tow. That made Charity feel she'd no right to complain about anything.

Pat had three children, ranging from thirteen to seven. Her pale face was the result of running herself ragged when her husband drifted from job to job. It was no wonder she never had time to wash her hair.

Jill might be simple but she worked like a demon. Now that Charity knew that Jill could neither read nor write, but was the sole provider for a mother of eighty, and that they lived in a two-roomed cottage with no electricity, how could she feel sorry for herself?

It struck Charity that it was a home for oddballs, at least in the kitchens. Even the other part-time women who came and went each day weren't exactly ordinary. Freda with a port-wine birthmark on her face. Janice who was expecting her seventh child, and Alice the quiet older lady who sang sad songs as she worked – they all had something unusual about them. It was like being back in the baths in Greenwich listening to the gossip.

These women had hard lives, their clothes were shabby and their families' survival depended on their small wage packets. Yet they kept their dignity, laughed at misfortune and were always optimistic, believing that things could only improve.

'Feeling better today?' Carol asked as she took off her apron at the end of her shift. Charity was sitting down at the kitchen table, having a cup of tea with Mrs Cod.

'Much better, thank you.' She was nervous at speaking out in front of cook.

'Carol knows what goes on here.' Mrs Cod smiled at the girl. 'She had it hard when she first started too, same as we all did. I thought I was going to drop dead my first couple of months. My Christopher was in a playpen out there beside the sinks and I had to keep the job because of him. But there was times when I'd have just walked out, left him an' all, I was so tired. But with a bit of a laugh and a joke with the other women, another pair of hands sharing the work, it ain't so bad.'

She asked Charity about her background and when she heard about the fire and the other children, her fat face clouded over.

'Well you've had your share of troubles love, and no mistake. But you've landed in a decent place, there's plenty of people here will give you a helping hand if you want it. It will get easier.'

'You aren't reading again are you, Swot?' Mrs Cod called back with laughter in her voice. 'If you are I'll take the ladle to your backside!'

Charity smiled. Mrs Cod had given her the nickname because she often had a book propped up in front of the sink and she insisted it was a better name than shortening her real one to Char. She pulled out the plug in the big sink, and idly watched the greasy

115

water gurgle down the drain. Today, however, there was no book; her mind had been on going home for Christmas.

Almost four months of working at the school had brought new maturity and sense of purpose to Charity. She still missed the children terribly, she still got very tired, but she'd learned to live with it and most of the time she actually enjoyed her work. All the other staff were impressed by her thirst for knowledge and her persistence with her studies. But perhaps Mrs Cod was the one who encouraged her the most.

'Read us a bit of poetry, Swot,' she'd shout out across the kitchen in a lull between meals. Charity got used to scouring books for a new passage, studying the words carefully so she had the full meaning at her fingertips should anyone ask, as they so often did. While the staff ate their lunch sometimes Charity read them a book as a serial and Jill would sit with her great long arms folded across her chest, drinking in every word.

Her confidence was growing daily. She began to look around her and ask questions – about everything from nutrition and recipes from Mrs Cod to childbirth and pregnancy from Janice and Pat. Her letters home were full of the characters she worked with, sparkling little anecdotes that Lou and Geoff informed her they read and reread.

But perhaps it was her friendship with Carol that opened her out the most.

There had never been time as a child in Greenwich to have close friendships. But each day the girls grew closer. At eight-thirty in the evening the one who had finished earlier in the day had tea and cake ready and then they either walked down the lane to the village in the darkness for one drink or, if it was wet and cold, curled up in one of their rooms just to chat. They examined each other's clothes, shared magazines, did

116

each other's hair and discussed the sixth-form boys in detail.

Although Carol was always talking about boys, she had no wish to find one and settle down. Her ideas were big: she planned to go to America as a nanny.

'I shan't stay, of course,' she said with a wicked twinkle in her eyes, running her fingers through her curly hair. 'I'm going to make my way to San Francisco and get a job as a secretary for someone important.'

To Charity's surprise she had it all worked out. She had been doing a home-study course for over a year, and practised typing on a portable.

'I've got nearly enough money saved for a six-week course in London,' Carol said, showing Charity a glossy brochure. 'I can type and do shorthand now, but they'll get my speeds up and give me a diploma. Then I go for the nanny's job and get my fare paid over there. I'll stay just long enough to learn how things work, then whoosh! I'll be off.'

She had this wonderful, simple philosophy that all ambition meant was writing down where you wanted to end up, then charting each step of how to get there.

'Doing typing at school was the first step,' she explained. 'Then I came here because I knew I could save and study with no distractions. London's the next step. I'll stay with my aunt there while I do the course.'

'But it will be awful again when you go,' Charity said wistfully.

'It won't, you've settled in now,' Carol insisted. 'We can write to one another. Who knows, you might want to come out and join me. You'd be a far better nanny than me!'

Charity swilled down the sink, wiped the draining boards then took off her apron. It was just after two, time for a quiet cup of tea round the kitchen table with the other women, then she'd walk into the village and look for some Christmas presents.

The school looked wonderfully Christmassy. A huge tree in the big hall, paper chains and foil lanterns in the classrooms, holly and ivy entwined round the banisters. Next week they would be cooking the Christmas dinner for the boys with turkey and all the trimmings. There was the Christmas play to see, a carol service and all the staff were to have a party in the refectory on the last night of term. But all these events were merely pleasant interludes to Charity, things that made the days pass quicker till she got home to Clapham.

At times she could hardly contain her excitement. Her first Christmas with Lou and Geoff, the first when she'd had money to buy presents. But most of all it was the thought of seeing the children. Of holding James in her arms again, kicking a ball with Toby and finding out how well Prue was doing at the grammar school.

Mrs Cod was turning out a huge slab of fruit cake on to a cooling tray as Charity got out the teacups, when Miss Hawkins came into the kitchen.

The staff called her Hawkeye behind her back. Certainly her sharp eyes missed nothing. But although her straight, skinny body didn't suggest there was a real human being beneath her starched uniform, Charity liked her.

She ran the housekeeping side of the school with an iron hand. If one pillowcase went missing, she knew. When the younger boys were using one of the top landings as a slide, she heard them. She checked every bill with meticulous care and was on to anyone wasting food or cleaning materials. Her cleaning staff all came in daily, and many of them grumbled about her high standards.

'Anyone would think it was Buckingham Palace instead of a school,' was a cry often heard. But Miss Hawkins just sniffed and claimed, 'Our boys come from good homes, their parents pay for the same standards.'

'Thank goodness you're still here,' Miss Hawkins said to Charity. 'I was afraid you'd already gone off duty when I got no reply at your room.'

'You get your money's worth out of our little Swot,' Mrs Cod joked. 'First here in the morning, last to leave. You don't get many of them to the pound!'

No alarm bells rang in Charity's head. Miss Hawkins often popped in to ask her to buy something in the village shop.

'I'm just making tea,' Charity said. 'Would you like a cup too?'

Miss Hawkins's eyes flitted round the kitchen, but seeing only Charity and Mrs Cod left behind, she nodded.

'I was going to suggest you came up to my sitting room,' she said rather hesitantly. 'But if you don't mind, we can talk here.'

Charity filled the big brown teapot with hot water and put it on the table. She knew she wasn't in trouble, as Miss Hawkins always sent a messenger with a summons for that kind of thing, but she was curious.

Odder still, Miss Hawkins poured the milk into the cups and took over the tea pouring.

'I've had a phone call from Mr Charles,' she said, handing Charity her tea and patting a chair for her to sit down at the big table. 'I'm afraid it's sad news, Charity, and he asked me to break it to you gently.'

Charity clutched her stomach with fear.

'Someone's hurt?'

'Not as serious as that, my dear.' Miss Hawkins looked terribly strained and the way she looked round at Mrs Cod suggested she was unsure if she should continue here. 'No, the children are well, it's just that your Uncle Stephen has taken them to his house.'

'For *Christmas*?' Charity asked. 'Without me?'

Miss Hawkins squirmed, hardly able to continue.

'Not just for Christmas. Permanently.'

For a moment Charity thought it was a bad dream. Only a week ago she'd had a letter from Toby saying they were putting up the Christmas decorations and he was to be Joseph in the Nativity play. It felt as if someone had opened a trapdoor beneath her and she was falling into a black hole.

'No!' Charity's cry was pure anguish. 'It can't be true. He can't take them!'

'James is still with Mr and Mrs Charles,' Miss Hawkins hastily added, hoping that would make it less painful. 'You'll be with him for Christmas.'

Charity was motionless, eyes brimming with tears.

'But why?' she asked, her voice shaking. 'Prue was settled at the grammar school. Toby was happy too. And what about James with everyone gone?'

Miss Hawkins felt ashamed of herself now for not realising just what a shock this would be to Charity. She certainly shouldn't have blurted it out in the kitchen.

'My dear, I'm not able to answer that. Mr Charles received a message only yesterday that Colonel Pennycuick was sending his driver for the children. He would've preferred to tell you himself, but he thought it would be worse if he wrote, or waited until you came home and found Prue and Toby already gone.' Miss Hawkins blinked fast behind her glasses. 'Of course Mr and Mrs Charles are terribly upset too. But as the colonel is the children's guardian there was nothing they could do.'

'I must go and see them,' Charity said and jumped up, pulling off her apron. 'I've got to warn them what our uncle's like.'

Miss Hawkins got up and put her hands on Charity's arms to restrain her.

'No Charity, you can't go. A letter will come tomorrow morning explaining everything.'

'You don't understand.' Charity's face had lost all its colour, her eyes dark with growing anger. 'Uncle Stephen's an evil man. I must go to them.'

Miss Hawkins sighed deeply. Mr Charles had predicted that Charity might attempt to go to London. But even he hadn't foreseen she might want to rush to Studley Priory.

'You will not leave the school now,' she said firmly. 'It's only ten days till the end of term, and meanwhile you'll calm down and wait for Mr Charles's letter. There is nothing to be gained by confronting your uncle. It could make things far more difficult for you in the long run.'

'Why has he done this?' Charity whispered, anger turning to utter dejection as tears streamed down her cheeks. 'Isn't it enough to lose our parents, without splitting us all up too? Uncle Stephen doesn't know anything about children, he's cruel and nasty. It was bad enough for me when I went there for a week. They'll be so unhappy.'

'Calm down, Charity.' Miss Hawkins put on her most officious voice. 'Wait and read Mr Charles's letter. It might not be as bad as you fear.'

Charity drew herself up and looked Miss Hawkins in the eye.

'Why is it that some adults are so stupid?' she said. 'My parents, social workers and Uncle Stephen – not one of them had any real idea what a child feels. They do what suits them, they lie and they cheat. And then they tell children to behave like they do.'

She turned and walked out of the kitchen. The two older women could only stare at one another blankly.

'She's right, of course.' Miss Hawkins broke the

silence first, picked up her tea and drank it in one large gulp. 'We are stupid and we do lie and cheat. I wish it were different.'

'She won't run away,' Mrs Cod said stoutly, her many chins wobbling with emotion. 'She'll sob upstairs all on her own and she'll be down to do breakfast tomorrow because that's the way she's made.'

'Can you keep a confidence?' Miss Hawkins leaned conspiratorially across the table.

'Of course,' Mrs Cod nodded. 'You know something more?'

'That uncle is as bad as she claims. The truth is he's told the Charleses not to allow Charity into their house, or he'll remove James too.'

Mrs Cod's mouth dropped open and she fumbled for a cigarette even though she wasn't allowed them in the kitchen.

'Thank goodness you didn't tell her that today.' She shook her head in bafflement. 'Is that what's in the letter?'

'No.' Miss Hawkins helped herself to a cigarette too, suddenly caring nothing for the rules she'd created. 'Mr Charles is prepared to defy the colonel on that count. At least until after Christmas.'

'Thank heavens for that,' Mrs Cod said, and inhaled deeply on her cigarette.

She had talked with Charity often about her family and listened to her dreams and plans. They were all about her brothers and sister, and her objective of finding a home one day they could all share. She showed no interest in boyfriends, dancing or parties. It was as if she wore blinkers and could only see straight ahead.

'No girl of her age should feel such a weight of responsibility.' Miss Hawkins puffed on her cigarette, her eyes full of anxiety. 'The trouble is, without her

122

brothers and sister, there's no telling what it might do to her. I've seen young girls go off the rails for far less reason.'

'Me too,' Mrs Cod agreed. 'Look at some of the girls we've had here in the past. Straight out of orphanages, never had any love and they throw themselves at the first man who comes along. I can tell you that if I hadn't had Christopher to care for when my Eric was killed, I might have gone the same way. But I can't understand that wicked uncle of hers. Why does he want to hurt her?'

'I don't know.' Miss Hawkins made a despairing gesture.

'Her goodness, I expect,' Mrs Cod snorted, wide nostrils flaring with anger. 'A man like him ought to be hung, drawn and quartered. I'd like ten minutes with him to tell a few home truths.'

Miss Hawkins got up from the table.

'Don't let's despair,' she sighed. 'Mr Charles has left the door open. He hopes the children will behave so badly over Christmas they might be sent back.'

'I do hope so.' Mrs Cod wiped her face with her apron. 'We'd all better offer up a few prayers for Charity. Not even sixteen and so much sadness in her young life already.'

Alone in her room Charity broke down completely. On her dressing-table was a pile of brightly wrapped presents for the children, and the new midnight blue dress she had bought to wear on Christmas Day hung on the wardrobe door, mocking her.

'I hate you, Colonel Bloody Pennycuick,' she said, thumping her fists into the pillow. 'But if you think you can break me down till I become like my mother, you're mistaken. I love them, and I'll get them back. However long it takes.'

Chapter Seven

1961

Charity lay on her back in the long grass, hands tucked behind her head, bare legs bent at the knees. The sun was so intense she could only peep at it through half-closed eyes, clouds wispy, like the net in her old can-can petticoat.

She was in what had once been the orchard. Two old apple trees flanked a small door set in the high stone wall that surrounded the school, but the rest of the trees had been uprooted and now it was a mere field, belonging to the neighbouring farm.

It was a good place to retreat to, as few masters or boys ever came this way. Further down the field, the ancient wall disappeared into the dense woodland which marked the boundary of the playing fields.

Sounds from the school were minimal here. The odd smack of cricket ball on willow, the occasional growled order from Giles, the head groundsman as he went in and out of his hut beyond the wall. But mostly there was only birdsong, grasshoppers and bees to break into the stillness.

Charity had got into the habit of going for a long walk each afternoon when she was on early duty. Through the small gate, across this field and then on to a footpath that led all the way to Mayfield. Each day she pushed herself to walk a little further, to make herself so tired she couldn't lie awake dwelling on how alone she was, or how much she hated Uncle Stephen.

It was July now, seven long months since the shattering news that Toby and Prue had been whisked away to Studley Priory. She might have forgiven her uncle for that, as by all accounts they were happy there. But when Geoff and Lou dropped the bombshell later that he wanted Charity cast out entirely, not even allowed to visit James at Clapham, she felt murderous.

Lou and Geoff assured her they would keep writing to her, pass on all the news they got of the children. But that could never make up for holding James in her arms, watching him grow or playing with him. Neither did letters match up to having a home to go to in the holidays. Never to have Lou sitting on her bed at night and chatting, or Geoff teasing her as she helped him in the garden. Did Uncle Stephen know how desperately abandoned she'd feel without them to run to? Is that why he did it?

As Geoff pointed out, they could take a chance and defy Stephen, as they already had at Christmas. But James was to be taken to Studley in future, for part of each holiday too, and no one could reasonably expect a three-year-old not to speak of seeing his older sister. But although Charity knew Geoff and Lou were only honouring Stephen's wishes because he might whisk James away from them too, it still felt a bit like they had joined the enemy camp.

Rage was the fuel that had kept her going in the last six months. As she washed dishes, laid tables and prepared vegetables, her mind was always on a single goal: to get the children back, with her.

Charity had no clear idea of how she was going to do this. She would need a well-paid job and a home of her own before she could even think of tackling Uncle Stephen. All she had on her side was determination. One day they would all be together, whatever Uncle Stephen said or did.

Loneliness was Charity's biggest enemy. In working hours she found solace in the other women, but once that was over she often found herself slipping into black despair.

Carol had left suddenly at Easter because a place came up for her in the college in London. A new maid called Deirdre had taken her job, but along with having a personality akin to a rice pudding, she lived in the village and ran off home the minute she'd finished her work. Now there was no one to share cocoa and cake with. No trips to the cinema or the pub. At night in her room Charity buried herself in a book, turning her radio on just to shut out the silence, and tried hard not to remember nights when the room had rung with laughter.

Carol's departure had become another deep loss. Her battered portable typewriter sat on the chest of drawers surrounded by photographs of the children, Geoff and Lou, like some kind of shrine to happier times.

But as Charity lay in the grass she wasn't reminiscing, or even planning, she was just seeing the whole month of August as some kind of black hole which she didn't know how to fill.

Every other member of staff was awaiting the holiday with happy anticipation. Mrs Cod had Christopher coming home, Pat was planning days out at Hastings with her children, even Miss Hawkins was going away to Eastbourne. Charity could stay at the school with the skeleton staff of groundsmen and a couple of masters and their wives, but who would she talk to? How would she pass the time?

Just a week till the end of term. Another week

clearing up after the boys and doing the big spring-clean. Then nothing.

Charity turned over on to her stomach and rested her head on her arms. She was wearing the pale blue shorts Mrs Cod had given her, that had once been Christopher's. Although she had put on a little weight and her legs and arms were turning brown, it gave her no pleasure to see that her body finally looked womanly. Not when she was so terribly alone.

'Hallo there!'

A male voice startled her and she sat up quickly, wrapping her arms instinctively round her bare legs.

'You work at the school, don't you?'

Despite her shock at being discovered, the boy's fresh, flushed face, the cricket whites and his tousled black hair made her smile. He was clearly as surprised to stumble on her as she was to be spoken to.

'Yes, in the kitchens.'

'What are you doing out here?'

This question might have been construed as a reproach at a humble kitchen maid lying around in a field just beyond the school wall, but his wide grin held nothing but interest.

'I've been for a long walk. It's so warm still I didn't want to go back.'

She didn't even consider the rule about not fraternising with the pupils. To ignore him would have been rude.

'I've seen you scuttling across the playing fields loads of times,' he said, flopping down on the grass beside her. 'I always wanted to get a better look at you. You're the only pretty member of staff.'

Charity blushed scarlet at such an unexpected compliment and shuffled back on the grass, away from him.

'Hey, don't be embarrassed,' he said. 'What's your name?'

127

His confidence was startling. Although some of the older boys could be quite cheeky when they were in groups, alone they were almost as nervous and tongue-tied as she was.

Charity had noticed this boy before, but then he was the kind of boy who would stand out anywhere. Jet black hair in need of a cut, dark blue eyes and golden shiny skin.

'Charity Stratton,' she said. 'But I shouldn't be talking to you. I'll get into trouble.'

'I'm Hugh Mainwaring,' he grinned. 'Don't you ever do anything you aren't supposed to?'

'Not often,' she replied, unable actually to remember when she had last broken a rule. 'I must go back now.'

'No you mustn't.' He shook his head in disbelief. 'I've watched you from the dorm window. You don't usually go back until six o'clock. It's only half-past four.'

It gave her the oddest sensation to know he was that familiar with her movements. But he was right. She didn't have to go back. It would be a long, dull evening just like all the others and she hadn't even got a book to read.

'But you have to be back for tea at five!' She smiled triumphantly. 'And you can't go in the refectory in cricket clothes.'

'Shows how much you know about the sixth form,' he retorted. 'We can make our own tea up in the study, any time we like. We can even go into the village and scoff in the café if we've got any money left.'

'But you aren't allowed to talk to kitchen maids, especially sitting in long grass outside the grounds?'

For a moment their eyes met and they both smiled.

'That's a silly rule,' he said. 'I'm leaving at the end of term. No one can see us from here and what harm is there in a little chat?'

There didn't seem to be any harm. Sitting in a field with the kitchen door just fifty yards the other side of the wall, afternoon sun burning into their skin, birds singing and the sweet smell of grass all around them.

He lay propped up on one elbow, some few yards from her, sucking a blade of grass as he talked.

He told her he came from Yorkshire, that his father was a lawyer and he planned to be one too. He had a place at Oxford for October, but he was spending most of the summer holiday at a friend's house nearby in Five Ash Down.

'There's a pub nearby that wants a couple of waiters,' he said gleefully. 'I worked there last summer and it's wild. Loads of students help out and they're a real crazy bunch. I've known my friend Rob since we were at prep school. He's a bit quiet, but this cottage his parents are letting us stay in is fantastic. We'll be able to have all-night parties, because his folks are clearing off on holiday and leaving us alone.'

Although she was nervous about being in such close proximity to a boy, something about his open and friendly manner made her relax, as if she were merely talking to an interesting person on a train or bus.

Yet the conversation wasn't a casual one. He spoke of his family as if he didn't care for them much. A neurotic mother who was always arranging dinner parties and whose schedule he upset when he came home. His father he described as 'distant'. He implied that his parents were snobs, only interested in their social standing and his achievements.

'I wish I had some brothers and sisters,' he said wistfully. 'Maybe my parents wouldn't expect so much of me then. I bet you've got a wonderful family?' he added, with a woebegone expression that reminded her curiously of Toby.

'Not now,' she said and to her surprise found herself telling him everything.

It just came out. If anyone had told her she would spill everything out to a stranger, she would have laughed. She felt a little self-conscious about her London accent and the huge divide between her poor background and his wealthy one. Yet she found herself revealing it all as if she'd known him for years.

'Oh shit, Charity.' He shook his head in almost disbelief. 'That's terrible!'

'I don't know why I told you.' She tried to laugh and make light of it, feeling faintly ridiculous.

His teeth were even and brilliantly white, lips beautifully shaped and plump. Although he must be almost eighteen and his voice was deep, his skin had the peachy softness of a younger boy.

'Everyone needs someone.' He reached out and touched her hand. 'My first year at Bowes Court was hell. When I went home my parents were always rowing. I was so miserable I could have jumped off the tower. But that's nothing compared with what you've had to live with. Have you got any friends?'

She looked down at his hand and he removed it immediately, dropping his eyes from hers almost apologetically.

'Not really. There was a girl called Carol here until recently. We used to spend our time together, but there's no one now.'

'The big redhead!' he nodded. 'But why do you stay?'

She explained that for now she had no real choice, that she needed experience before she could look for a better job. But then she admitted that the thought of the long summer holiday was worrying her.

'You could get a job at the pub I was talking about,' he suggested. 'It's great there, always packed out, I could ask for you!'

She wasn't sure Geoff and Lou would approve of

130

this, yet a vision of spending the long holiday with other young people and him, made bubbles of excitement rise within her.

'Would you? I'd love it, I'm sure I'd be good at it!' she said impulsively.

'Of course you would,' he grinned broadly. 'Besides it would mean I could see you too.'

All at once she remembered her position and the danger of being caught talking to him. He was, after all, a pupil and an attractive one at that. She was flattered by his interest in her, but she had to get away now, before someone saw her with him.

She jumped up quickly. 'Look I must go. I really liked talking to you Hugh. But you know how it is.'

'It's an archaic and snobbish rule banning us from mixing with the staff,' he said indignantly, getting up from the grass.

Hugh had more experience with girls than most of the other boys. Last summer he'd done some heavy petting with an older barmaid called Angela and in the Christmas hols there'd been Wendy who worked in the local grocer's. The sort of girls his parents would approve of wouldn't let him get closer than a chaste kiss. But in the last few months, fired by stories from other boys and pin-up pictures in magazines, he had found himself dwelling on girls constantly and he was desperate to get some real experience before going on to Oxford.

He wasn't the only boy in the sixth year to notice Charity. Duncan Gooding raved about her blonde hair; Antony Curlew went into raptures about her blue eyes and her wide mouth. But while other boys merely observed her from a distance and fantasised about kissing, or even screwing her, Hugh had been determined to get to know her. Running into her today wasn't an accident. He'd planned it: he'd been watching her movements for weeks, waiting for an

131

opportunity. If he was honest, all he'd wanted until now was to score points. If he'd been able to go back to the sixth form and boast that he'd kissed her, that would've been enough. He hadn't for one moment expected her to be so well spoken, or so intelligent. He certainly hadn't expected to really like her.

'Another week and I won't be a pupil any more,' he said, frantically trying to think of some way to persuade her to see him again. 'Couldn't you meet me one evening?'

He didn't know how he could get out unseen, but he was desperate enough now to try.

Charity just stood there looking at him. Something stirred within her. It was like goosebumps, butterflies in her tummy and a faint electric shock all at once. It was tempting to agree, but she remembered Carol telling her how it was always the staff who got punished, while the boys only got a telling off. She'd also pointed out that public schoolboys used kitchen maids for practice at seduction. They wouldn't dream of having one as a real girlfriend.

'I daren't.' She dropped her eyes from his and backed away. 'If Miss Hawkins found out I'd be sacked immediately.'

For all his lack of experience, Hugh noticed the 'I daren't' rather than I don't want to, or I can't. He felt as if there was already a bond between them and he wasn't going to give up easily.

'Then I'll have to think of something else,' he grinned. The sun was behind her, turning her hair to a fuzzy gold halo, and he longed to reach out and stroke it. 'I can't see how they can make something of us running into one another accidentally.'

'I must go now,' she murmured faintly.

She turned and ran to the side gate into the school grounds, but as she pushed the gate open a low whistle made her turn.

He had sprinted right down to the other end of the wall, obviously intending to climb over into the wood. He raised one hand to say goodbye and disappeared out of sight.

It rained solidly for the next two days and the forlorn view of green and grey landscape from the window seemed to heighten the feelings growing inside her. Try as she might, Charity couldn't banish Hugh from her mind. No book could hold her attention and the clock hands seemed to move even more slowly than usual.

On Friday morning the rain had stopped, and watery sunshine was trying to peep through the clouds, but as Charity washed the last of the pots and pans she had made up her mind to forget Hugh and walk to the library that afternoon to find some new books.

It was just before three when she emerged from the staff door. She had changed her overall for jeans and a sweater, and her library books were in a shoulderbag. Pausing for a second at the top of the steps from the kitchen, she glanced at the sky.

Black clouds were gathering. Could she get to the village and back before the rain came? Undecided she hesitated. The thought of another afternoon indoors held no appeal, but neither did a soaking.

To her left was the path round the school towards the drive and the main gates. That was the way to Heathfield and the library, yet some strange instinct was urging her to walk over the grass, open that side gate and slip out across the fields towards Mayfield.

She turned back, ran down the steps and dumped her bag of books just inside the kitchen door. Then before she could change her mind again she ran back up again and straight across the still wet grass to the gate.

Once in the old orchard she noticed the patch of flattened grass where she'd sat with Hugh two days ago. Her heart fluttered, her plimsolls were soaked and it felt cold, but still she walked on straight across the field, over the stile and on to the footpath that led through the woods, hoping against hope he would appear.

'Charity!'

Startled by his voice, she turned to see him bounding across the roughly ploughed field on her right. To her surprise he was dressed in running shorts, a school striped rugby shirt and plimsolls.

Joy surged through her, making her forget the school rules, the imminent rain and the cold.

'Miss Hawkins might be looking out her window,' she blurted out, looking back towards the school down the hill.

'She went into Heathfield,' he rasped out, bending over and clutching his stomach as if he had a stitch. 'I saw her get in the car with Giles, they overtook me up the lane. That's when I doubled back over the fields. I hoped you'd come.'

His clothes suggested that this meeting was pure chance and Charity felt oddly hurt by his casualness.

'Perfect cover, eh!' He looked down at his bare legs splattered with mud. 'No one would suspect me of meeting a girl like this! You aren't embarrassed by me being dressed like this, are you?'

'No.' She felt a sense of kinship with him now and, as he said, it was the perfect cover.

'I came out yesterday and the day before,' he said as he walked briskly up the hill beside her, into the wood, peering round at her face. 'I didn't think you'd come, really. Not when it was raining so hard. But I hoped you would.'

That admission sounded as if his feelings were the

134

same as hers, and as they reached the far end of the wood Charity felt safer. From the old log where she'd often sat to rest there was a clear view down the hill. Even if someone did come up the path, they would have more than enough time to separate before they were seen.

'It was nice talking to you the other day,' she said hesitantly as she sat down. 'But I – ' She stopped short not knowing what to say.

He stood in front of her, looking down at her, muscular tanned legs slightly apart, hands on his hips.

'Don't say you don't like me?'

His expression made her feel odd. There was hurt in his dark blue eyes.

'No. I'm just scared of getting the sack,' she said.

The clouds were growing darker and thicker by the minute. Mayfield in the distance was shrouded in mist and it was getting colder.

Hugh sat down next to her, his legs stretched out in front of him. He wiped some of the mud from them with a clump of grass.

'If you met me after I'd left the school, say at a pub or a party, no one could say anything!'

Carol would have known how to handle this. Charity had no experience to fall back on. Was he trying to say he wanted her as a girlfriend? Or was he merely looking for someone to talk to?

'I feel awkward,' she stammered. 'I'm not used to boys, apart from my brothers.'

'We're just people,' he shrugged. 'Besides, I like you!'

She giggled with embarrassment and felt slightly less intimidated.

'Lots of the other boys have got girlfriends,' Hugh said. 'I've often wanted to ask them how you go about it, but you can't ask things like that, can you?'

'Carol used to know about all that,' Charity volunteered. 'She was very good at talking to people.'

'So are you.' He turned to her, his face thoughtful. 'And you're much prettier than her, lots of the other boys fancy you.'

'None of them ever see me,' she laughed, liking the flattery but not believing it.

'We see you going up and down the stairs. We watch you laying the tables.' He grinned. He couldn't possibly admit that Jackson, one of the other sixth-formers, claimed he always thought of Charity when he masturbated. Or indeed that the sight of her small bottom and slim legs in her shorts had kept him wide awake for the past two nights. It seemed to Hugh that there had to be something special here. He hadn't told anyone he'd spoken to her, even though it would have boosted his image in the other boys' eyes. She was his secret, and a deliciously sweet one.

Hugh glanced through his eyelashes at her. She had the most adorable wide mouth, with plump full lips, and he longed to touch her silky hair.

'Don't you ever notice any of the boys?'

'Not really.' Charity smiled. 'Some of the little ones, because they make me think of Toby, but the big ones make me nervous.'

The conversation moved away from personal things, on to his running, the cricket team and his intended career.

'I've bent to Dad's wishes to a certain extent. But I'm going to be a criminal lawyer,' he told her. 'My father's into company law, acting for unscrupulous rich men who want to screw someone else to make a few more thousands. I intend to help people, not grind them further into the dirt.'

It was touching to find he was idealistic, that his stuffy parents hadn't managed to turn him into a carbon copy of themselves.

She talked about her need to get a better job and one day find a home she could share with her brothers and sister.

'They'll be almost grown up by the time I make enough money,' she sighed. 'I miss them so much, you can't imagine what it's like.'

'I can't believe anyone would be so cruel as to keep you apart,' Hugh said in sympathy. 'Maybe I could ask my father about the legal position. Surely if your uncle is your guardian too then he's being derelict in his duty by ignoring you?'

'The way I see it, adults can do what they like.' Charity's voice shook. 'What really hurts is that he's probably told lies about me and I can't talk to the children to make them understand that.'

It was as they walked back through the wood that Hugh took her hand as naturally as the children would. But as his fingers closed round hers she felt a strange sense of elation.

'I'd better go on alone from here,' she said as they approached the end of the wood.

'Will you meet me here tomorrow?' he asked, turning to stand right in front of her.

'We shouldn't do this,' she whispered, hanging her head. 'I can't afford to lose my job. Lou and Geoff would be disappointed in me too.'

With one hand still holding hers, he lifted the other to her cheek and stroked it lightly and she was forced to look up at him. His dark blue eyes held no danger, only tenderness.

'I want to see you in the hols,' he whispered. 'They can't stop us doing that. But I can't wait that long. I've got to see you before, to make arrangements. We'll make certain no one sees us. I won't breathe a word to anyone at school.'

His hand on her face felt so good . . . she was aware

137

he had stepped closer, and that he was slowly bending down to her and all at once his lips were on hers.

Carol had often spoken of kissing, but Charity hadn't expected it to be anything like this.

His lips were warm and soft, and a shiver of pleasure ran down her spine as he drew her closer. Not a practised kiss like ones in films, their noses got in the way and she could hardly breathe, but still it had some strange magic that made her shut her eyes, arms moving round his slim body.

It was beginning to rain, just a few drops at first, which they ignored as they held one another, heads bent together. She could feel his heart beating through his shirt and his breath warm on her skin.

Trees were all around, forming a green canopy above them and the path was muddy beneath their feet. As the rain became heavier, the drumming on leaves made them look up.

'Run back,' he whispered, kissing her one more time. 'You'll get soaked without a coat. I'll meet you here tomorrow at three.'

She ran then. Out of the woods, down the footpath and on without stopping or looking back till she reached the stile.

Pat was in the kitchen buttering slices of bread as Charity ran in through the door. Her hair was plastered to her head, rain running down her face.

'You're soaked,' Pat reproved her. 'Look at your jeans! What on earth have you been doing?'

Rain had penetrated right through to her underwear, and her saturated jeans were making puddles on the kitchen floor as she paused to get her breath back.

'I went for a walk,' she said lamely. 'I didn't think it would rain.'

Pat frowned. Charity had long since stopped calling

her the Viper. Her sharpness was just a manner brought about by her good-for-nothing husband and the responsibility of providing for her three children. Now her long, pale face showed concern, perhaps even suspicion that Charity had been up to something.

'Out of those wet clothes,' she said reprovingly. 'You'll get pneumonia!'

Charity stripped off her clothes in her room and put on her dressing-gown, shivering now. From her window she could see Hugh in the distance, running up the playing fields, his brown legs shiny with rain, and her heart contracted painfully.

That night she couldn't sleep. She could see Hugh, feel the warmth of his hand on her cheek, the softness of his lips on hers. She wanted to see him again, wanted it more than anything. Yet terrible fear came with the wanting.

She knew nothing of kissing, of courtship and cuddling. All she knew was the part that it all led to and that meant pain and humiliation. Yet even though her heart was hammering with fear, she knew she'd risk everything to see him again.

Chapter Eight

Charity stood emotionally on the bottom of the main staircase listening to the boys singing, her eyes prickling.

The anthem was 'I Vow to Thee My Country' and the sentiments it expressed had never seemed more appropriate or moving.

Seven days since Hugh first kissed her, long nights of lying awake thinking of him.

The wide front door was open to let in a welcome breeze, and sunshine danced on the polished wood floor turning it into a gleaming pool. Beyond the steps outside was just a fragment of England's beauty, the sweeping green lawn speckled with daisies, a majestic chestnut tree, then the larch and beech trees by the boundary wall, planted a century ago.

Smells of steak-and-kidney pudding mingled with chalk and polish and if she stood on tiptoe she could just see into the assembly hall through a high pane of glass on the door. Two hundred boys. The youngest at the front by the stage; at the back the older ones who were almost men. A sea of blue blazers, voices raised in patriotic fervour. To the right of the stage was the roll of honour, a reminder of old boys who had made the ultimate sacrifice for their country in both world wars.

'Stirring, isn't it?' Miss Hawkins's voice behind her made Charity jump. 'Especially now when so many of them are leaving. They came as little boys; now they are ready to take their places as men in the outside world.'

Charity hastily wiped her eyes with the back of her hand and smiled.

'I was just going to help Matron,' she said quickly, feeling guilty because her tears were for Hugh alone. 'I got sidetracked!'

'Is everything all right?' Miss Hawkins's sharp features softened with concern. 'You've seemed very jumpy these last few days.'

'Just tired, I expect.' Charity blushed.

'Well you make sure you get a good rest during the holidays.' The older woman patted Charity's bottom affectionately. 'Now off you go, Matron will be wondering how she's ever going to get finished.'

Charity had been more than jumpy in the last week, she'd been unable to eat, sleep or even think clearly. The price for meeting Hugh in secret was high – instant dismissal with no reference – but she had willingly gambled everything for just an hour in his arms.

All day she thought of nothing but him, washing and drying dishes at astonishing speed, mouth dry, heart pounding. When their eyes met in the refectory, she had to rush away in confusion. If he strolled past the kitchen door in an effort to catch a glimpse of her, she wanted to shout and sing because it meant he shared her feelings. One moment she believed they could have a future together; the next she was sure he was merely playing with her.

'Look at those cars!' Pat leaned on the windowsill of the refectory and gazed out at the cavalcade of vehicles scrunching their way up the drive. 'All that money and they still pack their kids off to boarding-school! If I was in their shoes I'd be taking mine on picnics every day.'

Charity heard the envy in the older woman's voice and finished polishing the last table before she joined her to watch.

Since ten that morning the noise hadn't ceased. Trunks being bumped down the stairs, excited voices calling out last frantic messages. Matron, who was normally almost invisible, had been up and down sorting out lost property, admonishing boys to go out into the quadrangle to await their parents and soothing younger ones who were fearful they'd been forgotten.

'Look at 'er.' Pat waved a work-reddened hand at a woman getting out of a chauffeur-driven Daimler. 'I bet that bleedin' outfit costs more than I earn in a year!'

The woman in question looked like a film star, in a rose pink silk suit with matching wide-brimmed hat. One of the smaller boys ran out to hug her, but she neatly sidestepped him and merely offered a cool cheek for his kiss.

'Poor kid.' Pat shook her head in dismay. 'If she feels like that she shoulda given him away at birth.'

Charity's mind wasn't on the woman in the pink suit. Hugh was walking towards the front door with a man who could only be his father, and as he saw her looking out of the window he gave her a secret smile that meant he had to go home to Yorkshire for ten days, but he'd be back for his bar job, the cottage and her.

His father was shorter than Hugh, stockily built with a perspiring red face and gold-rimmed spectacles. His hair was streaked with grey and although his well-cut grey suit hid it well, Charity suspected he had a fat stomach.

Just a few minutes later they came in sight again, carrying Hugh's trunk between them.

'He's a nice boy,' Pat said. 'Took him some time to

settle down when he was a new boy, but now he's off to Oxford after the holidays.'

Charity was tempted to take Pat into her confidence, but knew that if she did Pat would point out that young gentlemen like Hugh Mainwaring would choose someone of a higher status than kitchen maid for a girlfriend.

As the cars purred off down the drive and through the school gates, Charity was even more aware of the divide between her in a blue nylon overall, a polishing cloth in her hands, and Hugh sitting in that luxurious red Jaguar.

The agony of separation was soothed by the air of joviality that spread through the school once the last boy had left. There was a mountain of work to be done. Beds to be stripped, washed down with disinfectant. Curtains taken down for cleaning, desks emptied and classrooms cleared of rubbish. A smell of varnish, blackboard paint and turpentine took over from the aroma of baking pies and cakes.

When the first letter came from Hugh she wanted to sing with joy. He said Yorkshire was dull and lonely without her; when he looked at the cornflowers in the garden he saw her eyes and he dreamed of her nightly, counting the days till he got back to Sussex.

She sped through her tasks now with a new fervour. Each polished floor was as if he was to walk on it, and when she found old exercise books with his name on them, she clutched them to her chest with love.

His second letter confirmed he would be arriving at the cottage on 29 July. He promised to meet her that evening by the crossroads.

Lou and Geoff had written too. They were taking James away for a holiday to the seaside, followed by a couple of days at Studley so that James could see Prue and Toby. Their assurances that they would do their best to persuade Stephen to change his mind about Charity were comforting, but more importantly they would be able to give her a first-hand report later on how all three children were reacting to the changes in their lives.

'Has my taxi arrived yet?' Miss Hawkins came down the stairs, carrying a small case in one hand.

Charity's work was over now. The rest of the staff gone, she had been waiting to see the housekeeper off before taking a bath in preparation for seeing Hugh. The school was silent: benches stacked on the refectory tables, revarnished desks gleaming in sun-filled classrooms, dormitories almost ghostly with bare iron beds, lockers waiting for their new owners in September. Not even the sound of Giles mowing the grass, or Mrs Cod banging pots and dishes. Just blissful silence, birdsong and the buzzing of insects.

'It's just turned into the drive,' Charity informed her, looking at Miss Hawkins in some astonishment. She wore a pale blue costume and a small feathered hat, even a touch of lipstick and powder. It had transformed her from a formidable middle-aged matron into a younger, attractive lady. 'You look lovely!'

'Well thank you, dear.' The older woman smiled warmly. 'It's good to get out of my uniform. I think we all tend to forget there is a world beyond the school walls. Now mind you have a good rest this holiday, you've been looking a bit peaky lately. Mrs Cod will be in and out, but make sure you leave the kitchen tidy when you make your food, it's her holiday too. I've asked Giles to dig you out a bicycle so you can get out and about a bit.'

'Thank you,' Charity blushed. Everyone was a little concerned that she would be alone during the holidays. Pat had even invited her to join her family on outings. Now she felt guilty at not admitting she had other plans. 'Let me take your case!'

'Off with you.' Miss Hawkins waved her aside. 'You're on holiday now, enjoy it.'

Charity waved until Miss Hawkins was out of sight, feeling dwarfed by the big, empty school behind her and the expanse of lawn in front. But she didn't feel isolated or lonely today. Bubbles of excitement were fizzing up inside her, banishing even thoughts of the children.

Charity had thought about what she was going to wear to meet Hugh all week. But as she rushed up the hill at seven-thirty, she felt she'd made the right choice. One of the masters' wives had given her the sleeveless lilac shift dress and it was a far more expensive one than she could have considered buying herself. With her hair freshly washed, loose on her shoulders and her bare feet in new white sandals, she felt she looked as good as the models in teenage magazines.

It was still very warm. Even on the hill over-shadowed by thick hedges and trees she had no need for the cardigan she was carrying. The balmy air was full of country smells: meadowsweet, damp earth and privet. In darkness this part of the road was a little scary, but now the rustlings in bushes were clearly only the odd rabbit or birds and the joyful expectancy of seeing Hugh again made her hurry to reach the crossroads.

She saw him as she reached the brow of the hill. He was sitting on a grass bank by the signpost, his bicycle thrown down beside him and as he jumped up to run to her, her heart turned somersaults.

He was wearing faded blue jeans and a white short-sleeved shirt. His golden skin was tanned still darker since he left school over a week ago.

145

'Charity,' he said throwing his arms wide as he ran to her. 'I thought you'd never get here!'

She had rehearsed this meeting a hundred times in the past few days, but again and again she'd reminded herself he might not show the same degree of enthusiasm now he was free of the school. But as his arms went round her and his lips came down on hers with passion, she was sure he really did love her.

'Oh Charity!' he gasped, holding her to him tightly, his lips on her hair. 'I've missed you so much.'

They sat in a pub garden drinking cider and he barely let go of her hand as he told her about the cottage, his friend Robert Cuthbertson and his plans for the holiday.

'We've both got a job for four nights a week at the pub,' he said, barely suppressed excitement dancing in his eyes. 'But we'll have the days free.'

Charity told him about Giles fixing up a bike for her, omitting the fact that her only attempt at riding one had been a wobbly ride down Easton Street several years before.

'Great,' he beamed. 'I'll meet you here tomorrow at ten and take you to the cottage. Then I'll introduce you to Sonia and Angus at the pub. I'm sure they'll give you a job too.'

Hugh was a great talker. He told her about the students who worked at the pub, many of whom he'd met the previous year. He painted a vivid, sometimes frightening, picture of heavy drinkers, wild parties and girls who seemed to have all the confidence she lacked.

As fascinated as Charity was by these revelations about his friends, she was scared. She might just be well-spoken enough to pass muster with these privileged, wild people, but could she hope to hold on to

Hugh when she was seen next to girls from the same background as him?

'What about Robert's parents?' she asked nervously. 'Won't they mind me visiting the cottage?'

'They've gone off to Italy for six weeks,' Hugh grinned. 'It's just a holiday cottage, on their estate. They certainly wouldn't let us stay in the big house, they'd be scared we'd mess it up.'

'Why don't they take him on holiday with them?' Charity asked, puzzled by such parental indifference.

Hugh looked bemused.

'I doubt he wanted to go. His mother's even weirder than mine, she's been in and out of loony bins.'

Charity frowned, not quite liking such a callous remark.

'Well she's had at least two breakdowns.' Hugh saw the disapproval and tried to appease her. 'Besides, his dad is an ogre. He sent him off to Rugby instead of letting him come to Bowes Court with me. To "toughen him up" was his excuse. Even now he keeps on at him because Rob's going to study English literature rather than law. I thought my parents were bad enough, but his are much worse.'

He gave Charity a crossbar back to the school gates soon after ten. He had no lights and the swoop down the narrow winding lane in pitch darkness was terrifying, even with his arms round her. But the promise he would meet her in the morning and his lingering kisses more than made up for it.

Charity was up the next morning at six. It was a beautiful day, early mist quickly clearing and a promise in the air it would be very hot later. The school was so quiet it was eerie, her footsteps echoing around the empty building as she ran downstairs.

She wheeled the bike out of the shed and walked with it round to the quadrangle. Giles had oiled it

147

and pumped up the tyres. It was an old-fashioned black one, quite different from the lightweight, blue racing bike Hugh had, but Charity was determined that by ten she would be able to ride it properly.

Pushing herself off from a low wall round a flowerbed, she tried again and again. She fell off several times, grazed her knee and ended up with oil all over her legs, but by the time it was eight she'd managed to ride a complete circuit of the quad.

'Use your brakes!' Hugh yelled up at her in greeting as she came hurtling towards him at the crossroads, using her sandalled feet as brakes. 'You'll hurt your toes!'

She was so proud of herself she didn't mind admitting now she'd only just learned to ride. As they sped down the hill together towards Five Ash Down her main fear was not passing cars, or the brakes, but wishing she'd had the sense to put on a pair of shorts like Hugh, instead of a summer dress that kept whipping back and showing her knickers.

'That's Rob's parents' house.' Hugh pulled up to point out an old house partly concealed by trees. 'Nice, isn't it?'

'Nice' was inadequate. Splendid or magnificent would have been more appropriate. The house was partly sixteenth century, one end being half-timbered, the rest covered in white weatherboarding, with a rich red-tiled roof and tall chimneys. Charity had seen many picturesque cottages around Heathfield, but none so big or so perfect as this one. A dovecote on the lawn, the graceful trees grouped around the house, beds of carefully tended roses and small, manicured low hedges all created an impression of extreme wealth.

'It's even bigger than it looks,' Hugh said almost casually as he made off down a narrow rutted lane a little further along. 'They've got an indoor swimming pool built in an extension at the back and a billiard room.'

'What does his father do?' Charity called out as she rode.

'I don't know exactly,' Hugh replied. 'He's some sort of tycoon, buys and sells companies I think. All this belongs to him too.' He pointed out a farm in the distance. 'He doesn't work it himself, he's got a tenant farmer in to run it.'

Then just when Charity was despairing of ever getting to the cottage, Hugh pointed in front of them. 'That's it!' he shouted back to her. 'What do you think?'

Charity could only gape in amazement. Just a tiny cottage backing on to a wood, covered in the white weatherboarding so common in this area, two windows up, two down and a central wooden porch covered in an abundance of honeysuckle. White picket fencing completed the picture of something right out of a child's fairytale book. Pink and red hollyhocks rose up above the downstairs windows.

Hugh tinkled his bell and a boy appeared in the open doorway.

'Hallo there,' he yelled out.

Charity had imagined this friend of Hugh's as big, confident and possibly resentful that his friend had a girl in tow, but as they rested their bikes against the picket fence and he came forward to greet them, she felt the oddest sensation of instant kinship.

For one thing he was small, only marginally taller than herself and very skinny. He had the worst acne she'd ever seen, floppy fair hair, and a warm, if shy smile.

'You're even prettier than he said,' Robert said awkwardly, looking down at his bare feet, as Hugh introduced them. 'Come on in.'

149

The front door led straight into a kitchen. Although it was fitted with honey-coloured modern units, it had the feel of a farmhouse with its central pine table and chairs. With windows at both back and front it was very light and cheery, yellow gingham curtains bringing in more sunshine.

'It was just a farm labourer's cottage,' Robert explained, clearly pleased by Charity's gasps of delight. 'There's three altogether on the estate. Dad had this done up as a holiday place, but he hardly ever bothers to let it. This is the sitting room,' he said, putting one hand on her elbow and drawing her into the other room downstairs.

Charity felt a stab of real envy that some people considered this a holiday home, when she would die to live in it for ever. Like the kitchen it was furnished simply, but the grass-green carpet, the beautiful old stone fireplace with its tub of beech leaves and the chintz-covered armchairs all looked so perfectly in place. Beneath an open pine staircase was an old desk and bookshelves stuffed with paperbacks. The walls were white apart from two black beams across the ceiling, and carefully chosen small watercolours and pretty plates broke up the starkness.

'It's wonderful,' she enthused, amazed that the boys seemed so casual. 'Can I see upstairs?'

Robert stayed in the kitchen to make a cup of tea, and Hugh dragged Charity up the open staircase making jokes about Robert not forgetting to cut cucumber sandwiches.

There were only two bedrooms, with the bathroom slotted in between. They contained old-fashioned double beds, big chests of drawers and tiled washstands as dressing-tables.

The windows were set low to the floor, the ceilings curving down to meet them. Charity dropped to her knees in the room Hugh said was his, to look at the view.

'It's like a doll's house, isn't it?' Hugh said behind her.

Charity was struck speechless. It wasn't a doll's house to her, but a dream of a house for happy ever after. Across the lane in a meadow were a herd of black and white cows grazing on the lush grass. Birds sang in the trees that came right up to the back of the cottage and it was so quiet and still she could hear the buzzing of bees.

'You do like it?' Hugh said coming up behind her and kneeling to hold her. 'You will stay here too? It's a long way back to the school.'

'I love it.' She smiled hesitantly. That double bed with its thick white cover was too close and she hadn't quite realised that they would be so isolated, or that Hugh intended her to sleep here. 'But of course I can't stay, Hugh. It wouldn't be right.'

He kissed her then, kneeling before the window. The sun was hot on her arms and face, he smelt of fresh air and soap and the way his tongue insinuated its way into her mouth in turn thrilled and frightened her.

'I could sleep downstairs,' he said at length as he paused to nuzzle into her neck. 'There's a chair that makes into a bed. I didn't mean –' he stopped short.

Charity covered his face with soft little kisses.

'I have to go back. Mrs Cod'll send out a search party,' she said quickly. 'But we must go downstairs again and see Rob, we can't make him feel awkward by me being here.'

The day passed all too quickly. They rode down to the village shop and brought groceries and ice-cream, explored the woods behind the cottage and later Charity cooked them sausages and mash, but as the hands of the clock got nearer to eight and the pub was mentioned, Charity made her excuses.

'I'll go home,' she said. 'You go and meet all your old friends.'

Hugh looked a bit sulky. She sensed he was dying to get down to the pub but at the same time he didn't want her to go.

'I'll come back in the morning,' she suggested, 'but I must go now.'

'Stay tomorrow?' Rob suggested and she was sure it wasn't prompted by Hugh, but because he liked her. A day in the sun had brought out a few freckles across his nose and she noticed for the first time how lovely his eyes were, a kind of browny greeny colour with tiny flecks of amber. 'It's such a long way for you to ride alone, and besides you want to work at the pub too, don't you?'

'I don't know, Rob.' She wished she could fully explain her fears. 'If your mother was near it might be different.'

'I don't see why,' he said. 'It's more dangerous riding home on a bike in the dark than staying with us. We'll look after you. Hugh will sleep downstairs, or even with me.'

Rob had a gentlemanly quality which Hugh didn't share. He showed his appreciation when she cooked their meal, he helped her wash up and now he was concerned about the danger of her riding home alone.

'I'll see.' She looked across at Hugh, hoping he'd suggest at least going part of the way with her. 'I'd have to think up something to tell Mrs Cod anyway.'

'Just say you've got a job at the pub.' Rob's face broke into a wide grin. 'She'll just assume you're staying there, some of the students do.'

It was a long way back. Much further than Charity had realised, and most of it uphill. Worse still, it got dark before she'd even got to the halfway point. Without lights she couldn't be seen by cars, and once she had to throw herself into a ditch. Branches struck her face and arms and the soreness she'd felt that morning in her bottom was now real pain. By the time she reached the school gates she'd already decided: if she wanted to spend time with Hugh, she had to stay at the cottage.

Hugh's eyes lit up when he saw her sponge bag and a change of clothing in the basket the next morning.

'Yippee!' he yelled. 'You're going to stay!'

'You will behave, and sleep downstairs?' she begged him, wishing she knew how other girls behaved at times like this. 'I'll go home if you don't.'

'Scout's honour.' He did a mock salute. 'Now come on in, we thought we'd have a picnic today.'

'No Hugh, you can't!' Charity pushed him towards the bedroom door.

'Please! I only want to cuddle you,' he pleaded.

She was in her cotton nightdress brushing her hair when Hugh came in. He wore nothing but a pair of jeans and in the soft lamplight his bare golden chest looked all too inviting.

The first night she'd stayed at the cottage Hugh had been very well behaved. He'd kissed her goodnight downstairs and even when he came up to use the bathroom he hadn't attempted to come into the bedroom.

But this afternoon while Rob was out checking everything was all right over at the big house, Hugh had got a bit heated while they lay sunbathing in the garden.

Charity didn't know how to explain she wasn't prepared to do anything more than kiss and cuddle.

Aside from being certain it was wrong to go any further, she had her period.

Yet each time he held her, strange, wonderful sensations crept over her and she was beginning to understand why Carol had spoken of 'getting carried away'.

'I'm scared it might lead to more,' she insisted, her eyes wide in panic as she pushed him back towards the door. 'Please go downstairs!'

'Don't you trust me?' He put his hands on her shoulders and forced her to look up at him. 'I love you, Charity. Why should it be wrong to hold you in my arms all night?'

She remembered Carol telling her that boys always said that, quickly followed by 'you would if you loved me'. He was so close now his bare chest was just touching her nipples and it brought back all those confused feelings.

'No.' She held her ground. 'I can't take the risk.'

To her surprise he backed away.

'OK.' He sighed deeply and looked hurt. 'I just thought –' he broke off and opened the door, leaving as quickly as he came in.

Charity shut the door behind him and leaned against it, closing her eyes.

She understood exactly. They hadn't worked at the pub tonight, just stayed in and watched television, but even though Rob was with them she sensed that Hugh was desperate to hold her. The heat from his thigh pressed against her as they sat together, his deep sighs, the secret messages from his hand in hers were all proof of how he felt. Each time Rob went out of the room Hugh pulled her to him for a kiss and although she welcomed his lips, it was the feeling of losing control that scared her.

Back in the baths at Greenwich she'd overheard women talking about men and sex so often. 'All men are the same. They want only one thing. Once they've been with a girl they don't respect her.' She wished she could ask for reassurance that this wasn't how he would react, but she was too embarrassed to talk about anything like that.

Although she was exhausted she couldn't sleep. It was hot and sticky, no breeze came in the open window and her feelings were completely confused.

Every magazine she'd ever read urged girls not to fall into the trap of sex without marriage. Hugh might say he loved her, but did he really? He hadn't spoken of the future once: was this because he knew she wouldn't fit into his life once he was at university?

But on top of all this were those terrible memories of her father. Until now it was something she'd managed to forget, and now it had come back she felt dirty.

Yet despite all that, she wanted Hugh. Her body throbbed at the mere thought of his hands touching her; each kiss made her shiver with pleasure. She wished now she hadn't closed her ears when Carol spoke of her old boyfriend in Devon. She might have learned if what she felt now was commonplace, or was she a slut to think such things?

She turned over on to her stomach and tried to sleep, but all she could think of was Hugh kissing her. How much longer would she be able to hold out? Maybe she should go back to the school at nights.

But she didn't return to the school, not at night. Sometimes during the day the three of them cycled near there and she popped in to get a change of clothing, hoping she wouldn't run into Mrs Cod, who might question her about her accommodation at the pub. She left cheery notes, waved to Giles out in the grounds, but never stayed more than a few minutes.

Long lazy days of lying in the sun, bike rides, walks and picnics, then the pub in the evenings.

Day by day she was falling deeper and deeper under Hugh's spell. He was the one with the ideas, the enthusiasm. From the moment he woke in the morning he expected her and Robert to fall in with his plans. But how much longer could she hope Hugh would be satisfied with a few passionate kisses that led nowhere?

'What's up, Chas?' Rob asked one afternoon as they lay on a rug together out in the small back garden. 'You aren't fed up, are you?'

'No of course not.' She laughed lightly, glancing over to Hugh who was practising archery with a handmade bow and arrows. He couldn't just bask in the sun, or read companionably as she and Rob could, he had to be doing something all the time. It was Rob she talked to, Rob who helped prepare meals and clean up, yet she couldn't admit this private fear, not to him when he was Hugh's best friend. 'Just thinking about working tonight. I hope it's not as hot in the kitchen as it was yesterday,' she lied.

Sonia and Angus took Charity up on an offer to help one night when they were very busy and once they'd seen how efficient she was, they'd given her a job too in the kitchen. Although she was glad of the extra money and the opportunity to be working while Rob and Hugh were, somehow it marked even more clearly the divide between her world and theirs.

Charity was back in an apron, standing over a hot grill, washing dishes and pans, while they were clowning at tables and behind the bar. The White Swan was a mecca for upper-crust people and though it had an atmosphere of jollity, the voices were all braying public school ones and some of the customers were insufferably rude and snobbish.

Angus was a huge, red-haired Scot with a fearsome bushy beard and muscles like a docker. Sonia his wife was a tiny blonde who tripped into the bar in four-inch heels and expensive couture clothes. Although Angus could bodily throw out any troublemakers, Sonia was the real force. She could rip a member of staff who misbehaved to shreds in five seconds with her caustic tongue, and her sharp eyes missed nothing.

It was Sonia who had pointed out Hugh's deficiencies. Whether this was meant as a warning to Charity, or was just a casual observation, Charity couldn't help but see truth in her words.

'He's an arrogant young pup,' Sonia said. 'Don't get yourself in over your head, Charity, because that lad is entirely self-centred. He'll forge his way to the top and he won't let anyone stop him, not even a pretty little thing like you. To be honest, Charity, you'd have done better going for young Rob.'

Charity had kept these words to herself, but as the days passed she saw there was a great deal of truth in them. Hugh was arrogant, he saw himself as a superior being and he laughed at those less fortunate. He made jokes about farm workers 'who bred like rabbits', he sneered at the pretentiousness of suburbia. He even hid crumbs behind chairs to catch the cleaning lady out.

Rob's parents allowed him to run up a slate in the grocer's to be paid when they got back. Hugh saw nothing wrong in adding a bottle of whisky or steak, even though this was blatant greed. In the same way he'd drink all the milk at night, leaving nothing for the morning. One pint of beer was never enough, he had to have six; he'd take the largest cake, the last potato, the biggest share of everything. He didn't help around the cottage, leaving it all to Charity and Rob. His attitude was that he was special and lesser mortals were there for his convenience.

Rob was quite different, despite coming from an even wealthier background than Hugh. He was shy, liked books rather than sport and he had real affection for the staff who worked for his parents. He could easily afford to throw his weight around as everyone knew he was the heir to the Cuthbertson fortunes, but not once had Charity heard him boast about anything.

Even though she found herself liking Rob more and more as the days passed, it was the easy familiarity of two people alike in spirit. She could tell Rob a little of her days in Greenwich, of her mother's depression and her father's parishioners. He seemed to understand exactly how she felt about not seeing the children. He knew what loneliness was and for all his family's wealth he was as insecure as her.

With Hugh it was fireworks, birthdays, Christmas and Easter all in one day. He made things such good fun. Rowdy, talkative, affectionate and so full of life, yet she couldn't be certain his feelings for her ran as deeply as hers for him.

'Angus and Sonia think you're wonderful,' Rob said shyly. He was wearing only swimming trunks and his bare chest was underdeveloped and pale compared with Hugh's bronzed muscles. 'Hugh's a lucky chap. I wish I could find a girl like you.'

The feeling of kinship she'd felt with Rob the first day at the cottage had deepened as he told her about his parents. Hugh's rather callous remark about his mother going to a 'loony bin' was in fact true. She was alternately high as a kite, or so depressed she wouldn't get out of bed. His father was pompous and overbearing, a man who'd flaunted scores of mistresses in front of his wife. Rob's childhood had been as miserable as Charity's own: beatings from his father, lack of interest from his mother – he even hinted at unpleasant experiences with older boys at school. His family home reminded her of Studley and Uncle Stephen – more evidence of how rich, influential people manipulated everyone, even children.

'Do you think Hugh will still care about me once he gets to Oxford?' she asked in a whisper, taking care to make sure Hugh was still engrossed in his archery.

Rob didn't answer for a moment, his speckly eyes thoughtful.

Rob had looked up to Hugh from the first day they met as two seven-year-olds in prep school. Hugh was always quicker, braver and tougher, and Rob knew their friendship had survived only because Hugh actively sought out companions who wouldn't steal his limelight. Yet despite always being in his friend's shadow, he'd never felt jealous of him until he met Charity.

She was the sort of girl Rob's dreams were made of. Dainty, pretty, and with the kind of warmth and kindness he'd never encountered before. Although he had no experience with girls he could sense her vulnerability. A few kind words and promises from someone as charismatic as Hugh and she'd follow him blindly.

'As long as you don't make too many demands,' he said at length, running his fingers through his straggly fair hair. 'He's like a big kid, Chas, he wants everything now. Although he's my best friend and I've known him since prep school he does tend to be a taker rather than a giver.'

Out of loyalty he couldn't admit how Hugh had boasted that he intended to shag her: the crude expression his friend had used made him smart with anger. Neither could he spell out that Hugh would lose interest the moment he got to Oxford because he was incapable of sustaining an interest in anything or anyone for long.

Charity didn't press Rob further; he was loyal and she didn't want to put him on a spot. Anyway there was over two weeks left of the holidays, enough time to make Hugh feel the way she did.

'Here she comes! I can smell Miss Chip Pan!'

Charity stopped dead in the kitchen doorway, a tray loaded with baskets of chicken and chips in her hands. Hugh had bellowed out the insulting remark and a flush of anger and hurt turned her face red.

He was serving drinks, cool in a white shirt and grey trousers. Along the bar were those leggy, classy girls with their long hair, tight sun-tops and shorts, all of them laughing at her discomfort.

It was true she smelt of fried food. But then she had been standing over a chip pan for hours in blazing heat. She was prettier than any one of those stupid girls with their plummy accents and she could more than compete if she was on their side of the bar. But not with stringy hair, covered in a huge white apron, and with sweat glistening on her brow.

She took a deep breath and handed the tray silently to Rob, aware that he too had heard the remark and was shamed by it. Without even looking at Hugh she disappeared back into the kitchen.

At half-past ten as she cleaned the kitchen the noise from the bar was growing louder. Saturday night and the usual group of locals swollen by people coming in on the way back from day trips to the coast. Hugh and Rob normally joined her for a break soon after ten, bringing a pint for them and a cider for her, but she hadn't seen either of them since the incident earlier.

'Rob's drunk,' Sonia snapped as she came in fleetingly. She wore a turquoise halter-neck dress tonight, her blonde hair piled up on top of her head in loose curls, her nails and makeup as immaculate as if she'd just stepped out of a beauty parlour instead of pulling pints and waiting at tables since five-thirty. 'I don't know what's got into him, he's just invited half the bar back to the cottage for a party.'

Charity groaned. Hugh was always suggesting parties, but Rob usually had more sense. Another time she would've gone out there and talked him out of it, but she was reluctant to appear again until all those girls had left.

'What did Hugh say?' Charity asked.

'He's every bit as bad.' Sonia frowned with irritation. 'He's reminded everyone to buy a bottle. It might be good for business but already someone's thrown up in the garden and some stupid girl's crying her eyes out because her boyfriend says she can't go. A party is all right if you arrange it sober and pick your guests, a nightmare when it's just a drunken binge.'

Charity stood on the open staircase looking down at the crowd in the sitting room and saw exactly what Sonia had meant.

'Summertime Blues' by Eddie Cochran was blaring out, for the sixth time in succession. It was three in the morning and the hordes of people showed no sign of leaving.

They were a mixed bunch, mostly not even friends of Rob's or Hugh's. A group of young Londoners in sharp suits on their way home, hoping to pick up a girl or two *en route*. Two older women who claimed to be happy divorcees, three married salesmen who were staying overnight in the next village, all in their forties, then the gaggle of leggy girls in shorts who'd spent the whole time flirting with Hugh. Added to these unknown quantities were the regulars, at least a dozen male students, some local girls in party frocks and three or four men who'd started the evening on a stag night and lost the groom along the way.

The common denominator was the desire to get as drunk as possible and make as much noise as they could in the process.

She had tried to talk both Rob and Hugh out of it, but they said she was a killjoy. Rob was out cold now, lying on the settee clutching an empty pipkin of Red Barrel. Hugh was dancing drunkenly with one of those snooty girls who'd laughed at her. People were lying on the floor and sprawled drunkenly on the chairs; a divorcee was practically devouring one of the London men sitting astride his lap on a chair in the corner.

The kitchen was awash with beer: a pile of empty half-gallon party packs almost up to the ceiling, and enough bottles to start a winemaking business. Burn holes in the carpet and on the coffee table. Someone had been sick on the floor of the bathroom and the toilet was blocked up.

'Come on, Charlotte, do a strip!' Hugh bellowed out, staggering back to lean against the wall. 'Show us your tits!'

Wild anger rose up inside Charity as the girl began to sway her hips suggestively in time to the music. There was a couple making love in her bed. Someone lying asleep in the flowerbed out the front and she'd seen men using the picket fence as a urinal.

She'd had enough! No one could accuse her of not attempting to join in. She'd come home, washed and changed and tried to be friendly. But that girl Charlotte had made some remark about her 'shacking up with Hugh and Rob' and even went as far as asking who had the biggest cock!

Charity stamped down the stairs, switched off the record player and turned to face the stunned crowd.

'It's over. Time to go home,' she shouted. 'Go now or I'll call the police!'

'Who on earth is that?' A girl in a tight red dress with the straps hanging off her shoulders leaned on Hugh provocatively.

'The maid,' Hugh said, bursting into laughter.

If Rob hadn't chosen that moment to be violently sick right across the floor, splattering everyone within a three-yard range, Charity might have reached Hugh and slapped his face. But Charlotte did up the buttons on her blouse, another couple of girls ran to the door holding out stained dresses and Charity knew this would finish the party.

'Go.' Charity pointed a finger towards the door. Rob was beyond help: he lay green-faced and groaning and the last few men edged away in disgust.

Once a few made their way out, the exodus began in earnest. She heard plaintive cries about how far away their homes were, but would have none of it.

'No one is staying,' she insisted. 'Go!'

Anger made her stronger as she stepped through broken glasses and bottles. She stamped upstairs again, pulled back the covers from the couple in her bed and ordered them out too.

'Don't be like this.' Hugh tried to put his arms round her as she finally shut the front door when everyone had gone. 'I love you.'

'You don't love anyone but yourself,' she said as she flounced away. 'And as soon as it's light I'm going back to the school.'

It was just after seven when Charity came downstairs again. She had locked herself in Rob's room intending to wait until the sun came out, but she'd dropped off to sleep despite her anger. Hugh had slunk into her bed and through the open door she could see Rob in beside him.

But as she paused in the filthy kitchen her resolve vanished. The boys would never be able to clean the cottage properly and she had visions of the little cleaning lady being asked to tackle it.

Rob appeared first, around ten, holding his head and groaning. Even through his drunken stupor he'd known how wild the party was, and how badly he'd behaved. He had woken some time ago but had been afraid to view the damage. Now, miraculously, every trace of the party had vanished. The windows were open, a smell of cleaning fluid taking the place of beer and cigarettes. He noted a couple of small burns in the carpet and the dampness which showed that Charity had scrubbed it, but it was as clean and fresh as it had been on their arrival.

'I'm so sorry,' he whispered. He could see marks of tears on her cheeks and remembered only too well how insulting Hugh had been the night before in the bar. 'You shouldn't have cleaned it up.'

'You couldn't have coped,' she said tartly. 'I didn't do it for you two anyway, but for your mother and the cleaning lady.'

Rob slunk away. He was ashamed for getting drunk and inviting people back, but even more of his feelings for Charity. Hugh was his best friend, but all Rob could think of was his girl.

He went outside, walking aimlessly down the lane. He could never compete with Hugh: not at sport, in company or in looks. He certainly had no chance of getting Charity!

Charity didn't really understand why she couldn't bring herself to go back to the school. She refused to speak to Hugh when he staggered down the stairs smelling of stale beer and went out into the back garden to sunbathe.

She fell asleep, waking later to hear someone crushing tins around the side of the cottage. Then she heard

Hugh's voice and guessed that the pair of them were trying to make the mountain of empties less obvious.

'You shouldn't have called her Miss Chip Pan, it must have been so humiliating.'

Charity pricked up her ears.

'It was just a joke. I didn't mean to be cruel,' Hugh replied.

'You did, you were showing off,' Rob insisted. 'You don't deserve someone as nice as her. Now take her some tea and apologise. I'm going out on my bike.'

Charity pretended to be asleep as Hugh approached her. It was the first cup of tea he'd ever made and she was surprised he knew how to do it.

'I'm sorry, Charlie,' he said, using the pet name to soften her up. 'I was thoughtless, but I thought you'd just laugh it off.'

She turned over on to her back and sat up, taking the tea from him. A few minutes ago she'd been determined to make him grovel a bit, but seeing his face so strained and apologetic, dark blue eyes soft with remorse, her resolve left her. Besides, he looked so beautiful in only a pair of shorts, his chest golden and hard. Maybe he'd learned his lesson now.

'Don't ever do that to me again,' she implored him. 'I can't bear it.'

He lay down on the rug and slipped his arms around her. He smelt of soap now, his face smooth and golden again.

'I love you so much,' he whispered. 'I want us to be together for ever. Let's start all over again.'

His kisses had new tenderness, and knowing Rob had gone out made Charity respond as never before. Hugh's body fitted against her so perfectly, the softness of his lips and the sensuality of his tongue made her belly contract and her breasts throb. She had never allowed him to go further than kissing before but as his fingers crept up under her loose blouse she found herself powerless to stop him.

'I love you,' he whispered as he cupped her small breast in his hand. 'You feel so wonderful.'

As he stroked her nipples Charity forgot how cross she'd been. She moved into a timeless, beautiful world where only his lips on hers mattered, the sensation of holding and being held, lost in love.

He unbuttoned her blouse, moving down to kiss her breasts and his hard young body pressed closer still to hers. His breath fiery and heavy on her nipples and the feel of his skin against hers sent her into a state of abandonment. Every caress seemed to move her closer to something more and though several times she made an effort to move away, he drew her back with more kisses.

Slowly his hand crept up her leg and now it was she who was quivering with desire, pulling him closer still as his tongue licked at her nipples.

The hard lump in his shorts frightened her. One moment she was lost in the bliss of petting, then he moved and she felt it.

'That's enough.' She struggled to get free. 'Rob will be back any minute!'

Hugh leaned back from her, the lower half of his body still pinning her to the ground. His eyes looked soft and sleepy, lips very red from kissing.

'He's not coming back for a while,' he said softly, one hand still on her breast. 'Let me love you, Charlie?'

The tenderness in his face was almost enough to sway her, but a glance down brought back the fear she thought was forgotten.

His penis was peeping over the top of his shorts, red tipped and shiny.

'No.' Her voice was a croak of alarm and she wriggled out from under him in alarm. 'It's not right.'

'But it is,' he insisted, lying on his stomach and leaning up on his elbows. 'It is when you love someone.'

Charity pulled her knees up against her chest and hugged them tightly, dropping her head down so she couldn't see him. She felt him move and then his hand come down on her shoulder.

'I wasn't going to force you,' he said quietly behind her. 'I only wanted to show how much I love you, that's all. If you really cared for me, you'd want to too.'

Chapter Nine

'It's hot.' Hugh was sitting on the doorstep in the sunshine. He wore only an old pair of shorts and his feet were bare. 'We should have got up early and got the train to Brighton.'

'We could take a picnic somewhere,' Charity suggested. It was hard to tell if Hugh's quietness this morning was disappointment because Rob had gone to see his grandmother, or if he was still brooding about yesterday's events.

To her surprise his face broke into a wide smile.

'I know where we could go – ' he took a couple of steps towards her and reached out to hug her. 'It's quite a long ride but it's lovely. Put some shorts on.'

'I thought you were cross with me,' she said, burying her head against his shoulder. Last night he'd come up to her bedroom and he'd been sullen when she sent him away.

'How can I be?' He stroked her hair tenderly and lifted her face up to kiss her. 'I get mad because you don't trust me, but I still like you.'

'How much further is it?' Charity staggered up the hill pushing her bike, red in the face and so hot she felt she might collapse.

'Only a little way.' Hugh grabbed her bike and pushed both up the last bit of the hill. 'It will be easier going home, it's all downhill.'

The last cottage they passed was at least a mile back

and this lane was so narrow and steep Charity felt they must be going to the top of the world.

'Here we are.' Hugh steered them towards a stile and footpath. 'I'll just hump the bikes over and we'll leave them there and walk the rest of the way.'

Hugh took the bag with the picnic and the blanket. The path led them along the edge of a wheatfield which sloped steeply on their left down to a thatched cottage at the bottom.

'Isn't it gorgeous!' Charity stopped to look at the view. From the golden wheat in front of them to a thick wood on the horizon, the fields stretched for miles like a vast patchwork quilt, golden, green and brown. There was a little church with a square tower far away on their right, surrounded by a clutch of cottages, but only birdsong and the buzzing of insects broke the silence.

'Not as gorgeous as you.' Hugh slumped down on the path and just looked at her.

She stood with one hand shielding her eyes: slender legs tanned a golden brown, her bottom small and taut in faded blue outgrown shorts of Rob's and a white sleeveless blouse. Small pert breasts pushed out the front of her top, and her hair, bleached white by the sun, shimmered over her slim shoulders. But it was her profile he studied, struck by its perfection. Her skin was the colour of honey, a sprinkling of freckles across the bridge of her small nose. Lips pink and pouty, eyebrows a feathering of gold above such beautiful blue eyes.

Last night he had lain awake for hours thinking about her. He wanted Charity so much it made him quiver inside. Yet as Rob had pointed out, there would be trouble if his parents found out about her.

'I'm too thin to be gorgeous,' Charity laughed as she turned back to him, her eyes dancing with delight.

She bent over and kissed his forehead, her hair tickling his face.

Hugh caught hold of her waist, pulling her down into his arms, and they rolled together on the grassy path.

'You're slender, not thin,' he reproved her, kissing her eyes, her nose and finally her mouth. 'I thought you were pretty when I first saw you, but now you're beautiful!'

He wasn't going to let his parents throw a shadow over the day. Let them do and say what they liked. Now was the important thing, not next month or even tomorrow.

The path led to another stile, then on down another hill, but Hugh lifted a barbed-wire fence for Charity to crawl under and they made their way upwards through long grass towards a small wood.

'Not much further now.' He took her hand and smiled encouragingly.

'This place had better be worth it!' She was panting and beads of perspiration were running down her forehead. 'Are you sure you aren't lost?'

'Do I look lost?' he said as they walked down towards a wood nestling in a dip. 'You just be patient.'

A wire fence surrounded the wood and Hugh stopped at a place where it was broken and climbed over, holding out his arms for Charity.

'Almost there,' he grinned wickedly. 'But the wood's thicker than I remembered. Just follow me.'

He pushed through the trees, holding back branches for her to follow. It was much cooler now in the shade and it smelt of rotting leaves, but just as Charity was about to complain at branches and brambles scratching her, they came to a narrow path with logs set in it for steps.

'Now close your eyes and don't open them until I say.'

She giggled as he made her follow him, both hands on his waist, her eyes obediently shut. The path was steep and uneven under her sandals, and the smell of steamy vegetation was almost overpowering. She could hear a trickle of water somewhere to her right and leaves brushed against her legs and arms.

'You can open them now.' He stood still, taking her hand.

Charity opened her eyes and gasped in surprise.

'Was it worth the long walk?' Hugh asked.

She couldn't speak: the beauty of the scene in front of her brought a lump to her throat. The steep path had brought them to a grassy glade, hemmed in by thick bushes. In front of them was a pond, its surface almost entirely covered in water lilies, with thick waxy white flowers. On the other side stood a small hut with a tiled roof and a wooden landing stage. Purple clematis climbed up over it, mingling with jasmine.

'Oh Hugh! Who does it belong to?' Charity said in hushed tones. Clematis and jasmine didn't grow wild and there were foxgloves and tall fiery red plants which suggested cultivation. The trickle of water was from a tiny stream, running over big stones to fill the pond.

'Some people Robert's parents know,' he said casually. 'Their place is over the back.' He pointed to his right. 'But they're old and they don't come up here any longer.'

It was so peaceful. Birds sang in the bushes, dragonflies hovered and darted about the water lilies and they saw a kingfisher swoop down, a flash of turquoise as he grabbed a small fish.

'It's like finding buried treasure.' Charity was unable to find the right words to describe how the place made her feel. 'I'm stunned.'

Closer inspection confirmed that it had been

cultivated, for hidden amongst the bushes were a couple of cherub statues, old urns covered with weeds and even small terraces with dainty alpine flowers still managing to grow despite the choking weeds.

'I wish we could tidy it up,' Charity said and pulled a clump of bindweed from a little purple flower.

'We didn't come here to do other people's gardening.' Hugh sank down on to the grass. 'Besides, part of its charm is that it's a secret place. I like it just the way it is.'

'But how big *is* their place if this is hidden away in it?' she asked.

'Well it's an estate.' He waved his hand towards the far side of the pond. 'Beyond the wood that way is a mile or so of grazing land and the farmhouse. Beyond that the big house. There's a tennis court, stables, the whole bit. The grandfather of the people who own it got one of those famous landscape designers to do this back in early Victorian times. In those days they had big house parties and the guests would come out here for picnics.'

'I shouldn't think anyone's been here for twenty or so years,' Charity said thoughtfully. She could see bits of path, but ivy and creeping ground weeds had choked most of them.

'Robert said he came here once when he was around five,' Hugh offered. 'A while later the family's only son was killed in a riding accident and they stopped having guests and became like hermits. The couple must be eighty or so now; heaven knows what will happen to it when they die.'

They spread the blanket out on the only clear stretch of grass and lay down side by side.

For a while Hugh said nothing, just lay gazing at the sky, but when Charity looked across at him she had a feeling he was thinking about her.

'What is it?' she asked, propping herself up on one elbow.

'I was just wondering if you could come to Oxford,' he said softly, lifting one hand and stroking her face. 'You see I can't imagine how we'll get to see one another unless you do.'

'Do you mean live there?'

'Well yes. Get a job there.'

'What kind of job? Like I do at the school?'

Hugh frowned.

'No. I meant in an office or something. You could get a flat, maybe go to night school and learn typing.'

A thrill ran down Charity's spine. His suggestion implied he wanted her close to him, that he was looking ahead and planning.

'But I can't do anything except cook and clean.'

'You can learn,' he insisted. 'You're really quick.'

She was prepared to walk on heated coals if it meant being near him and she loved him even more just for thinking she was capable of getting a good job.

Hugh smiled, seeing that he had found a way round the problem of his parents. Once Charity was in a good job, with a flat of her own, there was no reason why they should object to her. Her uncle was a colonel, after all: maybe they'd even approve of her! The job of kitchen maid was the only stumbling block, but once he'd moved her on from that everything would look different.

'It will work out,' he said, drawing her into his arms to kiss her. 'I just know it will.'

His words soothed the troubled place in Charity's heart, and now instead of anxiety there was only the desire to please. In the garden there had been the threat of someone seeing them, but here, surrounded by woods, hidden from the outside world, she felt secure. Each kiss was deeper and longer, till they were panting and writhing against each other. Somehow her blouse came off and his lips were on her nipples.

Slowly he pulled her shorts down, covering her lips with his as she protested.

'Just let me touch you,' he whispered. 'I want to learn to make it nice for you. I won't put it in you.'

As he kissed her again she could feel the boundaries she'd made in her head becoming blurred. Her body was arching to his involuntarily, she wanted more despite herself. As his fingers stroked her inner thigh, slowly moving closer and closer, her breath was as hard and heavy as his.

'I love you,' he whispered as his fingers found their way into her. 'I want to make you feel like I do.'

All fear was banished by his gentle probes. Wave after wave of delicious sensations went through her body, drowning any small voices that were trying to call a halt. She was on fire, aware only of his lips, his smooth skin against hers and love flowing between them.

'Hold me too,' he whispered, taking her hand and putting it on him. 'I'll burst if you don't.'

There was a moment of hesitation, but he overcame it by stroking her more and more. Her fingers closed round his erect penis and his groan of pleasure pushed away the last vestiges of repugnance.

The sun was burning down on them, birds sang and the trickle of water over stones made a perfect soundtrack. Her nipples were hard against his smooth chest, mouths devouring one another.

She could feel the tip of his penis against her inner thigh as she caressed it, and involuntarily she moved closer still, fear entirely gone now.

'It's so wonderful,' he whispered. 'You are all I ever wanted. I love you.'

His fingers moved faster and faster in and out and she moaned aloud and rubbed him harder. He

174

groaned deeply, rolling on to her, clutching her hand round him tighter.

'Oh darling,' he called out. 'I'm coming.'

She was still moving under him, but his fingers inside her were still now as he lay panting on her breasts. The stickiness was on her belly and as he moved slightly it made a sucking noise.

'When we're married we'll be able to go the whole way,' he said softly into her breasts. 'Just imagine what that must be like.'

Charity felt tears of happiness welling up in her eyes as she lay there holding him. The cloudless blue sky, the ring of trees surrounding them, it was all so beautiful. But it was his words that made her heart throb. He had banished any shame, wiped out the past. He loved her and wanted to marry her and she knew in that moment that she had stepped out of girlhood to become a woman.

'Let's swim,' he whispered. 'Let the water cool us down and wash it all away and then we'll do it again.'

Charity smiled sleepily. She was soaked in sweat, her shoulders red hot from the sun, yet she felt unable to move. Hugh jumped up and leapt the couple of yards into the water, showering her with icy spray.

'Come on,' he yelled back. 'It's wonderful.'

She sat up then, watching him dive under the water and turn a somersault. He came up, shaking his head violently like a dog, spraying her again.

'I can't swim,' she laughed, covering her small breasts with her hands.

'You don't have to, it isn't deep here.' Hugh stood up to show her, and the water only reached his navel.

Charity stood up nervously, embarrassed by her nakedness, but Hugh was looking at her with adoring eyes and his hands were held out for her.

She edged in, squealing as the icy water gradually crept up her sun-hot body. Hugh bounded up to her, caught her round the waist and pulled her back into deeper water.

'No, I'm scared!' she yelled, clutching at his arms.

'I won't let you go,' he assured her, kissing her shoulders and letting her head lean back on him. 'Isn't that good?'

Until today their time had been spent like innocent children, romping, laughing and playing. But it was different now; a new maturity, a kind of wisdom flowed between them, that made each touch like a caress.

It was good to be cool again. The water felt like silk as he swished her round and round and splashed more on to her face. They moved back into the shallow water, Charity kneeling on the bottom while Hugh floated beside her.

'This is heaven,' he said, turning his face towards her. 'And you look like an angel.'

A feeling of exquisite tenderness welled up inside him as he looked at Charity. Her wet hair hung in thick strands over her shoulders and her eyes were like cornflowers. Such small slender shoulders, tanned golden brown with pure white strap marks from a sun-top. Her breasts were just above the water, small, firm and up-tilted with nipples the colour of crushed raspberries.

He swam then, flashing out across the pond and climbing out on the landing stage by the hut. He struck a pose like Rodin's 'Thinker', water glistening on his polished smooth skin like a million raindrops.

'What do you think of that?' he yelled back. 'Want to see me dive?'

Charity could only laugh. His naked body wasn't frightening now: he looked as perfect and right here as the kingfisher and the water lilies.

The dive was as graceful as everything about him. A leap, a perfect curve and he disappeared under the water, barely causing a ripple. She could see his white buttocks beneath the green water and he swam right across the pond under the water lilies without coming up for air.

Charity bobbed up and down in the water, too nervous to move in case she got out of her depth. Hugh emerged from the water, bringing up a clump of lilies on his shoulders.

'Was it a good dive?' he shouted.

'The best,' she called back.

Later he tried to teach her to swim, holding her under the stomach and floating her on the water. 'Make your legs go like a frog and push away with your hands,' he commanded.

She tried, but each time she just sank under the water.

'I'll get you a rubber ring,' he laughed. 'I won't give up! Now let's have the picnic, I'm starving.'

Cheese and pickle sandwiches had never tasted so good and Charity even forgot she was entirely naked, her hair hanging dripping down her back, as they wolfed the food down and drank deeply from the warm lemonade.

'What if someone comes along?' she asked, as Hugh wiped a smear of pickle from her cheek.

'They won't,' he said. 'It's a secret place, no one knows about it but us and those old dears.'

They dried sitting in the sun, and when Hugh kissed her again, passion flared up like a match on dry straw.

This time it was even more sensuous and lingering: each touch savoured as if it was the last, legs wrapped round one another, fingers more exploratory and bolder. Hugh lay beside her, mouth on her breast, touching and stroking until she cried out with desire. Even when he moved down on to her belly and she knew he was looking at her pussy as his fingers slipped in and out, she felt no shame, only bliss. It was she who drew him on top of her, losing all control. Some urge from deep within her made her open her legs wider still, wrapping them round him. She felt the hard tip of his penis pressing against her pubic bone and she arched her back, digging her fingernails into his shoulders.

Suddenly he was inside her, moving in and out so naturally she felt no sense of panic, only the need for more. His hands moved down to her buttocks and he held her firmly, driving into her, and all the time she could only think of how much she loved him.

It was only as his movements became harder, his breath hot and violent on her neck, that she remembered what this was and she wriggled, trying to get him off.

'No Hugh.' She pushed at him. 'No!'

But he was immersed in the act now, oblivious to anything but his own needs until with a great groan, he slumped down on her.

'I love you,' he murmured, his eyes shut and beads of perspiration on his forehead. 'That was so wonderful.'

'I didn't mean you to.' Tears welled up in Charity's eyes.

His head shot up, eyes full of alarm when he saw her tears. 'Did I hurt you?'

She almost blurted it out. All the suppressed anger, the guilt and shame, but as her mouth opened she saw the fright in his eyes and she choked it back.

It would only hurt him. She mustn't speak of it now, or ever. Hugh wasn't responsible for what had happened, it was she who had lost control and instigated it.

'I meant to stop,' he said, looking horrified. 'Oh God, you'd better get back in the water and wash it all away.'

She couldn't be angry with him. He was thinking of pregnancy, which hadn't even occurred to her. He washed her so tenderly and promised to get some Durex on the way home.

'It had to happen sooner or later,' he said as he kissed her. 'We love one another and that makes it right. Tonight in bed we'll do it all properly. I'll make it beautiful for you too.'

She watched him as he swam again later. The water glistened on his brown shoulders and his black hair was slicked back so he reminded her of the seals she'd seen in London Zoo. He dived under the water lilies, coming up further back with one hanging on his head and she knew she would love him for ever.

Charity woke early on her last day at the cottage. Rain was gushing down a drainpipe and splashing down the side of the cottage. She turned her head to see Hugh still sound asleep, one arm curled round his dark head.

She never got tired of looking at him, but now she could see he had changed from a boy to a man in their month here. Faint dark stubble on his chin, a stronger, more mature look about his mouth. His bare shoulders looked almost black against the white sheets and his lashes were as thick and long as brushes.

This was the last time she'd lie in bed with him for some time. No more bliss-filled nights as they discovered one another, no more days of fun and laughter. He'd replaced ugly memories by beautiful ones and even if they split up one day, she'd have those to sustain her.

Tonight she would be back in her room at Bowes Court, while Hugh had one last night at the pub with Rob. Tomorrow she would be making beds, polishing floors in her overall and Hugh would be travelling back to Yorkshire wearing his dark suit. Rob would move back to the big house to await his parents' return.

It would be weeks before she tasted Hugh's kisses again. Perhaps months before she found a flat so they could lie in each other's arms and do again all those things they had learned together. Sadness overwhelmed her and a tear trickled down her cheek.

'What's up?' he whispered in the murky light.

'Just thinking about tomorrow.' She let him draw her into his arms and savoured that warm, musky smell of his skin.

'I wish I could take you home with me,' he said softly.

He had avoided the subject of his parents and in her heart she knew why.

'You will write to me?' she asked. 'You won't find someone else?'

She knew he was dreading the six weeks before university, and she still hoped he'd invite her to Yorkshire.

'Of course I won't.' He turned her face to his, a look of surprise in his eyes. 'Do you think I'd forget you so easily?'

He sighed then and she knew the time had come when he was going to talk about his parents.

'I wish I could ask you home,' he said gently. 'But I can't, Charity, because they'd be against you from the start. I've got to be really casual about you. If they found out they'd be looking for ways to end it.'

His words said everything she feared, and tears welled up again.

'Don't cry.' He wiped the tears away and kissed her nose. 'It isn't that I'm not proud of you. Just that I don't want them making life difficult for us. You do understand, don't you?'

'Yes.' She bit back the tears, loving him still more

180

because he had been so diplomatic. She must get a good job, develop a patina of sophistication, become like Tania and Charlotte, the student waitresses at the pub who spoke of riding, balls and 'drinkies', before she was presented to the Mainwarings.

Charity rolled over until she was on top of him. She knew that scenes now wouldn't help either of them. She had to convince him first that she was the only one for him. His parents she'd work on later.

'We've got lots of fun ahead too,' she smiled down at him.

She memorised every last thing about the cottage, as she got her things together. The smells, the feels, the sounds. The aroma of ground coffee, sheets damp with lovemaking, the perfume from the jasmine outside the door and even the grass. The sounds of birds, Chuck Berry records. She would see in her mind's eye for ever the dalhias in the garden, the white picket fence and the gleam of sunshine on old pine furniture. She would feel the wind in her hair as they rode their bikes, and moss under their feet in the woods. Relive the sensation of cool night breezes on passion-heated bodies. Remember how it felt to wake and and find him looking at her with lazy deep blue eyes.

Hugh wanted her to get a taxi back to school, but she insisted on riding the bike. He and Rob packed a box with the new clothes Hugh had bought her on a trip to Brighton and tied it firmly to the carrier on the back.

The earlier rain had cooled the air and brightened the flowers in the garden. The lane was full of puddles and the air smelt of wet grass. Across the meadow the red tiles on Robert's home stood out behind the dark green trees, but the sky was as grey and sad as she felt.

'Hugh's a lucky chap,' Rob said quietly as Hugh went back into the cottage to collect the sponge bag she'd forgotten. He held the handlebars of her bike and his eyes couldn't quite meet hers. He looked far better now than a month ago. Sun had almost banished his acne, he had a sturdier appearance and a more confident air.

Charity had become aware how Rob felt about her, ever since he'd come back from his grandmother's and discovered Hugh and her in bed together. His bleak expression in the days that followed made it clear he'd had a crush on her for some time. She'd tried to include him as before, but it hadn't really worked. He worked longer hours and backed away from picnics and bike rides with her and Hugh.

'He's lucky to have a friend like you, certainly.' She smiled, reaching out to touch his face. She would miss him too, all those chats about books, her brothers and sister and his time at school. Hugh was her love, but Rob had become her closest friend and now they were parting she wished she could tell him that. 'Thank you for letting me stay, Rob. I hope I didn't spoil things for you?'

'You made the holiday.' He smiled but his eyes looked sad. 'Hugh would've picked on me the whole time without you. Maybe if things work out for you in Oxford you could both come down at Christmas?'

Rob didn't share Hugh's confidence that it would all work out for them. His own mother might understand, but Clarissa Mainwaring was a calculating, heartless woman and if she suspected her son had left his heart in the hands of a girl she'd consider 'common', she would find a way to spoil it. Loyalty to Hugh wouldn't allow Rob to speak of this; he didn't even dare suggest Charity kept in touch with him in case it was seen as trying to muscle in on her.

'Good luck with university.' Charity managed a wobbly smile for Rob. 'Find yourself a nice girlfriend and have fun.'

Rob could barely meet her eyes. She was the first person he'd ever felt this close to and he wished more than anything that she loved him. Hugh might be stronger in most ways, but if Rob had a girl like Charity, nothing and no one would stop him taking care of her.

'Don't you forget all those ambitions.' Rob forced himself to use a light tone. 'A good job, getting your family back together again. And don't let that pig of an uncle wear you down.'

Hugh rode with her most of the way, but they were silent, wrapped in sadness.

'I'll think of you every night,' Charity said at the crossroads where they'd agreed to part. 'Promise me you won't forget me?'

His last kiss was so painful. She felt no passion; tenderness and sorrow had taken its place. Clinging to him desperately, she wished she had the words to say what she felt.

He was still standing by the crossroads when she took the final bend out of sight. She stopped and waved, soaking up the way he looked. His legs like mahogany, his teeth flashing white against his brown face as he smiled. One hand to his lips, blowing a kiss.

It was such an odd sensation being back at school. Only this time last year she'd been a frightened child thrown into an adult world. Frightened of Miss Hawkins, intimidated by the size of dormitories and classrooms. Now she was a woman, showing a new girl how to hang curtains and polish floors ready for the boys' arrival.

Mrs Cod was a little cool with her, perhaps waiting for a more complete explanation as to where she'd been. But Charity didn't care. Her mind was on Hugh and she was counting the days until his first letter would arrive.

It was rather disappointing, although he had enclosed some photographs he'd taken at the cottage. He recalled some of the times they'd shared, reassured her he would help her find a flat in Oxford, and that he missed her badly. But if he shared the almost unbearable desperation she felt at being apart, he didn't say.

The boys arrived back at school. The new ones looked so small and frightened that Charity's heart went out to them. Sometimes in the morning when she saw Matron with an armful of wet sheets it was a reminder of Toby and how even now he was going through the same trauma at Wellington College.

It was a whole year now since she had last seen Toby and Prue. Although Lou reported Prue had made friends locally and was having music and dancing lessons, and that Toby couldn't wait to get to Wellington, her letter too seemed to lack something. What exactly did she mean when she said 'You need have no fear about Toby and Prue. They are more in danger of being spoiled than of being neglected'? The remarks about Prue being 'a little madam' and Toby running rings round his uncle held a tone of disapproval and perhaps anxiety. Lou said she had made no headway regarding Charity's position. Stephen maintained he'd given her the same opportunities as the other children and he didn't want her undermining his authority now.

But although this letter wasn't encouraging, Charity was able to accept it. If she found a job in Oxford it might be possible to see Toby and Prue in secret. Daydreams of finding a little flat and making it pretty filled the long working days and at night-time she could imagine cooking meals for Hugh, and cosy nights by a fire.

To fill the lonely evenings, Charity turned to writing. Hugh had asked her not to write often because too many letters would make his mother suspicious. So instead she wrote stories. Some were fantasy, projecting her experiences into what she'd like to happen, some were reminiscences of the holiday. She bought a large notepad, with the idea that she could store them away for the future, when she could look back and laugh about these fears, hopes and feelings.

The diary Uncle Geoff gave her was of some help, although there were only scanty entries in August; it was while leafing through it that she found an entry on the third of August.

'Bad tummy ache. Hugh keeps asking what's wrong, but how do you explain that to a boy?'

Charity kept looking at it, a sick feeling welling up in her stomach. She remembered exactly what that tummy ache was caused by – it had been her last period. She counted the days feverishly on a calendar. However hard she tried not to be alarmed, she was ten days late!

Common sense told her she needn't worry. Her cycle had never been very regular and anyway Hugh had used Durex every time, except for that first time at the pool. An article in a magazine claimed that any unusual excitement or upheaval could delay a period . . . but still it niggled at her like a toothache.

She wrote to Hugh as usual, but didn't mention it. They had agreed she mustn't write anything too personal for fear of his mother reading it, and anyway she was sure she would start her period any day.

But the days crept by and still nothing happened. Sometimes she woke in the night with a tummy ache, jumped out of bed – but it was always a false alarm.

The leaves on the trees were slowly turning gold.

In the morning and evening there was a nip in the air and at times heavy rain lashed down for days. But Charity barely noticed the passing of summer as her anxiety grew.

Hugh's letters were becoming shorter and further apart. Was that because he'd stopped thinking of her, or was he busy studying? She stopped counting the days, and turned instead to weeks. Two weeks late, three, and then four. Hugh must be busy getting ready for Oxford because she hadn't had a letter for over a week. She couldn't really be pregnant, could she?

'What's up love?' Mrs Cod called from the kitchen as Charity ran out into the scullery as they were preparing breakfast. 'Are you ill?'

Charity didn't answer. She held on to the sink so hard her knuckles were white. It was the smell of the grilling bacon, and any minute she was going to be sick.

Taking deep breaths helped. The feeling of nausea stayed, but it went no further. She had beads of perspiration on her forehead yet she was shivering, and then she remembered how the women had been discussing pregnancy one day and the subject of morning sickness had come up.

'I couldn't abide the smell of meat,' Pat had said. 'I could eat it once it was cooked, but the smell of it raw turned my stomach. And tea! I couldn't keep it down. Drank nothing but water till I was seven months gone.'

Janice said it was eggs that made her bad, but it was Mrs Cod who couldn't bear the smell of bacon.

'Charity!' Mrs Cod's big hand touched her shoulder. 'What's wrong? This isn't like you. You're as white as a sheet.'

'A tummy upset.' Charity managed a weak smile. 'I had a pain in the night and it's just come back.'

186

'You'd better go and lie down then,' she said. 'Go on, I can manage.'

Lying on her bed Charity faced up to what was happening.

She was five weeks overdue and that attack downstairs had been morning sickness, however much she hoped otherwise. Now she thought about it, her breasts were tender, something she remembered her mother complaining about when she was expecting James.

The prospect was too awful to contemplate. If she confided in anyone it would soon get back to Miss Hawkins and she knew she'd get the sack immediately.

She got off the bed and went over to the window. The big chestnut tree at the bottom of the playing field was shaking in the wind, golden leaves fluttering down like scraps of paper from a bonfire. A group of boys in shorts and singlets running round the grounds reminded her sharply of Hugh.

'Just keep calm,' she told herself as she turned away and opened the drawer to take out her writing paper. 'You aren't the first girl in the world to get pregnant out of marriage, and he loves you.'

Chapter Ten

'There's a letter for you, Charity,' Mrs Cod yelled over the roar of the potato peeler.

Charity's heart leapt. She dropped the porridge pan she was scouring into the sink with a clatter and ran into the kitchen, tearing off her rubber gloves.

'A boyfriend?' Pat enquired, her long face bright with curiosity as she peeled apples for pies.

'It's over there!' Mrs Cod nodded her head in the direction of a work surface by the door. She was rolling out pastry on the table, her red face frosted with flour. 'Miss Hawkins brought it in.'

Charity snatched up the familiar blue envelope.

'Aren't we going to hear who it's from?' Mrs Cod asked as Charity disappeared back into the scullery.

'She don't share anything with us these days,' Pat said teasingly. 'Our little Swot's got herself a fella!'

Although Charity heard the women's familiar banter her mind was only on Hugh's handwriting. Trembling with excitement she pulled out the single sheet of paper and leaned back against the sink.

But as her eyes scanned the lines, her legs seemed to turn to jelly and an involuntary gasp of horror escaped from her lips.

She read it through again, sure she must be mistaken, but as his words slowly sank in, the colour drained from her face.

It was hot and steamy in the scullery, but all at once she was shivering.

'Come on, out with it.' Mrs Cod's voice seemed to come out of nowhere. Charity glanced up and saw the woman standing in the doorway, her hands on her wide hips. 'Anything to tell us?'

'No.' Charity shoved the letter into her pocket. 'It's nothing.'

'Not bad news, is it?' The older woman moved nearer, a frown of concern on her big florid face.

Charity wanted to scream, knock pans round the kitchen, cry in someone's arms, but she could say nothing – at least not until she'd thought it through.

'No, it's all right.' She turned back to the sink, willing Mrs Cod to clear off and leave her. 'Just a note from someone who worked at the pub this summer.'

The morning seemed interminable as she tried to bottle up her grief. She avoided contact with the other women, knowing that one affectionate remark, any attempt at drawing her out, would make her confess everything.

But as she reached her room at two-thirty, the pain of rejection hit her. She fell on to her narrow bed and sobbed until the tears ran dry.

'But *why*, Hugh?' she whispered. 'Why did you say all those things if you never meant them?'

She read the letter again, trying desperately to make his words sound less final.

Dear Charity,

I'm sorry, but I have to break it off with you. My mother found out from Rob's mother that you'd been staying at the cottage and she went ape. At first I thought she might calm down and forget about it. But she's threatened to write to the school and tell them about us, unless I promise to stop seeing you. I don't want you getting the sack on my account and anyway, Mother's right, it wouldn't work out.

I've got years of studying ahead of me and I'm too young to go steady. It was a great summer, we had a lot of fun and I'll never forget you. But I can't go against my parents, not now. Sorry, I hope you aren't too upset.

Love, Hugh.

Bitterness rose up in her as she analysed exactly what he was saying. Faced with the possibility of his parents' cutting off their financial support, Hugh found he didn't care tuppence about the girl he said he loved. She was just a kitchen maid, an embarrassment, an unnecessary burden.

If he'd meant only half of the things he'd said back in the cottage, he could've suggested they pretend to break it off and meet in secret. But it was clear he wanted nothing more to do with her. She would figure in his boasts to friends as the girl he bedded in the summer hols, along with how many pints of beer he drank in one night and the escapades of the other student bar staff. But he didn't love her, now or then.

Alone in her room, six weeks after she had said goodbye to him, she could look back and see pointers which showed that his feelings had never run as deep as hers. His letters had never been as passionate as hers, and until that day at the pool he'd never spoken of the future. Even his farewell wave didn't have the same sadness as her own.

Everyone always said men only wanted one thing. While she'd been looking at love and marriage, his mind had just been on sex.

She couldn't go back downstairs to get her tea at five. If anyone saw her swollen eyes they'd guess.

Lying on the bed staring at the ceiling she knew she had to leave. If she stayed until her pregnancy was obvious she'd get the sack anyway.

But how would she manage? She'd been relying on Hugh's help. Fear brought a fresh flood of tears and although she tried to think calmly all she could see was her stomach growing larger and larger until the baby arrived.

A woman at the baths in Greenwich had once talked about visiting someone to get rid of an unwanted baby. That was the answer! But how would she find someone?

One thing was certain: there was no one here at Bowes Court who would know such things. She would have to go to London.

The pain inside her welled up until it consumed her. There was no one up here to hear her sobs, no one anywhere that truly cared. She had trusted him, given him everything she had to offer and now she was rejected.

'I'm having your baby,' she cried as she held Hugh's photograph to her heart. 'Do you know what you've done to me?'

Sleeping on her problems didn't ease the pain, but in the early hours she came up with a plan. She would say she was going for an interview for a job on her day off, then come back and announce she was handing in her notice.

She was glad now she hadn't told Hugh about her pregnancy in her letters. If he didn't want her without knowing his child was growing inside her, he certainly wasn't going to help her now.

'Are you quite sure this is what you want?' Miss Hawkins looked at Charity's handwritten notice, then back at her face.

She had heard Charity's story that she'd landed a job at an insurance company in London and how she intended to find a room in a shared flat with some other girls, but somehow it didn't ring true. Was she making it all up?

It was Charity's expression that worried her. There was a dead look in her eyes, no warmth in her smile. Where was the excitement that young girls usually showed when they were on their way to a more thrilling job?

'Quite sure,' Charity said evenly, avoiding the housekeeper's direct glance. 'I get lonely here and I want some new experience.'

Then Miss Hawkins remembered those letters. For the whole first year the only ones Charity got were from Mr and Mrs Charles. But since the holiday there had been three or four from a different source. Maybe Charity had found herself a boyfriend during the holidays, as Mrs Cod suggested. But it wasn't her business to pry.

'I'm sorry to see you go, Charity.' Miss Hawkins was sincere about this, she liked the girl. 'You've been one of the best workers we've ever had here and all the staff will miss you. But if this is what you really want, then I can't stop you.'

Charity longed to tell Miss Hawkins what she really wanted. For Hugh to write again and say it was all a big mistake and he still loved her. Or that she'd wake one morning and find the pregnancy was a false alarm. But no one could give her those things. Leaving was the only way to keep her good name.

'Well if you're sure I'll have your cards and a reference ready on Friday.' Miss Hawkins sighed. 'But if you change your mind, you're quite welcome to stay.'

It was very odd saying goodbyes. She felt little emotion, even though every one of the kitchen staff had come to mean a great deal. She went through the ritual of taking their addresses and small gifts, promising she'd write as soon as she was settled, knowing she would never contact anyone again.

But the oddest thing of all was leaving by the front door. In a whole year she'd never been out that way and it seemed strangely symbolic that her last memory of Bowes Court should be stepping out of the brightly lit hall into darkness. All this school meant to her was Hugh, and she was never going to see either of them again.

As Charity came up the steps from the underground at Hammersmith she felt as if she'd arrived in a different country. Although it was nearly eleven at night it was bustling with people, and so noisy she was instantly intimidated. Traffic roared around the Broadway, there were cafés and restaurants still open and music blasted out from at least five public houses.

'Could you tell me the way to Shepherd's Bush Road?' she asked a couple of girls. They were dressed as if going dancing or to a party, their hair up in beehives, coats open to show sparkly dresses.

'You ain't going to the Palais with that lot, are you?' one giggled, looking down at Charity's case and holdall.

'No I'm looking for a place called Greystones,' she said, not understanding what the girl meant by the Palais.

'Dunno where that is.' The second girl blew a bubble of gum thoughtfully. Her eyes were heavily lined with black, giving her a menacing look. 'But this is Shepherd's Bush Road.' She pointed to the road round the corner where much of the traffic was heading.

'It's a long bleedin' road,' the other one volunteered.

Charity thanked them, picked up her case again and as she turned the corner saw the Palais for herself. Dozens of girls just like the ones she'd spoken to were making their way in there and even more men, all in suits with winklepickers and slicked-down hair. She had to step into the road to get past them all and she saw it was a dance hall, with men on the door wearing dinner jackets and bow ties.

Had she not been so exhausted and strung out by the day's events, she might have felt a twinge of excitement at coming to such a busy place, but instead all these people out enjoying themselves heightened her sense of isolation.

She had a picture in her head of Greystones girls' hostel as a place something like a hotel. She'd got the number out of the classified telephone directory. Four other hostels had said they were full, so when she'd heard this one had a spare bed she booked it there and then. But as she made her way along the road and saw one long terrace of tall, dilapidated houses, her expectations slowly shrank. The basement rooms she glimpsed below the level of the railings were grim. Some were kitchens which evoked memories of Easton Street in Greenwich; in others she could see little more than a flickering television and the legs of people watching it. But even those rooms which had tidy, closed curtains held that air of poverty she once thought she'd escaped for good.

Drunks staggered across the busy road; teenage boys stood in groups, cigarettes dangling from their lips, collars turned up against the cold wind. From time to time music wafted out from an upstairs window.

Finally, just when she thought her arms would break with the heavy case, she saw Greystones House. If there had been any alternative she would have turned back.

She hesitated at the steps up to the front door, knowing instinctively this was a bad place. Someone had broken one of the glass panels in the front door and it had been replaced by a hastily tacked on sheet of hardboard. A glance down into the basement showed a group of girls watching television in a gloomy, smoke-filled room, but it was too late and she was too tired to go another step.

Tentatively she rang the bell. A strong smell of cabbage was wafting out and with it the sounds of music and people shouting. When no one came she rang again.

'All right, I'm coming!' a voice yelled out and seconds later the door opened.

Charity stepped back in alarm at the apparition in front of her. The woman was grotesque, enormously fat with bulging dark eyes and greasy hair loose on her shoulders.

'Yes,' she snapped.

'I'm Charity Stratton.' Her voice wavered. The woman was wearing something akin to a navy uniform, but it was so stained with spilt food she could have been an inmate of a lunatic asylum. 'I rang earlier.'

'Fine time this is to arrive,' the woman said, opening the door marginally wider. 'I thought you'd changed your mind.'

'I had to come up from Sussex,' Charity said weakly, afraid to actually step over the threshold. 'I'm sorry if I kept you up.'

'Come in then,' the woman snapped again, then as wild laughter came from upstairs she turned back. 'Stop that row you lot, and one of you come down here and see to the new girl.'

Charity picked up her case again and slipped in. She was appalled by the place; even the air seemed to be filled with grease and nicotine. The hall was painted a murky green, scuffed at elbow height, grease marks at shoulder. The carpet had been patterned but it was reduced to a dull brown by count-less feet.

'I'm Miss Gullick.' The woman looked back at Charity with a look intended to freeze. 'I'm the warden and while you live here you abide by my rules. As you've left it so late tonight I'll take all your particulars in the morning. Just give me the advance rent now and you can get off to bed.'

'How much is it?' Charity had to focus only on the thought of bed, otherwise she might have burst into tears. She hadn't expected a welcome exactly, but a bit of friendly warmth would be a help.

'Three pounds, five shillings. That includes break-fast and a cooked tea. I don't give any reduction if you choose not to eat it.'

As Charity took out her purse, a big dark-haired girl appeared on the stairs. She wore jeans and a striped sweater and she looked Charity up and down as if she had three heads and four legs.

Something warned Charity not to let either of these people see how much money she had. She pulled out three pound notes and five shillings in change and quickly put the purse back in her bag.

'Take her up now, Joan,' Miss Gullick said and looked sharply at the other girl. 'She's in your room. Make sure she knows the rules and don't go teaching her your bad habits.'

Charity lay in the lumpy, narrow bed too scared even to sleep. She hadn't expected to share a room with three other girls, especially girls who viewed her with such suspicion. The room smelt of sweat and feet, the sheets were grey with careless washing and she hadn't dared to check on the mattress for fear of finding something worse. Even now in the darkness the girls were whispering and giggling and she knew it was directed at her. Despite her promise that she wouldn't cry, she couldn't control herself and an audible sob slipped out.

'It gets worse,' Joan called out. 'You wait till you see the breakfast!'

Charity turned on to her stomach, sliding her hand under her pillow to make sure her purse was still there. This place was dangerous and she must get out of it as quickly as possible.

Chapter Eleven

'Someone's taken my cardigan,' Charity ventured nervously to Miss Gullick.

Charity had been at Greystones for ten days and it was a hellhole. Once a gracious family home with servants living in the basement, now all semblance of family life had gone and the rooms were stark and cheaply furnished. Twenty-four girls shared six bedrooms, with only two bathrooms between them. She heard Miss Gullick telling someone on the telephone that it was 'a home from home' and it made her wonder what sort of home she'd been brought up in.

The dingy basement held the dining room, the kitchen and what passed as a sitting room. This had a small television with very bad reception, about twelve fireside chairs with scratched arms and damaged webbing beneath the worn cushions, and a radio which was on all day and evening too.

Four bedrooms on the ground floor, with bars across the window because girls had been known to go out after eleven at night that way. Two on the first floor, of which one was Charity's, and the bathrooms and toilets. The top floor was Miss Gullick's domain and no one dared, or wanted, to go up there.

The baths were always filthy because the girls were supposed to clean them after use, but never did. The toilets were even worse, and one day Charity found that someone had done her business on the floor.

It was odious. Evil smells from the toilets, overcooked cabbage and girls who hadn't the slightest idea of personal hygiene, mingled with constant noise. Shouting, crying, radio and television and from outside the barrage of traffic which kept her awake at night. She had given up trying to eat the stodgy, flavourless food as soon as she found work as a waitress in a small restaurant nearby.

Charity was speaking to Miss Gullick by the 'Office' in the basement. In reality it was merely a store-room full of giant tins of baked beans, tinned fruit and washing powder. Presumably it had got its name because it housed a tall stool at a small bench under the barred window and Miss Gullick kept her records here.

'You should have looked after it.' The warden's wheezy voice had more than a trace of irritation. 'Don't come bothering me. I've got more than enough to worry about.

'Well, what are you waiting for?' Miss Gullick turned to see Charity still hovering in the doorway. She stuck her face up close to Charity's, blasting her with foul breath. 'I thought you had a job to go to?'

Charity recoiled. The woman was gross: greasy skin peppered with blackheads, bulging frog-like eyes and a wet slack mouth with a dark moustache.

'I haven't got to be there until ten,' Charity said, trying to smile pleasantly, because she wanted this fearsome woman on her side. 'I wondered how much notice I had to give if I find a flat or a room somewhere?'

'Not good enough for you here?' Miss Gullick sneered. 'Or have you got a bloke you want to shack up with?'

Charity's eyes widened, appalled by the woman's crudity.

Her first night's impression of Greystones as a

dangerous place was uncannily accurate. It was a dumping ground for severely disturbed and difficult girls. She'd been right to hide her purse too. Her manicure set went the next morning, and now there was the cardigan. Daily she heard the wails of girls who'd lost sweets, clothes, cigarettes and money. Charity now kept her money tucked into her blouse pocket, and photographs and letters she wanted to keep she'd sewn into the lining of her handbag for safety.

On her second day, after she'd found a job, she took the precaution of packing everything she valued into her case and took it to the left luggage office in Hammersmith Broadway for safe keeping.

Social workers and police called frequently. Each night when she got home from work she would hear whispers about someone going to court or being arrested. Words like 'store detectives', 'bail', 'fines' and 'prison' seemed an integral part of each girl's conversation, along with talk of men they'd 'been with'. Arguments turned to violence in seconds. Joan, the big dark girl who'd spoken about the breakfast on her first night, was the most terrifying. Only a couple of nights earlier she'd gone for another girl with a fork and scraped it down her cheek.

She was certain some of the girls here would know how to get an abortion, but she couldn't ask. Even if Hugh had rejected her she felt too much loyalty to him and his child to bandy around intimate details.

But as Charity heard whispered malicious remarks about her clothes, accent and looks, she sensed she was a target. All they were waiting for was an excuse and an opportunity to hurt her.

Perhaps she ought to feel some affinity: after all, she was as unwanted as any of them. But a stronger voice told her that each person had to fight to keep their dignity, not wallow in self-pity and degrade themselves further.

'We don't go much on notice here,' Miss Gullick gave her a withering look. 'But don't expect a refund of your rent if you leave before the end of the week.'

'I'll tell you this evening, is that all right?' Charity wondered if she'd even bother to change the sheets before a new girl came. They hadn't looked clean when she got here.

The woman didn't reply, just slouched off into the kitchen.

Charity made her way down Shepherd's Bush Road towards Hammersmith Broadway, her mind on Lou and Geoff. Their comfortable home, their wisdom and kindness felt like a magnet, drawing her towards the tube station. But she knew she didn't dare go there, or even telephone them. This was something she had to handle alone.

'Do you know anywhere I could get a room?' Charity asked Marjorie, her employer, soon after she got to work.

Bell's Diner, in King Street, just two minutes' walk from Hammersmith Broadway, was a very popular place because it was cheap and the food good, plain cooking. It was somewhere between a transport café and a tea shop in its appearance, with net curtains on the windows, as many tables and chairs as they could squeeze in, but the tablecloths were always clean and you did get waitress service.

Martin, Marjorie's husband did all the cooking. Roasts, shepherd's pie, toad in the hole and braised steak. Majorie was always trying to vary the menu, with curry or salads, but day after day most of the customers ordered what Martin did best: great piles of meat and vegetables with a river of gravy around them.

During the afternoon they did snacks, then in the evening most of the food was fried to order, anything from beefburgers to steak. But from twelve until two they were rushed off their feet and quite often there was a queue of people waiting for tables.

Marjorie was a frayed-looking woman of forty with dyed red hair and pale skin which reflected a lack of fresh air. The day Charity had come in for the job advertised on the window, Marjorie had asked her few questions and given the reference only a cursory glance. At the time Charity had seen this as indifference, but during her first week she found she was mistaken.

Marjorie was a diplomat. She gleaned a great deal of information about her regulars, but never passed it on as gossip. She was the kind of person who bided her time and waited for others to open up.

'Is the hostel that bad?' she asked, sitting down at one of the tables and indicating that Charity should join her.

She'd probably been pretty as a girl. Her eyes were bluey green and her nose turned up at the tip. Even now if she was to get her hair cut and styled properly, instead of just tying it back with a rubber band, and put on a little makeup she could be attractive. Hard work had kept her slim, and her black skirt and white blouse were always spotless. Yet it was the weariness people noticed, not her good points.

'Make us a couple of cups of coffee, love?' she yelled back to Martin in the kitchen. 'Charity's got a problem.'

'It's awful.' Charity gave her a quick rundown of the stealing, the filth and her general fear. 'I can't bear it another minute.'

Time and again since starting here she'd thought of taking Marjorie into her confidence to ask for advice. But even though she knew she was pregnant, somehow it didn't seem real. Finding somewhere to live was the first priority. Maybe once she was over that hurdle, she could face the next.

Marjorie lit a cigarette and drew in reflectively.

'Always been a bad place, that.' She shook her head. 'I thought it had improved when you said you lived there. I've had girls from there ordering a dinner then do a runner on me.'

Charity sensed as she looked into those calm eyes that Majorie would give her good advice. She was blunt, never dressed things up, and above all she could be trusted.

'There's a place on the Broadway that's got proper flats in its window. Do you think they do just rooms?'

It hadn't taken Charity long to cotton on to the reality of life in London. Just a glimpse of the advertisements in the evening paper proved that decent flats at low rent were as difficult to find as nice people.

Hammersmith was so dingy: rows of houses once as smart as those on Clapham Common, but falling into neglect as the owners let them out. The Broadway shops must once have been select establishments, but they had gone the same way as the houses. Soot blackened their fancy brickwork and they now catered just for the constantly changing population. Rubbish lay in the subways uncleared. Drunks staggered about at night clutching bottles. Pubs blasted out pop music and the traffic roared round in a never-ending stream.

'I've just thought.' Marjorie smiled, suddenly animated. 'There's a bloke comes in here every day that runs a flat letting agency, we could ask him. But rooms cost a few bob, love! You ain't gonna get much change out of three quid. That only leaves you two to live on.'

'I haven't any choice.' Charity made a glum face. 'If I stay in Greystones I'll probably get everything stolen. Besides if I'm too hard up I could get another job in the evenings.'

'You could work a few more hours for me.' Marjorie looked round at her husband as he came in with the coffee. 'Thanks, love, we'll be out in a minute, but Charity's just been telling me what that Greystones is like. We must get her out of it.'

'I'm sorry to hear that,' he said and sat down next to Charity, glancing first at his wife for approval.

Martin Bell was a small, tubby man with hazel eyes and a gentle voice. Although he was only around forty like his wife, he'd lost most of his hair and the bald patch on top gleamed under the lights. He was the more outgoing of the couple, given to bursting into song in the kitchen sometimes. He had worked as a chef for many of the leading London hotels before taking on this business, and as they prepared the vegetables he often amused Charity with hilarious disaster tales.

The three of them discussed Charity's plight and Martin offered to go straight away to the man's office and ask him.

'I wish we could offer you a bed.' He smiled at Charity. 'But you've seen how crowded it is up there.'

They were living in a two-roomed flat above the restaurant while they saved enough money to buy a house. There was barely enough room for them because an aunt had given them a whole load of furniture ready for the house.

'I wouldn't expect you to.' Charity smiled weakly. 'But it's nice of you to think it.'

'Well you're the first girl we've had for a long time that's got any idea.' Marjorie smiled. 'We don't want to lose you.'

Martin scuttled out, still in his striped chef's trousers and white jacket.

'He'll see you all right,' Majorie assured her. 'Now, how much money have you got? They'll probably want a deposit and that agency bloke gets a cut.'

'About twelve pounds,' Charity replied. 'I paid for

204

the hostel in advance. So if I leave on Friday I don't have to give them anything more.'

'If he says you can move in tomorrow, you do it.' Marjorie patted Charity's hand. 'You haven't told us much about yourself, love. Perhaps one day you'll feel like opening up. When you do, I'm here.'

Those few kind words brought a lump to Charity's throat. If there hadn't been a rush of people coming in for coffee, she might have spilled out everything. But past experience told her that people didn't always react as she expected and it didn't do to trust completely.

'I'd like to tell you the whole story,' she said, getting up to go into the kitchen. 'One wet afternoon when there's nothing to do!'

'You've got a date,' Marjorie laughed and suddenly looked pretty.

'You're in luck, little girl.' Martin beamed as he came back in. 'He's got a room just a few doors down from here. It's not too smart, he says, but it's only two quid, including the electric light. He says you can have it if you bung him a quid, it will save him advertising it.'

'When could I move in?' Charity's pulse quickened with sheer relief.

'He suggested tomorrow. He's coming in for his dinner anyway and then he'll take you along to see it. So put on a bright smile, darling, and you might earn a few tips today.'

Charity's heart plummeted once more as she saw the miserable room, but she knew she'd have to take it.

It was just along King Street, only four doors from the Bells' dining rooms, at the back of the house on the second floor.

'It's grimmer than I realised,' Mr Rose the agency man said, embarrassed. Charity had served him every day at the restaurant. He looked as smart as a bank manager with his pin-striped navy suit and sparkling white shirt, so he obviously made lots of money. 'But it's cheap, Charity, and you can always tart it up.'

The room was perhaps twelve by nine. An ancient gas fire stuck into an old fireplace, a single bed under the window. The wardrobe was merely a rod fixed across the chimney-breast and a disgusting-looking two-ring burner sat on a rickety table. A washbasin in the corner smelt as if it had been used as a toilet and the chest of drawers had most of its handles gone. Everything was dirty, though to be fair to Mr Rose, he had told her the last tenant had done a moonlight and he hadn't had time to send someone in to clean it.

Charity picked up one of the blankets with two fingers. They were so dirty she could never lie under them and she had no sheets or pillowcases.

'I'll throw those out.' Mr Rose chucked her under the chin. 'Cheer up, girl, I'll bet anything you like Marge has got a few spare ones. If she hasn't I'll dig some out.'

The bathroom next door was cleanish, though antiquated, with a huge sort of geyser on the wall above the bath.

'On the plus side the other tenants are a jolly bunch,' he grinned at her. 'To be honest with you, the people here usually introduce their friends. I don't think I've ever had to advertise for someone here. This fella that skipped out owing rent conned me. I thought he was OK.'

'I'll take it,' Charity said, more because he was straight than anything else. 'But the *mattress*!'

He sighed. 'I hoped you wouldn't notice that.' Not only was a spring coming through it, but it was stained as if someone had wet on it. Charity imagined bugs crawling everywhere. 'Yeah, I'll get that dumped. I've got a couple of new ones in my office.

But you do me a favour too. You clean it up. I don't think anyone I know would do a good enough job for you anyway.'

'OK.' Charity was pleased that he saw her as a fastidious person. 'So how much do I have to pay you?'

'Two quid deposit and a quid for the introduction, that's half-price as you're a friend of Martin's. I'll start the rent from Friday night, because that's when I collect from everyone. If you aren't here, leave it on the table for me. I get nasty if you forget.'

He handed her two keys.

'Don't lose them.' He smiled. 'And I'll dump the stuff later today.'

Charity ran back to Greystones on winged feet when she finished work. She intended to pack the few clothes she had there and go back to the room to start cleaning. Majorie had sorted out sheets, blankets and pillows for her and even promised to find her a pair of curtains once she'd got settled.

Finding a room was a start. She had stopped feeling sick in the mornings too. Once she was settled then she could think about all her other problems, like finding someone who knew about abortions.

The moment she got in she went down to the basement to look for Miss Gullick.

The evening meal was always served at six-thirty and the entire house smelt of cabbage and burnt sausages.

Miss Gullick was mashing grey-looking potato in a big pan and the kitchen was full of steam. She looked up as Charity came in.

'I've found a room.' Charity tried to give a warm smile, hoping to endear herself to the woman even at this last stage. 'I can move in tomorrow.'

'I'm not giving you a refund!'

'No, of course not,' Charity shot back, backing away. 'I'm going round there now to clean up.'

The radio was booming out from the sitting room and, judging by the wreaths of smoke coming out the door, most of the girls were in there waiting for their tea, which meant she wouldn't have to run into anyone.

Her bag was packed, she had changed into jeans and a sweater, and her plain navy skirt and blouse for work were folded on the chair ready for tomorrow.

At the sound of feet on the stairs, she reached out for her coat, anxious to avoid any confrontation. But suddenly Joan was coming through the door, followed by Sue and Denise, and she knew from their faces it meant trouble.

'Leaving, are we?' Joan asked in a nasty tone, folding her arms across her chest, flanked by her sidekicks.

Joan was big with wide, masculine shoulders. As always, she wore men's jeans and a skinny rib red sweater that showed off her big bust. As she stood there she tapped the lino with the tip of her long black winklepickers.

'Tomorrow.' Charity tried to smile, but she was scared. 'I'm just going round to clean the room, it's filthy.'

The other two girls were known troublemakers too. Sue was a gangly simple-minded girl, with bad skin and lank, greasy brown hair.

Denise was a small bleached blonde, one of the girls who went with men for money. She was clearly dressed ready to go out in a skin-tight white pencil skirt and short boxy navy jacket, her hair done up in a beehive.

'Lady Muck!' She gave one of her hysterical giggles. 'Even Buck 'ouse wouldn't suit you.'

Charity noticed the oddest things about the girls.

208

Denise's suspenders sticking through her tight skirt, a yellow-headed spot on Sue's chin and a huge love bite on Joan's neck.

Joan sauntered over, the cigarette dangling from her lips. She put one hand on Charity's bag. 'You ain't nicked nuffin, 'ave you?'

'Of course not!' Charity backed away.

'Well let's just check, shall we?' Joan flipped the bag up and over, tipping the contents out on her bed.

Sue leapt forward like a hyena, big rough hands picking up Charity's underwear.

'Look at 'er fancy knickers!' she taunted, holding up a pair of dainty briefs. 'No skid marks in those. Bet her shit even smells like fuckin' roses.'

'Please don't,' Charity begged them. 'I must get going.'

'Oh you must, must you!' Joan leapt forward before Charity had a chance to move away, handing her cigarette to Denise. 'You fuckin' poncey cow. You think you're better than all of us, don't you?'

She got Charity by the throat, her big hands squeezing her windpipe. Charity could feel her eyes popping almost out of her head and she desperately clutched the girl's arms.

'You think you're so pretty, don't you?' Denise came forward, braver now her big friend had Charity in a stranglehold. Her small sharp features were alight with spite. 'Well I'm going to cut off your bloody hair and mark your face.'

Charity had lived with people making fun of her all her childhood and had learned at an early age just to laugh it off. But she couldn't laugh now. These three girls with their evil, grinning faces were like something from her worst nightmares.

She screamed, but a blow on her cheek silenced her momentarily. She didn't see it come, just a flash of fist

209

and the impact of bone on bone. It threw her back against the door, slamming it behind her.

'Shut up, you evil little slag,' Joan commanded. 'Bring those scissors here, Sue!'

'No!' Charity yelled. 'No, please don't!'

Denise came forward to hold her head as Sue danced from one foot to the other like a mad thing.

'No, please don't,' Sue mimicked. 'Go on Joan, cut it off, the lot of it.'

Hank after hank came away in Joan's hand.

Charity screamed again, her arms flailing around, trying frantically to protect herself.

At last she heard running footsteps on the stairs, and someone pushing against the door. Joan took a step back, the scissors still in her hand.

Charity moved to let the person in, still screaming in terror, but Joan ran at her, the scissors pointing right at her face.

Covering it was a reflex, but as the door burst open, taking her with it, Joan made a final lunge and the point of the scissors went right through her fingers into her cheek.

'What's going on?' Miss Gullick shouted.

Blood was running through Charity's fingers and dripping down her hands but she didn't dare remove them from her face for fear of what had been done to her. She was aware that other girls had come in, and someone put a comforting arm round her shoulders.

'Ring the police,' Miss Gullick ordered. 'You, Pat! Don't just stand there.'

Charity slowly lowered her hands. Miss Gullick had Joan pushed back on to a bed and was restraining her by sitting on her. Sue stood over by the window smirking, Denise bent over the end of Charity's bed shoving the clothes back into the bag as if her life depended on it. Five or six other girls were elbowing their way into the room, faces alight with curiosity.

'Look what they've done to her lovely hair,' a voice piped up.

Tears came then. Charity saw the hanks of hair, white gold on the dark brown lino, and felt with horror the shorn stumps on one side of her head. Her face stung, not just from the cut, but from the punch before it. She didn't have to look to know she would have a black eye by the morning. But it wasn't spoiled looks that made her cry, it was a feeling of utter desolation.

She was pregnant, Hugh didn't want her, and now this!

She wouldn't stay the night, even though the police who came begged her to. She let them bathe her face, but she insisted on going to her new room, even if there would be no sheets or blankets.

'You can't stay here, it's filthy,' said the police-woman who had come up the stairs with her at King Street.

Charity looked round at the woman's sympathetic face.

'It's not as filthy as Greystones,' she retorted. 'But if you're really worried about me, you could go along to Bell's dining room four doors down and explain. My boss Marjorie has some sheets and blankets for me and a box of cleaning things I bought today. She'll give them to you.'

The policewoman came back ten minutes later with Martin carrying the stuff.

He took one look at Charity's face and hair, put down the pile on the bed and held out his arms.

'That place ought to be closed down.' He shook his head in shock as Charity leaned against him. 'And that woman who runs it should be locked up for not warning you it was a hostel for disturbed girls.'

Martin tried to make her go home with him, but Charity would have none of it.

'This is my home now,' she said, needing to hold on to her last vestiges of pride. 'When I lock that door no one can hurt me, or steal from me. It's kind of you to offer but this is where I stay.'

It was after eleven when she finally got to bed. The room smelt of bleach and cleaning fluid and it was as bare and comfortless as a monk's cell.

She had only a tiny handbag mirror in her bag, but it was big enough for her to see her face was a mess. The cut was deep, though small, and it would probably leave a scar. The other cheek was swollen, the eye above it half closed and turning black. Thumbprints on her neck were clearly visible, but it was her hair that concerned her most. On the right side of her face it was cut jagged right up past her ear and there was no alternative but to have it cut short all round.

She was exhausted now, shaking with delayed shock and the punishing cleaning she'd forced herself to do. But the sheets and blankets were clean and aired, and the new mattress was softer than the one at Greystones.

'Why, Hugh?' for the millionth time she asked herself. 'What did I do wrong?'

Chapter Twelve

'A bit further to the left.' Marjorie stood back while Charity reached up on the stepladder to pin a gold foil ball to the ceiling. 'That's perfect. Make certain it's fixed, we don't want it falling into someone's dinner.'

It was the beginning of December and the restaurant was closed for a couple of hours in the afternoon while they put up the decorations. A big box on the floor was spilling over with paper garlands, tinsel and damaged Chinese lanterns, the tables were stacked in pairs to make more room, and draped over some of them were plastic snowmen and Father Christmases which Marjorie was attempting to sort out.

'So many of these are broken,' Majorie sighed. 'Every year we say we'll buy new ones for next year, and each December we find we've forgotten once again. Remind me, Charity, to throw this lot out when they come down.'

Charity smiled down at her employer.

'Well throw all the bad ones away now,' she suggested, pointing to one of the snowmen. 'He's only got half a hat for a start and those lanterns are so decrepit no one would even pinch them if you left them outside the door.'

'It's memories, you see,' Martin chimed in as he struggled to stand the tree in the window. 'We got those lanterns when we first got married. Did up our one room like a little grotto, didn't we sweetheart?'

Charity knew exactly what Martin meant. Each one of these decorations had reminded her of past Christmases. Making paper chains with Toby and Prue, arranging the Nativity scene that father brought out of the attic every year. Decorating Babylon Hall with some of the parishioners and putting the special Christmas cloth over the altar.

This year there would be no children to watch opening stockings. Lou and Geoff would be alone with James; Toby and Prue sitting at the big dining table at Studley Priory. Would they talk about her? Did they feel the same sense of loss she did?

Marjorie heard her husband's remark about their old memories but she didn't respond. She was looking at Charity up on the stepladder. A light caught her sideways on, and to her surprise she could see a pot belly.

'You're putting on weight, my girl,' Marjorie exclaimed.

'Don't be so personal,' Martin chuckled. The tree just wouldn't stand up, however hard he ground it into the bucket of sand. 'It's my fault, I'm always pushing food on to her.'

Marjorie opened her mouth to apologise for being so blunt, but her words were halted by the expression on Charity's face. Not embarrassment, but fear!

'You'd better check the fairy lights, dear.' Marjorie turned to her husband and away from Charity. She could feel a blush spreading over her pale face and suddenly she understood everything.

The night when the police came in to tell them Charity had been attacked had been a turning point in the relationship between the three of them. Staff came and went, rarely putting much effort into the job; they could be sly, dishonest and most were plain lazy. The Bells had never felt involved with anyone before, but when Charity came in on time that next morning with a sticking plaster over her cheek, and makeup over her black eye, their hearts went out to her for her courage and singlemindedness.

They packed her off to the hairdresser's to get her hair sorted out, let her work behind the scenes until her face returned to normal and encouraged her to put the nasty experience behind her.

Since then Charity had told them bits of the events that led up to her arrival in Hammersmith. It came out that she and her brothers and sister were orphaned and their uncle had become their guardian. Later she admitted her distress that she wasn't allowed to see the children. She had never explained why she left the public school she worked in, or why she ended up in Greystones House, but Marjorie was sure there was a boy at the bottom of it.

She didn't complain about anything. She worked hard and cheerfully, painted her room to make it as pretty and cosy as possible, but Marjorie often wondered why such an attractive girl had no friends. Now that Marjorie had spotted that tummy everything fell into place. The drawn, anxious look on the girl's face, the way she rarely spent any money, and the way she never spoke of the future.

'Give us a hand folding these serviettes,' Marjorie said. She sat down at a table with a pile in front of her, nodding at Martin to make himself scarce. He had finally got the tree upright, wedged between two bricks, and the fairy lights flashed cheerily, reflecting off the decorations.

Charity sat down opposite Marjorie and began folding the serviettes in triangles. 'I could make some table decorations for the evening,' she suggested. 'A candlestick in plasticine with a bit of holly and glitter. I did some at the school last year.'

215

'That would be nice.' Marjorie looked up at Charity and knew she had to tackle her now.

It was obvious, really; she didn't understand why she hadn't realised sooner. Charity's face was plumper, with a rosy glow about it, and her breasts were bigger too. Of course the new haircut had altered her a great deal. Maybe that was what had distracted her.

The short feather cut emphasised her dainty small features and focused on her big blue eyes. She looked like an elf with all those little tendrils round her face. At a casual glance it was nothing more than a few gained pounds, but Marjorie was certain she was right.

'Are you pregnant, Charity?' she said in a low voice.

Charity looked up quickly, fear widening her blue eyes.

'It's all right. I'm not asking because I intend to sack you or anything like that,' Marjorie reassured her. 'But if you are, you need help, and quickly.'

Charity had wanted to tell Marjorie so many times. Alone in her room at night she worked out what she would say, but the next morning she found she couldn't. Day by day as she felt her tummy getting bigger she became more scared, but now with Marjorie looking at her in sympathy she felt nothing but relief.

'Yes. I wanted to tell you before, but I didn't know how to,' she admitted, trying hard not to cry.

She had come to like and respect Martin and Marjorie. They were hard-working people. Almost always cheerful, sincere and fair, they had built up a good trade by treating every customer as if he or she were important. The time was right to reveal everything now.

Charity told Marjorie everything: how she had met Hugh, and the summer holiday at the cottage.

216

'When he wrote and said he'd had second thoughts I wanted to die.'

'But you didn't,' Marjorie pointed out. 'And you'll get through this because you're brave and sensible. But you can't just ignore what's happening.'

'Do you know anything about abortions?' Charity whispered.

Marjorie looked shocked.

'Not much, love, but I know you're too far gone to even consider that.'

Charity's lips trembled.

'Come on, love,' Marjorie wheedled. 'You couldn't have gone through that anyway. What about writing to Hugh again and telling him how things are?'

'No.' Charity blanched. 'If he doesn't want me I'm not going to try and blackmail him to help.'

Marjorie shook her head in bewilderment. The kid was made of stern stuff, that much was certain; more pride than the changing of the Guard.

'But it's his responsibility too!' she argued.

'No, I couldn't,' Charity insisted. 'I'd rather have a baby all on my own than have him hating me for showing him up. If I was to see him again I know I'd try and plead with him to love me again.'

'Then you've got to handle this alone, I'm afraid. But we're here and you aren't the first girl to fall for a handsome face and a few empty promises. Now, have you been to a doctor yet?'

'No.' Charity shook her head. 'I've been too scared to.'

The plaintive look on Charity's face made Marjorie's heart prickle with tenderness. She wasn't one to get involved with other people's problems, she had enough of her own. The restaurant wasn't the little gold mine people supposed. A thirteen-hour day, cramped living conditions, health inspectors who thought they were the Gestapo and a mountain of paperwork left very little time even to wash her hair. But Charity was the only girl they'd ever employed who actually made life easier for them, and Marjorie was very fond of her.

'There's no need to be scared. The moment you face up to it, the better you'll feel,' she said sensibly. 'I'll ring my doctor now and make an appointment for you after work.'

'But my job! I've got to keep working.' Charity was close to crying now with the release of tension.

'There's no reason why you shouldn't go on working for quite some time.' Marjorie saw how close she was to breaking down and didn't want to make things worse. 'But you must stop carrying heavy things, and wear some flat shoes.'

Everything Marjorie knew about pregnancy had been gleaned from younger sisters and customers. She had never wanted a baby herself; until she met Charity she hadn't even been aware she had any maternal instincts.

Charity looked down at her three-inch heels. They made her feel older and she was loath to give them up.

'I mean it.' Marjorie smiled. 'And perhaps you should get a looser skirt. That way no one will notice for some time.'

'You are indeed pregnant.'

Dr Thomas washed his hands at his sink, looking over his shoulder as Charity scuttled back behind the screen to get dressed. 'Almost four months, which means the baby will arrive in the middle of May.'

Dr Thomas's surgery was in the basement of a house in Brook Green, reached by a flight of steep stairs with rusting railings. Once inside, leaving behind a faint whiff of dustbins, it was a surprisingly antiseptic place with black and white tiled floor and walls that appeared to have been painted pale green only days before.

The doctor sat down at his desk and waited for the young girl to reappear. He knew she was crying and his heart went out to her. He studied the few notes he'd made. She'd be seventeen when the baby arrived, no husband, no parents and from what he gathered the father had deserted her.

Dr Thomas was well over sixty and in the thirty years he'd been a GP he must have seen thousands of pregnant women. Telling a happily married woman such news was a time for joy, but for girls like Charity there would be no happy ending.

Charity came from behind the screen, dabbing at her eyes.

'Sit down for a moment,' he said gently. He might be an old man with white hair, but he couldn't fail to be moved by such a pretty girl's distress. 'Now, I've written a letter to Hammersmith hospital, that's not the one across the road, it's by Wormwood Scrubs. You must take it there and they'll sort out your ante-natal visits. This is a prescription for some iron tablets, take one with each meal.'

He paused, wishing he could tell her something to ease her mind.

'Now Charity, there is an almoner at the hospital, she's the person who will put you in touch with people to help you.'

Charity silently put the letter and prescription into her bag, trying to control a desire to break down.

'Thank you, Doctor,' she whispered.

'You can come and see me if you have any problems,' he said gently. 'Try and eat sensibly, get plenty of fresh air and exercise to make sure you have a healthy baby. Try not to worry too much, there are people out there to help you.'

219

'Miss Stratton!' A beefy, red-faced nurse called out her name, making a point of the 'Miss' bit.

Charity got up, blushing. It had been bad enough sitting amongst twenty or so older married women, without having her predicament advertised.

The nurse handed her a tall glass.

'A specimen please!'

Charity didn't know what the nurse meant and stared blankly.

'Go in the toilet and pass some urine in here.' The nurse seemed to think she was deaf as well as stupid. 'When you've done that put it on the table outside and go into the cubicle and undress. There's a gown inside to put on. Take off everything.'

It seemed to be one humiliation after another. So many questions, so much embarrassment. A whole group of men and women stood around watching while the doctor gave her an internal examination. It wasn't just the delicate probing that Dr Thomas done, either: they pushed a huge metal shoehorn-type thing into her, prised her open then peered in. One by one they listened to the baby's heart through a metal trumpet, just as if she was a side of meat, not a human being.

They took blood from her arm and made her cry. They said she was underweight, as if that was her fault. The doctor said she would have to be checked for venereal diseases because she wasn't married. When she began to cry the big nurse curtly informed her that she should have thought of the consequences before she had sex.

She felt lower than a prostitute. Unclean, unwanted.

Finally at twelve, after being there since before nine, they sent her to see the almoner.

Dr Thomas had said this was the person who would help, so she began to cheer up while she waited on a row of chairs in a long corridor. But two hours later she was still there and no one seemed to care.

She was bursting to go to the lavatory when finally the door opened.

'Come in, Miss Stratton.' A tall thin woman in a tweed suit popped her head out the door.

She just sat behind her desk, drinking coffee and reading notes in front of her. Charity didn't like the look of her one bit. She had a bony, heavily lined face and a row of pearls round a scraggy neck and the way she avoided looking at Charity suggested she was going to be unpleasant.

'I'm Mrs Perkins. From what I gather,' she said in a plummy voice, peering over her glasses, 'you are unmarried. Four months pregnant, without any parents. Is that so?'

'Yes,' Charity murmured.

'Your job?'

'A waitress.'

'What sort of accommodation do you have?'

'A bedsitter in Hammersmith,' Charity said weakly. The woman tutted.

Charity thought Mrs Perkins was the kind Lou despised: middle class, with no experience of hardship in her own life to draw on. Such a woman would put people into categories. Charity was probably labelled 'delinquent'.

'The father has deserted you, I suppose?'

Charity could only nod.

'His name and address?'

'Why do you want that?' Charity was immediately on her guard.

The woman looked askance at her. 'So we can take him to court to make paternity payments, of course.'

'I don't know his address.'

The woman looked hard at Charity.

'When will you girls learn some sense?' She sighed. 'Does he know you're pregnant?'

'No.' Charity was sure that was a trick question. 'I couldn't tell him because I don't know where to write.'

Mrs Perkins scribbled down what seemed to be far more than Charity had told her.

'What had you in mind to do when the baby arrives?' The almoner fired the question as if from a gun.

Charity didn't know what to say.

'Well, were you thinking of taking the baby back to your room? Have you a job in mind? Do you have any idea how much it costs to bring up a child? Or were you hoping someone would miraculously solve these problems for you?'

'I don't know.' Charity hung her head. 'I mean, I haven't thought that far ahead.' How could she explain to this woman that she'd been in a state of numbness since Hugh's last letter?

'Well you should, my girl. And quick!' Mrs Perkins pointed her pen towards Charity. 'Let me make a couple of points. One is that a new baby requires not only money to buy food and clothes, but a great deal of care and attention. You can't shut it in a bedsitter on King Street for long because if it cries it will disturb your neighbours. You can claim National Assistance to live on, but believe me they will give you precious little.'

'I'll get a job.' Charity imagined a baby in her poky room, and shuddered.

'What sort of job? Waitressing? How much do you earn at that?'

'Five pounds a week.' Charity's voice began to shake.

'But where would the baby be while you were at work?'

Charity could see what Mrs Perkins was getting at.

'You haven't thought about it, dear, have you?' Suddenly the older woman's voice softened. 'I don't mean to be harsh, but I see so many girls like you, Charity. Reality is wheeling a pram through the streets in the early morning and leaving your baby at a nursery all day while you work. Then going to collect it at night when you are exhausted. By the time you've bathed and fed it, it's time for bed, then the whole thing starts again the next day. You'll have no time for friends, no nice clothes for yourself, it will be work and still more work, washing nappies at midnight, wondering where you'll get the next shilling for the gas. Every decision has to be made by you. If the baby's sick you can't go to work. If you can't work you get no money.'

Charity's stricken face proved Mrs Perkins's point.

'There is of course an alternative,' the almoner said gently, her pale eyes fixed on Charity. 'That is adoption. At this stage in your pregnancy it often sounds like the perfect solution and one most girls are eager to grasp.'

'Give the baby away?' Charity's eyes flew open in horror. 'Oh no, I couldn't do that.'

'Don't be too hasty.' Mrs Perkins took off her glasses and polished them. 'I have never yet met a girl who gave her baby up easily, however much she claimed before its birth that she would. But in the end it is the bravest, the most caring mothers who do, because they can see beyond their own pain and want the best for their child.'

Charity shook her head.

'No, I couldn't.'

'No one is asking you to. No one will force your hand, Charity. The final decision will be up to you, and you alone. But I can tell you now there are couples out there desperate for a child to love, people who have beautiful homes, stable marriages and everything in the world to offer. Every adoptive couple is checked and rechecked for suitability. It's a lucky child who ends up in one of these homes, a child matched to its new parents by what is known about the real ones. Nothing is left to chance.'

She didn't tell Charity she worked on a committee for an adoption society, or that she was one of the people who vetted prospective adoptive parents. Instead she paused and took a small booklet out of her desk.

'Take this home and read it,' she said, and passed it over. 'Meanwhile I'll get in touch with someone from the Moral Welfare Association, they are a group of people who help girls such as yourself. A lady called Miss Frost will be in touch with you soon.'

Charity found herself just wandering around Shepherd's Bush instead of going home. Darkness had descended without her noticing; the air was damp with a slight hint of fog.

Christmas was on everyone's mind. Women struggling with heavy baskets of shopping. Men in suits carrying carrier bags along with their briefcases and umbrellas. Schoolchildren dawdling home in groups, pausing to look into shops bright with tinsel, decorations and coloured lights, but Charity felt nothing but apathy.

A huge Christmas tree had been erected on the green, lit up with hundreds of coloured bulbs. A greengrocer's wares spilt out on to the pavement: piles of tangerines, cupped in silver paper, pineapples, nuts, apples and bananas. A toy shop on a corner had a working model of Santa Claus waving his arms in its brightly lit window and two small children stood with their noses pressed up against the glass, faces bright with excitement.

Was it only two years ago she'd been like one of those children? She could remember taking Prue and

Toby into Lewisham one afternoon on the bus and seeing Santa Claus at Chiesman's in his grotto. He had given her a hand mirror, only pink plastic with a lady in a crinoline painted on the back, but she'd thought it wonderful. Just a few weeks later the fire had burned everything – that mirror, her parents, their home – and finished her childhood for good.

Next Christmas her child would be over six months old. It seemed only minutes since James was that age. Mrs Perkins didn't have to tell her how hard it was to bring up a child. She knew.

She walked back past Greystones and glanced down into the basement. They had a tree in the window and she could see Joan sprawled out in a chair, smoking a cigarette while she watched television.

Once she'd considered herself better than those other girls, but now she could see there was little difference. They were all in trouble in one way or another.

She read the little booklet that night. Not once but four times. It spelled out in simple language exactly what being an unmarried mother meant and the stigma on the child. It explained there were benefits she could claim and National Assistance for her and her baby, but it underlined the message that few landlords would give her a flat and the Council rarely considered unmarried mothers on their waiting lists.

Adoption was explained fully, and mother and baby homes. Charity put the booklet down and sobbed into her pillow. She had lost everything she cared for now. The children, Hugh and even Lou and Geoff. She daren't pass on her new London address in case Geoff took it into his head to pop over and see her. However much she wanted their sympathy and kindness, she wasn't going to risk Uncle Stephen discovering her predicament, or bringing shame to her brothers and sister.

'So this Miss Frost is coming to see you here?' Marjorie looked surprised. 'Was that her idea or yours?'

'Mine.' Charity hung her head. 'I thought if she saw the house I was living in she'd turn against me straight away.'

'But you've made your room so pretty,' Marjorie said. 'Half the bedsitters in London are as grotty as your house. She'll have seen far worse.'

'But it's smarter here.' Charity glanced round the restaurant with its snowy tablecloths, gleaming cutlery and smart Regency striped wallpaper. 'I feel safer with you around.'

Christmas had passed painfully. She accepted the invitation from Marjorie and Martin because there was nowhere else, and although they did their best to make it a jolly occasion, Charity was relieved when it was over.

Charity lay awake as 1962 came in. She could hear people singing Auld Lang Syne out in King Street and the sound of their revelry made her want to cry with loneliness. Now it was twelfth night and they were taking down the Christmas decorations.

Hammersmith Broadway looked even more mucky and dismal than usual as Charity walked to work that morning. It had begun to snow yesterday and for a short while everything looked magical, but now the snow had been shovelled up into black heaps on the pavement and a further frost had made it as hard as concrete.

'Miss Frost might not be like her name,' Martin said and slung an arm round Charity's shoulder when he overheard the news of the intended visit. 'But just in case she is, you want us to thaw her out?'

Charity giggled.

Martin was very astute. That was exactly what she meant, but she couldn't have put it into words.

'We'll support you,' Marjorie said stoutly. 'If she gives me a chance I'll tell her what a little gem you are. Now stop worrying, she might be nice.'

Charity just knew the woman in the dark blue pork pie hat was Miss Frost, even before she spoke. She was a big woman; not fat, but big-boned and angular. Her coat was shabby, a different shade of blue from the hat, and she wore thick brown lisle stockings and fur-lined boots with a zip up the front.

Charity approached the woman as soon as she sat down.

'Are you Miss Frost?' she said, hoping she was mistaken and it was just another customer after tea and a cake.

'I am.' The woman unwound a thick grey scarf from her neck and peeled off fur-lined leather gloves. 'You must be Charity Stratton?'

Charity nodded. 'I'll just get you some tea,' she said in a small voice. 'Would you like a toasted teacake too?'

Marjorie, who had watched the interchange from the kitchen door, swept over to the table.

'Good afternoon. It is Miss Frost, isn't it?' She smiled down pleasantly as Charity hovered, not knowing whether to sit, stand or run. 'I call Charity my little gem; goodness knows how we're going to manage once she leaves. Do sit down and talk, Charity.' She winked at her carefully so the older woman didn't see. 'I'll get you a tray of tea myself.'

Charity had no choice but to sit down now, but Marjorie had at least shown the woman that her employers were aware of her predicament.

Miss Frost had the most piercing eyes, a chilly

bright blue. At first glance Charity had thought her old, but this was mainly because of her dress. Close up she saw she was mistaken. The woman was in her late thirties and she had smooth unlined skin, stretched over prominent cheekbones. 'It's always much easier for my girls when they have an ally.' The way she pronounced 'girls' as 'gels' made Charity think of Joyce Grenfell.

'Mr and Mr Bell have been very kind to me,' Charity said.

Miss Frost didn't reply to this, just gave Charity a long stare.

'Have you any plans you would like to air with me?'

Charity wasn't sure what this meant.

'Well, is there any family who would help you?' Miss Frost prompted. 'Any chance of marriage with the father?'

Charity shook her head on both counts.

'Well in that case I recommend a mother and baby home,' Miss Frost said carefully as Marjorie brought the tea. 'We have one home in Hampstead which I think you would fit into very well. I would book you in there for the beginning of April and you would stay in total twelve or thirteen weeks, depending on whether baby arrives on time.'

'Is there any alternative?' Marjorie asked. She had appeared with the tea just in time to hear about the home. 'You see when Charity first came to London someone sent her to Greystones House. She had some very nasty experiences there.'

Miss Frost turned her piercing eyes on to Marjorie.

'That hostel is an abomination,' she said indignantly. 'The Moral Welfare Association does not run its homes along those lines. We are a charitable organisation, our committee members have worked hard to provide good, clean, comfortable homes and all our staff are fully qualified in this work. Daleham Gardens, for example, is a beautiful house with a delightful garden. In the six weeks antenatal period, the girls learn mothering skills, while sharing the running of the house. During this time Charity will be fully counselled about both keeping her baby and giving it up for adoption. When her time comes, she will go outside the home to have her baby at Queen Mary's on Hampstead Heath, then return ten days later.'

Miss Frost never faltered once in this long, glossy description of the home, almost as if she were reciting it from a brochure. Yet behind her stern face and piercing eyes Charity recognised a woman with a kind spirit.

'May I sit down and join you?' Marjorie said. 'Please say if you think I'm butting in, but I really want to hear.'

Charity threw her a grateful glance.

'Of course, Mrs Bell. As someone close to Charity it is admirable that you should know the procedure.'

Marjorie sat down and poured the tea.

'The final six weeks are when the girls have to make their minds up.' Miss Frost lowered her voice just a little. There were only two couples in the restaurant, both deep in their own conversation, but she realised that Charity didn't want her position made public. 'At one time adoptive babies were taken at birth from their mothers. Although to the uninitiated this may sound less painful, it is in fact storing up trouble for the mother. By staying with her child for a full six weeks, not only do we discover any problems the baby may have, but the mother has time to make the right decision.'

'But six weeks – it sounds so cruel!' Marjorie looked horrified.

'No so, quite the reverse. The young mothers have

a taste of what hard work a new baby is; they learn it isn't a doll they can put away and forget about when they are tired. Sometimes the fathers come forward at this stage and very often parents who claimed once they didn't even want to see their grandchild, step in. We have many happy endings, I assure you.'

'But that isn't going to happen to me,' Charity said at last.

'Maybe not.' Miss Frost took a bite of her teacake and smiled approvingly.

'And what if Charity decides on adoption?' Marjorie asked.

Miss Frost sniffed and wiped her mouth delicately with a man's handkerchief. 'The wheels are put in motion at four weeks, and providing we have suitable parents, the baby will be handed over at six weeks, almost always away from the home.'

'What happens to me then?' Charity took a deep breath.

'You leave the home, find a job, get on with your life,' Miss Frost said, patting her hand on the table. 'For several months you will get reports on your baby, photographs and letters from the adoptive parents, though of course we don't let you know who they are, or where. At six months the baby is taken to court and legally made over to the parents with a new birth certificate, etcetera. You no longer have any rights in the child.'

'Could I get the baby back during that time?' Charity asked. 'I mean, if I found I could look after it?'

Miss Frost was taken with Charity. She liked her gentle yet straightforward manner, her cleanliness and her obvious intelligence. So many girls she interviewed for the first time were belligerent; even more seemed dim-witted. In her time she had dealt with hysteria, blatant lies and girls who refused to co-operate, so to find someone who appreciated her help, listened to what she said and would act on her advice was unexpectedly pleasant.

'Legally yes, though it is ill-advised to do so. The baby's well-being is of paramount importance. Once he or she has settled down, it would be cruel to take it back. You must make the lasting decision at six weeks and stick by it.'

Marjorie had to get back to work. Once she'd gone Miss Frost took a large form out of her bag.

'I have to ask you some questions now,' she said to Charity. 'This forms the basis of looking into finding the right parents for your child, should that be the option you choose to take. Therefore you must be truthful, Charity. If your boyfriend was of mixed blood, if you knew him to have any disease, you must tell me now.'

Charity gave a false name, but every other detail of Hugh's build, colouring and background was correct. On her side of the family Miss Frost wanted her to go right back to her grandparents, and it was only when she got to the point of her uncle being legal guardian that she got frightened.

'You won't contact him, will you?' she begged.

'Of course not, Charity,' Miss Frost said firmly. 'We understand these things. Many of our girls don't even tell their parents. The only time someone would be contacted is if you needed an emergency operation such as a Caesarean when we would have to get permission.'

The form seemed endless; every last detail was recorded painstakingly.

'What happens now?' Charity asked finally.

'Nothing.' Miss Frost smiled. 'I keep in touch with you, call round from time to time. Meanwhile I book you into Daleham Gardens. Next time I'll call to see your room. I usually do that unannounced, to keep my girls on their toes.' She handed Charity a card with a phone number and address. 'If something unexpected comes up – if you are ill, move, leave your job – get in touch with me immediately.'

It stayed freezing all through January and February too. Charity bought a girdle to hold her stomach in at work and Marjorie gave her a frilly white overall and a matching cap that concealed her shape completely. Every evening Charity climbed into her bed to keep warm and every morning even the insides of the windows were iced up.

Taking up knitting helped the long evenings pass, and she was soon mastering the most complicated patterns. Her list for the home only asked for three of everything, but Charity made dozens of little jackets, bootees and a big shawl.

At night as she lay in her bed she thought of Hugh and relived each moment of that bliss-filled holiday. She could forget the cold when she imagined that hot day by the pond. She tucked her hands round her swollen belly and felt the baby move.

Love stirred within her, and she began to stop thinking of the baby as a problem as it became part of her. She would trudge through the snow to look in baby shops, wishing she was lucky enough to be able to choose a pram, a cot or a playpen. She read every book she could find on childbirth and babies, and with a Woolworth's wedding ring she could pretend in shops that she was planning a nursery for her child.

Sometimes in a wild fantasy she imagined Hugh coming for her, driving up in his father's car and scooping her into his arms. She could project it further to him taking her to a tiny thatched cottage like Rob's parents', where Hugh and herself would walk down a sunfilled lane pushing the baby in a pram.

There were times when she thought of writing to

232

him, even of going to Oxford and confronting him, but each time she squashed the thoughts and reread his last letter to remind herself that he had betrayed her trust.

Love for Hugh took second place to her baby. When her heart ached with sorrow, when tears trickled down her cheeks, she'd put her hands on her tummy and turn the love inside to him. Her brothers and sister had trained her for this, she'd turned to them when there was nothing else and one day, when all this was over, she'd see them again.

March came in with a thaw. Everyone who came into the restaurant had a horror story of burst pipes, but Martin and Marjorie were lucky: their flat and the kitchens were so constantly warm they had no trouble.

Charity too had a burst pipe in her house. She arrived home one evening to find water gushing down the stairs from the bathroom and all the tenants shrieking about damaged carpets. In her room it was only a puddle by the door and she found it ironic that soon the entire house would be recarpeted and the hall and stairway decorated, now her time there was almost up.

She was tired now in the evenings, her ankles swollen with standing all day. Sometimes she went to bed the moment she got in from work, sleep blotting out the fear of leaving Marjorie and Martin.

Only one case was allowed at Daleham Gardens, so bit by bit she packed everything else in boxes and Martin put them away in his store-room. Cheap posters came down from the walls, little ornaments were wrapped in newspaper and finally the room was bare and characterless again.

'Well, this is it,' Martin said on the April morning when the taxi finally came to collect her. 'We'll try and get over to see you, but you know how we're fixed.'

Marjorie was struggling not to cry. Charity's tummy had grown suddenly in the last two weeks and there was no disguising her position any longer. She was a woman now, in the full flower of motherhood, with rosy cheeks and a calm steadfast look in those big blue eyes.

'We'll be thinking about you constantly.' Marjorie's voice shook as she embraced Charity. 'Whatever you decide, we'll be behind you. Let us know the moment he's born.'

Charity saw the concern in their eyes. She knew that if they had the room, they would offer it to her willingly.

'Don't worry about me,' she whispered into Marjorie's neck, which smelt of soap and cooked food. 'I'll be fine. I'm a big girl now.'

She wanted to tell them just how much they meant to her, how she dreaded a day without their faces, their laughter and their warmth. She had a carrier bag full of little presents from them, and from the many customers who'd got to know her over the months.

'We'll send on any letters,' Martin said. He removed his wife's arms from her and offered his own. 'We won't let on to anyone where you are without first contacting you. And there's a job to come back to, any time you want it.'

'Thank you for everything,' Charity said against his shoulder, breathing in deeply his smell of sweat, mingled with onions and roasted meat. 'You are the kindest, nicest people in the world.'

She had to go quickly then. Tears were springing up in her eyes and threatening to overflow.

Hammersmith Broadway didn't look dingy any longer as the taxi sped her away. There was a tub of daffodils outside the flat-letting agency, Mr Harris the greengrocer was sweeping the pavement outside his shop, the windows seemed to sparkle in the spring sunshine and now she was leaving, it looked like home.

Chapter Thirteen

'Charity! What sort of a handle is that to give to a girl?'

If the girl hadn't had such dancing brown eyes, such a preposterously large belly and such flaming red hair, Charity might have been offended. But there was nothing but cheekiness and good humour in her pleasant face. Charity giggled.

'I've abandoned all faith and hope,' she said.

'Ah but the greatest of these is Charity!' The girl's mischievous eyes twinkled. 'You've got the bed next to mine. I hope you don't live to regret it.'

Charity looked round the six-bedded sunny room and smiled.

'It's much nicer than I expected!'

'That's what I thought too, though most of the others moan like hell. I'm Rita, by the way. Want some help with unpacking?'

Number sixteen Daleham Gardens was as far removed from Greystones House as Buckingham Palace was from a slum in Paddington.

As the taxi sped through St John's Wood and into Swiss Cottage, Charity's spirits had lifted slightly. She didn't know this part of London, and the wide tree-lined roads with smart houses were an unexpected bonus. But as they turned off the main road into Daleham Gardens and stopped, her heart turned somersaults.

Not a dustbin in sight, no funny old men shuffling past with bottles in their hands. Just big, fine houses with front gardens full of trees and spring flowers.

Number 16 was semidetached, with a wooden veranda across the ground floor and six wide stone steps up to a bright red front door. There were no signs advertising the fact that it was a 'home'. If Charity hadn't happened to glance down to the basement, and seen what looked like a sluice room and laundry, she would have believed it to be a wealthy family's house.

The door was opened by another heavily pregnant girl with long dark hair, who scuttled off to find Miss Mansell, the matron and Charity was left to stand in the spacious hall and marvel.

To her right was a flight of wide stairs, with a stained-glass window on a half-landing that cast twinkling patches of red and blue on to apple green walls. Straight ahead she saw a nursery, and through the open door she could see small canvas cots and a couple of girls cradling babies in their arms. Next to that was a sunny sitting room where she caught a glimpse of another pregnant girl sitting knitting.

The overall impression was one of brightness.

'Charity!' A petite older woman emerged from up the basement stairs, beaming a welcome. 'I'm Miss Mansell, the matron. That was Holly who opened the door. Leave your case there and come into my office a minute. Then I'll get one of the girls to show you round.'

Charity liked Miss Mansell that first moment, even before she took her into the room behind the closed door. Her gentle voice implied strength and kindness.

The office confirmed this. It was orderly, yet homely, and doubled as a private sitting room. Framed family photographs shared space with many of girls and babies. Notelets and letters were pinned to a notice-board, presumably from girls who'd written to thank her for their stay here.

'Do sit down, Charity.' Miss Mansell waved a small hand to one of the two armchairs by the window. She glanced down at Charity's feet. 'Oh dear, your ankles are very swollen. I must take your blood pressure! How are you feeling?'

'Fine.' Charity smiled, suddenly feeling much less exhausted. 'I did a lot of going up and down stairs this morning. They'll soon go down again.' She looked at her fat ankles.

'Yes I expect so, dear.' Miss Mansell perched on the edge of the other chair like a little bird. She had a gentle face and looked nothing like Charity's idea of a matron. 'You've been waitressing, haven't you? Very hard on the feet for a mother-to-be.'

Although she had a file on her big desk with Charity's name on it, she didn't consult it once, proving she had read and remembered everything.

'For now I just want to welcome you. I'll let the other girls fill you in on all their horror stories later. But basically all you really need to know is that this is your home for the next three months and I'm Mother.' She smiled warmly at her little joke. 'The few rules we have must be followed because they were made for your safety and well-being. In the mornings we have a rota of work, none of which will come hard to you, though many of the girls complain. After lunch you may go out, sit in the garden or the lounge, whatever you like. Tea is served at five-thirty, but if you have friends taking you out you may skip that as long as you are home by six-thirty and you let me know. I pack you pregnant girls off to bed at nine. On Sundays you all go to church.'

She paused to let that sink in.

'Now, each week you will go to your antenatal classes up on the Heath. Most of the girls enjoy that, as it's a pretty walk even if it is uphill all the way. When you go into labour you come and tell me, even if it is during the night. I get an ambulance and see you off.'

She went on to explain that Charity must sign the back of her benefit book, which she would cash for her and give her back fifteen shillings a week pocket money.

'Most of the girls smoke,' Miss Mansell said disapprovingly. 'Many of them stuff themselves with sweets, but whatever you blow your money on, once it's gone you have to wait another week for more. I don't give subs.'

Charity had assumed she would have to hand over every penny of her maternity allowance. This and the news that she could go out in the afternoons came as a pleasant surprise.

They chatted for a little longer about Charity's job and her uncertainty about the future. Miss Mansell listened carefully to her anxiety about her brothers and sister.

'My dear, you must put them aside for the time being. All that matters now is you and your baby's health. I'm here to listen, to advise and help you young mothers, but the feelings you will have when your baby is put into your arms may very well drive out everything you have thought beforehand.'

'You mean I might want to keep him?' Charity always thought of her baby as 'him'.

'I *know* you will want to keep him.' A flicker of sadness crossed the older woman's face. 'You will want it so fiercely you will think it's impossible to do otherwise. I never met a girl who wanted anything else in all my years here.'

'But they do give them up, don't they?' Charity wanted reassurance that she could manage it too if she had to.

239

'It's very often the most loving, caring girls who do,' said Miss Mansell. Her eyes held a strange expression. 'It isn't lack of love which prompts them, believe me. Your grief will be another couple's joy if you give him up. But that, my dear, has to be your choice, made only with love and a great deal of soul-searching.'

'There's the bathrooms.' Rita pointed out three baths in cubicles just outside their dormitory. 'There's a bog on each floor too. Yesterday some of the girls in the other dorm got tough with a girl who smelt. They bundled her in here and shoved her in the bath.'

Charity immediately felt nervous.

'She *was* a bit pongy.' Rita grinned. 'But I'm glad I'm not in that room, there's some right dragons in there. They don't like me much. They think I'm weird.'

Charity thought there was nothing weird about Rita at all, unless you counted being outspoken and friendly.

'It's because a lot of them have never been away from home before.' Rita dropped her voice to a whisper as she showed Charity the other dormitory. 'You see some of them were sent away by their parents, to stop the neighbours finding out. They've had pampered lives, they hate scrubbing floors and polishing. They moan about everything.'

'Do we have to scrub floors?' Charity wasn't concerned, just surprised. The floors were all covered in shiny brown lino which hardly warranted scrubbing.

'Yes we do. Miss Mansell says it's good exercise, keeps our muscles supple. We scrub Monday, polish Tuesday. I quite enjoy it.'

The dorm was an airy room overlooking the big rear garden, with six white-painted iron beds, a locker apiece and two large chests of drawers and one small wardrobe and a washbasin. Personal belongings were everywhere: teddy bears on beds, makeup, perfume and even handbags gaping open.

'That's asking for trouble,' Rita said, pointing out one bag. 'Stealing isn't a problem here, but I'd be a bit more careful than that.'

The attic floor had sloping ceilings and small windows. Here there were only four beds to each of the two rooms, and in one a girl lay sleeping.

'Fiona's been up all night with her baby,' Rita whispered.

They went downstairs to see the nursery.

Charity was overcome with tenderness as she peered into each cot. All the babies were different – dark ones, fair ones, some bald and big, one so tiny it looked like a doll.

Eight babies in eight cots. Eight piles of nappies in square pigeonholes with another beneath holding a basket of talc, bottom cream and sponges. A nappy bucket for each, and eight low chairs for feeding, around a white-painted table, its legs cut short.

It was a lovely room, with a pale grey and white tiled floor and huge windows looking on to the garden. Mobiles hung from the ceiling and a big jolly nursery frieze ran along one wall.

'I love coming in here,' Rita said and stroked her stomach. 'I was never interested in babies before, but now I'm always popping in to lend a hand.'

'Are you getting married or anything?' Charity hardly dared to ask, but didn't think somehow she'd be rebuffed.

'No, he scarpered the moment I mentioned I was late,' Rita grinned. 'I'm going to have mine adopted. I can't see any alternative.'

Rita, as it turned out, was in much the same boat as Charity. Her mother and father didn't know about the baby and wouldn't help if they did. Until coming here she'd worked as a chambermaid.

'My folks are snobs.' Rita picked up a crying baby and held him against her shoulder. 'They sent me to a good school, then secretarial college and hoped I would marry someone presentable soon after. But I moved into a flat in Earls Court with some mates and that's when I got into this mess. The girls asked me to leave. So I got the job in the hotel, lay low and let my parents think I'm working up in Edinburgh.'

'But how?' Charity held her back and stretched slightly to relieve the pressure caused by standing for so long.

'A friend I knew in school works there. I post her a letter every week. She posts it to my parents and sends their replies back to me. I'm terrified Dad might spot me one day. They live in Hampstead Garden Suburb, you see, which isn't a million miles from here.' She giggled.

'Let me have him.' Charity held out her arms for the baby which Rita couldn't silence.

Rita sat down heavily on one of the low chairs, tucking her hands round her tummy. 'Tell me about yourself,' she said.

Charity sat down too. It was easy to talk to Rita, as if they were old friends already. She passed quickly over her parents' death, but explained about Hugh and her brothers and sister.

'I'm never going to be a mug when it comes to men again,' Rita declared. 'I don't intend to make the same mistake again. But you've had it tougher than any of us here. It makes me feel guilty whining on about my parents.'

'This is Charity,' Rita announced as they entered the dining room in the basement, in answer to the gong for tea.

242

Aside from the eighteen girls already sitting at the table, Miss Mansell and two women helpers were there too. It was a sea of faces and as Rita reeled off the list of names Charity felt certain she could never learn them all.

She was surprised at the family atmosphere as bread and butter was passed round, cups of tea, jam and honey, then cake.

She saw at once how the girls split into two groups: those with babies and those still pregnant. Not that there was any animosity; they just had different values. The pregnant ones talked about pop records, clothes, even what they would do when they left; the mothers chatted about feeds, of getting up at night and babies' weights.

The dining room was a semi-basement and the sun came right in. There was a television down here too but no one seemed to be interested in it.

'We aren't allowed to smoke anywhere but the lounge,' Rita whispered. 'We all watch *Ready, Steady, Go!*, but nothing else much.'

By the time Charity got to bed at nine she knew a little about each of the girls in her dormitory. Anne was a quiet, dark-haired girl from Romford. Sally, the extrovert with pretty auburn corkscrew curls, made them laugh with tales of her 'Sugar Daddy' who wrote to her all the time. Then there was Linda, a moon-faced girl who had a book of poetry by her bed, and Dorothy.

Dorothy was the one Charity found herself liking the most. She was tall and strikingly beautiful with a perfect oval face and dark lustrous eyes. Her dark brown hair she wore parted in the middle and plaited at each side of her head like a Red Indian squaw. She came from Devon and spoke with a cultured accent. She referred to the girls in the other dorm as 'the peasants' without any malice, and cut up a large chocolate cake to share out.

'Mother sent it,' she said. 'It's her way of grovelling a bit because Pop called me a whore. As I pointed out to him, if I'd been a whore I'd not only have a wedge in the bank, but I wouldn't be stupid enough to have ended up here.'

She mentioned working for the FO, which Charity later discovered was the Foreign Office, and at nineteen she was the eldest here by six months.

'What are you going to do, then?' Charity asked her, sitting up in bed and wolfing down the cake.

'Give the little blighter away, of course,' Dorothy said. 'I expect the jungle drums are beating round the adoption societies right now: "Dorothy Heywood, latterly of the FO, begat with Roger Turnball, also of the same office, a son or daughter, which is up for grabs. This child comes with an immaculate pedigree on both sides, despite the mother being a whore and the father a lily-livered creep of the first order." '

All the girls laughed, but Charity guessed what was going on behind that cool beautiful façade.

Charity lay awake long after the other girls had fallen asleep. The bed was hard and lumpy. She could hear Sally by the window snoring softly, and someone else grinding her teeth, but it was good to feel the presence of five other girls all in the same position as herself.

'I'm not polishing any bloody floors.' The small blonde girl glowered at Charity, her sharp features alight with spite.

'Come on, it's fun,' Charity wheedled. 'You'll only get into trouble and we have a laugh while we're doing it.'

'I can't see any fun in polishing a bloody floor that

doesn't need it.' The girl sat down on a bed, arms folded in defiance.

Anne, the dark girl from Romford, had gone into hospital only two days after Charity's arrival. She had been replaced by Dee, this hard-faced blonde, just a couple of days later and already she'd managed to upset almost everyone.

Dee seemed like a fish out of water. She swore constantly and talked about men in the way the girls at Greystones had. Her parents were elderly and it was quite obvious she'd run a bit wild.

'Look, Dee, there's a rota.' Dorothy put her hands on her hips and glowered at the smaller girl. 'You, me, Charity and Rita do the floors. There's worse jobs here than this, I assure you. And if you won't toe the line then we aren't going to cover for you.'

With that Dorothy got down on all fours, tucked a duster under each knee and, starting from the end wall, began to rub in polish. Charity took up a position next to her, with Rita alongside, leaving a strip at the end for Dee.

'We won't do your bit,' Dorothy said, looking round over her shoulder, then switched the radio on.

All three of them began singing along with the music as they worked backwards, rubbing the polish in, wriggling their bottoms in time to the beat.

Dee watched them on the floor, trying hard not to laugh.

It was a hilarious sight. They all looked like Humpty Dumpty with their big tummies and their dresses tucked into their knickers to keep them from dragging on the floor.

Dee didn't want to be in this place, but her mother insisted her neighbours in Hornsey must never find out about her 'accident'. She had always been in control, wherever she was, by being tougher, ruder and nastier than any other girl.

245

Maybe she shouldn't have thrown that box of cutlery at Janice for saying her hair was bleached. It had been pretty stupid to say she hated babies and put everyone's back up. Now they were all nervous about her and Miss Mansell had said if she didn't stop upsetting people she would be sent away to a different home.

She was torn two ways. Maybe if she behaved really badly her parents would take her home, but on the other hand, watching Charity larking about with Dorothy and Rita she wanted to be part of that too.

'She was just seventeen, you know what I mean,' they sang along loudly to the Beatles number. 'And the way she looked was way beyond compare!'

Rita knelt up and did a ridiculous wobble of her tits which had all three of them creased up with laughter.

'How could I dance with another?' She got up and continued the demented dance. 'When I saw – her – standing . . . there.'

Dee laughed despite herself. Charity turned round and smiled.

'Come on, we can be the Four Seasons all together!'

It wasn't the words, but the pleading note in Charity's voice that did it. It was a sound that said she knew how Dee felt and she'd be happier if they were all friends.

Dee picked up the fourth tin of polish and the dusters and moved over to the far edge by the wall.

'Don't put too much on!' Charity yelled over the music. 'It's hard to polish off.'

The beds and lockers were moved right back at the end of the room. When they reached them the girls got up.

'Go on, tell me, now the hard work starts!' Dee wiped a sweaty forehead with the back of her hand.

'Not at all.' Dorothy grinned. 'This, my dear, is the fun bit.' She dropped her two dusters on the floor, put one foot on each and started to do a kind of shuffle forward in time to the music.

The other girls followed, Dee included. They pretended to be skaters, ballerinas and made up a routine together to a kind of cha-cha. When Chubby Checker's 'Let's Twist Again' came on, all four of them went wild.

They didn't see the door open, just felt a presence and one by one they stopped in their tracks.

It was Miss Mansell.

She just looked, at their bare feet covered in dusters, at the maternity smocks rucked up in their knickers and the shiny floor.

'You've missed some bits around the edges,' she said drily. 'Might I suggest the veleta, there's some good sliding movements in that.'

She left without another word. The girls shrieked with laughter as they tried her suggestion.

As the days passed there was always something to laugh about. To watch each other washing in the morning, stripped off, big tummies stopping them from reaching the basin properly, started them off. Dorothy would go to the wardrobe and pretend to flick through dozens of dresses.

'What shall I wear today? Will it be the blue silk, the Norman Hartnell, the Jaeger costume? Or shall I wear this snazzy little number again?'

She would bring out her one and only dress, a striped smock in dark browns and blues, fling it over her head and mince around the room like a model.

'Dorothy is modelling a number equally stunning on the fuller figure. Note the four yards of handprinted Indian cotton, the flattering square neckline, full sleeves and pockets big enough for dusters.'

Some of the other girls gave them shirty looks, but

Miss Mansell just smiled and said nothing as she passed them.

In the afternoons they went out, usually down to John Lewis in the Finchley Road where they sometimes posed as rich women out shopping.

Rita would pick out the most expensive dress, jumper or skirt, note the colours it came in, then ask for it in something else.

'I would've loved it in olive green,' she'd say with sincerity. 'My husband insisted I buy something to cheer myself up, but I just can't wear any of those colours.'

The assistants were clearly puzzled by four girls in an equally advanced state of pregnancy out shopping together.

'We're Mormons,' Dorothy once said in her clear voice that carried around the whole floor. 'We share a husband. We don't believe in monogamy.' It didn't matter whether the dumbstruck salesgirls believed them. It was enough to send all four girls into hysterical giggling.

'What is it, Dot?' Charity heard her friend tossing and turning and climbed out of bed to go across the room to her.

'It's started.' Dorothy's face was a pale oval in the dark. 'I was hoping I wouldn't disturb anyone.'

'How often are the pains?' Charity whispered.

'About five minutes apart.'

'Get up then and we'll go downstairs.' Charity fumbled in the dark for Dorothy's dressing-gown and the ready-packed bag beneath the bed. 'Here we are. Now where's your slippers?'

The pair of them crept out of the room, Charity carrying the bag. Once in the hall, she sat Dorothy down. Another contraction started almost immediately.

Charity looked hard at her friend. Dorothy was tough, but it must be fierce for her to screw her face up like that. She sat down on the couch next to her, rubbing Dorothy's back until the pain stopped, watching the clock all the time. It was three minutes later that the next pain started.

'I must get Miss Mansell,' Charity said. 'Just hold on, I'll come straight back.' She flew up the stairs to the top floor and knocked on the door.

'Miss Mansell,' she whispered, opening the door a crack. 'It's Dorothy, she's gone into labour.'

'I'll be right down.' Miss Mansell's voice sounded heavy with sleep. 'Go on back to her.'

Another contraction came before Miss Mansell arrived: only two and a half minutes since the last, and very strong.

Miss Mansell arrived, put one hand on Dorothy's stomach, then moved down to listen too.

'I'll call the ambulance,' she said. 'Go back to bed Charity, I'll look after her.'

'Can't she come with me?' Dorothy sounded desperate. 'Please!'

'To the hospital!' The matron had her professional midwife face on now, stern and no nonsense. 'It's not allowed.'

'But other women have their mothers or sisters there,' Dorothy pleaded.

Charity was surprised by Dorothy. She'd have laid bets that this girl would creep out in the night without waking a soul, much less ask for a companion.

'Let me go, Miss Mansell.' She caught hold of the matron's arm. 'She's scared and she'll be better with me there.'

Miss Mansell saw the terror in Dorothy's eyes.

'OK, run and get dressed, but don't be surprised if they give you a frosty reception up on the Heath.'

Charity stood by the bed rubbing Dorothy's back. It was getting light now outside and her friend's contractions were only seconds apart.

She did get the frosty reception Miss Mansell had anticipated, but when they took Dorothy away to be shaved and given an enema, her cries of terror soon persuaded them that Charity might be useful.

'Rub her back with each contraction,' the nurse said, once they'd got Dorothy back into bed. 'We're so busy tonight we can't spare someone to stay with her all the time. Ring the bell if you notice anything unusual.'

Charity's back ached with leaning over the bed, her arms throbbed with rubbing and her ankles were swollen, but she felt nothing beyond the need to relieve her friend's pain. Dorothy was stoic as long as Charity's hands were there on her back reassuring her she wasn't alone. Her face contorted with agony at each contraction, and under her hands Charity could almost feel the baby as it moved further down.

'I want to push now,' Dorothy croaked.

'Don't until the midwife says it's all right,' Charity said gently, pushing the button, then turning her friend on to her back. 'It won't be long now!'

The midwife, a sweaty-looking, stout woman in a dark green uniform, came running in.

'She wants to push now,' Charity told her. 'I said to wait until you came.'

The midwife put Dorothy's legs up and examined her.

'My word, Dorothy, you're fully dilated.' She smiled at the girl in front of her. 'You can go ahead at the next pain. Bear down hard, push for the whole of the contraction, use it.'

'Can I stay?' Charity asked, gripping Dorothy's hand.

The midwife saw the gesture, and nodded.

'Stay up that end,' she said firmly. 'Talk to her, tell her to push.'

Charity braced herself as another contraction came. Dorothy groaned deeply as she pushed. Water gushed out from between her legs and the midwife mopped it up quickly.

'That's good,' she praised Dorothy. 'Your waters have broken at last, it'll be over soon now. Push!'

Again and again Dorothy looked as if she was giving up, but Charity urged her and so did the midwife.

'Push!' they shouted in unison. 'Push harder!'

'Ring the bell, Charity,' the midwife said suddenly. 'I can see the head and it's coming fast!'

Charity rang, then wiped Dorothy's face with a wet cloth.

'He's got black hair, lots of it,' the midwife said exultantly. 'Come on! Another *huge* push!'

Charity saw it happen before her eyes, just as a second nurse rushed in. A mass of black hair caked to its tiny head, a little screwed-up angry face – Dorothy's baby made its entrance.

'Now pant,' the midwife said. 'Just the rest of him to come.'

Charity could see Dorothy's stomach gradually caving in, and with a squelch the baby was caught in the midwife's hands.

'It's a girl,' Charity exclaimed, tears of joy running down her cheeks. 'Oh Dotty, it's a little girl!'

She had to sit down then. She watched the nurse cut the cord, heard the baby's first angry scream, and her whole being longed to hold it herself.

'I'm going to call her Samantha.' Dorothy's voice sounded near normal now, clear and confident. She lay back on the pillow, her face gleaming with sweat, as calmly as if the agony a few seconds ago had happened to someone else.

The moment when they wrapped the baby in a towel and put it into her friend's arms was one that Charity felt she would never forget.

Dorothy's face was serene, glowing with a strange light as she looked tenderly at the tiny black-haired child cradled against the white hospital gown. It reminded her of the Madonna picture in her father's study and confirmed in her heart that there was a God after all, even if sometimes it felt like he'd deserted them.

'You'd better go now.' The midwife turned to Charity and saw the naked longing in her big blue eyes. 'You know, Charity, you should go in for this work, you're made for it. We couldn't have managed without you tonight.'

Someone drove her back to the home, but Charity's mind was focused on the baby and Dorothy.

'It was so beautiful,' she breathed as Miss Mansell opened the door to her. 'A miracle, a wonderful, wonderful miracle.'

Rita went into labour the following night, but she didn't wake Charity, just slipped out and got Miss Mansell on her own. She had a little boy she called Warren, and now Charity had both friends to visit.

She went every afternoon, sometimes with Sally, sometimes with Dee, but mostly alone. Suddenly she realised it was her turn next and except for Dee all the girls in her dormitory were new ones.

The laughter prompted by Charity and her close friends continued even though two of the ringleaders were gone, but Charity's role in the home shifted slightly. She had one foot in the mothers' camp now her time was so close.

Two girls left after handing over their babies for adoption. It was Charity who hugged them, reassured

252

them they had made the right choice. But as she dried their tears and searched for the right soothing words she wondered who would be there for her if she had to face such agony.

The first pain came when she was in the garden, hanging out nappies. It wasn't her job, but she'd been awake early and came downstairs to help the mothers with the laundry.

It was a beautiful day, as if overnight it had been decided that summer was here. A lilac tree was thick with sweet perfumed blossom, the grass twinkling with dewdrops and the sun on the back of her neck warmed her as she stretched up to the clothes line.

Not a pain, but rather a sensation in her belly and she put her hands down to stroke it.

'Are you coming, baby?' she whispered. 'It's a beautiful day for it and I'm dying to see you.'

She said nothing at breakfast, but listened to the girls discussing the post and the usual banter about the work rota.

'Are you all right, Charity?' Miss Mansell stopped her as she got up from her chair, holding on to her back.

'I think it's started,' Charity said. 'But it's nothing much.'

'Go and sit upstairs with a book, then,' the older woman said, and put her arm round Charity. 'Call me if you want help.'

Charity sat on the veranda in the sunshine. The pains were growing stronger now, but she felt a kind of peace within her. From upstairs she could hear the sounds of the girls larking about as they cleaned. Someone was singing Cliff Richard's song 'The Young Ones' at the top of her voice.

Mrs Coombes the cook, who came in daily to prepare lunch, was in the store-room just below the veranda; her voice mingled with Miss Mansell's comfortingly. Charity wanted to hold on to this day, remember all the sights and sounds, so one day she could tell him all about it.

She thought of Hugh, imagined his dark head bent over books as he studied. In a few hours his child would be in her arms. Would Hugh sense something was happening? Did he ever think of her?

Chapter Fourteen

Pain washed over her so fiercely she thought she might die, but still she didn't cry out.

It was noon when she left Daleham Gardens and now in more lucid moments she sensed it was early evening. The white-painted room, the clock on the wall, even the shiny steel lamp above her head had disappeared. She was engulfed in agony that had no place or time.

She felt, but barely saw, hands touching her and taking her blood pressure. She heard voices as if from another room reassuring her that all was well, but she wished they would stay with her, instead of going out and leaving her alone with nightmares.

Her father's face was visible, even though she knew her eyes were closed. It was the face she remembered when he came to her at night, contorted, ugly.

She saw the fire again, but now she was in it, feeling it licking across her body, waiting to consume her too.

Water gushed from her, but she couldn't get up or even move, and pain welled up again, so strong she had to grit her teeth not to call out.

But then the pain changed. It was every bit as bad, but it had a kind of significant feel to it, and she realised her baby wanted to be pushed out.

Her hand groped for the bell. They had put it beside her earlier on, but it had fallen over the edge of the bed and the pain was too bad for her to stretch out.

Her fingers contacted the rubber lead, scrabbling down it to find the button and push it.

Drawing her knees up, she put her feet firmly on the bed and reached up behind her to grab the bed rail.

They had been taught to wait before pushing until the midwife said it was time. But Charity's instinct told her it felt right. As the next pain crashed over her, she drew in a breath, then breathed out slowly, bearing down.

Still no nurse came, but another pain did.

Again a breath in, then a slow exhale as she pushed down hard with her bottom.

She remembered thinking that someone should switch the light on above her, someone should be there helping her do this, but there was no one, so she would have to do it alone.

The door opened and the midwife rushed in, followed by a nurse.

Vaguely she recognised the same midwife who'd delivered Dorothy's baby, but a face meant nothing now.

'My goodness, Charity!' the familiar voice said. 'You've almost done it all by yourself.'

Someone was wiping her forehead and neck, she felt sheets being changed underneath her and another pillow being put under her head.

'Use all the pain,' the voice said very close by. 'Push and keep pushing, I can see his head.'

She made herself think of the fire, focusing only on the need to get the baby out and pushed so hard she felt torn apart.

'It's coming. One more little one!'

The agony was sharply cut off and she found she could raise herself slightly, enough to see a small dark head between her legs.

'Baby!' she uttered and she felt a slithering, fluid feeling as the midwife drew him out.

'A boy!'

She heard the midwife's exclamation and slumped back on to the pillow, exhausted but triumphant.

He looked so crumpled, so red and cross, and as she watched his cry filled the air. First the mew of a kitten, quickly changing to an angry roar, and she lay back and laughed.

'He's a fine, handsome big boy.' The midwife laughed too as she handed the baby to the nurse momentarily.

'Let me hold him now?' Charity begged. 'Straight away.'

'First things first,' the nurse said, swiftly wrapping him in a towel.

It was the best and purest thing Charity had ever known. They tucked him on to her chest, his cheek against her neck, and she breathed in the smell of him, the sound of his breathing and the feel of his tiny body, so recently torn from hers.

'Isn't he beautiful!' she whispered.

The midwife came close, her big, plain face made lovely by her reverence.

'He is indeed, but then I expected you to have an extra special one.'

After so much pain, nothing hurt or indeed embarrassed Charity now. Not the doctor sitting before her stitching her up and asking how such a little girl had managed to produce an eight-pounder. Or the midwife stripping off her gown and washing her all over like a helpless child. She just lay back and kept her eye on her baby, watching them putting tags on his ankle and wrist, washing him gently and putting him into a tiny gown.

His cot was wheeled right up beside her. Cocooned tightly in a blanket, he reminded her of the clothes-

257

peg dolls she used to make for Prudence. She thought he looked like Hugh. He had the same jet black hair, wide cheekbones and she was sure once he opened his eyes they would be a deep, dark blue.

'He'll make a good rugby player.' The doctor was back examining her baby. He was young and thickset, with fair hair and a rugged jawline. 'A fine pair of thighs and I'll bet he's got lungs to match.'

It was strangely touching to see such a big man gently handling such a tiny baby.

He smiled round at Charity and said, 'I never get tired of this bit.' Picking up the baby, he rewrapped him and tucked him into Charity's eager arms. 'He's a handsome little chap. What are you going to call him?'

'Daniel.' She smiled. 'Do you think that suits him?'

'Perfectly,' the doctor said. 'Now just a five-minute cuddle then Nurse will pack you off to bed. Don't worry about him, he'll be in good hands.'

For the first five days Charity was in a small four-bedded room on the first floor of the maternity hospital, and for three of those days she was made to stay in bed.

The room overlooked the garden and beyond the hospital wall she could see Whitestone pond. Children came to sail boats there and it reminded her of Blackheath. The other three women in the room were wives of wealthy businessmen. They had congratulatory telegrams, dozens of cards covered their lockers and spilled over to the windowsill, and bouquets of flowers arrived. Their husbands came in with their arms full of presents, fruit and chocolates, sat on the beds and cuddled their wives and babies while Charity kept her nose buried in a book.

She had one bouquet of flowers from Marjorie and

Martin. Miss Mansell came to visit on the second day, but apart from Dorothy and Rita slipping in for five minutes before they left the hospital to go back to the home, she had no visitors.

It was so tempting to write and tell Lou and Geoff the truth. She so much wanted to share her baby with them. But she'd already written from Marjorie and Martin's address telling them she was employed by a catering agency that sent her to different temporary jobs. And she'd compounded that lie by getting Rita's friend in Scotland to post another letter from there. Besides, it would make things so difficult for them.

'Write to Hugh one last time,' Dorothy urged her. 'If he doesn't write back or come you'll know once and for all he doesn't care. But give him a chance. He has a right to know about Daniel.'

'Have you written to Roger?' Charity asked. It was funny to see Dorothy slim again: she wore a honey-coloured sleeveless shift dress and her thick brown hair cascaded down her back, sleek and shiny.

'Yes.' Dorothy's dark eyes were oblique. 'I had a letter and a cheque from him. But though he's prepared to pay maintenance, he doesn't want to know.'

'I'm sorry.' Charity squeezed her friend's hand.

'Perhaps it's just as well,' Dorothy said. 'I see things in him now I couldn't live with. I don't think I could bear to marry him, not even for Samantha.'

Charity knew better than to press her further about her decision. The hospital was no place for that.

'We'll talk when I get back,' she said. 'Try and save me a bed in the same room as you and Rita.'

On the fifth day Charity was moved down to a room on the ground floor, which was known as 'Toddlers'. It was much bigger, with french windows opening out on to the walled garden.

Apart from women in dressing-gowns and slippers,

it didn't feel like a hospital. They could wander out into the garden with visitors, they ate their meals at a table all together, even watched television in the evenings in a small lounge.

Marjorie managed a brief visit, bringing fruit, cake and a teddy bear for Daniel. She held him in that awkward way people did who weren't used to babies and she promised Charity a job if and when she wanted it.

Charity kept her distance from the other women. Their chatter about nurseries, prams and their homes was a reminder she didn't need about the choices open to her. Many of them were Jewish, with large extended families who visited in droves, and though these women were kindly, offering her more cake and fruit, she was too immersed in Daniel to need or want their friendship.

Feeding, bathing and changing his nappies was everything. She steeled herself against thinking beyond the next day, treasuring each moment.

Now that Daniel had lost his early redness she saw his skin had the same golden glow as Hugh's and his eyes were an identical blue. At night most women opted for the nurses to feed their baby, but Charity never did. At the first bleat she was awake, padding down the corridor before even a nurse had heard him, and however long he took to finish his bottle, she didn't mind.

His little button nose, the downy hair on his spine, each tiny finger and toe was a constant delight. She brushed his dark hair up into a quiff and laughed and sang with him.

Her midwife, Mrs Evans, came to see her the day before she left and they went out into the garden.

'Do you know what you're going to do?' she asked as they sat down on a bench in the sunshine.

'I keep hoping for a miracle,' Charity said. 'What

can I offer him? Sleeping in a pram in a bedsitter! Struggling on National Assistance!'

'Don't try to plan yet.' The midwife took Charity's hand in her two. 'These six weeks are very important for both of you. Don't hold back love because you're afraid of the pain that comes with it. Even if you have to give Daniel up he'll take that love with him to his new mother and you'll never need to reproach yourself that you didn't give him the finest start in life.'

'How will I be able to bear it?' Charity asked, leaning her head against the older woman's shoulder.

'Because of him,' the midwife said and in an uncharacteristic gesture kissed Charity on the forehead. 'You'll think of him with all those things you couldn't give him. You'll remember the joy you've given to a childless couple and that will sustain you.'

It was so good to go back to Daleham Gardens. To be among girls who felt just as she did: no need to hide her predicament, no fear of judgements being made.

Dorothy and Rita had kept her a bed in their room and talk of the future was suspended in the delight of being together again.

The three of them got up earlier than was necessary, starting the boiler for the nappies and sharing the chores eagerly. June came in with a heat wave and before breakfast they would run barefoot over the lawn, hanging up the washing, laughing and joking as if they were three girls without a care in the world.

Yet the laughter and jokes were tempered with a new maturity. In the nursery the songs were gentle lullabies, the chatter was babies, feeds and the lack of sleep. Later, their work done, they lay on blankets out in the garden, soaking up the sun, in easy, companionable silence.

Charity's letter to Hugh came back marked 'Not known at this address'. Dorothy's parents remained

261

unmoved by her plight and Rita couldn't bring herself to ask for help from hers.

Sometimes they discussed the possibility of finding a flat all together. But after many phone calls to landlords, even with help from Miss Mansell, they began to see that no one out there wanted three unmarried mothers with babies.

Rita and Dorothy got to the four-week deadline, were individually ushered into the office and when they came out they were pale and silent.

They heard that a solicitor and his wife in Wales wanted Samantha, that Rita's baby Warren's new home would be in Devon with a doctor. All three of them tried to pretend they were relieved.

'I'll be out dancing in two weeks,' Dorothy said. 'I'll blow all my money on a fabulous dress and knock everyone dead.'

'I'm going back home,' Rita said, her eyes downcast. 'I'll let Dad buy me loads of new clothes. I'll go out and get very drunk and find a man to tell me lots of pretty lies. Then I'll find a decent job and try to settle down to what my parents want.'

The windows were all wide open to catch the breeze; often the babies lay out in their cots on the veranda in just vests and nappies. The girls no longer wanted to go down to John Lewis and look at clothes or try makeup. Instead they prepared a box each for their baby's clothes. Dorothy covered hers in imitation crocodile-skin paper.

'They'll know by that she had a classy mum.' She laughed, but it sounded hollow. 'I wonder if they'll keep these things to show her when she's grown up?' she said, tying a little bell on pink ribbon round the neck of a teddy bear.

Charity saw her kiss the bear as she put it in the box, saw her tears as she unpicked her initials from the pile of nappies, and wondered if she could be so brave when her time came.

Charity's two friends left on the same day, Dorothy with her social worker, Rita with Miss Frost. Their cases were packed into the car boot: both were going home to their parents, straight after handing over the babies.

Dorothy left first.

'Don't come out to the car,' she said to Charity as they dressed Samantha the final time. 'I couldn't bear it.'

Samantha had a pink frilly dress with matching bootees and Charity put the white shawl round her and laid her in the cot so she could hug her friend.

'Write and tell me what you decide.' Dorothy struggled not to cry as they embraced. 'I wish I could tell you what I feel about you and how much I wish we were leaving together.'

She broke away and picked up Samantha.

'I'll never forget anything,' she said. 'You do know what I mean, don't you?'

Charity watched from the veranda as Dorothy climbed into the car and saw that little spiky-haired dark head nestled against her friend's breast. Tears crept down her cheeks.

Rita's leaving was more emotional.

'I couldn't have coped without you,' she sobbed. 'It's not fair I won't be here to help you. Ring me the minute you get out of here. If you keep Daniel, I'll help you.'

Her face was blotchy, but her red hair shone like burnished copper as she walked down the steps with Warren in her arms. She had a new expensive emerald green dress with a pleated skirt and tonight she would be sitting down to dinner in Hampstead Garden

Suburb, trying to pretend the past few months 'working in Scotland' had been thrilling.

One pale hand raised in farewell as she got in the car and Miss Frost's head obscured her. Charity turned away and went back to Daniel in the nursery.

The nursery didn't fill up again. Dee had a little girl called Frances and her parents came and took her straight home from hospital, despite everything they'd said. Sally's boyfriend turned up and gave her an engagement ring and two days later she went home.

There was the full complement of pregnant girls, but Charity's last three weeks were shared only by Janice, a big quiet girl who said little, and Ruth who was going home with her baby to stay with her grandparents.

Charity was glad of the peace. She got up alone to do the laundry, and slept every night in the nursery instead of going upstairs. She wanted to savour every moment with Daniel so waking the other girls for their babies was such a little price to pay.

'Miss Frost's coming tomorrow,' Miss Mansell told her late one evening. 'She'll be wanting to know your decision, Charity.'

It was in the middle of the night as she fed Daniel that Charity finally made up her mind. As he lay in her arms, one hand curled round her finger, eyes drooping, she knew she must give him up.

She owed him more than a bedsitter and a day nursery while she worked. In Daleham Gardens it was easy to forget how grim London was, but she forced herself to remember trailing James in the pram down to the baths to do the washing. She made herself see her old room in Hammersmith, the dirty stairs, the continual noise from her neighbours.

Instead she saw a proper home, with Daniel riding a bike round a garden, and a father coming home from work and scooping him up in his arms. She saw him in a smart school uniform, holding a woman's hand as he walked down a tree-lined avenue.

There was no real contest. All she had on her side was love – and would that be enough to counteract the humiliation of poverty, a childhood in one squalid room?

'Well, Charity?' Miss Frost in a lemon yellow dress looked surprisingly feminine.

'I'm giving him up,' Charity said. Her voice sounded too loud to her own ears. 'Find him nice parents!'

Miss Frost and the matron exchanged glances.

'Are you sure?' Miss Mansell said.

Charity looked up and saw deep compassion in both pairs of eyes.

'I'm sure. I won't back down.'

Charity covered her box with teddy-bear paper alone. Each small garment was folded, each ribbon pressed smooth. The pile of nappies were gleaming white, still with tiny specks of the blue initials 'C.S.' she had picked out carefully.

She had no spare money to spend on an expensive outfit to dress him in, but she'd spent the last four evenings making a little blue and white romper suit on Miss Mansell's sewing machine.

Daniel was the only baby left in the nursery. The other girls had left. Seven empty chairs, cots and nappy pails, disinfected ready for the three girls due home tomorrow soon after she left.

It meant she could pretend that this was her room. As she stood at the window rocking him in her arms and watching darkness fall, she was just another mother getting her child to sleep.

He had smiled today for the first time, and the width of it reminded her even more of Hugh.

Next door in the lounge someone was playing 'When the Saints Go Marching In'. The new girls didn't lark about as her friends had done; they sat, mainly smoking and knitting, many with sour faces because they hated being here.

But she'd loved it. So many good memories to store away and bring out in the future.

Daniel was asleep now, making funny little huffing sounds against her neck. His small arms reminded her of sausages and she stroked the soft flesh tenderly. She wrapped a blanket round him later, but didn't put him down.

It was almost eleven. Another nine hours and Miss Frost would call to collect her. By teatime she would be in the Regent Palace Hotel in Piccadilly as their new chambermaid and all this would be put aside.

She was grateful to Miss Frost for arranging this job for her, but she couldn't feel any enthusiasm to get back to work, or even the faintest curiosity about what life in a big hotel would be like. It was just a wage and a room, a stopgap until she could get back on her feet.

'I won't ever forget you.' She kissed Daniel's soft cheek, breathing in deeply that warm, sweet baby smell. 'Wherever I am I'll be thinking of you, every day, every birthday and Christmas. Don't ever think otherwise.'

'Miss Frost's here, Charity,' Miss Mansell said as she came into the nursery. Charity was wearing a new pale blue dress, her hair, so much longer than when she came, shining from a recent wash.

266

But her eyes had dark circles beneath them, and it was clear she'd been awake all night.

Charity went to the cot and picked up Daniel, wrapping his shawl round him.

'Come back to see me?' Miss Mansell wanted to embrace the girl, but she had to try and keep things as matter of fact as possible. 'You can call me any time, just for a chat.'

Charity's smile was bleak.

'Thank you for everything,' she said in a small voice.

'It will get easier.' The older woman put one hand on Charity's shoulder. 'I've got scores of letters from girls to prove it. You must look onwards and upwards now.'

Charity didn't look out the window as the car drew away. She didn't want to see the waving hands at the window or remember past laughter. Instead she kept her eyes on Daniel, photographing his face on her mind indelibly.

The adoption society offices were close to Baker Street. Aside from a discreet plaque on the wall, it was just another Georgian terraced house with black iron railings.

Charity and Miss Frost were ushered into a waiting room towards the back of the house. A heavy old-fashioned lace curtain covered the window; a few wooden-armed chairs were the only furniture. A tank of goldfish stood against one wall and Charity stood looking into it with unseeing eyes, rocking Daniel.

They had been in there for perhaps five minutes when a big lady came in. She wore a bright pink blouse under a grey suit and she smiled brightly.

'What a beautiful baby,' she said, holding out her arms. 'Let me look at you, you handsome boy.'

Charity smiled, pleased at her reaction and let the

267

woman hold him. But to her horror the woman turned and walked with him straight out of the door.

She went to run after him, but Miss Frost was quicker. She moved to the door, shut it and leaned hard against it.

All at once Charity knew. That was it. They'd taken him.

'But I haven't kissed him goodbye!' she cried and lunged at Miss Frost, thumping her with her fists.

'Charity, shush.' Miss Frost caught hold of her hands to calm her. 'Listen. Just listen!'

Tears were still streaming down Charity's face, but she stood very still.

In the distance she heard the tapping of a type-writer, the hum of traffic in Baker Street and the sound of the woman holding Daniel ascending the stairs.

'Any moment now she'll show Daniel to his new parents,' Miss Frost said. 'Listen!' She opened the door a crack, holding firmly on to Charity with one hand.

Suddenly Charity heard laughter. It was laughter that sprang from absolute joy.

The male voice was deep, echoing round the carpet-less landing, but above that she heard the sound of a woman's voice, and it was as pure as water running over stones.

Miss Frost held out her arms and pulled Charity to her. 'Listen to that joyful sound and be glad for Daniel.'

Chapter Fifteen

January 1963

Beyond the closed door Charity could hear the sounds
of the other chambermaids getting ready for a night
out. Radios playing, bathwater running and voices
calling to one another to borrow a jumper or a hair-
drier. She could smell nail varnish, perfume and
coffee, but none of these sounds and smells stimulated
in her the desire to move from her bed.

There was no evidence she'd been here six whole
months. None of the accumulated clutter common to
all teenage girls – no makeup, jewellery, pictures of
pop stars, magazines or strewn clothing. Aside from
a framed photograph of the children taken back at
Clapham, talcum powder, shampoo and a pile of
library books on the dressing-table it had the severity
of a monk's cell.

It was a narrow room, gloomy with only the strip
light above her washbasin. Snow piled up against the
small, high window, but there was nothing out there
to see except more snow covering rooftops, water
tanks and coloured flashes from the neon lights in
Piccadilly Circus.

People said it was the worst winter since 1947. Daily
reports came in of villages cut off by snow, mail and
milk being delivered by helicopter and old people
dying of cold, but the bitter weather meant little to
Charity, as she seldom went outside the hotel. During

her few solitary walks around the West End, picking her way through blackened piles of hard snow, Charity observed that fashion had changed since the summer. The 'Mod' craze was under way, fired by the music of The Who. Girls now wore tight, longer skirts, bobbed their hair and winklepickers had been replaced by round-toed, clumpy shoes. The young men seemed to favour sharp suits and drive Lambrettas, but these changes only served to bring on a still deeper sense of isolation.

Her eighteenth birthday a few days earlier had passed unnoticed. That evening all the other chambermaids went dancing at the Empire in Leicester Square. Charity had heard their excited giggles as they set each other's hair and swapped clothes, but she stayed in her room, immersed in a book.

Charity lifted her head just enough to see her clock. Another five minutes and she must go downstairs to turn down the guests' beds. She had extra rooms to do tonight so Maureen and Judy could get out earlier.

None of the girls would bang on her door and ask her to join them later. Charity had become almost invisible.

She cleaned her allocated rooms silently, took her meals alone and her spare time was spent up here reading. So deep was she in a black pit of desolation she'd forgotten that life wasn't always like this. Unopened letters were tucked away in a drawer, belongings still uncollected from Marjorie and Martin. Grief had turned to emptiness; solitude was easier than attempting to get back into the mainstream of life.

Charity had been too numb on her arrival at the hotel to take in anything but her duties. Those first few weeks of July and August were hot, and the ceaseless noise of traffic around Piccadilly kept her awake at night. Sometimes in the afternoons she would walk down to Trafalgar Square, but instead of feeling stimulated by the jostling tourists, the hustle and bustle of a big city, it just made her withdraw further into herself.

She sat up, swung her legs over the side of the bed and slid her feet into shoes. Standing up, she smoothed down the dark red overall with REGENT PALACE HOTEL embroidered in gold above her right breast, and tied the small white frilly apron round her waist.

Moving over to the washbasin she brushed her hair, then dragged it back, fastening it at her neck with a rubber band. It was over a year since she'd had it cut in Hammersmith; now the urchin cut had grown long and untidy, but she didn't notice. The white cap went on next. Without bothering to look if it was straight, she picked up her bunch of keys and opened the door.

She'd heard the other chambermaids call her 'weird', 'snooty' and 'barmy' but she hardly registered their giggles and whispers. She'd grown a protective shield that nothing could penetrate.

Miss Frost had given her a lecture only two days earlier when Charity visited her office to sign the final adoption papers. She'd spoken brusquely about her appearance, implored her to pull herself together, but she didn't seem to understand that the old Charity had died that day they took Daniel from her arms.

Opening the door to the guests' part of the hotel was like leaving a slum and entering a palace. The staff bedrooms were tiny, furnished with cast-out pieces that guests had ruined. No new decoration had taken place up on the top floor for years, the carpets were so worn you could see the lines in the floor-boards; even the lighting was dingy.

Now Charity felt thick red and gold carpet beneath her feet, breathed in that smell of opulence that came with flock wallpaper, soft wall lights, cigars, expensive perfume and people that had some purpose in their lives.

The other chambermaids had a great deal of curiosity about the guests. They whispered amongst themselves about the expensive clothes, jewellery and the amount these people ate and drank. Charity felt nothing: she picked up clothing, tidied cosmetics and cleaned, almost like a blind person. The other girls might help themselves to chocolates, giggle at naughty underwear and spray themselves with perfume, but she was only interested in keeping the rooms immaculate.

Knocking on doors, then using her pass key when no one answered, Charity went from room to room. She drew curtains, picked up wet towels, turned the beds down neatly, then passed on.

She knocked on number 212 and waited longer than usual, because Mr Marshall was often in his room at this time. He was one of the few guests she knew by name; in fact she had spoken to him several times during his two-week stay here.

John Marshall was a photographer. According to the hotel gossip, a well-known one whose pictures often appeared in *National Geographic*. She'd seen him polishing the lenses in his cameras once and out of politeness had asked him about his work. Rather shyly he had shown her some stunning photographs of a stampede of wildebeest in Africa.

But aside from his profession that made him a little more intriguing than the other guests, Mr Marshall was a real gentleman. She guessed his age to be around the mid-forties. He was tall and slim with a permanent suntan and the kind of leather luggage and good shoes that suggested a man of taste. He never made suggestive remarks as many other businessmen did, he kept his room tidy and he was unfailingly courteous, opening doors for her and generally making her workload a little easier.

Getting no answer, she used her key. As she opened the door a blast of icy wind and the roar of traffic surprised her. Assuming that Mr Marshall had opened the windows, perhaps to clear smoky air, and had then forgotten to close them before going out earlier in the day, she switched on the light and moved in.

She had taken only two steps when she saw his naked legs and feet protruding from behind the bed.

'Mr Marshall?' she called, nervousness taking the place of apathy. She had often walked in on drunks, once even finding one asleep in a cold bath, but nothing she'd seen of this man had suggested he was a drinker. 'Mr Marshall, are you all right?'

It was a bit early for anyone to be drunk enough to fall on the floor. Besides, why was he in the dark?

The curtains were flapping, his bed was rumpled as if he'd been in it, yet a quick glance round showed no bottle, just an empty glass on the cabinet by the bed. She shivered and moved forward to close the windows.

As she reached the end of the bed, she gasped, clasping her hand to her mouth involuntarily. Mr Marshall was stark naked.

He lay twisted, halfway between face down and sideways, his naked bottom startlingly white compared with his deep brown back and legs.

Pulling the windows shut quickly, Charity dropped on to her knees beside him, pulling the bedspread down with her to cover him.

'Mr Marshall,' she called again, putting one hand gingerly on his shoulder. 'It's me, Charity, the chambermaid. Are you ill?'

His skin was icy cold to the touch. Worse still, she saw an open bottle of pills that had rolled under the edge of the bed, a few white tablets gleaming against the dark carpet.

'Oh no,' she gasped, grabbing the phone above her. 'Hold on, I'll get help.'

'Mr Marshall in room 212,' she said urgently to the girl that answered. 'He's collapsed in his room, get a doctor quickly.'

Now help was on its way Charity took his hand and felt for a pulse. She had no idea if it was fast or slow, it was just a relief to find there was one.

'Help's coming,' she said, bending close to his ear.

His lips moved and his eyelids flickered but nothing more.

Seen close up without his specs, Mr Marshall looked far younger than Charity had thought. Of course he was pallid now, his lips blue from cold, but his curly brown hair was thick and soft to her touch, with just a sprinkling of grey at the temples.

As she waited, Charity felt an odd sense of comradeship towards the man whose room she had cleaned so often. Perhaps it was merely those tablets on the floor that reminded her of times when she'd been tempted to swallow a whole bottle of aspirin, but his room had the same stark quality as her own. His jacket was hung neatly on the back of the trouser press. Three pairs of shoes were lined up in a row under the dressing-table, even his shirt and underclothes were folded on the chair. There were no personal belongings strewn about, aside from his cameras, nothing to indicate that he'd been staying for some time, or that he was a regular visitor to the hotel.

Every other guest had carrier bags from the big stores, postcards to send to their families and friends, brochures for everything from theatres to car hire, evidence that they were here for pleasure or business. She had been relieved that his room held no such clutter while she was cleaning it, but now she wondered if, like her, he had faced some crisis during his time here.

The assistant manager Mr Cox came barging into the room suddenly, quickly followed by the house doctor.

Charity jumped up, told them how she'd found Mr Marshall, and moved back to let the doctor examine him.

'You can go,' Mr Cox said dismissively. 'And don't bandy this around.'

Mr Cox was always unpleasant. A tall, gangly man, he had sharp features and a bad temper. She got the impression he was annoyed at being interrupted drinking and toadying with the guests downstairs.

'Thank you, Charity.' The doctor looked up from where he knelt beside Mr Marshall, aware the little chambermaid was deeply concerned. 'It must have been quite a shock to you finding someone like this. I'll let you know later how he is.'

It was after ten when Charity heard a knock on her door. She'd had a bath and washed her hair and was wearing her pink dressing-gown, but finding Mr Marshall like that had shaken her out of her usual apathy, and she'd been waiting anxiously for news.

'How is he?' she asked when she opened the door and saw Dr Cole. 'Has he gone to hospital?'

'May I come in for a moment? I don't want to talk out here.'

Charity let him in and he sat down on the one chair, while she perched on the bed.

Dr Cole was rumoured to be an alcoholic. He was over sixty, small and worn looking.

'He's sleeping it off now.' The doctor smiled wearily at Charity. 'I didn't think he needed hospital, he hadn't taken enough pills for that. He'll wake up in the morning with a hangover, but that's all.'

Charity sighed with relief. She'd been thinking about Mr Marshall all the time while she had a bath, remembering how pleasant he'd been. She had learned to freeze out male guests who made provocative suggestions, avert her eyes from saucy magazines and nudity, but with Mr Marshall there had never been any kind of threat, only a desire to make her job easier.

'Did he mean to kill himself?' she blurted out.

The doctor looked hard at Charity. He'd used this incident as an excuse to speak to her, because he'd been worried about her for some time. He sensed she'd had some sort of disaster prior to taking up this job and he'd tried to get her to open up on several occasions. She was far too pale and thin, and he knew she never went out or mixed with the other girls.

'I don't think so,' he said. 'From what I can gather he'd just hit a rut in the road.'

Charity frowned, not understanding.

'It happens to us all at times.' Dr Cole shrugged his shoulders in a gesture of sympathy. 'Grief, private worries, a feeling of hopelessness. In Mr Marshall's case I think he took a couple of pills to sleep, then woke and took some more without knowing what he was doing. Maybe that's why the window was open when you found him. I think he must have felt ill, got up to open it, then collapsed. It was a good job you found him, he could have died of cold.'

'I'm so glad he's all right,' Charity said. 'He's a nice man.'

'And what about you, young lady?' Dr Cole looked at her over his glasses.

Charity dropped her gaze.

The doctor rapped one finger on her pile of books. 'What's this? Studying, or just for pleasure?'

He was surprised to see Jane Austen, Dickens and Trollope. Most of the girls who worked here would be hard pressed to read an Enid Blyton.

'I had an uncle once who called it "improving my mind",' Charity said and smiled despite herself.

'In my time I've met a psychopathic chef, a house-keeper who claimed she was a witch, chambermaids hiding from violent husbands and several barmen who'd been in prison at some time. Now I can add a bluestocking to the list. It seems to me the work attracts the lonely, the sad and even the mad. That's probably why I'm here too.'

Charity's lips twitched.

'Go on, laugh.' Dr Cole's pale eyes twinkled.

'Is Mr Marshall lonely?' Charity knew the doctor was trying to probe into her past and she wanted to lead him away from it.

'I suspect he's got a great deal in common with you,' the doctor said unexpectedly. Charity jerked her head up in surprise. 'Someone who has chosen to isolate himself while he tries to sort out where his life has gone wrong.'

Dr Cole observed the flush that spread up from the girl's slim neck, the way her fingers picked nervously at her dressing-gown.

'Do you mind if I go to bed now?' Charity said. She was touched by his interest and compassion, but she had no intention of admitting anything for fear a confession might open gates she could never close again. 'I have to be up early in the morning.'

'Of course, my dear.' He got up to leave. 'I think Mr Marshall would like to thank you personally for rescuing him, so try and find time to pop in and see him tomorrow. If you want to talk to someone any time, don't forget me. Goodnight.'

Charity woke as usual at six-thirty to alarm clocks

going off all down the corridor. She'd lied to the doctor last night; she didn't have to get up early as it was her day off. She could hear doors open, lavatories flushing and the usual moaning banter between the girls.

Normally she felt a certain dread on her day off – all those spare hours with nothing to fill them – but for once she felt slightly more alive, even curious about the other girls.

She could hear Judy talking about a man she'd met at a Soho club last night and she leaned up on her elbow to listen.

'I told him I was a guest here.' Judy giggled. 'He wanted to come in for a drink and I didn't know what to do. So I told him I had a business meeting early this morning and I had to get my beauty sleep. I suppose I'd better tell him the truth tonight when I meet him.'

Her voice tailed off as she moved away to go downstairs and Charity lay down again to try and go back to sleep. But for some odd reason her mind kept turning back to Mr Marshall.

It was just after eleven when Charity knocked at his door, balancing a tea tray on one hip. She was aware that this was the first time since she arrived at the hotel she'd felt any interest in anyone, and the sensation was quite pleasant.

'Come in.' His voice sounded weak; in the past it had always been quite commanding.

'It's Charity. I thought you might like some tea.'

'That's very thoughtful of you.' All she could see of him was a dark shape against the white sheets. 'I was hoping to run into you at some time today. I believe I've you to thank for my rescue?'

'No thanks necessary,' she said, putting the tray down on the dressing-table. 'How do you feel this morning?'

278

'A bit woozy.'

'Shall I open the curtains a little, then I can pour you the tea?'

'Fine,' he said and she heard a movement as if he was trying to sit up. 'I have to warn you I'm not a pretty sight!'

Charity pulled the curtain cord and weak sunshine spilled into the room. The window overlooked Piccadilly Circus and as always at this time of day it was choked with traffic and milling with thousands of people, though through double glass the noise was a mere dull drone.

When she turned she found he had pulled himself up in bed and was leaning back against the headboard. His deeply tanned chest was bare, but aside from a dark shadow on his chin and slightly puffy eyes he looked normal enough.

'Have a cup with me?' he said unexpectedly as she poured his. 'I feel I owe you an explanation.'

Charity turned to him, his cup in her hands and for some inexplicable reason knew she had to stay, even though visiting guests in their rooms was frowned on.

'Don't feel you've got to,' she said, putting the cup right into his hands. 'If you want to talk, that's fine, but I'm not sitting in judgement.'

There was an empty coffee cup on the dressing-table, presumably brought to him last night. She rinsed it out in his bathroom and came back to fill it.

'Have you finished your work for the morning?' he asked. 'You aren't wearing your uniform.'

'It's my day off,' she explained, looking down at her jeans and sweater. 'I'd get shot if I worked like this.'

As she looked at him sitting up in bed she realised his long face was attractive. He had a small, almost pretty nose and beautifully shaped lips. His body too was youthful, slender, yet strong looking and muscular. Although he had the covers well over his stomach, she could see it was taut and flat like that of a far younger man and his curly hair was endearingly tousled. Suddenly she felt rather self-conscious.

'You look nice in jeans,' he said. 'Your uniform makes you look like a Victorian maid. So what prompted a girl on her day off to bring me tea? Curiosity or a touch of the Florence Nightingales?'

Charity wasn't sure what to make of his remarks. Was it sarcasm, joviality or just plain interest? She perched on the edge of the dressing-table and sipped her tea.

'A bit of both,' she admitted. 'Dr Cole told me last night he hadn't sent you to hospital, but hotels can be very lonely places, especially if you don't feel quite yourself.'

'I had no intention of doing away with myself,' Mr Marshall said. His eyes were brown and very sad looking. 'At least not consciously, anyway. I had some terrible news yesterday and I think I just tried to shut out the pain.'

He paused and tears sprang to his eyes.

'Can you understand that?'

'Yes I can, very well.' Charity put down her cup. 'It might help to talk about it.'

She could see he was struggling to compose himself, a nerve twitching in his cheek.

'I heard my daughter had been killed in a car crash yesterday,' he said hoarsely, wiping his eyes with the back of his hand. 'She was only twenty-one. She died and was buried and I didn't even know about it.'

Instinctively Charity moved across to him and sat down on the bed, compassion wiping out all hesitancy.

'I'm so sorry,' she said, taking his hand in hers and squeezing it. 'How terrible!'

Her small hand on his felt cool and comforting. Minutes before she came into the room he'd been steeling himself to get up, pack and leave without telling anyone. This little chambermaid was only a child, several years younger than Susie, yet he had an overwhelming desire to pour it all out to her.

'I'd been an absentee husband and father, always off on another assignment,' he said gruffly. 'I suppose I deserve punishment for neglecting my family, but I loved Susie so much and I never got the chance to tell her.'

'What about your wife?'

'We were all washed up.' He turned away so Charity couldn't see his expression. 'The last time I came home she'd got another man and she'd changed the locks on the door. I resigned myself to that, she deserved more than a husband who was never there. But I was angry because she turned the girls against me too. So I went back to Africa on another assignment for the *National Geographic*.'

Charity nodded.

'I shouldn't have gone. I should've stayed longer and tried to talk to her properly. Once I was in Africa I could see that. So I cut the job short, intending to handle it better this time, give her the divorce she wanted and make my peace with her and the girls. That's why I've been staying here, trying to get through to her. I rang, and rang, our home in Norfolk, but there was no reply. I thought maybe she had taken a holiday, then I wondered if she'd moved. Then finally yesterday I rang our family solicitor and he told me what had happened.'

Charity could think of nothing to say. She felt it all – the first time since parting with Daniel that she'd felt anything for anyone. But she couldn't find the words to say it.

'I shouldn't be telling you all this.' He tried to smile, but it came out as a grimace. 'You're too young.'

'I'm not,' she whispered. 'I'm the right person to tell, age has nothing to do with it. I know how you feel. You must talk about it.'

He looked at her, really looked this time because her words had a ring of complete understanding. Now he saw for the first time that her eyes were sad, he remembered one of the other chambermaids telling him she was strange because she had nothing to do with anyone, and he knew suddenly she'd been to the same dark place as him.

'You do know, don't you?' he whispered.

She nodded.

Outside the wind had dropped, watery January sun played on the windows and traffic hummed. But all Charity was aware of was this man's pain, the sound of muffled sobbing and a feeling that there was more to this meeting than pure chance.

She wanted to make him tell her all about his daughter, but sensed that he couldn't, not yet, just as she couldn't speak of Daniel.

His sobs gradually subsided.

'I haven't cried since I was a child,' he said. 'Whatever must you think of me!'

'I think you are a very honest man,' she replied, stroking his hair just the way she used to do with the children. 'Crying is good at times like this, nothing to be ashamed of.'

He moved back from her as if suddenly recalling where they were and how it would look to someone else. 'Will you meet me later for lunch?'

Charity looked at him slumped against the pillows. She was touched that even in grief he was concerned about her reputation and job.

'OK.' She smiled. 'If you feel up to it. Where shall I meet you?'

282

He thought for a moment.

'Outside Swan and Edgar's at one. I'll take you to the Ritz.'

It was only back in her room that she panicked. If he'd suggested a walk in St James's Park, or even going to the Wimpy bar that would have been all right. But the Ritz!

As she stood by the wardrobe mirror she saw for the first time what she had become. There was no shine in her bedraggled hair, no colour in her thin face and she knew she had nothing suitable to wear. But he needed someone. If she turned him down now when he was at a low ebb, anything might happen.

She opened the wardrobe door and flicked through the few clothes hanging there. The blue dress she had worn to hand over Daniel and came here wearing was too summery; a pink wool dress she'd worn in the earlier part of her pregnancy was too stretched.

Faced with embarrassing herself and him she suddenly realised how far she'd let herself go. All her underwear was grey and worn, she hadn't bought one new item since coming here, even her shoes were down at the heel. The only things that weren't too bad were a navy blue skirt and a pale blue sweater. Maybe if she polished her shoes they wouldn't look too bad.

John Marshall stood outside Swan and Edgar's, warm in a navy blue cashmere overcoat over a dark grey suit. To his surprise he felt much better for getting up. A bath, a shave and a brisk walk through the snow in Green Park had blown away his headache.

Out here with all the hustle and bustle of Piccadilly Circus going on around him he felt less fraught. It was good to see shoppers flocking to the January sales, undeterred by ice and snow or reports that half the country had come to a standstill. Little office girls were rushing in and out of sandwich bars, swathed in scarves and hats. Tourists photographed each other against Eros, just as they did day in and day out all year, and cars, buses and taxis forced their way round the busy Circus with their usual aggressiveness.

A gypsy woman was trying to force tiny bunches of purple heather on to people who tried to sidestep her. Somehow the busy scene was comforting, a reminder that life went on, even though at present he found it impossible to look forward.

John Marshall was tall, over six feet, and he could see over the heads of the crowds of people milling across the bottom of Regent Street. He spotted Charity at once.

She hesitated by the lights, afraid to run once they'd turned amber and to his dismay he saw that she looked as forlorn and waiflike as she did in her uniform. She was wearing a shabby blue coat which was too big on the shoulders, clutching a shiny plastic handbag and her shoes slopped on her feet. She looked so young.

John Marshall's world was one of smart hotels, airport lounges, beautiful, well-groomed women and good restaurants. An acclaimed photographer, he'd made his name taking compelling pictures of famines, earthquakes and floods. But he observed poverty and suffering only through a lens and until yesterday he'd never known heartbreak.

The lights turned to green and Charity hurried across the road. As he watched her she suddenly caught sight of him, smiled and raised a hand in greeting.

Only then did he see the effort she'd made. Her white-blonde hair was tied back with a ribbon the colour of her eyes. Her rundown shoes were polished and she wore pink lipstick and a touch of rouge.

Suddenly he was ashamed that he'd even noticed her clothes.

'Hallo,' she said shyly as she approached him. 'I almost didn't recognise you, you look so different.'

'In clothes?' He smiled down at her, noting her perfect white teeth and the clarity of her complexion.

She blushed and dropped her eyes from his. In fact she was stunned at how smart and almost handsome he looked. Much taller than she'd realised, with the straight back of a guardsman; but even though he looked young, he had to be at least forty-five, she thought.

'Let's go then.' He put one hand on her arm.

She didn't move, but looked up at him with fear-filled eyes.

'Not the Ritz,' she stammered. 'It's too posh and I don't look right. Can we go somewhere else?'

'I'd gone off that idea myself,' he reassured her, all at once seeing the place he usually went for celebration lunches as inappropriate. 'Not because you don't look right, but because it's stuffy. I know a place in Chelsea that's much nicer.'

In the taxi John made small talk, pointing out landmarks and telling her about restaurants he'd visited. When Susie was Charity's age she'd been full of chatter about records, clothes and boys, and he wondered again what had driven such an obviously intelligent girl, who spoke so well, into a job as a chambermaid.

The Marco Polo, an Italian restaurant just off King's Road, wasn't quite as intimidating as Charity had expected. Very simply decorated with plain white walls and red and white checked tablecloths, it had a jolly atmosphere. There were a great many businessmen lunching there, but at the next table to the one the waiter ushered them to in a corner, there was a family with two children and that took the edge off Charity's fear.

Faced with a menu in Italian, she could only stare in horror.

'Do you like Italian food?' John asked gently, sensing her dilemma.

'I've only ever had spaghetti.'

'Well that's a bit hard to eat in public. Shall I order for you? Chicken, perhaps?'

He rattled off an order to the waiter in a stream of Italian, and Charity listened in awe.

'Have you lived there, Mr Marshall?' she asked.

'You can't call me Mr Marshall after what we've been through,' he said. 'It's John, and no I've never lived in Italy, but I've worked there quite a bit. That Italian might sound impressive to you, but believe me I only know enough to order a meal, or book a hotel room.'

She sipped the red wine the waiter poured into her glass. She had only ever tasted red wine once before and that was at the cottage. Compared with that vinegary stuff, this was nice!

A few more sips and she felt easier. No one could see her shoes tucked under the table and her awful coat was hung up out of sight.

'Tell me all about you,' she said. 'From the beginning.'

'I'll tell you everything if afterwards you promise to tell me all about you! We've met under unfortunate circumstances, so we're pals. That means we both have to be truthful.'

'OK.' She shrugged her shoulders and folded her arms on the table, looking earnestly at him. She could see that many of his facial lines were from a lifetime of laughter before he'd hit what Dr Cole called 'his rut in the road'. Two deep ones ran from his nose

286

to his mouth and there was something undeniably attractive about such a lived-in face. 'You start.'

'Well,' he fidgeted with the stem of his glass, 'I was born in 1913. To my horror, that makes me almost fifty. I was born in London, Highgate, the youngest of three and I was fortunate enough to have a wonderful childhood. My father was something of an explorer, always off to far-flung places, coming back with thrilling stories and strange artefacts. I went to Uppingham, a public school in Rutland, but I never ever thought of getting a "proper" job or entering the professions. I was interested in photography even then and I drifted off to Paris as a young man to starve in a garret.'

Charity's eyes widened.

'I didn't starve,' he added. 'Instead I found a job in an art gallery. But when my father died in 1938 I had to face up to the real world. He left very little money and Mother had to sell the house and move out to a cottage in the country. Next thing was the war and I joined the air force. They channelled me into aerial photography because I was useless at everything else. I met Hester in 1940 at a dance and we got married in 1941, Susie was born a year later, Anna my second daughter in '44.'

Charity saw pain flicker into his eyes and again wondered whether they'd done the right thing to come to such a public place. But it was too late now to change their minds.

'Were you happy together then?' something prompted her to ask.

'Yes,' he said thoughtfully as if he wasn't sure. 'I have to admit with hindsight it was more a marriage of companionship than deep love, but I suppose the war distorted things. Hester moved out of London to Sussex when she was expecting Susie and I couldn't get home very much. I missed so much of the girls when they were small, but then so did every other father at that time.'

The waiter brought their food. Charity had never tasted anything so wonderful as the chicken filled with garlic butter.

'But after the war?'

'I began travelling,' John said, filling her glass yet again. 'I spent a great deal of time in Germany and Poland and my first successes came then through pictures of Birkenau that I took for the *National Geographic*.'

'And your wife and girls stayed at home?'

John nodded.

'I was making very little money in those days. I wasn't motivated by money anyway, and Hester inherited a small amount of money from her family. I suppose while I was away we were growing further and further apart. Hester could never really understand my need to travel, or my love for my job.'

'You mean you didn't consider your family important?'

John had the grace to look slightly sheepish. 'I thought children were women's work and my father had always been a wanderer, so I saw nothing wrong in what I was doing. Mother had always been delighted when Father came home, she made a fuss of him, and I suppose I thought this was the way all marriages should be.'

'I bet your wife got fed up with you.'

'She did,' John agreed. 'But each time she brought up the subject I whisked her and the girls off with me for a bit, and I thought that kept her happy. About ten years ago I started to make a name for myself and commissions began to pour in. I'd be home for a week, then suddenly I'd be off to India or Africa. Anyway, to cut a long story short, I was in Mexico last year when I got a letter from Hester asking for a divorce.

She'd met someone else. I should have flown home there and then, but I didn't, I stayed another three months to finish what I was doing and wrote to her saying we'd discuss it when I got back.'

Privately Charity was amazed that he could be so thoughtless and self-centred.

'I know,' he agreed, seeing her expression. 'I deserved everything. That was when I got home to find Hester had changed the locks.'

'And you were angry?'

'Male pride!' He bit his lip hard, as if remembering something he'd rather forget. 'She'd turned the girls against me too, that was the real shock. But after I'd returned to Africa and calmed down I realised it was really all my fault. Who could blame the girls for taking her part? That, my dear, is where you found me, on my way home to offer the final olive branch: a divorce, and an apology. Whatever it took to make peace.'

'And you found Susie had been killed?' Charity said gently.

'She was in a car with some friends, driving back to her flat after a pre-Christmas party.' John's voice sounded flat.

'And no one managed to get a message to you?'

'They tried,' he admitted, 'but I was travelling overland, on my way to Nairobi. Susie's funeral was on December 23rd, they delayed it in the hope that I'd arrive. When they didn't hear from me I suppose they just had to go ahead.'

'So where are Hester and Anna now?'

'At Hester's parents' in Wales,' John said sadly.

'Poor John,' Charity said. 'And poor Hester too.'

'She'd got her new man with her.' John's face convulsed as if he might cry again. He blinked hard.

'You must write to them,' Charity said. 'Explain

how it was, apologise for the past. Don't make things worse by withdrawing from them.'

'You're very wise.' John was touched by Charity's sincerity and obvious concern. He ordered another bottle of wine. 'Your turn now,' he said.

If she hadn't drunk three glasses of wine, Charity might not have been able to tell a virtual stranger as much as she did. She started by telling him how she had come to be working at the Regent Palace, then suddenly the dam burst and she began to tell him all about Daniel.

Now and again John had to stop her and make her backtrack so he could take it all in, but in the end her sad story was clear. 'No wonder you look so sad,' he said, stunned that someone so young could have had so much thrown at her in life. 'But you've got to do exactly what you told me to do. Sort out your life, put this behind you.' He looked at her. She had become prettier and prettier as they talked; she had a pink glow in her cheeks now, even her eyes looked less haunted. If he could just take her and get her hair cut, buy her a few decent clothes, she could be stunning. He wondered if he dared suggest it.

'Look,' he said, 'I hope we'll stay friends. I'm leaving the hotel this evening. I was going straight to Paris, but now I think I'll go down to Wales first. I should be back in early February. Can I see you again then?'

'Do you really want to?' Charity wondered if he was just being polite.

'Of course I do.' At the moment John felt as if she was the only friend he had in the world; that just knowing where she was and that he could see her again would help him through the next few weeks. 'We'll have to compare notes on how we're getting on.'

As they walked up the King's Road John looked down at Charity.

'Let me buy you a present,' he said impulsively. 'Let's get you a new coat.'

Charity stopped short, frowning up at him.

'Of course not.' She blushed furiously.

'Only as a thank you,' he said, aware he'd embarrassed her.

She gave him a long stare.

'I know my coat's shabby,' she said with some dignity, 'but I've got money in the bank, John. I just haven't felt like buying new clothes. Lunch was enough of a thank you.'

'I didn't mean to hurt your feelings,' he said quickly. 'It's just that I always used to treat my daughters.'

'But I'm not your daughter,' Charity replied. 'Only a friend.'

'Does a friend get a hug then?' He smiled.

For a moment she froze. Suddenly she found herself acutely aware of him as a man, not just another troubled soul.

He looked down at her anxious face and ran his thumbs across her cheekbones.

'Thank you for lunch,' she stammered. 'Look after yourself.'

The hug came naturally then. Their ages and station in life were unimportant. Just two people clinging to one another for comfort.

Chapter Sixteen

'You look fabulous!' Sonia gaped in shocked surprise as Charity came in through the staff door laden with carrier bags. 'I can't believe it's you!'

Sonia was a petite dark-haired girl with sharp features and an even sharper tongue. Although Charity didn't feel she ever wanted to be friends with this particular girl, her compliment was very welcome.

'Just a haircut.' She shrugged her shoulders. 'Not before time either!'

'Cor blimey.' Albert, one of the porters, stuck his head through the pigeonhole from the porters' room, a wide grin stretched across his narrow, lined face. 'You look a million dollars, babe.'

'Thank you.' Charity smiled shyly and walked on, leaving Sonia and Albert to start more gossip.

It was six days since John Marshall had taken her out to lunch, and she couldn't thank him enough for helping her pull herself together again.

Today she'd left the Regent Palace at nine o'clock, taken some money out of the post office, then gone straight to the hairdresser's in Selfridges. An hour later she had emerged with her hair in the latest style, a sleek bob which swung forward on to her cheeks, like Cilla Black's.

Admiring wolf whistles from a couple of workmen lifted her spirits still further and from there she did a tour of the Oxford Street shops, hunting for bargains in the sales.

She had bought a royal blue swagger coat, reduced to half price because it was so tiny, a smart black dress, two skirts, a jumper, some new underwear and a pair of shoes. Halfway through the morning she had gone into the powder room in John Lewis and changed, dumping her shabby old clothes by some dustbins on her way out.

Charity opened her door, threw her bags into the chair and flung herself down on the bed, sighing with relief as she kicked off her shoes. She'd begun to put her life in order again.

She had taken the first step during the evening after her lunch with John when she finally opened all those letters she'd left in a drawer unread. To her surprise, not one of them evoked more painful memories, but instead a warm feeling of being cared for.

From Marjorie and Martin there were no recriminations that she hadn't been in touch, only understanding and concern. They enclosed two letters from Lou and Geoff sent to their address and urged her to call at the restaurant soon.

Lou and Geoff were anxious at not hearing from her for so many months. But although they begged her to write or telephone it was apparent they assumed her silence was due more to being a scatterbrained and preoccupied teenager than to any disaster.

But although the replies to the Charleses and the Bells would take some thinking out, the letters from Dorothy and Rita confirmed that she wasn't alone in feeling depressed and isolated.

Dorothy's letter was a bright and cynical report of her escapades in Devon, but however funny she made the stories of being 'The Scarlet Woman' of Ilfracombe, it was clear she had immersed herself in several affairs with married men out of desperation. Rita too spoke of drinking too much, of feeling worthless, and of her bitterness that her parents shut their eyes and ears to everything rather than allow her to tell them something they couldn't accept.

Putting pen to paper was tough, but Charity began with the simplest letter: to Miss Mansell, telling her she was feeling better and thanking her for her kindness. Next, Majorie and Martin; the long overdue explanation that she couldn't face anyone until now, but would ring in a day or two and arrange to collect her belongings from them.

Writing these letters had a therapeutic effect. While she was choosing words to make light of the miserable last months, she found she was thinking deeply and ultimately coming to terms with the need to put it all behind her. By the time she replied to Dorothy's and Rita's letters she found she was feeling positive, even making jokes about the sorry state she'd fallen into.

Finally it was time to tackle Geoff and Lou. She apologised for her lack of communication with the excuse that she worked such long hours, and explained she was now back in London working at the hotel as a temporary measure until she found something better. She begged for news of the children and some photographs and gave them a rundown on the books she'd read in her spare time so they wouldn't think she'd forgotten her plans to better herself.

All this week she'd thought about Daniel just as often as she had before, but she believed now that the acute pain would lessen with time. As Miss Frost had said when she signed the final adoption papers, it was done now. The only road was forward.

She looked good again. Tonight she would collect her belongings from Majorie and Martin, and soon she would arrange to see both Rita and Dorothy.

Writing letters was one step towards getting back to normal, but Charity knew that the next step had to be making new friends. This proved more difficult.

Each evening after work she left her door open, looked up and smiled when any of the girls went past, and even went along to the tiny kitchen at the end of the passage and made herself coffee hoping someone would stop to speak.

She couldn't reproach the other girls for not rushing in to befriend her, or inviting her into their rooms. She'd shown no interest in them all this time, and who could blame them for thinking she was weird!

Ironically, it was a postcard from John in Paris that finally broke the ice. Staff letters were always put in the porters' room and just about everyone must have picked the card up and read it before she even knew it had arrived.

It wasn't a view of the Eiffel Tower, but an arty black and white photograph of two street urchins sitting on a kerb eating ice-cream.

'That's not from that bloke who tried to top 'imself, is it?' Albert the porter asked as he handed it to Charity.

'He didn't try to kill himself,' Charity retorted, for a moment tempted to tell him to mind his own business. 'He was feeling miserable and a bit confused, that's all. He'd just heard his daughter had been killed in a road accident.'

'Poor bugger.' Albert's lined face contorted with sympathy. 'Lucky you found 'im, wasn't it? 'E's a famous photographer, what's won prizes and stuff. Took you out to lunch, did he?'

'Yes, he was nice.' Charity wasn't pleased that Albert had read the postcard before she'd even got a chance to, but she was loath to bite his head off. 'I expect I made him think of his daughter.'

'Well he obviously got more chat out of you than we've ever had.' Albert grinned.

By lunchtime the news that John Marshall had written to Charity had spread around the hotel, elevating her to almost celebrity status. It dawned on her that John Marshall was a great deal more famous than he'd let on to her and this lack of conceit on his part heightened his image in her mind. Although she felt concern that John's personal problems were being bandied around, the sense that people were intrigued by her friendship with him gave her a warm glow.

Charity had a reply to her letter from Rita within the week and they arranged a meeting. When the evening came she was so excited as she changed out of her uniform that she could barely manage to put her lipstick on straight. Her excitement wasn't only due to the reunion. Rita said she had a plan she wanted to share with both Charity and Dorothy.

'Charity!'

She turned at hearing her name yelled out and to her surprise it wasn't the girl she remembered with tousled curls and a nappy pin stuck in the front of her dress, but a glamorous redhead tottering towards her on four-inch heels, arms open wide.

It was half-past eight on a Wednesday night. More snow was expected and Oxford Street was almost deserted. Courting couples lingered in the warmth of shop doorways and there was only a handful of people like herself, waiting for someone.

'Rita! You look so different,' Charity gasped, returning the warm hug that said the packaging might be different but the product was the same. 'Let me look at you.'

Rita was wearing a camel coat with a huge fox-fur collar turned up around her face. She had lost weight dramatically and her hair was piled up on top of her head in fat, shiny curls. Long glittery earrings, false eyelashes and a face made up like a model's wiped out the image of a young mother.

'You look different too,' Rita giggled. 'But let's find a warm place to go and chat. I'm freezing.'

They found a pub round by the London Palladium and over a couple of Babychams everything came out.

'It's been hell at home,' Rita admitted. 'Both Mum and Dad knew something serious had happened, but they didn't care enough to force me into an admission. Mum kept buying me things to cheer me up, when all I wanted was a shoulder to cry on. She went on and on about me being fat. How can parents be so cruel?'

It was good to be able to talk about their feelings, to share the painful secret they'd locked away.

'I didn't want anyone to come near me,' Charity said. 'I felt so empty that nothing but solitude and silence helped.'

'I found myself crying all the time,' Rita confessed. 'Anything would bring it on – the sight of a baby in a pram, a child holding its mother's hand . . .'

She went on to tell Charity how she'd found work doing promotions. 'I just threw myself into it,' she said with a wry smile. 'The other girls are all hard-drinking men chasers, so I made out I was the same. After a bit it became second nature.'

Rita's life sounded very racy: wild parties, married men, drinking herself stupid most evenings.

'But I'm on the mend now.' She squeezed Charity's hand, her eyes glistening with tears. 'I've calmed down.'

Charity told her friend that if she hadn't met John Marshall she might still be sitting alone in her room. 'I want to find a better job and leave the hotel,' she said. 'But I can't imagine what I'd do. I don't know how to do anything other than skivvying.'

'You could do promotions too,' Rita bubbled up with all her old warmth. 'It's a doddle of a job, you only have to look good and like chatting to people. There's a job coming up in a couple of weeks for beauty consultants for a new cosmetics firm. They want lots of girls and it could lead to something permanent.'

This was all progressing a bit too fast for Charity. She had put one toe in the water in getting her hair cut and thinking about the future, but now Rita was getting carried away.

Rita, like Dorothy, came from a wealthy middle-class background; they were both only children who'd been brought up in luxurious homes. Neither of them suffered from feelings of inadequacy, they could launch themselves into the beauty world with the assurance they belonged there.

The pub was cosy and by the time they were on their third Babycham Charity was beginning to warm to Rita's lifestyle.

It all sounded so exciting – staying in hotels with other girls, making more money than Charity had ever dreamed of, and all the perks like clothes allowances and free makeup and perfume. But then Rita moved on to talk about getting a flat.

'I know of one coming up in Earls Court,' she insisted. 'Dad will give me a deposit if we need one. He's dying to get rid of me, I cramp their style on bridge nights. Think of it, Charity – you, me and Dorothy. We could have such a good time.'

'Will Dorothy want to come to London?'

'Want to! She can't wait,' Rita grinned mischievously. 'She phoned last night to say she had a case packed ready.

'Tell me more about this John.' Rita looked attentively at her friend. Charity had mentioned John only in passing, but Rita sensed there was more to tell. 'How long have you been going out with him?'

'He isn't a *boyfriend*.' Charity looked shocked, then proceeded to talk about John Marshall for twenty minutes.

Rita missed nothing. She thought her friend was smitten. 'John Marshall! He's bloody famous, Charity. Even *I've* heard of him.'

'Hold on.' Charity saw Rita was reading more into this than she wanted her to. 'He's fifty and it's not the way you think.'

'The best lover I ever had was fifty. He did things to me that make me go weak at the knees just thinking about it.' Rita's eyes went all dreamy. 'Of course he was married and nothing could come of it. But this guy is on his own. He'll pamper you, teach you all sorts of things. Grab the chance while you can.'

'I don't suppose he thinks that way for a minute.' Charity giggled at her friend's audacity. 'He's lost his daughter, I'm just a substitute, that's all.'

Rita looked carefully at Charity. She was very thin and pale compared with how she remembered her at Daleham Gardens and her clothes, though new, weren't exactly fashionable. But Charity was a natural beauty, her skin was as clear as a child's and her blonde hair gleamed under the lights.

'Charity, you're gorgeous,' she insisted. 'I don't believe that any man could fail to notice that, even if you were wearing a sack. He must be interested if he's written and says he wants to see you again. Men aren't like women, they don't collect substitutes for their own kids.'

Charity felt a pang of guilt as she thought of her own father. 'He's old enough to be my dad.'

'But he *isn't* your dad.' Rita smiled triumphantly. 'He's a rich, famous man who also happens to be free. Start thinking about him in that way. You like him, you said yourself he's handsome and easy to talk to. What else do you want?'

Charity wanted what she had had with Hugh, only for it to last for ever. She wanted the security of knowing she was loved, a man's arms around her, a man who would never lie to her.

'I want love, I suppose,' she said.

'Look where love got the three of us!' Rita gave a tight little laugh. 'I'll settle for fun from now on, men who adore me and show their appreciation with more than a quick screw in the back of their car. I don't ever want the pain of caring too much, and I don't think you do either.'

They parted after the pub closed. The last thing Rita said was that she was going out to look for a flat the next day and she'd be in touch as soon as she'd found the right one.

'Promise me you won't let me down?' she said as she got into a taxi. 'I'm relying on you.'

Charity had spent many nights lying awake in the Regent Palace, but this was the first that her thoughts were entirely happy ones.

Only one tiny thing bothered her. Was Rita being entirely truthful? Her new glamorous appearance, that kind of hard-bitten confidence she'd acquired, was that really entirely due to promotions work she was doing? She hadn't actually mentioned any of the companies she worked for by name. Charity felt uneasy, despite herself.

It was snowing again on the first of February. Charity woke to find the roof outside her window glimmering in the darkness and still more snow falling. She'd scarely noticed it in the first few weeks, yet now for some reason she felt a wild elation as she got into her uniform, as if something wonderful was about to happen.

She skipped through taking early morning tea round to the guests, laughed at Cyril the breakfast chef's little jokes when normally she ignored them, and when the mail came and she found a letter from John, her heart turned somersaults.

Just a few lines on one piece of thick hotel paper from Paris:

I'm flying back into London on the evening of February 1st. I'll stay at the Hilton because I don't want to make things awkward for you. Can you ring me there on the morning of the 2nd? I'm looking forward to seeing you again.

The letter was enough to send her flying through her work doing the bedrooms. An American businessman had left her a five-pound tip and then just as she was going off duty for the afternoon, Rita rang her.

'I've found the flat,' she gasped down the phone. 'It's wonderful, Chas, Dad's paid the key money for us and the first month's rent.'

'Where is it?' Charity felt a surge of wild excitement.

'In Earls Court, Barkston Gardens,' Rita gabbled out. 'It's not a grotty place, though it needs a bit of painting. It's in one of those proper blocks with heating and everything. You wait till you see it. You'll be jumping up and down with glee.'

'When *can* I see it?' Charity said eagerly.

'Meet me at Earls Court tube tonight at eight,' Rita said. 'Dad's signing the lease today and picking up the keys. I'm going to phone Dot at teatime. I bet she'll be on the next train.'

It was all so sudden that Charity couldn't think straight. 'But what about my job?' she blurted out.

'Hand in your notice,' Rita said impatiently. 'Do it

301

now, otherwise you'll be agonising over it. I'll get you a job straight away. They need loads of girls right now. By the way, it's the Earls Court Road side of the station, not the bit by the exhibition hall. Look, I've got to go. See you there at eight.'

There was no time to ask how she'd get there if snow stopped the tubes, no time for reassurance that she really would get another job, or even to tell Rita about John. But the elation she'd felt earlier that morning was enough to tell her that her future was about to change dramatically.

'I didn't expect it to be as posh as this,' Charity gasped as Rita stopped at Barkston Mansions.

There could have been no better way to see the private gardens in the centre of the square than in the golden glow of the Victorian street lamps: grass hidden under a blanket of thick, untrampled snow, trees weighed down with sparkling frosting. Black railings and a lone snowman turned it into a scene of serenity and beauty straight from a Christmas card, hiding the fact that this area was the heart of rather squalid bedsitter land.

A couple of wide white marble steps led up to half-glassed double doors and beyond the spacious hall was an old wrought-iron lift, the staircase winding round it, with a red carpet and gleaming brass stair rods.

Charity looked up. The building had at least five floors, as did all the houses, and the porch was supported by stone pillars. Across the square most of the other houses had damaged stonework and peeling paint, but this was red brick and the lower flats had leaded windows.

'Ours isn't all that grand,' Rita said, dragging Charity up the steps. 'Dad gave me a warning about wild parties. Apparently there's quite a lot of old fogies living here.'

Their flat was on the fourth floor to the right of the stairs. A big square hall, with all the other rooms leading off.

'An old lady lived here,' Rita explained as she led Charity into the hall. 'Apparently her son whisked her off into a home and he's sold off all her good stuff, but he told Dad we could have the rest.'

Charity stood still and just stared. A scratched table and four unmatching chairs stood in the middle of the hall, the dark green carpet had deep dents where heavier furniture had stood and there were clean marks on the faded wallpaper where pictures had been removed.

A faint whiff of old ladies and mothballs lingered, but even at that first glance Charity knew it had great potential.

'It's so warm,' she gasped, taking off her coat and flinging it down on the table before she went to explore.

'The heating and hot water is thrown in with the rent,' Rita said as she followed her. 'I was a bit disappointed because it's only got two bedrooms and when I saw it the first time there was a lot more furniture.'

A sitting room overlooking the street held only a large shabby sofa and two armchairs. Next to this was a small bedroom with an old-fashioned bed like something from 'Goldilocks and the Three Bears'. The second bedroom was at the back, sandwiched between the kitchen and bathroom.

'We could make the hall the lounge,' Charity suggested. She moved the table and chairs back against the wall between the bedroom and kitchen. The carpet was the best in the entire flat, with only one worn part. 'If we put the sofa over that to hide it.'

She could see it repainted, with bright pictures on

the wall and a couple of lamps. The doors were all lovely mahogany ones with brass knobs and at night it wouldn't matter that there were no windows.

Silence from Rita made her look round.

Rita was standing by the small pine table, two pretty china plates in her hands, and to Charity's amazement she was crying.

'What on earth's the matter?' Charity went over to her friend and put her arms round her.

'Just being silly,' Rita sniffed. 'I've pretended for so long that everything was fine. I put on my makeup, tart myself up and show off.' She didn't have to add that if her father had helped her like this six months ago, all three of them might have been able to keep their babies.

Charity held Rita tightly. She too was never going to mention what might have been, or allow herself any bitter backward glances. 'It's all going to be wonderful from now on. We three are going to be a family, looking out for one another. Together we can be happy.'

It was only as they travelled back on the Piccadilly line together that Charity remembered to tell Rita that John would be in London in the morning.

'At the Hilton, eh?' Rita winked suggestively. 'Well have a good time. Dorothy's got some bloke to drive her up on Thursday. Can you meet us at the flat in the evening to do some cleaning? Then we can all move in on Saturday. Try and nick us some sheets and towels!'

Charity approached the Hilton with butterflies in her stomach and her heart fluttering. It was all very well the other chambermaids telling her she looked like a model in her new black dress, and dabbing some Chanel number 5 on her neck and wrists; inside she felt like the maid dressed up in her mistress's clothes. Her feet were like ice, shoes already wet with snow and even the new coat offered little protection from the icy wind.

She ought to have got a taxi instead of walking down Piccadilly and now she was scared stiff of going into somewhere so grand. Suppose John didn't really want to see her? It was three weeks since that lunch and he'd been upset enough to agree to anything then. It would be too awful if she found he was only meeting her out of politeness.

Park Lane looked very pretty. Although the road had been cleared, snow hung on the trees and beyond the railings Hyde Park was one glorious sweep of winter wonderland lit up by the street lamps.

The liveried doorman was flagging down a cab for a couple in evening dress standing under the hotel canopy and it took all Charity's courage to walk past them and through the big doors.

John had said he would be waiting in reception, but she couldn't see him.

A porter looked round from the desk where he was talking to one of the clerks, and Charity blushed scarlet. At the Regent Palace they had to be very careful about prostitutes using the hotel and she wondered if they might suspect her of being one.

Then she saw John and a hot tingle surged through her veins.

He came towards her smiling, caught hold of her arms and kissed her cheek. 'It's so good to see you again. For a moment I didn't recognise you.'

'I had my hair cut,' she said in little more than a whisper, feeling flustered as if every one of the dozens of people milling round the foyer were watching them.

'Come and have a drink,' he said and led her towards the bar.

John looked so handsome and distinguished in his grey suit and striped tie. His face had a healthy glow that hadn't been there at their last meeting and Charity found herself gazing at his strong features.

'You look better,' she said softly as they sat down. 'How are you feeling?'

'Calmer.' He smiled. 'A bit ashamed of myself for letting my emotions get the better of me.'

Over a drink Charity told him about the flat.

'Well, good for you.' He reached across the table and put his hand over hers. 'I wish you every happiness in your new home, it sounds marvellous.'

Later he took her to another Italian restaurant at the back of Oxford Street and over a leisurely meal he told her about his work and all the countries he'd been to.

It was like being taken on a magic carpet ride as he talked of palaces in India, the wildlife in Africa, mountains of Nepal and the people in China. He mentioned he was hoping to go back to Africa before long to finish the job he had abandoned when he cut short his last trip.

'Travelling is a love affair for me.' He smiled. 'I wish I could settle down in one place, but as soon as I've unpacked my bags I start hankering for wide open spaces, for new sights, sounds and smells. Sometimes I think I've spent more time in airport lounges than anyone else in the world.'

Charity studied his face as he was speaking: the way his eyes crinkled up when he laughed, the curve of his lips. She had the desire to run a finger down the deep lines in his cheeks, to touch those springy, grey-frosted brown curls.

Rita's words about older men were pricking at her. John had a youthful exuberance that years and experience hadn't diluted and she found herself wishing she could be with him on one of these trips.

She told him all about Dorothy and Rita and talked of the flat again, describing it in minute detail.

'It will be the first time I've ever been really free,' she said. 'I can't quite imagine being able to come and go as I like with no one to ask questions.'

'I know how it will be for you if you aren't careful,' John said gently. 'You'll turn that flat into a real home, you'll collect possessions and be a mother to the other girls, even though you're the youngest. Try not to do that. Enjoy the fun and be irresponsible.'

'We *will* have fun,' she said. 'But what's wrong with painting the place and making it nice?'

'Nothing at all.' He patted her cheek. 'But supposing someone came along and asked you to drop everything and go on a trip with them. What would your answer be?'

'It would depend who it was, and when they wanted me to go,' she said.

'Well, for argument's sake, suppose I asked you to come to Italy with me at the end of next week. Would you come?'

Charity's heart turned over. 'I couldn't,' she replied. 'I've got the flat to paint, interviews for jobs, Dorothy and Rita to consider.'

John looked at Charity and smiled.

He knew she hadn't realised his question was a real invitation. She didn't look like a little waif tonight. The black sheath dress and her new hairstyle gave her a veneer of sophistication, and new-found happiness had made her eyes sparkle. But she had no experience of anything other than drudgery and suddenly he wanted to lift her away from all that, show her the world was a big, beautiful place.

'I've got to go to Florence at the end of next week,' he said. 'Come with me?'

Charity just stared in surprise.

'I can't,' she said faintly.

'I know. You've got the painting and unpacking, the interviews and being with your friends,' John said.

'But I'm only talking about a few days, a week at most. All that can wait.'

Later Charity thought it odd that she hadn't even considered whether he was asking her to share his bed, or hadn't even been shocked at the suggestion that he might be.

'I can't just go like that.' She giggled, embarrassed now by the intensity in his eyes.

'You can.' He took her hand and lifted it to his lips, gently kissing the tips of her fingers. 'You told me yourself it is the first time you've been free.'

He could hardly believe what he was saying. A man of fifty suddenly asking an eighteen-year-old to go away with him. It was madness!

'But Rita and Dorothy – '

Her flushed face throbbed and the touch of his lips on her fingers was making her feel very peculiar.

'I bet *they'd* go.' He laughed softly and continued to nibble at her fingers. 'Come on, be daring. Say yes.'

'But I hardly know you!' She thought she ought to remove her hand from his, but she so wanted to keep it there. She felt very confused.

John had enough experience for both of them. There had been many women in his life, of all nationalities, brief affairs in the main because of the nature of his work. He knew Charity's becoming blush was a prickle of sexual attraction, even if she didn't.

'But – ' she stopped short unable to find the right words.

Her face was so beautiful John had a desire to pull her into his arms there and then, regardless of the other customers. But he knew he mustn't frighten her.

'It can be however you want it to be,' he said. 'As friends with separate rooms, if that's what you want. I won't push you into anything you aren't happy about.'

'I'll have to think about it.' She looked down at the table. 'It's a big step.'

'It's not such a big step,' he said. 'I'll look after you, take you back home afterwards. It's just for fun, Charity, a holiday.' He didn't know if he was speaking the truth or not.

All through coffee Charity kept stealing glances at John. He was speaking in fluent Italian to the waiter and she watched his expressive hands, so long and slender, his smile, the way his lips curled at the corners. She wondered what he would be like to kiss.

He took her back to the hotel in a taxi and jumped out with her. Piccadilly was a blaze of lights, hundreds of people milling around just the way it always was.

'I'll walk back to my hotel,' he said catching her hand in his in a firm grip. 'But how long have I got to wait for my reply? Have you got a passport? We'll have to get that organised.'

Charity stopped just far enough away from the hotel not to be spotted by the doorman.

'If you turn me down we'll still be friends Charity,' he said. 'No strings!'

He took a step back from her, leaving her with her lips slightly apart waiting for the kiss that never materialised.

The next day Charity called in to Central Promotions in Oxford Street, at Rita's suggestion. Almost the moment she stepped into the smart, glossy office she lost her confidence. Anne Rushton, a hard-looking blonde in her thirties, looked Charity up and down, then raised one eyebrow when she saw on the application form where Charity was working. Even the fact that she was a friend of Rita's didn't seem to impress her.

'As I said, I'm only interviewing now to make a

short list of girls I consider suitable for Glamour Girl Cosmetics' promotion. Bearing in mind your lack of experience in this field I don't want to build your hopes up. But call in again. I'm sure I shall be able to slot you into some other, less high-profile promotion job.'

Charity's heart sank. It sounded very much like total rejection.

'Thank you for seeing me, Miss Rushton.' She forced a smile. 'I'll pop in again soon.'

Outside the office, Charity turned up the collar of her coat against the cold wind and walked back down Regent Street towards the hotel.

She was riddled with self-doubt now, wondering if she'd been a little hasty handing in her notice and letting Rita convince her the agency would jump at taking her on. Tonight she was meeting the girls at the flat and though she couldn't wait to see Dorothy again, and to move in there, she had looked upon getting this job lined up as the deciding factor in whether she went with John to Florence or not.

'Chas!' Dorothy came hurtling across the box-strewn hall and flung her arms round Charity. 'I thought you'd never get here.'

Charity just held her friend tightly for a moment, overcome. 'I can't really believe this,' she said breathlessly. 'Our flat, us all together again. It's too much.'

Rita's giggle made them both turn to her. She was brandishing a bottle of gin.

'Celebration time,' she said. 'I helped myself to this from Dad's drinks cabinet. It ought to be champagne, but it'll have to do.'

Charity took off her coat and perched on the arm of the settee. All three of them were in jeans for the cleaning, but Dorothy looked even more devastatingly lovely than she remembered.

She was much slimmer and her fine features even more pronounced. Even though she was wearing no makeup and her long, dark brown hair was tied back with an elastic band, she had that enviable elegant look Charity would have died to possess.

'How did the interview go?' Rita asked as she poured liberal quantities of gin into three tumblers.

Charity dolefully recounted it.

'I don't think Anne Rushton was very impressed with me,' she said finally.

'The girls call her Ratty Rushton,' Rita said with a smile. 'I'll put in a good word for you. Don't worry.'

'She's stupid if she doesn't take us,' Dorothy said with that supreme confidence Charity had always been so impressed by. 'Where else is she going to find a job lot with such fabulous faces, stunning figures and such charisma?'

Charity giggled, at once forgetting her anxiety. Rita topped up their glasses with lemonade and passed them round.

'To our future,' she said, raising hers for a toast. 'May every party we throw be the wildest. May all our men be stinking rich!'

It was *so* good to be together again. They talked non stop, giggling about everything and anything.

Charity told them a little of her date with John, but held back about his invitation to Florence. She would make up her own mind about that and she knew if she told them they would insist she went.

Not a duster or broom was lifted, despite that being the intention of the evening. They moved Dorothy's belongings into her room, unpacked a box of tinned food her mother had sent with her and discussed the need for paint and new curtains, but nothing more.

'We'll do it at the weekend.' Rita's words were slurred now with the gin. 'Besides, we've all got next week free. Here's to doing what we want, when *we* want to do it!'

John Marshall waited at the reception desk for his key. He had spent the day seeing publishers, but his mind had been on Charity and her decision.

'There's a letter for you.' The tall brunette smiled. 'A young lady dropped it in this afternoon while you were out.'

He opened the envelope, convinced she had found some polite excuse. To his amazement a couple of small photographs fell out.

'You little darling,' he said to himself as he bent to pick them up.

She had filled out the entire form herself, even enclosed the money for the passport and there was a letter . . .

> Dear John,
>   I would like to come if you still want me to. We aren't on the phone at the new flat yet, but I've put the address at the bottom. Thank you for the lovely meal last night. I'm going to buy a book on Florence so I know all about it.
>   Love, Charity.

Chapter Seventeen

'My ears have gone all funny,' Charity whispered to John. There was a stern-looking businessman sitting on the other side of him and she didn't want to show John up.

'Hold your nose and gulp,' John suggested. 'It always happens in takeoff.'

Charity did as he said and smiled as she found it worked. She had been in a state of nervous anticipation for the last three days, unable to eat or sleep. So many new experiences ahead of her – flying, going abroad, staying in a hotel as a guest instead of as a chambermaid, to say nothing of being with a man she'd only been out with twice.

'Excited?' John asked, leaning closer to her to share the view from the window. It was a surprisingly clear day for February and the panoramic view of London wreathed in snow beneath them was as compelling for him as it was for her. 'The first time I flew was in the RAF and I was scared stiff.'

'Very excited,' Charity said. She wished she could be honest and tell him how awkward she felt. At times in the airport lounge she was sure from his long silences that he was already regretting asking her. 'What time will we get there?'

'Around three, their time.' John altered his watch. 'Then we catch a train from Milan to Florence. With luck we'll be at the hotel in good time for dinner.'

Charity watched as John bought a bottle of Bacardi

from the duty-free trolley. He had asked what spirits she liked to drink and she hadn't known what to say. But Dorothy drank Bacardi, so it must be all right.

She wished she could get over this ridiculous shyness. Both times she'd gone out with him before it had been so easy to talk, but now he seemed strained too. If it was this difficult in a plane full of businessmen, what would it be like when they were alone in a hotel?

Perhaps she shouldn't have come. Especially as she hadn't managed to arrange a job for when she got back. Anne Rushton had sounded marginally warmer when she called back to Central Promotions, but hadn't offered anything definite. Rita and Dot kept urging her not to worry and she'd spent the week painting and arranging the flat, but maybe she should've been a bit more conscientious about finding a job?

'Quest' è la camera, signorina,' the porter said as he opened the door. Charity followed as he put her case on a low bench.

'Isn't it wonderful?' Charity gasped, looking round at John.

The Hotel Berchielli was an old merchant's house built in the fourteenth century right on the River Arno, placed between the Ponte Vecchio and Ponte St Trinità. All Charity had seen of it so far was the impressive entrance with huge studded oak doors and a reception area which John said was typically Florentine. It looked to her much like some of the pictures of palaces in her guidebook, with heavy carved furniture, red leather and a painted ceiling that could have been done by one of Michelangelo's apprentices.

Charity's room was decorated in a more feminine 1930s style, with light shiny walnut furniture, all pastel greens and pinks.

The porter showed them the adjoining bathroom, with a huge cast-iron bath on clawed feet, mirrored walls and a washbasin set in marble, then went on to open another door through to John's room.

Charity stood awkwardly as John spoke to the porter in rapid Italian. Did the elderly porter think they were father and daughter? Or lovers?

John's room was distinctly masculine. The same red and gold decoration as downstairs, with a vast, dark wood carved bed with matching wardrobe and dressing-table.

'Well what do you think?' John asked once the porter had left. Charity was still standing in the bath-room doorway and he could see that she was tense and apprehensive.

'It's absolutely marvellous,' she said, determined to show John she wasn't intimidated by such a grand place. She moved over to the window and pushed the heavy curtains aside. 'Look at this!'

It was dark now. The river was black, twinkling with reflected lights like diamonds on a jeweller's tray. A hodgepodge of houses seemed to grow right out of the river on the far bank and to her left she could see the Ponte Vecchio with all its medieval shops lit up brightly.

She hadn't caught more than a glimpse of Florence during the taxi ride from the station. They seemed to be hurtling through the narrowest of dark alleys at sixty miles an hour, narrowly missing many scooters and mopeds.

John put one hand lightly on her shoulder. 'Beauti-ful, isn't it,' he said. 'I'm sure you're dying to see more of it. Why don't you have a bath and change? Then we'll go out and have a few drinks before dinner.'

Charity's nervousness grew while she was in the

bathroom, very aware of John just the other side of the door. She gulped down the glass of Bacardi and Coke he'd poured for her, hoping she could quickly acquire the taste as it might make her feel calmer.

Dot and Rita would be green with envy, she said to herself as she got dressed again. They had both been quite shocked when she'd finally told them about this holiday. Although they'd agreed that they'd jump at the opportunity, Charity got the impression they thought she'd been a bit hasty. Now she wished she'd asked for some advice about how to handle it. Did John want her? He hadn't so much as held her hand so far. What would happen when they got back tonight after dinner?

Charity's nervousness was replaced by enchantment as they strolled through the streets an hour later. One moment they were in dark, narrow alleyways, the next plunged into brightly lit shopping streets packed with people and noise. Listening to Italians speaking was like hearing music. Tiny delicatessens festooned with strange-looking sausages on big hooks and different kinds of pasta displayed in huge trays vied with chic shoe shops and tiny boutiques for her attention. So many restaurants and bars, all so much more colourful than anything she'd seen in England. She had to keep stopping John to let her look.

They shared a bottle of wine in the Piazza del Duomo, sitting outside a café so she could watch the people passing through the busy square beside the magnificent green and white cathedral.

'It's so warm,' Charity remarked, unable to believe anyone would sit outside at night in February, even if they were wearing coats. 'And so exciting. I can't wait to see everything.'

John looked at her rapt face, felt her excitement and knew he'd been right to bring her here.

'Come on,' he said, taking a few lire notes and

leaving them on the table. 'I know just the thing for you.'

He didn't let go of her hand, but led her round the cathedral towards a row of horse-drawn carriages.

'Are we going in one of those?' she gasped. Many of the horses wore bells on their reins and the carriages had red leather upholstery.

John just grinned and broke into a volley of Italian to the driver.

'I've never been in one before either,' he admitted as the driver flicked his reins and the horse lurched the carriage forward. 'It's one of those romantic things you only do with a special lady.'

Charity felt as if she was in heaven. It wasn't just the jogging along the narrow streets, like a queen, but John's words and his hand still holding hers.

He pointed out many important places as they passed and seemed to know every art treasure in every building. She had lost all sense of direction soon after they left the hotel, and this ride confused her still further, but she was only too happy to sit back in comfort and enjoy the experience.

The carriage stopped at the Ponte Vecchio. John got out first, holding out his hand to help her down. He paid the driver, then slipped one arm round her, drawing her on to the bridge.

Charity was spellbound. The bridge was packed with tiny glittering jewellers' shops on both sides. The combination of the night sky above, the brilliance of the shop lights and the dazzling jewels on display was like stepping into Aladdin's cave, or a Christmas grotto.

She pressed her nose up against the windows, excitedly pointing out first one thing, then another, then moved on to the next shop.

'Do you like that?' John pointed out a small gold bow brooch studded with tiny diamonds.

'Umm, it's lovely,' Charity agreed, too enthralled to notice that the question had some significance.

She was so engrossed in the window displays she wasn't aware that he'd disappeared, but as she turned to show something to him, she found he was gone.

The bridge was crowded with people, but it didn't feel frightening in any way. She stood still, waiting, then she saw him come out of a shop.

'I thought you'd abandoned me,' she joked, rushing up to him. 'Did you buy something?'

'Yes, for you,' he said. Reaching into his coat pocket he brought out a small black velvet box.

It was the bow brooch.

'Oh John,' she gasped. 'You shouldn't have.'

He took it from the box and bent to pin it to the lapel of her coat. 'I want to shower you with presents,' he said softly. 'You make me feel so young and happy.'

A tingle ran down Charity's spine and she raised one hand to stroke his cheek, overwhelmed not only by the unexpected and expensive gift but by the feelings he aroused in her.

'Thank you,' she said, letting her hand linger on him. 'I'll treasure it for ever.'

The intimacy increased as the evening wore on. They ate at a crowded trattoria close to their hotel, a gay, noisy place which was nevertheless romantically candlelit.

Charity was aware of people looking at them with interest, perhaps wondering about their relationship because of the huge age gap, but she didn't care. Each time John's hand brushed hers, or his knee met hers under the table, she found herself anticipating his first kiss which she was sure would come later.

It was after twelve when they left. A stillness had fallen on the city, just faint music from here and there

318

and the odd passing car. The earlier crowds thronging the pavements had gone.

Charity's heels sounded like castanets on the cobbled street and the wind had got up, ruffling her hair. She stopped to look down at the river, leaning forward on the wall.

The moon cut a silver swath across the dark water and the only lights on the Ponte Vecchio were dim street lamps. John stood very close to her, just touching and Charity hoped he would kiss her now.

She glanced round at him. He was looking into the distance as if deep in thought, his back straight, both hands on the wall in front of him.

'What are you thinking about?' she asked.

He smiled faintly.

'Nothing much. Just about tomorrow and what to show you first. I hope you've got some sensible shoes with you. You can walk miles round all the galleries and museums.'

Her excitement fizzled out like a damp firework. She had expected him to say he was thinking of her, maybe even ask how she felt about him.

Charity stood at the window looking out at the river. Even though they'd been in Florence for two days, she felt she could never grow tired of the view. By day the water was dark green, busy with rowers scudding along at great speed, but at this time of night she liked it best, when it looked like black tar studded with diamonds.

The Hotel Berchielli was a very chic place to stay and John was very much at home amongst the stylish guests, conversing easily in Italian, French and German. Even so, he hadn't left Charity out of anything, taking great pains to act as an interpreter for her and introducing her with pride, despite her youth and cheap clothes.

319

But though Charity admired his suave sophistication and appreciated his gentlemanly qualities, she was finding him increasingly baffling.

Why didn't he attempt to kiss her? Didn't he find her attractive?

All day long he took pictures of her. Sometimes as he tilted her face or smoothed back her hair, the urge to hold him was so intense she could barely control it.

On both previous nights he'd come into her room for a nightcap, and left ten minutes later after only a peck on the cheek, leaving her feeling let down and wanting him desperately.

But today there'd been moments when she was sure he felt as she did. They had gone to see the Palazzo Pitti, where the Medici family once lived. Several times when he wanted to show her something especially beautiful like one of the wonderful ceilings, he took her hand, often caressing her fingers.

This closeness had increased as the day wore on. Charity found herself forgetting how much older he was than her, leaning against him companionably, reaching out to touch his face, ruffling his hair, laughing with him about anything and everything.

But again tonight, even after another romantic and memorable meal at Roberto's trattoria, he had disappeared to make a phone call. He would almost certainly come back into her room in a minute with another drink, but right now she felt she might cry if he didn't take her in his arms tonight.

'A penny for them?' John's deep voice surprised her. She hadn't heard him come in.

'I wonder if I'll ever travel as much as you have,' she said, still staring out the window. She could see John reflected in the glass, and was again moved by how distinguished he looked.

'I hadn't been anywhere much at your age,' John

said as he moved closer to her back. Her hair stopped short of the nape of her neck and the inch or two of vulnerable white flesh gave him an irresistible urge to kiss it.

She was wearing a pale blue cardigan back to front. He'd observed from other girls in London that this was the fashion. Either side of the row of small pearl buttons her shoulderblades stuck out like tiny wings. A broad black belt made her waist a mere hand span and the tight skirt accentuated the slender curve of her young buttocks.

His hand crept out to her shoulder, his thumb lightly touching skin. She didn't flinch as he expected; in fact she leaned back towards him and he could feel goosepimples on her neck.

Still holding her shoulder he bent towards her and as his mouth touched her neck she sighed, leaning back into his arms.

John slid his right hand round her waist and kept his lips on her neck, teasing her with the tip of his tongue.

'That's nice,' she whispered, putting her hand on his just below her breast.

'Oh Charity,' he said hoarsely. 'You make me feel I'm eighteen again.'

She turned to face him, running her thumbs down the deep lines in his cheeks.

His age was immaterial now. His soul was young. Fate had brought them together for some purpose and suddenly Charity knew they were going to become lovers.

'I want you to kiss me,' she whispered.

He crushed her into his arms but then drew back to lightly touch her lips with his. She was surprised to find that he was shaking.

Her lips parted under his, sweet and pliant, as her firm young body pressed into his.

'Don't you want me?' She looked at him with those big sad eyes, fear of rejection written in them.

'Of course I do,' he said, forcing himself to smile when already he could feel stabs of tenderness he couldn't control. 'I'm just not sure you know what you're doing.'

Her answer was to kiss him again. She closed her eyes and offered her lips and this time John couldn't hold back. His arms went round her, drawing her tightly against him and as her tongue flickered into his mouth, passion flared up, blotting out all thought but to possess.

He could feel her breasts pushing into his chest, her belly moving unconsciously against his hardness. He wanted to rip off her clothes, to enter her immediately, but everything he knew about lovemaking said he must hold back and make certain this really was what she wanted.

'It's not too late to stop.'

'It is,' she murmured, arching her body against his.

John caught her up in his arms and carried her through the bathroom to his room.

Only the night before he had imagined this very scene. He'd mentally taken off each garment, kissing each piece of flesh as it became exposed. But he hadn't imagined that he would be trembling, that just the sight of an inch of white skin above stocking tops would arouse him so much. He hadn't expected either that Charity would claw at his shirt buttons so feverishly, that her mouth would suck at his so wantonly.

They rolled together, locked in a fierce embrace. It was she who flung off her belt and unzipped her tight skirt. But as he pulled it off and saw the curve of her belly beneath those white lacy panties, the thin garter belt defining her slender shape, frantic desire overtook him.

He pulled her sweater over her head, moving down

322

to her breasts with such savagery that she cried out. His fingers fumbled to unclasp her bra, frustrated by being unable to control their shaking, and when finally it came loose in his hands he could only sink down on to her breasts, biting instead of stroking.

In the intensity of the moment, his head reeling with the smell, taste and feel of her young flesh, he didn't feel the difference between an involuntary arching of her body and a wince of pain. It was only as he dragged down her panties and thrust his fingers into her that he sensed she was no longer responding and to his horror he found she was crying.

His erection vanished as speedily as it had come.

'Oh Charity,' he said, taking his hand away from her breast. 'What have I done?'

She lay there naked apart from her garter belt and stockings, as small and vulnerable as a child.

'It's all right,' she sobbed. 'It's my fault. It's not you.' She tried to form the words. 'It's something else . . .' she stopped, unable to voice it.

John wiped away her tears with the edge of the sheet, then got up and slipped through the bathroom to her room, returning a minute later wearing pyjama trousers, with her nightie over his arm.

'Put it on,' he said gently. 'I want you to stay here with me. Perhaps we can make it better.'

As John turned out the light and drew her into his arms, she fought back the desire to tell him the truth. Better to let him think she'd just panicked for a moment, or that she was reminded of Hugh and Daniel. A man as sensitive as John, still grieving for his own daughter, didn't need her shameful childhood secrets thrust on to him.

She woke later to find John curled round her back, his hand on her hip. He was sound asleep, his breath warm on the back of her neck and it felt snug and comfortable. But as she lay there trying to go back to sleep she felt those prickles of desire for him again.

The hand on her hip was heavy. She moved it up till it was on her waist and pressed her back against him. She could feel the heat from his chest through her nightie; his thighs against the backs of hers were hard and hot. Moving gently against them sent shivers of pleasure down her spine and slowly she moved his hand up till it covered one breast. Instantly her nipple reacted, hardening against his fingers, even through the nylon of her nightie.

John stirred and Charity held her breath as his fingers moved sleepily on her. He cupped his hand round her breast and nuzzled into the back of her neck.

She knew he was awake now by his breathing, and slowly he began to caress her, rolling her hardened nipple between his fingers.

Charity feigned sleep as his hand slid down her body on to her thigh and then slipped under her nightie, but as his hand smoothed over the bare skin on her belly, she sighed involuntarily.

His touch was so sensuous she had to turn towards him, offering her lips without even opening her eyes, pulling him closer to her, and pressing her body against his.

That kiss went on and on, slowly growing in passion as his hands caressed her gently. Slowly he moved her on to her back and, lifting her nightdress up, he pulled it over her head then moved down to her breasts.

He showed no haste this time, licking, sucking and squeezing until she found herself writhing against him and throwing her arms out wide.

'Such perfect little breasts,' he murmured. 'So sweet and delicious.'

She had never felt anything as thrilling as this with

324

Hugh. Although she was aware no man could be such a skilful lover without vast experience, John made her feel as if he was doing all this for the first time. His gasps of pleasure as he probed inside her, the endearments he murmured and the sweetness of his kisses, moved her almost to tears.

It felt so right being loved by him. The warmth of his hard body, the tenderness in his caresses, drove out all thoughts of what had gone before. There was nothing dirty or shameful in the way he made her feel, no reminders of the past, only ecstasy and a deep need for fulfilment.

When he moved down her body to kiss her inner thighs she stiffened momentarily.

'Let me kiss you there,' he whispered, his fingers parting her vagina lips in a way that made her feel shocked, apprehensive yet thrilled all at once. 'I want to taste you, to show you how beautiful it can be. Trust me, darling.'

Never before had she felt anything so overpoweringly wonderful as his tongue flitted over her. Wave after wave of intense pleasure that made her toss from side to side and call out his name and clutch his head closer to her. The intensity increased with such ferocity she lost all sense of time or place and finally it erupted in an orgasm.

Her body was still shuddering as he moved back to enfold her in his arms. She wanted to gasp out that she'd never felt anything like that before, to ask what she could do to him that would make him feel as wonderful.

Was it just because he was more mature? Hugh had never managed to make anything like that happen. Is that what Rita meant when she said her older lover made her weak at the knees?

'I want you,' John whispered hoarsely and only then was she aware he still had his pyjama trousers

325

on and that his need was as great as hers had been seconds before. 'Can you bear it?'

'Of course.' She giggled softly, touched by his sensitivity. 'I want you too.'

He didn't let go of her for an instant, yet somehow he managed to strip off his pyjamas and rip open a packet of Durex while still murmuring endearments. Her hands reached out to help him eagerly, loving him still more for not making this moment coarse as Hugh had often done.

'It's so hot and wet in there,' John gasped as he slipped into her, his lips reaching for hers with sweet sensuality. 'Oh my darling, you are wonderful.'

His shuddering moan as he came moved her to a second climax and as they clung together wordlessly, she felt reborn, as if her life was just starting and all the pain and sadness of her childhood was washed away.

It was nearly eight when they woke again. John drew the curtains back so the weak sunshine spilled over the bed. Below in the street they could hear traffic and Charity had never felt more at peace as she lay in his arms.

'I'm starving,' John said. 'I think I'll ring and ask them for our breakfast in bed.'

'I'd be embarrassed if they brought breakfast in,' she said, torn between hunger and the need to stay in bed. 'They'd know what we'd been up to.'

'Who cares,' John laughed. 'You can hide in the bathroom anyway. I'll even put my pyjamas on and make it look respectable.'

Charity scooted away when the waiter brought the tray, but the moment he'd gone she came leaping in again to join John in bed.

'Croissants and jam.' John rolled his eyes in blissful delight as he buttered one for her. 'This is heaven!'

They ate every last thing on the tray, even the salami

and ham they'd turned their noses up at before in the dining room.

'Now for a bath,' John said once the last crumb had gone. 'And then I'm going to start all over again.'

Charity covered her naked body with her hands as John came into the bathroom while she was testing the water. A glimpse of her boyish figure in the big gilt-framed mirror just seconds before John came in had wiped out her new-found confidence.

'Don't hide yourself from me,' he said gently, taking her hands in his and drawing her into his arms.

'I'm too skinny.' She blushed scarlet as his eyes travelled down her.

He shook his head.

'Tiny and exquisite, not skinny.'

Charity lay back in the deep water watching while John shaved. His back was deeply tanned, speckled with tiny freckles. His skin was as smooth as her own and her eyes travelled down over his taut buttocks to his muscular thighs and calves. He turned, perhaps sensing her watching and smiled, one half of his face still covered in shaving soap.

'What are you thinking?' he asked.

'What a nice shape you are,' she said. 'If you'd been fat I'd probably have left you on the hotel floor that night.'

In fact she had been considering his penis, though she couldn't bring herself to admit that. She had expected men's penises to be much the same size. John's and Hugh's while they were limp were similar, yet erect John's was almost twice as big as Hugh's.

John grinned and shook his head, turning back to finish shaving.

'You need glasses,' he joked.

'Did you do this with your wife?' Charity asked as

327

she leaned back on John in the bath, while he played with her breasts.

'Don't ask me things about her,' he said and although she couldn't see his expression she felt it might be one of hurt.

'I just hoped it might've been the first time you'd ever had a bath with a girl,' she said in a small voice, jealousy creeping up on her unawares. 'I didn't want to know your secrets.'

'Now is the only important thing.' He nuzzled his lips against Charity's neck. 'And if you must know, there aren't a great deal of young pretty girls queuing up to share a bath with me.'

Charity turned to face him, moving over on her stomach between his legs and resting her chin on his chest.

'I don't understand how any woman could resist you.'

His face was becoming increasingly dear to her; she wanted to photograph permanently in her mind every line. The way his lips curled slightly at the corners, each freckle, every tiny flaw. But the way he looked now, his curls damp, naked and boyish sent a stab of love through her heart.

'What do you want from a woman?' she asked.

He didn't answer for a moment, and when he spoke he sounded very sad and hesitant to Charity's ears.

'I want a woman who desires me as much as I desire her. Someone who can be my friend, who makes me laugh and wants to share everything. A woman I don't have to pretend with, who doesn't give a toss about tomorrow, or even the world outside.'

'Am I that person?' Charity was terrified of the answer, but she had to ask.

'Charity,' John said softly. 'It's too soon to speak about those things and you're so very young. Let's just enjoy what we've got now.'

328

She felt a sudden chill, as abandoned and frightened for a second as she had when she listened to her father's footsteps on the stairs.

They made love again later, even though they could hear the maids coming up the corridor to clean the rooms. Charity found she was losing all her inhibitions, wallowing in the sensual delights John introduced her to.

Later they got dressed and went out, but instead of taking her to the Uffizi Gallery as she'd expected, John led her to the smart shops in the Via de' Calzaiuoli.

'Don't even think of protesting,' he said as she looked wary. 'I want to buy you some beautiful clothes and I won't take no for an answer.'

He seemed to know as much about clothes as he did about everything else. In a volley of rapid Italian he had the elegant assistants jumping to it and bringing out one exquisite dress, jacket and skirt after another.

Back home she wouldn't even have dared look in such shops, much less allow herself to be divested of her clothes and pushed into trying such wonderful things on. In the first shop he bought her a pale blue soft leather jacket that toned perfectly with a checked straight skirt and a silk shirt. In the next he bought a black chiffon cocktail dress with sequins round the high collar.

Charity was torn between delight and suspicion. Was he buying her things out of guilt because he didn't feel the way she did about him?

'But where will I wear it?' she said helplessly as she stood in front of the mirror. Beneath the billowing sheer chiffon there was a slinky slip that clung to her like a second skin; as impractical as it was, she loved it.

'Don't worry,' John grinned. 'Girls who look like you always get the opportunities.'

He went on and on. First one shop for sweaters, then another for a couple of day dresses and shoes. Only when the shops began to close for the afternoon did he seem satisfied.

They stopped for a bottle of wine and a pizza in an open-air café in the Piazza della Signoria. It was warm in the sunshine, like an early summer's day at home and Charity found it hard to believe it was only February.

'Shall we go back to the hotel now for a rest?' John said, taking her hand in his and playing with her fingers.

'Rest!' she exclaimed. 'I had more than that in mind.'

'Sei una fica affamata,' he smiled.

'What does that mean?' she asked.

He leaned forward to whisper in her ear. 'You have a hungry pussy.'

Charity giggled.

'Very hungry,' she agreed. 'And if you don't get me back there quickly it might claw you.'

They could hardly wait until the bedroom door was closed behind them before they were tearing each other's clothes off.

'Go easy on me,' John protested at one point. 'I told you I'm an old man. At this rate there'll only be a husk of John Marshall escorting you home. They might have to put me in a wheelchair.'

Knowledge of each other made it sweeter still. Lingering caresses added a new dimension to their lovemaking, both feeling so much they wanted it to last and last.

'I love you,' Charity heard herself cry out at the moment of climax, but it was only later she realised he hadn't reciprocated.

Yet as they lay in the afterglow, arms and legs wrap-

330

ped around one another, Charity was sure he must feel the same. His eyes spoke of love even though his lips didn't – surely no man could make love that way and not give his heart too?

Next day she broached the subject that had been on her mind. They were sitting in a sunny spot outside their favourite café in the Piazza della Signoria, sheltered from the breeze by bushes and Charity was tipsy enough after a bottle of wine not to mind being the initiator.

'I'm falling in love with you,' she said.

He smiled tenderly, brushing the back of his hand across her cheek.

'It's just this place,' he said. 'When we get back to England you'll find it's like a touch of flu. A few more sniffles, then it'll be gone.'

'I don't believe that.' Charity felt a desperate pang. 'It doesn't feel that way.'

'Don't talk about love,' John said, looking away.

'Why not?' she asked, catching hold of his hand and holding it in both of hers. 'Because I'm too young? Do you think I don't know what I feel?'

She had to get up and run away then, hurtling through the piazza, startling a flock of pigeons.

John watched her running, but he made himself stay and finish his wine. Her hair swayed from side to side, a platinum pennant signalling rejection; her bottom wiggled with the effort of running in high-heeled shoes.

She was lying on the bed crying when he got back to the hotel.

Saying nothing, he just sat on the bed beside her and stroked her back.

'I didn't mean it quite the way it sounded,' he said

331

eventually as her sobs subsided. 'Don't cry, Charity, please don't cry.'

'Don't I mean anything to you at all?' She lifted a tear-stained face to his.

'I want you to see me, and all this – ' he waved one hand at the room – 'as a wonderful experience, a stepping stone forward. You must learn from it, from good food, the nice clothes, aim to achieve something for yourself. You don't want to be saddled with an old man.'

'But I do,' she whispered. 'I want to be your love, to be that friend you spoke of, have your babies.'

He made love to her again, long and hard.

Later he looked down at Charity lying asleep in his arms. It was getting dark outside, but there was still light enough to see her clearly. Her hair was tousled, smears of mascara on her cheeks rosy from love-making, slightly squashed as she lay on his shoulder. One slender leg was thrown over his, her small buttocks very white and smooth as if carved from marble. One breast was pushed outwards on to his chest, the nipple soft again like a crushed raspberry, and her hand lay relaxed on his stomach.

He had the power to keep her. If he was to wake her now, tell her he loved her and ask her to marry him, he knew she would.

John sighed deeply because in his heart he knew it wouldn't work. He must encourage her to find a good job, to make something of her own life, and wait and see how she felt then.

The days passed so quickly, yet in an indolent, lazy glow of sightseeing, shopping, drinking, eating and making love. Charity's natural sensuality grew deeper every day. She no longer became embarrassed when he whispered erotic things to her, but flushed with excitement.

One evening they were coming back to the hotel from a restaurant, slipping through the narrow dark alleys, when Charity kissed him.

'What's this about?' He laughed, delighted by the intensity of her probing tongue.

'It's the hungry pussy again,' she whispered, undulating her belly against him and giving him an erection. 'Feel me?'

He slid his hand up her skirt and to his surprise found that she was wearing no knickers and she was hot and wet. He pressed her up against the wall, not caring if anyone came along.

'You naughty girl,' he murmured, pushing his fingers deep inside her. 'Fancy letting a man do this to you.'

'Make me come here,' she whispered. 'I can't wait.'

He couldn't describe how she made him feel. It was like being a teenager again with all the thrill of heavy petting. She dug her fingernails into his neck and clung to him as he played with her. Her breathing was laboured and her knees quivered against his.

She unzipped his trousers and took out his penis, holding it against her belly, groaning and writhing, her lips reaching for his.

'I'm coming,' she moaned. 'Do it harder!'

He was tempted to fuck her now, even though he was nervous about being caught. But Charity moved him round, pushed him up against the wall, bent down and took him in her mouth.

John could hardly believe she was doing this. She had attempted it for the first time only the day before and he'd thought she didn't really like it.

There was only one dim lantern at the end of the cobbled alley. Two windows with iron bars looked down on to it and in both there was faint light which could be a staircase where someone was standing watching them. But he didn't care now; all he could

333

think of was her lips around him, the feelings welling up inside him and how hot her pussy had been seconds before.

'Oh God,' he groaned as he came, his legs turning to indiarubber so he had to lean forward on her.

They ran back to the hotel hand in hand, laughing like a couple of school children.

It was after one when they got back to their room, having stopped for a few more drinks in the bar downstairs. Charity was so drunk now she could barely manage the stairs.

'I love you,' Charity flopped down on the bed, stretching her hands out wide, her skirt rising up to show her lack of underwear. 'Please come and do wicked things to me.'

'My father always said gentlemen mustn't take advantage of drunken women.' John looked down at her, putting on an air of mock disgust. 'And tomorrow morning you must go down to the bar and apologise for sitting there without knickers. You are insatiable. I must've aged ten years in these few days.'

In the time it took to clean his teeth, John found she had fallen asleep, still dressed. He rolled her over, unzipped her dress and took off her stockings, leaning to kiss the soft skin on the inside of her thighs.

'I love you,' he murmured, rubbing his face on her belly and drinking in the musky smell that reminded him again of the incident in the alley.

He wished he dared expose everything that was in his heart, but he daren't. There was a place and time for them here. But what about in ten or twenty years' time, when he was growing frail and she was still young and beautiful? He couldn't bear to see her going to meet a lover, to see irritation on her face instead of desire. Most of his life had been spent happily alone. He wanted that kind of peace now, not this raging in his heart that would stop him from working or even thinking.

But as he looked down at her sleeping face, the pain of knowing what he must do was unbearable. She was in his heart, his skin – even his soul. He had never loved any woman as deeply as this and he knew, with utter certainty, that he never would again.

'Only one more day.' John sighed as they stood on the top of the dome of the Duomo looking down over Florence. He had climbed the four hundred stairs often before, marvelled at the panoramic view in all four seasons. But it had never looked quite so beautiful as today.

The sun was warm, lighting up the red of the rough tiles of roofs below. Churches, houses and palaces huddled together in a patchwork of terracotta, pink, grey, yellow and cream. Here and there small roof gardens were bright with mimosa and polyanthus, and in the distance tall thin cypress trees stood sentinel on the green hills.

'Do we have to go back?' Charity couldn't imagine London now. Even going back to her new flat and seeing Dorothy and Rita had no appeal.

'Of course we do.' John looked off into the distance. 'You've got to find a job and I've got an assignment for the *Sunday Times* in Germany.'

Charity wanted to ask him so much, but she couldn't. She found it was odd that she could talk about everything else – about sex, her family, even experiences while she was having Daniel – yet she couldn't quite put her feelings towards him into words.

'I love you' didn't cover it. She needed him, adored him and she wanted to wake every morning with him beside her. How could she explain adequately to such a sophisticated man how much she wished she could cook his dinner, iron his shirts and care for him? He'd be appalled if he knew she had hoped one of those Durex had broken and she was pregnant.

In these few days she'd thought of Daniel often, but her feelings were less intense. She'd even stopped to look at a tiny Italian baby in a pram without wanting to snatch it up and hold it. But she needed the security of knowing John felt at least a little like she did; then she could go back to London and pick up her life.

'But what about us?' was all she managed to say.

'I'll be in and out of London.' He smiled down at her but his eyes looked distant. 'You must go back to your life and your friends.'

'I can't bear the thought of being apart from you,' she gulped, ignoring a horde of noisy Americans clicking cameras and shouting to each other. 'I love you, John.'

'You don't really love me, Charity.' He forced himself to laugh lightly. 'It's been wonderful, but what we've got here will fade back in England. Just think of me as a good friend. Wear those new clothes with pride and don't look back. You are like Michelangelo's David – small in stature, young and smart, and you can take on all those Goliaths now. Remember that when you think of Florence: the past is done, only the future is important.'

Charity bit back her tears. She wasn't going to beg him to say he loved her and she would show him she could be strong.

'I do love you, John Marshall,' she said with a toss of her head, turning to the narrow winding staircase. 'Just remember it was you who turned me down, when you're old and lonely.'

John stayed another minute or two. He would never come back here again; he had to impress it on his memory now, for all time. If he lived to be a hundred,

Florence and Charity would remain inseparable and he had to try and leave his heart and love for her here.

Chapter Eighteen

A smell of stale cigarettes and fried food assaulted Charity's nostrils as she opened the front door. She dropped her case and stared in disgust.

The coffee table was awash with spilt tea, mugs and a loaded ashtray stuck to it. Dirty plates and clothing were strewn on the floor; a saucepan congealed with dried baked beans lay on one of the armchairs.

She had expected the girls to be at work, but seeing this kind of squalid mess after the luxury of the hotel in Florence brought on a feeling of total desolation.

Charity closed her eyes for a moment. When she opened them she made herself switch on the light to brighten the gloom and see the flat through the same eyes as she had before she went away.

They had painted the lounge white that first weekend. Dorothy had brought the two big Renoir prints back from Devon, Rita's mother had given them the wall unit that housed the television and record player. Charity had contributed the bright Mexican-type rug they'd flung over the old settee and the lace cloth on the table. All three of them had sat here gloating over how good it looked and vowed never to turn it into a pigsty.

With a sigh, Charity began to stack up the dirty dishes and carried them through to the kitchen. She avoided looking at the mess in there. She took a wet cloth and went back to the coffee table, wiped it clean, and made an attempt at picking up all the clothes.

'You knew they were untidy,' she said aloud, switching on the radio for company. 'At least it gives you something to do until they get home.'

Charity wasn't sure whether John even intended to contact her again. He'd held her hand so tightly as he put her in the taxi at London airport. But he still kept insisting she would forget him as soon as she was back here.

How could he think that? Her whole body was aching for him, she was sure she couldn't live without him. Did all those wonderful experiences in Florence mean nothing to him?

It was over an hour before she found the letter from Central Promotions tucked up by the sugar jar in the kitchen.

'Dear Miss Stratton,' she read. 'I have now selected a short list of girls for the Glamour Girl Cosmetics promotion and I would like you to attend a second interview with two of the company directors on Monday, 22 February at 10 a.m. at this office. If you are unable to attend, please contact me as soon as possible.

'Yours sincerely, Anne Rushton.'

The feeling of dejection left Charity suddenly. If she hadn't been alone she might have whooped with glee. She had convinced herself Miss Rushton hadn't liked her but now she had a second chance to impress her.

'Chas!' Rita shrieked as she opened the front door. 'Look, she's home, Dot, the flat's all clean!'

If Charity had harboured any thoughts of grumbling they were forgotten in the joy she felt at the sound of Rita's voice. She ran out of her bedroom, arms wide to hug her friends.

'We've missed you so much.' Rita's coat was soaked with rain but she embraced Charity fiercely. 'What was it like?'

'It was wonderful,' Charity said, but disengaged herself to look at her friends. Both were wet right through, icy to the touch. 'But I'll tell you everything when you're dry. Let me take those coats!'

'You're not our mother!' Dorothy admonished her. Her eyes sparkled with pleasure at seeing Charity even though she was too cool to go in for Rita's exuberant hugging. 'I'm sorry about the mess we left. We didn't expect you back till tomorrow.'

Despite the apology, both girls stripped off their coats, flung them down on the floor, kicked off their shoes and ran to get towels for their wet hair.

'Come on, we want the dirt,' Dorothy yelled out from the bathroom. 'We've spent the whole week guessing what you were up to. We want the complete, unexpurgated version now.'

Charity made them a cup of coffee, hanging up their coats at the same time. By the time she got back into the lounge Dorothy was wearing a towelling bathrobe and was perched on the end of the settee filing her nails.

'It was the most beautiful place I've ever seen,' Charity said.

'We're not interested in the scenery.' Dorothy grinned. 'We want to know about you-know-what!'

Rita threw herself into an armchair, her legs over the arm. Her red hair had gone into corkscrew curls from the rain, she had mascara smears down her cheeks and a huge hole in the knee of her stocking.

'Well! Did you sleep with him?' Her brown eyes danced with mischief.

'Don't ask such personal questions,' Charity said haughtily. She had expected the girls would want to know everything and until this minute she'd thought she could tell them; but now found she couldn't.

Dorothy sensed that Charity was upset.

'Later, eh?' she said, patting Charity's shoulder in

340

understanding. 'We've got a date tonight so we'll have to have a bath and get ready. But tomorrow we'll have a long talk.'

'You're both going out?' Charity's heart sank. It was bad enough spending the afternoon alone but she had comforted herself with the thought that her friends would be home tonight.

She saw the girls exchange glances and knew instinctively that something had happened while she was away.

'Oh hell, Chas.' Rita looked oddly embarrassed. 'We wouldn't have arranged anything if we'd known.'

'It's OK.' Charity switched on a smile. 'I've got some washing to do and sleep to catch up with. Did you know I've got a second interview for Glamour Girl on Monday?'

'Yes, Ratty Rushton told me.' Rita looked pleased at the opportunity to change the subject. 'Dorothy's started working there with me already.'

'I didn't think she liked me,' Charity admitted. 'In fact I'd convinced myself she thought I was dowdy, stupid and plain. She asked if I always wore such long skirts and suggested that I get a padded bra!'

'It was your skin she was interested in, she couldn't fault that.' Rita balked at admitting Charity had sensed Miss Rushton's real opinion of her: the only reason she'd finally agreed to give Charity a second chance was because Rita had promised to work on her. 'Now if you'd gone for the first interview looking like you do today! . . .'

In all the excitement it was only now that the girls noticed a change had taken place in Charity. Her dress was of turquoise wool crêpe, with a deep scoop neckline and long sleeves. It clung to her slim shape like a second skin and it had obviously been very expensive. Not only that, but she had the most exquisite black suede shoes with four-inch stilettos.

341

'Where did you get that outfit?' Rita got up from the settee and touched Charity's dress reverently.

'John bought it for me,' Charity blushed. 'He bought me so much, he just wouldn't stop. Do you like it?'

'Like it! I'd die for it.' Dorothy shook her head in wonder. 'Shame you're so small, I could have borrowed it tonight. Let's see the rest of the stuff then!'

Dorothy and Rita stared in amazement at the heap of clothes on her bed. 'He bought you all *that*?' Rita gasped.

Charity nodded. 'I hate to think what it cost! I kept telling him not to, but the more I said it, the more he bought.'

Rita began to sift through the dainty underwear, blouses, skirts and sweaters as if she were at the first day of the sales, clucking and squeaking with excitement.

Dorothy picked up a black chiffon evening dress with a sequinned collar and held it against herself.

'It must have cost over a hundred quid!' she said in awe. 'And look at that!' She dropped the dress and picked up a pale blue leather jacket. 'Tell me your secret. I never got more from a man than a bunch of flowers.'

A sob made the girls turn to look at Charity. Tears were running down her cheeks.

'Oh I see, it's like that, is it?' Dorothy put her arm round Charity. 'Didn't we manage to teach you anything?'

The three girls had a cup of coffee together. Charity told them a little of how things were between her and John, but when she asked who they were going out with tonight and how the girls had met these men, Rita disappeared into her bedroom and Dorothy rushed for the bathroom.

Charity followed Dorothy. 'What's going on?' she asked.

Dorothy took off her dressing-gown and climbed into the bath. Her hesitancy confirmed Charity's fears that something wasn't quite right.

'It's just a date with a couple of chaps we met at the agricultural show,' Dorothy said too quickly, moving on to tell Charity how Miss Rushton had sent them both out to help on one of the stands.

Charity knew this much was true. She'd seen some leaflets about tractors lying around when she cleared up. But the girls were holding something back.

'Don't shut me out,' she said, sitting down on the toilet and folding her arms. 'I had a funny feeling Rita was doing more than just promotion work before I went away. Is this something to do with that?'

Dorothy blurted it out then and Charity's eyes opened wide with shock.

Rita wasn't just working at promotions. She was an escort for lonely businessmen at night. For each man she went out with she got a fee of ten pounds. Now Dorothy had joined her and they were getting the contacts from a woman called Carmel Connor.

'Rita didn't tell you straight away because she thought you wouldn't approve,' Dorothy explained. 'I thought it sounded a bit dodgy too, until I met Carmel.'

Charity just listened as Dorothy went on to explain how she had been initiated.

'We had a double date because I refused to go alone with anyone,' she said. 'I was dead scared, but we had a whale of a time. The two men took us to the Beachcomber Club. We had a fantastic meal, all the drinks we could guzzle down and then they put us in a taxi home. Tonight we're going to a show, then on to another club.'

Charity wasn't surprised that a couple of business-men would want to pay for the privilege of taking the girls out. They were funny, intelligent, well bred

343

and stunning. Even lying back in a bath, Dorothy was gorgeous: long brown hair slicked back from a face devoid of makeup, golden satiny skin, breasts like two bouncy tennis balls, a small waist, shapely hips and long, long legs. Her oval face, aquiline nose and lips with a perfect Cupid's bow had all the hallmarks of classic beauty, but her almond-shaped tawny eyes gave her something special that would make anyone turn to look at her.

'It sounds dangerously like prostitution to me,' Charity said in alarm. 'And I'm shocked at you not talking Rita out of it.'

'You've got it all wrong.' Dorothy's eyes sparked with indignation. 'Look there's hundreds of lonely men stuck in London overnight. They aren't looking for sex – most of them are happily married. All they want is a bit of fun with a pretty girl on their arm. These two we went out with were typical. Middle-aged, fat and balding, but they were nice guys. We just made sure they had a good time. We didn't even kiss them. As for Rita, well why should I talk her out of something so harmless?'

Dorothy had put together a good case, but just the same, Charity didn't like the sound of it.

'But you might have been lucky so far,' she argued, understanding now why Rita had got out of the way. 'Next time it could be different. They might whisk you off to a hotel. They could be nut cases or perverts!'

'We told Carmel that we'd only do double dates.' Dorothy had that snooty look she always put on when someone criticised her. 'She's a really nice woman, not a brothel keeper, if that's what you're thinking. She sacks girls who take money for sex, it's purely an escort agency.'

Charity shrugged her slim shoulders.

'If you want to do it then that's up to you,' she said. 'Just don't try to drag me into it too.'

Dorothy's eyes narrowed.

'But that's the whole point,' she wheedled. 'You see, Carmel's got enough jobs to keep us out six nights a week. We'd be exhausted if we did that many. But if you joined us too, we could work a rota.'

'I couldn't,' Charity said point blank, holding out a warm towel to her friend. 'Any man spending a lot of money on a girl hopes for something in return.'

'Did John?' Dorothy smirked.

'No. He isn't like that,' Charity said indignantly. 'If I'd said no he'd have been just as nice.'

Dorothy smiled in triumph.

'It's just the same with these men. You make the ground rules right from the start,' Dorothy said as she pulled out the plug and swished the bathwater round. 'You don't go back to their hotel room. You steer the conversation away from sexy things and if they do try anything, you put them down firmly.'

'No.' Charity turned away to the door. 'You two do it if that's what you want, but don't include me.'

'You could make about forty quid a week,' Dorothy called after her. 'Think what that would mean on top of your daytime wages!'

Charity closed her ears to temptation. The only job she wanted was the one for Glamour Girl Cosmetics.

Charity was nervous. She knew she looked good in her blue jacket and toning plaid skirt; Rita had helped with her hair and makeup. But although the girls had play-acted interviews with her last night, they couldn't prepare her for the close scrutiny these two men were putting her under.

The man right in front of her had introduced himself as Mr Burgess, the sales director. Around forty, he was a suave-looking man in a pin-striped suit, and had thick dark eyebrows. He had done all the talking so far, explaining how he intended to make his products market leaders.

The other man was older, with grey hair and glasses, but he hadn't spoken and he seemed to be just an observer.

Miss Rushton, who made up the trio, sat at the side of the desk, presumably there to give the two men guidance about the interviewees.

'Well Miss Stratton,' Mr Burgess looked down at her application form and then back at Charity, 'I'm a little puzzled as to why a girl who looks as good as you has only experience of domestic work.'

He couldn't fault Charity's appearance. With her clear skin, shining, well-cut hair and that blue leather jacket and skirt she had the chic of a French girl.

Fortunately this was one question Dorothy had anticipated.

'I had to find a living-in job when my parents died,' she explained, looking him straight in the eye as Dorothy had said she must. 'I would've preferred something more challenging, but that was all there was. I studied in my spare time and I've just been waiting for a chance to break into the beauty world.'

'I see.' He was surprised too by her voice and confidence. 'We give training, of course, as a beautician, but the job also requires selling ability. Now just suppose Miss Rushton came to your stand, how would you persuade her to change her brand of cosmetics?'

Charity looked across at Miss Rushton. She was an elegant blonde in her thirties, with faultless makeup.

'I'd start off by admiring her appearance.' She gulped hard, unsure of herself. 'Clearly I couldn't claim to improve on her makeup, but once I'd discovered what she used already, I could maybe point out that Glamour Girl products were less expensive, yet of a similar quality.'

'Very good, Miss Stratton.' He smiled. 'But is talking enough?'

'I think I'd try and get her to let me smooth some of your face cream into her hand,' Charity said. 'Once she felt how nice it was she'd be tempted. Or I could show her the colours of the lipsticks and nail varnish. Every woman wants a new colour now and again.'

The two men exchanged glances and the older man nodded.

'Are you free to start two weeks' training next Monday, Miss Stratton?' Mr Burgess asked.

Charity was stunned for a moment. She had expected a far longer grilling.

'Yes please,' she said eagerly, assuming this meant she'd been selected. 'I mean, yes sir,' she said, blushing.

Mr Burgess stood up and held out his hand, smiling at last.

'Welcome aboard, Miss Stratton,' he said. 'Keep that enthusiasm, it's the salesgirl's best weapon. Miss Rushton will give you all the company rules, explain the uniform and so on. Providing you prove satisfactory during training, we will allocate you to a stand in a London department store to start mid-March.'

'Thank you sir.' Charity shook his hand, her smile as wide as the office windows.

'That'll be Carmel,' Dorothy called out to Charity as the doorbell rang. 'Let her in and make her a cup of coffee, will you?'

It was four weeks since Charity had returned from Florence. She had joined another seventeen girls for two weeks' intensive training and now each of the girls on the course had been sent to a store in London or the Home Counties as a beauty consultant. Charity was at Barker's in Kensington High Street, and after only one week her sales had been impressive enough for the floor manager to extend the intended four-week promotion for another month.

During this time Rita and Dorothy had continued to act as escorts, three or four times a week. Charity's feelings swung between disapproval and envy. They were making a great deal of money, and having a good time, but Charity was still concerned for their safety.

'Carmel?' Charity asked as she opened the door and found a big but elegant woman standing there.

'I am.' The woman smiled knowingly. 'Not what you expected?'

Charity blushed. She had pictured the owner of the escort agency as a brassy blonde, but she could hardly admit that.

She had hoped her friends would drop this night-time work now they had a good job. But neither Rita nor Dorothy seemed as committed to Glamour Girl as herself and they never missed an opportunity to try and get her to join them as an escort. She suspected they'd invited Carmel to the flat as further persuasion.

'You're much younger than I imagined,' Charity said diplomatically. 'Do come in. Dorothy and Rita are dressing.'

The woman was undeniably attractive. Although stout, she carried it well. Her complexion was flawless, her dark hair worn in a becoming bouffant style and her emerald green suit was impeccably cut.

'How kind.' Carmel chuckled, dark eyes sparkling with youthful mischief. 'I won't see fifty again, but I do try to keep old age at bay.'

Despite Charity's convictions that this woman was nothing short of a procurer of young girls, she liked her instantly. Although she was glamorous in her stilettos and her beautiful suit, her face was comfortingly maternal.

'Are you enjoying your job?' she asked Charity, as

she sat down on the settee. 'Dorothy and Rita said you're outshining all the other girls!'

'I don't know about that.' Charity blushed modestly. 'I'm still learning. But I do love it.'

From the first time she'd nervously asked a woman customer to come on to her stand for a facial and makeup demonstration, Charity had discovered the creativity there could be in selling.

'Your own skin is the best advertisement,' Carmel said, looking at her critically. 'If I was to walk into a store and see you offering advice on makeup, I'd assume it was entirely due to your products.'

'I learned a lot of handy hints in the training,' Charity admitted. 'I was hopeless at makeup before.'

Learning about beauty had added to the confidence John had boosted. Now she'd lost her timidity and every day seemed an exciting new challenge.

'Well, you look wonderful,' Carmel said firmly. 'I wish you'd join Rita and Dottie working for me. Some of my gentlemen would be thrilled to take you out.'

'I can't,' Charity said firmly. But she was tempted. The girls seemed to go to such swish clubs and restaurants and she was getting fed up with staying in alone at nights, thinking about John and jumping every time the phone rang. But deep down she still felt it was immoral.

Carmel studied Charity carefully. Running a marriage bureau was her main business; the escort work was a lucrative sideline which was gradually taking over. But finding the right girls was tough. They had to be attractive, intelligent and well mannered, with enough poise and sophistication not to show her gentlemen up in smart places.

'I understand your fears,' she said gently. 'I know many escort agencies are just a front for prostitution. But not mine. I vet each client carefully. I know about

349

men, Charity, and when I say mine are all gentlemen, I mean it.'

'I'm sure they are,' Charity said. She was reassured slightly now she'd met the woman Dorothy and Rita spoke so highly of, but she was still hoping that John would be back from Germany soon and he certainly wouldn't approve of her doing such a thing. 'It's just not my scene.'

She was saved from further persuasion by Dorothy appearing.

'What've you got for us tonight, Carmel?' she asked, eyes sparkling with anticipation. 'David Niven look-alikes, or a roly-poly midget?'

Charity reached the safety of her bedroom just in time to hear Carmel's answer.

'Yours is almost a Rock Hudson, Rita's more Peter Cushing, but they are both directors of an international stationery company and they want to see a show, then dinner afterwards.'

Charity felt rather lonely once the others had left, and phoned Lou for a chat. Now she almost wished she hadn't. Toby was in trouble.

It was Lou's reluctance to talk about anything other than Charity's job that made her suspicious. But she had kept probing until finally Lou blurted it all out.

It was serious – not minor naughtiness or disobedience. Toby had stolen money from another boy at Wellington and he was found to have a huge amount of sweets and chocolate hidden in his locker. Only Uncle Stephen's powers of persuasion had prevented his being expelled.

'But I thought he was happy,' Charity said. 'Why is he doing this? Why would he want so many sweets?'

'I can't say. He has more than enough pocket money of his own.' Lou sounded distressed. 'I suspect though he has been trying to buy other boys' friendship with

350

the sweets. That's a fairly classic symptom in a child who feels isolated.'

'But Toby was always good at mixing with other boys,' Charity said, her anxiety mounting.

'He still is,' Lou assured her. 'He keeps up with his schoolwork, he's very good at sport, but he's had a great many changes in his life, dramatic ones. Moving from a terraced house in Greenwich to Studley Priory and discovering he's to inherit it one day is enough to disturb any child. Your uncle overindulges him during the holidays and he's constantly reminding the boy he has to excel.'

'And I don't suppose he gets any love or affection,' Charity said, a lump coming up in her throat.

'Oddly enough, from what I can see, I think Stephen has grown rather fond of him,' Lou said. 'He may not be the ideal guardian, and perhaps Toby needs more demonstrative affection, but they are quite close. Geoff and I are taking James there at Easter. We're going to try and talk to the colonel then and to your grand-mother. Maybe we can make him see sense about you.'

'Me!'

'You know both Geoff and I totally disapprove of him keeping you from the children,' Lou said. 'I hope we can make him see you might be able to help Toby.'

'Do Toby and Prue talk about me?' Charity asked. She couldn't stop a tear trickling down her face, and her voice was breaking.

'Yes, when they are alone with Geoff and me.' Charity felt Lou was choosing her words carefully. 'We've tried to make them understand that you had no choice but to take the job at Bowes Court. Unfortu-nately Stephen has managed to paint a rather different picture.'

'They don't think I abandoned them?' Charity's voice rose in alarm.

'Not exactly,' Lou said too quickly. 'But they choose to believe you were given the opportunity to live at Studley too. Geoff and I have done our best to explain your side of it, but you must understand we're in a difficult position. If Stephen was to think we were undermining or opposing him in any way, he could very well take James from us.'

After Charity had put the phone down she just sat there, overwhelmed by what she'd heard.

'They think I deserted them,' she said to herself.

Even in the blackest moments in the past three years this had never occurred to her. She had worried about them being ill treated, imagined every kind of horror from illness to neglect. But always she'd believed they had understood why she'd had to leave them.

She had thought Uncle Stephen had done his worst when he cut her off from the children, and the fear they would forget her had been the biggest worry. But now she saw that Stephen was even more vindictive than she supposed: he hadn't been satisfied until he'd poisoned their minds against her too.

Everything was going so well – or so she'd thought until she phoned Lou. Today she'd been told her sales figures were the highest on the team. John was flying back from Hanover tomorrow and she'd just received her first commission cheque from Glamour Girl. But now all that happiness had been wiped out by one phone call.

Prue and Toby now had an enviable life with good schools and nice clothes. Toby was riding, Prue having dancing and piano lessons and Stephen had convinced them that she could have had the same. Who could blame them for reaching the conclusion that their elder sister had run out on them for selfish reasons?

Charity climbed into bed and lay there brooding.

She wanted to think about John coming back tomorrow and what she was going to wear when he took her out to dinner. But all she could think of was how much she'd lost.

There was hardly a day when she didn't think about Daniel, trying to imagine how big he was, how many teeth he had, whether he crawled, or shuffled around on his bottom as James did. Daniel was ten months old now, happily unaware there had ever been anyone else in his life but the woman who now fed and changed him. But her brothers and sister *did* remember her: she had been a major part of their lives from the moment they were born, and they carried that inside them. How could she let them know that her love for them was still just as strong and that the promises she'd made to find a home one day so they could all be together hadn't been abandoned?

'I'm going back to Africa, Charity,' John said, his eyes on the tablecloth.

'For how long?' she asked, reaching out across the table to touch his hand.

'For good.'

Charity knew by his expression and the finality of his words that he hadn't come back from Germany for her.

'You mean, that's it?'

John shifted in his seat. He had chosen the restaurant in Queensway purposely. It was crowded with people of all nationalities, noisy and busy. He had let her eat her dinner, heard about her job and her worries about the children, how she'd painted her room pink and white and made new curtains. Now he knew he had to come to the point.

'I wanted to say goodbye for good when we parted at the airport,' he said in a low voice, 'but I couldn't do it. I thought of writing it in a letter, but that seemed cowardly.'

'Why?' she asked. She was begging him with her eyes to say he didn't mean it. 'We're so good together.'

'We might be now,' he said gently. 'But in another ten years it will be different. I'm too old for you, Charity. You need a young man who can give you children. Not a rootless wanderer like me.'

All the time he'd been in Germany his mind had been in turmoil. So many times he'd been tempted to let his love for her override caution, to come back and sweep her off with him. But it was madness to think that way. She had the job she wanted now, her flat and her friends; he couldn't offer her a secure home with his lifestyle.

'Without you I don't have anything,' she said, wiping a tear from her cheek.

'That's not so.' He took her hand and squeezed it. 'You've got far more here than I could give you. You've got a career now, you're young and beautiful and the world is at your feet. Trust Geoff and Lou to help you get to see your brothers and sister. Toby and Prue are teenagers now and your uncle can't keep them away from you for ever. Find a young man to love and one day soon you'll look back on this and be glad I left you.'

'I'll never, ever love anyone but you.' She held on to his hand tightly. 'You don't know how I feel inside.'

'I do,' he said, his eyes full of understanding. 'But I know it will fade.'

He poured Charity another glass of wine. Everything he felt was mirrored in her eyes and the pain inside him was so intense he had to look away. He wanted to run, to get to the airport and catch the first plane out of London – anything but see the heartbreak in her face.

Charity pushed her chair back and stood up, trembling and white-faced. 'I think you're cruel, selfish and cowardly. Go back to Africa, John. But if you think I'm going to say I hope you'll be happy, then you're mistaken. I hope you'll be as miserable as you've made me.'

She turned and ran out of the restaurant. People looked up in surprise as she passed.

Charity sat by the open window painting her nails bright red. It was her day off, she'd just arrived back from the hairdresser's and the afternoon sun was warm on her face.

It was a month since John left for good and until today the weather had been as miserable as she'd felt. Strong winds and rain, fog, ice and even snow. Rushing off to work in gloom, arriving home in darkness, Sundays spent hugging the fire or staying in bed, continually thinking of John. One moment she was sobbing because she wanted him so much, the next she was angry and bitter.

He was too old. He didn't really want children. Maybe she'd only been a substitute for his daughter Susie ... However many excuses she offered, it didn't make it stop hurting. She began to think that if she couldn't manage to make a relationship work for love she might as well do it for money.

But today she'd woken to April sunshine, and as she looked down at the garden in the square the sudden change from winter to spring seemed reassuringly symbolic.

An almond tree was in blossom; beneath it a massed choir of daffodils opening their golden trumpets as if to herald the arrival of spring. The grass glistened, a couple of pigeons perched companionably on a bare branch and a lone blackbird kept a vigil for worms.

All day she had told herself she had only agreed to go with Dorothy as an escort tonight because Rita had flu. Even a couple of hours ago under the drier in the hairdresser's she had told herself it was only one date. But in the last hour as she'd sat here by the window she'd made up her mind. Maybe accepting money just for being a lonely man's partner wasn't an ideal, or moral, way to start the wheels of success rolling, but right now she couldn't think of a better way.

'Are you going to sit up or have I got to pour this soup up your nose?' Charity joked as she went into Rita's bedroom.

Rita looked awful, her face white except for a bright red nose, her red hair lank and dull, tied into two bunches.

'I don't suppose I'll be able to taste it.' Rita slowly hauled herself up to a sitting position, her voice thick with cold. 'I feel so bloody awful I'd be quite happy to die.'

Charity placed the tray across her friend's lap. Rita smelt ill, that peculiar sour, musty smell that evoked memories in Charity of her mother. She was wearing an old beige cardigan over her nightdress and her bedside table was littered with Vick, cough mixture, Beecham's Powders and tissues.

Rita was scatterbrained, noisy and vivacious, but the moment she felt ill she became morose, wallowing in neurotic self-pity. When she had merely a hangover she was convinced it was something more dramatic, like food poisoning. She would wrap herself in the most unbecoming garments, refuse to comb her hair or even wash her face. But perhaps this was all a cry for attention.

'You'll feel better tomorrow,' Charity soothed her. 'Would you like me to refill your hot-water bottle?'

Rita dipped the spoon in the tomato soup and gingerly tried it. 'You're still going to take my place tonight?' she asked.

356

'I promised, didn't I?' Charity said. 'Look, I've even had my hair done!'

'It looks lovely.' Rita sniffed. 'I thought you might chicken out. You're such a prude sometimes.'

'I'm not a prude,' she retorted. 'I was only worried about you both.'

'Are you feeling better about John now?' Rita asked anxiously.

Charity shrugged her shoulders.

'I suppose so. Life goes on, doesn't it?'

She wasn't going to admit she doubted she could ever love again, or that if John called her from outer Mongolia and asked her to join him, she'd swim there if necessary.

'Before you came in I was thinking about us at Daleham Gardens,' Rita said in a small voice. 'Our babies will be having their first birthdays soon. How are we going to get through that?'

Charity was surprised. By tacit agreement they'd drawn a curtain over that part of their lives. She sat down on the bed.

'Same as we get through everything else,' she said. 'A bottle of wine, a few sad records, looking at their photographs and reminiscing.'

'We all pretend we've forgotten, don't we?' Rita wiped away a stray tear. 'Sometimes I even believe I have, then wallop, it comes back.'

'I suspect it will never leave us,' Charity said thoughtfully. 'It's the same with my brothers and sister. I want the feeling I have for them to fade, but it's still just as sharp.'

'I wish your uncle knew what a good person you are,' Rita retorted, a spark of indignation in her eyes.

'Not that good.' Charity half smiled. 'If he knew I was going out as an escort tonight, he'd claim he was right about me all along.'

'So why did you suddenly change your mind?'

'To make my fortune,' Charity said lightly. 'Nothing bad has happened to either you or Dottie. I'm fed up with staying home like the ugly sister while you two have fun. Is that good enough?'

Charity opened the door to Rita's room an hour later, and struck a model-like pose. 'Will I do?' she asked.

Rita was propped up in the clean bed, a cardigan round her shoulders, reading Harold Robbins's *79 Park Avenue*. When she saw Charity she dropped it in surprise.

'Will you *do*?' she gasped. 'You look sensational!'

Charity was wearing the black dress John had bought her in Florence. Beneath the sheer billowing chiffon was a tightly fitting sheath that displayed her slender yet curvaceous body and cleavage. The sequinned choker collar gave her delicate features and blonde hair an ethereal look.

'You don't think I look too – well, brassy?' Charity frowned. She was pleased to see that Rita had washed her hair. It was curling over her shoulders like a Pre-Raphaelite beauty, a sure sign she was on the mend.

'Brassy! You!' Rita cackled. 'You couldn't manage to look like a tart if you were wearing a red and black basque! You look utterly delectable. Poor old Pinky will probably drop dead with shock.'

'You must stop calling him that,' Charity reprimanded her. 'I'll forget his real name.'

'It's Basil,' Rita reminded her. 'But he *is* pink! Bright pink – and when he's had a few he gets even pinker. But he's a nice guy, a real gent and I doubt when he's seen you he'll ever want me as an escort again.'

'How's the invalid?' Dorothy joined them, looking a dream in a cream crêpe dress with a cowl neckline, her hair up in a French roll.

'A bit better now.' Rita grinned. 'Doesn't Charity look the business?'

358

'Devastating.' Dorothy's luscious lips curved into a seductive smile. 'Don't wait up for us!'

Charity tried hard not to look too amazed at the Beachcomber Club. Even though she'd been told all about it many times by her flatmates, she was still staggered.

It was decorated to look like a tropical island, and apart from the smoky atmosphere instead of sunshine it succeeded. Tables stood on small wooden platforms at different heights and angles, each one with a straw umbrella, and were linked by rustic wooden and bamboo bridges. From a waterfall at one end of the club, the water ran into many small streams under the bridges, and above the central tiny dance floor a Hawaiian band played with a couple of girls dancing seductively in grass skirts and shell beads.

Beyond some realistic palm trees a film played on a blank wall, showing more palm trees, and turquoise sea breaking on white sand.

'Have you been here before?' Basil took Charity's arm and led her across one of the bridges to the reserved table.

'No, I haven't. But it's every bit as nice as I'd heard.'

In fact she couldn't believe what she was seeing. There were real crocodiles in the pools; she thought they were plastic ones until someone prodded one and it swished its tail. People were drinking huge exotic cocktails embellished with fruit and umbrellas, and the meals were vast. She was sure she wasn't fooling Basil with her portrayal of a sophisticated girl about town. She wanted to giggle and gawp, but Dorothy's stern eye on her prevented it.

Basil was a nice man. He did have a pink face, his eyes were very small behind his thick glasses and he was podgy and white-haired enough to play the part of Santa Claus, but he had a lovely deep voice and a good sense of humour.

Rita had said that he was inordinately proud of his twin sons, but Charity had let him tell her all about them as if she had no idea about his background. He and Gerald, Dorothy's date, were directors of a pet food company in Sheffield and they were down in London on a sales drive.

Gerald was obviously quite smitten with Dorothy. He had the well-rounded vowels of public school and the height and bearing of a military man. Charity was quite surprised by Dorothy's behaviour tonight. In men's company she was usually brittle and cold, or alternatively overly seductive, but with Gerald she was regally cool, yet listened to him speaking as if she was fascinated by every word he uttered.

A waitress in a grass skirt with a bare navel and a flower behind her ear came up with menus written on old parchment. 'Look at that!' Charity said, pointing to a storm coming up on the film on the wall. 'It looks real, doesn't it?'

If it hadn't been for Rita telling her about this scene and explaining it was a film, she might have thought it *was* real. The wind was bowing the palm trees and whipping up the waves, the sky growing dark and forbidding.

'When I was your age I wouldn't even have known that was Hawaii,' Basil smirked. 'But then you girls have been brought up in a different world from me.'

Gerald and Dorothy were in a deep whispered conversation as Basil told Charity about his childhood in Scunthorpe.

'I never had a new item of clothing until I started earning,' he said without a trace of self-pity. 'Even then I had to tip my wages up on a Friday night because Dad was out of work. Eight of us all crowded in that tiny house and often we went to bed hungry.

But I tell you, Charity, poverty in childhood can be the making of a man. You girls with your nice clothes and posh voices don't have that hunger to make something of yourselves.'

Charity was just about to retort that she knew exactly what poverty was like, when Dorothy kicked her foot under the table. She closed her mouth and caught her friend's warning eye.

'No, I suppose we don't.' She turned to Basil and smiled. 'It must have been awful!'

It was an enjoyable evening. The meal was superb, the huge cocktails even better, and later they danced a little drunkenly.

'Who would have thought that Arthur Braithwaite would ever go to places like this with a girl like a princess in his arms,' Basil said later.

'Who's Arthur Braithwaite?' Charity moved her head away from his too close lips and pushed him back from her slightly.

'That's me,' he grinned, his small blue eyes twinkling behind his thick glasses. 'I called myself Basil as it sounded more classy, and got a few elocution lessons. That's how I met my Mary: she was having them too.'

'Your wife?'

'Yes, my wife,' he sighed deeply. 'She'd be mad if she could see me carrying on like this. "Basil," she'd say, "those society lasses are no good to you, they give you ideas above your station."'

As the girls went home in a taxi, Charity told Dorothy what Basil had said.

'I don't know how I kept a straight face,' she giggled. 'Fancy him seeing me as a "Society lass"!'

'Well Gerald comes from a privileged background and you fooled him too.' Dorothy tucked her hand into Charity's arm. 'So think on that tonight, little one, and a tenner on top for a night of eating and drinking in a swish nightclub. Now are you going to do it again?'

'Why not?' Charity laughed. 'It beats flogging lipstick!'

Chapter Nineteen

'Hullo love!' Carmel said as Charity came into her office one wet afternoon in July. 'What on earth's the matter? You look like your dog just got run over.'

'I've got the sack,' Charity said.

Few people passing Carmel's tiny office in the Fulham Road would even notice there was activity behind the windows partially covered in brown paper. Sandwiched between a delicatessen and a dry cleaner's close to the ABC Cinema, the office displayed a small sign that only the most observant would spot: INTRODUCTIONS WITH A VIEW TO MARRIAGE. ALL ENQUIRIES TREATED WITH THE UTMOST CONFIDENTIALITY.

Charity had laughed on seeing it for the first time, assuming people would need to be desperate to step into such a seedy place. But now she knew Carmel used it only as a base, a store-room for hundreds of index card files, and to make arrangements by telephone. Interviews with clients took place either in Carmel's own home or over afternoon tea at Harrods. But then this warm-hearted woman was motivated more by helping people and making them happy than by financial gain.

Carmel's striking and smart appearance was at odds with her office. The floor hadn't been swept for years, ancient, browning wallpaper flapped in places and cobwebs hung from a central naked light bulb.

Charity often wondered how she could bear to work in such squalor.

'You've got the sack? But you were doing so well.' Carmel got up from her seat and gave Charity a comforting hug. 'Sit down and tell me all about it. I'll make us some tea.'

'It isn't just me.' Charity removed some bulging files from the only chair and sat down. 'It's all the girls. Glamour Girl are doing so well they don't need a promotion any longer.'

'Well that's not so bad,' Carmel said as she filled up a kettle and plugged it in at the back of the office. 'What did your boss at the agency say?'

'Oh they've got loads of other jobs we can do. I just liked being a beautician so much.'

Charity often popped in to see Carmel, on her day off or in her lunch hour. It wasn't just to see what escort jobs she had, but because she liked Carmel. She was funny, kind-hearted and very wise about things. Charity once told her all about John and Carmel had made her see that he was right, their relationship couldn't have worked for long.

The marriage bureau fascinated Charity too. Occasionally Carmel would show her photographs of some of her clients and she had been surprised to discover that few of them were ancient or actually desperate. In the main they were widows and widowers, often wealthy and well connected. Carmel's explanation as to how she paired off people with common interests and backgrounds made further sense of why it wouldn't have worked with John.

But the escort business provided Carmel's main income. The men came to Carmel by discreet advertisements and personal recommendation and she took a twenty-pound fee from them in advance, of which she kept half. Although Carmel never admitted just how many 'dates' she fixed up, Charity and her two flatmates usually did three or four between them each week, and there were at least ten other girls, so it was obviously a lucrative business.

Carmel handed Charity a mug of tea and sat down again at her desk. Close up, Charity could see she was far older than the fifty years she claimed to be. Her makeup stuck to the lines round her eyes and her neck was crêpey. Dressed up to go out, she always wore strong corsets, but today she had several large rolls of fat billowing beneath a loose cotton dress. Yet even though she'd abandoned her glamour, her black bouffant hairstyle was perfection and the office was full of her Tweed perfume.

'You mustn't see this as an end, but a chance for further experience,' Carmel said. 'You're good at selling. You'll find it doesn't matter a jot whether you're selling lipstick, clothes or saucepans. You'll still be meeting the public and the variety of products you work with can only enhance your career.'

Charity began to cheer up slightly.

'They offered me a job for next week selling a kitchen gadget,' she said. 'But I'm scared, Carmel. I have to do a proper demonstration with it, get a crowd round the stand and everything.'

Carmel's painted eyebrows rose into an inverted V.

'So! That's no different from hauling women up to have a facial. Central Promotions wouldn't suggest you unless they thought you could do it.'

Charity smiled weakly. 'You always make me feel better,' she said. 'I suppose I am being silly, and anyway I've got to go to the company tomorrow for a briefing. They're bound to show me how to go about it.'

'So what store are they sending you to?'

'Whiteley's in Queensway.'

'I tell you what, I'll pop in on Monday and pretend

365

to be a customer,' Carmel suggested. 'Once you've got the patter going and a few people round you interested you'll be selling those gadgets like hot cakes. Now, what about Dorothy and Rita?'

'They're both being sent to the motor show at Earls Court,' Charity said. 'I wish I was going with them.'

'They won't learn anything there, except how to flirt.' Carmel chuckled. 'They'll be bored to tears with all those car-mad men and watching the clock. You'll see I'm right.'

'How did you get to be so wise?' Charity asked, her depression suddenly leaving her.

'Through making a great many mistakes, my love,' Carmel said. 'Now what you've got to do is see every new job as a challenge and a learning process. Dorothy and Rita don't see anything but a pay packet at the end of the week, but I know you want more than that. Keep your eyes and ears open and you may find one of these temporary jobs leads to something special.'

'Have you got any dates for us this weekend?' Charity asked.

Carmel smiled. 'As it happens I've got a beaut lined up. All three of you for Saturday night. Three nice Yanks over here on a sales conference and they want to paint the town red. I met them at their hotel last night to check them out and they're real Southern gentlemen.'

'Rhett Butlers?' Charity said hopefully.

Carmel laughed. 'Not quite so dashing! A bit tubby and thin on top, but charming for all that. I suggested they book a table at Churchill's as there's always a cabaret on Saturday nights, so glam evening dresses, please.'

'What are you doing?' Dorothy asked as she came into the kitchen still in her nightdress on Sunday morning and found Charity cutting up a melon.

The date with the three Americans had been everything Carmel said it would be: dinner, champagne, dancing and such good fun the girls hadn't come home until four that morning.

'This is my gadget.' Charity grinned. 'Pretend you're a customer who's stopped to watch.'

Dorothy slumped on to a chair, yawning. She hadn't taken her makeup off when they got in and now smeared mascara and eyeliner made her look like a tousle-haired panda.

Charity pushed the small, stainless-steel scoop into the melon and drew out a perfect ball the size of a marble. She dropped it into a sundae dish, then added another, and another.

'Isn't that pretty, madam?' She giggled. 'Instead of serving melon in the usual boring manner one can make an artistic statement. It also makes the melon go further and it's a great deal easier to manage than slices.'

'OK, I'm impressed.' Dorothy yawned. She was half asleep but felt she had to humour Charity. 'So how much is it going to cost me?'

'The stainless-steel scoop is just nineteen and elevenpence,' Charity said. 'But today I'm prepared to offer you another amazing kitchen tool absolutely free.' She picked up a plastic board with a wavy blade attached and proceeded to slice it down through a raw potato, making thin wavy slices.

'Staggering!' Dorothy said. 'What am I supposed to do with those skinny chips?'

'Lightly fry them in oil and you have wonderful homemade crisps, or you can slice cucumber or carrots for dinner parties. Both items are indispensable for a hostess. Can you manage without them?'

Dorothy scratched her head.

'Very easily,' she said, trying not to laugh. 'I suppose

we've got to have bloody melon balls for breakfast now and crisps for lunch?'

'I haven't got around to showing you how you can make fake new potatoes yet,' Charity said. 'You just hold the scoop against the potato firmly, push in and then twist your wrist.'

'I'll twist your wrist if you don't shut up,' Dorothy said. 'Enthusiasm for work on a Sunday morning just isn't on.'

'Would you like a couple of wavy slices of cucumber to put over those bloodshot eyes?' Charity said, deftly cutting two almost transparent slices. 'You can lie on the settee with them and I'll drop melon balls in your mouth.'

'Balls to you too,' Dorothy sniggered. 'Now please can I have a cup of coffee?'

Whiteley's department store was quiet on Monday morning. Charity stood behind her small stand in the kitchenware department, adding embellishments to her display. She was pleased to see that hers was the only demonstration; Rita had warned her that sometimes a store ran two or three at the same time and then they had to vie for sales.

Her central display was a large dish of tiny potatoes garnished with parsley in the centre, surrounded by wavy slices of cucumber and carrots. She had made coleslaw, cutting the cabbage with her gadget, and several sundae dishes were filled with various fruits from melon to peaches made into balls. Beneath her stand was a whole box of wasted fruit, but she hoped no one would ask what they would do with the odd bits of squashed fruit left over.

It was lunchtime before she managed to entice a crowd. So far she had sold only two tools and she'd had to work hard to persuade these two women to buy. As a group of middle-aged women shoppers came in, she began frantically slicing carrots.

'Hallo,' she said brightly. 'I'm sure all of you are interested in items that help make cooking more interesting and fun?'

There was no response, but the women did stop at some distance from her stand. Undeterred by their lack of curiosity, Charity launched into her spiel, all the time keeping her hands moving as she scooped out perfect round melon balls.

'But melon isn't the only thing you can use it for,' she said, picking up a peeled potato. 'Tiny potatoes are so much more attractive, so much quicker to cook. You can have new potatoes in the middle of winter, make a melon go round a great many more people, and add a touch of flair to the presentation of a meal.'

The women edged closer, and soon she saw other people peering over their shoulders. Her heart beat faster; the patter became easier with their interest.

'At just nineteen and elevenpence the stainless-steel scoop is a bargain that will last you a lifetime. But today I'm giving away another essential kitchen item, the miracle slicer, absolutely free. Now I'm sure you'd all like these two products. Who's going to be first?'

Charity was amazed how quickly they got out their purses, pound notes fluttering in outstretched hands. As fast as she handed out the gadgets in their plastic bags and rang up the money on her till, more people were craning their necks to see what was on offer.

'Just hold on,' she called to the people at the back. 'I shall start another demonstration of the Miracle scoop in just two minutes.'

She managed to keep a crowd around her until well after two in the afternoon. Her box of tools was half empty and the pile of discarded potatoes and fruit beneath the stand was growing.

'You've done very well,' the floor manager said

369

when he came over to check on her till. 'Sixty-five items!'

Charity beamed at the round-faced portly man. Early this morning he had claimed she wouldn't sell ten!

'I've brought our tea home!' Charity said as she swept into the flat to find Dorothy and Rita lounging on the settee with their shoes off.

'What is it?' Dorothy looked at the two large plastic boxes. 'Cake?'

'No.' Charity giggled. 'We have a dieter's dream! Cucumber, carrot and cabbage coleslaw, followed by mushy fruit salad.'

'Get a job demonstrating chicken or steak next week,' Rita said opening one of the boxes and recoiling at the huge amount of coleslaw. 'I was never very keen on healthy food.'

'How did it go at the motor show?' Charity asked.

Dorothy pulled a face. 'Bloody boring,' she said. 'I thought we'd be on the Rolls-Royce or Mercedes stand. Instead we got lumbered with the Hillman one and had to talk to Normal Normans all day. They didn't even have booze on our stand!'

'Was it that bad, Rita?' Charity asked.

'I don't even want to discuss it.' She yawned. 'Let's just say I've had more fun at the library.'

'Thank God shops close at Christmas.' Dorothy came through the front door, slinging her coat in one direction and kicking her shoes off in another. 'I'm exhausted.'

Charity was lying on the floor, her legs stretched up the wall, vainly trying to reduce their swelling.

'Four days off,' she said dreamily. 'With absolutely nothing to do but eat and drink.'

Since the job with the Miracle scoop back in July

she'd been booked solidly every week. She'd promoted crisps, pork sausages, non-stick pans, soft drinks, cigarettes and vacuum cleaners, but for the whole of December she'd been in Selfridges' toy department as one of Santa's helpers.

At first this had seemed the most fun job of all, escorting children on to the sleigh ride through Santa's grotto dressed like a gnome. But wearing red tights and a green tunic and painting her nose bright red each day had worn thin, especially as some of the children were little horrors.

Hour after hour of being jolly, saying the same old clichés, holding sticky hands and looking at runny noses had almost put her off children. Every now and then she would get a pang of grief when she saw a toddler gazing in wonder at the mechanical elves making toys. Each time she heard 'Mary's Boy Child' a lump came to her throat and she wondered if Daniel had been to visit Santa Claus with his new parents.

Each blond-haired boy and girl looking at the displays of toys jolted her further. Prue was fourteen now, Toby almost thirteen – too old to believe in Santa Claus as James still did. Would Stephen and Grandmother make Christmas magical for them? Did they miss their big sister?

But it was Christmas Eve, work put aside for a few days. No more reminders of things she wanted to forget. She and Dorothy were going to Rita's parents' tomorrow. No more escort dates for a while, as all those businessmen were home with their families. Tonight she and her flatmates were going down to the Coleherne in Earls Court Road, and they'd get drunk and kiss anyone who was even vaguely presentable.

'Can I wear your white sweater tonight?' Rita said as she bent over Charity. She had her hair in rollers and a mud pack on her face.

'If you promise to wash it afterwards,' Charity said, suddenly feeling magnanimous. 'I'm going to wear my new pink dress and I'm going to flirt outrageously. I think my New Year's resolution will be to find myself a new man.'

There were many perks in promotion work. Left-over prepared food, free samples, and sometimes when they worked out of London they stayed in hotels. Dorothy and Rita tended to see the men that chatted them up as the major perk, but until this minute that had left Charity cold.

'Glad to hear it, prudy-pants,' Dorothy yelled from the kitchen. 'We'll hold you to that!'

Chapter Twenty

1964

'You want to give up?' Charity looked at Carmel in astonishment.

'I'm too old for all this.' Carmel waved her heavily jewelled hand at the tottering piles of files all around her. 'It was fun once, but not any longer. I like the marriage bureau side of it, but I could run that from home.'

It was October, a raw, windy day. Charity had popped in for a chat with Carmel in her break, partly to see if she had any escort work, but more importantly to talk.

Charity was promoting a new board game in Harrods' toy department, but although she'd been sublimely happy all year, in the last couple of months she'd felt her life had grown stagnant. Since January Central Promotions had sent her out on a different job almost every week. But though the varied work had given her a great deal of experience and she'd met many new and interesting people, a small voice inside her kept suggesting it was time she moved on to something more challenging.

Rita and Dorothy claimed she needed a lover. Perhaps they were right, but although Charity had been out with several men she'd met through promotions, not one of them had made her toes curl or her heart flutter. Yet a new man didn't seem to be the answer. Charity felt that a change of direction was needed.

Girls she'd worked with a year ago were talking about getting married, Marjorie and Martin over in Hammersmith were discussing selling their restaurant and starting up a frozen food company; even Rita, who once only lived for the day, had ideas about finding a job with more stability.

It was eighteen months since Charity had first met Carmel and their relationship had deepened into mutual respect and affection. Charity had grown fond of the grubby, chaotic office and the woman who maintained her glamorous appearance even in such surroundings. Today she was wearing a cream wool suit and a brown frilly blouse, her bulk contained by strong corsets. As always her hair was immaculate and her nails painted bright red, yet Charity could hear a new weariness in her voice.

'But what about the escort service?' Charity asked.

'Maybe I'll go through all these – ' Carmel's dark eyes sparkled mischievously. She patted the file nearest to her with one podgy hand. 'And blackmail the naughtiest ones!'

Charity laughed.

Carmel made it her business to know about each man who booked an escort, but as loyalty and discretion were her trademark, she used her knowledge only to help her clients. She took no moral stand, firmly believing a little lighthearted fun and flirtation while men were away on business sent them home to their wives refreshed and contented.

'You'd never divulge anything about anyone,' Charity said. 'You're too much of a romantic. You could've made a killing after the Profumo scandal with all the knowledge you've got about politicians, but you wouldn't dream of doing it.'

Charity had been out with two junior cabinet ministers and one eminent judge and although they had behaved themselves, she knew girls who would have taken advantage of them.

'I think of my clients as friends,' Carmel said gently. 'I see it as a privilege when they tell me little secrets. I couldn't betray their trust. That's why I'm still in business.'

'But what will they all do without you?' Charity moved nearer to the one-bar electric fire; a draught was whistling under the street door.

Carmel looked at Charity. The girl looked stunning as usual, today in a black fitted coat with a black and white checked minidress beneath and laced-up black granny boots. She moved with the fashion, but had a knack of interpreting it in a unique way. Other girls still backcombed their hair, but Charity's was cut to her shoulders, gleaming like ivory satin, the sort of hair one's fingers itched to touch. There was never any fear with Charity that she'd embarrass her dates. Even though she wasn't quite twenty, she knew the right outfit for the occasion, she knew how to behave. Sophisticated men didn't want anyone guessing they'd paid for the girl's services; nor did they want a brassy-looking piece who got drunk, talked too loudly and showed them up.

'It does seem a waste to burn all this.' Carmel sighed, waving a hand at the mountain of files. 'But what else can I do? Other agencies would probably offer me a great deal of money for my connections, but I couldn't trust them to find nice girls for my gentlemen. Worse still, my best girls, like you, might be tempted into accepting dates with seedy characters.'

Charity stifled a giggle.

Carmel fully believed that all her girls were above reproach, and in fact all of them were – in the beginning. But the offer of money did strange things to people and Charity knew quite well that some of the girls didn't stop at just dinner or a nightclub.

Charity had received at least ten offers of extra money herself, but not once had any of the men turned nasty when she'd refused.

'But you can't just drop everything.' Charity felt anxious now. She had made a great deal of money as an escort; Dorothy and Rita had made still more. They wouldn't want to work for anyone else, because they trusted Carmel. She vetted all her clients.

'I can't spend another winter in here – ' Carmel waved her hand round the dingy office. 'My arthritis is playing me up. Anyway, I've lost the drive to go out and find new clients. Once I used to attend all the trade fairs, I knew all the head porters in the good hotels. Now I just rely on word of mouth.'

'What will happen to the office then?' An idea suddenly presented itself to Charity.

'Well that's another problem.' Carmel sighed. 'There's at least another two years to run on the lease. Not long enough to get a good price for it, but too long for me to have to pay the rent if I close down.'

'Supposing someone offered to take it over?' Charity asked, trying to keep her tone casual.

'Who'd want to, dear?' Carmel shook her head as she picked up two cups and went over to the tiny sink to wash them.

'I would!'

Carmel turned, her thin pencilled eyebrows raised in surprise.

'I could run it.'

The tip of Carmel's tongue slid over her scarlet lips. She liked and trusted Charity. They were more than agent and escort. In many ways they were very alike: both had been brought up in poverty with responsibility for younger brothers and sisters, and Charity had that hunger for wealth she had once had.

Carmel told all the girls and her clients she was a widow. In fact she had never married, but had been the mistress of many rich men in her time. But her heyday was in the war and when her looks started to fade she had thrown herself into this business, using all the knowledge of men she'd picked up over the years to make it a success. She was happy to spend her old age alone. She had wonderful memories and didn't want reminders that she was fat and wrinkled now.

She could see that Charity had the intelligence and enthusiasm needed to run the office, and that she was also very good at keeping her distance from the clients. But should she encourage someone so young and vulnerable to take over such a risqué business?

'You could run into problems, being so young.' Carmel looked anxious. 'As you know, escort agencies have a bad name.'

'I'd be as careful as you are,' Charity insisted. 'Besides, I was thinking more of starting up a promotions agency, not expanding the escort side.'

Carmel felt a surge of admiration. Charity wasn't just a pretty face, but ambitious and creative. Perhaps she should give her the chance to prove herself?

'I'd have to ask for money for it,' she said. 'I couldn't just give it away, not even to you.'

'I wouldn't expect you to.' Charity's big blue eyes were full of excitement. 'How much?'

'I'd need at least five hundred,' Carmel said quickly. 'I couldn't let it go for less.'

Charity's heart sank. She had saved three hundred pounds over the last eighteen months. Should she take a gamble with it?

'I haven't got that much.'

'Well think it over.' Carmel resisted the urge to ask how much she *had* got. 'I'll hold fire for a couple of

377

weeks. You might get a bright idea if you're keen enough.'

Carmel made them tea and they discussed the rent, the rates and the clients. She could see Charity was burning to buy the business and if she really did know Charity as she thought she did, she'd find the rest of the money.

'You could do well.' Carmel squeezed Charity's hand as she left to go back to work. 'Where there's a will, there's a way.'

Charity went back to work that afternoon, but her heart wasn't in it. All she could think of was how she could find another two hundred pounds.

In the last year she'd been sent out to so many jobs she'd often thought she could run her own agency. She could easily train other girls: she had enough experience to spot reliable, hard-working girls and she knew all the angles and pitfalls. Now all those vague dreams and ambitions seemed to spring into focus with this new opportunity.

It was very quiet in Harrods. It was too early in October for the Christmas trade to get going. There was no new stock to arrange, no one even vaguely interested in board games, and she had to stay at her stand at all times.

A couple of smart middle-aged women were cooing over soft toys just over to her right and to her left a man was agonising between two very expensive dolls. But Charity barely saw them: she was wrapped up in her thoughts.

Carmel's office would be ideal. It had a good position and the rent was low. Although she had no real desire to keep the escort side going, she could use it to bring in money until she landed her first lucrative contracts. The phone, typewriter and duplicating machine were all there; all it needed was a coat of paint, a carpet and some decent lighting.

'Two hundred,' she murmured. 'It's not that much!'

Working as a promotions girl had given Charity the confidence and poise of a far older woman. Her romantic dreams of love and marriage had been replaced by a fierce desire for a successful career and independence.

John was just a beautiful memory, to be savoured late at night. It still hurt sometimes. If she thought too deeply she could torture herself imagining him with other women, but mostly he was the yardstick by which she measured other men and found them lacking.

If she ever felt a pang of guilt about taking money for nights out with lonely men, she reminded herself of her long-term plans. Her savings were increasing; the men had a good time.

But although she had reconciled herself to many things, her need for her brothers and sister never grew less. After each school holiday she would meet Lou for lunch, eager for all the news and the latest photographs.

Prue was nearly fifteen now, but so different from Charity at the same age. She was plump, with a bland, rather expressionless face and her father's overlarge forehead. Lou informed her that Prue 'was a little madam', but was too kindly to enlarge on that. Toby, at almost fourteen, was becoming even more like the young Uncle Stephen she remembered from her grandmother's photographs: tall, slender with perfect features, a very handsome boy. James, now seven, was a reminder of Toby at the same age – thin as a whippet, with an engaging grin and no front teeth. The only thing which still united them as a family was the white-blond hair and bright blue eyes.

Yet on each of these lunch dates which meant so

379

much to Charity, she sensed how much Lou was holding back. She spoke of the central heating put in at
Studley, of the walled garden being transformed into
an Italian garden complete with pergolas and fountain, and the redecoration of the children's rooms. She
admitted that staff came and went at an alarming rate
and said how frail Grandmother was becoming, but
she could never be pushed into revealing her real
feelings about Toby and Prue.

All Charity knew was that Prue was top of her class
in the nearby private school. She played the piano
well, still had dancing lessons and was now learning
both French and Italian. Toby was less academic: he
excelled at games and gymnastics and had learned to
ride, but somehow the absence of more detail suggested he was still in trouble one way or another. The
picture Charity was left with was that both children
had been spoiled.

Only James gave Charity real hope, as Lou was
effusive in his praise. She said he was quick, kind-
hearted, always laughing. Charity knew Lou was
frightened that he too might be whisked away to
Studley and that this was why she was so loath to go
against Stephen in any way.

One ray of hope kept Charity going. Lou in her
diplomatic way had managed to make both Toby and
Prue realise the truth of what had happened years
before. Each time she saw Charity she pointed out it
would only be a few more years before they'd be able
to defy their uncle and visit her.

Charity had learned to tuck her brothers and sister
away in the same special place she kept her memories
of Daniel. She celebrated each birthday silently,
bought them cards she couldn't send, and vowed to
herself that one day they'd be together again. Creating
a successful business would give her the ultimate
weapon to beat Uncle Stephen. What could be sweeter

than showing that chauvinistic old colonel that the girl he expected to clean for him now employed dozens of people?

'What's up, Chas?' Dorothy flung herself down on the sofa next to Charity. 'Counting your money again?'

It was just over a week since Carmel had offered her the office and since then Charity had thought of nothing else. But dreaming, scheming and wanting didn't make two hundred pounds appear.

Charity closed her notebook and smiled weakly. Dorothy had just got out of the bath and she wore only a slinky ivory satin housecoat. She rarely got up before midday now, spent all afternoon lying around doing her nails and hair, and never thought of cleaning up, offering to do some shopping, or even making coffee.

Rita might be scatterbrained and irresponsible, but she worked and played with enthusiasm. But sometimes it seemed Dorothy was going downhill fast.

'Just doing some sums,' Charity said.

She had spent her day off visiting the four main high street banks in an effort to raise a loan. But they all asked her for a business plan and she didn't know what that meant. Finally she'd come home around an hour ago to find Dorothy hogging the bathroom, a pile of unwashed dishes in the kitchen and her Beatles LP left on the floor, a coffee mug stuck to it.

It was hard not to let on to Dorothy and Rita about her plans, but she knew if she did they would want to be in on it. They might put up the money needed, but they would play at having a business for a couple of weeks, then lose interest and leave her to do everything while expecting their share of the profits.

'You aren't thinking about the kids again?' Dorothy leaned forward to get a cigarette, her naked breasts popping out of her housecoat. She was shameless these days, never thinking that other people might feel uncomfortable with a near-naked girl walking around the flat.

'Sort of,' Charity lied. 'Wondering why Lou won't tell me what's troubling her about them.'

'Well they're teenagers, aren't they? I was awful at that age,' Dorothy said sympathetically. 'Of course there's many people who don't think I've improved!'

'You should get a proper job,' Charity said archly. 'I worry about you too.'

Dorothy had dropped out of daytime work since the summer. She'd met an Australian called Neville and the temptation to laze around with him in the sun proved too much for Dorothy. After two weeks hitching round the South of France with him she came home alone, very subdued. She'd sneered at Neville, claimed it was the last time she'd let her heart rule her head, but she never divulged what had happened. It was only one night when she woke Charity to say she was bleeding heavily that it came out she'd been pregnant and had had an abortion that morning over in Paddington.

Charity and Rita still made allowances for Dorothy's inertia, her caustic remarks and her slovenly ways. They felt deeply for her being caught out a second time and the trauma the abortion must have caused. They even paid her share of the rent until she was better, assuming she'd get back to normal once her body had. But though Dorothy had returned to escort work, she made it clear she had no intention of getting a real job and she was much harder on men. She began to go alone on escort dates and often didn't come home at all. She always seemed to have plenty of money and Charity had to draw her own conclusions about how she came by it. But despite Dorothy's cynical attitude, her laziness and inability to take herself in hand, Charity still cared about her as much as ever.

'There are better things to do in life than be a wage slave.' Dorothy flashed a brilliant smile at Charity. 'You know your problem, Chas?'

'What's that?' Charity pulled her friend's housecoat back across her breasts.

'You're a doormat. You always consider everyone before yourself, and until you learn to be a bit more selfish people will always wipe their feet on you.'

Later, alone in her room, Charity consulted her little notebook again. She had an idea for raising the money, a little voice that wouldn't go away, but it was one which made her skin crawl. Yet Dorothy's words were echoing in her head. Was she really going to be a doormat all her life, or strike out now for what she wanted?

Surely she could justify it? She needed that money so badly. Even John had said she must make the most of opportunities. All week she'd hoped an alternative would present itself, but time and ideas had run out. Carmel wouldn't and couldn't wait. Everything and everyone had their price. The question was – would anyone consider her worth two hundred pounds?

It seemed like fate when Carmel rang the following day to ask if she would go out with Ted Parsloe. Of all the dozens of men she'd dated he was perhaps the only one she would agree to meet on her own. Normally when he was in town he had his sidekick Lawrence with him, and Charity certainly wouldn't even think of carrying out her plan with Rita there.

Ted had all the right credentials. His wealth was phenomenal, she knew he owned a string of garages in England and a chain of drug stores in the United States. On their previous five or six dates, she'd seen him win and lose hundreds at roulette without turning a hair.

But the best thing about Ted was that he'd made it plain before that he wanted her. He had been too much of a gentleman to push it, but it lay unspoken between them.

'Come back to my hotel for a nightcap?' Ted whispered in her ear as they danced.

Charity felt sick with apprehension yet she managed a bright smile. Ted Parsloe with his gold watch and Savile Row suit was playing right into her hands, just as she'd known he would, but it gave her no pleasure.

It was almost two o'clock, but Churchill's nightclub was in full swing and she knew most of the beautiful girls here tonight would offer sex at a price.

Maybe not hard cash, but a fur coat, a holiday or even just to be wined and dined in style. Why else would that leggy redhead with the sensational face be snuggled up to a fat, balding man? Would Patty, the girl with the huge soft dark eyes, have anything in common with that weedy little accountant if he didn't pay the rent on her mews cottage in Chelsea?

Charity had read so many articles in magazines that claimed women were attracted to powerful men, regardless of their looks. But the word 'power' was a euphemism: in her view it simply meant women were turned on by wealth.

Charity could see Mandy across the club. She was draped along a settee, her head on a man's knee, holding his face in her hands, her long cream evening dress slit to the thigh offering a glimpse of stocking top. Charity had met Mandy several months ago when they were working for a week in Barkers' department store on a perfume promotion. She was engaged to an engineering student then and didn't have a clue about anything. Just eighteen, wide-eyed and innocent with mousy long straight hair and her shapely body concealed by frumpy clothes.

One evening she had come back to the flat for a girls' evening of drink and chatter. Dorothy had suggested she lighten her hair while Charity showed her how to do her makeup.

A month later Charity bumped into her in Kensington High Street and if Mandy hadn't caught hold of her arm she wouldn't even have recognised her. She had blonde wavy hair and was poured into a shocking pink minidress that skimmed her crotch. She said she'd dropped the engagement to the engineer and moved in with two other girls in Kensington. Now she 'worked the clubs'.

Well, she'd be earning plenty tonight. No doubt that man leering down at her cleavage would provide enough money for a new dress and a week's rent. As a girl in the powder room had said earlier in the night, 'Well they get what they want and so do we. I can't see the sense in having sex for nothing when there's men out there willing to pay.'

Charity didn't agree with that philosophy. She remembered only too well making love to both Hugh and John, and no one could convince her it would be the same doing it for money.

But she had to get that two hundred pounds.

'A nightcap?' She looked right into Ted's eyes and let her lips curve into a seductive smile.

He was a good-looking man despite being overweight, with dark hair tinged with just the odd streak of grey and an attractive cleft chin. Charity couldn't work his age out. He could pass for late forties but she suspected he was closer to sixty because he'd made his original fortune in America during Prohibition.

It had been a lovely evening: a delicious Chinese meal in Soho, then on here to Churchill's for more drinks and dancing. Perhaps he even saw her agreement to a date on their own as a green flag.

'You know what I want, Charity.' He smiled back, soft dark eyes twinkling with merriment.

Even his voice was nice, a faint trace of Geordie with overtones of American. He had a good sense of humour and a straightforward approach to everything.

'Tell me, then.' She fluttered her eyelashes, knowing this was the moment she'd been waiting for.

'I want to screw you. I have from the first moment I saw you.'

She was glad he didn't say 'make love'; it was easier to handle that way.

'I don't know if you can afford me.' She kept her eyes on his, her tongue sliding nervously over her upper lip.

Ted recovered his composure very quickly.

'Come on now, Charity! I know you don't put it about. That's why I want you so much.'

'Everyone's got their price,' she said. She'd drunk enough to be this bold, and she'd had enough foresight to slip her diaphram in a while ago. 'Mine's very high.'

'How high?'

His hand in hers was sticky with sweat. Could she really do this? Wouldn't it be better to laugh now and tell Ted she'd been joking?

'Two hundred pounds.'

The room seemed to be spinning and she could feel sweat running down the middle of her back under her black chiffon dress. What if he laughed at her? Told her to get lost? How could she walk out of here and keep her dignity?

'You rate yourself very highly.' He looked down at her and his smile was cold.

'Well I'm special,' she smiled back. 'That's why I'm offering myself to you.'

In the beauty business she'd met countless people who believed that only something expensive was worth having. Why shouldn't she apply that sales ploy to herself?

'I could have any other girl in here for less than thirty pounds,' he said, but his voice was softer now, as if he were nibbling at the bait.

'I know, but you want me,' she said. 'And that's my price. No deals.'

He laughed then, taking her by surprise. His head rolled back and he let out a rich guffaw.

A strange thing happened inside her. She knew, then, that if she told him why she wanted the money, he would give it to her. She wouldn't have to sleep with him. But she wasn't going to beg. She would go through with it. Give him the time of his life and at the end she would have earned it.

'OK.' He moved his face closer to hers and kissed her cheek. She could smell how much he wanted her – it wafted out of him, stronger than his expensive aftershave. 'I've got that much back at the hotel. But you will stay till morning?'

'Of course.' She kissed him lightly on the lips. 'Take me there now!'

All the way to the Savoy she managed to think only of the money and the agency. But as the taxi pulled up and a liveried doorman leapt forward to open the cab door, she felt sick with fright.

His suite was luxurious, all gentle blues and greens, with the thickest, softest carpet Charity had ever seen and the sort of elegant furniture she imagined in stately homes. Ted pulled a cord to part the heavy brocade curtains so she could see the Thames.

'Isn't that something?' he said.

She stood transfixed by the view and a sharp pain shot through her heart. Her legs almost buckled under her as she looked down to see twinkling lights reflected in the black still water.

It was Florence all over again. How could she even think of taking money for sex when John had taught her the beauty of it, for love?

'What's wrong?' Ted's hand squeezed her shoulder.

'Nothing.' She tried to smile. 'Just the view, it reminded me of somewhere else for a moment.'

Ted looked down at Charity. She was so small and dainty next to his bulk, white-blonde hair showering over her slender shoulders.

'Reminds you of somewhere – or someone?' He turned away to open a small safe set in the wall and felt an unreasonable pang of jealousy. He took out a wad of notes and quickly counted out the two hundred. 'Here we are, put it away sweetheart and let's have some champagne.'

She drank the first glass of champagne quickly.

'Dutch courage?' Ted came up to her and took the empty glass from her hand, putting it down on the coffee table. 'How about a kiss?'

There was no going back now.

His kiss was tentative and gentle. She closed her eyes, and concentrated only on the sensation rather than thinking whose lips they were. To her surprise she found it wasn't unpleasant.

'Shall we take the champagne in with us?' she murmured against his shoulder.

'Best idea you've had all night,' he said and kissed her neck. He could feel the tension in her slender body, but maybe another drink or two would loosen her up.

As they reached the bedroom Ted put down the champagne on the bedside table and turned to her.

Charity was already reaching for the fastening at the back of her dress, her face contorted with nervousness.

'Let me do that,' he murmured, moving round behind her and parting her hair. Deftly he unfastened the two small buttons on the collar, then slowly peeled the chiffon away from her shoulders, bending to kiss her neck.

All she had to do was keep her eyes closed and pretend it was John. Maybe that way it wouldn't be so bad.

She wore nothing beneath her dress but tiny lace panties and a thin garter belt holding up her stockings. As his hands came round to cup her small breasts he gasped softly, increasing the pressure of his lips on her neck, and let her dress fall to the floor.

Charity looked down at his big hands: they were beautifully manicured and soft; sensitive, like John's. They couldn't possibly stir up passion in her the way John's had, but she could bear it.

'That's so nice.' She leaned back against him. One of his hands was sliding down to her belly, caressing and smoothing, but she could feel his soft flabby stomach even through all his clothes.

He turned her round, pulling her into his arms to kiss her again. She closed her eyes tightly, thinking only of how good he was at kissing, not of his girth or his age.

As he guided her towards the bed, she felt him shedding his jacket, and as he laid her down beside him, his shoes came off with a soft thud.

The only lights were from two small lamps on either side of the bed; the satin cover beneath her naked back was smooth, cool and sensuous. His fingers were in her hair, his tongue sliding round her lips but she felt nothing as her nipples touched his silk shirt.

'Your breasts are so beautiful,' he whispered,

moving down to take one nipple in his mouth. 'So little and firm, so sweet,' he groaned.

Charity ran her nails down his back, arching her body against his and moaning softly. She had to remember she was here for his pleasure: it was an acting job, nothing more.

His breathing was growing harder as he played with her nipples and his hand moved down towards her pussy. He groaned as he cupped her and she opened her legs obediently.

As his fingers caressed her gently she opened her eyes for a moment.

His mouth was on her breast, eyes closed, but his big face had a look of almost boyish wonder that touched something in her heart. 'Let me undress you,' she whispered, reaching out to take his face in her hands. 'I want to feel your skin against mine.'

She rolled him on to his back, kneeling beside him as she unfastened his shirt buttons. His chest and belly were covered in black hair and he was so fat she almost recoiled, but his expression was so tender that she bent to kiss him again.

'Oh Charity,' he breathed as her hands went down to his belt and zipper. 'You can't imagine how I feel!'

It was no good remembering how quickly and effortlessly both John and Hugh could shed their clothes, or how just the touch of their smooth skin against hers had made her feel. She mustn't dwell on Ted's quivering white thighs as she pulled down his trousers, but try to think only of pleasing him.

He looked like a beached whale lying there in huge white underpants. Even his feet, once she got his socks off, were as fat as the rest of him. But she knelt back at his side and unfastened her garter belt and stockings, then put her hands on both sides of him to lower his pants.

His penis rose up the second the white cotton had

passed over it. Alarmingly huge and purple tipped. She stripped the pants off his feet and moved back towards him, undulating her body against his.

A feeling of nausea washed over her as her fingers went round his penis. Dorothy had always claimed big men had small ones, but she was wrong about Ted. He lay back, arms stretched out, mouth open as she caressed him, and worst of all he was watching her every movement.

'Is that nice?' she whispered, wondering if this was what whores did. Would he come quickly and get it over? Could she hope he would fall asleep immediately?

'It's heaven,' he said raising himself on his elbows. 'Sit on me Charity. I can't wait.'

Charity gulped. The thought of trying to get that huge thing inside herself when she felt nothing was obscene, but she'd come this far – she couldn't back out now.

Slowly she moved to sit astride him, guiding him into her, blushing as he watched, embarrassed by his laboured breathing when all she could manage were fake sighs.

She was so dry and tight it hurt, but she made out her groans were pleasure and moved slowly up and down, gradually taking in the whole length.

His hands reached out for her breasts, she leaned forward to kiss him and thought only of how this had been with John. John's stomach, his chest and thighs were hard. He'd been agile enough to sit up and hold her tightly, stroking her back and buttocks, kissing her till she nearly fainted with ecstasy.

'It's like a little virgin's fanny,' Ted rasped. 'Oh my darling, it's so wonderful!'

Charity detached herself from reality, moved up and down, clawing at his chest with her fingernails, writhing against him until he was bucking beneath her, eyes closed and mouth open in delight. He came quickly, pulling her down towards him in a fierce embrace and all at once he was still.

'That was out of this world,' he croaked, panting with exertion. Beads of sweat glistened on his forehead, the heat from his body was roasting her and she longed to get up from him and rush to the bathroom to wash it away.

Her hope that he would fall asleep was dashed when he got up, put on a silk dressing-gown and filled their glasses with more champagne.

'Don't cover yourself up,' he said as Charity pulled his shirt over her nakedness. 'I want to look at you.'

She managed to get to the bathroom and wash, but when she came back he was sitting up in bed.

Her heart sank. She had expected him to be almost asleep, sure her night's work was over, but the expression on his face told her otherwise.

'Tell me about you,' she said, getting into bed beside him. She wanted to go home. To wipe the memory of this night for ever from her mind and her body. But she had made a deal with him.

'Why would you want to know about me?' he asked, smiling with real warmth.

'Because you're a good-looking man,' she said truthfully, stroking his chin and sliding one finger over the endearing cleft. 'And a nice one.'

Her heart ached for him and all the other lonely, unloved, good men in London. Real prostitutes were at least honest: they didn't pretend to care.

When Ted turned out the light, Charity was sure he would fall asleep, but instead his arms came round her tightly and his mouth moved back to her breasts.

In the darkness it was easy just to let him fondle her. His fingers had that practised manner of a man who knew exactly how women worked and he was so gentle, she found herself responding just enough to give plausibility to her deep sighs.

'It's wonderful,' she groaned, hoping she sounded sincere and that he'd enter her and get it over with. 'Fuck me now!'

But her hopes for a quick release were dashed once he moved on top of her. Not only was she almost crushed by his weight, but he was clearly prolonging it because he believed she was enjoying it. His fingers gripped her buttocks mercilessly as he drove into her with such force she wanted to scream out he was hurting her, but instead she submitted, still acting out the part of someone in the throes of passion.

His tongue writhed into her mouth, he was soaked in sweat and the hair on his chest was making her itch. An image of her father came into her mind, the first time since John had banished it. She felt sick, tears welled up in her eyes and she had to turn her head away to escape his mouth and tongue, yet still he went on and on driving into her with ever-increasing force.

She tried to make her mind go blank, to claw at him and go through the motions of pretended bliss, but he was making her sore now and the slap of his flesh against hers made her nauseous.

'I'm coming,' she gasped, hoping it would act as a spur to him. 'Come with me Ted, now.'

He finally came just at the point when she felt she might scream. With a shuddering moan he collapsed on to her, his big body going into a spasm of pleasure.

'Oh Charity.' He held her tightly. 'That was incredible!'

She had never felt more ashamed of anything than she did at that moment.

It was midday when Charity let herself into the flat. The needle of the record player was stuck on the

Rolling Stones record, 'Not Fade Away', the arm squeaking as it scraped backwards and forwards, and the hall was littered with debris. Dorothy and Rita had obviously had an impromptu party last night. A midnight blue satin cocktail dress of Dorothy's was lying on the floor, her black knickers, bra and suspender belt strewn in all directions, and the room stank of cigarettes and stale booze.

A glance into Rita's room revealed she hadn't been part of this. Her bed was made and a couple of dresses lying on it proved she hadn't been home since the night before.

Dorothy's door was open, and Charity peeped in.

Dorothy was lying naked across the bed, face down, and to Charity's disgust there was a pile of vomit on the floor.

'Dorothy!' she cried angrily. 'What on earth have you been doing?'

She strode forward and caught her friend by the hair, yanking her head up.

'Oh my God!' she gasped.

Dorothy's face was a mess, one eye half closed from a punch and an angry red swelling halfway down her cheek. Her lip was cut and swollen; dried blood and vomit stuck to her naked breasts.

'Who did this?' she said. 'Sit up and tell me!'

'A john,' Dorothy croaked. 'A bloke called Tony I've been with once before. He saw me in the Hilton cocktail bar with another guy and he asked me if he could meet me back here later.' She began to cry then, shivering and shaking so much Charity couldn't understand what she was saying.

'I'll run you a bath,' she said firmly, taking Dorothy's face between her hands and studying it. 'You'll be no oil painting for a while, but until you're clean I can't see your lips properly.'

As Charity ran a bath for Dorothy she realised she

was shaking. She had gone straight from the Savoy still dressed in her evening clothes to Carmel's office, to hand over the money. She didn't want to touch the notes any longer than she had to. From there they had gone on to a solicitor who would sign the documents and transfer the lease. Her pleasure at actually owning the business had almost succeeded in wiping out the shame of how she'd accomplished it, until this moment.

A couple of days ago Charity might have berated Dorothy for getting herself into such a situation. They had all agreed many times never to give any of their escort dates this address or even the phone number. Their flat was private, a place for invited friends only. But how could she take a high moral tone now?

While the bath was running Charity slipped into jeans and a sweater, then returning to Dorothy she helped her to the bathroom.

Haltingly Dorothy explained.

'I wanted to ignore him when he beckoned for me to come outside for a minute,' she said, tears running down her cheeks. 'He was a bit difficult, but eventually I said to meet me back here around two.

'I thought you and Rita would be here,' she sobbed. 'We had a few drinks, then he started telling me his marriage was over and he needed me. He raped me too.' Dorothy covered her face with both her hands. 'He hit me first, then he pulled off my clothes and raped me. When he'd finished he threw a ten-pound note at me.'

'Oh Dottie,' Charity said as she helped her friend out of the bath and wrapped a towel round her. She didn't know whether the man was a maniac or just another sad, lonely person who'd looked for Dorothy hoping she could offer him comfort. Many men had been on the receiving end of her friend's sharp tongue, but she'd picked on the wrong one this time.

She toyed with the idea of calling the police, but that was quickly dismissed. Girls like them wouldn't get police protection, and if the neighbours got wind of any of that they'd soon lose the flat too.

Charity got her own warm dressing-gown and led Dorothy into her bedroom, pulling back the bed-clothes for her.

It was a miserable, grey October day outside and in an effort to shut it out, Charity drew the curtains and switched on the bedside light. Then she looked down at her friend.

She wanted to confess her own prostitution more than anything in the world. It would be good to sob out her pain and they could find consolation in one another. But she forced herself to sound cold. If she was sympathetic, Dorothy would have no hope.

'I haven't got a great deal of sympathy,' she said coolly. 'That man shouldn't have hit you, or raped you. No one can condone that. But you play fast and loose with people's feelings, Dot; you had this coming.'

'Where are you going?' Dorothy looked round at her friend as she walked towards the door.

'To clear up before Rita has to see all this,' she said sharply. 'But I'm not cleaning your room. You can do that yourself later. Your face will mend, Dot, but if you go on like this you'll destroy yourself. Now, for once in your selfish little life, think about other people. Think about how lucky we were to get this flat, to have one another. Laziness and self-pity are slowly choking you. I'm ashamed of what you're becoming.'

In Dorothy's bedroom as she cleaned up the mess, despite what she'd said, Charity sobbed her heart out. They were both emotional cripples; they just used different crutches. Money and beautiful clothes wouldn't bring back their babies, or compensate for

396

lack of love. Both had gone right down to the gutter last night and perhaps the memory of it would prevent them ever rising up again.

Rita phoned later to say she was going over to see her parents after work and wouldn't be home. She asked why Charity sounded so odd, but all Charity could offer as an excuse was that she was tired.

She was tired, too. Tired of being an adult, when inside she wanted to be a little girl again. Tired of hoping that one day everything would be perfect. Tired of other people needing her when she had no one. Her brothers and sister lived in the lap of luxury, but even though they were old enough to know the truth about why she was exiled, they didn't care enough to phone, or write. Even Lou and Geoff told her half-truths.

As she heated up some soup for Dorothy and cut fingers of crustless bread and butter, tears trickled down her cheeks.

'Sit up Dot,' she said as she carried the tray into the bedroom. 'I'm sorry if I wasn't kinder when you needed it.'

Dorothy hauled herself up and leaned back against the head of the bed.

'You were right in what you said.' She shrugged her shoulders and tried to smile. 'I'm glad to see you being a bitch at last.'

Charity let Dorothy eat the soup, silently watching her. Even with a cut lip, black eye and bruised cheek she was still beautiful. She remembered all they'd been to one another at Daleham Gardens, sharing the birth of Samantha, the laughter and tears, and she knew that the bond between them was indestructible.

She could feel how much she had changed in the last twenty-four hours and knew too that she was never going to be the same again.

'I think I qualify for the title of bitch on all counts.

I've stopped being a doormat. I've gone behind your back and bought the agency from Carmel. I'm even going to refuse to clean up after you again.'

Dorothy's one good eye opened in surprise.

'Welcome to the bitches' club,' she said, holding on to her cut lip with one hand as if afraid a smile would open it again. 'Come into bed with me and give me a cuddle.'

Charity slipped in beside her friend and it was a moment or two before she realised it was Dorothy cuddling her, not the other way round.

Dorothy's voice was husky with emotion. 'I won't let you down again, Chas, promise.'

It was the strangest thing to find her friend acting as comforter to her for once. But perhaps that was what friendship was all about.

Chapter Twenty-One

Charity climbed down the stepladder as the phone rang and wiped her paint-covered hands on a rag.

'Chelsea 9367,' she said. 'Yes, you do have the right number, this is Carmel's agency. I've taken over her clients . . .'

Charity smiled as she put down the phone. That was the third booking she'd made today. Only one man had cried off when he found that Carmel had retired.

She jotted down the details on the booking sheet, then went back to her painting.

Carmel had moved her bulging old files out last Friday, and Charity had been working on the office all weekend. It had been a daunting, filthy job. Although the old wallpaper had been peeling off, beneath it the plaster came away in places too. Only the friendly intervention of the man in the sandwich bar next door had saved her, when he gave her a packet of Polyfilla and explained what was needed. But now it was nearly done: the ceiling and wood-work were white, the walls palest pink.

Later today the sandwich bar man had promised to send in a friend of his to put up some new lights, and a contact of Rita's was bringing round some old exhibition carpet which he said would be as good as new.

As Charity finished off the last bit of wall through

to the tiny kitchen at the back of the office, her mind was on money.

By the time she'd paid the electrician and the carpet man, she'd be cleaned out. But providing the men who wanted escorts did actually turn up tomorrow with their fees, she'd have enough to tide her over. She had to get the place straight by then. She couldn't expect anyone to take her seriously, unless it looked like a proper office.

It was only now she was nearly finished that other problems were presenting themselves, things she hadn't even thought of before. She didn't know how to work that duplicator. She couldn't even type!

'Hi busy bee!'

Charity turned quickly at Rita's voice. She had been cleaning the paintbrushes and hadn't heard her friend arrive.

Charity grinned. 'What a nice surprise: someone to admire my handiwork. Just don't look too closely, the finish is hardly professional.'

'I brought you a sandwich.' Rita put a bag down on the desk, gazing round appreciatively. 'It looks marvellous, Chas. I didn't realise this office was so big.'

Charity dried her hands on a towel. She wore an old shirt and jeans and they were daubed with paint.

'It's only because it's empty,' she said. 'It's still tiny, really. Fancy some tea?'

'I'll make it,' Rita offered. 'You look worn out. I can't stop long, I'm only on my lunch hour, but I wanted to see if you needed any help. I could come back after work.'

'Bless you,' Charity said, touched by Rita's interest. 'I don't suppose you know anything about duplicators?'

'A bit.' Rita took the cover off it and peered at it.

'We had one like this at college. You cut the stencils on the typewriter, wind it round, then – '

'Stop,' Charity said in alarm. 'I don't understand any of that!'

Rita shook her head in disbelief.

'Sit down,' she ordered. 'I'll make the tea and then you'd better tell me what else you don't understand.'

Half an hour later, Rita had made Charity even more anxious. She spoke of invoices, bookkeeping and contracts and the importance of making things look professional. Charity had forgotten that her friend had been to secretarial college before Daleham Gardens.

'Perhaps you'd better become my partner,' Charity suggested as Rita talked of accounts books and keeping proper records.

'It won't support two of us for some time,' Rita said. 'Besides, I wouldn't want that. But I'll help you when you get stuck and type stencils and things for you.'

Two weeks later Carmel came in to see how Charity was getting on, and found her sitting at her desk looking despondent.

'Why so glum?' she asked. 'It looks wonderful.'

Charity smiled weakly. The office did look good, if a little bare. The new lights and the grey carpet, a secondhand filing cabinet and a large plant on her desk all created an aura of success. But the new pink lettering on the windows reading STRATTON PROMOTIONS didn't mean clients were beating their way to her door.

'I haven't got one promotion job yet,' Charity admitted. 'I've rung dozens of companies I've worked for, but all of them use Central Promotions. Rita typed out a circular and I spent about twenty quid on postage sending them out, but not one reply. Other firms I've rung just say they'll be in touch if anything comes up.

If it wasn't for the escort service I wouldn't be earning a penny.'

'Rome wasn't built in a day,' Carmel said. 'Keep at it. Maybe you ought to change tactics and think up some scheme to put to companies.'

'Like what?' Charity said wearily.

'Well, Christmas for one.' Carmel shrugged. 'Look at a few store advertisements and consider how one or two of your girls might enhance sales over the Christmas period. How many girls have you got on your books?'

Charity gulped.

'None, really,' she said. 'I mean I was relying on getting the offer of jobs before I rang some of the girls I know. Rita and Dorothy will do them like a shot, and then there's the escort girls to call on.'

'Put a card in your window, now,' Carmel said firmly. 'Girls wanted for promotion work. Good wages, etcetera. They'll come in, there's hundreds of pretty girls walking up and down this road. Get them to fill in an application form and submit a photograph for your file. Meanwhile use your imagination.'

'When's this car coming then, Chas?' Dorothy shouted out from behind the screen hiding the kitchen. 'I'm dying to show off in this outfit. Maybe we could do a bit of carol singing outside the office?'

'Come out and let me see,' Charity shouted back.

Dorothy pranced out first, closely followed by Rita. Jane and Wendy, two newly recruited girls, were less enthusiastic and hung back.

'You all look marvellous!' Charity exclaimed.

All four girls were dressed as lady Santa Clauses in short fur-trimmed costumes with fishnet tights and hats worn at a jaunty angle.

Charity had taken Carmel's advice and at last she'd landed her first contract. The girls had been hired to add a touch of seasonal glamour to a new garage and car showroom opening this weekend in Tottenham Court Road. They were waiting now for the car to take them to the grand opening and Charity had been assured that the press would be there taking photographs.

'Do we really look all right?' Jane said nervously. She was one of the escort girls and she'd never done a promotion before.

'You all look beautiful.' Charity smiled. 'Sexy, gorgeous and utterly delectable. You'll stop the traffic in the Tottenham Court Road. But mind you behave properly. There'll be a lot of booze there, and randy salesmen. But I don't want any of you getting pickled. This job might lead us to many more if you charm everyone in the company.'

'Message received and understood, boss!' Dorothy clicked her heels and saluted. 'We'll behave with the utmost decorum.'

Dorothy had been very quiet and broody since the night she'd been beaten up and raped and Charity had been very concerned about her. But Dorothy was resilient: she'd taken on a promotional job as soon as her face was healed and she'd even insisted on Charity finding her escort dates, just as long as she was paired with Rita.

This Santa Claus job was the tonic they all needed. For Charity it meant she'd cracked the ice and launched her business; for Dorothy and Rita it meant three weeks of fun and a chance to show off in their brief and sexy costumes.

'Here's the car now.' Charity jumped up as she saw the limousine draw up outside. 'Now remember too that I have dozens of contracts,' she said with a wink. 'Stratton Promotions is *the* agency, with the brightest, best and most beautiful girls.'

But by the middle of February, things had got worse. Charity sat at her desk studying the paper, idly ringing round advertisements for companies who looked like prospects. She couldn't use the phone: it had been cut off that morning because she hadn't paid the bill, and she was trying to quell the panic rising inside her.

It was a bitterly cold, grey day and she didn't know where to turn next.

The Santa Claus job at the car showrooms had given her a false sense of security. Although she got a hefty fee and some free publicity from it, the escort business had gone quiet at the same time.

Carmel was right when she said girls would come into the office looking for work. They had. But what good was a file of girls' application forms without the jobs to send them to?

An electricity bill would plop through the door any day, the rent was due, and all the money she had was gone. Without the phone she was lost.

Charity had five bookings for escorts, but when the men found the phone wasn't working they'd assume she'd gone out of business, and although she was anxious to drop that side of her agency, at the moment it was her only lifeline.

On top of all this she was so lonely. She spent long days sitting in the office with little to occupy her other than practising two-fingered typing, with an even longer empty evening ahead of her.

Dorothy and Rita did glamorous, well-paid work by day, and divided their evenings between escort dates and boyfriends. From the day Charity took over the office she had vowed she'd never be an escort again. The image of Ted taunted her, a permanent reminder of a ruthless darker side of her nature, and it prevented her from even considering an innocent date with a man.

Even her twentieth birthday back in January had passed without celebration as Dorothy and Rita had both been out of town on jobs. She'd drunk a cheap bottle of wine alone and tried to think positively. After all, January was always a quiet month in any business.

But now she'd hit rock bottom and short of pawning the brooch John had given her, or asking the girls to lend her the money for the phone bill, she was finished.

A blast of cold air made her look up and to her absolute amazement there was John at the door.

Her heart hammered, her troubles instantly put aside.

'John!' she shrieked, getting up and rushing to him, flinging her arms round him. 'What a wonderful surprise. How did you know I was here?'

He didn't answer immediately, just held her tightly. She could feel how cold he was, even through his thick overcoat.

'I don't think I should have come, really,' he said into her neck. 'I went round to the flat, intending to put a book through your door. But Dorothy was there and insisted I went in. When she told me about the agency I tried to phone but there's something wrong with your number.'

Charity was hurt that he had intended to avoid her, but thought she'd better wait and hear him out before she said anything.

Over a cup of tea John explained he was back in London for just a couple of weeks to launch a book of his photographs, before going back to India. He sat hunched up over the electric fire and Charity saw he wasn't well. His face had always been thin, but now it was gaunt, his cheekbones sticking out prominently.

'Are you ill?' she said, kneeling down beside him and sliding her hands inside his coat. She could feel his ribs through his shirt and she saw he had lost perhaps two stone in weight.

'I got a dose of the Delhi belly.' He laughed but there was no humour in it and he moved her hands away from him, almost as if repulsed by her.

'What is it, John?' she asked anxiously. Seeing him again after so long brought back all the old feeling, but he was being very strange.

He didn't reply and his eyes wouldn't meet hers as she sat back on her heels by his feet.

'Come on!' she wheedled. 'We're old friends, aren't we? Are you in some sort of trouble?'

'I got married,' he blurted out.

'You got married?' She felt as if her blood was draining away.

He nodded, his eyes downcast.

Charity leapt up then, backing away.

'How could you be so cruel?' she shouted. 'Why come and tell me something like that?'

'I didn't mean to be cruel,' he said wearily. 'Like I said, if Dorothy hadn't been there I would just have left the book. There were some pictures of you in it, you see, and I had to give you a copy. But once I'd spoken to Dorothy, I knew I'd have to see you face to face.'

Charity began to shake uncontrollably. This seemed to be the last nail in the coffin, on top of all her other problems.

'Go, John.' She pointed towards the door. 'I'd like to say I'm happy for you, but it's just such a shock. Please don't come back again.'

'I'm not going until you've heard me out,' he said stubbornly. 'I hoped you'd found someone else. I thought I could exchange a few pleasantries with you, and be on my way.'

Charity turned away from him, struggling to control herself. John had always been honest to a fault.

But this time she would have preferred a little less directness.

She composed herself and turned back.

'Well get on with the pleasantries,' she said sarcastically. 'Who is it you've married? When and where?'

Charity listened as he explained, trying hard to control herself. Fifteen years ago on his first trip to India he had taken photographs for an illustrated animal book. The writer was a man called Martin Fellows; his wife was Nina. The three of them became good friends. He had stayed at their bungalow in the hills at the time, and on every subsequent visit to India he went back to see them.

He went on to say that he had met up with Nina again in Nairobi, some weeks after he last saw Charity. Martin had died two years earlier and she was in Africa doing research for a biography of her late husband.

'We were both lonely and heartsick,' he said. 'We leaned on one another. I dug out some old material of Martin's which had never been published. The African job I'd done led on to one in India, near where she lived. I knew then it was no good spending the rest of my life moping, and one thing led to another.'

It was obvious they had become lovers and just the thought of John making love to another woman made Charity feel intensely jealous.

'Are you happy with her?' she asked, wanting so much to hear it had all been a dreadful, hasty mistake.

'I'm content,' he said. 'Nina and I are the same age. We have the same interests. It's a peaceful relationship, Charity. We're both too old now for passion and fire.'

A picture of two calm, middle-aged people together was soothing. Charity fell silent for a moment, struggling with the need to wound him and yet knowing she still cared too much for him to do so.

'I'm glad then.' She put one hand on his shoulder. 'You were good for me, John, you deserve to be happy now.'

He stayed silent for a moment.

'And you?' he asked finally. 'Have you found happiness?'

'I think so.' Charity wished she could tell him how low she felt, but her pride wouldn't let her. 'Though I work too hard to think about it much.'

Over another cup of tea John asked her questions about the agency. Realising Dorothy had let it slip about how she came to buy it, she was forced to admit she still ran the escort service, and why the phone didn't work.

John's eyes were dark with reproach.

'It's no good you looking like that,' she said quickly, hoping he wouldn't press her about how she managed to save so much money. 'It was a good opportunity and I grabbed it. The only reason I still handle that side of it is because I have to.'

'Charity, listen to me,' he said, grabbing her hands, his eyes full of concern. 'I'm not concerned about you having a few dates with lonely businessmen, heaven knows I've hoped you'd find a man who could make you happy often enough. But it's running the service that concerns me. If just one of your girls takes money for sex and it comes out, you'll be in trouble. It's living on immoral earnings, a criminal offence. Do you think anyone will believe you didn't know?'

She had wrestled with this dozens of times, but always the need for money got the better of her.

'I would drop it immediately if I could get the promotions side off the ground.' She pouted defiantly, irritated by his remark about hoping she'd find someone to make her happy. 'You tell me how I'm going to get a few good contracts and I'll jack it in tomorrow.'

He took her to the Marco Polo where they'd had lunch the first time and over lasagne and a bottle of wine she blurted out her problems.

John let her talk. He was surprised by her knowledge of the promotion world, and impressed by her courage at taking on such a venture so young, with no backing. More than anything he wanted it to work for her.

'I'll pay the telephone,' he said immediately, getting out his chequebook. 'But to get the promotions agency off the ground, you've got to think more positively.'

'I have tried.' Charity sounded plaintive, a little irritated that he thought she hadn't worked hard at it and embarrassed by his cheque. 'I don't know what I'm doing wrong. I'm game for attempting anything to get me noticed, but advertising costs so much.'

'Not always,' he smiled. 'I'll come up with a plan. Meanwhile get that phone bill paid, stop worrying and come out to dinner with me tomorrow night.'

John turned on the light on his bedside table and looked at his watch. It was four in the morning and he couldn't sleep. He was shivering, even though the room was warm. His stomach kept churning and although it was partly due to the severe attack of dysentery, he knew most of the problem was Charity.

All through lunch he just hadn't been able to take his eyes off her. She had altered subtly – a few gained pounds which added curves to her slender shape – and her hair had lost that wispy, childish quality and now hung in one gleaming swing of white gold. He remembered wincing once at her hastily applied makeup. Now it enhanced the beauty already there. Her lustrous eyes, and those full lips were enough to draw any male eye. Her black suit could have come from Worth, the only decoration the bow brooch he'd bought her in Florence and a single string of pearls.

But these visible attractions were nothing to her new manner. She no longer giggled, she had looked at the menu with complete understanding and even suggested a red wine that was superb without being outrageously expensive. She had asked him intelligent questions about his work.

He had to help her get her business off the ground. She deserved it. Maybe, too, it would end that dull ache for her inside him and he could return to Nina and India knowing he'd finally severed the last strand.

They had dinner at John's hotel. He chose it because it was brightly lit and impersonal, yet comfortable enough to sit for a long talk.

Over coffee, he began to talk to her about Stratton Promotions.

'More than anything you need publicity,' he said forcefully. He'd given her business a great deal of thought during the day. 'You need the right girls, the right image and the good companies. Publicity will get all three.'

His plan was to run an advertisement for girls to come forward to enrol with her, the inducement being a chance to be photographed by Grant Meredith, the top fashion man who happened to owe John a favour.

'The girls will come running,' he replied firmly to her protestations. 'So will the media! Then we get a glossy brochure printed and you're halfway there.'

'Grant Meredith!' Charity could hardly believe he was serious. The man was legendary: to fashion what John was to scenic photography. 'He'll cost a fortune!'

John didn't deny or confirm this, just insisted he was going to see to it and the cost of the printing.

'You can't do this stuck behind a desk, Charity.' He spoke in the kind of bullying tone she knew he used with the magazines he worked for. 'You've got to get out there yourself, demand to see the top men and plonk down these images of glorious girls on their desks. You can sell, Charity, but now you've got something bigger than lipsticks or perfume. You're selling your company image and your expertise. You must convince yourself you are the best and convince them too.'

'Will you be around long enough to see all this happen?' she asked, suddenly aware he was speaking as if this was their last meeting.

'Long enough to set it up.' He half smiled, the lines on his face deeper than she remembered. 'I'll see to the finances and give you all the contacts. But I think it's better we only talk on the phone after tonight.'

John was as good as his word. All the next week he used his contacts, his keen mind and his powers of organisation to make the name of Stratton Promotions work.

He didn't have to tell her that she must drop the escort side of the business like a hot brick, she knew that. She paid the bill, and changed the number. The files of old clients were destroyed and a circular was sent out to all her legitimate business contacts informing them she was moving on to a higher profile.

Charity saw then just how John Marshall had become so successful. It wasn't just his creative photography, but his ability to motivate others. He booked a studio in Kensington for the following week and hired a public relations man to handle the publicity. The printers were standing by and the advertisement for girls was placed in several papers.

'This time tomorrow I'll be halfway back to India,' John said as they ate a last dinner together at the Marco Polo. They had both been uncertain about meeting again but it was unthinkable for him to leave with only another phone call after all he'd done.

411

'Don't look so anxious, Charity, you can handle everything now.'

The Marco Polo hadn't changed. Still the old red
and white checked tablecloths, white walls and
vibrant Italian pictures. Yet even though Charity had
changed immeasurably since that first lunch date two
years earlier, in many ways she felt the same. Scared,
excited, sad and happy all at once, with the same
sensation of standing on the threshold to a new orld.

There was a certain relief that John would soon be
gone. Each time he'd phoned the office, no matter how
businesslike he was, there was still the temptation to
try and make more of it. But now, faced with all the
frantic work to be done in the next few weeks, she
felt able to shut the door firmly for ever.

Yet as she she looked at his narrow, lined face, those
gentle eyes and his endearingly small nose, she still
wanted to touch him one last time. She itched to run
her fingers through his curls, to trace those deep lines,
to smell his skin and hold that hard lean body. But it
was more than just a physical need; the emotional
bond had to be severed too.

'If you ever really need me, you can get in touch
through my agent in London,' he said, sliding his
hand over hers. He didn't have to say he wasn't going
to write, or visit when he was in London, Charity
knew he would be too honourable to do that now
he'd committed himself to Nina.

'Just send me a postcard to tell me you are truly
happy,' she whispered, biting back tears. 'That's
enough for me. I'm a big girl now.'

John looked at her and remembered how she had
been the first day he brought her to this restaurant.
She'd been such a waif then, her eyes and mouth too
big for that little pale face, her hair straggly, her
clothes so shabby. She had given him back his life
and, despite the ache in his heart at saying goodbye

for good, he knew she had given him the power to be happy with Nina. Through her he had learned to truly love, to give of himself, and now he could look forward to a new phase of his life.

The money he had spent to launch her business was nothing to him; he felt he owed her far more. All he wished was that he could find the right words now to speed her on her way to fulfil all her ambitions.

'Are you coming home with me?' she asked as John opened the cab door for her.

King's Road was busy despite the late hour, girls in miniskirts, young men in jeans and denim jackets thronging to the Village Gate club. Cars were cruising, windows open and music blaring, and it seemed here that the night was just starting.

'No I want to leave you here, where it all started,' John said, pulling her to him for one last hug. 'Remember how I tried to hug you that day?'

'You scared me.' She smiled at the memory.

'Not enough.' He held her tightly, his lips on her hair. 'But you'll never be scared of anything again, will you?'

She released herself from his grip and took his face in her hands.

'Such an old face,' he said, guessing she was photographing it in her mind one last time just as he was hers.

'Such a dear face,' she said. 'No man will ever quite measure up to you, John.'

He took her hand and kissed the tips of her fingers. 'Go now angel. Don't look back.'

Alone in her bed in the darkness, Charity finally let the tears flow until she was drained. Yet they were healing tears. Now it was finally over she had to build on what he'd given her. She had tasted real love, plumbed the depths and soared with the eagles, and if it never came again, at least she knew what it was.

The name 'Grant Meredith' was like a magic key to open a locked door. Girls were soon beating a path to Charity's office on the chance of being photographed by the great man. Models between jobs, 'resting' actresses, shop assistants and office girls all wanted to put their names down on her books.

Charity vetted them carefully, dividing them into types. Ultra-glamour girls for jobs such as posing on cars at motor shows. Smart ones capable of real selling and then a huge heap of those more ordinary ones who could be allocated to appropriate slots.

Grant Meredith, according to the many articles about him, was supposed to be rude, temperamental and overbearing, but Charity found him to be none of these things. He diplomatically took shots of every one of the eighty girls who turned up, but handed cards only to those he thought the most photogenic to come again the next day, on an appointment system for more sensational shots.

By the afternoon of the last day, when he suggested Charity should pose for him, she liked him enough to be completely at her ease.

He looked extraordinary, with long greasy hair slicked back, somewhere between a Chicago gangster and a teddy boy. His leather jacket was falling apart, he wore motorcycle boots and she did wonder what he and John had in common.

'We go back a long way,' he said with a wicked grin as he packed away his cameras. 'Before you were born, love, in Paris, but he wouldn't want me to tell you all about that!'

Charity stared at the proofs in amazement. Even the

plainer girls looked fabulous: she would be proud to display these pictures anywhere.

'One of the girls is a real cracker,' Grant said, pulling out a couple of bigger prints to show her. 'I'd like to take some more of her, can you arrange for her to ring me?'

It was Dorothy. Grant had caught that fabulous enigmatic smile, the cool sensuality of her.

'That's my flatmate.' Charity's eyes lit up with pride and excitement. 'I can give you her number right now.'

The day she waited for Grant to come with the proofs was to be the last one of inactivity. From the very next day things began to happen. First Jackson Booth, the man John had asked to handle the public relations, rang to say that the *Evening News* wanted to interview her, and this was quickly followed by a call from the *Daily Express*, who were intrigued at a businesswoman being so young. Both articles were in print in two days with one of Grant's group photographs, and from then on the phone began to ring.

Asking Rita's help in those first heady days was natural. Rita knew the promotion game as well as Charity did and she had all the secretarial skills.

'I'll just help out for a couple of weeks,' Rita suggested. 'Then maybe you can get someone in part time.'

It was an uneasy alliance at first. Both Rita and Dorothy were missing the money from escort work and Charity doubted the wisdom of employing her flatmate, even as a temporary measure. But Rita surprised Charity. Once she sat down behind her desk, she really worked, creating an efficient system that Charity could follow.

The moment the first batch of brochures arrived, Charity started work with new fervour. She demanded an interview, wouldn't be fobbed off with secretaries or 'leave a brochure and we'll see what we can do'. Now she insisted on making an appointment to see the top man or woman and instead of meekly taking their 'we'll call you when something comes up', she made suggestions as to how her agency could enhance their image with direct promotions.

A soft drink promotion came first, quickly followed by one for tights. They were small companies and the contracts were only for a week each, but it was a breakthrough.

'It's going to work,' Charity said one afternoon as she returned from a meeting with the sales manager of a cosmetics company who had suggested a trial two-week job. 'It really is. Stay with me, Rita, be a partner.'

'I don't want to be a partner,' Rita said, with a wide grin which showed that she appreciated the thought. 'It wouldn't work long term and I haven't got any money to put into the business anyway. But if you can pay me the same as I earn at promotions and you increase it as the money comes rolling in, that's enough for me.'

The money didn't come rolling in. Companies weren't always as quick to pay as they were to arrange a promotion. Sometimes Rita had to go off and take the place of one of the girls when they didn't turn up, and several times Charity had to arrange an overdraft just to pay the girls' wages. But slowly and surely the business began to grow.

An eight-week contract with a new confectionery company kept her best girls in work. A nightclub promotion for Bacardi held the interest of the more glamorous girls and there were other smaller jobs with crisp and biscuits companies that filled in gaps between bigger promotions.

Rita was happy. She liked working with Charity,

her parents approved of her finally settling down in what they called 'a real job'. The office was only a short walk from the flat and she had escaped the regimentation and boredom of work in big stores.

Dorothy was as selfish and arrogant as ever. She bemoaned the loss of income as an escort, sniffed at most of the jobs Charity offered her and did as little around the flat as ever. But when the three girls saw the shots Grant had taken of her in his studio, they all knew it wouldn't be long before she moved on to modelling. She seemed to encapsulate the look of the moment, with her long straight hair, her beautiful eyes and chiselled bone structure.

In May she got her first job on the cover of a visitors' guide to London, quickly followed by one for *Honey* magazine. She found herself an agent who said he'd have her modelling furs in August with Grant taking the pictures, and discussed sending her to New York for a fashion show.

But if Rita and Dorothy were satisfied with their lot, Charity was still hankering for a prestigious promotion. She knew that until she landed one of the really big names she would always be struggling to pay her girls and the rent.

Ironically it was one of Carmel's clients who put her in touch with Marlboro cigarettes. Arnold Fear came to the office one day looking for Carmel and fortunately Charity didn't freeze him out as she did with most men who turned up at the door. He came in, studied the framed glossy prints of her girls on the wall and began to chat. He did tell Charity he worked for a cigarette company, but she didn't press him to tell her which one, or his position there. Instead she offered him a cup of tea while she found Carmel's number and chatted about her agency.

Two days later Arnold phoned and told her that he had recommended her to Marlboro.

'I just hope you can handle it,' he said. 'Mr Grimes, the chap who deals with promotions, is a hard cookie. But he's willing to see you.'

Charity had never been so nervous in her entire life as the day of her initial interview with Mr Grimes. He was in fact a director of Style and Design, an advertising agency in Regent Street that handled the Marlboro account, so more than one job might rest on the impression she gave him.

She went right through her wardrobe, discarding just about everything, and finally plumped for the black suit she'd been wearing when John came back and Dorothy's best white silk shirt. With three-inch heels, a manicure and her hair set that morning, she felt confident about her appearance, if nothing else. Rita had typed out details of all their other promotions, and along with the glossy brochure she had photographs of the best of her girls tucked into an expensive briefcase borrowed from Rita's father.

A severe-looking secretary ushered her into a spacious, plush office and she found Mr Grimes was almost as forbidding as his name.

He was very tall, which immediately put her at a disadvantage, and had the kind of stern, unsmiling face she expected from a bank manager.

Charity listened carefully as he laid out his plan for a cigarette promotion at Goodwood races, her heart racing, and immediately she added more money to the fee she'd planned. He wanted girls who were 'top drawer' types, well used to the kind of people who went to motor racing.

'As I'm sure you're aware,' he said, fixing her with penetrating dark eyes, 'a company like Marlboro isn't concerned with selling a few extra packets, but to create an image. Although the girls will be handing out cigarettes, and indeed selling some of our merchandise, the main object is that people link Marlboro with the smart set. Do you understand that?'

'Of course, Mr Grimes.' Charity smiled, clutching her hands together beneath the shelter of his desk. 'My girls are entirely part of that image – glamorous, sophisticated girls. But let me show you a few of them.'

She had brought eight pictures with her and she stood up and slowly put them down one by one, until she got to the final one of Dorothy, which she placed closest to him. As she expected, he focused only on Dorothy, barely glancing at the others again.

'I only need four,' he said. 'Are all these girls available for the whole of July?'

'Dorothy,' Charity tapped her picture, 'is modelling in August, but I'm almost certain I haven't booked her out yet for July. Jane is free then, Susie and Wendy I shall have to check on. Donna and Jackie have been booked, but if you would like them I can always juggle other girls into their places.'

Charity took a deep breath. She had learned enough about salesmanship to know she had to close this sale now.

'Which girls would you like?' she asked.

He fell for it, just as she hoped he would. 'This one, Dorothy did you say her name was? And these other three.'

'Dorothy, Donna, Jane and Susie,' she said, picking up the spare pictures and leaving the ones he'd chosen on the desk. 'Now shall we talk about dress? What did you have in mind?'

Charity was so excited once she was back in Regent Street that she flagged a taxi without even thinking of the expense. She couldn't wait to get back and tell Rita.

'Get out the contract!' she shouted as she burst

419

through the door. 'We'd better not celebrate until he signs it tomorrow, but it's as good as in the bag.'

Rita bounced out of her chair, quite forgetting the cool businesslike manner she'd struggled to create. She flung her arms round Charity and led her in a mad dance round the office. 'Who did he pick?' she finally managed breathlessly.

'Well, Dot of course! Donna, Susie and Jane.' Charity slumped back down on her chair, eyes shining.

'Did he agree to all the terms you wanted?' Rita asked.

'I didn't actually put mine forward. Everything he offered was better.' Charity giggled. 'I've got more money, the girls get snazzy dresses provided, and put up in a posh hotel. The only thing that's different is the hours because he wants them present at some evening do's – not that that'll be a hardship.'

'They'll have the time of their lives,' Rita said enviously, imagining all those dishy racing drivers. 'I wish we were going!'

'I can't wait to tell Dottie.' Charity giggled. 'She'll be like a dog with three tails.'

Rita went back to her desk, and loaded the contract form into her typewriter.

Charity sat for a moment in thought.

'We could go down there one weekend,' she said eventually. 'It might be good for business to show our faces.'

'Never mind business, think of the fun.' Rita grinned. 'All those men and powerful cars. We can't leave them all to Dottie. Besides, you spend too much time being serious.'

Charity didn't reply for a moment. Rita was right: since that night with Ted, work had become a substitute for fun. She hardly thought about Hugh any more. She was over John. All the old clichés were true, time did heal most wounds. She had learned to put aside what her father had done to her. She no longer blamed herself for her parents' death. Even Uncle Stephen worried her less – a lawyer-contact, a friend of Dot's, had recently suggested she might be able to take over the children's guardianship once she was twenty-one if she could prove her ability to take care of them. Giving up Daniel was the only thing that still hurt. Hardly a day passed without her wondering what he looked like, or what he was doing.

It was time she started living, really living, not merely marking time or dwelling on the past.

'We *will* go,' Charity said, a wide smile spreading across her face. 'What's more we'll have a new racy dress each on the business.'

Chapter Twenty-Two

1966

Charity couldn't sleep. It was too hot. The window was wide open, but there wasn't even the faintest breeze. It had been growing warmer each day throughout July and now in the last week the temperature hadn't dropped below eighty degrees.

It hardly seemed possible that last year she and Rita had been celebrating signing the Marlboro contract. Now they only got excited when they were pulling in jobs for over ten girls. The office wasn't big enough now, they even complained about how shabby the flat was and while Charity and Rita were sweltering in a poky office, working long hours, Dorothy was always jetting off to exotic locations on fashion shoots.

The phone rang, making Charity jump. She turned on her light and frowned.

It was ten past twelve. Only one of Dorothy's admirers could be phoning this late, and she was out.

Padding into the lounge in her nightdress, Charity saw Rita through her open door, lying on the top of her bed, fast asleep.

'Earls Court 3245.'

'Is that Charity?' a girl's voice asked.

'Yes.' Charity frowned. There was something familiar about the voice, but she couldn't place it. 'Who's this?'

'It's Prue!'

Charity's knees gave way in shock.

'My Prue?' she stammered out, afraid she was mistaken.

'Yes, your sister. I know it's late, but I couldn't think of anyone else to phone. Everything's so awful.'

Charity didn't even consider the words 'I couldn't think of anyone else'. All she could hear was her sister's voice rising in a plea for help.

'It's all right.' Charity recovered enough to sit down on the settee. 'You've just given me such a shock. I didn't know you had my number Prue, it's so wonderful to hear you.'

'Lou gave it to me ages ago,' Prue said quickly, as if that wasn't important. 'Please come down and help me.'

Charity's heart lurched. Flashes of everything from road accidents and rape to someone standing over her sister with a gun, were running through her head.

'Calm down and tell me, Prue,' she said. 'Now, where are you? What's happened?'

'I'm at home, at Studley.' Prue started to cry. 'Grandmother's ill and Uncle Stephen is being so horrid. I can't cope.'

Charity's mind slipped back six years. She saw herself in her uncle's room holding that enema pan, remembered how hateful and menacing Stephen had been.

'But Stephen won't let me near Studley,' Charity pointed out. 'What's actually the matter with Grandmother? Is it bad enough to call an ambulance? Where's the housekeeper?'

'Mr and Mrs Pitt left ages ago,' Prue sobbed down the phone. 'There's nobody here now. Mrs Williams who used to clean left yesterday too because Uncle was so awful to her. He expects me to do everything now. I even had to change Grandmother's sheets when she wet the bed.'

'You poor love,' Charity said sympathetically. 'I can imagine what it's like. But tell me what's wrong with Grandmother. Has the doctor been?'

'He came earlier, but he said she's just old and frail.'

Charity could see it all. Grandmother upstairs in bed, Stephen downstairs in his wheelchair and Prue running between the two.

'But what about Toby? Surely he's there, it's the summer holidays?'

'He doesn't help.' Prue sounded very sorry for herself. 'He said it's woman's work.'

Charity thought quickly. They were only teenagers, and Prue sounded distraught.

'Listen Prue, I'll come first thing in the morning. But you'll have to prepare Uncle Stephen. I don't want to walk in there and get thrown out.'

'Oh Chas.' Prue let out a huge sigh of relief. 'Don't worry about him, I'll explain.'

She rang off suddenly.

'Who was that?' Rita stood in her bedroom doorway rubbing her eyes.

'My sister.' Charity sank back on the settee, too overcome to even think straight.

'She rang you? How wonderful!' Rita was wide awake at once. 'What did she say? What made her phone?'

As Charity explained, Rita's face clouded over.

'You mean she never asked how you were? Just demanded that you come and sort things out?'

'She's only a kid,' Charity retorted. 'She was upset and probably exhausted.'

Rita frowned, brown eyes full of concern. She twisted one of her red curls round her fingers the way she always did when she was preparing to say her piece.

'Chas, she's almost sixteen. At her age you were working like a slave. She's had your phone number

424

for some time but she never bothered to ring you. Now when she's lumbered with a sick granny, she suddenly remembers she's got a sister. It sounds dangerously like she's using you.'

Charity caught the train to Oxford the next morning. She took a deep breath to calm the butterflies inside her as the taxi swept into the drive at Studley and round the circular lawn to the front door.

It all looked just as it had on her first visit six years ago, but now she wasn't intimidated by its size or grandeur.

'Nice place!' the taxi driver commented. 'Your folks?'

Charity smiled. Six years ago no one would have considered her likely to be related to the owners and it gave her a surge of new courage.

'My uncle's.' She smiled as she paid him.

The gravel scrunched as the taxi pulled away. Charity stood for a moment, her small case in her hands, surveying the house and grounds.

She could see changes. The stable roof was mended. The lawn was as smooth as a bowling green and the yew hedges were trimmed like boxes. Her eyes swept over the grey stone, the mullioned windows and pointed gables, then she took another deep breath before walking to the front door.

Six years ago she'd had Jackson's hand steadying her elbow, a frightened child in a green skirt and cheap jacket. Now she wore a Mary Quant black and white minidress; her makeup and hair were faultless. She must remember she was a businesswoman now, tough enough to deal with even the most crusty of company directors. She could handle her uncle.

The front door opened before she could ring the bell and there was Prue.

Charity dropped her case, joy at seeing her sister

wiping out all anxiety. She opened her arms, emotional tears springing to her eyes.

'I was afraid you wouldn't come,' Prue managed to say before being enveloped in a hug.

For a brief moment no words were necessary. Insects buzzed, sun warm on bare arms, cheek on damp cheek.

'Let me look at you.' Charity took a step back, her sister's two hands in hers. 'You're all grown up!'

It was a surprise to find Prue was much bigger than herself. A well-developed girl with broad hips and a country girl rosiness rather than her own delicate colouring. She wore an outdated shirtwaister print dress and her long blonde hair was tied carelessly back in a single clump at her neck.

'I look frightful,' Prue said breathlessly, releasing one hand to wipe at her eyes. 'But I'm so glad you've come.'

She had her father's large forehead but her mother's thin lips, and her childhood angelic prettiness was gone. But Charity wasn't looking critically, only savouring the moment.

'Where's Toby?' she asked, as Prue led her in.

'Upstairs somewhere,' Prue said, as if he wasn't important. 'You can't imagine how dreadful it's been.'

There were so many things Charity wanted to ask, but as her eyes swept round the hall she could see that things had been sliding here for some time. Cobwebs clung to the stone walls and the big carved chest was dull with dust and grime.

'Have you told Uncle Stephen I was coming?' she asked, looking down at the worn Persian rug and wondering how long it was since it had last been taken out for a beating.

'Yes.' Prue was chewing on her lip, as if unsure of herself. 'He said I had no business going over his head.'

Charity glanced into the drawing room, half expecting him to be sitting there in his wheelchair like an aggressive toad. He wasn't, but she could see signs of neglect there too: stuffing coming out of a rip on a settee, more dust and grime.

'Where is he?'

'In his room,' Prue replied. 'He must've seen your taxi come. He's probably sulking. Maybe you should see Grandmother first.'

'I'd like a cup of tea,' Charity said. 'And to see Toby. Will you get him and I'll make tea for all of us?'

Charity felt uneasy now. All this time she'd imagined that when she saw Prue again they would instantly pick up where they'd left off six years ago. But Prue wasn't a dainty little girl any longer, she was a hefty, rather plain teenager with a plummy accent, and Charity was a stranger . . .

As Prue went off upstairs, Charity made her way through the dining room to the kitchen. She noted that the silver was tarnished and the once gleaming table dull, but when she came to the kitchen she recoiled in horror.

Piles of unwashed dishes filled the big sink, the tiled floor was filthy, even the walls were caked with grease. As she filled the kettle, everything she touched was sticky and there were mouse droppings on the work surface.

Ellen the cook who had been here on her last visit had kept it spotless: scoured saucepans hung from hooks, the glass on the cabinets twinkling. Tentatively Charity opened cupboards and found them almost empty, more mouse droppings everywhere.

She washed up a few cups and saucers, wiped over the table and was just opening the fridge to get some milk when she heard footsteps.

'Toby!'

'Chas!'

427

She wanted to hug him, but she was rooted to the spot in astonishment.

Toby towered over her, but it was his looks not his height that stunned her.

'My little brother has turned into a man,' she said weakly.

He was so handsome. No trace of teenage acne spoilt his peachy skin. He had a wide, smiling mouth, big bright blue eyes framed by long golden lashes and an endearing tousled mop of white-blond hair.

'Can I still hug you?' she said, not knowing whether to laugh or cry. 'Or are you too big?'

He took two steps towards her and enveloped her in his arms, lifting her right off her feet.

'And you're so little and pretty,' he laughed. 'I thought you'd be a fat cow like Prue.'

'I'm not fat,' Prue retorted. 'At least I've got brains!'

Charity began to laugh. This sniping took her right back to Greenwich. They might have grown up, everything around them was different, but clearly their love-hate relationship had remained the same.

'What's so funny?' Toby said, putting her down and draping his arm round her.

'Just you two sparring,' Charity spluttered. 'Six years on and you're still at it.'

Beauty had been unevenly divided between them, their eyes, blond hair and height the only similarities. Toby's features were chiselled perfection, while Prue's face was flat and bland. His slender body was graceful, Prue's heavy and awkward. It seemed impossible these were the two children who had once passed for twins.

Over tea Charity was torn between delight and deepening unease. She loved the way Toby looked, his body as perfect as his face. Slim hips, wide shoulders, a hint of muscle showing through his thin shirt and jeans. His deep voice was beautifully modulated and he had the composure of a gentleman. Yet arrogance seeped out of him, he showed no real concern when she asked about his grandmother and no respect for anything or anyone.

Prue was almost as bad. She whined about the work she had to do, spoke of having no time to practise the piano or go out with her friends. Her grandmother's incontinence was 'disgusting', the housework 'not her job'. But Charity couldn't help being proud of how intelligent she was. She'd taken ten O levels, intended to stay on for As and then go to teacher training college.

Lou was right, they had been spoiled. No one, it seemed, had attempted to curb their selfishness or teach them compassion. While it was heartening to discover they had no fear of their uncle, Charity was disappointed they didn't seem to see this reunion with her as a momentous occasion. It was almost as if she was a distant relative who had dropped in unexpectedly. Their few questions were politely cool and Charity had the distinct impression Prue was already regretting her impulsive plea for help.

'You'd better take me to Uncle now,' Charity suggested eventually. She was dreading the meeting, but it had to come some time. 'I hope he won't be unpleasant.'

'He's always grumpy,' Toby said as he slung his arm round her shoulder. 'Just ignore it, that's what I do.'

As the three of them walked through the drawing room, Charity noticed that the fireplace was full of old ashes. Every surface was dusty. Prue had complained about housework, but to Charity it didn't look as if Studley had been touched for some time.

Outside Stephen's door, Charity braced herself,

silently repeating the promise she'd made to herself on the way here that she wouldn't let him upset her.

But at her first glimpse of Stephen and his book-lined room, all the grim memories came flooding back and her nerve almost failed her.

He was even more gross than she remembered. A shock of thick white hair emphasised his bloated face with its eyes cold pinpricks of blue almost embedded in folds of flesh. His sloppy wet lips were already curled in scorn and worse still was the sour odour that emanted from him. His shirt was grubby and creased, the grey trousers pinned up over his stumps were stained; even his hair needed cutting.

'How are you?' Charity said, disinclined to give him the title of uncle and resisting any desire to apologise for her presence.

'Couldn't resist the opportunity to come and poke your nose in things, eh!' he growled, looking her up and down scornfully.

His sarcasm made her forget how nervous she was.

'I have no wish to "poke my nose" in anything,' she said. 'I came because Prue begged me to.'

She was aware of Toby and Prue watching this exchange with interest, and she knew it was imperative that she keep the upper hand if she were not to lose face in their eyes.

'Well now you're here you'd better roll up your sleeves and get the place back in shape,' he said, wheeling his chair round as if to dismiss her.

Cold anger swept over her. 'Just a moment.' She caught hold of the handle on his chair, preventing him turning any further. 'I am not your lackey. I came to help in any way I can, but if you require a cleaning lady, you should ring an employment agency.'

'How dare you!' he roared, swelling up just the way she remembered. 'Who on earth do you think you are?'

'Charity Stratton,' she said, folding her arms defiantly and glowering back at him. 'I own an employment agency in London, I am also your niece. I'm not over-delighted at being related to you, but I assure you I'll be only too happy to call a taxi and get back to my office.'

Out of the corner of her eye she saw Toby and Prue's mouths drop open in astonishment and she knew she must hold her ground at all costs.

'I'm willing to go and see to my grandmother. Then I suggest I make a list of jobs which need doing and find you some new staff.'

Stephen's thick wet lips opened and closed like a fish, but she thought she saw a flicker of admiration in those chinks of blue glass which passed for eyes.

'Well?' she said, moving back to the door to push home her point. 'Do I go, or stay?'

'Stay, goddammit.' He turned his wheelchair round. 'Push off and do whatever!'

Back in the drawing room, Charity turned to her brother and sister. They were clearly astounded by her nerve.

'You were brave,' Prue gasped. 'I thought he was going to have a fit!'

Charity noted the way Toby slumped down on a settee, as if everything was now settled and his responsibilities were over.

'I shall expect you two to help,' she reminded them. 'I can find staff and a domestic agency to give this place a spring-clean. But I don't intend to do it alone.'

'Us?' Prue's flat face held shocked surprise.

'Yes, of course.' Charity looked at first one then the other. 'You live here, after all. Now you'd better take me up to Grandmother.'

'I can't.' Prue wrinkled her nose in distaste. 'It stinks

431

in her room. I was nearly sick this morning when I took her some tea.'

'She's an old lady and your grandmother, Prue,' Charity reprimanded her, shocked by her sister's callous attitude. 'How can you be so heartless?'

'Don't ask me,' Toby said quickly. 'I can't stomach it either.'

In a flash of blinding clarity, Charity realised why Lou was so reticent about discussing Toby and Prue. They weren't just spoiled, they were ruined!

'I can't believe what I'm hearing,' she said, flushing with shame for them. 'Go and clean up the kitchen, both of you. I'll go and see Grandmother alone. We'll discuss this later.'

A smell of urine and old age made Charity gag as she opened the door of the upstairs room. She remembered this wood-panelled room as gloomy but now it was dark with the curtains closed. At first glance she thought the half-tester bed was empty but a faint rustle indicated that her grandmother was not only there, but awake.

'Hallo, Grandmother,' she said, switching on the bedside light. 'It's Charity.'

The person lying in the big bed bore no resemblance to the pretty woman she remembered. Her face was so heavily lined she looked more like a chimpanzee than a human, wispy white hair clinging to her scalp. For a moment Charity understood Toby and Prue's reluctance to come in here.

'Charity?' The old lady's head turned to look at her, her eyes so faded there was almost no colour left. 'But Stephen won't allow her here.'

'It *is* me, Grandmother,' Charity said. 'Prue phoned and said you weren't well. I came to see what I could do.'

Charity thought her grandmother had become senile. She just lay there, staring.

'Can I sit you up?' Charity held her breath, slid her arm under the old lady's shoulder and lifted her. To her horror, the old woman was soaked right through, the smell of ammonia overpowering, and the body beneath the nightgown was like a bag of bones.

'I rang the bell but no one came.' Grandmother's wizened hands clutched at Charity's arm. 'I couldn't help it.'

'It doesn't matter,' Charity said, pity overtaking disgust. 'I'm here now and I'll soon get you sorted out.'

'I asked Prue to get me my sticks. I could get out if I had them. But she doesn't care.'

The acute embarrassment in her grandmother's voice proved she was in entire command of her faculties and Charity was shamed even further by her sister's neglect and indifference.

Washing and changing an old lady wasn't something Charity had any experience of. The only way she could handle the embarrassment of it was to pretend her grandmother was just a child. But as she sponged her almost skeletal body, rolling her on to a dry towel to wash her back and bottom, then helped her into a clean nightdress, she could see that a trained nurse was needed.

By supporting the old lady she managed to get her on to a chair; then she drew back the curtains, opened the window and stripped the bed. Fortunately a rubber sheet had been placed over the mattress, but the blankets were wet too.

'If I can find a commode could you manage to use that?' Charity asked.

The old lady nodded, pink with embarrassment.

Charity put a shawl round her shoulders.

'It's all right, Grandma,' she said gently. 'It isn't

433

your fault. Now I'll just go and find some dry bedding. Then I'll get you something to eat.'

'I don't know where my teeth or my glasses are.' Grandmother caught hold of Charity's hand, her faded eyes full of despair. 'I'm so sorry to be a nuisance.'

When Charity returned to the kitchen she found Prue standing at the sink, but aside from a few washed plates, no real inroads had been made on the mess. Toby was making a show of stacking up some saucepans but it was clear he'd only got up from his chair when he heard Charity coming.

Charity forgot all the sentimental daydreams she'd lapsed into on the train journey, all the sweet thoughts of being reunited with her brother and sister. They were two selfish, idle teenagers and at that moment she felt like striking them.

'I'm ashamed of you two,' she said angrily. 'How could you let *anyone*, let alone your grandmother, get in such a state? She was soaked, and she looks half starved.'

'You don't know what she's been like,' Prue whined. 'She doesn't eat the food I've given her. She rings her bell all day. Then she started peeing the bed.'

'She hasn't got her sticks, her glasses or even her teeth,' Charity snapped back. 'What can you expect? She's not senile, she's just frail. Haven't you two got any compassion?'

They both had the grace to look crestfallen. Toby shuffled from foot to foot. Prue began to cry.

Charity sighed.

'This isn't the way I planned our reunion,' she said. 'I want to sit and talk to both of you, to catch up on all I've missed. But we have an emergency here and you are both old enough to see that. Right now we have to pull together and get things done. Do you understand?'

They nodded.

Charity opened the cupboards and found a lone tin of tomato soup.

'I'll give Grandmother this,' she said. 'Now get the washing up done, then Toby can go to the village shop and get some groceries. What have you been living on?'

'Toast mostly.' Toby grinned. 'And fried eggs, that's all Prue can do. By the way, what are *we* having for lunch?'

'Toby!' Charity felt as if she might explode. 'For your information men also have the ability to cook, and clean. You won't even get dinner tonight unless you pull your weight. Now, is there any bread?'

Grandmother dunked the bread into the soup and sucked it down greedily as if she hadn't eaten in days. Charity had found her sticks in the drawing room, her teeth and glasses in the bathroom, and already the old lady looked a little better. Sunshine showed up the dust in the room, great balls of fluff lying on the polished bare boards, and a stickily unpleasant tray of old medicine bottles and spoons. But her first fear that the woman was seriously ill had faded: a few good meals and a little tender care was all she needed.

'I'm going to insist that Uncle Stephen hires a nurse for you both,' Charity said. She sat on the side of the bed, making a list of jobs that needed doing. 'Will you write a note for him and say you agree it's necessary?'

For a moment Charity thought her grandmother hadn't heard her. She swallowed down her soup, wiping the last piece of bread round the bowl, then leaned back on the pillows.

'Of course I will.' Her lined face broke into the first

smile since Charity had arrived. 'I'll tell him what a fool he's been, too. You always were the best of the bunch!'

By seven that evening Charity was exhausted. She'd been up and down the stairs to her grandmother umpteen times. She'd made ham sandwiches for Stephen for lunch, for which all she got for her pains was the barked demand: 'Where's the mustard?'

Between organising Toby to do the shopping, cleaning the kitchen, preparing a shepherd's pie for dinner and contacting cleaning and nursing agencies on the telephone, she'd had more than enough for one day.

But when Toby wheeled Uncle Stephen into the dining room for the meal she braced herself for further confrontation.

Stephen sat at the end of the table, Toby to his right, Charity and Prue on his left. Charity dished up the shepherd's pie silently, then passed round the vegetables.

Stephen was clearly very hungry, shovelling the food down with gusto. Toby and Prue were somewhat subdued. Charity had kept them busy all day, but she felt their silence had more to do with resentment than tiredness.

'This is good,' Stephen said, when his plate was nearly empty. 'Has my mother had any?'

'Yes I took hers up a while ago,' Charity said. 'I've bathed her, changed her and she's feeling a bit better. But she needs a nurse.'

'She doesn't need a nurse,' he said scornfully. 'She's as strong as an ox.'

'She isn't,' Charity said. 'She's very frail and she needs more attention than I can give her. Besides, a nurse could look after you too, Uncle. It isn't right to expect Toby and Prue to help you.'

During the afternoon Prue had admitted she would rather run away than face helping the district nurse with her uncle's weekly enema and bath. Toby was less disturbed by this and in fact did help Stephen dress and get him in and out of bed, but when he returned to school in September someone would have to take his place.

'Nonsense,' Stephen blustered, looking to both Prue and Toby. 'They don't mind helping me!'

'It isn't that they mind exactly.' Charity tried to be diplomatic. 'It just isn't right. I've got a nurse coming for an interview tomorrow.'

'Without consulting me?' Stephen roared, banging his cutlery down on the table.

'Yes, Uncle.' Charity put her knife and fork down. 'Furthermore I've also got a team of cleaners coming in. And I've put an advert in the local paper for permanent staff.'

'You've *what*?'

The only sound in the room was his rasping breath and for a moment Charity thought he was going to have a fit. He was swelling up, his face almost black with anger.

'You heard,' she said firmly, taking her grandmother's note from her pocket and sliding it across the table to him. 'Your mother is in agreement. Now it's up to you. But if you refuse, I shall just go back to London.'

As he added nothing more, Charity continued.

'Incidentally, the bill at the local shop hasn't been paid and I've ordered meat and vegetables to be delivered tomorrow, so I'll need the money for that. I'll stay and get everything organised if you wish. I leave it entirely up to you.'

Toby smirked, and glanced at his uncle. Prue looked scared.

Stephen inhaled noisily.

437

'You've got a cheek coming here and giving me orders.'

'Someone's got to.' Charity shrugged her shoulders and continued to eat her meal. 'I do run my own business these days, Uncle Stephen. I've become used to giving orders, not taking them.'

It felt sweet to get the better of him, especially knowing she could walk out if he put one foot wrong.

'What sort of permanent staff?' His tone was churlish now rather than hostile.

'You need a cook-cum-housekeeper,' she said calmly. 'And at least one daily woman for the cleaning.'

'And what will you be doing while all this is going on?' he spat at her.

'Making sure it's done properly,' she said calmly. 'And by the way, I think you should insist that Prue and Toby do more. I'm ashamed how lazy they are.'

'We aren't,' Toby and Prue said in unison.

Charity had thought long and hard before antagonising her brother and sister, but all day she'd become more and more aware of their shortcomings. They weren't small children any longer and she knew from experience with girls in her employ that gentleness was often taken as weakness.

'You are,' she insisted, noting their sullen expressions. Then, to Stephen: 'You've lied to Prue and Toby about me and overindulged them. I hope you're satisfied with what you've made them. Prue was happy to leave your mother lying in a wet bed and Toby is as arrogant and chauvinistic as you. I think you three deserve one another.'

She got up from the table and collected their plates, leaving them speechless. 'I shall leave the moment things are sorted here,' she said in a low voice. 'Meanwhile I'd be grateful for your co-operation.'

*

'I'm sorry, Charity.'

Charity turned in surprise at her sister's voice. She was standing in the doorway, her shoulders slumped miserably. 'I've made things worse for you, haven't I?'

'I'm not concerned about whether Stephen likes or dislikes me,' Charity said. 'I came here for one reason only: the chance to be reunited with you and Toby. But as much as I care for you both, I can't ignore things that are terribly wrong.'

Prudence moved closer to Charity, dropping her head on to her shoulder. 'Are we such a disappointment to you?' she asked.

Charity put her arms round her sister and held her tight.

'No of course not,' she said. 'But for six years I've carried the picture in my head of two small, sweet children. It takes some getting used to finding you've grown up, that's all. I don't like this feeling that we are strangers. We were once so close.'

'We can be like that again,' Prue murmured.

Charity tilted Prue's face up to hers.

'Yes, we can, if we work at it,' she said, kissing her sister's nose. 'It's been a long, tiring day, and tomorrow will probably be even worse. But if we talk and work together, we'll find the way back to where we left off.'

'I'm still glad I phoned you,' Prue said, tears glistening in her eyes.

'Not as glad as I was.' Charity hugged her tightly. 'Now help me with the washing up and you can tell me all about school and your friends.'

The next day the house was buzzing with noise, two vacuum cleaners going at once and voices calling to one another above them. Six women and one man had arrived to do the spring-cleaning and they were systematically working their way through the rooms.

Curtains had been taken down and collected by a dry-cleaning company, rugs had been carried outside for a beating in the garden. The whole house smelt of cleaning fluids: bleach, disinfectant, polish and carpet shampoo.

In the kitchen one woman stood on steps washing down the walls, tutting at the congealed grease while another woman scrubbed out the cupboards.

'I'm afraid the house is in an uproar,' Charity said as she ushered the nurse sent from the agency into the winter parlour which hadn't been used for years. She had moved Grandmother into Prue's room while her own was cleaned, and to Charity's surprise she found it tidied. Uncle Stephen was skulking in his room, still claiming that all this was unnecessary, but he'd agreed to be taken out into the garden later while his room was tackled.

'I'm Dawn Giles.' The woman took the offered chair opposite Charity and pulled a sheaf of letters out of her large handbag. 'These are references from all my old patients. As you will see, I've been in private nursing for many years.'

Charity felt an instant liking for this nurse, though she couldn't have said why. She was a big woman, with a round, plain face and dull brown hair cut in a severe, unflattering bob to her jaw level. She wore a navy blue dress and jacket, which, like her hair, did her no favours, but there was a kindly look about her and her big arms suggested physical strength.

'I'll be honest,' Charity said. 'My uncle is an amputee and a difficult, bad-tempered man. My grandmother is just old. I can't stay here and look after them, I have a business of my own in London, and my younger brother and sister haven't been used to doing a hand's turn. I'm telling you this now so you aren't under any illusions about the job. I am advertising for domestic help and I'll stay here until I get the right people.'

Charity went on to explain what she believed was needed.

'I haven't had any contact with my uncle in years until yesterday,' she admitted. 'Medically I don't know what's required, but he or the district nurse can tell you that. I'll show you the room I thought would be suitable for you if you decide to come. Then perhaps you can have a chat with the colonel.'

It was almost half-past eleven when Charity took Nurse Giles in to see Stephen, after introducing her to Grandmother and showing the nurse her room. Around ten minutes later she was surprised to see the woman wheeling Stephen outside in his chair.

They were gone for over an hour, and when Charity went out later to look for them she was delighted to find them in the walled garden talking earnestly.

This garden, which had been very neglected, was the one that had been restored in the manner of an Italian garden, with brick paths, pergolas, a couple of stone benches and a small fountain.

Charity didn't interrupt. The nurse and her uncle appeared to be getting along very well, so she went back in to prepare some lunch.

'Charity!' Stephen's voice boomed out from the hall just as she was laying the table.

'Miss Giles is coming back later today,' he said once Charity reached him in the hall. 'Get her room ready.'

Charity overlooked the curt order, she was so pleased he'd agreed to a nurse.

'She seems nice,' she said cautiously. 'Your mother liked her too.'

'Sensible, no-nonsense type,' he said, wheeling his chair back into the drawing room. 'Have they finished messing around in my room?'

'Yes, Uncle,' she said. 'But lunch is nearly ready. Would you like a cold drink or anything first?'

He turned his chair back to face her.

Stephen really did like Nurse Giles, and she had passed on to him how much Charity had done for his mother, but he didn't like the feeling of losing control in his own house.

'Don't try to be too clever,' he said, his eyes almost disappearing into folds of flesh. 'I've got you taped.'

'What's that supposed to mean?' Again her hackles rose at his rudeness.

'Trying to worm your way in,' he snapped. 'It won't wash, though. I know what you are.'

'I know what you are too,' she said coldly. 'And believe me, I've no desire to worm my way anywhere near you.'

'I don't want you to leave.' Grandmother's small wrinkled face looked plaintive. She sat in a button-back chair by the open window in the drawing room, the cup of tea Charity had brought her in her hands.

'I'll stay till after the weekend,' Charity replied. 'But I'm needed at the office and everything's running smoothly here now.'

Charity's week at Studley was an exhausting, exasperating one. Scores of women had turned up in answer to her advertisement, but most of them had been more interested in getting a glimpse of the inside of the house than in working there. But finally Charity had taken on Margaret, a plump, jolly middle-aged woman, as cook, and her cousin Pat to do the cleaning. As both of them were local there was no call for them to live in and already they were getting on well with Nurse Giles and Grandmother.

But getting staff and having the domestic agency spring-clean the house was the easy part. Acting as a buffer between Stephen and the new help, working out duties and making Toby and Prue see they couldn't lie around and do nothing for themselves, was the most onerous.

There had been moments of delight being back with Toby and Prue, but there were many more times when Charity was tempted to just walk away. Toby was easier. Despite his arrogance he could be very charming. He wanted to know about Charity's life, her friends and work. He tagged along with her, helping her clean silver and turn out cupboards cheerfully, and he was very good at acting as a mediator between her and Stephen.

Prue was more difficult. She resented being asked to do anything she considered 'servants' work' and her pointed, snobbish remarks made Charity cringe. She had an inflated idea of her own importance, constantly boasting of her marks at school, how much the teachers liked her and how talented she was. In fact she played the piano only passably, with no passion, and her dancing lessons had given her no grace or poise.

At times, when Charity looked at Toby and Prue, she felt their sexes should be reversed. Prue, had she been a boy, would be ideal material for the role Stephen had in mind for Toby. She had the strength of character to be an officer in the army, the determination and the qualities of leadership. Toby, with his beauty, charm and warmth, would be far more comfortable in a more feminine role. He took interest in all the old family treasures, he liked people more than his sister did and he was far more diplomatic.

But though Charity had made many observations about her brother and sister, discovered a great deal about their life in the past six years, it was disappointing to find she couldn't get close to either of them. It was as if a transparent membrane separated them: she could see and hear and touch them, but until she could find a way to break that membrane, they would always be aloof.

'I suspect Nurse Giles is a maneater,' Grandmother said to Charity. 'But time will tell, and you're right, she is making him more pleasant.'

Charity was tempted to ask the old lady to enlarge on this observation, but out of loyalty to the woman who had the patience to wash and set Grandmother's hair the previous day, she decided against it.

'She's a good nurse,' Charity said firmly. 'You look so much better since she's been here.'

Grandmother's hair was like a fluffy white halo, and her lined face had a pink glow again.

'I feel better.' She sighed deeply. 'But Toby worries me,' she whispered, as if afraid they'd be overheard. 'He's very charming, but there's something not quite right. He's too sure of himself, too ruthless for such a young man and he's dishonest.'

The old lady dropped her eyes. 'He tells lies as easily as he breathes. I even suspect him of stealing from me. Prue is far from perfect. She's a snob, selfish and very greedy. But she's honest and deep down I know she's a good girl. But Toby!'

Charity thought this over for a moment. Grandmother clearly loved both children; the tender way she looked at them was enough to prove that. She was one for making sweeping remarks about people, like the one about Nurse Giles being a maneater, but Charity had noticed she was remarkably astute.

'I'll try and talk to him.' Charity got up from her seat and bent down to tuck a blanket round her grandmother's knees. Don't you worry about the children, you've done a good job as their granny and they love you. Now why don't you have a little snooze before tea?'

The old lady smiled, reassured. 'I want to give you something,' she said.

Charity stared in surprise as her grandmother pulled out a small blue velvet drawstring bag from the pocket of her dress and tipped a pair of earrings on to her lap.

They were brilliant blue stones that sparkled in the sunshine. Three stones in all, the largest almost as big as a sixpence, intricately suspended from an old gold clip.

Even though Charity had no real knowledge of jewellery, it was obvious they were extremely valuable.

'They are sapphires,' Grandmother said, holding them up to the light. 'My mother gave them to me when I married. I always intended to give them to Gwen, but circumstances prevented me.'

'I can't take those!' Charity gasped.

'I might not be here when you marry,' the old lady said as she held them up to Charity's cheek. 'They go with your eyes and they never belonged to the Pennycuick family: that's enough reason to give them to you.'

It was their background that weakened Charity. She clipped them on to her ears and smiled down at her grandmother. 'How do I look?' she said, sweeping her hair up on top of her head.

'Like a duchess.' The old lady smiled. 'Now wear them with pride. My grandfather gave them to Grandmother on her wedding day.'

Charity looked at herself in the mirror above the fireplace. She loved them. They were dainty, they did match her eyes and they made her feel wonderful.

'I can't take them.' She took them off reluctantly and held them out to her grandmother. 'They are too valuable, I'd be afraid of losing them. Besides, Uncle Stephen wouldn't like it.'

445

'Nonsense,' Grandmother snapped. 'I told you why I want you to have them. They suit you just as they did me and my mother before that. My son will have everything else when I go, but he has no right to these.'

Chapter Twenty-Three

Charity walked into the kitchen to find Margaret filling Kilner jars with gooseberries on the kitchen table.

'Can I help?' she asked. 'I'm at a bit of a loose end, Toby and Prue have gone off to the riding stables and I'm not going back to London till this evening.'

'You can pour in the sugared water, if you like.' Margaret wiped her forehead with the back of her hand. 'But you should get on out in the sunshine, you'll be stuck behind your desk tomorrow.'

Although Margaret had been in her new job for only a few days she had already made a great many observations about the residents in the household. She was a lively and energetic fifty-year-old, her own two sons were grown up and recently emigrated to Canada, her husband Tom retired. She had already decided this was a position she could be happy in: she liked to keep busy and care for people, but more than that she'd taken these motherless children to her heart.

Charity lifted the big enamel jug and began to pour the liquid over the fruit. She liked Margaret. In many ways she reminded her of Mrs Cod at Bowes Court, with the same kind of brisk efficiency and jovial warmth. A short, stout woman with iron-grey permed hair, she had a youthful, unlined face. Although she waddled rather than walked and her big white apron emphasised her plump body, she accomplished her workload with remarkable calmness and speed. The cake tins were full of delicious homemade cakes and biscuits, and now she was looking ahead to the winter with bottled fruit. She'd even made the kitchen look more cheery with geraniums on the windowsill.

Margaret guessed that Charity had something on her mind and she was concerned that a girl of only twenty-one seemed to take on so much responsibility.

'Don't you go worrying about anything,' she said. 'Pat and me have got the house sorted now, and Nurse Giles is a brick.'

'I think you should ask Prue and Toby to help out sometimes,' Charity said.

Margaret glanced at Charity. Her blonde hair was so shiny and silky, her pale blue minidress the height of fashion, yet this pretty young girl seemed so much older than her years. She and Dawn Giles were puzzled about why the colonel had something against her: both of them would be proud to have her as a daughter, let alone a niece.

'I'll give them a few cookery lessons,' Margaret replied. 'Then they'll be able to cope on my day off.'

'I hope you can manage when James arrives later this month.' Charity smiled. 'He's only eight and I'm a bit concerned Toby and Prue will leave him to his own devices too much.'

'I'm well used to little boys.' Margaret's face glowed with pleasure at the prospect. 'He can come in here and play with a bit of pastry and things. If the other two had had a bit of that they wouldn't be such strangers to a kitchen now. But maybe you could come down for a weekend then and see him for yourself?'

'I haven't had an invitation yet.' Charity raised one eyebrow, knowing Margaret understood the situation very well.

Margaret lifted the loaded jars on to a tray ready to put it into the oven, then glanced up at the clock. 'It's nearly time for elevenses,' she said. 'Why don't you go and have a chat now with Mrs Pennycuick? I'll bring you in some coffee in a minute.'

As Charity walked into the drawing room she saw her grandmother had nodded off in her chair by the window. She looked so sweet and small, her head resting on the winged chair-back, her glasses sliding down her nose and the unread newspaper folded on her lap.

Charity stood at one of the long windows looking out, a feeling of peace filling her. A gap in the bushes by the railings on the far side of the drive gave a view over the fields right across to Beckley. It had rained constantly over the weekend, but now the sun had come out again and everything looked shiny and new. A couple of birds were bathing in a puddle on the drive and Morris the gardener was clipping the yew hedge, his pipe dangling from the corner of his mouth.

Stephen was listening to the morning story on his wireless in his room. Nurse Giles was out in the laundry. The hum of the vacuum cleaner suggested that Pat was cleaning Grandmother's room.

It was disappointing that Toby and Prue had scooted off so early this morning. Charity had hoped they would spend her last day with her, but they had been cooped up the whole weekend.

Charity felt content, even sorry to be leaving. Stephen had come round enough to offer a little grudging respect. Grandmother and she had become close. It would take a little longer perhaps to really find Prue and Toby again, but the first steps had been taken and Charity didn't think the door to Studley was going to close behind her for good when she left tonight.

Glancing round, she noticed her grandmother's nose was running and she moved over to her, taking a handkerchief from her pocket to wipe it.

But as she put her hand gently on the old lady's

cheek, the coldness of her skin sent a shudder of alarm down Charity's spine.

'Granny!' she said, caressing the old wrinkled face. 'Granny, you're cold.'

She knew at once, even though she'd never seen death before. It was no chill from a draught. Her grandmother was dead, even if she looked as if she was in a peaceful sleep.

She ran to her uncle's room next door, barging in without knocking.

He was sitting by the wireless, resting his head on one hand, his elbow on the arm of his chair.

'Uncle Stephen,' she cried, her eyes welling with tears. 'It's Grandmother. I think she's dead.'

He sat up straight, eyes widening in shock, his face blanching. Charity caught hold of his chair, turned it and pushed him towards the door.

'Get Nurse Giles, you fool!' he yelled at her, as they reached the drawing room, Charity propelling his chair towards his mother. 'Now!'

Charity had wished Stephen a thousand punishments in the past. But never this.

She heard his bellow of pain before she got to the hall and looked back to see him bent over in his chair, his head in his mother's lap, arms trying to enfold her small body.

Nurse Giles could do nothing but confirm what Charity already knew. They drew the heavy curtains between them, then Charity phoned the doctor while the nurse tried to prise the sobbing Stephen from his mother's body.

It had been eleven when Charity found her grandmother but time seemed to stand still from that moment. She remembered Prue and Toby returning from the stables on their bikes, seeing their flushed faces blanch and dissolve into tears as she broke the sad news.

'But I went in to see her this morning, and she was fine then,' Prue sobbed. 'We shouldn't have gone out riding.'

'She asked me to get her some chocolate,' Toby said, covering his face with his hands as if he didn't want anyone to see him cry. 'I forgot about it.'

'Don't blame yourselves for anything,' Charity said soothingly, herself crying for the old lady who had become dearer to her each day. 'The doctor said the heart attack struck her while she was asleep, she never knew a moment's pain.'

Over and above the sounds of Toby and Prue's grief was the terrifying noise of Stephen's anguish. Wailing, sobbing and incoherent ramblings to Nurse Giles from the drawing room seemed to fill the whole house, echoing eerily around the stone walls of the hall and sending cold shivers down Charity's spine.

'I'm so sorry uncle.' Charity lay one hand on Stephen's shoulder. The undertakers had carried Grandmother through to the cold, still room just across the passage from Stephen's room.

Charity wished she could do more to comfort Stephen. Nurse Giles had helped him on to his Chesterfield and given him a sedative, but he looked crumpled and old, his face yellow in the gloom. Yet even though she felt his loss and shared in his grief she couldn't hold him, or even find the right words.

Nothing much in Stephen's room had changed in six years. Charity's eyes were drawn to the mock battle scene, and she remembered him shouting at his mother just a few days earlier for knocking over a couple of lead soldiers.

'I've got nothing now.' His large head sunk to his

chest, all the power gone from his voice. 'I'm all alone.'

'No you aren't,' Charity said gently. 'You've got the children still, and your mother was so old and frail. Have a little sleep now. I'll come back later to see how you are.'

'No one understands,' he wept, great tears of self-pity rolling down his fat cheeks. 'I thought we had years together yet. I wanted to get the house restored so she could see it.'

'She was tired,' Charity soothed him. 'I think she was ready to go.'

She leaned forward and kissed his forehead, the closest she'd ever got to him.

'I'm here to take care of things,' she said. 'Ring your bell if you need anything.'

It was four in the afternoon, but it felt much later. Silence pressed in on Charity as she made her way through the house to the kitchen. Nurse Giles had gone to the village to collect a prescription, and Margaret had gone home for a couple of hours. Charity assumed Toby and Prue were up in their rooms, but she was too wrung out and tense to join them. She needed fresh air.

Charity slumped down on a bench just outside the kitchen door with a glass of orange squash, a hundred and one thoughts crowding into her mind. Someone ought to phone Lou and Geoff to prepare James. Could Rita manage the office alone for another week? Would Stephen pull himself together in the next day or two enough to make the funeral arrangements?

A giggle from the walled garden made her look up in surprise, but just as she was about to go and investigate, Toby's voice rung out clearly.

'She'd better have left us something after all the fetching and carrying we did for her.'

'I hope it's money. I don't want some mouldy old bit of jewellery,' Prue said, just as clearly. 'Trust the old bag to snuff it just as I'd planned to have Janice to come and stay.'

Charity stood up, stunned by such callousness.

'Let's hope the legless ogre dies of shock too,' Toby said. 'Just think, this would be all mine.'

Charity's blood ran cold. Just a couple of hours ago they had seemed inconsolable. Now their grand-mother's death was an irritation. They had no love for anyone but themselves.

Grandmother's whispered warnings about Toby and Prue came sharply into focus. Charity blushed with shame at their ingratitude and heartlessness.

She walked silently to the archway of the walled garden, anger surging through her. As she looked in she could see them both seated on the low wall surrounding the small fountain, their bare feet in the water. Somehow their long sun-tanned limbs, bright hair and smiling faces added further insult to that caring old lady.

All around Charity was evidence of what Stephen and his mother had done with these two in mind. The restored garden, redecoration, central heating. No one could deny these children had been fortunate, at least in the material sense. The least they could do was show some respect.

'How could you say such wicked things, she said in a low voice. 'I'm ashamed of you.'

Prue had the grace to blush and leap to her feet, but Toby just turned his head towards her and smiled lazily.

'You know what they say about people who listen at keyholes? You probably heard it all wrong, anyway.'

'I didn't get anything wrong,' Charity said, tempted to slap their faces. 'That old lady loved you both and

453

I thought you loved her. She isn't even cold yet and you speak of what she'll leave you.'

'Oh so holy, aren't we?' Toby sneered, standing up and fastening his open shirt. 'You only crept round Gran to see what you could get out of her. You've always hated Uncle Stephen and you're jealous of us.'

Charity's knees gave way at the malice in his voice. She stumbled to the stone bench and slumped down, tears springing to her eyes. For years she'd worried about these two. Each birthday noted, cards bought that she could never send. Now she realised they were as lost to her as Daniel was.

'Oh, I get it.' Prue's snooty voice shook her still further. 'You're scared you'll be out on your ear now Gran's dead.'

'Get out of my sight,' Charity hissed between her teeth. 'I don't give a damn about this place. All I cared about was you two and James, but I can see you two at least are a lost cause. You are despicable.'

They ran away then, and Charity sobbed into her hands, too overwhelmed by anger and desolation to move.

She was tempted just to pack her bag and leave. But for Grandmother's sake she had to stay and give her a peaceful funeral, without further gossip to shame her. She owed her that much.

Stephen was calmer the next morning. He called Charity into his room to discuss the funeral, which he wanted to arrange for the following Monday, and asked her help in contacting relatives and friends.

Charity didn't know whether his apparent recovery was due to Nurse Giles's patience with him last night, or whether it was because he'd discovered the rift between the children and her and guessed that Charity would soon be gone for good. But whatever the reason, he was remarkably benign and he actually thanked her, brusquely, for her help.

There was enough work to do in the next two days to avoid any close contact with Toby and Prue and she only spoke to them when necessary. Prue kept looking at her older sister with a kind of nervous pleading, and Charity felt she wanted to apologise, but her own heart remained stony.

Early on Thursday Charity went to London to spend a day in the office with Rita going over some urgent problems, and she didn't return until Friday. Toby was waiting in the hall as she got out of the taxi. He was suspiciously red-eyed.

'Please come up to my room to talk,' he pleaded with her. 'You don't know how bad I feel.'

'You feel bad,' Charity shrugged, walking right past him. 'Perhaps you should consider my feelings.'

He chased after her, talking all the time.

'We're both so sorry. We didn't think what we were saying. We didn't really mean any of it, especially the nasty things we said about you.'

A day back in London had mellowed Charity. Lou and Geoff were bringing James down on Monday and she had no wish to jeopardise her future relationship with him. Besides, talking to Toby alone might be a good thing, bearing in mind what Grandmother had said about him.

'OK,' she said, stopping at his door. 'I'll hear you out, though it's more than you deserve.'

Toby's room was in the Tudor part of the house, a spacious, low-ceilinged room overlooking the front drive. Stephen had clearly spared no expense making his heir comfortable. Charity sat down on the bed, with Toby cross-legged on the floor in front of her. He looked very young tonight, in shorts and a T-shirt, his arms and legs tanned a deep gold and a sorrowful expression in his eyes.

'What you said isn't really important,' Charity told him, after Toby had tried in a clumsy way to explain himself. 'The important thing is *why* you said it.'

Toby looked blank.

'Well, there must be some deep-rooted resentment, against me, Grandmother and Stephen,' Charity went on. 'Now let's get to the bottom of that, shall we?'

'I didn't resent Gran in any way,' he said, dropping his eyes from her. 'I was very fond of her.'

'Well, that leaves Stephen and me,' she said. 'What have you got against me? No one says such spiteful things as you did without meaning them, at least in part.'

Toby shrugged his shoulders. 'I suppose I did in a way. You came here ordering us around, making Gran like you.'

'I didn't, Toby. I came because I wanted to see you both again and someone had to take charge. Of course I wanted Gran to like me, she was my grandmother too.

Toby looked surly, his lips curling. 'You've got all the freedom.'

Charity almost laughed aloud. 'Freedom?'

'Yes, you can do what you like, go where you want.'

Charity shook her head at him. 'Toby, when I was your age I was scouring pots at Bowes Court. Totally alone and often frightened. I've had to work really hard to get where I am now. And I don't feel very free.'

'But you can choose what you want to do,' he insisted, looking up at her. 'I've got to go Wellington, then Sandhurst, then take a commission in the army. I can't choose anything.'

'What would you rather do, then?' she asked.

'I don't know.' He shrugged his shoulders. 'It's not that I'm against the idea of the army. I just feel I'm being pushed into it.'

'No one can force you to go in the army,' she said firmly. 'Not even Uncle Stephen, and you've got another couple of years at Wellington anyway. There isn't a great deal of point agonising over it when you don't know what you'd like instead, is there?'

'I suppose not.' Toby half smiled.

'What's more important is how you feel about people. How do you feel about Uncle Stephen, for instance?'

'I don't know,' he said, looking at his bare feet. 'I wish he was the way I tell people he is.'

Charity smiled. 'A sort of Douglas Bader?'

'I suppose so,' Toby smirked.

Charity digested this. 'What about our parents?' she asked. 'Do you tell people about them?'

He shook his head violently. 'I don't want anyone to know my father was a weird preacher. I only tell people about Uncle Stephen and Studley.'

In a flash of insight Charity understood. Toby had tried to wipe out all that went before, and created a glorious background for himself. Four generations of Pennycuicks in the Rifle Brigade, a dashing, brave and indulgent colonel uncle. A mansion and a fortune he would one day inherit. But an adolescent boy with the trauma of being orphaned behind him needed more than a romantic fantasy if he was to grow straight and true. He needed love and support. With only a bitter, manipulative man like Stephen to guide him, it was little wonder Toby's outlook on the world was becoming twisted.

'I don't tell many people about the past either,' she said gently. 'When people see my nice clothes and my business they might think I had rich parents and went to a good school. It's OK to let people form their own impression, but you mustn't tell lies about it There's nothing to be ashamed of in our background.'

457

Toby lifted his eyes to Charity's and the coldness chilled her. 'You know that's not true.'

Charity flushed, and her heart began to beat faster. Did he know what their father did to her? Is that what he meant?

'I know Father was very stern, sometimes cruel,' she stammered. He couldn't know, surely? He was only nine at the time of the fire – he would surely have said something before? 'OK, so we were scared of him and Mother was always ill. We were also desperately poor. But by the time you get to my age you find none of that matters.'

'Do you tell people about me?' Toby asked.

'Of course I do.' She laughed in relief, now her moment of panic had passed. 'I show people your photographs, talk about you all the time. When I get back to London I'll be boring everyone to death with how handsome and clever you are.'

'Will you forgive me now?' he asked, moving nearer to her and putting one hand on her knee. 'You see, I couldn't bear it if you went away and never saw us again.'

'Oh Toby.' She reached out and cupped his face in both hands. 'I might not like you and Prue all the time, but I'll always love you. I practically brought you both up. Love is like one of those trees out there in the drive, there for ever. We might have lots of disagreements, but when the roots go down as far as ours do, you can't kill it.'

'Will you come and see me at school next year?' Toby begged her with his eyes. 'Wear something beautiful so all the boys turn and stare?'

'Wild horses wouldn't keep me away,' she smiled. 'But I want you to promise me you'll be honest from now on. No more lies. Admit to your friends that your uncle is a crusty old buzzard and half the house is closed up. You'll feel better without so much pressure, and people will like you more.'

'She just looks as if she's asleep,' Charity said to Stephen as she stood by the open coffin looking down at her grandmother.

It was Saturday. All week people had trooped in to pay their last respects to Isobel Pennycuick, Stephen had spent many hours alone with her, but Charity had avoided coming in here until now.

She felt a little foolish that she'd been frightened of this moment. Grandmother's face seemed to have lost some of its deep lines, and there was a tranquil expression on her lips as if she'd died having a happy dream. Charity bent to kiss her cheek, and though her skin was icy cold, it wasn't an unpleasant experience.

'She had a good innings.' Stephen sighed. 'At least she didn't have to suffer pain and she kept all her faculties.'

'Would you like to be alone with her for a bit?' Charity said gently. This was the first time Stephen had really spoken to her as an equal and even in such sad circumstances it felt good. But she had a feeling he wanted to cry and she had no wish to prevent it.

'No, take me back to the library,' he said. 'Nurse Giles is waiting. I can come in again tomorrow.'

As Charity wheeled him back towards his room he turned his head round to her.

'Get my mother's jewel box,' he said, his customary brusqueness back. 'She kept it somewhere in her wardrobe. Prue probably knows where.'

It took Prue some time to find the box, which had been hidden beneath a pile of old nightdresses. When Charity got back to Stephen, he was in his dressing-gown and nightshirt. Nurse Giles was just leaving.

'I'll be back in half an hour,' she said, giving Stephen an almost affectionate pat on the cheek. She smiled at Charity, then swept out carrying some clothes.

Grandmother's remark about Dawn Giles being a maneater came back to Charity. Maybe it was the swing of her hips and her big breasts pushing out her starched apron, but there was something seductive and very worldly about her. She had been cloistered with Stephen a great deal since Grandmother died and the fact he'd rallied round the morning after his mother's death, becoming almost polite, was odd. But Charity wasn't concerned if the nurse had some secret way of making him more amenable. In fact, she applauded it.

'Here we are, Uncle,' she said, putting the box on Stephen's desk. 'By the way, Grandmother did tell you about giving me the earrings, didn't she?'

'She mentioned it.' He looked up at Charity and frowned.

'You don't mind, do you?' She was anxious now.

'I would rather she had consulted me first since they are very valuable. But they were hers to dispose of, if that was her wish,' he said looking away from her.

He unlocked the box and opened it before Charity had left the room and her eyes nearly popped out of her head. The top velvet tray was full of rings and as he lifted it out, she saw a layer of earrings and brooches.

'Some of these are three hundred years old,' Stephen said, glancing round at her hovering in the doorway. 'Passed down through the family.'

'May I see?' Charity asked. She had a feeling he wanted to share them and she was curious.

Stephen lifted out the final tray and put his hand in, bringing out a ruby necklace. 'This one is worth a king's ransom,' he said.

Charity gasped. It was an intricate web of gold

460

with rubies suspended from it the size and colour of pomegranate seeds.

'It's fantastic,' she said, moving closer. 'I can't believe Grandmother had that just lying in her wardrobe. You should put it in a bank vault, Uncle.'

'I don't need you to tell me how to look after my valuables,' he snapped, instantly severing any idea she might have had that they were beginning to establish a rapport. 'Now off with you, and make sure you look after those earrings.'

It rained the whole weekend, but though it should have been a sad and difficult time, for Charity it was almost joyful. She, Toby and Prue sat up in Toby's room playing board games and talking, and for the first time since Charity came to Studley she felt as if their defences were breaking down. As the weekend progressed she began to see Toby and Prue's characters unfolding. Prue was ambitious, but she also had a gentler, romantic side which sat uneasily with her plain appearance. Toby was far more vulnerable; he knew he wasn't as clever as Prue so he compensated by laying on charm with a trowel. His looks and his sporting ability had pushed him into the role of devil-may-care rabble-rouser at school, but underneath, Charity knew he wasn't sure of himself at all.

Yet despite everything, both Prue and Toby loved James. They spoke of him with pride and affection, getting out photographs and showing her his sweet, childish letters. Whatever else might be slightly awry in their lives, James was clearly not a cause for concern. They were looking forward to seeing him again, made long-term plans for his holiday with them later in the month, and to Charity that made up for a great deal.

Despite everyone's predictions that the rain would go on right through Monday, it was a beautiful day.

Charity had risen at six to get the food prepared for tea after the funeral service, but as an early mist slowly drifted away the sun came out and dried up the puddles. Now the weather seemed more suitable for a wedding.

The cypress and oak trees on the drive had never been more beautiful; each flower seemed more brilliant. Even the birdsong sounded like a massed choir paying their last respects to the old lady who had loved this place.

Prue and Toby were unusually co-operative, Prue helping Margaret in the kitchen, Toby rushing around finding extra chairs for the mourners.

Lou and Geoff arrived with James soon after eleven and although Charity couldn't give them the sort of joyous welcome she would have like to, she soon managed to get them out into the walled garden.

'I couldn't say what I wanted to with Stephen about,' she said, looking at James with shining eyes.

She could hardly believe this was the baby she had once done everything for. An eight-year-old boy in long grey trousers and a school blazer, with a wide grin and two missing front teeth.

'You're so big, James,' she said, wanting to hug him fiercely but afraid he would reject someone he didn't remember.

'Is this really my sister?' He looked from Lou to Geoff for confirmation. 'The one you tell me about?'

'That's her all right,' Geoff grinned. 'Pretty enough for you?'

Geoff and Lou looked odd in their sombre dark clothes. It was the first time Charity could recall seeing Lou in high-heeled shoes. Her red hair was restrained under a black hat that made her look much older. Geoff had even less hair, and he'd trimmed his beard hard back. But his eyes still twinkled.

'These are my first pair of long trousers,' James said

462

gleefully. 'Uncle Geoff says I have to lift them at the knees when I kneel in church. Auntie put a sixpence in the pocket too and I don't have to put it in the collection.'

Charity was lost for words. There was so much she wanted to ask, but all she could do was look at James. He was very like Toby and it was clear he was going to be tall too.

'Why have you got tears in your eyes?' James asked, looking up at Charity in surprise.

'Because I'm so pleased to see you again,' she said, with a wobbly smile. His mouth was still plump and childlike, cheeks soft and rosy. 'Can I hug you?'

'Course you can.' He threw himself at her with the happy enthusiasm of a child who'd known nothing but love and demonstrative affection all his life.

She felt his arms around her waist, his head resting on her shoulder, and she didn't know whether to laugh or cry she felt so happy.

'Come and see us as soon as you get back to London,' Lou said, smiling broadly. 'We can't talk properly here today, everything will be a bit stilted.'

Geoff grinned. 'You look marvellous, Charity,' he said. 'We're so proud of you. Everything will be different now, you'll see.'

The funeral service was more like a joyous tribute than a mournful goodbye. The sun peeped in at the small church windows, dancing on the flowers and polished wood. Everyone for miles around had come. Wealthy landowners standing shoulder to shoulder with shopkeepers, farm labourers and villagers. The vicar's words about Isobel Pennycuick were uplifting; she had been a great favourite of his. Even when the coffin was lowered into the grave on top of the brigadier's, the brilliant sunshine made it seem more poignant than sad.

Around twenty people came back to the house and the atmosphere verged on the jovial as relations who rarely met caught up with news of family events. Charity kept herself busy plying people with tea, sandwiches and cake, one ear pricked up to hear the gossip.

Nurse Giles bustled into the room bringing a tray of drinks, her large breasts quivering beneath her dress like two large blancmanges.

'I wouldn't say no to a bit of nursing from her myself,' Charity overheard one old gent say to another. She had to hide her face so people wouldn't see her struggling not to laugh.

Charity sat alone in the dining room the next morning and poured a cup of tea for herself. Her packed case was in the hall and Margaret had informed her that Toby and Prue had both gone out riding, but would be back before she left. It had been wonderful to see James, Lou and Geoff again, and as they'd left yesterday they'd urged her to come and see them in London soon.

But Charity was anxious now about saying goodbye to Stephen. He had been very upset last night and as she cleared away in the drawing room she'd heard him sobbing like a child in his room.

The dining room door opened and Nurse Giles came in. As she saw Charity she smiled.

'All ready to leave?' she asked.

'Have you got time for some tea?' Charity asked. 'I wanted to ask how you think Uncle Stephen is.'

The nurse sat down heavily beside Charity. 'He's feeling a bit poorly,' she said. 'Too much whisky and feeling sorry for himself.'

'Perhaps I should stay on till tomorrow?' Charity asked.

'You go.' Nurse Giles tossed her head, in a gesture

that said Stephen's temper wouldn't improve if Charity stayed. 'Don't you worry, Miss Charity, I'll soon get him settled down.'

Charity found herself studying the nurse as they drank tea and chatted. Dawn Giles was a very plain woman with a pale moon face which wasn't helped by straight hair cut off abruptly at her jawline. Her eyes were pale brown, her nose a little too big. Her mouth was her only redeeming feature: well-shaped lips curled up at the corners, giving the impression she was smiling. Yet there was something vivid about her that seemed to come from within, and Charity wished she'd taken the trouble to discover more about this intriguing woman.

'I'm nervous about saying goodbye,' Charity admitted.

Dawn Giles looked at Charity appraisingly for a moment, then patted her hand.

'He's just an old windbag,' she said, dropping her voice. 'But for all that, I'm intending to stay because there aren't many nice comfortable jobs around like this for a woman of my age and circumstances. But you, Miss Charity, you've got the world at your feet, if you don't think I'm being too personal.'

'Not at all,' Charity said, a little taken aback.

'Well take a bit of advice from a woman who's been around. Think of yourself, dear, not those kids, and not him. Get back to your business and your own life. I'll sort your uncle out.'

'I suppose I'm scared he'll slam the door in my face,' Charity said. She guessed Nurse Giles must know her position. 'Now that I've seen the children again after so many years I don't want to lose them a second time.'

'They're almost grown now. You're – what? Twenty-one? You've got a lifetime ahead of you to share with them, but the years when you're young and pretty go very quickly. Make the most of them.'

Charity had a feeling this advice came from personal experience and she appreciated it because of that.

'Good luck with Stephen.' Charity got up and put one hand on the plump nurse's shoulder. 'Thank you.'

'I just came to say goodbye, Uncle,' Charity said from his doorway.

Stephen was still in his dressing-gown, unshaven, and his eyes were puffy. His breakfast tray was untouched and she saw an empty Scotch bottle on his desk.

'Goodbye?' he frowned. 'Where're you going?'

'Back to London and my business,' she said. 'I can't take any more time off.'

'What does a slip of a girl know about business?' he snorted.

'I've been here almost three weeks,' she said. 'I must go.'

His face crumpled unexpectedly.

'Don't leave me all alone,' he said in a strangled voice. 'I can't manage.'

'You've got plenty of help now.' Charity was repulsed, but she tried to soothe him, even moving forward to pat his large, veiny hand. 'And you've got Prue and Toby.'

'What use are children to me?' he said. 'I need you here. This house needs a mistress.'

'I'm sorry, Uncle,' she said firmly. 'I have to go, but I'll come back.'

His head reared up and his eyes flashed.

'You minx!' he roared. 'You worm your way back in here, take my mother's earrings. What else have you got? Another few valuable trinkets, pieces of family silver?'

466

'I beg your pardon.' Charity felt anger rising inside her. 'How dare you suggest such a thing? You know perfectly well those earrings were a present!'

'Huh,' he snorted. 'You leave here now and you won't come back a second time.'

Charity turned away. She had hoped for so much, but she wasn't going to plead.

'I'm sorry for you, Uncle Stephen,' she said, turning as she reached the door. 'I thought we'd reached some sort of truce. I became very fond of your mother and I know this isn't how she'd have wanted it to be. But I can't take any more abuse from you.'

She waited, hoping for an apology.

'I won't let you see the children again.' His voice dropped, heavy with menace.

Charity sighed deeply.

'That won't wash this time,' she said, shrugging her shoulders. 'They're big enough to make up their own minds about me. Goodbye, sir. I've done all I can here.'

She didn't stop even to say goodbye to Margaret and Dawn Giles, though she suspected the nurse at least had overheard the whole conversation from the drawing room. Picking up her case from the hall, she marched out the front door and down the drive, her eyes smarting.

She kept walking, right down through the village and on towards Beckley. It was hot, her case was heavy but she was still hoping to see Prue and Toby before she hitched a ride into Oxford.

She paused for a moment by a five barred gate and looked back at the Priory on the hill. Sadness took the place of anger. It stood, so proud, on the brow of the hill, flanked by cypress trees almost as old as itself.

'Chas!'

She looked back up the road. Prue and Toby were flying down the hill towards her on their bikes. In shorts and T-shirts they looked very alike, Prue's hair floating out behind her.

Toby reached her first. He leapt off his bike and dropped it against the hedge. 'How could you go without saying goodbye?'

His arms were round her, hugging her so tight she could scarcely breathe. Prue joined them seconds later, her face flushed, her eyes troubled.

Charity explained briefly.

'I don't want to quarrel with Uncle.' She struggled to compose herself. 'I want you to remember that.'

They stood side by side in front of her and despite their increased height and the passing of six years, their expressions were the ones she remembered from Greenwich, when she had meant everything to them. The memory came back to her sharply. She reached out her hands to stroke both their faces. 'I have a home in London, and it's yours too whenever you want it. I'll come to your speech days Toby, with or without Uncle's permission. I'll meet you anywhere, Prue. But I can't and won't come here again.'

She hugged them both fiercely one last time, dried their eyes and kissed them.

'Go back now.' She tried to smile. 'Be good.'

Charity watched as they rode back up the hill. Toby stood up on the pedals, slender and graceful. Prue's plump bottom wobbled as she struggled to keep up with her brother and for a brief instant Charity was reminded of herself and Hugh that summer in Sussex.

Chapter Twenty-Four

'Nurse Giles!' Prue called out, pedalling her bike up the hill towards the nurse.

Dawn Giles turned at Prue's voice, sighing inwardly. She had come out for a walk to try and sort out what she was going to do. The last thing she needed was a sixteen-year-old questioning her.

Prue's face was red with exertion by the time she reached Nurse Giles. 'What's the matter with Uncle?' she said breathlessly. 'Is he ill?'

It was two days since Charity left Studley and Stephen hadn't come out of his room once during that time, not even for dinner. Prue and Toby had heard odd noises coming from the room – bellows of anger, banging and the sound of breaking glass. They'd been too scared to go and see him, so they'd stayed away when they could. When Prue spotted the nurse walking briskly up the hill away from Studley she thought for one horrible moment the woman was leaving for good.

'He's not exactly ill.' The nurse tried to keep her tone light as she didn't want to alarm Prue. 'He's just upset. People often get like it after they lose someone close to them.'

'I thought for a minute you were leaving too,' Prue said. It was sad enough seeing Charity leave, just when she and Toby were getting to rely on their older sister. But if the nurse left they might be forced to look after Uncle Stephen themselves and the thought was horrifying.

'Just getting a bit of exercise. In fact I'm on my way back now,' the nurse reassured Prue.

The day Dawn had arrived for her interview at Studley she knew this was the right job for her. She loved the beautiful house, the wages were fair and her room overlooking the garden was delightful. Furthermore, her sister lived only a bus ride away.

Dawn was appalled by the colonel's health. He was so frustrated, both mentally and physically. His diet was appalling: soft, pappy foods which did nothing to help his bowel problems, and so much starch it was no wonder he was grossly overweight.

Of course she had known it wasn't going to be easy looking after a grumpy amputee and his frail old mother, especially with those two uppity teenagers tearing round the house. But within days Dawn had discovered that Stephen Pennycuick had a great deal in common with many of the other older gentlemen she'd nursed. She had sensed his eyes on her bottom when she bent over and he was very quick to get an erection when she was bathing him. It had given her heart.

But since Mrs Pennycuick had died and Charity left, the colonel had been impossible. Dawn had put up with a lot from private patients in the past, but never anything like this.

For two days now Stephen had refused to get out of his bed, drinking Scotch continually. He had knocked over endless bedpans in his temper, thrown glasses across the room and hurled the kind of abuse at her she didn't intend to take from anyone.

All families had secrets tucked away, and certainly Stephen Pennycuick was carrying a heavy burden of guilt about something. Sometimes Dawn thought

Stephen confused Charity with his sister Gwen; the state he was in now was more than just grief for his mother and pique that his niece had left. But however much Dawn wanted to help the man and release him from his misery, she was coming to the end of her tether.

That's why she'd come out this afternoon. To think things over. Should she go, or stay? The trouble was she didn't have anywhere to go. Her sister Kate would put her up for a day or two, but that wouldn't help much.

Giving her charges a bit of loving was how Dawn had controlled her difficult patients in the past. But Stephen Pennycuick was such a brusque, unaffectionate man and Dawn was just like any other woman: she wanted a bit of tenderness in return.

Dawn was thirty-nine with a powerful sex drive which sat rather uneasily in such a strong, competent and compassionate woman. She had been sixteen in 1943 when she was seduced for the first time by an American airman but by the time she began her nursing training at eighteen she had lost track of how many lovers she'd had. Dawn had never been pretty; she was a big girl with the kind of face and lank hair that makeup and perms didn't seem to help. But she had a shapely body and she made men feel good.

Marriage and children held no appeal for her. She loved nursing too much. She wasn't glamorous enough to become a gentleman's mistress, and that only seemed to leave rough, working men. She had tried a couple of these, but once the novelty of new passion wore off, she found herself hating the dullness of the life, trapped in a tiny house, expected to clean, cook and wash their filthy clothes without even appreciation. It was after she had run away from the last one that she stumbled accidentally into private nursing and at once saw advantages in this new life that a hospital could never give her.

A decent place to live, a job with prestige – and so often a secret sex life with an appreciative gentleman.

Dawn let herself in at Studley and stood for a moment in the hall listening, before she took off her raincoat. She couldn't hear any noise coming from Stephen's room, so perhaps he'd fallen asleep.

Ten minutes later, with her cap and apron on, she opened the door of the colonel's room.

She heard his sobs before she saw him: great gasping ones that cut her in two. Worse still, he had turned himself on to his stomach and couldn't get back because he was too weak.

'Now, now, sir,' she said, advancing across the room. 'What sort of a state is this to get yourself into?'

He had vomited in the bed and lay there like a big messy baby.

'Go away,' he shouted, but his voice was muffled by the pillow. 'Get away from me!'

'I'm not going to put up with this, sir,' Dawn said, pulling back the covers. The air in the room was fetid with his body odour, vomit and whisky, but such things didn't bother Dawn Giles. She pulled back the curtain a little way, opened a window wide enough to let the smell out and pushed his chair up to the side of the bed. 'You, my boy, are going in the bath,' she snapped at him. 'And we'll have no more nonsense.'

She hauled him on to his side and practically dragged him into his wheelchair. 'I'll look after you, sir, but only if you behave like a human being,' she said.

'Leave me alone,' Stephen roared at her as she peeled off his nightshirt while the bath was running. 'I don't want a bloody bath.'

When he wouldn't co-operate by using his arms to swing across on to the bath seat as he usually did, she slapped him.

His look of shock made her giggle, despite her anger with him. The slap on his shoulder had left a bright red imprint on his white skin. His mouth hung open and his eyes were wide and almost innocent with surprise.

But he co-operated then, putting one hand on to the bath rail, the other on the wheelchair and hauled his fat body across on to the bath seat.

Stephen wasn't much to look at naked: a huge flabby belly almost hiding his private parts, arms surprisingly thin through lack of exercise, his back and buttocks still bearing scars from his war injuries, and those two pitiful stumps that once had been fine sturdy legs.

'That's better,' Dawn said tartly as she soaped and sponged him like a baby. 'From now on you're going to do as I say, otherwise I'll be off too and then you'll be put in a home.'

It was as Dawn dried him that he began to cry again and it was second nature to cuddle him.

'There, there,' she said comfortingly, letting his head rest against her big breasts. 'You've had a bad time, but I can make things a bit better. I'll show you how to do some things for yourself, I'll take you out for walks in your chair and we'll try to get you to lose a bit of that extra weight. It's only your legs that are gone, remember. The rest of the man is still there.'

As Stephen sat in his wheelchair in a clean nightshirt while she changed his bed, Dawn knew that their relationship was going to grow as it had with her other gentlemen. He'd had an erection several times before when she bathed him, but always she had given it the officious smack taught to her by an older nursing sister. It hadn't seemed right to take liberties, with his mother, nieces and nephew in the house.

But his mother was gone now, the children out and Stephen needed comfort.

She helped him from the wheelchair into the clean bed, but instead of letting him go once he was safely in, she kept her arms round him and let him lie with his head on her breasts.

'That's better,' she whispered, sliding her fingers underneath his face to fold down her apron and unbutton her striped uniform dress. 'We all need a bit of comfort now and then.'

Dawn was proud of her breasts: they were big, but firm and pink with plump brown nipples. It always gave her a thrill when a man saw them for the first time – that gasp of pleasure as they reached out for them, the hungry look in their eyes.

But Stephen's expression surpassed anything she'd ever known. His eyes widened and his mouth attacked them with such ferocity, it alarmed her. He took one in each hand, squeezing and biting till she had to stop him.

'Gently now,' she whispered. 'They're there for you any time, but I like them stroked and kissed, not that rough stuff.'

She made him sit up in his bed then, and held her breasts in her hands. She could see herself and Stephen reflected in the glass of a picture. Her breasts like two firm melons and his rapt face, enthralled by them.

'Have you got something you'd like to put between these, sir?' she said, licking her lips as she jiggled her breasts.

'Oh nursey,' he gasped, his breathing hard and heavy. His eyes were glazed with wanting and he pulled his nightshirt up to expose his erect penis.

'That's better.' She smiled lasciviously, guiding it

between her two breasts and squeezing them together round it. 'Nursey just wants you to be a happy boy.'

Stephen was sleeping like a baby when she left him later. Dawn had his promise there would be no more scenes, no more wild drinking and that he would stick to his diet.

She sat in the drawing room with a gin and tonic in her hand, waiting for the children to come home. She could stay here now. A week or two and she'd be able to put a stop to those dreadful enemas, even though he seemed to get some kinky pleasure from them. No more strapping him in at night; she'd teach him to get in and out of bed himself. A set of dumb-bells would improve the muscles in his arms and perhaps she'd get herself a nice new set of black undies to excite him.

'How's Uncle Stephen?' Prue asked as she came in, Toby close behind her.

'Much better now.' Dawn smiled warmly at the two blond teenagers. 'He'll be up for his meals tomorrow again. Now off you go to bed and don't worry any more.'

'Well Nurse Giles, you've done a fine job.' Dr Harris smiled appreciatively at the big nurse as saw him out the door. He had been the colonel's doctor for some twelve years and today's visit was the first time he'd seen a real smile on the man's face. 'Only a month since his mother died and you've worked a miracle.'

'Go on with you.' Nurse Giles beamed. She liked Dr Harris, he was a real gentleman, though a bit small and wiry for her taste. 'I'm only doing what I was trained to do.'

'Getting him to lose a stone, toning up his arm muscles, not to mention improving his disposition, is more than just nursing,' Dr Harris insisted. 'He looks good for another twenty years at least.'

'I hope so.' Nurse Giles smiled. 'I'm very happy here.'

'And the children?' Dr Harris raised one bushy eyebrow. 'How have they coped with losing their grandmother?'

'Very well,' the nurse reported. 'Young James came down to stay for a week and that cheered them up. Now Toby's back at Wellington College. Prue's studying hard for her exams next year. It's very peaceful at Studley now.'

'What about Charity?' the doctor asked. He'd only met her briefly when Isobel died and later at the funeral, but he'd been very taken with her and disappointed to hear the gossip flying round the village.

Nurse Giles sighed deeply.

'I haven't managed to make the colonel see how silly he's been about her. But I suspect the kids are keeping in touch. Charity won't give up on them, that girl's got a backbone of steel.'

Dr Harris turned to go, looking out for a minute across the drive.

'Autumn's on its way,' he said. 'I saw some kids collecting conkers on my way here. Maybe the long winter's nights will mellow the old chap still further. Keep up the good work, Nurse Giles. I'll see you next month.'

Dawn Giles closed the front door behind him and smiled to herself.

Margaret was baking an apple pie, the smell of cinnamon wafting through the house. Pat was polishing the furniture in the drawing room. Dawn had got what she wanted now: a beautiful home and security. Long cosy evenings by the fire, listening to Stephen talking about his army days, the places he'd been to and how Studley was when he was a boy.

Maybe Dr Harris wouldn't be quite so approving if he knew just how she'd achieved so much with Stephen, but Dawn knew the healing powers of a good sexual relationship.

And it was early days yet. She hadn't shown him all her little tricks, by a long way.

Chapter Twenty-Five

June 1968

'I can't really believe we're leaving here,' Rita said to Charity as she handed her last box to the taxi driver waiting in Barkston Gardens. 'I thought it was incredible when we moved the office to King's Road, but I never imagined being sensible enough to buy flats of our own.'

'Come back here a moment.' Charity ran back to the doorway to shelter from the rain. 'Give me a hug.'

Rita ran to her, rain already turning her hair into corkscrew curls.

'Don't be ridiculous.' Rita laughed. 'Anyone would think we were going to the opposite ends of the world. I'll see you on Monday at the office.'

Dorothy leaving for New York and the lease expiring on the flat in Barkston Gardens at the same time had been the deciding factor in moving out. It made better financial sense to buy a place of their own than rent again, and now Rita had found a minute studio apartment close to the office and Charity a flat in St John's Wood.

The new office had come about for similar reasons. A year ago, when the lease expired in Fulham Road, Charity had had to go cap in hand to the bank, for a loan to buy the lease of another office in King's Road, Chelsea. At the time it had been very worrying – the new place had much higher overheads – but the gamble had paid off: larger premises in a better area had increased Stratton Promotions' profile and with it came bigger and more lucrative contracts.

'This is the end of an era,' Charity said. 'We have to mark it with something.'

Rita hugged her friend exuberantly.

'I think we left enough marks on the flat and the neighbours,' she said. 'Now look, I've got to go. Simon's waiting for me to go and buy a bed.'

'I suppose you'll be testing it this afternoon,' Charity shouted as Rita ran back to her car.

'As the Aussies round here would say, "too right".' Rita grinned. 'Good luck settling in. Give the kids my love tomorrow. Next time they're in London I'll pop round to see them.'

Charity went back upstairs for her last few things, but as she stepped into the bare hall, alone, she suddenly felt an unexpected pang of sentiment.

Rain was drumming against the windows, obliterating the sound of traffic from the Earls Court Road. A dismal, yellowy light showed up all the marks of the last five years.

The carpet had always been threadbare under the settee. Now it was a hole. Stains as diverse as wine, nail varnish and spilt coffee made a joke of her leaving it for the next tenants. White shapes on the yellowing walls marked where pictures had been; paintwork was scuffed and peeling in places. Rita's room was bare now, the furniture she'd brought from her parents' home so long ago, sold to a man across the square. A whiff of Chanel still lingered in Dorothy's, but the many scratches on the dressing-table, stains of wine and tea splattered on the ivory walls, were far more evocative of her untidy nature. Dorothy had gone to the States a few weeks before on a modelling job, but as always she'd found a wealthy man and the girls guessed this one was keeping their friend between jobs.

Charity had been just eighteen when she first saw this flat. Now she was twenty-three and buying the kind of flat which had once been just a dream.

'So many memories,' Charity said aloud as she went back into her old room. The curtains were gone, given to Lou. A big blown-up photograph of her taken by John in Florence was already hanging in her new flat. The bed here looked saggy and uncomfortable, the small bamboo table was fit for nothing but a rubbish dump.

All her dreaming of John had been done here, lying awake night after night when they got back from Florence, wondering how she could feel so much pain yet still survive. Worrying about the children, so scared she might never see them again. She'd planned to get the agency here too, and devised the plot to get the money from Ted.

Then there were the thoughts of Daniel. How many times had she taken out his photographs and bootees and cried over them? A hundred? A thousand. He'd be six now, a little schoolboy. Did he look like her? Would he one day discover that his real mother had given him away?

'Enough of that,' she said out loud, the words echoing round the empty room. 'Remember the good times!'

She, Rita and Dorothy had turned from girls into women, shared dreams, sadness, fought and laughed here. Pinning up each other's skirts when the mini hit London, daring each other to be bold enough to wear crocheted dresses, swapping feather boas, velvet jackets and jewellery. All those records, now divided up, each with its own bittersweet memories. 'You've lost that lovin' feeling', 'River deep mountain high' ...

words and music that charted romances, periods of gloom, and left indelible marks on their souls.

Nights when the three of them were here alone, reminiscing about the past over bottles of cheap wine and vowing they'd always stay together.

Charity paused to look round one last time with the front door open. They would never live together again, but the bonds they had formed back in Daleham Gardens were strong ones and their friendship would last a lifetime. Dorothy had had her few moments of fame even if her modelling career hadn't turned out to be quite as lucrative as she expected. And there would always be a rich man, somewhere, prepared to share his money and life with her.

Rita and Charity were woven together now, like two cords in the same rope. Charity had the fire and drive, Rita the plodding diligence needed to keep the piles of paperwork under control. Rita still wouldn't accept a partnership; she maintained it wouldn't work, but at least she'd agreed to a profit-sharing arrangement which their accountant had sorted out each year.

A gust of wind made the naked light bulb quiver, a whiff of disinfectant and mustiness had taken the place of the smells Charity remembered of perfume, makeup and bacon sandwiches. The flat looked desolate and unloved as she slowly closed the door for the last time.

Charity had just finished stacking the last of her books on her shelves in her new flat when the buzzer went.

Since leaving Barkston Gardens yesterday at noon she'd worked tirelessly and now at last her brothers and sister were here to warm it properly.

Beech House was a modern block of flats on the tree-lined Finchley Road in St John's Wood. It took its name from two copper beeches in front of it, and though the flats were the least expensive in the area, Prue would no doubt approve of its air of quiet gentility.

Charity's plans of finding a home for all of them had become tempered by maturity and realism. The most she could expect was a weekend visit from one or the other of them. Toby and Prue still saw Studley Priory as home; James would stay with Lou and Geoff. So she'd chosen this flat for its central position, its modern, spacious design and the fabulous view from the balcony.

It was on the fourth floor, and she could see across the houses and gardens to Primrose Hill. To the right was Regent's Park, and the sound of traffic was just a faint purr in the background. The first time she'd seen the flat the sun was just going down and she'd waited until darkness fell and all those street lights sparkled like diamonds on black velvet before her.

Charity picked up the answerphone.

'Is that you, kids?' she said, laughing as she imagined their startled faces down there under the porch. 'I'm opening the door. Come up to the fourth floor in the lift.'

She glanced around before opening the flat door, pleased by what she saw. Cream carpet throughout, two new and expensive large floppy settees in pale blue velvet and a large teak wall unit to house her records, books and stereo. This room was a bit sparse yet, she needed a table and chairs, but the bedroom, the settees, curtains and carpets had cleaned her out and she'd need a few more good contracts before she dared splash out on anything else.

'Come in all of you!' Charity beamed at the three of them as she opened the door. 'Goodness me you're all soaked. Take your shoes off out there!'

'Houseproud already?' Toby retorted but abandoned his umbrella outside the door and removed his shoes. 'We thought it was right by Lord's Cricket Ground and we got off the bus at the wrong stop.'

James, the moment he'd abandoned his shoes, took a running leap at Charity, enveloping her in a frantic hug. He was ten now, but still didn't seem to be concerned with behaving in the same laid-back way as his older brother.

'Isn't it posh, Chas,' he squealed with delight, wriggling out of his coat and running over to the window. 'It's like being in space up here. You can see the whole world.'

'Not a very good view in the rain,' Charity said, collecting all the raincoats and hanging them over the bath. 'But maybe next time you come it will be sunny and we can sit out on the balcony.'

'I thought you'd have got a bigger place,' Prue said. 'There's only one bedroom.'

Charity ignored that remark. Prue had an unerring way of criticising everything, it was a rare occurrence when she wholeheartedly approved.

'The settees are big enough to sleep on,' Charity said. 'And if you want to stay, Prue, you can share my bed, it's big enough.'

'Wow!' Toby said as he peeped into the bedroom. It was very feminine with palest pink silky curtains with a pleated pelmet. A cream lace bedspread, lampshades to match on Oriental lamp bases and the dressing-table ivory coloured wood that appeared to have been bleached. 'And that huge bed! Have you got an orgy in mind?'

'Don't be silly.' Charity reached up to smack his ear playfully. Toby was seventeen now, well over six feet tall, and preoccupied with sex and girls. 'Now when you've all had a good poke round, perhaps we can have some tea?'

Charity busied herself putting cakes on plates,

laying out cups and saucers on the coffee table, but all the time she was watching her brothers and sister.

They were all so different in nature. Since Prue had started at teacher training college in Oxford she'd adopted a rather 'county' image with tweed skirts and sensible shoes, entirely at odds with the droves of flower children flocking around London. Prue's snobbishness hadn't left her: now she spoke of being 'at Oxford' so people assumed she meant the university. She almost took a pride in being plain. Sometimes Charity longed to get hold of her, show her how to use makeup effectively and make her have her hair cut instead of wearing it in one thick plait. But Prue wouldn't take advice from anyone; she knew everything.

Toby, on the other hand, was physical perfection. Still no spots on his peachy skin, a lean yet muscular body; even in need of a haircut and scowling he had that charismatic James Dean look. Intellectually he wasn't even close to Prue, he just scraped through exams, took no interest in books. Sport, cars and girls were the only things he showed any enthusiasm for. Toby still worried Charity. There was something dark and devious in his nature that she couldn't quite put out of her mind. She had bought him an expensive watch last Christmas and by Easter he wasn't wearing it. Toby said the strap had broken and he'd taken it to a shop to get it repaired, but she was sure he'd sold it, yet why, when he had more money than most boys of his age? There were many more instances of lies and subterfuge, but somehow he had only to flash that brilliant smile and she forgave him.

But if Toby and Prue gave her cause for concern, James more than made up for it. He was a delight – warm, affectionate, bright and sunny. He never asked for anything, and treasured each and every gift. Lou and Geoff had made a great job of bringing him up.

'Who took this picture of you?' Prue looked round at Charity, pointing to the large black and white framed print of her feeding the pigeons in the Piazza del Duomo. 'It's frightfully good!'

'It would be. John Marshall took it,' Charity said.

'*The* John Marshall?' Prue gasped. 'When on earth did you meet him?'

'When I was your age,' Charity smiled. 'He took me to Florence with him.'

'Gosh.' Prue blinked very fast. 'But he's old!'

'Too old, that's why it didn't last,' Charity said ruefully. 'Now come and have some tea.'

'You're a bit of a dark horse,' Toby said, throwing himself down on the opposite settee and helping himself to the largest of the cream cakes. 'Were you his mistress?'

'Use a plate please, Toby,' Charity said, handing him one. 'Don't drop cream on the settee.'

'Don't change the subject,' Toby said, as always picking up on an undercurrent. 'Were you?'

'I loved him, if that's what you mean.' Charity had always intended to tell them about this one day, but she hadn't expected it to come up now. 'But it didn't work out.'

'How frightfully romantic,' Prue said, leaning forward to grab a cake. 'Have you been pining for him ever since? Is that why you haven't got a boyfriend now?'

'Uncle Stephen's got a girlfriend,' James piped up.

Instantly everyone looked at him.

'Don't be ridiculous,' Prue said.

'You kiss girlfriends, don't you?' James went on, undeterred. 'Well I saw him kissing Nurse Giles.'

Toby, Prue and Charity all roared with laughter.

'Why is it funny?' James said, his blue eyes wide with innocence. 'When I told Uncle Geoff, he said maybe that was what made Uncle more animal.'

485

Another roar of laughter and James was indignant now.

'Do you think he said "amenable"?' Charity spluttered with laughter.

'He might have. I'm not sure. Anyway I did see them kissing. I was looking through his window and there they were.'

Charity hugged this snippet of information to herself. Both Toby and Prue had mentioned odd things too that led her to believe the nurse and the colonel were now lovers. It was an obscene thought, but one she often giggled over with Rita in the office, and it brought back nice memories of Grandmother claiming the woman was a maneater.

'Tell me,' Charity said a little later. 'Does your uncle know you see me from time to time?'

Toby shrugged and looked at Prue.

'He must do,' Prue said, blushing a little. 'But we've never actually said.'

'I have,' James piped up. 'I told him you took me to the pictures at half-term and bought me a cricket bat.'

'We told you to keep quiet about that,' Toby said, cuffing his brother round the ear.

'I'm not telling lies,' James said. 'Uncle was bowling balls to me at Studley and he asked where I got the bat because it was a good one. I had to tell him.'

'Quite right too,' Charity said.

'He didn't say anything to us,' Prue said. 'He must've decided to ignore it. He never asks where we go when we come up here to see James. Sometimes I think he's glad to see the back of us.'

'He's probably having it off with Nurse Giles,' Toby said, then roared with laughter. 'Anyway, I tell Margaret we see you. She's all for it.'

The afternoon passed too quickly. Prue told Charity

about her boyfriend Tim, who apparently had the brains of Einstein and the looks of Sean Connery. While Prue was in the bathroom Toby said he might have brains but he had terminal acne and he was a weed.

Toby told her about his driving lessons and said Uncle Stephen was going to buy him a sports car next year when he went to Sandhurst. All James could come up with was that he took a blackbird's nest into school for the nature table.

It was only when Charity had returned from seeing them off at the bus stop that a feeling of melancholy came over her. Without them the flat felt very empty and Prue's question about why she didn't have a boyfriend prickled at her.

Work had become her love, new contracts taking the place of passion. Men had come and gone; for brief moments they'd added zest to her life, like seasoning on a meal, but she'd never let anyone get close enough to become more.

The rain had stopped and the sun was making the tiles out on the balcony steam. Charity opened the doors and stepped outside, leaning on the railings.

People said she'd changed and grown hard. But she had to be tough with both her employees and the companies she dealt with because there was too much at stake for sentimentality. Yet out there in London other girls were going to rock concerts, wild all-night clubs and pop festivals. They wore beaded Indian smocks, velvet loons, painted flowers on their faces and stayed up all night smoking pot. Love and fun was everything to them.

In her wardrobe there were Ossie Clark evening dresses, Jaeger suits and many Mary Quant dresses, all so smart and even glamorous, but had she slipped into a kind of early middle age?

'Don't be ridiculous,' Charity murmured.

She had so much – a successful business, beautiful clothes, now this smart flat – and she remembered only too well what it was like to be poor and defenceless. Maybe material things wouldn't give her the kind of sweet moments of bliss she'd felt when she held Daniel in her arms, or bring back the joy of first love. But it beat the desolation of heartbreak, of being rejected because she was a poor kitchen maid.

'Hi there.' Rita came bounding out of the back office as Charity arrived for work on Monday. 'Settled in OK? How were the kids?'

'The kids were wonderful, the flat looks like home. How about yours?'

'I felt a bit lonely last night when Simon cleared off,' Rita admitted. 'I suppose we'll both have to get used to having no one around. Anyway I want you to come to dinner next weekend. You haven't met Simon properly and he's got a nice friend.'

Charity pulled a face.

'Don't look like that, he's lovely!'

'You said that about the last gargoyle you presented me with. I'd like to meet Simon and find out if he's all he's cracked up to be, but I hate being foisted on to strangers.'

'How on earth can anyone please you?' Rita put her hands on her hips and glared at Charity. 'Dorothy I understand. She's only interested in the size of men's wallets. I don't know what you want.'

'Love,' Charity grinned. 'But it just doesn't happen to me. Anyway let's get off this subject, there's work to do.'

The new office seemed huge in comparison to the old one. A small reception area behind the big plate-glass window held comfortable modern chairs and a smart

Italian black desk where Rita worked as office manager. Behind this three girls typed and manned the office machinery.

Charity's office was upstairs overlooking the King's Road. This was where she interviewed both promotion girls and prospective clients.

It was a far cry from Fulham Road in many ways. The soft grey carpet was expensive Wilton, the pink décor done by a professional decorator. They even had a proper kitchen now, with ice in the fridge for important clients' drinks.

Stratton Promotions was becoming well known in London. Charity had carved out a niche for herself by getting the right girls, keeping their loyalty by fairness, good jobs and paying them better than anyone else. But though the office was smarter, the contracts bigger and so much more money at stake, all the fundamental things remained the same. Rita might have passed on the more mundane typing, filing and checking time sheets, but she still handled the wages, bookkeeping and typing the contracts. Charity spent more time away from the office, seeing clients and checking that her girls were working properly, but she still followed up every new enquiry and attended all the briefings with her girls so she knew exactly what was expected of them. And there were still moments of blind panic when cheques didn't arrive in time to pay wages and the rent.

'Martin Bell would like to see you,' Rita said over the intercom later that morning. 'He's in the office now.'

'Send him right up.' Charity jumped up from her desk to meet him.

She felt a surge of happiness. It had been ages since she last had time to see Marjorie and Martin. Now they'd sold Bell's Diner in Hammersmith and moved out to Hertfordshire, Charity had grown used to a quick phone call once every six months.

She ran to the door, just as Martin came up the stairs.

He looked just the same: short and tubby, his bald spot shining.

'Oh Martin,' she gasped. 'It's so good to see you. How are you?'

'Doing very well,' he grinned, kissing her cheek. 'And it looks as if you are too.'

Only then did Charity notice his expensive suit.

'This is a bit flash for you,' she said, playfully pulling on the revers. 'Had a pools win?'

'Sort of.' He smiled. 'Let's talk about it.'

Over coffee Martin talked. He had lost still more hair, his face had a few more lines, but there was a new excitement in his voice, and greater confidence than he'd ever shown in the days when Charity worked as his waitress.

He spoke of expanding the frozen food business he'd started with just vegetables, into pies, hamburgers and sausages.

'The frozen food company has done fabulous business,' he said. 'Of course we didn't know when we started it that ordinary people would start buying freezers to have at home. We thought we'd only be supplying restaurants, canteens and hospitals. But suddenly business increased, the first frozen food shops started opening and supermarkets are stocking more and more lines. Now the sky's the limit.'

'Wonderful.' Charity was so pleased for him and Marjorie. She remembered how hard they had always worked. 'You deserve it. How's Marjorie coping with money and success?'

'As if born to it,' Martin beamed. 'She's a lady of leisure now, spending her time reading glossy magazines and thinking up ways to spend our money. She's really happy.'

'What brought you up here today then?' Charity asked.

'To see you, of course – and to put some business your way.'

'Really?' Charity was happy just to see him, but the offer of business was even better.

'I've bought a small share in a domestic freezer business,' Martin explained. 'Of course I know nothing about freezers themselves, only the grub you put in them, but it was suggested we got a few girls in major appliance shops to push them and I immediately thought of you.'

'My girls can sell anything.' Charity instantly switched from mere friend to saleswoman. 'Tell me more.'

They talked for some time, first the business, then switching back to more personal things. Finally Martin had to go.

As he was about to descend the stairs, he turned to her. 'We're so bloody proud of you,' he said. 'When I think what you've been through, and now you've got all this! But keep freezer and frozen food companies in mind. There's a revolution coming in food, and if you get in on the ground floor with it, you'll go right to the top.'

'You always were so good to me.' Charity hugged him. 'Thanks for the leads. I'll be on to them like a bloodhound. And I'll come and see you and Marjorie soon.'

Chapter Twenty-Six

1973

Charity leapt out of her Mini. She was late for an appointment with Martin Bell and although he would understand, Charity believed in punctuality.

She felt great, even though it was a grey, cold March day. She had returned just a few days earlier from a holiday in Florida with Dorothy, complete with a golden tan and a curly perm Dot had insisted on. But better still, she had an idea for Martin that could be brilliant for both of them.

Dorothy's thirtieth birthday party was the main reason Charity had gone to Florida. Her friend hadn't changed much: she moaned about her age, then advertised it by throwing an extravagant party. Of course there was a rich man in the background who paid the rent on her sumptuous apartment in Miami, and her Cadillac was a present from another, and her modelling still brought in enough work to keep her very comfortably. It had been a wonderful holiday, long lazy days on the beach, parties and fun; they'd even been to Disneyland like a couple of kids. Dorothy was hard with men, she'd grown even more self-centred, but alone with Charity it was just like their old flat-sharing days, giggling and gossiping till the early hours.

Charity shivered and clutched her black rabbit coat round her tighter as the cold wind caught her. She just hoped Martin was as impressed with her idea as she was and went for it. Things were getting a bit tight in London.

Property prices had gone sky high in the last year, inflation was out of control and she sensed that the economy was about to take a slide into a depression. For the moment Charity was holding her own, still taking a large slice of the pie in promotions work, but if the economy were to take a nose dive, she knew the first hit would be small businesses like hers.

Charity was twenty-eight now, still slender in size ten clothes, but curvier now than she had been as a girl. Unlike Dorothy who worried about her increasing age because it meant less modelling work for her, Charity was glad of maturity because in her business it meant she was taken more seriously.

Not that she was feeling mature today. Her new curly perm made her feel ridiculously young and giggly and she thought she might persuade Rita to go out somewhere tonight.

As Charity turned into King's Road she waved to Carla, the owner of the boutique, who was dressing her window and paused just long enough to admire the pale pink spring suit she was arranging.

'Good morning Miss Stratton,' Jaquintha put her phone down as Charity swept in. 'Mr Bell's here, he's waiting in your office. I gave him some coffee.'

Rita was tucked away in her own office upstairs now. This new receptionist was nineteen, a small pretty brunette straight out of secretarial college. She had only been with them for a few months but she was shaping up well.

'Thank you, Jaquintha.' Charity smiled at the girl, noting immediately that she was looking pale. 'What's the matter?'

Jaquintha blushed.

493

'Just a tummy ache,' she said in a low voice. 'It's . . . you know.'

Charity leaned closer over the desk.

'Go and take a couple of aspirin,' she suggested. 'If it doesn't go within an hour get one of the other girls to cover for you and go home.'

Charity had learned to be tough with both employees and clients over the years, otherwise they took advantage. But her sympathetic nature was easily tugged, especially by the young and vulnerable.

'Sorry to keep you waiting, Martin,' she said as she walked into her office. 'The traffic's appalling.'

Martin got up and kissed her cheek.

'For you I'd wait for ever,' he said. 'But it's only five minutes. You look fantastic, Charity, the holiday did you good. I like the hair too. It makes you look truly angelic.'

Martin had observed the changes in Charity over the eleven years he'd known her. He'd seen the frightened little girl, the giddy young thing about town, then the slow transformation into an astute business-woman. Yet there was still a sense of purity in her, something untouched, undefiled.

'Your old flattery.' Her wide mouth curved into a disarming smile. 'Dot called it Rabelaisian. I'm not quite sure what she meant by that. Does it mean I look like a good-time girl?'

The freezer promotion five years earlier was the start of a series of campaigns connected with Martin. They had been just small jobs: girls offering money-off vouchers for frozen food and occasionally cookery demonstrations. Martin had been right – frozen food and freezers had become more and more popular and he'd been smart enough to capitalise on it. Now Charity felt it was time for them to get together in a big joint venture.

Two years ago Martin had moved into the American

idea of frozen TV Dinners, but although the potential was enormous, so far the British public were hesitant about trying them. Martin had discussed this with Charity before she went away and now she felt sure she had the solution.

Charity had used her holiday in Miami to do some homework. She'd seen promotion girls handing out samples of such foods, and knew it could work here in England.

Martin looked prosperous now. Impeccably cut suits hid his increasing stoutness, even his balding head gave him an air of distinction. Playing golf at weekends had given him a healthy glow he never had back in Hammersmith, but it was the inner man that shone through. He had maintained his fairness and good humour, he wasn't ashamed of his background, but best of all to Charity was that he was faithful to Marjorie, even though his success gave him plenty of opportunity to stray.

'I think any man under sixty would like a good time with you, Charity.' Martin smiled, as always wondering why someone hadn't snapped up such a beautiful and caring woman. 'But we'd better get down to business, hadn't we? I'm sure you're as pushed for time as me.'

'I gave your convenience foods a great deal of thought while I was away,' Charity said, taking from her briefcase the notes she'd made. 'In-store sampling is the only thing that's really going to move them.'

'But that's so expensive,' Martin said. 'Wouldn't money-off vouchers do as well, backed up with advertising?'

Charity shook her head. 'You can't smell or taste a voucher.'

'It's worked with frozen veg,' Martin retorted.

'That's different. People know what frozen peas are all about; the concept of a complete, ready-made meal

495

is different. We have to overcome resistance to the high price by proving the product is worth it.'

Martin shrugged his shoulders. He didn't believe his meals were expensive.

'Just imagine yourself as a working woman for a moment,' Charity said. 'You rush into a store to get something for tea, you're hungry, you know when you get in the family will be clamouring for something quick. While you are rushing about grabbing tins of beans, sausages, you suddenly see a girl standing under a bright yellow and white awning, cooking something that smells wonderful. You stop for a second, just to look, and she offers you a dish of chicken and pasta, or beef and vegetables. In the time it takes to wolf down this delicious taster she is explaining that the dish comes ready made: all you have to do is pop it in the oven for twenty minutes.' Charity paused to let this sink in.

'Well what would you do, Martin?'

'Buy it of course.' He smiled.

'So would I.' Her eyes looked intently into his. 'But the point is: that woman wouldn't have picked it from the freezer, not even with a money-off voucher, because she couldn't see or smell the finished product. There she would weigh up its cost compared with sausages or fish fingers. But once she's committed herself to a couple of mouthfuls she knows little Johnny will eat it, and what's more there's no preparation, precious little washing up to do afterwards – and the extra cost ceases to be of any significance.'

'Put like that I have to agree.' Martin's nut-brown eyes twinkled with amusement at her enthusiasm. 'But the cost of running a promotion like that would be huge.'

'The cost would soon be recovered,' Charity wheedled. 'Once women have tried these foods once, they'll return to buy them again and again, and tell their friends how good they are. Can you afford *not* to offer a tasting?'

Charity saw Martin's eyes glinting and knew she was almost there.

'My partners are keen on the idea of television advertising,' he said.

'That's an excellent way of pointing out the quickness, the nutritional value and how labour saving these meals are. But it isn't as effective as offering a sample of delicious food to a hungry woman who is out buying food, and sticking the box in her shopping basket.'

'OK.' Martin knew when he was beaten. 'I agree that we ought to hit all the major supermarkets, but have you got any suggestions of ways we can slash the cost of the equipment needed?'

'Yes.' She pulled a sheet of paper from her folder. 'One girl with one set of equipment moves from shop to shop in a given area over a four-week period. I've got girls with their own cars and a couple of supervisors who can do the rounds to check everything is running smoothly. All I would need from you is the back-up of stock arriving at the stores, the equipment and of course the promotion briefing, which should be somewhere central.'

Martin knew it made sense. Although Charity had organised only small-scale promotions for his company in the past, he knew she wouldn't suggest such a big scheme unless she could handle it, and he trusted her judgement.

'Fair enough.' He held out his hand as a gesture of agreement. 'But you'll have to come out to the factory in Luton and give my partners a presentation.'

Charity shook his hand firmly, blue eyes dancing with delight.

'Get a sample stand made up and we could even

arrange a trial demonstration in a local store,' she suggested.

Martin stood up, pulling his jacket over his plump tummy.

'You aren't just a pretty face,' he grinned. 'Tell me – do you ever think about those days back in Hammersmith?'

Charity knew that Martin meant Daniel but couldn't bring himself to say it.

'Yes, all the time,' she said. 'He'll be eleven in May, going on to a big school in September.'

Martin saw her eyes cloud and wished he hadn't mentioned it.

'Marge and I wish we'd had a child now,' he said. 'All those years of struggling ... now we've got so much, yet we've got no one to share it with. Don't make that mistake, Charity, find someone to love again and have a child.'

'I do my best,' Charity said, standing up to kiss his cheek. 'Sometimes I think all the best men are spoken for.'

Charity let herself into her flat just after twelve that night and went straight to the bathroom. While the bath was filling, she walked over to the window and gazed thoughtfully at the view.

There was enough moonlight to see ghostly silhouettes of the trees on Primrose Hill against the backdrop of the night sky.

She had had a good evening with Rita, telling her all about Dorothy and Florida; they hadn't mentioned work once. But as always Charity was glad to get home, to shut the door and the world and people out.

She never really understood why she felt this way. She had essentially been on her own for the last few years. Prue had got the teaching job she wanted, and married Tim, a colleague, two years ago. It had hurt

Charity not to be invited to the wedding, but Prue had said she couldn't risk upsetting Stephen when he was footing the bill. Taking Prue and Tim out for a celebratory meal and looking at the photographs hadn't made up for not sharing the day with her only sister. But Charity was happy for Prue: she had a little house of her own just outside Oxford and mixed with the kind of intellectual and well-bred friends that meant so much to her.

James was fifteen now, and at Dulwich College. His sunny nature hadn't changed. Although he was good at almost everything he turned his hand to, from lessons and sport to playing the guitar, he hadn't a trace of Toby's and Prue's superiority.

He often spent weekends with Charity. Whether they went for a spin in her car, looked round the shops in Oxford Street or just lazed about chatting, he was happy. Now he said he wanted to be a doctor and as far as she could see, he'd be perfect – he had the brains, the persistence and the compassion.

On the face of it Toby was an even greater success story than the other two. He was twenty-two now and he'd gone on from Wellington College to Sandhurst, passed out with flying colours and got his commission in the army. Now, like his grandfather and uncle, he was in the Royal Green Jackets and Uncle Stephen was reported to be delighted.

Charity looked out at the twinkling lights of London for a moment longer, then pulled the curtain cord and shut out the view. She wondered, as she had so many times in the last few year, why she couldn't just see Toby as everyone else did. A charming, handsome young man who was just a little irresponsible and thoughtless. He was stationed in Winchester and when he had leave he treated her flat like a London hotel, turning up, taking a shower, then rushing off until the early hours of the morning, without the least concern for Charity's feelings.

He appeared to have it all – looks, the sporting ability and the charm – yet he never considered himself fortunate. There were always complaints. His officer's salary wasn't enough, his mess bills were huge, his car wasn't fast enough and other officers were always trying to do him down.

Time and again when he came here, she would look at him gracefully sprawled on her settee, listen to the lazy way he drawled out his complaints and wish she could smack that handsome face and point out that he was twenty-two, a man, and responsible for his own life.

There were other more hurtful things too. Toby never appreciated how hard she worked, or praised her for doing well. He carped about her flat being so small and asked why she hadn't bought a place with a spare room so he could be comfortable when he stayed the night. If she took him out for a meal he wanted to go somewhere ridiculously expensive and before he left he always asked her to lend him some money, which he never paid back.

But most of Charity's anxiety about her brother was just suspicion, based on little things Prue or James mentioned quite innocently.

Prue spoke of some silver disappearing from Studley and how Uncle Stephen believed it was taken by a 'walk-in' burglar one afternoon while he and Nurse Giles where out in the grounds. Charity didn't want to believe it was Toby who took it, but he did seem remarkably flush around that time.

James found Toby ill in his room one day and the symptoms he described sounded far more like a comedown from drugs than the dose of flu Toby claimed it was.

Another story was told to Charity by Annabel, one

of her promotion girls, and though it could quite possibly be pure spite because Toby had taken Annabel out a few times, then dropped her, Charity didn't think so.

Annabel said he picked up older women and conned them into buying him expensive presents and paying his mess bills. She hinted too that he hung around Soho on his leave, gambling and drinking with rough characters.

When Charity analysed her fears and suspicions, she found she never had enough evidence to confront Toby with anything. But the worry about drugs niggled at her like a sore tooth. Half the people of Toby's age in London were dabbling in drugs. It was all part of the hippie scene and in fact Charity had tried smoking pot and taking speed herself on a couple of occasions, so she wasn't naïve about it. But she knew that if Toby was caught with so much as a pinprick of cannabis, he would be thrown out of the army immediately.

The last couple of times Toby had visited her, she had thought his behaviour very odd. He had had no appetite and he seemed nervous. She'd tried to talk to him about it but he'd brushed it away as her imagination and gone off out again.

He never spoke about where he went when he was in London. He made brief phonecalls arranging to meet people, but he never said who. His visits always left her with a feeling of dissatisfaction and unease. He never seemed interested in her, or James and Prue. In fact, Toby was becoming almost a stranger.

Charity woke the next morning with a start when her alarm went off, feeling as if she'd only been in bed for an hour or so. She leapt up to get washed and dressed, mentally making a note to give Toby a good talking-to next time he turned up.

It was Friday, and as always it was the busiest day of the week with her girls phoning in their hours, queries about wages and last-minute arrangements for the next week's work.

By lunchtime Charity was feeling very optimistic. All her regular girls had work lined up for the next two months and only four of the casual ones had to be told there was nothing for next week. The campaign with Martin's company would be a big one and it could lead to still more opportunities.

'Your brother called a few minutes ago,' Jaquintha said as Charity came back into the office after nipping across the King's Road to Safeway for some groceries at lunchtime.

'James or Toby.' Charity asked, her hand reaching out for the phone.

'It was Toby.' Jaquintha smiled as all the girls did when her brother was mentioned. He charmed all of them, he had only to walk in and they were fluttering their eyelashes and offering him coffee. 'You can't phone him back. He's out on manoeuvres on Salisbury Plain. He just asked me to give you the message that he'd be up tonight.'

Charity frowned. She hadn't got anything on tonight, but it annoyed her the way Toby just presumed she would be free. He hadn't rung her to ask about her holiday, even though she'd been back a few days, and his insensitivity brought back last night's thoughts.

Toby let himself in with his key just after seven that evening. Charity had changed out of her suit into jeans and a sweater and was just about to make herself something to eat.

'Hallo,' she smiled, reaching up to kiss his cheek. 'I'm just going to cook something. What would you like?'

She thought Toby looked tired and drawn and although he was clean and tidy in jeans and a sweat-shirt, he needed a shave. Remembering that he'd been out on Salisbury Plain all day, followed by a long drive to London, she felt sympathetic.

'A sandwich will do,' Toby said, dumping a small holdall on the floor. 'I'm going out later.'

Her sympathy vanished.

'This isn't a hotel, Toby,' she said sharply. 'Don't you think it's a bit rude to just turn up here, then go out again? How about spending an evening with me for a change?'

Toby just flopped down on the settee and lit up a cigarette.

There were many times when Charity looked at Toby and marvelled at his physical perfection. He was an Adonis with his blond hair, classic features and his clear peachy skin. Yet now she saw a slyness in his eyes and petulance in his sensual lips; it was like seeing a beautiful flower with blight.

'Come on, sis.' His tone was jocular. 'You're the one who always said we must stick close to one another. I could easily stay with someone else. I thought you liked to see me?'

'I do,' she agreed. 'But I don't like being used.'

'Who's using you?' His blue eyes, so like her own, looked entirely innocent. 'What have I done to deserve the third degree?'

'I'm not cross-examining you,' Charity said as she went back into the kitchen. 'Just try being a little less arrogant.'

She made him a cup of tea and a sandwich and listened while he discussed his forthcoming posting to Celle in north Germany. This posting pleased her: if he was getting in with unsavoury characters in London, this might nip it in the bud. But he kept looking at his watch and she guessed he was waiting to make a phone call.

She ate her lasagne while they watched TV, but as the clock moved closer to eight she could feel the tension.

'I'm just going to sort out some urgent papers in the bedroom,' she said casually. 'I shan't be long.'

At exactly eight he picked up the receiver and began to dial. The moment she heard the sound, she picked up the bedside extension.

'Jim?' she heard Toby say. 'It's Strat!'

'The game's on.' The man's voice sounded gruff, certainly not the kind of voice she would expect from one of Toby's friends. 'OK your end?'

'Fine,' Toby replied. 'Usual stake?'

'Yup,' the gruff voice said. 'When can you get here?'

'Twenty minutes, half an hour. That OK?'

Charity carefully put the phone down just as her brother did. Toby stuck his head round the door and grinned at her.

'I'm just nipping over to a friend's. I won't be long.'

'Does that mean you won't be back till tomorrow?' Charity said sarcastically, tempted to warn him she wouldn't lend him another penny if he was gambling.

'No, sis.' Again he grinned disarmingly. 'Not tonight. I'll pick up a bottle of something on the way back and we can have a drink.'

She didn't really expect him to come back, so when she heard his key in the lock soon after nine, she was shocked.

'There you go.' Toby almost bounced in with a bottle of vodka in one hand and a bunch of rather wilted flowers in the other. 'They were all I could get at this time of night. But they're meant as an apology.'

A couple of drinks later Charity began to wonder if she'd misread Toby. He seemed totally relaxed, lying on the settee, chatting about Uncle Stephen with a warmth she hadn't felt in him for some time.

'He's changed so much,' he insisted. 'He's lost all that weight. He does exercises to make his arms strong and he can haul himself in and out of bed alone now. I haven't heard him yell at anyone in a long time, he trundles himself around the grounds, he's quite a happy man these days.'

'Are you happy in the army?' Charity ventured. 'Sometimes you seem so tense.'

'I suppose I've accepted it now,' he grinned. 'What else could I do really, sis? I'm not cut out for a job in the City. I haven't got the brains James has.'

'You would tell me if there was anything troubling you?' Charity said wistfully. His face looked softer tonight and she wished she dared be completely honest and tell him she'd listened in on his conversation. 'You've always been the brother I worry about, Toby.'

For just a second she thought she saw a tender expression in his eyes, and he looked the way he used to look when he was small and Charity helped hide his misdemeanours from their parents.

'You're a worryguts, sis.' He laughed. 'You ought to get married and have some kids of your own. I'm a grown man now, not your responsibility any longer.'

To Charity's surprise Toby was asleep on the settee the next morning and there was no sign that he'd slipped out during the night. They had breakfast together, then he showered and said he was going out for a paper.

'Anything you want?' he asked. 'I'll have to go about three but that leaves us time for lunch together, doesn't it?'

Charity asked him to get some more milk and he

was gone, leaving the jacket he'd been wearing the night before on the back of a chair.

Charity hated going through his pockets and when she found nothing to alarm her she felt very guilty. She went into the bathroom to clean the basin. Finding his razor, she took it back to the lounge to add it to his washing things in his holdall.

A quick flick through showed nothing but the shirt and underclothes he'd worn yesterday, an Ian Fleming paperback and his toilet bag. She unzipped it and popped in the razor on top of his face flannel without really looking. It was only as she started to zip it up again that she noticed how bulky the bag was and delved under the flannel.

Charity's fingers touched something odd. It felt almost like beans in a bean bag. Pulling out the flannel, she gasped.

Beneath it were two plastic bags, full of red and black capsules.

In horror she pulled one bag out. Even at a guess she thought it must hold well over a hundred pills.

Dimly she heard Toby's feet coming up the stairs, but she made no attempt to put the bag back.

'Snooping?' Toby's voice held a menacing note.

Charity dropped the bag, spilling the contents all over the floor, and turned to her brother in dismay. She felt faint with shock. Imagining him taking a few pills himself had been one thing, but finding this amount of amphetamines had to mean he was selling them.

'Why, Toby?' she asked.

'Money, my sweet, *innocent* sister.' Toby's eyes were terrifyingly cold.

'Get them out of my flat, and you with them,' she hissed. 'I've put up with a lot from you, but I won't tolerate drugs.'

'Don't come all that high and mighty stuff with

me,' Toby said as he leaned down almost casually to pick up the dropped pills. 'You didn't get where you are without sailing a bit close to the wind.'

Charity stared at him in amazement.

'Don't look at me like that.' He looked up at her and smirked. 'You know what I mean. I worked out how you got those nice clothes and your precious agency. Tell me, which is worse – to sell your body, or flog a few pills?'

She could feel herself growing hot and her stomach turned over.

'What?'

'You heard. I said selling your body!'

'I didn't sell my body,' Charity said.

'Come off it.' He stood up and sneered at her. 'I was only a kid but I knew what was going on when you lived in Earls Court with those two other tarts. That old guy John Marshall must have chucked you hundreds over the years.'

'I was in love with John.' Charity trembled with anger. The trouble was, Toby was partly right. 'Anything I did, I did because I had no choice.'

Toby gave a hollow, disbelieving laugh.

'You make me sick. I've had it with your lectures, the mealy-mouthed martyr bit. You make out Prue is strange with her snobby ways, but she's a darn sight more honest than you. Uncle Stephen is the only person aside from me who can see through that innocent façade. You're a whore, Charity, that's all and you've got no right to tell me I can't sell a few pills to make some money.'

Rage rose up in Charity like hot bubbling tar.

'You evil swine!' she shouted. 'I've never claimed to be perfect, but I'm not a whore and I worked my fingers to the bone to get where I am. Ever since our parents died in that fire I've done everything I could

507

for you three. Not because I was a martyr, but because I loved you.'

Toby smiled at her anger. A ridiculous thought flashed through her mind that he looked like an SS officer in an old Nazi war film.

'Father was fucking you, wasn't he? Is that how you learned to be a whore? I knew what was going on. I heard him creeping up the stairs on Friday nights, and don't tell me you didn't like it. You never even called out for help.'

Charity felt she was tumbling from a clifftop. To be confronted by something she'd buried years ago was bad enough. But to hear it from her own brother's lips!

He was gone before she could think of a reply. He snatched up his bag and his jacket and slammed the door behind him.

She cried then, bitter angry tears that scalded her cheeks, and her heart felt as if it had been shattered into a thousand pieces.

She drank a little brandy later to try and pull herself together, but instead of numbing the pain it burned her throat and made her nauseous. Somehow she managed to crawl to the bathroom and knelt in front of the toilet vomiting until there was nothing left but green bile. The smell of brandy was everywhere, like the ghost of her father come back to haunt her, and she wished she could die.

Chapter Twenty-Seven

'Charity, whatever's the matter with you?' Rita put her hands on Charity's shoulders as she sat slumped at her desk. 'You've been getting stranger and stranger for weeks. Please tell me.'

'It's nothing.' Charity sat up straight and opened the file Rita had brought her, but the words and figures were meaningless. 'I think I need a tonic, that's all.'

Rita caught hold of Charity's chair and swivelled it round so she could see her friend's face.

It was very pale, with mauve circles beneath dull eyes, and thinner as if she'd lost weight. Although her makeup and hair would pass as normal to anyone else, Rita could tell that the usual care hadn't been taken with them.

'I know you almost as well as myself,' Rita said as she pulled another chair close and caught hold of her friend's hands. 'We've shared everything. The loss of our babies, building this business. I was there when John left you. You've heard my innermost thoughts about the men I loved. Surely you can tell me about this?'

'I can't explain because I don't know myself,' Charity said in a weary voice.

Rita didn't want to bring up how distant Charity had been with clients, the missed appointments or the days she hadn't come in at all; her only concern was for her friend.

'Well I believe you're heading for a nervous breakdown,' Rita said gently. 'You need help, and quickly. Now why don't you go home, call your doctor? I can cope with everything here.'

Charity knew she needed help. She'd been this way before, after Daniel's adoption. She was in a dark world where even old friends like Rita couldn't break through. Nothing mattered to her any more: not the business, not friends, not herself.

'There's Martin's promotion to sort out,' Charity said bleakly. 'I just can't seem to get my head round that.'

'The girls and I can handle it,' Rita said firmly. 'You're just making yourself worse by trying too hard.'

'OK.' Charity got up from her chair. She knew if she stayed in the office Rita would keep on digging. She didn't want to be at home either, but solitude was preferable to questions. 'Maybe a couple of days in bed will sort me out.'

'The doctor first,' Rita reminded her. 'Now put the business out of your mind and just rest. I'll pop round after work tomorrow to see how you are.'

Rita sat with Charity's address book in front of her. Charity wouldn't approve of her worrying Prue, but in Rita's view she was the right person to help.

Rita had quietened down a great deal in the past few years, in both appearance and personality. In working hours her curly hair was tied back, she favoured smart dark suits rather than the vivid mini-dresses she once loved. Deep down within her she knew the conscientious and committed way she handled her job was due to Charity's influence. Without her friend's affectionate support over the years she had no doubt she would've gone off the rails, and for that she would always be deeply grateful. But now

Charity needed help and Rita intended to see that she got it.

Prue answered the phone breathlessly, as if she'd just run down the stairs.

'Hallo Prudence.' Rita felt a little awkward. She had met the girl perhaps nine or ten times in all, but they'd never established any real rapport. She was a cold fish, quite unlike the boys and Charity. 'It's Rita Simpson, Charity's friend. I hope I'm not interrupting anything important, but I felt I must speak to you about your sister.'

Prue's guarded tones made it difficult. She wasn't an easy person to talk to at any time, but as Rita launched into an explanation, she could almost hear the girl bristling.

'I don't know what you expect me to do,' she said coldly. 'I have a job too, you know.'

'I understand that.' Rita felt a cold shudder go down her spine, remembering how Charity had skimped herself to give this girl a deposit for a house as a wedding present, even though she wasn't welcome at the ceremony because of that monstrous uncle. 'But Charity would take time off her work for any one of you.'

'I don't feel I have to explain myself to you,' Prue said in an icy voice. 'This is family business.'

Rita knew she couldn't continue this conversation without becoming rude.

'I'll leave the ball in your court,' she said crisply. 'I shall go and see her tomorrow of course, but perhaps you'd like to pass on the message to Toby if he contacts you.'

'Toby's in Germany,' Prue snapped back. 'But I will tell him if he calls.'

Rita put the phone down, her hands trembling. In her mind's eye she could see Charity's face some seven years earlier when Prue called from Studley for help. She remembered too all those Christmases when Charity came staggering through the office doors laden with presents for the children. Weekends given up willingly for them.

'You don't deserve a sister like her,' Rita said between clenched teeth. 'I hope one day you're in serious trouble and that she turns her back on you.'

'Was it Toby?' Stephen pushed his way into the drawing room, his face bright with expectancy. 'Is he coming home?'

He had heard the phone ring while he was outside. Nurse Giles had just put the receiver down and as she stood at the window the morning sun through the leaded panes made a criss-cross pattern on her pale, round face. Her striped uniform and starched white cap suited her buxom shape, giving her an air of confidence she didn't appear to have in her off-duty clothes.

'No Stephen, it was Charity.' She paused just long enough for this to sink in, then smiled. 'It's more than you deserve. But she's coming down tonight.'

Disappointment flooded Stephen's face. He had been waiting for word from Toby for some time – not a letter or phone call in six or eight weeks.

Stephen could pass for a forty-year-old now. He was three stone lighter, and a new diet and long hours spent outdoors had turned his face brown. Dawn was responsible for his new appearance. Her arm exercises had made him strong enough to lift himself, giving him a degree of independence. Her company made the days fly by, but it was their sexual relationship that made him feel like a real man again.

Stephen wasn't ashamed to look in a mirror now. No huge belly flopping over his trousers. His chin was clearly defined. Dawn trimmed his hair herself and it had lost that wild bushy look. But perhaps the

512

most startling feature now was his eyes: losing so much weight meant that they were no longer embedded in flesh and they shone out like blue glass marbles, making him look almost handsome.

Stephen no longer spent hours in his study playing with his soldiers and reading. He trundled his chair out into the grounds, and he'd discovered many tasks he could manage there: pruning roses, weeding the raised flowerbeds in the walled garden, even a bit of hedge trimming.

With stronger arm muscles he could even get up the stairs occasionally to look around. It was a slow, laborious job, hauling himself up on his bottom, but worth it when he explored rooms he hadn't seen in nearly thirty years.

'Why didn't you call me to speak to her? I was only outside.'

'I was afraid you'd put her off,' Dawn retorted. For a big woman her voice was unexpectedly soft, but then Stephen knew only too well there were many inconsistencies in Dawn Giles. Those big muscular arms which could easily support him gave the impression of masculinity, yet she favoured frilly underwear. She maintained an air of starchy sternness in her professional role, yet when alone she often had all the warmth and gaiety of a chorus girl. 'So I said how pleased you'd be to see her, how much happier you are now, and how nice it will be for me to have a night off.'

'How dare you presume so much.' Stephen immediately puffed up with indignation and waved a warning finger at her. 'I'm not senile yet, I can still make decisions for myself.'

Stephen was aware that he was utterly dependent on this woman, both physically and mentally. The thought of someone having so much power over him scared him and he never missed an opportunity to try and put her back in her place.

'No, you aren't senile.' Dawn smiled at him affectionately. 'But you are tactless and somebody had to take you in hand. Besides, I know you've been hoping she'd bury the hatchet and this is proof she wants to.'

He didn't reply for a moment as if chewing it over in his mind.

'Why should she just decide to come out of the blue like this? I don't trust her, she wants something.'

An improvement in his looks and health hadn't changed his suspicious nature, especially where women and money were concerned. Neither had he learned to apologise, not even when he knew he was in the wrong.

'Oh Stephen.' Dawn sat down on the settee next to his wheelchair, shaking her head as if he were a small, stubborn boy. 'Has she ever asked anything of you before?'

Stephen was torn. He didn't approve of bossy women and Dawn had no business to be sticking her nose into family affairs. But he had been considering how he could get Charity back into the fold again. He wasn't exactly surprised that Dawn knew his private thoughts; at times she appeared to have taken him over entirely, mind and body.

'Has she heard anything from Toby?' He was anxious now, afraid Charity might bring bad news.

'She didn't say, but then that will give you something to chat about. She's driving down later this afternoon, she should be here about seven.'

'I still don't understand why she should suddenly have a change of heart.' Stephen turned his wheelchair round and began moving towards the door. 'It's been six years since my mother died and not a letter or a phone call. She did her best to turn Toby and Prudence against me and she influences James.'

514

'For the good,' Dawn said as she followed him to the door. 'He's a kind-hearted, considerate boy and she's more than partially responsible for that. Charity's the one who encourages him to work hard at school, she takes him to lovely places and not once has he ever said anything to me that would lead me to believe she makes you out to be an ogre. That's a good enough reason to make peace, isn't it?'

'I suppose so,' he said reluctantly.

Dawn pushed him into the library.

'Well that's settled then! I must go now and make up a bed for her and ask Margaret to leave some supper for her. You won't need me here so I'll catch the seven o'clock bus.'

Stephen jerked his head round sharply.

'You aren't leaving me here alone with her?'

'Why on earth not!' Dawn put her hands on her hips and glared at him. 'She's your niece, not a fire-eating dragon, and I haven't had an evening with my sister for weeks. I'd only be in the way. You can talk much better without me here.'

'But –' he started to launch into his old routine about needing help.

'You can easily get into that bed alone,' she snapped. 'I'll leave you your medicine by the bed and the bottle in case you need it in the night. I'll be back on the first bus in the morning and Charity will be here if there is an emergency.'

In the past few years, Stephen had become completely dependent on Dawn. And to her surprise, the years with Stephen had been some of the happiest in Dawn's whole life. It had been unexpectedly rewarding stripping the old crusty layers from the man and finding a much younger, virile one buried beneath that surplus weight. His capacity for sexy games surprised her: hardly a day went by without him thinking

515

up a new variation. He loved her striped uniform and black stockings and a glimpse of her white thighs was enough to give him an erection. Sometimes she strapped him down in his bed and teased him with her big breasts; sometimes it was a massage.

But Stephen had learned how to please her too. At times she would pretend to be reading a book sitting on his bed and he'd wheel his chair up in front of her and slide his hands up her knicker legs, then once she was fully aroused she'd sit astride him and he would go on and on for ever until she had several orgasms. Yet it wasn't just the wonderful sex they had together, but sharing things that meant the most.

They would sit together in the evenings, listening to music, watching the television or doing jigsaws. By day she helped him in the garden, took him for long walks or just sat companionably reading. She might have given him back his health and vigour, but Stephen was the first man who had ever made her feel wanted, needed and loved.

Dawn didn't go straight back to him when she'd finished preparing Charity's room; she packed an overnight bag and checked that all the upstairs rooms looked nice.

She was curious about what Charity wanted too. Perhaps Charity thought it was time everyone was open about the children seeing her. It had been very silly for the first couple of years when Stephen pretended he didn't know. But Charity hadn't sounded quite herself on the phone; at least it wasn't the clear, assertive voice Dawn remembered. Dawn hoped it wasn't more trouble.

She was wary of both Prue and Toby. Prue because she looked down her nose at Dawn, and sucked up to her uncle when she really cared nothing for him. It had been a relief when she got married and left Studley.

Toby was far more lovable, but underneath that charming exterior she knew he was a rogue. As a boy he stole money from her purse, though Stephen hotly denied it. She was absolutely certain it was Toby who took the photo frames and she suspected other things had gone too, over the years.

But he had been in the army for a year now; maybe that would sort him out. Dawn just wished he'd phone Stephen now and again. It didn't take much to keep Stephen happy.

Such a big house just for us two, she thought as she paused at the top of the wide oak staircase. Stephen had told her once that this house had been built in 1184 as a nunnery, something which always made her smile. Charles I had stayed here during the civil war and she loved to imagine those Cavaliers with long curling hair, velvet doublets and swords at their sides, striding around in the great hall.

Dawn went out into the kitchen and made a pot of tea. As she came back in carrying the tray, she saw that Stephen had dropped the side of his wheelchair and hoisted himself out on to the Chesterfield.

'Come and sit beside me,' he said in a plaintive voice.

Dawn put the tray down on a small table and drew it closer. 'What's the matter?' she asked.

Once that sort of question would have prompted a sharp retort, but instead he put his arm around her and drew her close.

'Do you ever regret things you've said and done?' he asked.

'Often,' she said, turning to face him. 'Sometimes I lie awake thinking about them and wish I could apologise to the people involved.'

'You are a good woman, Dawn,' he murmured, his fingers reaching for the buttons on her dress. 'Thank goodness you've stayed with me all these years.'

His fingers found her right nipple and the way he rolled it between his fingers made her belly contract with desire.

He moved his head down to her breasts, pulling her brassière down beneath them so they rose up to his face like two firm melons.

'I can never get enough of these,' he murmured, rubbing his lips from one nipple to the other and squeezing them gently. 'I used to look at my dirty books and dream of having a pair in my hands. I never thought it would happen though, and even in my wildest dreams I never imagined being able to fuck someone again.'

Dawn arched her back and let him suck at her nipples. If she closed her eyes she could imagine Stephen as he was in all those photographs of him when he was young: a green uniform with black buttons, a hard young body inside it. Just the thought of it made the blood rush to her head and her insides turn to jelly.

'You must promise me you'll be nice to Charity,' she said, as his hand crept up her thigh over her stocking tops. 'And tomorrow night when she's gone I'll put on that naughty underwear you bought me and give you a really good seeing to.'

'I can't wait that long,' he pleaded. 'Sit on my chair and let me look at you.'

She knew exactly what he meant; this was a game he loved to play. Sometimes she had to pretend she was asleep across his bed, sometimes he got her to perch on his desk just in front of him.

One of his hands was already fumbling at the zip of his trousers.

'It's broad daylight and the curtains are open,' she said, licking her full lips, excited herself now at the thought of the pleasure he would give her.

'No one's likely to look in my window.' He grinned wolfishly. 'Come on, Dawnie, show me your pussy!'

She couldn't resist him when he looked so hungry for her. She stood up, lifted her dress and pulled down her knickers, stuffing them under a cushion, then sat in his wheelchair facing him with her legs splayed apart.

'You're a naughty boy,' she said reprovingly. 'I've got a good mind to give you a spanking for making me do this.'

Stephen forgot about his disappointment that Toby hadn't written or phoned, and forgot too that Charity was coming later. All he could think of was that mound of dark pubic hair, the contrast of white belly and thighs against her black stockings and suspenders and how good it was to have a real woman to feel again.

'I hoped she'd be here by now.' Dawn stood at the window with her dark blue coat on. 'I'll have to go if I'm to catch the bus.'

She had given Stephen his supper, leaving Charity's on a low heat, and the fire was lit in the drawing room. Out of uniform Dawn looked like any other middle-aged woman, with her greying hair and sensible stout shoes.

'Go and catch the bus,' Stephen said with a smile. 'Leave the door on the latch for Charity. I'll see you tomorrow.'

Dawn bent to kiss him. It made her sad to think of what he had been and a little ashamed she didn't really love him. But they were friends, she looked after him well and she knew she'd made him happier.

'Goodnight,' she said, ruffling his hair with affection. 'Now just you be nice to Charity – or else!'

Stephen watched as she walked down the drive. She wasn't graceful, she walked with a curious flat-footed plod and she had thick ankles. Before his accident he wouldn't have looked twice at her. But he knew he loved her far more than he'd ever loved any other woman.

It began to rain soon after eight, lightly at first, but growing heavier as he sat waiting for the sound of car tyres on the gravel.

By nine it was torrential, wind bending the big cypress tree till it creaked and groaned.

Stephen checked that the spark guard was in front of the fire in the drawing room. Dawn had picked dozens of tulips earlier in the day and the sight of the red and yellow flowers in the old pottery vase made her seem closer. She never went in for dainty arrangements, just picked flowers for their bright colours and plonked them in a vase. They looked more cheery like that, a vivid splash of colour in a sombre room.

It was half-past ten when Stephen decided to go to bed. He poured himself a large tumbler of whisky, downed the two sleeping pills Dawn had left out for him, then lowered the side of his wheelchair and hoisted himself on to his bed.

Of all the things Dawn had done for him, this one act of teaching him to get in and out of bed alone humbled him most. It reminded him of how he had wallowed in self-pity for years after his amputation, refusing the offer of artificial legs until it was too late.

To think they once said he wouldn't live beyond fifty! He'd show everyone – he'd still be around for his ninetieth birthday.

The pills and the whisky began to work almost as soon as his head touched the pillow. He closed his eyes and thought about Dawn while the storm lashed around the house in fury.

Stephen felt the softness of the pillow on his face, but

in his dreams it was just Dawn's big breasts comforting him.

It was only when his hands tried to reach for her that he felt the restraints across his chest and knew this was no dream.

He fought hard and long, bucking, thrashing and head-butting, his fingers clenching at the bedcovers, unable to reach his silent assailant.

A sharp pain in his chest arrested any further movement. He could hear fluid bubbling in his lungs and all the time the pressure over his nose and mouth grew stronger.

Dawn he tried to shout, but the word was only in his head and he knew this was the end.

Charity bent over the steering wheel, her hands clenching it so hard her knuckles were white. By the time she'd got to Henley's Corner on the North Circular Road the traffic was thinning and all she could see clearly was the road ahead in the beam of her lights. The rain was driven sideways by the strong wind, wipers having a hard job to clear it fast enough, and the impression was of being in a boat.

Once on the dual carriageway she felt herself relaxing slightly. There were no more lights from houses, few other cars on the road and the speed was exhilarating. On and on she drove, past the turn-off to Beaconsfield, then on past High Wycombe. It was only when she saw signs ahead for Oxford that it dawned on her she had run out of her flat and driven this far without really knowing what she was doing.

Why had she come out? Was it a crazy idea to go to Studley Priory, or to see Prue?

To her further dismay she saw she was almost out of petrol, so she took the road to Cowley. It was another ten minutes before she saw a garage up ahead, but as she got closer she saw it was shut. She went on and on, with no idea where she was. She saw a sign saying 'Iffley' but this meant nothing and once again she only saw a closed garage. By the time she reached a still busy intersection Charity had lost all sense of direction and she turned right, thinking that led towards the centre of Oxford, but within minutes she became aware she was going further away from the town. Panic overtook her, she gripped the steering wheel harder still, peering through the rain-lashed windscreen, unable to see more than thirty feet ahead.

At last she saw a brightly lit garage. Sighing with relief she pulled in and stopped. But as she turned to the passenger seat and saw no handbag the feeling of panic came back.

She put her arms on the steering wheel, her head dropping on to them in bleak despair, tears welling up inside her.

Her watch said ten past twelve. The hours between leaving the office and now were hazy. She had left her flat without knowing where she was going, or why, and she had no money with her. Was she going mad?

A tap on the window made her look up. A man in a yellow oilskin coat was peering in. Charity sat up, wiped her eyes and opened the window.

'What's up, love? Lost yer way?' the man said.

'I need petrol,' she said. 'But I've just found I left my purse at home.'

'Ain't you got a cheque?' he asked.

'No,' she shook her head. 'Could you let me have petrol and I'll send you one tomorrow.'

The man sucked in his breath. The woman looked honest enough, too young and pretty to be trying it on and she'd been crying. But if she didn't send a cheque on, he'd have to pay.

'Can't do that,' he said. 'You could leave yer watch as security.'

Charity would have given him anything just then. She pulled it off her wrist and handed it to him.

'OK, love,' he said. 'Fill 'er up then come over to the office for a receipt.'

Anger took the place of apathy as Charity found she'd taken a wrong turning and ended up in the middle of a council estate. She would do as Rita said and see a doctor; maybe with help she could put all this hurt behind her. As for Toby, he could look out for himself from now on. At this moment she never wanted to see him again.

She found her way back on to the right road eventually and now she wanted nothing more than to be home, back in her little flat, safe within her own four walls. Round the roundabout she'd started off from and at last the signs showed she was back on the A40. The empty road seemed to go on and on for ever and she stepped harder on the gas to get home quicker.

There was nothing to indicate she was approaching London. Lights had gone out in houses; even the street lamps appeared dull in the driving rain. With her foot hard on the accelerator, concentrating only on the road in front of her, she wasn't aware she was approaching Hanger Lane. All she saw was the clear road ahead in the arc of her wipers. Not the red light.

Bob and Janet Robinson were coming down from Ealing on their way home to Wembley in their Ford. Bob had his foot down and he was laughing at Janet's tale about another guest at the dinner party. Their light was green and they belted across the crossroads.

'Christ Almighty!' Bob yelled as the black Mini appeared from nowhere right across their path.

Stan Meadows lived in a flat above the shops that overlooked the crossroads. He was just going to bed when he heard the squeal of brakes and leapt to the window to see what was happening.

The two cars collided with an almighty crash just as he looked out. The black car spun round in a complete circle and crashed into the barrier outside the tube station. The light-coloured one spun in the opposite direction, right round into the path of oncoming traffic.

Sodium lamps made the scene as light as day. Rain lashing down turned the road to a river, a Belisha beacon on a pedestrian crossing making dozens of golden moon shapes in the water.

For a moment he could only stare. He could see someone hanging halfway out of the black car's windscreen, blonde hair vivid against the gleaming paintwork and steam or smoke rising from the smashed bonnet. When he looked back to the other car he saw there were two passengers, both slumped forward.

He grabbed the phone and dialled 999.

It was just after seven in the morning when Dawn Giles arrived back at Studley Priory, stepping past the huge puddles on the drive.

'Fancy forgetting to lock the door,' she muttered as she found it still on the latch. She paused in the hall, looking across the drawing room to the library and glanced at her watch.

It was too early to wake Stephen, so she turned into the dining room to make her way to the kitchen to make herself a cup of tea.

She frowned at the cooker. It was still on a low heat. Opening the door she found Charity's supper, now a dark brown mass.

'Perhaps Stephen forgot to tell her.' She sighed, scraping it into the bin and leaving the plate to soak. Waiting for the kettle to boil, she returned to the drawing room and pulled back the curtains. Only then did she notice that there was no car in the drive.

Puzzled, she went upstairs, taking her coat off as she went. Quietly she opened the door of the room Charity was intended to sleep in, only to find the bed empty.

'Oh dear,' she sighed. 'I suppose she decided not to come with the storm and all. He'll have that to hold against her now.'

Dawn hung up her coat, changed into her uniform and brushed her hair before going downstairs again.

It was eight o'clock when she went into Stephen's room with the tea tray. In the gloom she could see him lying asleep on his back just as he always did. She put the tray down on the desk and went to draw back the curtains.

As light flooded into the room, she screamed, clutching her apron between her hands.

His face was blue, eyes bulging out of his head like azure marbles and his mouth gaping open.

Despite all Dawn's training and her familiarity with death she was rooted to the spot with horror.

It was the worst day Dawn Giles had ever experienced. First Dr Harris arrived, then the local police, then a police doctor, who confirmed Dr Harris's opinion that Stephen had been strapped down securely while still sleeping, then suffocated with a pillow.

Margaret arrived for work at nine, but instead of being allowed the comfort of talking to another woman, a policeman ordered Dawn curtly to stay in the drawing room until she'd been questioned.

Suddenly the house was crawling with men. Some in uniform, some plain clothes, and not one of them seemed to realise just how upset Dawn was. They took over the house, poking into every drawer, every cupboard and asking so many questions.

They took Charity's, Prue's and Toby's telephone numbers but didn't tell Dawn whether or not they'd been able to contact any of them.

Stephen's body was photographed, then later taken away for a post-mortem and she still wasn't allowed to move. Worse still, Dawn realised with ever growing horror that she was a prime suspect.

At five in the afternoon the police got the message that Charity Stratton had been found in a hospital in Ealing. Admitted seriously injured less than two hours after the time of Stephen's death, her car had crashed as she came off the Oxford road.

Dawn didn't know how to react to this further tragedy in the family, and it didn't help that the police wouldn't explain anything. Had Charity been here? Was it possible that she had killed Stephen? Or was it just coincidence?

At ten Dawn went to bed, but knew she wouldn't sleep. All alone in the big house, she was scared. Not just of all the strange creaking sounds the Priory made at night, but of the future.

She had been told by the police not to leave the house, or to gossip with anyone about the investigation. They'd locked Stephen's room and taken away the key.

Everything she'd worked for these seven years – gone. Who would want to employ her as a nurse when it got out that she'd left her last patient all alone?

The police were informing both Prudence and Toby about the murder and soon they'd be here, doubtless blaming her for everything. Neither of them would give her a reference now.

Charity was aware of someone sitting beside her, though she couldn't see them, just as she'd been aware of people handling her on and off for some time. She had memories of terrible pain, but could feel nothing now.

Her right arm wouldn't move, it seemed to be held fast, but her left fingers were touching something bumpy and soft. She moved them slightly, like a blind person reading Braille, but no message came back to her. Slowly she lifted them up to her face.

'Miss Stratton?' A deep male voice spoke.

She tried to move her head in the direction of the voice, but a sharp pain in her neck prevented her. Slowly she lowered her hand to her mouth. It felt so strange, something like after having an injection at the dentist, puffy, yet numb, then as she felt upwards towards her eyes her fingers touched a bandage.

'What's happened to me?' Her voice came out as a croak, her hand feverishly discovering that her entire head seemed to be bandaged.

'You're in Ealing hospital. You had a bad accident in your car. Do you remember?'

'My car?'

She could picture herself in her car. She was in a traffic jam just by Lord's Cricket Ground and someone was honking a horn at her because she hadn't moved when the car in front did. She moved the memory frame forward and saw herself getting out at her flat, locking the car and going in.

She could hear the man telling her about an accident at Hanger Lane, about the passengers in another car she hit, but it meant nothing.

'Am I blind?' she whispered.

She could tell he'd moved closer to her; she could feel his breath on her cheek.

'No. Your eyes and head are bandaged because of bad cuts, and your arm's broken. But the doctor will come and tell you about it.'

'Who are you, then?' Her lips were sore and her tongue felt too big for her mouth.

'I'm a policeman,' he said. 'Jim Baker. I've been sitting here waiting for you to wake up. How do you feel?'

She couldn't answer that question accurately. Maybe if she could see how bad her injuries were she'd be able to make an assessment. She felt numb, her mind cloudy, and apart from her fingers touching the blanket she had no real feeling.

'Am I paralysed?' she asked weakly.

'I don't know,' he replied and she heard sympathy in his voice. 'But the doctor will come any minute.'

She felt herself drifting off again, and even though she was aware the man was speaking to her, it meant nothing.

'She woke for a minute or two.' Jim Baker got up and moved towards the policeman who'd come to relieve him. 'But she didn't say much.'

Charity had been admitted to the intensive care unit of the hospital thirty-six hours earlier but once it was discovered she was the niece of the wealthy man who had been murdered in Oxford the day before, she had been moved up to a private room on the second floor. The two policemen had been sitting with her in shifts since then, waiting for her to come round.

PC James Baker was stout, prematurely balding even though he was only thirty. Unambitious, he usually ended up being given jobs like this because of his patient, caring nature. Martin Cox was the same age, and they had joined the force at the same time, twelve years ago. Already their sympathies were

528

aroused by the patient, regardless of whether or not she'd played some part in the murder. Lying in that bed she looked so small and helpless, like a child.

Chapter Twenty-Eight

Hugh Mainwaring stared at the newspaper in front
of him. He had a client waiting to see him, a pile of
briefs that needed checking through and there were
letters he should dictate for his typist, but he was
stunned by all the memories thrusting their way back
into his mind.

'*Charity,*' he muttered to himself.

His office was small and cluttered. A gloomy room
which befitted his status as a junior partner in the
firm of solicitors, tucked away on the second floor of
their chambers in the Temple.

Today had started as uneventfully as all other days.
He caught the eight-fifteen train from Staines, just as
he did every morning. In his pin-striped dark suit,
bowler hat, furled umbrella and briefcase, he blended
in with all the other City gents who flocked to the
City daily. He nodded to men he saw each morning
and resigned himself to folding his copy of *The
Times* and attempting to read it standing up, as it was
a rare day when he managed to get a seat.

It was doubtful he'd have even noticed the small
item about a retired colonel found dead in his bed
if it hadn't happened in Oxford. He idly wondered
whether 'suspicious circumstances' meant the man
had been poisoned, shot or strangled, then moved on
to something else.

Had it not been for Simon, one of the articled clerks,

he probably wouldn't have heard anything more about the case for a day or two.

'Wouldn't mind a bedside vigil with her myself!' Simon was saying, to giggles from the typing pool, hanging over a copy of the *Daily Mirror*. Simon fancied himself as a ladies' man, despite the fact that he was only five foot three with a round, chubby face. Hugh paused, more from amusement at Simon's schoolboy-ish glee than interest in the object of his admiration.

'Blonde or brunette?' he asked, fully expecting Simon to report rapturously on the girl's vital stat-istics. 'Has she got big ones?'

'You men are so insensitive.' Judy the older of the two typists, a bookish girl with glasses, looked offended. 'The poor girl's in hospital fighting for her life. How can you treat it so lightly?'

Hugh moved closer to the paper on the desk, but even as he read the headline POLICE IN BEDSIDE VIGIL, the picture beneath it of a beautiful blonde woman made his head spin. He sat down with a bump on a typing stool.

'I say Hugh, you've gone as white as a sheet!' Simon said. 'Do you know her?'

Denial was instinctive.

'Just for a moment I thought I did.' Hugh forced himself to smile. 'One too many drinks last night!'

He left the typing pool seconds later, but instead of going to his office went out into the street to buy another copy of the paper.

It was like having twelve years stripped away. Hugh's heart was pumping and his palms were sweaty. In his head Charity had stayed as she'd been when he saw her ride off on her bike that last day at the cottage, boyishly slender in little blue shorts, her hair long and straight, her sweet innocent face dis-torted by tears.

This other Charity looked to be a beautiful woman,

531

with a coolly distant expression and a harder look in her eyes.

It was five in the afternoon before he had time to get his thoughts together. All day between court appearances, reading briefs and interviewing two clients, Charity had been flitting through his mind. He could recall every detail about that summer romance. He'd often relived it in his mind and had been surprised at how long she stayed with him, despite the number of other girls he'd slept with at Oxford.

Hugh had always been considered a lucky chap. He had breezed through school and Oxford effortlessly, liked by almost all his tutors, looked up to by other students and very successful with women. But somehow, somewhere along the line a light had gone out, and he'd lost his glow.

Marrying Sophie Alton had been perhaps slightly influenced by the fact that Beresford, her father, was a High Court judge, but Hugh had honestly thought he loved her at the time.

The temptation, based on his teenage memory, was too strong. His hand strayed to the phone. The least he could do was check out how badly hurt she was and maybe discover how involved she was in the death of her uncle.

Half an hour later Hugh was still in his office. He was aware he'd missed his usual train home and that Charles Sommerville, a colleague, was coming to dinner. His police contact said she was badly injured, that she had no memory of driving anywhere.

'Oh Hugh, I'm furious. You are naughty being late tonight.' Sophie came out of the kitchen as he stepped into the hall. 'Charles and Hilary will be here in five minutes and I was expecting some help.'

'I'm sorry.' Hugh put his umbrella in the stand

by the door and kissed her proffered cheek. He was tempted to say that she'd had all day to prepare dinner. Cooking for two old friends wasn't exactly beyond a woman who boasted she could knock up a cordon bleu meal in half an hour, and she had a daily woman in anyway. 'What needs doing?'

'Nothing now,' she sulked. 'I've even opened the claret. You'd better get changed.'

Sophie's prettiness was of the chocolate-box variety: strawberry blonde, with pink and white skin and a hint of freckles on her slightly upturned nose. In a long, pintuck-bodiced Laura Ashley dress, she was a real Home Counties girl. She liked everything to be perfect, a kind of romantic dream in soft focus. Ruffles on every flower-sprigged curtain, a profusion of cream lace and gentility.

Hugh had made no protests as each room in their mock-Georgian house was transformed into pretty feminine perfection. Sophie scoured antique shops for the stripped pine furniture, studied the glossy magazines for further inspiration to create an image of Edwardian fussiness. But tonight as he went into their bedroom and saw the satin and lace-trimmed pillows strewn on the canopied bed, he had a desire to sweep them all off. Open the window to let out the smell of pot-pourri, and untidy those perfectly placed bottles of expensive perfume.

A dark blue velvet frame trimmed with ribbon on his chest of drawers held a photograph of Sophie in her wedding dress, with beside it a small crystal vase of freesia. He took out his gold cufflinks, put them into the tiny tray left for the purpose and winced at the photograph.

Their wedding day had been the first time he had realised how entirely self-centred Sophie was. Everything from her ridiculously expensive dress to his top hat and tails, the open-topped vintage car and even her lace parasol had been designed to show herself off. He had been well down her list of priorities that day.

'Damn you,' Hugh muttered as he went into the bathroom for a shower. He wasn't sure if he meant Charity for invading his thoughts again, or Sophie for not turning out to be quite the loving partner he'd expected.

Hugh slipped away to his study while Sophie was showing Charles and his wife some holiday snaps, using the excuse that he had to telephone a client urgently.

'How the hell are you, Rob?' he said, quite forgetting he had neglected his old chum shamefully over the past ten years. 'It's Hugh! Long time no see!'

He kept up the lighthearted banter for some minutes before he began to realise that Rob didn't sound particularly pleased to hear from him.

'Look, I'll get to the point, old man,' he said, having the grace to blush a little. 'Have you seen the papers today? Charity – you remember her, don't you? – Well she's had a bad car accident, and you being a doctor, well I thought you'd be well placed to find out how she is.'

Dr Robert Cuthbertson put the phone down and for a moment he was too stunned by the news from Hugh to even think.

'Charity,' he said aloud.

He could recall a picture of her as clearly as if he'd seen her this afternoon. Yet it was twelve years ago when he'd stood at the cottage door and seen her for the first time.

She'd been wearing a pink cotton dress that day; her legs and arms bare and her long blonde hair windswept from riding her bike. Her smile was as shy as his own and he remembered being acutely aware of

534

his acne and his weedy frame, next to Hugh's teen idol perfection.

Charity had stayed in Rob's head and heart long after his tan from that summer had faded and he couldn't count the times he'd ridden his bike up past Bowes Court school with the faint hope he might just run into her.

He stood up, leaving his sitting room to get the telephone directory from the hall, but as he saw his reflection in the hall mirror he was again reminded of how much time had passed and the changes that must have taken place in all three of them.

Rob had had a spurt of growth after that summer. Now he was a presentable five feet ten, and no one, not even wonderboy Hugh Mainwaring, could accuse him of being a weed any longer. Rob could never have been described as handsome – his fair hair flopped, he got freckles in the sun and there wasn't one remarkable feature in his face – but his patients responded to him, nurses claimed he had a kissable mouth, and it was a face that seemed to improve with maturity.

Rob's life hadn't turned out a bit as he'd supposed it would that summer in the cottage. He didn't even get to Oxford. When his mother came back from Italy she'd collapsed with a nervous breakdown and attempted suicide, so Rob stayed at home instead. It was during this time as he helped look after his mother that his whole outlook changed and he decided to become a doctor. He got a place later in a pre-medical course at St Bart's in London, but it wasn't until six years later, still at St Bart's doing his pre-registration year, that he realised medical or surgical work wasn't for him, but psychiatry. Now he was a senior registrar at Colney Hatch mental hospital.

Rob lived at Albemarle Mansions, a quaintly Victorian block of flats just off Baker Street. His grand-

535

mother had bought the flat for him for his twenty-first birthday, though she never understood why he wanted such an odd, old-fashioned place, aside from it being a smart address.

But then Rob loved the odd, the unexplained, even the bizarre; that was why he liked psychiatry. His flat was like a rabbit warren: long narrow passages, peculiar shaped rooms, an impractical place with great character.

He'd furnished it with antiques from his grandmother, not because they were valuable, but because he loved to have memories of her and they looked right here. Girlfriends said the place was creepy, but that was because he seldom remembered to replace light bulbs. His work at the hospital didn't give him much time for tidying up. In his sitting room books were piled on the floor, a mountain of papers spilled over his desk, and his bedroom was even worse.

After Rob had rung the Ealing hospital he sat at his piano and began to play. He had been working his way through Beatles numbers for some weeks, but he found it ironic that the one he picked tonight was 'Girl'.

'She's the kind of girl you want so much it makes you sorry, but you don't regret a single day,' he sang softly.

PC Jim Baker was bored stiff. He couldn't think why they were still mounting a twenty-four-hour guard on Charity Stratton as it was patently obvious she had neither the strength nor the inclination to run away.

The sound of feet made Baker turn in his seat, stifling yet another yawn. A man was walking purposefully along the corridor towards him carrying a huge bunch of flowers.

He stopped, looking at the door of the private room, then back at Baker.

'May I see Miss Stratton?'

'Who are you?' Baker asked. The man was around the same age as himself, with fair hair neither fashionably long nor a decent short cut, and a worn brown leather jacket but for some reason the clipped public school voice irritated him. Maybe it wasn't the voice so much, more that the man looked far more youthful than he felt himself.

'Dr Cuthbertson. May I see her?'

The title 'doctor' immediately made Baker feel intimidated, yet at the same time the bunch of flowers and the man's leather jacket meant he wasn't visiting in a professional capacity.

'I've had instructions not to let anyone in but close relatives.' Baker's tone was a little churlish.

Since Miss Stratton regained consciousness, Baker often went in for little chats with her. At first they had been pure duty: questions designed to get her to open up, maybe even get a confession. Detective Inspector Fleming didn't believe she remembered nothing about the evening prior to her accident, but Baker did, now.

As unprofessional as he knew it was, Baker saw himself as a friend, not a gaoler. Fleming and some of the other officers involved with the case might see her as a high-flying businesswoman who'd cracked and killed her uncle because of some family feud. But Baker's gut reaction was that she was merely a lonely, disturbed woman who just happened to crash her car in the wrong place, at the wrong time.

'Have any of her close relatives been?' Robert asked, his question worded in such a way it sounded like a challenge.

'Well no,' Baker admitted reluctantly. 'Not yet anyway. Only Rita Simpson who works for her.'

'I'm quite safe,' Robert said, picking up that this burly policeman had become protective towards his charge, just as he did with many of his troubled patients. 'Look, if you're doubtful about me, contact Dr Mead the registrar, I spoke to him last night. I'm not just a doctor, but an old friend of Charity's.'

'OK, go on in.' Baker nodded his head towards the door. 'But you'd better give me your name and address.'

Robert gave the information.

'How is she doing?' he asked, his hand on the door.

'Up and down.' Baker shrugged his shoulders. 'She tries to keep a brave face, but since she heard about her uncle – ' he paused, unable to admit how often he'd heard her crying when she thought no one was around.

Robert stood for a moment just inside the door, overcome by an unexpected rush of emotion.

He had seen countless patients with far worse injuries than he knew Charity's to be. But she was unrecognisable. Her entire face, neck and the parts of her arms and hands not hidden by either her nightdress or plaster were covered with cuts and both her eyes were blackened and swollen. Her head was swathed in bandage and the plastered arm held still on a rest; even her shape was concealed by a frame over her legs.

There was a basket of flowers on the windowsill, a vase of carnations on the locker and just two get-well cards beside it, a pitifully bleak collection.

'Hallo Charity,' he said, approaching the bed. 'Remember me?'

One swollen eye opened a little wider and he saw a flash of brilliant blue.

'Is this a trick question?' Her voice was barely recognisable. 'Should I know you?'

'No tricks.' He held his hands wide, waving the

flowers, suddenly feeling just as shy as he had at their first meeting. 'It's just a very long time ago.'

Charity studied him. There was something vaguely familiar about him, but she couldn't place him. The man had a comfortably pleasant sort of face, nice brown eyes, and his voice was ringing distant bells.

'Give us a clue?' she said.

'A cottage at Five Ash Down...' Rob lifted one eyebrow questioningly.

Her one free hand flew up to her mouth.

'Rob?'

'The very same.' He smiled. 'May I stay?'

'Yes of course,' she said hurriedly, yet at the same time she had a desire to pull the sheet over her face and hide from him. 'How on earth did you find me?'

Rob put the flowers in the washbasin and pulled up a chair, giving himself time to present the story as Hugh had suggested.

'I saw a bit about you in the paper, and I just had to come. I thought you might need a friend.'

He could see no more of her eyes than a chink of blue embedded in swollen flesh, but a tear glinted on her eyelashes.

'You don't need someone like me as a friend,' she murmured. 'But I appreciate the thought, and the flowers.'

'Allow me to be the judge of whether I need you as a friend.' Rob smiled and reached out to touch her bandaged hand.

There had been many moments since Charity regained consciousness when she wished she'd died in that crash. Apart from the times when her dressings were being changed, or when Jim came in to talk to her, the days and nights were endless. Again and again she'd tried to focus on happy moments in her life, forcing herself to believe this was just a bad patch which she could get over. But she felt as if she was in

539

quicksand, clutching on to a weak branch that would eventually break and she'd be swallowed up by thick slime.

But now Rob had appeared out of nowhere, a boy she retained sweet memories of. He looked so bright and cheery, his hand on hers, warm and capable, and it felt strangely as if she was being offered a hand to help her out.

He was so different from how she remembered. Twelve years ago he'd been small and thin, just like her. Now he was tall, and although still slender he had the kind of robust fitness of a sportsman. She didn't remember Rob having such a square, strong jaw, or such well-shaped lips. But it was his manner that had changed the most: the young Rob had dropped his eyes from direct stares, this Rob looked into her eyes unwaveringly. She recalled how they used to talk together, how much she'd revealed to him about her childhood that she never told Hugh.

'I'm glad you came,' she said. 'Tell me about yourself.'

'But you're the patient,' he smiled. 'I want to know how you are, how you feel?'

'You sound like a doctor.' She tried to smile but it was just a twitch of the lips.

'I suppose I can't switch it off,' Rob said. 'I am a doctor.'

Again her eyes widened enough for him to see blue.

'But you were going to study English literature?'

'I had a change of heart,' he explained. He gave her a brief rundown, omitting to tell her he was in fact a psychiatrist now. 'And to be truthful I phoned the registrar here last night, so I know your spine isn't broken, just your arm. You had a lucky escape, Charity. Most people that fly through windscreens come off much worse than you.'

Charity studied his face as he spoke and liked what

she saw. He had a lovely mobile and expressive mouth, when he smiled it lit up his whole face, and those brown speckly eyes she had liked all those years ago had a wealth of understanding in them now, almost as if he'd seen everything, as she sometimes felt she had.

'I suppose you know too that I'm rumoured to be a bit of a crackpot?' she said, guessing that Dr Mead would tell another doctor everything he knew. 'You must know too I'm a murder suspect.'

'I like to make my own diagnosis.' Rob smiled. 'And from what I remember of you, you aren't capable of murder.'

Robert hadn't had the wonderful childhood most people credited him with. He was a very lonely boy trapped between a hard, ruthless father who was only interested in making money and a highly strung mother who fluctuated between neglecting him and smothering him. For as far back as Rob could remember there had always been fights and slanging matches and as a small boy he'd been convinced he was the reason for the strife.

It was only when his mother had had that breakdown, that Rob had begun to see the fault didn't lie with him. And once his mother had claimed that if she'd had one good friend to talk to, she might not have ended up sedated in hospital. It was a painful memory. Perhaps his experience would help Charity – and do some good.

'I'm not the girl you used to know,' Charity said in a small voice. 'So much has happened.'

'That's true of me too,' Rob said. Charity's injuries prevented him from reading her facial expressions. It was like trying to make an assessment of someone over the phone. All he had to go on was a twelve-year-old memory. 'But I believed we were good friends that summer and I think we could be again, don't you?'

Charity just looked at him for a moment.

She had learned to weigh up people over the years and even if she'd never met Rob before in her life she would instinctively trust him. He'd come not out of curiosity, but with a genuine desire to help her.

'I always liked you, Rob,' she admitted, remembering now with a prickle of guilt that he'd had a crush on her and it must have been painful for him watching Hugh and her together. 'We were good friends, weren't we?'

Rob wondered why she didn't lead on from that remark to ask about Hugh.

'You know, I always imagined you being married, with a parcel of kids,' Rob said with a smile. 'Now I hear you're a successful businesswoman. I'd love to know how that came about.'

'A long story.' Charity tried to smile back, suddenly feeling warmer inside. 'But what about you? Are you married?'

Rob shook his head. 'I failed in that department.'

'A big love that went wrong?' Charity asked.

'Sort of.' Rob looked rueful. 'How about you?'

'Colossal failure,' she said and for the first time in a very long time she actually wanted to laugh. 'So we've got something in common.'

'You know, I think we've got a great deal in common.' Rob smiled. 'But you must rest, and I've got to get back to my own hospital in north London and my own patients. Can I come and see you again?'

'Please do.' Charity felt sad that he was leaving.

Rob stood up, hesitating before saying what had sprung into his mind.

'Look, Charity,' he said. 'I know from Dr Mead that you were in a low state before the accident. I'd like

542

to help. When I come again do you think you could bring yourself to talk to me?'

He sensed rather than saw her pain; it was almost like a grey aura round her.

'I don't know if I can,' she stammered.

'Think it over.' His voice was gentle. 'I came as a friend, that's all, but I am a doctor too and I work with people's problems every day. I can help you if you want me to.'

'Dr Mead said he was going to arrange for a psychiatrist to speak to me,' she said in a low voice. 'Is that what you mean?'

'I am a psychiatrist,' Rob said, putting one hand on hers. This was the last thing he'd intended to admit; he'd found people were wary of psychiatrists. 'Talk to Dr Mead. If you'd rather see someone else, that's fine. I'll still come and visit you.'

The feeling Charity had had earlier that Rob was offering a hand to pull her out of this pit she was in came back, and was stronger now. Her sense of isolation was suddenly lessened.

Her eyes were closing with weariness, but now there was a glimmer of hope. 'Please come back, Rob.'

Robert sat in an armchair deep in thought. It was nearly midnight and he knew he ought to get to bed as he had full schedule of patients to see tomorrow, but Charity was on his mind.

He couldn't see her as just a patient, and that troubled him. Neither could he view her as just a friend in trouble: it had become quite clear to him she needed professional help.

Rob had already made several wrong moves. The first had been in allowing Hugh to manipulate him. The second had been in putting himself forward as a psychiatrist; the third, being unprofessional enough

543

to go and see Charity's friend and employee Rita Simpson.

Hugh was reasonably simple to sort out: he'd just phone him tomorrow and pass on the kind of detached information he usually gave to enquiring friends or relatives. Once Hugh heard Charity hadn't even asked about him he would probably lose interest, as the man had an ego the size of a football pitch.

The second and third moves were now entwined, and at least Rita was wholeheartedly in agreement that Charity needed his help. Rita had given him a great deal of background information – on their flat-sharing days, the building of the business, and the brothers and sister Rob remembered Charity being so concerned about all those years ago. He learned to his dismay that none of these siblings had been to see Charity and this seemed to be a pointer to what caused her depression prior to the crash.

Rita had said that another friend, Dorothy, was coming back from America as soon as she could arrange it. That was a good sign; there didn't seem to be anyone else of importance in Charity's life.

Perhaps the thing which jarred Rob the most about today's events was coming up with direct parallels to his own life. Although there were great gaps in his knowledge about Charity's past, her character and personality, he'd formed a partial picture.

Rob was content with his bachelor life. He had a job which enthralled him, a good salary and, when he needed it, a busy social life. But like Charity, he too had become engrossed in his work and the years had slipped by without him noticing, until now he was becoming a bit of a hermit.

There had been women, lots of them. Nurses he'd dated, a couple of lady doctors and many more bright social butterflies who were attracted to him because of his profession. Charity might have been driven to succeed because of her childhood poverty. Rob was driven by a need for personal recognition.

Right from a small boy Rob had known that people accepted him only because he was rich. If he'd been the son of a farm labourer, no one would have invited a shy kid like him to parties or asked him to play with their children. Hugh was a fine example of this attitude, though it was some years before Rob realised it. At medical school it was the same: he got asked to dinner parties, even though he was frequently tongue-tied with shyness, just so his hosts could boast they knew the heir to the Cuthbertson fortune.

He had been twenty-three when his father lost everything. He'd always been a speculator, starting in the post-war years, but though in the late Fifties and early Sixties he couldn't go wrong with buying and selling land, by 1970 other speculators sharper than himself emerged. It transpired that his father had been robbing Peter to pay Paul for some time and when one of his schemes crashed, it brought the others down too.

Rob had been happily in love with Polly then, a pretty and vivacious girl he'd met at a smart party in Knightsbridge and he believed she loved him for himself. But the night he went to her for comfort when his mother committed suicide following the financial crash, her coolness and lack of sympathy made him see her for what she was.

Rob's mother's death still haunted him, even though he had the experience now to know she had always been a deeply troubled soul. It hurt to see friends like Hugh drop away too, now Rob couldn't splash his money around. Yet being cut adrift from a fortune had been the making of Rob. He found new friends, real ones who liked him for himself, and slowly the personality that had been swamped by his family's wealth and by people who treated him as inferior, began to develop.

Rob had only just taken up his position at Colney Hatch hospital when his grandmother died. She left her house to Rob's father, but all her investments to Rob. To Rob this meant nothing more than the security of knowing he could choose to stay in the field of work he cared deeply about, without financial considerations. To make sure people continued to like him for himself, Rob told no one about his inheritance.

Bridget, a middle-aged Irish woman, came in twice a week to clean up. Though she despaired of a kitchen that showed no signs of cooked meals and a bedroom that looked like a war zone, she managed to keep on top of it. Once Rob had let friends stay in one of the two spare bedrooms, but male companions could be even more trying than female ones, and now these two rooms had the doors firmly shut, except for odd nights when he allowed someone to sleep off a drunken stupor.

I wonder what Charity would make of it? he thought to himself?

'Go to bed, you silly sod,' he said, hauling himself out of the chair. 'Rescue the damsel in distress if you must, but don't look for happy ever after.'

Chapter Twenty-Nine

Charity woke and lay listening to the birdsong from the garden beneath. The curtains were pale blue with a white cloud design, almost like looking at a summer sky. But then there was no indication in the room that this was a nursing home. Aside from the bed, which was higher than a normal one. A television, two comfortable high-backed armchairs, even the white units of drawers, shelves and a desk implied a hotel, not an institution. This was Charity's fourth morning in Holly Bush House, and the first since the accident, nearly three weeks ago, that she hadn't woken out of a nightmare.

She had tried to rationalise what exactly happened in these nightmares so she could tell Rob, but apart from a feeling of terrifying menace there was nothing to hang on to.

Rolling over on to her side, she gripped the mattress with her one good hand and manoeuvred her legs towards the floor. The pain in her back and neck made it impossible to haul herself up to a sitting position, but yesterday she'd mastered this way of getting out of bed. Once her feet touched the hard surface it was comparatively easy to stand.

Her legs were undamaged, but walking jarred her spine. She reached out for her stick and, wincing with the pain, slowly crept towards the en-suite bathroom.

Charity stared dispassionately at herself in the mirror. Her facial scars were still shocking to anyone seeing her for the first time: the one on her right cheek was jagged and ugly and another across her forehead had needed four stitches. But bad as they were, it was her hair that concerned her most. It looked and felt disgusting! Stitching the bad gash on the side of her head had necessitated shaving the immediate area. Now with her hair lank and greasy, this bald patch showed up vividly.

Charity felt no bitterness. Each time she looked in the mirror it was a reminder that she could have killed those two other people. Fortunately their injuries hadn't been as serious as hers and they'd been discharged from hospital within a week.

Ten minutes later she came out of the bathroom and hobbled over to the window to draw back the curtains. The windowsill was just the right height to lean on with her good arm and the slight stretch seemed to help the pain in her back.

It was a beautiful morning. Dew glistened on the grass, a lilac bush was in full bloom, the many rose bushes in the biggest flowerbed were just budding and she could see the Thames beyond the garden wall.

Holly Bush House was in Walton-on-Thames, a large and gracious 1930s house with sunray designs on the front windows, and a wide central staircase and imposing hall. Rob had arranged for her to come here to convalesce.

Rob's visits were the most important thing in her life now; sometimes, she felt, the only thing. Gradually, as the days went past Charity began to feel as if a heavy burden was being lifted from her shoulders. Day after day, she and Rob sat, putting pieces into the jigsaw.

The day she told him about Daniel he sat very quiet and still, his legs crossed, listening attentively.

'Hugh has become the sort of man you wouldn't

like,' he said carefully. 'I believe he really did love you, Charity, but he loved himself more. I'm so sorry about Daniel. I wish I could take away the hurt.'

She told him how low she sank after the adoption, then moved on to lighter things, about how she had met up with Dorothy and Rita again.

She knew she was glossing over other areas in her life. When she talked about sharing the flat she made no mention of the escort service. She spoke of the fire which killed her parents, but couldn't bring herself to explain to him why she didn't grieve for them. Yet she longed to confide in him.

There were many times after these sessions that she wondered about Rob. She wanted to build up a picture of his life, of where and how he lived, but once Rob had taken her on as a patient, he became very skilful at keeping her as the main subject. Charity didn't know whether this desire to know about him was just her natural curiosity, or a wish to redress the balance. After all, he knew so much about her.

She liked his sensitivity, the way he could turn things she'd said around and make her laugh about them. But there was something tantalisingly untouchable about him which intrigued her.

It worried her slightly that she spent so much time dwelling on him. Once or twice she'd even lapsed into imagining how it might have been if she'd fallen for him that summer, instead of Hugh, or indeed if she'd run into him before this breakdown began.

The door opened behind her.

'Good morning, Charity! How are we feeling today?'

Charity turned and smiled at the nurse coming in with her breakfast.

Molly Burke was her favourite nurse, a West Indian woman with a wonderful sense of humour and a delightful singsong voice. She was tall and slender, with curly hair like a fuzzy halo, huge dark brown eyes and a wide, wide smile.

'Pretty good,' Charity said, picking up her stick again and making her way over to the small table where Molly was putting her breakfast.

'Well that's good,' Molly said. 'Because I've got a surprise for you.'

'Give us a clue?' Charity laughed. Molly liked to play games. She often kept meals covered until Charity guessed what was under the lid.

'Tall! Beautiful enough to make most of us give up.'

'Not Dorothy!' Charity's eyes lit up and her smile almost split her face in two.

'The very same.' Molly giggled. 'She turned up late last night, but you were already asleep. She's checked into a hotel and unless I've read her wrong, she'll be rushing back here any minute.'

'Oh Molly.' Charity's spoon stopped halfway to her mouth. 'She came all this way just to see me?'

'Eat that breakfast,' Molly commanded. 'Then we'll attempt to wash your hair.'

The hair washing was finally accomplished between bouts of helpless giggling and groans of pain.

'This is like some medieval torture,' Charity gasped. 'Do I really need clean hair?'

'Where's your pride, you floozie?' Molly reproached her as she pummelled away at her scalp. 'Cleanliness is next to godliness, so my aunt used to say. If you could see the filth coming out of your locks you'd be ashamed of yourself.'

Charity was sitting in a chair when she heard Dorothy's voice wafting along the landing outside her door. She felt a hundred times better in clothes and with her hair washed. As long as she didn't try to move or look at her plastered arm, she could almost pretend she was her old self again.

'Hallo babe!'

The resonant contralto voice brought back so many images from the past. Charity couldn't even attempt to get up; instead, to her embarrassment, tears filled her eyes.

'It's so good to see you, Dot,' was all she managed to get out.

'Now don't start blubbing,' Dorothy said as she paused in the open doorway, 'or I'll be on the next plane back.'

She looked harder and thinner than Charity had noticed when they were in Florida, but still sensational in a cream silk maxidress, deeply tanned and with her hair in a chignon.

For a moment the two girls just looked at one another, then Dorothy moved swiftly to her side, dropped down on to her knees and enveloped Charity in a hug.

'You poor darling,' she whispered and to Charity's surprise her friend's heavily mascaraed eyes were swimming with tears. 'But I'm here now and I'm not leaving.'

Charity had almost forgotten that the bond between them was still so strong. Just one telephone call and Dorothy had abandoned her lovers, her social life in Florida, and jumped on a plane.

Rita had brought Dorothy up to date with all the news last night. Although Charity had been the police's main suspect at first, a petrol receipt found amongst the wreckage of her car proved that she had stopped at a garage on the Abingdon Road, miles away from Studley, at around the time of Stephen's murder. But because of her disturbed mental state and lack of memory, they still hadn't ruled Charity out entirely as an accessory. Toby was another strong suspect, but he had a cast-iron alibi: he'd been drinking in the mess in Germany with at least six other officers. Prue and Nurse Giles had been struck off the police list but they were still vigorously investigating every avenue from ex-employees with a grudge, to random burglary.

At Charity's request Rita had rung friends, Lou and Geoff, Martin and Marjorie to ask them not to visit because she wasn't up to it, but they had all sent flowers and cards. Both Dorothy and Rita were puzzled as to why there had been no enquiries, cards or flowers from Toby or Prue.

Dorothy had never been diplomatic or subtle. The only way she knew how to tackle things was head on. She talked about her work in America, made Charity laugh with heartless tales about her lovers, examined her friend's scars, but all the time she knew she had to strike at the real issue.

'Come on, Chas,' she said. 'What brought all this on?'

Charity shrugged.

'You do know,' Dorothy insisted. 'You might not remember the events just before the accident, but Rita said you were moping about for weeks before that night. She said the last time you were your old self was when you and she went out for a drink together, soon after you came back from Florida.'

Charity felt as if she was being cornered. She did, of course, remember only too clearly what had started it all, even if she couldn't recall the hours before the accident.

Shielding her brothers and sister was so deeply ingrained in her, she couldn't bring herself to admit to Toby and the drugs. The thought of him being thrown out of the army or, worse still, police involvement terrified her. On top of that was the deep sense of shame she felt, for herself and Toby.

'I can't remember,' she said. 'It's all hazy.'

Charity had never been a good liar. Dorothy was pleased to see she wasn't as transparent as she'd once been, but all the same she wasn't quite convincing enough.

'Don't lie to me,' she said reprovingly. 'We've always been honest with one another. I think this must have something to do with Toby.'

Charity knew she'd have to say something or Dorothy would keep on and on.

'We did have a row,' she admitted.

'About what?'

Dorothy had never liked Toby; he was too sly, too sparing with the truth. Last night Rita had told her a story gleaned from one of the office girls and if it was even partially true, Toby had some explaining to do.

'He said I was a prostitute.'

Dorothy wanted to laugh, but she didn't dare.

'That's ridiculous,' she said. 'Are you sure he wasn't getting you mixed up with me?'

'But I was, Dot.' Charity's eyes dropped and a blush stained her face. 'How do you think I got the money to buy the agency from Carmel?'

Dorothy was shocked now. She never felt guilty about her own past: it was something she'd done, and she saw no point in agonising over it. But *Charity*! She always seemed so pure, so unworldly.

'That night the man beat you up,' Charity whispered, 'I didn't come home – remember? I was with Ted Parsloe, I got him to pay me two hundred pounds.'

Dorothy bit back the desire to cheer anyone getting so much.

'So what, Chas! We were all a bit wild then.'

'But I came back and laid into you, didn't I? I was such a hypocrite.'

'If you hadn't laid into me, I'd probably be touting

my diseased fanny around Soho now.' Dorothy's voice wobbled. 'You know I've done far worse and boasted about it too.'

Charity was crying now, big tears rolling down her cheeks, and Dorothy was at a loss as to how to comfort her.

'Oh Chas,' she caressed her friend's scarred cheek tenderly, 'can't you see that brother of yours is poisonous? Why do you go on letting yourself be hurt by your family?'

'Because I love them, because I haven't got anything else.' Charity swiped at her tears with the back of her hand and tried to smile. 'Maybe now I've told you it will help.'

'And Prue? Where does she fit into this?' Dorothy asked.

'You know how starchy she is,' Charity said bleakly. 'I expect Toby told her and she's ashamed of me.'

'Let me try and rustle up some coffee.' Dorothy stood up and smoothed down her silk dress. 'Then we'll have a chat about jollier subjects, like this dishy shrink Rita keeps raving about.'

It was just after nine that night when Dorothy stepped out of a taxi in Greek Street, Soho. She had changed her silk dress for a beige linen trouser suit and her hair was tied back at the nape of her neck with a wide brown velvet ribbon.

Daylight was just fading and all around her neon lights were being switched on, but it was a little early in the evening to be really busy. A bunch of American tourists were outside a strip club. One man in a white suit was posing next to a lifesized cutout nude girl, one of his hands on her breast, while his wife was taking his photograph.

Dorothy felt distaste, not just at them but the whole sordid scene. It had been some years since she was last in Soho and it all looked so dirty and seedy. There were far more sex shops and strip clubs than she remembered and though it was too early for prostitutes to be out and about, every doorway seemed to be covered with cards offering the services of girls upstairs.

The worst of it was, she might have ended up like that, putting out a card offering 'French Lessons' or 'Strict Tuition'. It had all seemed such a joke seven or eight years ago when she thought her beauty and youth would last for ever. She had Charity to thank for stopping her running over that particular clifftop.

Dorothy hurried on up the dingy staircase. Scuffed cream paint, the stairs littered with scraps of paper and balls of fluff. At the top a steel-plated door bore the sign BAYLISS ENTERPRISES in black lettering. She knocked and waited.

She felt rather than heard someone looking through a spyhole at her. The door opened.

'Hallo, George,' she said. 'Remember me?'

George had been one of her first escort dates. He stuck in her mind because he'd informed her he didn't normally pay to take a girl out, but he needed someone classy with him that night because he was out to impress a guy he was going to do a deal with. After that night she was given similar excuses by many men, but George was the only one she ever really believed.

His slight frame, thinning hair and small greying moustache made him an unlikely candidate to run a string of clubs in Soho. But what he lacked in physical presence he made up for in his clothes. His suit was silver grey, a four or five hundred pound hand-tailored job, and he had enough gold jewellery to buy a house in the suburbs.

'As if I could forget a face like that!' He smiled. 'It's Dorothy! What on earth brings you to my door?'

His firm handshake and the instant recognition gave Dorothy new heart. She hadn't really expected him to be around Soho still. She'd also thought he'd be much seedier and older by now.

He led her into an inner office. After the dingy staircase it seemed almost palatial, with leather chairs and a mahogany desk. If it hadn't been for a view through the small window of chimneypots, dirty windows and tiny yards packed with beer crates, she might have thought they were in Mayfair.

'Do sit down, Dorothy.' He was as polite as she remembered, and it impressed her. 'Can I get you a drink?'

'Not now.' She gave him a long look. Nine years ago he had seemed ancient. Now she saw he was possibly fifty, but moustaches often made men look older. 'Maybe later. I came to see you, George because I thought you might be able to help me.'

Dorothy's name and her face had stayed in George's memory for more than her beauty. She had amused him all those years ago because she was so open about being a gold-digger. George appreciated honesty; it was a rare commodity in his world.

'I want you to find out anything you can about this man. I'll pay you for the information.'

She pulled out a photograph of Toby Stratton in uniform that Charity had once given her. George picked it up and looked at it hard.

'An officer in Her Majesty's eh? What's this all about?'

'I can't tell you that,' Dorothy said.

'Can you just give a rough idea of what he's done? Anything,' George said. 'It's a bit like looking for the proverbial whatsit.'

'I can't, George,' she said again. 'All I can say is he's a bit flash, he might use some of the clubs round here. I seem to remember you know everyone.'

'The important people.' He smiled, and for a moment he reminded Dorothy of David Niven.

'Show it to them, then,' she said arching her eyebrows delicately. 'I'm sure I don't have to ask you to be discreet?'

'I'll do my best.'

To her surprise, Dorothy discovered that she found the older man rather attractive.

'I want to know everything about him. Absolutely everything.'

'I'll put one of my contacts on to it right away.' George smiled with his eyes. 'Where can I get hold of you?'

'You can't.' Dorothy stood up. 'I'll contact you!'

'And when we've got the full picture, what then?' George asked.

'That all depends on what you find.' Dorothy made towards the door. 'I'll be in touch. And George – thanks! I had a feeling I was right coming to you.'

Chapter Thirty

Toby sat at the small desk in the drawing room, Nurse Giles a few feet away in a wing-backed armchair. His chequebook was in front of him and his pen, but he was trying to ascertain how little he could give to her whilst still appearing to be generous.

In a blazer, grey slacks and a white open-necked shirt he looked very much like the young Stephen in old photographs, and by the way Nurse Giles looked at Toby on occasions he guessed she wouldn't mind offering him a little of her 'nursing' skills too.

Toby felt he was walking a tightrope. He was anxious to get rid of anyone who knew the Pennycuicks and their history and this nurse knew more than anyone. But at the same time he wanted her complete sympathy, to make sure she retained some loyalty to the family.

'You do understand I don't want to let you go.' He gave her the concerned, anxious look he had perfected with women. 'You were so good with my uncle and I know you've come to see Studley as your home. But I don't know what else to do, Dawn. You see until the estate has gone through probate, I don't have the money to keep you on.'

Toby had big plans. He would turn the old place into a country club eventually. But it was only a few weeks since he'd buried his uncle and until the police stopped probing and digging, he wasn't going to do anything to raise anyone's suspicions about anything.

'I understand.' Dawn Giles hung her head. She had been expecting this for weeks and was touched that Toby had been so kind and considerate to have kept her on with full pay all this time. But his compassionate leave from the army was up and he had to rejoin his regiment; apart from a bit of cleaning there was no place for her now. 'You've been more than fair with me and I can stay with my sister until I find another job.'

'The death of the colonel has left a big hole in both our lives.' Toby sighed deeply, smoothing back his hair as if deeply concerned for her. 'I thought he'd be around for years to guide me in my career and I feel too young for all this responsibility. I try so hard to believe in Charity's innocence too, but she's torn the family apart.'

'You've got to try and put it aside,' Dawn said, her maternal feelings aroused by Toby's obvious grief.

Toby poured himself a large glass of whisky and sat down again once Nurse Giles had left. One more night here and back to his regiment to play soldiers and in a year or so, once the estate was finally his, he could buy himself out of the army.

He was just about to start on a second glass when he saw Prue's car turn into the drive.

The Morris Minor estate she drove said all there was to say about her. Boringly practical and yawningly dull. He could almost bet she had a 'Ban the bomb' sticker on its back window. Toby got up quickly, tucked the glass under the settee and went to open the front door.

'What a nice surprise!' He tried to look delighted as Prue stepped out of her car. She looked halfway between a hippie and a frumpy housewife. Her long hair was scraped back from her wide face and held with a rubber band. She wore no makeup, a long smock-type dress and the kind of Jesus sandals only favoured by intense librarians. Toby often wondered why she made no effort to make the best of herself, but Prue was full of feminist claptrap these days and perhaps she thought by making herself look as unattractive as possible she would never be mistaken for a sex object. 'What brings you here?'

'I want to talk to you,' Prue said with that tight-lipped look he remembered so well from when they were children. 'I've got things to say to you, Toby. Where are the servants?'

'If you mean Margaret, she's doing some shopping.' Prue had some wonderful expressions, but then she belonged in another century. 'Dawn Giles has left now. So we're all alone.'

Prue stormed past him leaving in her wake a faint hint of lavender water. Toby followed her into the drawing room and flopped down on the settee.

At closer inspection he could see she looked quite demented. Her usually pale face was flushed and he noticed at once she'd bitten all her nails. She didn't sit down, but leaned one hand on the mantelpiece as if bracing herself for something unpleasant.

'Tea or coffee?' he asked. 'And do sit down.'

'I don't want a drink,' Prue snapped. 'And I'd rather stand. I've had that friend of Charity's down today.'

'What friend?' Toby's stomach churned alarmingly. 'Dorothy.'

'Oh that old slag.' Toby felt relieved. 'I thought she'd gone off to America with some old man?'

'She is actually a very charming woman, Toby. I think you've been leading me up the garden path.'

'I don't get you.'

'You've been turning me against Charity. You told me Charity bought her promotions business with money earned from prostitution.'

'So she did.' Toby rearranged his long legs more

comfortably and leaned back with his hands behind his head.

'No she didn't.' Anger flashed in Prue's blue eyes, turning them into accusing lasers. 'Dorothy was very candid with me. There's a world of difference between getting a friend to help out and going on the streets.'

'Come on now!' Toby laughed awkwardly and cursed inwardly. It looked as if Prue and this woman had had a real heart to heart. 'You've often said yourself how odd it was that she got the money together.'

'Yes I have,' Prue admitted. 'And I'm ashamed of that now.'

Toby couldn't find anything to fight back with.

'I was a louse,' he said feebly. 'I was just mad with Chas and I threw up a few things to get at her. When you're angry you don't think of what you're saying. I'm sorry.'

He knew he had lost his grip on Prue now. She had many faults, but she had integrity. No amount of charm and sweet talking was going to bring her round.

'Do you know, Charity has never once said anything bad about you to me?' Prue slumped into a chair, and put her hands over her face. 'I've been a selfish bitch. But the biggest mistake I ever made was not to suspect your motives when you said Charity was a whore. I should have gone straight to her and found out what your row with her was about. Maybe then she wouldn't have cracked up, with someone on her side.'

She got up quickly and strode towards the door, then turned, her face like stone.

'Don't try and contact me again, Toby, not ever – and I shall make sure James doesn't come near you either.'

She was gone before Toby could think of a reply. By the time he'd risen from his chair she was already pulling away in the drive.

He couldn't sleep that night. The house creaked and rustled and he was scared, so scared he was shivering.

Suddenly he felt terribly alone. The old house didn't seem so attractive a proposition and he still had that one last job to do before he would be free.

'Oh Prue, let me look at you!' Charity was on her feet the moment her door opened and she saw her sister standing there shamefaced. She didn't feel the stab of pain in her back; she forgot too just how long it had taken for her sister to visit. All that mattered was that Prue was here now.

Prue had clearly made a great effort with her appearance. In a pink Laura Ashley dress, her hair loose on her shoulders, she looked like a rosy milkmaid.

'I'm so sorry,' Prue managed to get out before she burst into tears.

Charity put her one good arm round her sister and hugged her awkwardly. 'It doesn't matter,' she murmured. 'Come and sit down and tell me all your news.'

Prue found it even harder to bear the fact that Charity only wanted to hear about her. No angry questions, no recriminations.

'I've been such a bitch,' Prue sobbed. 'I shouldn't have let Toby turn me against you. How can you ever forgive me?'

'Because you're my sister, and I love you,' Charity said evenly. 'Because all of us have scars from the past and we all have different ways of dealing with them. You've been a good girl, you used your brains to better yourself. I would have scolded you if you'd done any of the things I did.'

'Scolded me!' Prue managed a weak laugh. 'That just about sums your attitude up. "Laid into me",

562

"whacked me", that's the way we were brought up – yet you use words like "scold"!'

'I was always a bit feeble.' Charity let go of Prue's hand and caressed her cheek. 'Don't let's go over the past though, it's done with.'

'But it isn't,' Prue insisted. 'Look at your face. If I'd come to you when Rita asked me to, maybe I could've prevented that. I hate Toby. I'll never speak to him again.'

'Hush now.' Charity put her finger to Prue's lips. Prue brushed them away, looking at Charity in astonishment.

'He's a rotter, Chas, and you know it deep down. Stop protecting him.'

'I'll think about it,' Charity smiled. 'But it comes hard to let any one of you three go. I've been holding on to you all for so long.'

'Tell me about seeing Prue again?' Rob asked.

It was the afternoon of the following day and Rob had arrived to find Charity looking very peaceful. She was lying on her bed because her back was hurting and he'd insisted she stayed that way.

'She was so different,' Charity said. 'More like she was when she was little, sort of warm and caring. We talked about so much, about the kids she teaches, Tim, her husband and about the times back in Greenwich.'

'Tell me about things you did together when they were small,' Rob said.

Charity told him about the trips to Greenwich Park, doing the washing on Saturdays with James sitting between the bags of laundry.

She couldn't see Rob without twisting her head round and in some odd way it made it easier for all the images to come back. She saw Easton Street, smelt the smell of the baths.

'I used to tell them stories about the house I'd find

563

for us all one day,' she said. 'I'd tell Prue she could wear her hair loose and have a blue velvet dress, and Toby could go out to play football whenever he wanted to.'

Rob listened carefully as Charity described Babylon Hall, her school and the chores she had to do. She had never spoken this fluently before; now her bleak childhood was spilling out, making him see and feel how it was.

But again and again she returned to the part about this fantasy house.

'Why did you want to live away from your parents, Charity?' he said softly.

'To keep them safe,' she said. 'So Father – ' she stopped suddenly.

'So Father – what, Charity?' Rob held his breath for a moment.

'So he couldn't hurt Prue,' she blurted out.

Rob waited. He could see that her neck and cheek were flushed, and her breathing was faster.

'Like he hurt you?'

It was raining outside, a sudden violent shower that would soon be over and it had made the room darker.

'Yes,' she whispered.

Her voice changed as she began to tell him, it rasped in her throat, laboured and in pain.

Rob heard the stairs creak in the darkness, heard the wind coming off the river and experienced the pain with her.

Graphic descriptions with nothing held back. He could see the big man coming towards Charity's small skinny body in the narrow bed, hear his panting as the terrified child cowered away from him.

'I felt so dirty all the time,' she croaked. 'I couldn't take in my lessons at school and they called me a dunce.'

Rob had this desire to take her in his arms, but he

564

knew he must suppress it, because there was more to come.

'When he said I was to leave and he'd find a job for me I was scared for Prue. I asked God to help me – and then the fire came.'

Charity had told him about the fire before, but never like this. He could feel her indecision on the stairs, hear Prue screaming, see the flames as they engulfed the house.

'I was glad when I woke up in the hospital,' she sobbed. 'I heard the nurse telling me they were dead, but all I could think of was that I'd never have to see Father again.'

'Have a sleep now,' Rob said gently when she finally stopped crying. He put a blanket over her and stepped back. 'You'll feel better soon.'

Her eyes seemed to beg him to stay. Rob sat down on the chair by the bed and waited till she fell asleep.

He felt like crying himself now. He could remember the sixth-form boy who called him into his study at school when he was just twelve. The pain and dirtiness of that had never quite left him either. He'd tried to tell his father once, but he wouldn't listen.

As Charity finally fell asleep, Rob stood up and looked at her. He could remember looking down once before like this, when she was asleep in the garden of the cottage. She was wearing his old blue shorts and a white blouse, her long silky hair white-gold against the deep green of the grass. His heart seemed to swell that day, just as it was doing now, and he knew the seeds she'd planted so long ago had begun to grow.

Chapter Thirty-One

Hugh hesitated outside Holly Bush House, a bunch of red roses in one hand, his briefcase in the other.

It hadn't taken much detective work to find out where Rob had tucked Charity away: all Hugh had had to do was phone Stratton Promotions and say he wanted to send Charity some flowers. It was a smarter place than he'd expected, though. A big detached house in a tree-lined quiet cul-de-sac, backing on to the river. From what he knew about most of Rob's patients, few of them could afford even a day out in Brighton.

Hugh almost wished now that he hadn't seen Charity's picture in the paper. For some odd reason he couldn't get her out of his mind, and Sophie was starting to notice how distracted he was. Only last night she'd asked him if he was having an affair.

The trouble was, he was finding fault constantly with Sophie, comparing her unfavourably to a girl he hadn't seen for twelve years. What sort of madness was it that made a man in his position start dreaming about sunlit pools, walks in woods and bike rides, and what made him feel he'd missed out somewhere along the line?

'I'd like to see Miss Stratton, please,' he said to the black nurse who answered the door.

'I'm afraid she doesn't have visitors unless by prior arrangement,' the nurse replied starchily.

'I'm a solicitor, and an old friend of Miss Stratton's.' Hugh smiled engagingly, removing his bowler hat. 'I wanted to surprise her. But if you're unsure you could always stay in the room with us.'

He took out his business card and handed it to her. Molly read it, looked up at his smooth, handsome face and weakened.

'I should ask her first,' she said.

'That would spoil the surprise,' Hugh said. 'Go on, let me just see her for a few minutes. As I said, you can stay in the room if you think I look a bit dodgy.'

Molly was a romantic at heart. She looked at his dark blue eyes, then at the roses. Matron wouldn't approve, but then she was out for the evening. Besides a solicitor wasn't just anyone, it was as safe as a doctor.

'For you I'll bend the rules,' she said. 'But if Charity's upset I'll throw you out.'

Hugh followed the nurse up the stairs. He was impressed by the place, it was more like a good hotel than a nursing home, airy and bright, with thick plain carpets and pastel walls.

Molly stopped before a door at the end of a passage and turned to Hugh. 'Miss Stratton is easily upset,' she whispered. 'Please be very tactful.'

'Of course,' Hugh assured her. 'Now don't tell her my name, just say it's an old friend.'

He stood back.

'You've got a surprise visitor,' he heard her say. 'Shall I ask him to come in?'

'Him?' Hugh heard Charity reply and just that one word brought her image back to him and made his heart lurch.

'He doesn't want me to tell you who he is,' the nurse replied in a low voice. 'But he looks nice.'

Hugh heard Charity giggle and he could wait no longer. He stepped inside the door.

Her one good hand flew up to cover her mouth and her eyes opened wide as if she'd been slapped.

'Are you all right, Charity?' Molly leaned down towards her patient, who was sitting in the chair. She had registered the shock, but couldn't tell if there was pleasure there too.

Charity could only stare. Although she hadn't recognised Rob immediately, she would have known Hugh anywhere. He was stockier, and his hair was longer. Twelve years ago his cheeks were almost as smooth as hers; now he had the dark shadow of a beard and a few lines around his eyes. But his dark blue eyes were instantly recognisable, just like Daniel's.

'What a surprise,' she managed to get out at last. 'Yes Molly, it's OK. Mr Mainwaring can stay for a while.'

Molly paused before she left. She wasn't entirely happy about this. Charity looked as if she'd seen a ghost.

'Ring the bell if you need me,' she said nervously. 'I won't be far away.'

Once Molly had closed the door behind her, Charity struggled to compose herself. Her heart was crashing painfully against her ribs.

'Well I never expected to see you again,' she said. 'I'm astounded at your cheek.'

Hugh put the flowers down on the table. He was chilled by the ice in her voice, and shocked by her scars. If the photograph in the paper had been of her like this, he would never have known her. Setting aside the scars, her eyes were hard and cold now, even the long straight hair was curly, all that was left was her wide mouth, and that wasn't smiling.

'I don't really know where to start,' he said. 'I was a bit of a louse, wasn't I?'

'You'd better sit down,' Charity said, her voice shaking. The casual way Hugh had breezed in without even phoning first suggested he had no idea how much he'd hurt her. She wasn't sure whether she could even speak to someone so grossly insensitive.

'You were a louse,' she said coldly. 'I expect you still are.'

'Not completely unredeemable.' He flashed his most winning smile. 'When I read about your accident I was terribly concerned about you. I found I kept thinking about you.'

It was like playing a game of ping-pong. She airily told him she now lived in London. He spoke of his university days. Charity went on to talk about her promotions agency; he told her about becoming a solicitor.

'Hell, Charity,' he smiled with all his old charm, maybe it was a good thing my parents twisted my arm to break it off with you. I expect if you'd come to Oxford neither of us would have got any work done.'

She smiled and let him go on about his days in Oxford. He always had been a good talker, but now she heard the emptiness in his words. He spoke of the parties, the drunken binges, even some of the students she'd met at the pub that summer. She could see just how it had been. His parents had bribed him with the sports car he spoke of and in no time at all he had forgotten there was a girl who had nothing in her life but him.

Glib phrases tripped off his tongue: he'd 'missed her', he'd been 'worried' about her, all weak phrases, considering what she had been through. He told her about his wife, his hopes to start his own firm of solicitors.

As Charity sat listening to him she remembered the other side of him, not the one she once loved. The way he had goaded the cleaning lady, his snobbish attitude, how he'd added bottles of drinks to the Cuthbertsons' account and humiliated her at the pub.

A fire began to kindle inside, growing fiercer by the minute.

'What was it exactly that made you come here?' she said eventually. 'Idle curiosity, a do-gooding venture, or a combination of both? Or did you want to be able to dine out on the inside information you'd obtained about a suspected murderess? I bet your heart raced a bit faster when you recognised my face in the paper. I bet you thought "My God, I slept with that woman" and it gave you the kind of thrill your boring wife can't.'

'No Charity!' He jumped up, his face bright red. 'I loved you, for Christ's sake. I didn't get over you for years.'

'Fat lot you know about love,' she screamed, the fire within her out of control. 'I was *pregnant*, Hugh. I was carrying your child when you dumped me.'

The colour drained from his face.

The nursing home was silent, not even the sound of a television in the distance. Charity could hear her heart pumping hard with rage.

'Our son was born in May of the following year, after I'd been through the kind of hell someone like you could never imagine. I had to give him up for adoption because I had no money or home to take him to. Have you *any* idea what that does to a woman?

'What were you doing on the 7th of May? Swanning around a May Ball in a tuxedo, with some horsy girl your parents approved of?'

Hugh felt faint. All the time they'd been talking he'd been waiting to hear sentimental words from those lovely lips. He'd sensed the chilly reception, but was sure he could charm her round. But a *baby*! Not once had he ever imagined anything like that.

'Oh Charity.' He sighed, moving over to her chair, wanting to reach out and touch her but not daring to. 'I had no idea. If I'd known!'

'If you'd known you would have run for it anyway. They bribed you with a car, didn't they? I can tell you now I was well rid of you. I wouldn't want to be part of a family like yours. Clear off now to your socially acceptable wife. You can brighten up your evening by telling her about me.'

'I can't believe you're saying such things,' he said weakly. 'You've changed so much. The Charity I knew was never like this.'

She laughed then. He looked like a little lost boy who'd had his ice-cream snatched out of his hands, all wide-eyed innocence and naïvety.

'I'm not the same girl now.' She leaned forward in her seat and her eyes were icy. 'These scars on my face are nothing to the ones inside me. There hasn't been a day in eleven years I haven't thought about our son – he had his eleventh birthday just before my accident. The ache for him never goes away, and it never will. I loved you Hugh, I believed in you and if the truth was known I'd have been a better wife than the one you married because if you'd stayed with me, you wouldn't be wanting to look for a bit on the side now!'

Hugh backed away, frightened by the fury in her. But she was right. He *had* been gutless – and if his life didn't shine quite as brightly as he'd hoped for, he only had himself to blame.

The door opened and Rob stood there panting from running up the stairs. His face was white, with two red spots on his cheeks.

'You had to come, didn't you?' he yelled at Hugh. 'You couldn't leave well alone, could you?'

Charity tried to haul herself out of her chair, frightened by the sparks flying between the two men.

'Enough!' she shouted. 'I'm glad Hugh came, Rob. At least I've been able to tell him about Daniel. But he's going now. We've nothing more to say to one another.'

Charity watched the sun come up through her window. Rob had put her to bed soon after Hugh left, but she was aware of him sitting silently beside her for some time, just holding her hand. It was dark when she woke and she had reached out for him blindly. But it was three in the morning and she couldn't expect him still to be sitting there. She hadn't slept since.

Seeing Hugh again had been like opening long-closed doors in her mind. Through them she could see herself and him at that secret pool, the water lilies, the overgrown garden. She could feel the sun hot on her back as they lay naked in each other's arms and she could hear him whispering how much he loved her.

Yet it meant nothing now, just a pretty out-of-focus picture. What was real was the scene in the adoption society, seeing that woman walk out of the room with Daniel in her arms, and knowing that a part of herself was lost for ever.

Her anger was gone. She'd thrown it all at Hugh and the knowledge that he now held the burden of guilt and remorse left her with a trace of pity for him.

The sun was bright red, as it came up over the roofs of the houses behind the river. Slowly it pushed away the darkness, black turning to grey and then to pink. She focused her eyes on the black part of the sky, finding it oddly similar to that dark part in her mind which she couldn't reach into. The sun was the truth, pushing until it banished all the black. Today she would tell Rob those last few dark secrets, clear them out once and for all.

'Hallo George,' Dorothy's voice purred down the phone, rich and sensual. 'It's Dorothy, have you got anything for me yet?'

'Not a great deal,' he said warily. 'People don't want to open up.'

'Then lean on them, George,' she said. 'I need some information quickly.'

'Look, come round to my office,' George said. 'There's one or two things that might interest you.'

'I'll be there in thirty minutes.'

Soho by day was very different from Soho by night. The strip clubs and dirty book shops seemed to disappear without their neon lights and the streets were full of office workers going to lunch. Dorothy caught a taxi to Tottenham Court Road and as she passed through Soho Square there were groups of people sunbathing on the central green and eating sandwiches. It reminded her fleetingly of Barkston Gardens and how the three of them used to lie outside all day on hot Sundays, gossiping and laughing.

Between visiting Charity, going to see Prudence, and giving Rita a hand at the agency she had barely thought about herself since she stepped off the plane at London airport. Now she could see this is how life had been for Charity: always doing things for other people, thinking how her actions would affect everyone, employees and family. No wonder she had no private life, no peace of mind.

Robert Cuthbertson was in love with Charity, that to Dorothy was as plain as a pikestaff. She had met him for a quick supper last night and he hadn't fooled her for a minute. Dorothy knew about men, if nothing else. Of course it was hard to gauge how Charity felt about Rob, she wasn't in a fit state to think about romance, but surely Robert Cuthbertson was the kind of man any sane woman would want? He had integrity, a sense of humour, he was far more interested in others than in himself. Dorothy had listened while he talked about his work at the mental hospital at Colney Hatch. Even with all her cynicism, she could see the man was an idealist, a carer. He and Charity were designed for one another.

I'll make sure you end up happy, Chas, if it's the last thing I do, she thought grimly as she approached George's office. You deserve it more than any of us.

'Drink?' George said as she sat down. It was very hot in his office, a small fan merely moving the air about. Dorothy sat in the chair nearest to the open window.

'Gin and tonic please,' she said, taking off her jacket and flinging it over another chair. 'Christ, it's hot in here!'

George looked round at her as he poured the drinks. She looked serenely cool in a pale blue silk dress, her hair twisted up loosely on the top of her head. He thought she was quite the most beautiful woman he'd ever seen with those sensational almond eyes and that glowing olive skin. He wondered if there was a man in her life, but didn't dare to ask.

'I keep thinking of moving my office somewhere a bit smarter,' he said with a smile. 'But Soho is where it all happens and I can't be too far away from my interests. Do you live in London still?'

'Part of the time,' she said vaguely. Men always wanted to question her and she usually only told the truth when she couldn't think of a lie. She liked to appear mysterious, it kept men on their toes. 'Now, what have you got for me?'

'Strat is the name he's known by, but his real one's Toby Stratton,' George said, handing her a large drink. 'He's the nephew of Colonel Pennycuick who quite coincidentally was murdered a while ago.'

Dorothy nodded.

574

George looked askance at her.

'You knew that already?'

'I know the family part,' she said carefully. 'What I want to know is how other people see him, the people who call him Strat. Who he hangs out with, what he's told them about himself.'

'The one thing that comes out is that young Toby, or Strat, isn't as smart as he likes to make out,' George grinned. 'It's no secret that he's been spending far more than he earns in the army, and until quite recently he owed money all over the place. The interesting thing is that he fobbed people off with tales that he would soon be getting his inheritance.'

Dorothy smiled.

'He was saying that *before* his uncle died?'

'He was saying it from the moment he hit London.' George raised an eyebrow. 'That's what I mean about him not being so smart. He uses part truth, part fiction. Even the name he uses is an abbreviation of his real one.'

'But you said he had debts "until recently". When did he pay them off?'

'Before the colonel died.' George smirked. 'So I asked myself where he got the money.'

Dorothy was warming to George by the minute.

'And what did you come up with?'

'Drugs. One of the girls told me he was into speed. Once people start using that they often go on to selling it, if only to support the habit. My guess is that he dabbled in dealing for a bit, made a few bob, then moved on to becoming a courier for heroin or cocaine.'

Dorothy felt a fizz of excitement rising inside her. So this was what Charity was keeping quiet about!

'What's your gut reaction to the murder of the old colonel?' she asked.

George sighed.

'You'd be a fool not to suspect him,' he said. 'If

he's picking up drugs in Rotterdam or Hamburg as I suspect, then it would be a doddle to find a hit man too. I certainly don't believe his sister did it, not unless she's in it with him.'

'She isn't,' Dorothy blurted out before she could stop herself.

George's face broke into a wide smile, his brown eyes twinkling.

'So that's it! You're working for her?'

'Not working for her. Just trying to unravel a few things,' Dorothy snapped. 'She's my best friend, but she'd have a fit if she knew I was poking around into her dear little brother's affairs.'

George looked speculatively at Dorothy.

He couldn't remember the last time he'd felt really drawn to a woman. It wasn't just her beauty, but something inside her. He'd dug around about Charity Stratton too and discovered that she'd bought Carmel Connor's old escort agency. Now it was all slotting into place.

'Look, Dorothy, I've stuck my neck out quite a bit asking around about all this. If Strat, Toby, whatever you like to call him is doing what I suspect, there's other people involved who are a darn sight more dangerous than he is. I don't want to be found in a back alley with a knife between my ribs, even for you. Now suppose you tell me the whole story over lunch? Then maybe we can work out where we go from here.'

Dorothy looked at him appraisingly. In the old days she would have surveyed his expensive suit, calculated how rich he was and how much of his money he would lavish on her. Then if the stakes were high enough, she'd go out with him, whether she liked him or not.

She knew George was wealthy already, but she was surprised to find she really liked him.

He wasn't even handsome or tall, his hair was thin

and she didn't care much for moustaches. But he had eyes that laughed even when his mouth didn't. He didn't take himself too seriously, which was unusual for a man involved with nightclubs. George was a good sort.

'As long as you let me buy the lunch,' she said.

His mouth broke into an endearing, boyish smile.

'I didn't expect that – the lunch, I mean.'

'I don't make a habit of paying for men,' Dorothy said with a wry smile.

A bit of Charity seemed to have rubbed off in the last couple of days, Dorothy thought. She might even change the habits of a lifetime if she stayed a little longer.

Chapter Thirty-Two

'I thought I told you never to contact me here,' Toby whispered hoarsely down the phone, kicking the drawing-room door shut in case Pat or Margaret were listening. 'I told you I'd be in touch.'

'I can't wait for that,' the voice replied. 'Catch the eleven o'clock train this morning, I'll meet you at Paddington.'

'I'm rejoining my regiment today.' Toby felt a little faint. He wanted to ask what it was about but didn't dare – not over the phone.

'I know that. But you have to get to Paddington. Be on that train!'

The line went dead, leaving Toby staring at the receiver. It was just after eight and he'd planned to spend the morning showing Tom, Margaret's husband, around the place; they were to move in while Toby was away. Now he wouldn't have time.

'Shit,' he exclaimed, putting the phone down. 'No wonder they call him Weasel.'

'Breakfast's ready,' Margaret called out from the hall.

'Coming.'

'I thought you were hungry?' Margaret looked down at Toby's plate of bacon and eggs disapprovingly.

'I was, earlier,' Toby gave her the plaintive look that invariably brought out the mother in all women. 'I think it's due to remembering what army food's like.'

He liked Margaret, really liked her. She wasn't false like most women. Plump and wholesome with soft grey hair and laughing eyes, she was never cross about anything. She loved to cook and feed people, but best of all she offered him the kind of uncritical affection that made him feel snug.

'I've made a nice fruit cake for you to take back with you,' she said. 'I'm going to miss you, sir. It will be very quiet with just me and Tom here.'

Toby knew Margaret wanted to ask why he'd fallen out with Prudence. But even though he now had his meals in the kitchen and discussed many things with her, she was always aware of her place.

'You've been a brick, Margaret.' Toby grinned up at her as she took his plate away. 'Now are you sure you two will be all right? I'll have to leave earlier than I intended.'

Margaret had refused extra money to live in because she said there'd be less work, but Toby knew she'd press Tom into service, helping the gardener, chopping up logs and doing dozens of other jobs.

'Don't you worry about a thing,' she said as she cleared the table. 'We can take care of everything.'

Toby left her washing up.

'I wish you could take care of Weasel,' he murmured as he went upstairs to change.

Margaret stood at the sink washing the breakfast dishes, thinking about Toby. Gossip was still rife in the village about the colonel's death and there were many who asked how she could bear to stay in a house where a murder had taken place.

But Margaret prided herself on being a realist. The dead couldn't come back and someone had to look after the house and the family's interests.

She liked all the children, but Toby was her pet. Her heart went out to him more than the others because in her opinion, he was the one who had suffered most through being orphaned. Toby had missed out on family life: shoved into public school, holidays here with old folk, and always his uncle manipulating him to become what he wanted.

Yet Toby had risen above it in the last year or so. He had become a real gentleman, kind, considerate and so very charming. First the trauma of his uncle's death and now the burden of the estate thrust on to him. He looked so troubled and anxious, the poor lamb.

She could see him now, blond hair shining in the sun as he strode across the kitchen garden to speak to Tom. He had changed into grey slacks and a blazer, ready to leave, and he looked so handsome it was no wonder girls fell over themselves to speak to him. He didn't really like the army, even though he always pretended to his uncle he did. What a burden for a young lad to carry!

It would have been a pleasant journey up to London if it hadn't been for meeting Weasel. A girl who introduced herself as Hazel sat opposite him in a short skirt and every time she crossed and uncrossed her legs he had a flash of pink knickers. He might have chatted her up if he hadn't been so preoccupied, but he could only make the weakest attempt at flirtation.

As he got to the barrier Weasel sidled up beside him out of nowhere.

His nickname couldn't be more appropriate. He was skinny, small with bright little dark eyes that were constantly on the move, and vicious. Personal hygiene wasn't his strong point either. He had a couple of days' growth of beard, his teeth were stained from chain-smoking and Toby could smell sweat. His clothes appeared to have been picked up in a jumble sale. A navy blue suit jacket which was too big and stained on the lapels, with brown trousers which hung over his dirty, rundown shoes. Next to Toby with his height, military bearing and tailored blazer, he looked like a tramp.

Toby had never learned his real name. All he knew of the man was his reputation for doing anything for a price, and until now he'd thought he could control him.

'What's this all about?' Toby said irritably. 'I've paid you the first half and you agreed to wait for the second.'

'That's the word of an officer and a gentleman, is it?' Weasel's voice was high, almost like a girl's, and the sarcasm was obvious.

'Of course,' Toby sniffed. 'What reason could you have to doubt me?'

'Plenty.' Weasel caught at the handle of Toby's suitcase. 'Come over here and we'll discuss it.'

Toby looked all around. He had been paranoid about being followed most of the time since he flew back from Germany to Studley, although he hadn't once seen anyone suspicious. Police had been countless times to Studley, picking over this and that. But they'd called less often in the last couple of weeks and he was sure they'd run out of steam.

'There's no one interested in us,' Weasel snapped and led him over to the side of the station where the mail trucks were loaded and unloaded. It was quieter away from the milling passengers. A few pigeons gathered round an abandoned sandwich and a couple of old ladies were sitting on the only seat.

Weasel sat down on the edge of a luggage trolley and motioned for Toby to join him, pulling a tobacco tin out of his pocket.

Toby brushed off the wooden slats and sat down gingerly, lifting the knees of his grey slacks.

'Come on then, out with it, you've clearly got a grievance.'

'I want the rest of my money, now,' Weasel said in a subdued voice, rolling a cigarette expertly.

'You know I don't have it yet,' Toby said haughtily. 'What are you going to do about it? Go to the police?'

He felt smug; the little shit couldn't do a thing to him, he didn't know why he'd worried in the first place.

Weasel hadn't had much of an education, he could only just about read, but he was respected as being fearless and shrewd. Burglary had been his game until recently. He could strip a bedroom while the occupants slept on.

'Disposing' of people had started only two years ago, when he was asked to stage an accident for a man whose wife had grown tired of him. She was well away at her sister's, and the wiring in their thatched cottage was ancient. All it took was smearing an already overloaded electrical point with some white spirit after the man had staggered home from the pub witlessly drunk and plugged in a kettle with no safety cutout. He then let himself out the front door. The next morning he read in the papers that the cottage had burnt to the ground due to an electrical fault. She got the insurance, a widow's pension and her freedom – and Weasel got three thousand pounds for a two-minute job.

But the colonel was different. It was all very well Toby telling him he was sick in the head as well as being a cripple. But actually creeping up to the man while he was snoring, strapping him down, then holding a pillow over his face, that was just a bit too personal. He'd taken so long to die too. Bucking and heaving like a rhinoceros on heat.

Weasel wanted out. To put as many miles as possible between himself and Toby Stratton.

'Don't come it with me,' Weasel snapped back. 'For one thing you can't do nothing to me without landing yourself in the shit. For another just remember I'm the bloke who makes "accidents" happen.'

'There's no need to talk like that.' Toby used an aggrieved tone, but Weasel's veiled threat frightened him.

'I 'appen to know you've got a deal coming up.' Weasel's eyes narrowed. 'You can pay me out of that.'

Toby's gut contracted with fear. He couldn't imagine how Weasel had found out about his sideline. Sweat was popping out all over him; he touched his upper lip and found it was wet.

'Put the money in the account, soon's the job's done,' Weasel said and got up from the trolley, his bright eyes cold and knowing. 'Or else.'

Toby had to agree.

'You promise you won't contact me again?'

'I've got no interest in you once I get the bread.' Weasel looked Toby up and down with a sneer. 'For all yer fancy school, yer looks and family estate, you're a maggot, Stratton. Lowest of the low.'

He had disappeared into a crowd of people before Toby could think of a reply.

George Bayliss had never been one to stay in bed after seven in the morning. He normally jumped out, went down to his indoor pool and swam thirty lengths, showered and shaved, ate his breakfast and was out of his house in Essex by eight-thirty at the latest. But today George had no desire to get up. He was thinking about Dorothy.

She had everything he ever wanted in a woman: looks, brains, sensuality, and above all she was honest.

He doubted most men would agree with that but they were just fooling themselves. Dorothy laid her cards on the table at the outset, and if they couldn't read them, they were fools. So she wanted rich men! Well that was honest. What woman actually planned to get a poor one? She traded her body, her company for a few comforts, but he would bet she never told anyone she loved them when she didn't!

He had driven Dorothy back to her friend's flat after a long lunch. They had talked easily, as if they'd known each other for years. He felt no need to try and impress her, she seemed comfortable enough with him just being himself.

Outside the flat she turned to him and kissed his cheek.

'I hope we can be lovers,' she said, without any coyness. 'I like you more than any man I've met for years and we'd be good for one another.'

For once he was lost for words. Her words mirrored his own thoughts, though he wouldn't have dared voice them. He sensed she meant after Charity was better and when Dorothy was in command of her own life again. He liked her even more because she wouldn't embark on an affair while her friend was in so much trouble.

George was forty-eight, he'd married young and lived to regret it. Since his divorce a few years ago he'd never wanted a permanent woman in his life, but Dorothy was the kind of woman he'd make an exception for.

'Ring me when you're ready,' was all he could say and as he drove away he felt like a dog with three tails.

He felt he knew Charity now from what Dorothy had told him. A woman who had guts and compassion, and had been driven by a fierce love for her family to make it in the hard world of business.

Getting information on Toby Stratton had been his brief, and he'd already accomplished that, but what Dorothy wanted – enough evidence to hand to the police – was more difficult. He had never been an informer and he wasn't going to start now, but there was nothing in the code he lived by to say he couldn't trip a man up.

George got up and stretched. He had a couple of good contacts in Hamburg. It shouldn't be too difficult to arrange a double-cross with Toby Stratton right in the firing line.

'What are we going to talk about this afternoon?' Rob asked Charity.

'Can't we talk about you for a change?' she countered. 'I'm a fraud, I don't need to be in this place any longer.'

'Charity, you are in here just until your body's mended. As I see it, you are still in pain when you walk and there's plaster on your arm.'

'Yes but mentally I'm OK now. Aren't I?'

'You are the best judge of that,' Rob said.

'Why are you smiling?'

'When my patients start wanting to escape it usually means my work's over.'

'I don't like the thought of not seeing you,' she said in a small voice.

'You can still see me when you get home if you want to,' Rob said quietly. 'I don't cut off my patients until they're ready.'

'I don't think I'll ever be ready for that.'

'Why?'

'Because I depend on you,' she blurted out.

Rob remained silent, as he always did when he wanted her to explain herself. But she couldn't explain it, everything was mixed up in her head. Telling him about the escort agency and Ted Parsloe had been tougher than she'd expected. Rob and she had had many sessions discussing her father and she'd found those difficult, but at least she didn't feel responsible.

But having sex for money was cold-blooded and calculating; however she looked at it, it stayed the same.

How could they just be social friends when he knew all this about her? But she couldn't continue to see a psychiatrist when it was no longer necessary.

'You depend on me for what?' he said. 'I don't bring you food, help you dress.'

'You know,' she said stubbornly.

'That you'll be alone again?'

Rob did know exactly what she meant. He felt it too. He had never put himself in a position where he wanted to hang on to a patient before, and this time he hadn't got the right answers to give her.

'Yes, and no,' she said shaking her head in frustration. 'I've got friends, I'm not scared of being alone in my flat. I just can't imagine not having you around.'

She had dreamed last night that she was making love with Rob. It was one of those vivid dreams that stayed long after she woke. In normal circumstances if she had such a dream about a man, she'd go out with him and see what happened.

But these weren't normal circumstances. Rob was her doctor . . . and wasn't she just influenced because both Dorothy and Rita had suggested he was in love with her? All her life she'd been looking and hoping for the big love affair that would last. What if she was only building up a kind of fantasy around Rob? After all, she knew so little about him.

'I'm waiting,' Rob said. 'Remember how I once told you to use the words "I feel". Let's try that once again.'

'I feel . . .' Charity paused, unable to say anything.

'What?' Rob raised one eyebrow. 'Happy, sad, gloomy, tense, angry?'

'Frustrated,' she said defiantly, hoping to get a reaction. 'I feel frustrated.'

'Physically, mentally, or sexually?' he said.

'All of them.'

'Well the first and last are understandable.' Rob smiled. 'With a bad back and a broken arm, it's hard to jump a fence, run a mile, and the last requires an imaginative lover and you've had few male visitors. So in what way are you mentally frustrated?'

'Because you only talk about me! I want to know about you.'

Rob leaned forward in his chair. He knew he was losing the battle to remain detached.

'What do you want to know?'

Charity looked at him. She knew she was better and she had this terrible desire to be naughty and shocking. Rob's face was getting more and more desirable. She kept looking at his lips, wanting to trace her finger round the shape, to hold that square chin and ruffle his already untidy hair.

'What you kiss like.'

He didn't say a word, just those speckly eyes looking right into hers. His hand reached out and took hers, and lifted it to his lips.

A delicious sensation ran down her spine as he kissed the tips of her fingers.

'It's too soon to even think about going down that path,' he said softly.

Chapter Thirty-Three

Toby leaned on the rail of the cross-channel ferry watching white foam curl back as the bows cut through the inky water.

It was pitch dark, not even the moon visible. Sea and sky merged into one sweep of blackness giving the impression that they were motionless despite the wind whipping back his hair and the noise of the engines.

Adrenalin and a snort of amphetamine sulphate had kept fear at bay on the long drive down through Germany, Belgium and France. But in front of him, as yet unseen, was Dover.

'Nothing to it,' he whispered. Raucous laughter wafted up from the bar below, reminding him that he was just one of dozens of men who would walk through the customs within the hour.

He turned away from the rail, opening his jacket to shield a cigarette as he lit it. Dragging deeply on it he looked towards the stern of the ship, noting faint pinpricks of lights from other vessels.

There was no one else on deck despite the warm, balmy air. Earlier there had been a couple of students up here; he had smelt the pungent cannabis they were smoking and sensed they too were nervous about the approaching customs. But they had gone now, mingling with all those lorry drivers who stood five deep at the bar, drinking with the camaraderie of men who anticipated the end of a long trip away from home.

In the past Toby had scorned these jovial, nomadic men with their beer bellies, grubby clothes and the smell of sweat and diesel that clung to them. But just now he almost wished he was one of them. They at least had wives and girlfriends anxiously waiting for their return.

Just remember it's the last time, he thought, sighing deeply as he dropped the cigarette butt over the rail. You don't have to go through this again.

Conscience was a concept he hadn't understood until recently. He'd felt no guilt at arranging his uncle's death; after all, the man had manipulated him since he was a small boy. Nor did he trouble himself about the ethics of drug running. Even when he heard that Charity had been discharged from the nursing home he'd seen it only as the perfect excuse to ask for compassionate leave; there had been no real relief that she was well again. But as he drove away from Hamburg guilt prickled at him like the strapping on his chest, and for the first time ever he felt ashamed of what he was.

Even the knowledge that he would inherit somewhere in the region of two hundred thousand pounds after the death duties, that Studley Priory and its contents were probably worth as much again, didn't make up for the emptiness inside him. For some strange reason he kept thinking of all those other Pennycuicks, his grandfather and his great-grandfather who had put family honour before everything.

The lights of Dover appeared. Silver threads reflected in the black water. Within minutes he'd see the white cliffs, that symbol of hope and glory for all those countless soldiers who'd fought in France in both world wars. Yet here he was approaching them with only greed in his heart and blood on his hands.

Toby sniffed, swiped angrily at a stray tear. It had been something of a shock to find he actually minded not getting letters from his sisters. Girls, drink, and his fellow officers filled some of the emptiness, but not all of it. He felt now as he did when he was first sent away to school: isolated and unwanted.

He could see Dover clearly now, the cliffs looming up behind the town, the bright lights of the harbour reflecting off the chalk. Just half an hour or so, and it would be over. He would drive up as far as Canterbury, then find a hotel for the night.

Toby leapt out of his green MG Midget on the customs bay, reached into the back for his holdall and the plastic bag containing his duty-free bottle of whisky and cigarettes and nonchalantly strolled into the customs room.

It was quieter than he'd ever seen it before, but then his car had been one of the first few off the ferry. A group of long-haired student types with backpacks who'd been larking about on the boat were subdued as they filed through, and he idly wondered if they were carrying something too.

A young couple were in front of him, the woman carrying a sleeping toddler in her arms while her husband struggled with two huge suitcases. Behind him the doors swung open again and a group of chattering French teenagers broke the silence.

One of the customs men waved through the young couple without so much as a cursory glance at their luggage, but another one was zealously raking through one of the students' rucksacks.

'Is this your only bag, sir?' The officer who had let the young couple go beckoned him over and unzipped the bag the second Toby put it down on the counter.

The man had a polished, bland face and his eyes

590

looked right into Toby's with that penetrating look that suggested he had X-ray vision.

'Yes, only home on a forty-eight-hour pass.' Toby had a strong desire to scratch his chest and hoped that wasn't really sweat forming on his upper lip, but he didn't dare lift a hand to check it.

The man went right down to the bottom of the bag, even checking his leather toiletries case. Then he zipped it up again and smiled.

'Have a good leave, sir,' he said and turned to the next person.

Another customs man was checking his car as he got back outside, but as Toby walked up he closed the door and waved him to drive on.

It wasn't until Toby was out of the town, driving up the steep hill by Dover Castle that he dared relax and reach for his cigarettes. The cool breeze coming through the open window was soothing, the road ahead of him was clear and at last he felt exhilarated rather than fearful.

Switching on his cassette recorder, he punched a Pink Floyd tape in. It made him smile as the track 'Money' was the first to blast out and he drummed his fingers on the steering wheel in time to the music. He wouldn't do any more trips again, whatever inducements he was offered. By tomorrow he would be free of Weasel and debt. His life was just taking off.

The strapping was itching like crazy under his shirt, but he always kept it on until the moment of delivery, for safety. The road was deserted and very dark, he put his headlights on full beam and stepped on the accelerator.

His mind was on Studley. On his next leave he could invite a few friends down, show off all the treasures, discuss his plans to convert it into a country club. He could almost smell the roses in the Italian garden, feel the sun on his bare chest. So the police were still sniffing around. Maybe they'd never give up entirely, but as long as he kept his nose clean from now on, there was no way they could touch him.

He was about halfway to Canterbury. As he spun round a sharp bend, he saw a white car ahead stopped in the middle of the road. He stepped on the brake, and just as he swerved to avoid it he saw a girl in a white dress waving her arms at him.

'Shit,' he exclaimed, indignant that anyone should leave a car in such a perilous position. There was no choice but to stop; no one could cruise past, leaving her alone on such a dark, deserted stretch of road without at least enquiring what was wrong.

The girl ran towards him. 'Thank goodness you stopped,' she said breathlessly as he opened his window. 'I was afraid I'd be here all night. I've broken down and I don't know what to do.'

She was the sort of girl few men would avoid offering assistance to. Long, dark hair cascaded over tanned, bare shoulders, and she had big soulful eyes and a wide, luscious mouth. She was well spoken, perhaps in her mid-twenties, and as she leaned closer he could smell Apple Blossom perfume that evoked an old girlfriend.

The only light came from his headlights; high hedges lined both sides of the road. Another car came up behind them and veered round them, shooting off into the distance, reminding Toby he must at least push her car in closer to the hedge.

'You've got petrol in it, I assume?' Toby asked as he got out to look. Girls never seemed to think of this.

'Yes I put some in before I left Dover,' she said. 'Do you know anything about cars?'

'A bit,' he said, opening his own boot and taking

out a torch. 'It might be the plugs. Have you got a rag for me to clean them on?'

She was even prettier closer up, and as she bent into her car he noticed she had a tight little bottom and good legs. All at once he hoped he couldn't get it going. Maybe he could give her a lift into Canterbury!

'This is terrible,' she said, looking at him as if she might cry. 'What will I do if it won't go? There's no garages open at this time of night.'

Toby took the duster she offered him and opened the bonnet. He cleaned the plugs and fiddled around with everything else, shining his torch around as if he knew what he was doing.

'Try it again,' he said after he'd put the plugs back in.

She got in and he could hear her turning the key, but the engine was completely dead.

'I think it's something electrical,' he said, putting the bonnet down and coming round to her. 'I can't do anything more in this darkness. Where are you going?'

'To London.' Her eyes were wide with panic and her lips were quivering. 'I wish I'd come earlier when it was light or waited till the morning.'

Few men would be callous enough to leave any woman alone in such circumstances, but Toby was moved more by her face, body and what could come out of gratitude than by protective instinct.

'Well I was only going as far as Canterbury,' he said, looking at his watch. 'I'm going to find a hotel there for the night. You could come there with me and we could ring a garage in the morning?'

'I can't afford to stay in a hotel,' she said wistfully. 'I'd better stay here with the car until it's light.'

'I'll pay for you,' he said impulsively. 'Come on, you can't stay here. It will be freezing and anyway it's not safe to be out here all alone.'

She smiled, a wide, warm smile as if touched by the gallant gesture, but then she shook her head.

'I can't.' She shrugged her shoulders. 'It's very sweet of you, but I can't go off to a hotel with a man I don't know.'

Toby flashed on his most brilliant smile.

'I'm an officer in the army,' he said. 'You can look in my passport if you like. Toby Stratton's the name and I assure you I'm only concerned about you being alone out here in the dark.'

Telling girls he was an officer always had the same effect: their eyes widened, tension vanished, almost as if he'd flashed a police identity card.

'Well if you're sure.' Her smile came back, as trusting as a child's. 'I'm Carla Clayton. I could phone my dad from the hotel. He'll come for me in the morning and he'll give you the money then.'

'Don't worry about that.' Toby grinned. 'Now let's push this off the road and lock it up. I've driven all the way from Germany and I'm tired.'

He couldn't believe his luck once she was tucked into his car beside him. She said she worked as a dental nurse in London, and she was going back to her flat in Chelsea after spending a few days at home with her parents.

'I share with a couple of other girls,' she said. 'My dad's always saying I should join the AA if I'm going to drive long distances, but I never thought something like this would happen.'

'It's fate,' Toby laughed, putting the music back on. 'I wanted some company and now I've got it.'

'You really are nice, Toby,' she said, putting her hand on his thigh. 'I've never met an officer before, only squaddies.'

'I think you're the prettiest girl I've seen in a long time.' He liked the feel of her hand on his leg, the

594

smell of her and that long black hair tumbling over her shoulders. 'The girls in Germany are all big beefy types.'

'I thought men liked girls like that,' she said, seductively batting her eyelashes. 'You know, big bosoms and stuff.'

'Not me.' He put his hand down on top of hers. 'I like them small and dainty.'

Carla was easy to talk to. She seemed to know a great deal about astrology and suggested that Arians like him were well suited to the army life and compatible with her sign of Leo.

'Then we were fated to meet?' Toby smiled, flattered by her opinion that he was courageous, tough and headstrong, as well as terribly handsome.

'There are no chance encounters,' she said seriously. 'I believe our lives are mapped out for us at birth, and there is a purpose for everything.'

Toby pulled up outside the County, a commercial hotel in Canterbury. One of the attractions of this place was that they employed a night porter, and they didn't ask too many questions.

'I'll just go and see if they've got rooms,' he said. 'Won't be a minute!'

He came back a few minutes later and opened her door.

'They've only got a double room.' He made himself look anxious. 'I said we'd take it because I doubt whether there's anywhere else open now. I'll sleep on the floor if it's a double bed.'

He expected her to protest or at least to look perturbed, but instead she smiled at him.

'Our fate!' she said, her small, perfect teeth very white against the red of her lips. 'I don't think I'm cruel enough to make you sleep on the floor!'

Toby's heart quickened as they walked in. To him

the way she'd slung her tapestry overnight bag over her shoulder, her leggy, self-assured stride, were indications she wasn't a timid virgin and that she was used to decent hotels. He liked the fact that she was a little older than him, that her dress and shoes were of the expensive kind. She was his kind of girl!

It was an old-style hotel, with thick traditional carpets, prints of hunting scenes on the oak panelling and a small bar just off the reception area with leather armchairs and highly polished low tables. The bar was closed and a grille pulled down on it. Even the lights had been dimmed.

'Room 202,' the porter said. He was a portly man in a dark suit and as he handed over the key and told them the room was on the second floor, he looked over to Carla and smiled warmly. 'I'm afraid you're too late for room service now. But there are tea-making facilities in the room.'

'I'll just phone home,' Carla said as she came up to Toby and handed him her bag with almost wifely poise. 'You go on up. I'll join you in a moment.'

Toby was glad of an excuse to go on ahead; he needed to get the strapping off his chest. As Carla went off towards the phone booth, he bounded up the wide staircase.

The room was comfortably ordinary. Pleasant enough not to be seedy with an orange candlewick bedspread that smacked of cosy familiarity. A wide double bed, a desk-cum-dressing-table, a small alcove with a rail and coat hangers, and a washbasin. He dumped both their bags on the bed and went out again to find the bathroom, leaving the key in the door.

He was ecstatic. It was easy enough to pull a girl but often he had nowhere to take them. A double bed was luxury and it had been weeks since he'd last had a woman. Just the thought of unzipping that white

596

dress, her slim body and her long legs, sent shivers down his spine.

It hurt to pull off the plaster and it left an angry red mark across his chest. He used the toilet, buttoned up his shirt again, tucking it into his slacks, and put the bags of heroin into his jacket pockets.

In the room he hung his jacket up on a hanger, and he was just drawing the curtains and switching on the light by the bed, when Carla came in.

'Dad was grumpy with me,' she said with an impish grin that implied she didn't care. 'But he said he'd meet me here at seven in the morning and take me back to the car. I'd better not let him meet you, though. I lied and just said a married couple had dropped me off here. I'll nip back and give you half the money for the bill.'

'You needn't worry about that.' Toby went over to her and put his hands on her shoulders. 'Your company is enough.'

'Oh Toby,' she sighed, leaning against him. 'You are nice. I don't know what I'd have done without you.'

Her words made him feel good. She was grateful, yet not gushing, happy to be in his company.

Toby put one hand under her chin and lifted her face to kiss her. As his lips met hers he felt an instant surge of passion and knew this was going to be a night to remember.

'You kiss beautifully,' she murmured, moving her head back just far enough to look into his eyes. 'I've been a very lucky girl tonight.'

'It's me that's lucky,' Toby said, elated by her lack of coyness. Her dark eyes glowed in the soft light and her wide mouth was asking to be kissed again. He drew her close to him, savouring the warmth of her slim body against his as he ran his fingers down her long silky hair. 'You can't imagine how good it feels to hold a woman in my arms after months of being shut up with other men.'

He kissed her again and she melted into him, her mouth as eager as his own, hips undulating with pleasure. As his fingers reached for the zip of her dress, she purred and pressed herself closer still and when he touched her bare back she shuddered sensuously.

'I ought to be ashamed of myself.' Carla laughed softly as her dress fell to the floor, revealing nothing beneath it but the tiniest pair of white lace panties. Her breasts were firm and round with big dark nipples and she took his hands and placed them on them, sighing with delight. 'But I'm not ashamed. I want you.'

She arched her back and purred as he cupped her breasts, her nipples hard beneath his fingers as if demanding more. As he bent to kiss them, she caught his head between her hands and groaned in delight, her hips gyrating against his pelvis, making him so hard it was almost painful.

'I love having my breasts sucked,' she said huskily. 'Do it harder, it makes me all wet.'

He moved with her back to the bed, lowering her on to it and unfastening his trousers.

Carla's moans were becoming louder, her hands scrabbling to pull his shirt from his trousers as he feasted on her breasts.

'I want to feel your skin against mine,' she murmured in his ear, hands pushing at the waistband of his trousers. 'Take your clothes off.'

Toby tore his shirt over his head without unbuttoning it. He had never wanted a woman more – the sight of her breasts, the slight curve of her belly, dark pubic hair nestling beneath the sheer lace of her panties and her tongue flickering over her lips inflamed him. He had to stand to unlace his shoes and step out of his trousers and pants and she was looking at him lasciviously, the way girls did in blue movies.

'It's so big,' Carla gasped, reaching out to touch his cock with reverence.

Toby closed his eyes and knelt on the bed as she stroked it. She had the kind of touch that belonged in wet dreams: sure, practised and so sensual he was afraid he just might disgrace himself by ejaculating at any minute.

'What's that?' Carla reached up one hand and touched the mark on his chest where the strapping had been.

If nothing else, it broke the spell in the nick of time.

'I had a broken rib,' he lied. 'I only got the strapping off this morning.'

'Poor Toby.' She laughed softly, sitting up on the bed and kissing the mark, at the same time removing her panties in one swift movement. 'I shall be very gentle with you, then!'

Lying down again, she drew him down beside her and placed his hand on her pussy.

'Touch me there,' she said huskily, arching her back towards him.

Girls were usually a disappointment to Toby. They flirted and teased, but often backed off at the last moment. Not once had he ever met anyone who took the initiative as she did. But as his fingers slid into her and she groaned deeply, the slippery heat proved too much and he had to enter her. In just a few strokes he came, and as he lay on top of her he felt that same sense of shame he often felt with women.

He could hear her still panting. She was moving under him in that so familiar way and though he had never concerned himself before with women's satisfaction, this time it made him feel guilty.

'I'm sorry,' he whispered against her neck. 'I was too fast.'

599

He waited for the usual lie – that it was good for her, or he was the best she'd ever known – but to his surprise she just purred in his ear.

'We've got all night,' she whispered. 'I'll show you ways to please me and I'll make you hard again.'

Toby was in heaven.

Other officers had spoken dreamily of women like Carla, but he'd never truly believed they existed. She was sensual, loving and giving, yet bold enough to insist on what she wanted.

She took his cock in her mouth and sucked it till he was hard again, then sat astride him, only letting the tip of him inside her.

'Rub me here,' she said, taking his hand and showing him where she meant. 'Gently, it's very sensitive. Oh that's nice!'

She moved away from him each time he got too excited. She lay beside him and made him watch as she masturbated herself, then got him to do it for her. The smell of her was driving him wild, each kiss sending him further and further into oblivion, but now he wanted to please her more than he wanted release himself.

'Lick me there now,' she said fiercely, catching hold of his head and drawing it down to her pussy. 'That's wonderful. More, more.'

It was a thrill being the one to give pleasure and, spurred by her moans and sighs of delight, Toby found a new dimension in lovemaking which until now had eluded him. Carla was bucking beneath him, saying the kind of things he'd only ever heard men boasting of and when she shouted out she was coming, he knew she really was.

'Fuck me now,' she lay back panting, her arms reaching out for him. 'You were wonderful and I want that big cock inside me.'

He had never felt such heat before, or such closeness

with another person. Each kiss was longer and deeper; her legs and arms held him so tightly he never wanted it to end. It was like a volcano erupting when he finally came and spasms of exquisite pleasure brought tears to his eyes.

'That was the best, the most wonderful – ' Toby shut his eyes tightly, trying to hold back his tears, wanting to tell her he loved her because no other girl had made him feel the way she had. He rolled off her and pulled her into his arms, tenderness welling up inside him, the need to explain so great, but he couldn't find the words.

Her body fitted into his so perfectly. He still wanted to touch and stroke, to kiss her. But most of all he wanted to ask if it was the same for her.

Carla knew how it was for him. She could feel it coming through his silky skin, the touch of his fingers and his lips. She wished this wasn't just a job to her, that she didn't know he was a shit of the first water who had to be taken down.

Putting her heart and soul into lovemaking came naturally: she'd been working as a call girl for five years. But she didn't get many men as physically perfect as Toby Stratton and she wished she hadn't sensed that deep need in him.

She lay in his arms, feeling his fingers gently playing with her nipple, and wondered why a man with so much going for him should have become such a bastard.

But George had paid her good money for this job and she mustn't start feeling sorry for Toby now. Once he was asleep, as he soon would be, she must get up and find the heroin, put it in her bag and be ready when George arrived at seven.

'I've never felt like this before,' Toby whispered against her hair. 'It's like a door opening and showing me something beautiful I didn't know was there.'

'You must have done.' She laughed softly. 'A man like you!'

Those were practised words she'd said to many men, said glibly while inside she was laughing at herself for stoking their vanity. The public school ones like Toby were usually hopeless cases, so proud of their background, their superior education and so hidebound by warped morality and unhappy childhoods that there was no way to get through to them. The most she could achieve from such men was the certainty that they'd keep call girls like her busy for years.

But Toby was different. He was still so young, innocent enough to think she was just an ordinary girl, naïve enough to believe this was dawning love. If she had met him in different circumstances she might be tempted to try and hold on to him, but that was out of the question.

Carla's home wasn't in Dover, with a loving father who would pick her up in the morning. She was Carol Muckle, a girl from Dagenham who had run away from home to avoid the attentions of her mother's latest boyfriend when she was only fifteen. If anyone had told her ten years ago that she would one day fool men into thinking she came out of the top drawer, she would've laughed at them. Secondhand clothes, a hideous cockney accent – she couldn't even hold a knife and fork correctly. All she had in her favour was a pretty face, a good body and a hatred of poverty.

It was Donald Withers who had changed her into Carla Clayton. A forty-year-old accountant whose passion for young girls was equal to hers for money and luxury, he may have thought of her as a sex slave when he set her up in a little flat in Stoke Newington, but three years later she had reversed their roles. True, she still put on a gym slip and navy blue knickers for his pleasure, plaited her hair and let him play out schoolroom games, but he was the slave, not her. She made sure she got a big allowance each week, or he didn't get so much as a finger in her knicker elastic. He paid for her to have elocution lessons and she insisted on eating out in good restaurants, and weekends away in smart hotels. By the time Donald was ready to trade her in for a younger, less worldly model, Carla had savings, a wardrobe full of expensive clothes and the equivalent of a degree in lovemaking. A couple of years as a receptionist in several top London hotels gave her all the confidence and inside information she needed; then she branched out on her own, doing the job she had trained for, pleasing men and getting paid for it.

But now as Toby nuzzled into her neck, she was reminded of times when she too had wished for the kind of love which would wash away all her more shameful memories.

'I've just used women,' he said softly, his voice full of regret. 'But perhaps it's not too late to change.'

'Of course it's not.' She ran her hand over his smooth chest. She knew of course that anything he felt tonight, whatever painful confessions he made, would be wiped out when he discovered he'd been set up. But all the same she wanted to reach inside him and discover what made a man with so much going for him resort to drug smuggling and even murder.

'Tell me about yourself,' she said softly, stroking his face. 'Lovemaking is a good time for sharing secrets. If you're embarrassed tomorrow you don't have to see me again.'

Toby had already forgotten the image he had cultivated over the years. Carla had peeled a layer of his act away and he rather liked the naked sensation.

'You don't want to know about me,' he whispered.

'I do,' she insisted.

'I'm not a very nice person,' he said, blushing slightly. 'Mind you, I think I inherited that from my father. He was cruel to my mother and to us kids.'

'Go on,' she prompted.

Toby smirked, stroking back her hair.

'I don't know why I've even told you that!'

'Making love can do lots of things to people.' She lifted herself up on one elbow and looked down at him, letting her long hair trail across his chest.

Toby's eyes were the clearest blue she'd ever seen, his hair white-blond like a Swede's or a German's. Undoubtedly he was the most handsome man she'd ever seen. But there was pain in those eyes, and she was sure it was those childhood memories that had twisted his mind.

'Making love can make you feel pure again. It can make you feel more for someone else than you do for yourself. It relaxes, stimulates so many different things. But I think in your case it's touched a part of you that was locked away – maybe your father.'

'He was a preacher,' he said turning his face away. 'Even as a little boy I knew it was all a sham. He was a liar, a hypocrite, he loved no one but himself, and worst of all he was a pervert.'

Carla had heard many such admissions from men. Whatever was going to happen to Toby after tonight she felt duty bound to let him unburden himself and maybe exorcise at least one of his demons.

'Tell me?' she said softly. She sat up and pulled him close to her so his head was resting on her breasts. She stroked his hair away from his face and waited.

'He screwed my sister,' he muttered into her flesh. 'One night I heard this noise and I went upstairs. I looked round the door and he was there, doing it to her. She must have been thirteen then and I was too young to really know what it was. But the noises he was making frightened me and I went away.'

'Did you ever tell your sister you knew?' She felt so sorry for him; it wasn't hard to imagine how such a scene could torment a boy once he reached adolescence and understood what he'd witnessed.

He didn't answer right away, just buried his face closer into her.

'Did you, Toby?'

'Yes.' He made an odd sound in his throat, like a half-swallowed sob. 'But I was as cruel as my father. I threw it at her, knowing it would hurt her.'

Carla closed her eyes. Somehow she understood everything, even though she knew no more of his background than George had needed to tell her. He loved this sister – perhaps she was the only person he'd ever loved – and he'd hurt her deliberately because of his own pain.

'You must tell her, Toby,' she said, smoothing his head gently. 'All of it. Don't let this thing grow between you like a cancer.'

He lifted his head from her breast and she saw tears in his eyes.

'You're very wise.' He tried to smile. 'How come you couldn't fix your car?'

'I'm better at fixing people.' She smiled back, wiping at his eyes with one finger. 'Suppose I make us a cup of tea, have a wash and then we start all over again?'

It wasn't until five that he eventually fell so sound asleep that she was able to wriggle out of his arms. She lay still for several minutes listening to his deep breathing, then slipped out of bed and over to his bag.

Enough faint light filtered through the curtains for her to see. Hardly daring to breathe she rummaged through it and when she found nothing but clothes and toiletries, her heart began to thump.

Could he have left it in the car? There was no way

she could go in and out of the hotel at this hour without arousing suspicion. But then she remembered the red marks on his chest. Of course, he'd taken it off once he got up here!

She glanced under the bed, and as she straightened up she saw his jacket. Keeping her eyes on Toby she crept towards it. He was sound asleep, one arm curled round his face like a small child, his half-covered body golden against the white sheets.

Holding the hanger still with one hand, she delved into the pockets and breathed a sigh of relief as she felt the packets.

It showed his real innocence that he hadn't suspected a set-up. Most men in his position wouldn't have stopped in a lonely road, even for a girl on her own. If they had been foolhardy enough to stop, they would have found a safer place to hide the drugs: in the hotel safe, even under the mattress.

In a minute she swapped his packets for ones of talcum powder she'd brought in her bag, then got back into bed beside him.

Carla knew there was no danger of falling asleep; she was much too tense now. She was being paid for a job, just as he was. They were both people who lived by their wits and it wasn't her responsibility to decide whether her actions were any more reprehensible than his.

He woke just as she got back from the bathroom. She had changed into jeans and a shirt.

'I've got to go,' she said and bent over to kiss him.

This was the dangerous time. Ruthless he might be, but he was brought up a gentleman and he would find it hard to let her go without escorting her downstairs.

'But – ' he sat up in bed, ready to jump up.

'Don't come down, Dad might be waiting in the foyer.' She kissed his forehead and pushed him gently back on the pillows.

'When will I see you again?' he said and his eyes looked sorrowful.

She took a sheet of hotel writing paper from the dressing-table and wrote down a number in London. It was a made-up one, but it was kinder than the truth.

'Ring me soon.' She kissed him again, for a moment letting herself sink into his arms. 'It was a wonderful night, Toby. You're the best lover I've ever had.'

She left then, running down the stairs with her bag in her hand and across the foyer to the street.

The black Jaguar was waiting just a few yards up the road. As she approached George leaned across and opened the door.

'You got it?'

'Of course.' She wanted to smile, to laugh and tell him how easy it had been, but all she could think of was that lonely, lost man lying there wrapped in rosy dreams while she was running out on him.

Toby felt like a new man as he drove back into London. Traffic was pouring down towards the coast, for a Sunday at the seaside, but there was little going into London. Despite only a few hours' sleep he was rested and relaxed. He had the hood down, the sun was shining and he couldn't wait to see Carla again. No girl had ever made him feel like this before. It was better than speed or coke, better even than money.

Maybe he shouldn't have told her about his father, but then maybe this good feeling inside him was a result of that confession?

As he drove up the Old Kent Road he saw a row of telephone boxes and on an impulse he pulled up outside.

As he dialled Charity's number he had a pang of anxiety that she would blank him off, but he knew he'd got to try and make amends.

607

'Hallo.'

Her voice sounded sweet; once again pangs of remorse came back.

'It's me, Chas,' he said. 'Toby!'

Once just the sound of his voice would have brought a note of delight into her voice, but instead she hesitated before speaking.

'Don't hang up on me,' he begged her. 'Let me just say my piece?'

'Go on then,' she said coolly.

'I got leave to come and see you. I'm so sorry about what I said and what I've done, Chas.' His words tumbled over one another. 'I know there isn't any excuse for any of it, particularly the cruel things I said.'

'I forgive you for what you said, Toby,' she said so quietly he had to listen hard to catch it. 'But I won't stand by and see you ruin your life with drugs and until I have your assurance that that part of your life is over I won't see you.'

'It *is* over,' he said. 'All this trouble with you has made me see it was stupid. Let me come round later today and see you.'

'I'm going out today,' she said gently. 'But tomorrow is fine. Come over for lunch and we'll talk.'

Toby had a lump in his throat. He swallowed hard but still it was there.

'You don't hate me?'

'I could never hate you, Toby. I don't like you sometimes, but I'll always love you.'

Toby put the phone down and went back to the car. He felt guilty that he still had the packages to deliver and he wished he hadn't agreed to this last trip, but he couldn't put the clock back now.

It was three in the afternoon as he parked his car in Cinnamon Street in Wapping. He had driven round the block of old warehouses, checking to see the place wasn't under police surveillance, then, satisfied it was safe, he transferred the heroin from his jacket pocket into a brown paper bag. It took a couple of minutes to put up the hood. Even though the street was deserted and he didn't intend to stay more than a few minutes, it was the sort of area that made him cautious.

Tucking the brown bag under his arm, he crossed the narrow cobbled street to the warehouse. The grass outside the seedy pre-war block of flats behind him was was brown and scrubby, the one lone tree laden with dust.

The few shops at the end of the street looked equally bleak: wire grilles over the windows, peeling paint and crumbling stone. A rancid smell filled the warm air, a mixture of river, rotting ancient buildings and neglect.

Ringing the bell above the green door, Toby glanced nervously over his shoulder. An old lady was leaning on the top-floor balcony looking down at him, but almost all the other balconies were hung with washing. He could smell spice wafting out of the brickwork, a reminder of what the warehouse had been built for. He never dared ask what they used it for now. Albert and Jim Tooley weren't the kind of men you questioned.

The sound of clonking boots on the stairs made him glance round again. He had changed this morning into jeans and a white T-shirt, but his short hair and sports car made him stand out in an area where men were tough, with tattoos, bulging muscles and beer bellies.

He sensed someone looking through the spyhole and then the door opened.

'Come in, mate.' Albert's big face registered nothing. Not pleasure, not even dislike. Toby had

609

never seen him smile, or show any other kind of emotion.

Albert was huge: over six feet, with a body like a tank. His brother Jim was the brain, at least he handed over the money and arranged things. Albert appeared to be there just to terrify people.

His nose was flat, as if it had been squashed on to his face by a sledgehammer and his nasal tones showed that he had difficulty breathing; hair cut to a mere brown fuzz and black stubble on his heavy jowls.

'Lovely day,' Toby said brightly as he went up the bare wooden stairs with Albert close behind him. He hated himself for trying to ingratiate himself with these brothers, he could tell they regarded him as an upper-class twit, however often he reminded them that he'd been born in Greenwich.

A snort was the only reply. They had reached the second floor, where the brothers camped out.

It was a mere open space, heavy rough wood beams slanting up from the centre to support the roof. Opposite the door was an open hatch with a huge rusting chain dangling in front of it from a pulley. A couple of mattresses lay behind one set of beams. Army blankets and a few grubby pillows gave the impression that the brothers slept here. On the far side some tea chests stacked on their sides held a couple of cracked mugs, a few beer bottles and what seemed to be car spares.

Jim was sitting on an upturned wooden box, wearing a grubby vest and jeans. Although he was neither as huge as Albert nor quite so ugly, there was something more chilling about him.

His eyes were like those of dead fish on a fishmonger's slab, staring and blank, and he had the thinnest lips Toby had ever seen. Muscles stood out like ropes in his neck and arms and the belly hidden beneath that vest was iron hard. Alf's skin was mottled red from the sun; Jim's was a deep, dark brown and shiny as if rubbed with oil.

Toby had once met Jim in a club when he was wearing a dicky bow and dark suit, but even discovering the man had some social graces, that his voice was well modulated and even pleasant, didn't quite wipe out the suspicion that he was an exceptionally dangerous animal.

'I expected you sooner,' Jim said, fixing Toby with those strange fish eyes. 'Did you miss the boat?'

'No, I was right on schedule.' Toby sat down on the empty box Jim waved his hand towards. 'But it's a long drive, so I stayed overnight on the way up.'

Another disturbing thing about Jim was the way he mimicked the accent of the person he was speaking to. With his brother it was pure cockney, but he could lapse into Scouse, Birmingham or even Toby's Sandhurst at will.

'Any trouble at the customs?'

Toby shook his head, holding out the brown paper package.

'They searched my bag and car, but not me.' Toby always had the desire to lie to this man. Claim he'd head-butted someone and run for it, or slipped the package into someone else's bag – anything to make himself look braver, or smarter. But he curbed it; perhaps Jim might just have a spy on the route. 'Plain sailing, really.'

Jim took the three packages out of the paper bag and rested them on his knee for a moment, looking at them reflectively. It was hard to read his emotions. Toby couldn't tell if it was the pleasure of knowing how much money this little lot would fetch, or regret that Toby hadn't bought more.

He took a Swiss Army knife from his pocket, pulled out the smallest blade and poked it through the plastic. Toby's guts churned. They always did at this moment, though why he didn't understand. He watched as Jim licked one finger, dipped it in the bag, then lifted it to his lips.

But this time Jim's expression changed. He frowned, licked his lips and his eyes shot up to glare at Toby.

'It's fuckin' talcum powder!'

'Don't be ridiculous!' Toby jumped up instinctively as Jim prodded the other two bags in quick succession, tasting a sample from each.

'Don't you call me fuckin' ridiculous!' Jim said, pushing the bags to the floor.

'I didn't mean *you* were,' Toby said hastily. He moved over to the bags spilling out on to the floor and tried them himself. 'Shit! They are, too. They've bloody seen us off!'

For a moment there was total silence. Toby saw Alf move in closer, but he was thinking only of Hans back in Hamburg who'd strapped the packets to his chest in the bathroom beyond his office, just as he'd done each time before.

'Not "they".' Jim stood up, blocking out the light from the open hatch, his eyes suddenly alive, burning with dark anger. 'You!'

Chapter Thirty-Four

'Toby phoned this morning,' Charity suddenly blurted out as Rob poured her a second glass of wine.

They were sitting in the tiny walled garden at the back of a restaurant in Hampstead village. They had ordered their lunch and Charity was determined to steer their conversation away from her problems, but she had to tell Rob this latest development.

It was another beautiful day. A cloudless sky, hot sunshine and the garden of the restaurant made Charity think of the courtyards in Florence. Climbing shrubs covered the walls, a stone lion's head in one corner dripped water into a tiny pool, and tubs of vivid petunias and geraniums stood between the four cast-iron tables.

Ten days ago Charity had been discharged from Holly Bush House and her recovery was almost complete. Two days ago the plaster had been removed from her arm and each day she could walk a little further. She still had pain in her back, but daily physiotherapy was easing it. Her facial scars were improving too; the smaller ones had almost gone. Charity was waiting now to see a plastic surgeon about the two bigger scars.

But for Charity her physical condition was unimportant. In herself she felt so well. For days now she'd woken each morning with an exhilarating lightness, the kind of feeling she could only liken to opening a window and seeing spring after a long, cold winter.

Deep inside her she knew this was due to her deepening relationship with Rob.

His daily visits now weren't psychiatrist and patient sessions, but visits from a caring friend, as he dropped in to see her on his way home from the hospital. The emphasis had changed: now Rob talked about people at the hospital, his friends and his outside interests and slowly Charity was seeing the whole man.

She knew that he played squash, and that he swam at least twice a week. He could cook, he spoke French and Italian fluently and he played the piano. Charity hoped that this lunch date would reveal still more.

He looked different today. It wasn't just his white open-necked shirt or the fact that he'd had his hair cut. Freckles had come out on his nose, as they had that summer in Sussex, and there was a sort of shine to him, as if he was excited about something. Charity wondered if he saw this lunch as their first real date, a lead up to something more. She hoped so.

'What did Toby have to say for himself?' Rob resisted the desire to word the question in his professional manner.

'He wanted to come round,' Charity said, smiling a little uncertainly. 'I'm improving! I said I was going out for lunch and suggested he come tomorrow. How should I play it with him now?' she asked.

Rob smiled at her. 'We both know you'll forgive him, even if I was to say you shouldn't. Just try to distance yourself, Charity, that's all I can suggest. Make Toby see he has to earn your respect.'

Over lunch they moved on to lighter subjects. They talked about Martin and Marjorie, who had invited Charity down for a weekend at their house in Hertfordshire; about Rita's latest boyfriend, Charity's thoughts about going back to work, and Dorothy.

'She's got some new man,' Charity giggled. 'She's

being very cagey about him too, which is unusual for her. He must be rich of course, because she said something about a swimming pool. Why do you think she's not telling Rita and me everything?'

'Maybe Dorothy's fallen in love with him,' Rob grinned. 'That's when most of us clam up.'

Charity looked puzzled.

'We get scared to say too much in case it doesn't work out,' Rob said. 'All our feelings are heightened, we start to act and think irrationally, and it can be very threatening.'

'That sounds like personal experience,' Charity said.

His eyes met hers and the intensity of his expression startled her. 'It is,' he said.

There were at least ten other people in the garden eating and drinking, but all at once it was as if they were totally alone. Charity wanted to slide her hand over his, to flirt and push him a little. But suddenly she was shy and uncertain.

'What happened to her, then?' she asked instead, looking away at the other diners.

'I didn't know how she felt,' he said, and his voice had a kind of plea in it. 'We talked about everything else, but I sort of hedged the last fence.'

Charity looked back at him. She knew with utter certainty he was talking about them, but the right words failed her.

'Another glass of wine?' She picked up the bottle and poured him a glass. 'If you haven't got anything on this afternoon maybe we could go back to my place and sit in the sun on the balcony.'

Rob sat up on the sun lounger and looked at his watch, horrified to find it was almost five-thirty. They'd had two bottles of wine with lunch and then come back here. He'd taken his shirt off, Charity had put on a bikini, but after chatting for a short while they had both fallen asleep in the sun.

Charity was still sound asleep, lying on her stomach, her head resting on one curled-up arm, hair hiding her remaining scars.

Rob tried hard not to stare at her body, but her pert firm buttocks, tiny waist and slender legs drew his eyes. There were tiny golden hairs on her spine and just above the pants of her polka-dotted bikini she had a kind of indentation, like a dimple. Temptation proved too much: he reached out and stroked her back.

Charity woke with a start at his touch.

'I was just making sure it wasn't burning,' he said guiltily. 'We've been asleep for a couple of hours.'

'What time is it?' Charity yawned, but made no attempt to get up. The last thing she remembered was Rob telling her a story about one of the junior doctors being caught making love to a nurse in a disused ward at Colney Hatch. Obviously the food, wine and sun had zonked them both out.

'Half-past five.' Rob slid his hands over her shoulderblades, making her tingle.

'That's nice,' she said sleepily. 'More!'

Rob moved then to sit up, his legs between the two sun loungers, and used both hands to massage her.

'Does it help the pain?' he asked after a few seconds.

'Um,' she muttered. She wasn't in any pain, but she was enjoying the sensation of being stroked.

With her head resting on her hands she found herself looking at Rob's stomach. It was flat and taut, lightly tanned with just a hint of golden hair around his navel. Her fingers itched to reach out and touch it.

'Kiss me,' she said softly, closing her eyes.

Although he bent closer, his lips didn't find hers as she expected. Instead he kissed her right down her spine, his tongue darting out with light yet sensual butterfly touches.

'That's wonderful,' Charity murmured, feeling a quivering starting inside her. She wanted to turn and touch him, but the sensation was too good to interrupt.

She slid out one arm, reaching for the part of him which was nearest, and ran her fingers down over his thigh. He was wearing light cotton trousers but she could feel muscles and heat through the thin fabric.

Rob's lips moved back up to her shoulders, hands parting her hair to kiss her neck, and she had to turn and pull him to her.

The shuddering started inside her the moment their lips met, growing stronger as his tongue flickered against hers. Her body was arching up towards him, fingers stroking his neck; suddenly vague wanting became fierce desire.

'Oh Charity,' Rob gasped, moving back a little, still kneeling beside her, his hands cupping her face. 'I've wanted to do that for so long.'

Of all the men she'd ever kissed, she had never felt such erotic sensitivity before, or encountered such a deep need in anyone. All at once she realised this had been pent up inside him for weeks and the knowledge that he'd managed to suppress it was humbling.

As he kissed her again and again, Charity felt her own need matching his, passion flaring up, demanding more.

'Let's go inside,' she whispered. 'You can't kneel on that stone any longer.'

Rob didn't move instantly as she expected, but held her tightly, his face burrowing into her neck.

'I've got to go back to the hospital,' he murmured.

'On a Sunday?' She moved her face and lifted his up to check if he was joking.

But Rob's eyes were sorrowful.

'Patients don't have weekends off.' He sighed deeply, stroking her face tenderly. 'I never thought I'd be tempted to call in sick, but I am now.'

He didn't look like a doctor now. His bare chest, his fair tousled hair and the sleepy look in his speckly eyes were boyishly endearing. Lips swollen with kissing, the freckles on his nose and the smell of sunbaked smooth skin were unbearably erotic. Charity wanted him. To hold that lean slender body against hers, to reach behind all those masks he put on and find the entire Robert Cuthbertson.

'Come back later,' she urged.

'No, not tonight.' He pressed his forehead against hers, kissing her nose. 'It'll be very late and that's no way to start a romance.'

'A romance?' she whispered. 'Is that what it's going to be?'

He disentangled himself from her arms and stood up, reaching for his shirt.

'The biggest,' he said, looking down at her with an expression so naked she felt goosebumps come up all over her. 'But I want everything to be right. We've taken so long to get to this point, a little longer won't hurt.'

Charity knew exactly what he meant. He wanted wine, soft music and an unhurried night to remember, not racing back here to find her half asleep. But although she agreed in principle, the wonderful feeling fizzing inside her was tempting her to insist.

Rob saw the desire in her eyes and he could feel himself weakening.

'Look, Toby's coming tomorrow,' he said, pulling her to her feet and hugging her tightly. 'You need a good night's sleep before seeing him, and I won't give you one,' he said, nuzzling her neck. 'I'll pop in on my way back from the hospital. I'd like to meet him at last, then we can make some plans. Maybe I can go sick on Tuesday!'

'I won't be that rough on you,' she said, raising her eyebrows in mock horror. 'What's more I'll give my little brother his marching orders long before he sees the feast I'm going to prepare for you.'

Rob bent his head and took a playful bite at her right breast.

'That's the only feast I want!'

She giggled, wriggling away.

'Tomorrow,' she said. 'I just wish I was the patient you're going to see.'

'No you don't.' Rob smiled, running his hand up her. An image of the pitiful, often violent schizophrenic young patient waiting for him wasn't one he wanted to conjure up just now. 'Just one more kiss to keep me going?'

Charity sank into his arms, happiness welling up inside her, washing away the last grey doubts in her mind.

'I shan't be able to concentrate on anything.' She sighed, kissing his eyes, his nose and his mouth. 'I'll be counting the hours till you come back.'

Chapter Thirty-Five

Toby didn't even see the punch that knocked him down. One moment Jim was standing there glowering at him, the next he felt the impact of fist on cheekbone and he was flying backwards.

It wasn't the first punch that had ever knocked Toby off his feet, but it was the only one that had been so fast he got no warning. His vision went for a second and fiery Catherine wheels spun before his eyes.

'Where's the real stuff, you shitbag?' Jim yelled at him.

Toby couldn't focus; all he saw was a dark shape leaning over him.

'I don't know.' Toby could barely move his mouth to speak and the pain was as if he'd been hit with a red hot iron. 'That's what Hans strapped to my chest. He's set you up, not me.'

A kick in his ribs sent him skidding two feet along the rough floor. As he scrabbled to get to his feet, Alf put one big boot on his wrist, pinning him in place.

'Don't hit me,' Toby pleaded. He had never seen any similarity between the brothers before, but now he noticed the identical cruel lips. 'This is all some terrible mistake. That's what I was given, I didn't even open the bags.'

'Fix 'im.' Jim made a gesture to his brother.

When Alf bent down and caught hold of both Toby's wrists, he thought he was going to kill him.

'No, please!' he yelled, the heels of his shoes scraping on the floor as he was hauled backwards to the corner of the room. 'I promise you I didn't take it. Do you think I'd have the front to walk in here with talcum power when I knew you'd test it?'

Something cold was clamped to both his wrists above his head; the click that followed told him they were handcuffs.

'Up,' Alf said in his guttural voice, dragging Toby to his feet by pulling on the cuffs.

Toby couldn't escape. The handcuffs tore into his skin and his arms felt as if they were being pulled from their sockets. Within seconds Alf had him secured to a length of heavy chain hanging in the corner of the room.

'Tie 'is feet,' Jim said, turning away and lighting a cigarette. 'Any yelling, give 'im a whack.'

Toby was beside himself with fear, and confused. He didn't understand why Hans had given him worthless powder instead of heroin. Jim disappeared downstairs without saying another word. Alf sat on a box, his back against a beam, calmly smoking. The rope round Toby's ankles was cutting into his skin, and already he had cramp in both arms.

'Look, Alf.' Toby tried to reason with the big man, even though he suspected it was futile. 'Those packages were still on my chest till just before I got here.'

As the words came out of his mouth, Toby saw the truth in a blinding flash.

Carla!

Every other trip the strapping had remained in place until he arrived here in the warehouse. Even when he'd broken his journey in a hotel he hadn't taken it off.

Despite the pain in his cheek, a throbbing around his left eye and his severely kicked rib he made himself think back to where she'd been standing by her car.

A lonely stretch of road enclosed by hedges! The perfect spot for an ambush – and whoever had planned it knew the only thing that would get him to stop was a girl.

He'd played right into her hands, too.

Why hadn't he been suspicious? How many girls would go to a hotel with a strange man in the middle of the night as readily as she did? All that bullshit she'd given him about fate! Only a conceited prat would believe that!

Toby felt sick at his stupidity.

He thought hard. How did anyone know he would be on that road, at that time?

Again he groaned mentally as he recalled a conversation while he was waiting to board the ferry in Calais.

It was just like every other trip. Dozens of cars and lorries waiting patiently on the dock for the signal to drive on. Many of the drivers were wandering around, chatting and passing out cigarettes. Although it was dark it was a hot night with scarcely a breeze; some of the drivers wore nothing but shorts and sandals.

'Nice car!' the man said. Stopping beside Toby, he ran his hand appreciatively over the gleaming paint-work. 'I always fancied one myself.'

He appeared to be a lorry driver, thickset, around forty, in a grubby shirt, big boots, and with half an inch of stubble on a weatherbeaten face.

There was nothing unusual about the man, or his friendly interest. Just a working man stretching his legs and having a smoke and a chat while he waited to drive on. Toby told him amongst other things that he was intending to stop overnight in Canterbury.

Now Toby came to think about it, he hadn't seen that man again on the ferry; if he had he might have bought him a drink. Maybe he didn't even have a lorry at all. He could have followed him all the way from Hamburg for all Toby knew, then once he knew Toby's plans he nipped off to a phone and relayed the message.

But to whom? No one knew about this trip other than Hans in Hamburg, Alf, Jim and Stubbs.

Except for Weasel.

But he couldn't know details of times and places. And why should he do it anyway when he stood to be paid off?

Jim came back up the stairs and waited in the doorway.

'Jim, listen to me,' Toby pleaded, taking the silence as a slight change of heart. 'I didn't – '

'Don't come out with all that crap again,' Jim cut him short, striding towards him and punching him in the ribs as if he were a punchbag in a gymnasium. 'I've rung Hans in Hamburg and he's assured me the bags he gave you were kosher. I've known him for years, he wouldn't stitch me up.'

The punch winded Toby, making him swing helplessly on the chain.

'Jim, listen to me,' he gasped. 'I'll tell you everything that happened, just undo me!'

'You'll tell me tied up,' Jim roared, slapping his fist into his other hand. 'Come on, spit it out!'

'There was this girl in a broken-down car,' Toby said haltingly, his eyes running with the pain in his ribs and belly. Even as he told the story he knew Jim wouldn't just accept it. He was all set to distribute the drugs that night, wanting to turn his investment around fast. Men like him didn't take kindly to any hitches.

'You stupid bastard,' Jim snarled as Toby finished the story, punching him yet again. 'You think I'm gonna believe that load of drivel?'

Alf came lumbering across the room.

623

'Want me to take over, bruv?' he said, his big face contorting into almost a smile.

Toby felt sick as he saw Alf pull a knuckleduster from his pocket. It was dull gunmetal, with protruding lumps as big as thimbles. He slid it over his big fingers, his eyes glinting with malice.

'Give it to 'im.' Jim turned away, a sly smile playing at the corners of his lips. 'I reckon ten should get the truth.'

Alf stood in front of Toby and braced himself. The muscles in Alf's neck and shoulders stood out like hosepipes, but it was the cruel look in his eyes that made Toby's bowels turn to water.

He didn't appear to put any effort into the first blow, just his elbow lifting slightly and the fist coming forward as his other hand reached out to grab the belt on Toby's jeans to hold him still. But the gentle movement had all the force of a bus doing sixty miles an hour and Toby heard a rib crack on impact.

'No!' Toby yelled, but before the pain even registered, another blow followed it, then another. Each hit a different spot till it seemed his whole abdomen and chest was stripped of flesh. The pain was too great to even think and by the fifth blow he wasn't just crying, but screaming in agony.

'Six,' he faintly heard Jim say. Toby looked down to see blood spurting out through his shirt. He willed himself to pass out, but no welcome blackness came. Instead he felt warm blood running down his arms where the handcuffs dug into his wrists and to his further shame, he wet himself.

'Peed our pants, 'ave we?' Alf grinned, spinning him round to strike out at his back with even greater force. 'You'll shit yerself too before I'm finished with you.'

If Toby had known anything more he would have told them.

624

'Stop!' he screamed. 'I'll give you anything. Just stop!'

By the tenth blow Toby was beyond screaming. He was twitching as if he was wired to the mains, his body screaming out that it could take no more.

'That's a taster,' Jim said from across the room. 'Now let's 'ave the truth.'

'I've told you,' Toby sobbed. 'There *is* nothing more. Ring the hotel, they'll tell you about the girl.'

He didn't see Alf lift his boot. Just a crunch in the knee, the sound of splintering bone and more intense agony.

'I'll give you anything,' Toby pleaded. 'I've got money coming to me. I'll pay you double what you've lost.'

'We want the stuff.' Jim barely lifted his head as he lit a cigarette, but his voice held terrifying menace. 'And we want names of people in with you.'

'Weasel's the only person who could've done something,' Toby said weakly. The room was swirling and growing dark. His chest and back were on fire and his leg felt as if it was dipped in boiling jam.

He tried to explain how he owed Weasel money, but the words sounded incoherent, even to him. He didn't know if he was really telling them about paying the man to kill his uncle, or if it was just a nightmare.

Jim looked at the prone body on the floor then back to his brother.

They had taken Toby down when he blacked out and laid him on the floor. His T-shirt was congealed with blood; more was seeping out through the knee of his jeans.

'I reckon he's told us the truth,' Jim said in a low voice. 'I'll 'ave to ring Guv.'

Jim Tooley didn't like many people, and he'd disliked Toby Stratton the moment he clapped eyes on him. When the boss had insisted he was the perfect

625

courier, reluctantly Jim had agreed. But he never had got to like him; in fact every trip when Toby tried to make out he was some kind of hero, he found himself resenting the cocky bastard still more.

Just looking at Toby made him want to puke. Even with a swollen eye, his shirt congealed with blood, he was still handsome.

'Whatcha reckon the governor will do?' Alf cupped his big hand round a cigarette and inhaled deeply. Although Alf was the older of the two, Jim always made the decisions because he was smart. He never discussed who they worked for, but Alf was bright enough to know that big money was riding on this deal. A whole chain of people were waiting for their cut and they weren't going to be happy when they knew they'd been cheated.

'Blind 'im, cut 'is balls off,' Jim said almost cheerfully. 'Reckon he'll send us after this Weasel too, but I'd better go on down and phone 'im.'

Jim came back up the stairs some twenty minutes later looking troubled. Although he knew Stratton deserved the injuries they'd already inflicted on him, he hadn't expected Stubbs to insist they finish him off.

Violence was in Jim's blood; he came from a long line of bare-knuckle fighters. But giving someone a caning for stepping out of line was one thing – cold-blooded killing was something else.

'What'd Guv say?' Alf's big face registered equal concern. His body was taut with anxiety, wide shoulders hunched, hands braced on his splayed knees.

Checking that Toby was still out cold, he moved over to his brother.

'We've got to get him out of 'ere,' he whispered. 'We'll carry 'im down to the van. You can drive it. I'll take 'is car.'

626

Alf looked up questioningly, making a slashing sign across his throat.

Jim nodded glumly. Wasting an army officer wasn't like tossing some thug in the Thames; the whole police force would be on to it. But as Stubbs said, there was no alternative. Stratton knew too much. If he'd been one of the lads, capable of keeping his trap shut, they might have taken a chance. But he'd squeal, loud and clear, and the whole set-up would be blown right open.

Jim's main anxiety right now was Alf. His simple-minded brother would do whatever he was told unquestioningly and he felt a deep sense of shame that he was dragging him into this.

'The word's gone out to pull in this bloke Weasel too. Guv knows who he is. All we gotta do is get shot of 'im – ' Jim inclined his head towards Toby.

Jim had a rough plan, but he could see great gaping holes in it even before he put it into action. Stratton's MG was the sort of car people remembered, especially in an area like Wapping where sports cars were as rare as unicorns. But if he drove it back down towards Canterbury, with a bit of luck the police wouldn't ask questions around here.

Toby groaned as they lifted him up to carry him down the stairs.

'It's OK,' Jim said brusquely. He was holding Toby's thighs while Alf had his shoulders and it was quite obvious Stratton's knee was shattered. 'We're taking you somewhere to get you fixed up.'

Toby heard the words as if from a great distance but the intense pain of being moved blotted out all thought or the ability to speak. Each step the men took brought on fresh stabs of agony which seemed to be centred around his leg, and he could feel tears scalding a raw place on his cheek.

'He's gone again,' Jim remarked as they laid him
down by the black transit van garaged in the bottom
of the warehouse. 'Get us a couple of those old
blankets to lay him on.'

The ground floor was gloomy, the only light coming
through a window up on the stairs and small grilles
high up on the double doors. Around the van in the
centre were stacked cardboard boxes and tea chests
of secondhand household equipment, evidence of the
brothers' legitimate house-clearing business. The
smell of spice was strongest here, overpowering the
mildew. Cobwebs hung from the ceiling and a thick
layer of black, gritty dust covered everything.

Jim opened the back doors of the van, pulled out a
couple of old chairs and a bookcase and made a crude
bed in the back with a pile of blankets. He worked in
silence punctuated only by the odd grunt, but his
mind was working overtime.

'Let's have him now.' He crouched down in the
van, holding out his hands.

Toby groaned again as they laid him down.

'Find 'is car keys,' Jim said, climbing out of the van
for some old cushions to wedge him in with. 'I'll get a
bottle of whisky and give him some to keep him quiet.'

Jim ran back upstairs with a bucket of water. There
was no time now to scrub up the blood on the floor,
but he sloshed the water over it and checked that
nothing of Toby's was left behind.

Rummaging through an upturned orange box he
pulled out his knife kept in a leather sheath. It had
been some years since he'd last used it for anything
more than a threat, but he'd kept it razor sharp. He
studied it for a moment, running his thumb down the
glinting blade, then pushed it back into its sheath,
wrapped it in an old black sweater and tucked it
under his arm.

When he came back down the stairs with a half-bottle of whisky, Alf was standing looking at a sheet of paper.

'The bird's telephone number,' he said, handing the sheet of hotel writing paper to his brother. ''Ere's 'is wallet too.'

Jim put on a pair of thin leather driving gloves. The brown pigskin wallet was stuffed with notes, some English but mostly German marks. He took out thirty pounds, left the rest and checked through the photos of three different girls. Two were obviously Stratton's sisters, blond like him; the third was a dark-haired girl in a bikini. Amongst a bunch of receipts there was one for petrol bought earlier in the day. He took that out, tore it into shreds and shoved the rest back.

'That should do it,' he said, wiping the wallet carefully with a cloth, then clambered into the van. He replaced the wallet in Stratton's hip pocket, then, lifting his head up, signalled for his brother to pass the whisky.

Toby bucked violently as the bottle touched his lips, his one undamaged eye flying open in alarm.

'Don't be fuckin' stupid,' Jim said. 'It ain't poison, only Scotch. Drink it, you berk, it'll 'elp the pain.'

As the fiery liquid dripped on to his tongue it brought Toby round enough to be aware that the arm holding him was gentle, the threat gone. He had no fight left in him: he drank greedily, wanting only relief from the pain.

'That's it,' Jim said encouragingly, watching as the whisky level went down, some of it spilling down over Toby's chin and neck. 'Now just you keep quiet, otherwise we'll 'ave to gag yer.'

'Whatcha going to do wiv the number?' Alf asked, pointing to the hotel writing paper abandoned on a box, his big face furrowed with frown lines.

629

'I'll stick it in his car.' Jim wiped it clean, but made a note of the number on the back of his hand. 'Don't suppose it's a real number anyway, but it'll give the filth something to chase.'

'Where we goin'?' Alf said in a whisper.

'Down to Kent,' Jim muttered, picking up his sweater with the weapon concealed inside it. 'You follow me.'

'I don't like this.' Alf's voice was even more nasal than usual. 'Ain't there another way?'

'No bruv', there ain't.' Jim shrugged his shoulders. 'Now get in the van and drive out when I open the doors. If he starts shouting or you need me, flash yer lights.'

Toby flitted in and out of consciousness. Each bump in the road, each jerk as the van braked, sent excruciating spasms of pain through his leg and spine. It was almost dark now, which must mean they had driven a long way but he no longer cared where he was being taken; all he could do was focus on Jim's promise that he'd get him fixed up.

Charity's face danced before him. He could see her long white-gold hair, soft blue eyes and gentle mouth, and he felt deep, agonising shame. Tomorrow she would worry when he didn't turn up. She might even get a call from a hospital.

How would he explain away his injuries? What if the police got wind of it? He'd told Jim and Alf about Uncle Stephen, suppose they told someone else?

But the thought of prison and losing his inheritance was nowhere near as bad as imagining what it would do to Charity when she discovered the whole truth about him.

It was only as Jim drove through the Blackwall Tunnel that he thought of Dungeness. It was a long way from

Canterbury, but far more isolated. He and Alf had been fishing there ever since they'd been kids and they knew their way around it better than anywhere. He signalled to Alf to pull into a petrol station in Shooters Hill and while they were filling up told him their destination.

It was dark when they reached Ashford. Jim was thirsty, he wanted something to eat and some more fags but didn't dare stop anywhere now. In London a man in jeans and a grubby vest might not be noticed driving a sports car, but down here he would be.

Why hadn't he thought to bring them both a change of clothing? Suppose they were stopped on the way back by the police? How would they explain the blood on their clothes?

Jim was sweating like a pig, yet he felt cold. His stomach was churning, his back ached but he knew he couldn't run from it. If the governor didn't read about Stratton's body being found in a day or two, it would be him and Alf for the chop.

Once out of Ashford on the familiar road to Ham Street Jim slipped into thinking about the past. He and Alf and a couple of mates would load up their old Consul on a Saturday afternoon with crates of beer, sandwiches and their tackle and stay out all night, fishing by the light of an old hurricane lamp. Those were the good old days: clearing houses all week, flogging it off to the junk shops, and weekends spent down here. If only they hadn't been tempted by the big money! He might have known it would lead to something like this.

Inky darkness hid the marshes on either side of the narrow concrete strip that led towards the lighthouse. Past the old railway carriage where the barmy old couple lived then on towards the sea.

By day this part of the marsh was desolate enough

to deter all but nature freaks and fishermen. Miles of shingle, with hillocks of marram grass and gorse bushes here and there, the only sounds the calling of seabirds and the wind. But by night it was eerie. The power station a couple of miles away was lit by arc lights like a forbidden city in a science fiction film.

Jim signalled to Alf that he was going to stop, and pulled up on to the shingle. He turned off his lights and immediately Alf did likewise.

The wind bombarded Jim as he got out of the car. He could taste salt on his lips and smell seaweed. Taking a few big gulps he scanned the area nervously. The road they'd taken was a disused one leading to nothing but the lighthouse; all the same, it was an ideal place for courting couples.

He could see no parked cars. Just black emptiness and the sound of waves breaking on the beach in the distance. Even a scream would be muffled by the strong wind.

Toby came to the moment the back doors of the van were opened. He could smell the sea, feel the loneliness of the spot and all at once knew what was going to happen.

'You can't kill me!' he shouted. He couldn't see their faces, but he could smell their sweat as they hauled him out. As the wind hit his damp trousers he wet himself again in terror. 'Please let go,' he pleaded, suddenly entirely conscious. 'I'll give you everything I've got.'

He knew it was futile, but still he struggled. Every nerve-ending jangled with pain and as he opened his mouth to scream, a rag was shoved roughly into his mouth.

'We didn't want this,' Jim said in his ear. 'But there's no choice now.'

Toby couldn't move. Even bucking as they carried him like a sack of flour did nothing but hurt him more. His feet were still tied, the handcuffs still on his wrists and though he screamed again and again, the sound was muffled by the rag.

Stones scrunching underfoot, wind whistling. Jim was leading the way, holding Toby's legs, his back in the white vest formidably wide. Toby jerked his head back towards Alf's chest, his eyes nearly out of their sockets straining to see. But all he could make out was Alf's teeth and the outline of his nostrils.

'This'll do,' Jim said in a low voice and at once Toby was dropped to the stones.

'No, please no!' Toby shouted through the rag, trying to force it out with his tongue. Silently they rolled him over on to his stomach.

Toby waited for gunshot, his face pressed into the stones. Surprisingly the pain had gone and he could feel how smooth the pebbles were, taste the salt on them, smell the cool, fresh air.

He felt a hand go round his forehead. It was warm and rough, and smelt of tobacco. The other hand moved over his ear, holding his head tightly and jerked it back sharply, exposing his neck. It was Jim holding him; Toby could see Alf was at his side and in the darkness he saw the glint of the knife.

Odd things came to Toby in those few seconds. An instructor at Sandhurst demonstrating a similar hold. His mother forcing him to open his mouth to give him medicine and Charity holding him tightly against her chest as they waited for the car to take them to their parents' funeral. Somehow all three memories had great significance.

'Do it, Jim,' Alf said. There was no spite in his voice, only urgency, as if the pair of them were preparing to put a sick dog out of its misery.

The pain in his leg came back hard and strong. His bowels evacuated just as he'd been told they did when

633

men were executed. He was crying, but he could no longer make any sound come out.

Toby felt the light touch of the blade cold against his skin. Then the sudden slash, which was surprisingly painless. For just one moment he didn't think they'd actually done it, but then he smelt blood and felt the warmth of it spurt up on to his chin.

Jim and Alf stared down at the body at their feet. Despite the width of his shoulders and muscular arms Stratton's back and lean hips looked disturbingly boyish, blond hair as bright as a lantern in the darkness. Blood flowed either side of his neck, black against the light-coloured pebbles. They couldn't see the yawning slash mark, but there was a faint bubbling sound, like air in a pipe.

'Is he – ' Alf whispered, clamping a hand over his mouth, knowing that any moment he would vomit.

'Not quite, but he soon will be,' Jim whispered back as he bent to unlock the handcuffs and cut the rope round Toby's ankles. 'Come on, let's go!'

Toby could hear a roaring noise in his ears, feel his life draining away. His own blood made his face warm, but nothing mattered any more. Charity's face appeared before him, he felt her soft hands caressing his cheek.

'I'm so sorry,' he said silently. 'Forgive me.'

Chapter Thirty-Six

Charity was laying the table for her dinner with Rob when the door buzzed.

All last night and earlier today she had been in a state of blissful anticipation. Her entire body tingled, her mind only on Rob. Even when she'd first met Hugh and John, she had never felt quite as giddy and deliriously happy as this. But when Toby failed to arrive for lunch, with no explanatory phone call, her glow slowly faded and anxiety took its place.

'Yes,' she said curtly into the receiver, fully expecting it to be Toby. It was just like him to turn up now she had bathed and dressed and prepared a meal for Rob.

'Miss Stratton.' The porter sounded hesitant. 'There's a couple of police officers here to see you. Can they come up?'

Charity winced with further irritation. She'd thought she was finished with questions from them!

'OK,' she said wearily. 'Send them up.'

The blue silky flared trousers and matching top she'd put on for Rob's benefit seemed a little too seductive to talk to the police, but it was too late to change now.

It was still very warm; the doors on to the balcony were wide open. Between irritation at Toby and anticipation at seeing Rob, the last thing she wanted was more cross-examination from the police.

She knew she would have to face a dangerous

driving charge at some stage. Perhaps that was what they were calling about. Or perhaps they'd found some fresh evidence about Stephen's killer?

She opened her door when she heard the lift but smiled when she saw two familiar faces.

One was the freshfaced WPC Bailey, the other burly Sergeant Searle. They were the two officers who had called to tell her about finding the petrol receipt in her wrecked car.

'Have you got my watch back yet?' she asked. 'I did send the garage a cheque.'

But as she spoke they exchanged glances and instantly Charity felt a pang of fear.

'What is it?' she asked.

Sergeant Searle hesitated. Charity's scarred face was flushed from the sun, her pretty hair tumbling over her shoulders. She looked almost recovered from her accident and now the news he had to give her would bring her further pain and anguish.

'I'm sorry, Miss Stratton,' he said, moving closer, quickly followed by Bailey. 'It's bad news, I'm afraid.'

Charity backed away and let them come in and shut the door.

'What now?' Charity clasped her hands together nervously. 'You haven't come to arrest me?'

'No, of course not.' Sergeant Searle put his hand on her arm and led her over to the settee. He had sad eyes like a spaniel. Now unsmiling, they seemed even larger and more mournful. 'I'm sorry to add to the unhappiness you've already been through, Miss Stratton, but it's your brother.'

'Toby! What's happened?' Charity said in alarm.

Again they exchanged glances and the woman sat down beside Charity, taking her hand in both of hers.

Sergeant Searle bent towards Charity, lightly touching her shoulder. 'He's dead, Miss Stratton. We're so very sorry.'

For a moment Charity was too stunned to take this in. She looked up at Searle, then back to Bailey.

'An accident in his car?' she whispered.

'No.' The sergeant paused for a moment as if trying to find the right words. 'He was murdered, I'm afraid.'

'I beg your pardon?' She leaned forward, thinking she had misheard him.

'He was murdered,' he repeated, lowering his voice to match her soft one. 'His body was found at Dungeness in Kent this morning.'

Charity felt the room start to spin. Her eyes ceased to focus and a hot flush was creeping up all over her.

'Put your head down between your knees,' Charity heard dimly and felt a hand on the back of her neck pushing her down.

Something cold on her forehead brought her out of the faint. She lifted her head and found Bailey on her knees in front of her pressing a wet flannel to Charity's forehead. Sergeant Searle held out a glass of water.

'Take a few sips,' he suggested and his eyes showed deep sympathy.

Charity heard them speaking but it was almost as if they spoke in a different language.

'Why would anyone murder Toby?' she heard herself ask.

'We don't know that yet,' Bailey said as she held the cold flannel to Charity's wrists. 'We only got a message about where he was found. His passport, uniform and other belongings were all in his car. When the Kent police contacted his regiment in Germany they were told he had leave to come and see you. The task of informing you was passed on to our station.'

'But he phoned me yesterday morning,' Charity said in some bewilderment. 'He was coming to lunch today.'

Sergeant Searle sat down on the other settee,

opposite the two women. He was aware that Miss Stratton hadn't fully taken in the news, and he wanted to get in his questions before she broke down entirely.

'Where did he phone from?'

'He didn't say. But I got the impression he was in London.'

'Did he say so?'

'No. But he spoke as if he could be with me in minutes. I was going out – ' she stopped short, her hand covering her mouth.

A terrible wail of anguish came from deep inside her and though Bailey moved nearer to hold her, Charity began to rock backwards and forwards, her arms clasped around her chest.

Sergeant Searle looked at the policewoman and shrugged. He didn't want to question Charity, not now while she was like this. But this was different from road traffic accidents and from the brief he'd received less than an hour ago he knew it was imperative that they move swiftly to discover the victim's last movements.

'Charity,' he said more firmly. 'I'm so sorry, but I have to know a few things. Do you know a girl called Carla Clayton?'

Charity shook her head, eyes wide with shock, huge tears streaming down her face in a torrent.

'Can you tell us any girlfriends' names?' he went on. 'Girls Toby saw recently.'

Charity had only one word in her head. It was going round and round, spinning faster and faster.

'Murdered!'

The letters were blood red, surrounded by blackness. She wanted to ask questions, but she was scared, terribly scared.

Bailey caught hold of Charity firmly, drawing her tight against her chest.

'There, there,' she said soothingly, looking up at

Searle and inclining her head towards the kitchen. 'Sergeant Searle will make you a cup of tea while we talk. I know you are in shock but you must try to tell us about Toby's friends because it's important we see them tonight.'

Searle wanted to walk out on that balcony and take some deep breaths. Any moment now he or Bailey would be forced to admit just how Miss Stratton's brother died and tell her of their suspicions that he'd been involved in serious crime, but for once he found it impossible to be dispassionate.

He switched the kettle on, then ran his wrists under the cold tap to cool himself down. Everything about the flat showed the woman's character. It was classy, with its soft greens and blues, but there was nothing ostentatious. Large vases of flowers stood on the table and on the bookcase. Photographs of her brothers and sister everywhere showed her priorities in life.

Sergeant Searle knew all the facts: the hotel where Stratton spent the night – even the torn-off Elastoplast – had been found. Whether the girl who stayed at the hotel with Stratton was another courier wasn't known yet, but the customs officer at Dover had said Stratton was alone.

There were no fingerprints except Stratton's in the car. Only one clear print which wasn't his had been found, and that was on his shoe, along with a black gritty dust which wasn't consistent with the kind found in country areas, but both those had yet to be checked out.

As Searle came back with the tea he found Bailey telling Charity how Toby had died, and their suspicions that he was a drugs courier.

He put the tea silently on the coffee table and sat down to watch Miss Stratton. On the point of how he met his death, the woman's reaction was entirely

639

predictable: shock, horror, colour draining from her face and wild sobs. But as Bailey spoke of drugs he saw acceptance in Miss Stratton's face, as if she half expected it.

'You knew, didn't you,' he said.

She lifted her face to his and her beautiful blue eyes swam.

'Not that he was a courier.' She tried to halt her sobs, swiping at the tears with the back of her hand. 'But he had some pills once. He promised me yesterday he was through with it. Do you think that's why they killed him – because he wanted out?'

'Maybe.' Searle knew this was unlikely, but if it gave her some comfort he wasn't going to deny her it.

The intercom buzzed. The two police looked at one another and back to Charity sitting motionless, head bowed with grief.

'Shall I answer it?' Bailey asked.

A faint nod.

'If it's Robert, ask him to come up,' she said faintly.

'Oh, Rob. Where did I go wrong with Toby?' Charity cried later.

The police had left soon after Rob arrived and he had cradled her in his arms until the wild sobbing slowed down.

Rob had counselled hundreds of grieving relatives over the last couple of years, for dozens of different reasons, but he was finding it hard to say the right words to Charity.

He'd cried with her, unable to stop himself.

'You didn't go wrong,' he said soothingly. 'Your parents, uncle, the school and even the army made him what he was, not you.'

'But I should've handled it differently when I found those pills,' she sobbed again. Her face was swollen with crying, her scars puckered and angry.

'No, Charity,' he said gently. 'You must accept he was a man, responsible for his own destiny. You gave him your love, no one could do more.'

Rob let her pour out so many stories about Toby, all of them tinged with her belief that she had let him down in some way. It was tempting to give her a new perspective, show her that Toby had always been a greedy little sneak, a user and a taker, but Rob couldn't bring himself to shatter the few comforting illusions she had left.

'How can I tell Prue and James?' she said, fresh tears running down her cheeks, as she finally remembered what this all really meant. 'What will this do to them?'

'I'll tell them,' he said firmly, lifting her up in his arms and carrying her towards the bedroom. 'I'm going to give you a sedative and pop you into bed. Then I'll phone them. You are doing nothing more tonight.'

Charity lay in bed, her eyes drooping. Rob was speaking on the telephone and although she wanted to stay awake long enough to hear the outcome, she was losing the battle against the pills.

As she drifted off, she was back in Greenwich Park. She could see Toby as clearly as if it were yesterday in his long grey flannel shorts and a threadbare navy blazer, kicking a football. His grey woolly socks were festooned round stick-thin ankles, his face pinched and pale, but his white-blond hair shone like a beacon against a backdrop of dark green trees.

Charity woke with a start, soaked in sweat. She had dreamed she was tied up, and her heart was hammering. She found it was only the sheet tightly wrapped round her, but the fear still made her stomach contract painfully.

Grey early morning light was coming through the curtains, and as she lay there trying to calm the rising panic inside her, faces danced before her.

Suddenly she knew what had happened in those missing hours before the accident. She'd been like this then. She had come home from the office, lain on the settee and then it had begun – a long, slow torture of memories.

Her father standing in his pulpit in a white surplice, arms stretched wide as he roared out his views on sin.

Mother bowed over in a chair, holding baby Jacob, lifeless in her arms, wailing in grief, tears raining down on his tiny face.

She saw Daniel's first smile as she bent over to change his nappy, that last morning at Daleham Gardens, remembered how his tiny hand had reached out to tug her hair.

John on the dome of the Duomo in Florence.

Grandmother was there too, sitting in the chair and holding out those sapphire earrings. Uncle Stephen glowered at Charity from his wheelchair.

More and more images kept coming, briefer now, flashing before her eyes like a slide show. Mrs Cod and Miss Hawkins at the kitchen table at Bowes Court. Hugh, Miss Mansell and Miss Frost.

Charity understood the significance of the images when Toby joined the ranks. She saw herself looking down from her balcony, watching him drive his car into the car park turning his face up to her to wave.

All of them were gone now, wiped out of her life. Now Toby was with them.

Time had run out before she could admit to Toby all the mistakes she'd made and forgive him for his. She would never see him again in his uniform, her heart swelling with pride at that straight back, broad shoulders and handsome face. There would be no

642

honourable military funeral with his fellow officers in
their green jackets, a Union Jack covering his coffin,
only shame that Toby had besmirched a proud family's history and his regiment.

Charity buried her face in the pillow and wept.
There was anger that Toby had chosen a short cut to
riches, bitterness that his actions would hurt Prue and
James, but most of all sorrow because in her heart she
knew Toby had always been a troubled soul, cast in
a role he couldn't handle.

Rob leaned on one elbow listening to Charity's sobs.
He hadn't slept at all; it was too hot, the settee too
soft.

He knew now with utter certainty that from the
first day at the cottage their paths were meant to
intertwine. In helping Charity through her past Rob
had come to terms with his own and all along that
long and winding path he had found remarkable similarities.

While Charity was pushing a pram of washing to
the baths, he was at a top school. But they both had
cruel fathers and mothers sunk in depression. Charity
bore the scars of incest, while Rob's were hideous
ones caused by bigger boys. They both shared the
feeling of being worthless and tainted, then misplaced
love, betrayal and heartache had forged sheets of steel
over their emotions.

He understood Charity because their motivations
were the same. Two people with a great deal of love
to give, yet who needed so much to have it returned.

Just last night Rob had believed the loneliness was
over for both of them. He'd imagined being in that
pink and cream bedroom, making love to Charity. The
words of love were all there in his head, waiting for
the right moment. But now she was lying in there

643

alone and sobbing, maybe slowly sliding into the same kind of insanity that had taken his mother.

'No, I won't let you,' Rob murmured, pulling on his trousers, his love for Charity stronger than his fear of rejection. 'We've come too far together to back away now.'

He stood in the doorway. In the dawn light creeping through the bedroom window Charity's small shoulderblades stood out like wings as she buried her face in the pillow.

Silently Rob moved to the bed, lay down beside her and gently drew her into his arms.

'I'm here,' he whispered against her hair. 'And I'm here for ever.'

'There is no for ever,' she sobbed. 'I can't keep anyone by me.'

'I can.' He kissed her damp forehead and held her shaking body. 'I'm here. I'm never going to leave you. The past is done, Charity, but there is a future with me.'

'Can you sit up and eat some breakfast?' Rob put a tray of scrambled eggs, toast and marmalade down on the bed and opened the curtains.

Charity had woken just moments before he came in. She sat up cautiously, expecting to find herself in physical pain.

'What time is it?' she asked, rather surprised to find she felt nothing but dull aches.

'Almost nine,' Rob said. 'How do you feel?'

'As if something sucked out all my blood in the night.' Charity winced at the food on the tray. 'I couldn't eat anything.'

'You must,' he said firmly. 'Try the orange juice first. My gran said you could do anything once you had food inside you.'

Charity looked up at Rob. The smell of soap and

644

shampoo, his clean white shirt and clean-shaven face were reminders of how he'd arrived the previous evening anticipating a night of love, not further trauma.

'You look nice.' She felt she ought to tell him how much he'd helped her, reassure him that she remembered his tender words, but she didn't know how to. 'I'm sorry if I disturbed your sleep,' she said, her eyes dropping from his with embarrassment.

'It's OK.' Rob smiled and sat down on the end of the bed. 'Now eat. Prue will be here soon.'

'How is she?' A look of alarm came back into Charity's face as she realised that the worst was yet to come. 'What did she say?'

'You can talk about that when she gets here,' Rob said gently, reaching out to smooth the frown on her forehead. 'I have to pop out to the hospital, but you can phone me there if you need me.'

Charity drank the orange juice, then tried the eggs tentatively. This time yesterday she had woken looking forward to lovemaking. Now she and Rob were doctor and patient again.

'Rob – ' she paused, unable to say what she wanted to.

He looked at her enquiringly.

Charity blushed.

'I'm sorry.'

'For what?' His smile was tender. 'There's – ' The buzzer on the door interrupted him.

Moments later Prue swept into the bedroom, bringing an air of country freshness with her long dress, her hair plaited into two thick gold skeins.

'Oh Chas,' she said, dropping a huge straw basket on the floor and enveloping Charity in a desperate hug. 'What do we do now?'

Charity could say nothing for a moment, just hugged her sister back, more glad to see her than she'd ever felt before.

645

'We try and be tough, I suppose,' she whispered eventually. 'I'm so glad you're here, Prue. Maybe you, me and James can salvage something together.'

Rob hovered in the doorway.

'Would you like some breakfast, Prue?' he asked. He felt uncertain about his role now. Last night he'd been comforter and organiser, but now Charity's family, who he knew so much about yet had never met, would take over.

'Just tea, please.' Prue let go of Charity and turned to Rob. 'Thank you so much for staying with Chas. But I'm here now.'

Charity felt that prickle of irritation she had always felt with Prue. Her flat, bland face was full of bossiness; she always assumed no one was as capable as she was.

'Rob's my doctor and a dear friend,' she said firmly, wanting to put the record straight immediately. 'And I'm not ill any longer, Prue, I'm perfectly able to look after myself.'

Rob smiled at Charity with a slightly quizzical look as if recalling everything Charity had ever told him about Prue. 'I'll pop in later,' he said. 'Phone me if you need me before.'

It was only after Rob had gone to work and Charity had showered and dressed that Prue let down her defences.

She had rushed around washing the breakfast things, straightening cushions, dusting the coffee table and putting food she'd brought into the cupboards. Finally she sat down on the settee and her eyes filled with tears.

'I didn't mean to dismiss Rob,' she said in a small voice. 'He's obviously a very kind man. I always seem to say the wrong thing.'

'It's all right.'

Charity had put on a dark blue dress and tied her hair back. She felt strained now, not knowing what to do exactly. It seemed wrong to behave normally, to sit outside in the sun, even to talk of anything other than Toby. She knew that Prue had expected to find her an invalid and that now she felt obsolete.

'Neither of us knows what to do or say. I did all my crying last night, and I'm sure you did too. Now it's like being in limbo.'

'I don't even know how I feel,' Prue said, her blue eyes full of despair. 'I can't forget all the awful things Toby's done. But on the other hand I can't believe I'm never going to see him again.'

Charity's heart went out to her sister. Prue and Toby were so close in age and as small children they had been inseparable, but after their parents' death Prue was the one who distanced herself. Toby had sniped at her continually, teased and laughed at her, yet there had been deep affection too. During holidays at Studley they'd come to rediscover one another. Now Prue was struggling with conflicting emotions.

'James will be here soon.' Charity sat down beside her sister and took her hands. 'We've got to walk a tightrope with him. We can't make out Toby was a hero, but neither must we dwell on the bad parts.'

'I expected to find you in a terrible state,' Prue admitted. 'I suppose I thought you cared more for Toby than me.'

'I love all three of you in different ways.' Charity shrugged her shoulders. 'You never seemed to need me as much as Toby did, you were always so independent and singleminded. If it seemed I cared more for the boys, I'm sorry.'

'I'm sure Toby killed Uncle Stephen,' Prue blurted out as if it had been on her mind constantly and she could no longer bear it. 'I think he paid someone to do it for him. That's why he's been killed, to silence him for good.'

'Please don't say such things.' Charity's eyes welled up with tears. 'I can't bear it.'

'You just wait and see,' Prue said darkly.

James arrived with Geoff and Lou soon after eleven. He was pink-eyed and very pale. While Prue made yet more tea James showed Charity a copy of a tabloid newspaper with the headline, ARMY OFFICER MURDERED. GANGLAND REVENGE.

'Was Toby doing something bad?' he asked plaintively.

To look at James was to see Toby at fifteen: a little blond fluff coming above his upper lip, the same achingly beautiful face. But with his innocent and guileless blue eyes, James was just a schoolboy too old and big to be cuddled and fobbed off with a kindly meant lie, yet not old enough to comprehend any of this.

Charity looked to Geoff and Lou for support and guidance. Both their faces were drawn with anxiety, as uncertain as Charity was.

'Tell him the truth, Charity,' Geoff said in a low voice. 'It hurts less in the long run.'

It was mid-afternoon when the police came. Geoff and Lou had gone home an hour earlier, taking James with them; there was nothing further any of them could do for now.

These two policeman were from the murder squad: two hard-faced plain-clothes men who looked like villains themselves. Scruffily dressed, they had cockney accents and pockmarked skin.

'We're sorry to intrude on you at such a time,' the older man who introduced himself as Detective Inspector Rudge said. 'But we need to know if either of you knew a Michael Bagshawe?'

The second man took a seat by the window. Clearly he was there only as a witness.

Charity shook her head and looked at Prue.

'Was he in the army too?' Prue asked. 'I've never heard that name.'

Rudge held out a black and white photograph. Charity felt a twinge of unease as she saw it was a picture taken by the police for their records. It showed a narrow-faced man with dark hair.

'I've never seen him,' Prue said and Charity agreed. 'Why do you want to know?'

'He's dead too,' Rudge said bluntly. 'He was found in Epping Forest, shot through the heart.'

'Are you implying our brother did it?' Prue's voice wavered slightly, but her eyes stayed steadily on the policeman's.

'No. He was killed some time after your brother. But we're sure the deaths are connected.'

Rudge opened up a small black holdall and pulled out a statuette of a silver pheasant. It was about twelve inches long and although badly tarnished it had obviously been made by a craftsman.

Prue gasped.

'You recognise this?' Rudge asked.

Charity looked at her younger sister in surprise. Charity had never seen the pheasant before, but it seemed that Prue had.

'Yes,' Prue said. 'It was our uncle's.'

'When did you last see it, and where?' Rudge asked.

'Oh I don't know,' Prue said, flustered. 'It was in Uncle's room. I cleaned it once for him. But that was ages ago and he had so much silver.'

The police explained they had found the pheasant in Michael Bagshawe's home. The dead man, who was known as Weasel, had a police record for burglary, Rudge said, but information received suggested he would do anything for a price, including murder.

The pheasant, plus Toby Stratton's army address and phone number found in Bagshawe's home, led them to believe that Toby had paid him to kill the colonel.

'No! Toby wouldn't do that,' Charity said, bursting into tears. 'I don't believe it.'

'Look at this.' Rudge took a piece of paper out of the bag. 'Study it and tell me what it is, and whose writing it is.'

Charity and Prue looked at it together. Even at a quick glance they knew what it was and who had drawn it. It was map of the interior of Studley Priory. Uncle Stephen's room was coloured in red, with a dotted line leading from it to the front door. The writing was Toby's.

'Well?' Inspector Rudge looked at the girls' stricken faces. 'It is your brother's, isn't it?'

Charity felt faint. She knew what they said was true, there was no other explanation, but still she wanted to protect Toby.

'But you said this man was a burglar,' she said desperately. 'Maybe Toby only plotted with him to burgle the house and – '

'No,' Rudge interrupted. 'We have evidence of a financial arrangement between the two men. Had Bagshawe gone to the Priory to burgle it, he would have stripped the place. We think he only took the pheasant that night because old habits die hard. I'm afraid, Miss Stratton, you have to accept your brother paid this man to kill your uncle.'

'I *can't* accept that.' Charity shook her head forcefully. Prue moved closer to her sister and put her arm round her comfortingly.

'You accepted that your brother was a drug dealer,' Rudge said, getting up from his seat to leave. 'You knew that, yet you concealed it from us during your uncle's murder inquiry. Had you told us the truth then, your brother might not be dead now, or Bagshawe. We might even have the entire drug ring in custody.'

Prue had listened to all this silently. Although she was mortified to discover her suspicions about her brother were true, something snapped inside her at this policeman's barbed comments.

She sprang to her feet, eyes blazing.

'Don't you even *think* my sister is to blame!' she shouted. 'Charity's loved all three of us like a mother and if she shielded Toby it was only because she was unable to see what a rotter he was. I'm more to blame than she is. *I* knew.'

'Don't, Prue,' Charity said weakly.

'Don't try and stop me telling the truth now.' Prue faltered only momentarily when she saw her sister's stricken face. 'Even as a kid Toby was a liar and a thief. Going to Sandhurst and joining the army was only to suck up to Uncle Stephen. I was just as bad, I loathed our uncle. I only tolerated him for what I could get out of him.'

Prue paused, white-faced and shaking, looking hard at both the astonished policemen.

'Don't try to pillory Charity because she's still got some shreds of loyalty to our worthless brother. She has loved and protected us all our lives and that's to be admired, not scorned.'

Detective Inspector Rudge was taken aback by this fiery outburst, but he recognised the truth in it.

'OK,' he said wearily, backing towards the door. 'We've a great deal more to investigate still, but we hope to make an arrest within twenty-four hours. We'll leave you alone now.' He looked down at Charity slumped in her chair. 'I am very sorry about your brother, Miss Stratton. I hope this will soon be over and your family can settle down again.'

*

Once the door closed Charity got up and moved towards Prue.

'I'm sorry.' Prue hung her head. 'Maybe I shouldn't have said all that.'

Charity's heart melted. For Prue to admit her own shortcomings and guilt took real courage.

'You spoke the truth.' Charity took a step towards Prue and held out her arms. 'They say it sets you free. But come here and give me a hug. I loved you for defending me.'

'What do we do now?' Prue buried her face in Charity's neck and began to sob wildly. 'All the disgrace ... people talking about us. I can't go back to work after this, not when my brother's a murderer. And what about James? How's he going to manage at school?'

'We try and hold our heads up.' Charity lifted Prue's face in her two hands and kissed away her tears. 'If necessary we'll move away where no one knows us. We stand together.'

'Tim doesn't like it.' Prue's voice shook. 'Ever since Uncle died he's been funny with me. I don't think our marriage can stand any more.'

Charity suspected that Tim had always been overpowered by Prue and that he might be using this as an excuse to get out. But she couldn't tell her that.

'Ring him,' she said. 'Tell him you love him and need him. I'll bet you haven't told him that often enough.'

'You're the only one of us that knows how to show love,' Prue sniffed. 'I wish I did.'

'You showed it when you defended me. There's nothing hard about it, Prue – you just say what your heart tells you, without holding anything back.'

Chapter Thirty-Seven

Charity heard the soft whirring noise even over the vicar's voice. Her eyes moved from the vicar to the coffin as it slowly disappeared through a hatch in the wall. Soon Toby would be nothing more than ashes and just another painful memory.

James squeezed Charity's hand. He had been a great source of comfort to both sisters since Toby's death. He seemed to have become a man overnight, his warmth, loyalty and strength of character uniting and sustaining them all.

Rain drummed down on the roof of the crematorium chapel and the patches of sky visible through the high slit windows were dark grey.

Lou and Geoff were just behind them; Margaret and Tom from Studley Priory, Rita and Rob. Charity had hoped some of Toby's friends might have turned up, but it seemed they were all distancing themselves from any involvement. It was a pitifully small gathering, but better just a few staunch, caring people than idly curious spectators who would sit in judgement rather than feel sorrow.

To ask that Toby could be laid to rest in the parish church at Studley-cum-Norton with his grandparents and uncle was unthinkable. A cremation service at Golders Green removed the fear of gossip-mongering neighbours and absolved them all from the hypocrisy of a church service. The vicar who had never met Toby spoke gently of the sadness of a man taken before he reached full maturity and read a moving poem instead of attempting to glorify Toby.

There had been few letters of condolence, yet each one had been a link with the past. Marjorie and Martin, Miss Mansell, Miss Hawkins from Bowes Court, and Carmel. Each one showed understanding of what Charity, Prue and James were going through and urged them to pick up their lives again, to hold close to one another and not blame themselves for what their brother had become.

Dorothy had gone back to the States soon after Charity left the nursing home. When Charity phoned her with the news of Toby's death she burst into uncharacteristic tears. Since then she had phoned several times offering all kinds of help, from the suggestion Charity join her for a holiday later, to the name of a brilliant plastic surgeon, yet she hadn't felt able to come to the funeral.

'I'll be with you in spirit,' she had said in a strangely detached manner. 'But it would be hypocritical for me to come when I feel so angry about everything Toby put you through. But I'll be back in England as soon as I've wound up things here. I'm going to marry George.'

Charity appreciated Dorothy's honesty. She didn't want anyone at the funeral who couldn't mourn Toby. At the same time she found it rather odd that Dorothy was planning to marry a man she had avoided introducing her friends to, and that she should announce it at such a sad time.

But the message that had meant most to Charity was from John Marshall. He had moved with his wife Nina to the Seychelles and had learned what had happened to Toby from his agent in London.

'My heart goes out to you, Charity,' he wrote. 'I have watched your success in business from a distance, many times wishing I dared write and say how proud I was of you. Now as I imagine your heartbreak I cannot hold back the rush of emotions and I had to communicate with you. You are in my thoughts and prayers, just as you always have been all these years, and I have to believe that out of all this tragedy, something good will come to you.'

John couldn't have known that his letter would give her such comfort. In his few words he managed to convey hope for the future and give meaning to the past. The funeral was the last hurdle. She, Prue and James had mourned Toby in private, drained their tears together, shared treasured memories. Prayers and hymns gave the occasion an air of dignified finality, and maybe they would give them the strength to rise above the gossip.

A clear thumb and forefinger print on Toby's shoe had led the police to Alf Tooley at an old warehouse in Wapping. Samples of grit embedded in Toby's clothes and shoes matched those found on the floor of the garage. Alf and his brother Jim were arrested.

The two brothers had confessed to Toby's murder, but as yet they remained stubbornly silent about the rest of the drug network and the man who organised it all. Charity didn't care: as far as she was concerned, the police had Toby's murderer and the mystery of her uncle's death was solved. That was enough.

Charity took Prue's arm as they filed out of the chapel. Prue was trembling, biting her lip to stop herself crying. Her moods had swung like a pendulum during the last two weeks. One moment she was claiming Toby's death was a relief and a blessing; almost lighthearted, she cleaned out cupboards for Charity and went shopping in the West End. The next she plunged into wild sobbing, saying her career as a teacher was finished, as was her marriage to Tim and that Toby had been led astray.

Today Prue was drained of all colour, her pallor made worse by her severe black dress and hat. Tim's continuing lack of support and his absence today seemed to confirm Prue's claim that he didn't care about her. Privately Charity thought her sister would be better off without such an insensitive man.

James was the rock. He constantly spoke of Toby's good points, refusing to bow down to the darker side of his brother's character. He encouraged them to reminisce about their childhood, even events before he was born, drawing the three of them into a tight unit.

Looking at James now in his neat dark suit and highly polished shoes was to see Toby again at the same age. But James had no chip on his shoulder, or hunger for wealth. In time, Charity knew, he'd give their family back a sense of pride.

'What do we do now?' Prue whispered as they walked slowly past the few wreaths lying in the porch.

Rain coming down like stair rods reduced visibility to a few yards, and mourners for the next funeral were scurrying through the car park in a sea of black umbrellas.

'We all go home to my flat, of course,' Charity said, thinking for a moment that Prue was losing her grip. 'We have tea and sandwiches, then it's over.'

'I didn't mean this minute.' Prue sighed deeply. 'I meant, how do we cope?'

'We take it one step at a time.' Charity put her arm through her sister's and smiled weakly at Lou and Geoff who were waiting to speak to her. 'First the tea. Don't try to look ahead just now, things can only get better.'

Charity stood at her window watching the rain beating down. Her pansies and petunias in their tubs looked as battered as she felt. It was just after four and everyone had left. James had gone home with Lou and Geoff to pack for a holiday in Cornwall. Prue had offered to drive Margaret and Tom back to Studley where they were still looking after things. Then Prue was going home to see Tim to attempt to patch up her marriage. Rita had returned to the office.

Rob hadn't wanted to leave. He'd suggested that Charity go back for a break to his flat in Baker Street, but Charity had refused: she wanted some time alone.

It was a great comfort that both Prue and James liked Rob. In the last two long weeks he'd taken James out swimming and to the squash club, lightening the long wait till the funeral. With Prue he'd sat and talked about her work, and listened to her fears that her career as a teacher was over. He'd even mentioned other fields she could move into if necessary.

Charity was glad to be alone. Two weeks of being surrounded by people, the constant buzz of conversation, drained emotions and even cooking and clearing up for others, made solitude welcome.

Grief was a strange thing, she decided: huge waves, almost drowning her, then long periods of calm and resignation. Now she felt empty. Maybe another wave would overwhelm her again soon, but for now there was peace.

The clearing up was done; uneaten sandwiches had been thrown away, plates washed and the carpet hoovered. She had some serious thinking to do and despite the rain she wanted to do it outside in the fresh air.

As she walked into her bedroom to collect her raincoat and a pair of stouter shoes, she was thinking about Rita.

'This is no time to discuss business,' Rita had said just before she left. 'But if in a couple of weeks' time you still can't face the office, perhaps we should talk about me buying it from you.'

657

There was Studley Priory to consider too. According to Uncle Stephen's solicitors, the estate would pass on to Charity, Prue and James jointly. Then there was Rob.

Their relationship had been put on hold. It hadn't seemed right even to kiss him or hold him while Prue and James had been there. But Charity could feel the need in him, the unasked questions, and several times today she'd caught those anxious glances that meant Rob was unsure of how and when to attempt picking up the threads again.

Should she take the initiative? Did she even want lovemaking so soon after such tragedy? One part of her said it would be the healer, but another voice was urging caution.

Charity was glad Frank the porter wasn't behind his desk when she got down to the foyer. He would probably have asked her solicitous questions about the funeral and though he meant well she'd had enough of people's condolences. She pulled her hood over her head and slipped out into the rain, walking briskly down Finchley Road towards Swiss Cottage.

Alec Stubbs dialled Charity's number, drumming his fingers on the callbox glass while he waited to see if she was in. He left it ringing for five minutes and smiled in triumph.

'At fuckin' last.' He sighed with relief.

He had been checking the number daily since Stratton's death, but every time there'd been someone there. Now the funeral was over Stratton's sister had obviously gone away, and there couldn't be a better time to check out her flat.

Just a few weeks ago Alec Stubbs wouldn't even have considered doing a job like this himself, but there was no one left he could trust now. Jim and Alf nicked, and all the others so nervous they wouldn't put their noses outside the door.

The moment Stubbs found out Toby was in league with Weasel he felt certain Toby had stashed the heroin somewhere. Once Weasel knew his life was on the line he'd had verbal dysentery, pouring out poison in an endless stream. Stubbs hadn't been particularly interested in Stratton hiring Weasel to kill his uncle, but if he could go that far for money he certainly wouldn't have any qualms about snatching thousands of pounds' worth of heroin.

Stashing it at his sister's was so obvious Stratton probably thought no one would bother to check it out. It was a good thing Jim had brought the keys from the MG back after their night at Dungeness. An odd-shaped one turned out to open the outer door of the block of flats, so it stood to reason the other one belonged to her apartment. The girl probably had no idea her brother had hidden the stuff there.

Alec Stubbs prided himself on being invincible. He'd got his big house down in Kent by using his brains and keeping the people who worked for him afraid. If he'd let Stratton get away with robbing him, it would soon get around. Shooting Weasel had had to be done; the man knew too much. But once Stubbs had retrieved the heroin he'd take a holiday and maybe plan a new line of business which gave him less headaches.

Returning to his car, Stubbs drove it to Cochrane Street and parked it. In his youth when burglary was his game, he'd liked areas like this. Plenty of old ladies with wads of money tucked under their mattresses, nice jewellery and tons of silver. A great many of the big houses had grilles on the windows now, a sign of the times, like safes and alarms. Charity Stratton's modern block was like Fort Knox too with its intercom and the porter. But when you had keys, had done your homework and found out when the porter went off for his tea, it was a doddle.

Stubbs wasn't nervous. In his view it raised less suspicion going into a place in broad daylight. Under an umbrella, wearing a suit and carrying a briefcase, he just looked like any other businessman going home.

It took two minutes to reach the front doors of the flats, just one second to slip in the key and turn it. He hesitated momentarily between the lift and the stairs, but took the lift as calmly as if he lived there.

Charity reached Swiss Cottage tube station and paused for a moment, trying to decide if she really wanted to go to Hampstead Heath in such heavy rain.

She would sell the business to Rita. Charity had no heart for it any more. It was time to sweep away the past, maybe take a holiday with Prue, live a little.

A tube map caught her attention and she moved closer to it, looking at the stations which had memories for her.

Hammersmith! She could see it so clearly in the snow that winter of '62. Hiding her ever-enlarging stomach under layers of baggy clothes, sidestepping the mounds of black ice building up on the kerbs. Her small, cold room, just a hole to crawl into while she waited for spring and her baby.

Piccadilly. Meeting John there for their first lunch date. A thin little waif in rundown shoes and a threadbare coat, frightened because John had suggested taking her to the Ritz.

Earls Court. Memories of Rita and Dorothy. Dolly-birds, that was the word people used then. Charity could see the three of them so clearly in their mini-skirts, long boots and fluttering false eyelashes.

Sloane Square, Marble Arch, Bond Street and Oxford Street were where she made her ambitions happen. All those department stores where she worked and later negotiated contracts.

Memories of the tubes ended when she got her first car. Once hurtling through tunnels staring at her own reflection in the dark windows had been a time to dream and plan. She had looked at all those little people scurrying to and from work like ants in a nest and vowed she'd rise beyond that.

Somehow moving away from public transport had removed her from the pulse of London. She forgot that those ants were happy, they had time to live and love, to get married and have children. While Charity was struggling to reach her goal, she'd failed to see that the posts had been moved.

She'd got the home she dreamed of, but it was an empty ivory tower which had never become the family haven she'd intended. There were so few times when all four of them had been together at one time. Now Toby was gone, Prue had a home and a life of her own and James wasn't the kind to lean on anyone.

It was time to find what *she* wanted now and she knew it wasn't riches, clothes with smart labels, or being looked up to as a successful businesswoman.

Charity wanted to love again and be loved. Nothing more.

She looked up and the rain ran down her face. The sky was still black, but over towards Hampstead it was lighter. Tomorrow the sun would be back and however empty she felt now, time could heal her.

Resolutely she turned back. She wasn't going to walk up Daleham Gardens and brood about Daniel. She'd made the decision to give him up because she loved him. The past was done, she couldn't change any of it, and it was time to start afresh.

She was soaked right through by the time she got back to Beech House. Charity smiled at her reflection

661

in the lift mirror. The scar on her cheek seemed less livid at last, small wet ringlets framed her face and she had colour back in her cheeks. Her eyes still looked sad, but they'd lost that haunted look.

As she pushed open her door she was thinking of Rob. Tomorrow morning she would phone him and ask him to come to dinner. Her new life would start from there, and he was part of it.

A rustle startled Charity as she shut the door. She wheeled round to see the contents of drawers strewn around the floor. For a moment she was rooted to the spot. Then she saw the man standing beside her drinks cabinet.

A man little taller than herself, but with broad shoulders and a receding hairline. He was wearing a dark business suit and just for a second she thought he was a policeman.

'How dare you!' she snapped. 'Don't you need a warrant to search someone's home?'

The man was as startled as she was. As Charity spoke his gloved hand disappeared inside his jacket and came out with a long, thin knife. His eyes had the look of a trapped animal. She knew then he was no policeman and her legs buckled under her.

Charity turned, in panic fumbling with the door catch, but he sprang forward and caught her shoulder.

'Don't try to run, lady,' he snarled, pulling her back against his chest. The knife came up to her throat. 'Don't scream, or I'll cut your throat soon as look at you.'

Charity hadn't had time to get more than a brief impression of him but his voice bore out what she'd gathered. A man who'd fought his way out of back streets, his broken nose a testimony to many fights. The suit was hand tailored, the kind wealthy business-men wore, but beneath it was an animal.

All at once she knew this was the man the police

were looking for. The man at the top who killed people who got in his way!

Charity's heart began to thump, terror clutched at her and she felt herself grow wet with sweat as the cold steel pressed against her windpipe.

'What do you want?' she stammered out.

'What's mine.' He pushed his face over her shoulder, the knife blade dangerously close. She could smell a distinctive aftershave, mingled with the fetid breath of a heavy smoker. His cheek against hers was close shaven, yet his skin was pitted and coarse. 'Your brother left some packages here.'

'No,' Charity whimpered, so scared she couldn't even think. 'Toby's dead.'

'D'you think I don't know that,' he smirked, catching hold of her wet hair. He pulled her round to face him, forcing her away from the door and back up against the wall. He lifted the knife up to her cheek, holding it like a razor as if to prove how sharp it was.

'But before he died he stashed the stuff, and I want it.'

Seen in a nightclub the man might pass as ruggedly handsome. His eyes were a pale, cold blue and his cleft chin reminded her of Kirk Douglas. But as close as she was and as terrified, she could focus only on his thin lips and the glint of the knife edge.

She didn't think Toby had been here – after all, she was only out at lunch with Rob that Sunday for a couple of hours. But maybe by pretending he had, she'd gain a little time.

Even at a glance Charity could tell the man had already searched extensively. Through the door that led to her bedroom and bathroom she saw handbags, belts and an upturned drawer on the floor.

'If Toby came here I wasn't aware of it,' she said, struggling to regain some composure. 'You can go on searching if you like. I'll help you.'

663

Charity didn't anticipate the blow. The man let go of her hair for a moment, then smashed her across the face with the flat of his hand.

'That's just to remind you I'm in charge, scarface,' he hissed at her. 'Don't come that high and mighty manner with me! Your bastard of a brother stitched me up.'

The sting of his slap brought home to Charity that she was in mortal danger. This man hadn't expected to be caught here, but now he had, there was no way he was going to let her go so she could give his description to the police. Even if she co-operated he would have to silence her permanently.

'I'm not being high and mighty,' Charity pleaded. 'I don't think there's anything in here, but I'll help you look. I've been through so much, don't hurt me.'

The man's eyes were reptilian, with no trace of humanity. It horrified her that Toby had thrown in his lot with such a brute.

'Shut it!' he snapped, grabbing her hair again. Using one of his knees to push her along, he forced her across the lounge towards the bedroom. The room was ransacked: dressing-table pulled away from the wall, books swiped from a shelf under the window. Wardrobe doors hung open, the contents thrown on to her bed and floor after he'd stripped the bed of covers. Kicking aside a drawer he tossed her on the bed on top of the clothes. Before she could attempt to move he had picked up a leather belt and a scarf.

'First a gag,' he said with menace, pulling her up by the shoulders, his knee in the small of her back. The knife was still in his hand, and she felt it graze over the collar of her raincoat, then drop as he bent to pick up a pair of knickers. He shoved these into her mouth, then tied the scarf round so tightly she was struggling for breath.

In one desperate move Charity tried to buck away

664

from him, her hand reaching out for the knife. But the man pounced: he picked up the knife and slashed the back of her hand with it.

'You ain't quick enough for me,' he snarled. 'Now shut up and keep still.'

Charity saw her hand only momentarily before he yanked both arms tightly behind her back. But it was enough to see a gash and blood spurting out. She heard the jingle of the belt buckle and felt him tightening the belt like a noose. He pulled it so tightly it hurt and immediately bent to find something else to secure her feet.

Tins rolling to the floor, cutlery rattling as the man ransacked the kitchen mingled with the rain splattering on the patio outside. It sounded like a mad symphony, with her own heart the beat of drums.

Panic robbed Charity of the ability to think. She knew by the state of her flat that he'd almost completed his search and once that was over he'd be back to finish her off.

'Think!' she ordered herself, lifting her face from a green chiffon evening dress. 'You can't just lie here and wait to die.'

Straining her head up Charity looked around the room for something that would help, but her reflection in the dressing-table mirror showed how helpless she was.

'God help me,' she prayed silently, feeling she might choke on the knickers in her mouth. 'Show me a way!'

A resounding crash of saucepans being knocked to the floor made her jump involuntarily, bending her back like a banana, but in that split second she saw enough of the belt and buckle in the mirror to glimpse a possibility. There was no hole in the belt so close to the buckle! The man had only slipped the leather like a noose through the buckle without securing it with the central prong.

Taking a deep breath, Charity lay still, clenching her wrists closer together, then quickly pushed them back against the leather. Feeling the faintest movement in her bonds, she repeated the action, closing her eyes to concentrate her energy. Again another small movement, and even over the noise of the man scrabbling in her fridge, she heard the rasp of stiff leather.

The cut on her hand stung and the blood made her hands sticky, but as the leather reached the cut, making her want to scream with pain, she knew she was getting there.

One more sharp thrust and the noose slipped off her hands. In one swift movement she rolled over and sat up, reaching down to her ankles to untie them. There was no time to fiddle with the gag. She needed a weapon!

Charity's eyes swept the room. There were paperback books, hairbrushes, handbags and shoes strewn all over the floor but nothing capable of inflicting a blow strong enough to floor him.

She stood still to listen. The man had moved back into the lounge and was pulling out her records and files from the wall unit. If she ran for the door he could easily catch her.

Charity picked up the bedside lamp, but it weighed too little. She put it down and picked up her briefcase. It was heavy with papers, but too unwieldy.

Then she remembered.

On the floor just inside the lounge doorway was a heavy cast-iron cat doorstop. Charity used it sometimes when the windows were open to stop the door banging. It was eighteen inches high and weighed a ton. The trouble was, the man might see her reaching for it.

Blood was dripping everywhere. Frantically she picked up a scarf and wrapped it round her hand, then, getting down on her hands and knees, she crawled out of the bedroom into the tiny lobby which led to the bathroom.

Charity knew exactly where he was from the sounds: just three feet to the right of the lounge, behind the open door, searching through a small cupboard at the bottom of the wall unit. The cat was two feet away on her left. All she could hope for was that he was facing towards the window and as she reached the doorway her arm snaked round until it touched the cat.

Her fingers closed round it and she held her breath as she gently pulled it towards her.

'Fuck!'

His exclamation unnerved her for a moment. He was closer than she'd thought – only the open door separated them. She guessed he had caught his hand on the sharp edge of an old toffee tin she kept photographs in, which meant he was almost through with his search. Desperation gave her a surge of new courage and she caught the cat still tighter, slowly pulling it towards her.

The last few inches to the doorpost she didn't dare to breathe. Slowly she edged back, clasping the cat in both hands, aware that if the man moved across the room now he could see she was no longer on the bed.

Once she was enclosed by the open door of the wardrobe, she stood up, lifting the cat above her head in readiness. It was so heavy it made her arms ache immediately and the cut in her hand was throbbing, but she shut that out of her mind.

All noise from the lounge stopped. Had he found something? Could Toby have been here at some time? What was the man doing? The thick carpet prevented her from hearing footsteps. Was he already creeping towards her with that knife in his hands?

A click told her he was. She knew that sound of her old blue handbag clasp; he'd trodden on it as he passed the bathroom.

Bracing herself she waited, legs apart, the cat poised in her hands, anger wiping out her fear. He wasn't going to kill her, not after all she'd been through. If she had to dash his brains out she'd do it, never mind that knife and what it might cost her.

She smelt his aftershave. He wasn't making a sound, but he couldn't disguise his smell. He was only inches from her, on the other side of the wardrobe door, probably waiting there silently hoping she'd make some movement to show where she was hidden.

Her eyes smarted and her arms ached intolerably. Blood was running from her hand right up the sleeve of her raincoat. She could hear her heart pounding but at last he moved silently forward and she could see first just his shoulder, then his back as he bent down to peer under the bed.

Charity leapt forward, thundering the doorstop down on his skull with every last vestige of strength she could muster. She heard a dull thud, a cry of surprise, and she lifted it to hit him again.

The man half turned as he pitched forward, an expression of outrage on his face, one hand catching the edge of the dressing-table and bringing a china lamp down with him. Charity threw the cat at him and leapt from her hiding place and out into the lounge.

Her fingers fumbled at the lock on her front door and she didn't dare to look round to see if he was following. At last it opened and she ran for the stairs.

She rushed headlong down, taking them two at a time. Every step she fully expected to be grabbed, convinced the man was right behind her, but at last she was in the foyer.

The porter wasn't there. She looked at the phone but then realised she was still gagged. Opening the front door she ran like the wind out into the drive, her fingers grappling with the gag.

She ran straight into a man on the pavement. A sedate businessman with a dark suit, under an umbrella. He stared at her in astonishment as she caught hold of his arms, gesticulating wildly up at her flat and her gag.

'Police!' she shouted, but her voice was just a grunt. She snatched his umbrella and put his hands on to the tightly knotted scarf to undo it.

As it came free, she pulled the knickers from her mouth.

'Get the police!' she yelled at him. 'There's a man in my flat. He wants to kill me.'

Charity was shaking so badly she couldn't hold the cup of tea offered to her.

'It's all right, you're quite safe now,' a soothing voice was saying as if from a great way off. 'They'll have him out of there in no time. Let me hold the cup for you.'

Charity was in a ground-floor flat identical in shape to hers, overlooking the road. The events that had led her there were hazy, but she remembered the man putting his arm round her and half carrying her across the lawn at the front of the building.

Presumably he'd used the phone here. One moment the only sound was her sobbing and the murmur of traffic from the main road, then suddenly car tyres were screeching on to the gravel drive, doors banging, men shouting and heavy feet charging up the stairs in the adjoining block.

'Why don't you lie down, dear?' the soothing voice asked. 'Let's take off that raincoat, it's soaking.'

Charity came to enough to see it was the middle-aged widow Mrs Andrews with a blue rinse who was always complaining about people making too much noise.

'I'm so sorry,' Charity managed to say. Mrs Andrews's flat was all creams and beige and she saw spots of blood on the carpet.

'Don't you worry about anything.' The woman took Charity's arm to help her out of the coat. 'You've had a terrible shock from what I gather, and a few spots of blood are easily cleaned. Now let me get a towel to wrap that poor hand in.'

A siren blared suddenly, making Charity jump and an ambulance joined the two police cars in the drive.

Mrs Andrews moved quickly to the window.

'Looks like you hurt him,' she said gleefully. 'Let's hope you finished him off!'

Charity shuddered, suddenly aware of her own aching body, how cold and wet she was and how badly her hand hurt.

'Oh my dear,' Mrs Andrews exclaimed. 'I'm being so tactless and forgetting the shock you've had. Let's get you warm and comfortable. The police will come down any minute now and then we can get your hand seen to.'

Mrs Andrews found a towel and wrapped it round Charity's hand, then put a blanket round her, tucking her feet up.

'Is there anyone I can phone for you?' she asked.

'Could you try ringing Dr Robert Cuthbertson?' Charity asked, stammering out the hospital number. 'Tell him I'm all in one piece so he doesn't panic.'

'Of course, my dear,' Mrs Andrews clucked in sympathy. 'That hand of yours will need stitches – and after all you've been through already!'

It occurred to Charity that Mrs Andrews probably knew almost as much about her as she did herself and she would be dining out on today's incidents for the next few weeks.

Charity had just got the message that Rob was on his way, when two policemen came in.

She smiled weakly at Detective Inspector Rudge, very glad to see his face. The other man was a lanky young constable who stood by the door as if guarding it.

'Well, Miss Stratton.' Inspector Rudge gave a sympathetic smile and pulled up a chair by her settee. 'You've been in the wars again. Can you tell me what happened exactly?'

Charity gave him a rundown on the events. She could see Mrs Andrews out of the corner of her eye, her mouth hanging open in shock.

'You didn't kill him.' Rudge half smiled. 'Knocked him out and he'll need a few stitches, but his skull must be made of cement. Remind me never to tangle with you! He's under arrest, and it looks as if we've finally nailed the man at the top. But we ought to get you off to hospital and get that hand looked at.'

Blood had soaked right through the towel now and Charity's hand throbbed mercilessly.

'Robert's coming, he'll see to it,' she said. 'What happens now?'

'Well, we'll need a statement from you, but that can wait until tomorrow. You can't stay up there now, it looks like World War Three's broken out.'

'Is this going to be the end of it?' Charity asked. Now it was over she wanted to cry and she hoped she could be away from here before she started.

'I think so.' Inspector Rudge placed one big hand over hers and smiled in sympathy. 'You've done us all a favour today. We had drawn a blank about who was behind all this. You've given us what we needed.'

'What a brave girl she was,' Mrs Andrews piped up from across the room. 'Who would think a little thing like her could get the better of a man?'

'Appearances are deceptive, Mrs Andrews.' Rudge chuckled. 'She's certainly tougher than she looks.'

'We have to stop this,' Charity said as Rob came in with scrambled eggs and toast for her.

'Stop what?'

'You waiting on me. Cooking me scrambled eggs. I was brought up to think women waited on men.'

'Well eggs are the only thing I have in the fridge,' he said and gave her a smile. 'Besides, I like looking after you and you can't do anything with that hand bandaged up.'

Dependable as ever, Rob had arrived within ten minutes of Mrs Andrews's call. He'd gone upstairs to Charity's flat to make sure everything was secured and came back down with a small case packed with a few clothes, cosmetics and shoes. Within an hour they were in and out of the Middlesex hospital. Fortunately the cut wasn't as deep as they'd feared, only requiring two stitches. Although it was still throbbing, the casualty doctor assured her it would feel easier by morning.

Rob hadn't asked if Charity wanted to be brought to his flat in Albermarle Mansions; he just took her there.

'But I'm OK,' she insisted as he helped her up the iron stairs to his third-floor landing. 'I could go back to my flat.'

'Don't be ridiculous,' he said firmly, as he opened his door and led her in. 'You've had a tremendous shock and even though you seem calm now, the effects might hit you like a sledgehammer later on.'

There was nothing for it but to sit obediently while he brought tea, then the eggs and toast. Maybe Rob put her silence down to delayed shock, but in fact Charity's thoughts were all centred on Rob, not her assailant, or her brother's funeral.

For some inexplicable reason Rob's flat felt like home, even though it was so different from her own. It was clearly a bachelor's residence: piles of books were dumped by his chair, the desk under a window was strewn with papers. Charity hadn't seen all of it yet, but it seemed to be all long passages with doors leading off. This room overlooked a central courtyard, the flats opening out on to long balconies with old-fashioned iron stairscases zigzagging down. The red Regency-striped wallpaper and antique furniture had a cosy quality she hadn't expected.

There was no feeling of walking into a minefield of memories. It was just Rob: a squash racket balanced on top of a bookcase, a dilapidated sad-looking teddy bear sitting astride a toy red engine. Shoe brushes abandoned on the mantelpiece next to a Waterford crystal decanter. An upright piano against one wall, the sheet music of Beatles songs open on it. An exquisite Persian rug and a chiffonier finer than anything at Studley standing by a hideous plastic-covered tea trolley.

'I made that at school,' Rob said when he saw her looking at it. 'My gran put the plastic on it for some reason. I keep it because it's handy, not for aesthetic value.'

'It's nice here,' she smiled. 'Not what I expected.'

'So what did you expect?' He put one hand on his hip in a ridiculous camp gesture. 'Frilly cushions, mirrors on ceilings, or Gothic horror?'

'I don't know,' she giggled. 'Sort of unlived-in, I suppose, arty.'

'It could do with a woman's touch.' He chuckled, removing a pair of socks from an armchair and waving his hand towards a dying plant. 'But I don't want you attempting anything with that bandaged hand.'

'I can do some things.' She got up from her chair and stood on tiptoe to kiss him, but instead of just a touch to his cheek she kissed him lingeringly on the lips.

'Thank you,' she said, letting her hand stay on his cheek. 'Thank you for being there whenever I need you, for making me feel whole again.'

He caught hold of the hand on his cheek, pressing it with his, and his eyes told her everything.

Love shone in them. Not that look she'd had from so many men when they just wanted her body, or even the kind of admiration she'd come to accept as normal. John had looked at her that way when she was too young to understand such an expression, and seeing it again sent shivers down her spine.

Charity didn't move away. She couldn't. Lifting her lips to his again arose from a deep urge inside her, a thirst that had to be quenched.

'Oh Charity.' Rob sighed, sliding his arms around her. 'You've made me feel whole again too.'

His kiss was tentative, as if he didn't dare believe this was any more than gratitude. But Charity slid her bandaged hand round his neck and drew him closer still.

Emotions that had lain dormant for so long stirred inside her. Nothing existed but the warmth of his lips, the need to hold and be held.

It was Rob who moved first, still holding her but dropping his head into her neck and sighing deeply.

'What is it?' she said, knowing, but needing to hear him say it.

'I want you,' he whispered, his voice muffled on her neck. 'For now, for always, but – ' he stopped short and as she looked down at his neck she saw it was red.

'But you're afraid this is too soon?' she asked, taking his head in her hands and lifting it up so she could look at him.

If she'd had any doubts before, they flew away. A bubble of joy was rising inside her, a feeling that however mixed up everything else was, this was right. She admired this man for his patience, compassion, intelligence; he had become her confidant and friend. Now that she felt sharp desire, she knew it was meant to be.

'I know you think I'm in shock,' she said, stroking his face tenderly with her unbandaged hand. 'But this afternoon before I found that man in my flat, I knew you and I had something special.'

He smiled down at her, a dazed kind of look as if he was hearing words he'd been dreaming of.

'I mean it,' she said. 'You do believe me, don't you?'

She was a little scared now, remembering how in one of their sessions at the nursing home she'd told him the way she used to play with men, and their feelings.

'I believe in you,' he said softly. 'I did from the first day I met you, and nothing you've told me has changed that.'

'Oh Rob.' She leaned against him, burying her face in his chest. 'It's been such a long, terrible day, but I feel as if I've just stepped into a new one.'

'Sit down,' he said, leading her back to the settee. Charity looked round in surprise as he disappeared through the door and she heard his footsteps going down the corridor. He returned with a bottle of wine and two glasses.

'My plan was to ask you to go away with me for a weekend, in a couple of weeks,' Rob said, stopping in the doorway and smiling down at her. 'I intended to woo you with champagne, a wonderful meal and dancing. But this will do until then!'

It was quite the most beautiful evening she'd ever spent with a man. They drank, talked and kissed with music playing softly in the background as relaxed as if Charity had spent the day in a park with Rob, not attending her brother's funeral then narrowly escaping murder. But Charity sensed he had no intention of making love tonight, and such sensitivity aroused her still more.

They talked of the future generally and Charity told him of her plan to sell her business to Rita.

'I want a new start,' she said, smiling in a way she'd almost forgotten she could. 'I think I'll sell the flat too after what happened there today. Do you think that's sensible?'

'I think I do.' He smiled, stroking back her hair. 'I'm amazed at how resilient you are sometimes.'

'I don't want to be high-powered again.' Charity frowned. 'It stops you from seeing what's going on around you. I think I'd rather work for someone else, with no responsibility.'

'There'll be Studley to think about soon,' he reminded her. 'How do you feel about that?'

'I can't cope with that yet.' Charity sighed. 'Someone will have to live there, I suppose. What would you do?'

'Nothing for now.' He smiled lazily. 'I never make decisions until I have to. Sometimes things alter all on their own, I've found, so why waste time and energy worrying about them?'

'That's a sound bit of philosophy,' she said cuddling into his chest. 'All I want at the moment is more kisses.'

'I should get up and put some sheets on the bed in the spare room,' he said, turning her face to his. Charity lost herself in the kiss, pressing her body close to his.

She wanted to sleep with him, not so much to make love as to feel his skin against hers, the security of his arms. But to ask that of him was expecting too much.

While Rob was making up her bed, Charity took a bath. The nurse in casualty had cleaned up the blood from her hands and arms, but she felt sticky after the long, exhausting day. The bathroom was surprisingly luxurious: a big tub set in a dark wood surround, a separate shower in a cubicle and a washbasin sunk into a vanity unit with a marble top. She lay back in the hot water, her bandaged hand dangling over the edge, looking up at Rob's shaving tackle sitting on a glass shelf and thought of that first bath in Florence with John.

There was a time when such memories had brought back stabs of pain, but now there was nothing but sweetness, as if she was recalling something which had happened in a previous life. She could never go back to such innocence, and she didn't want to. This time she was meeting a man on equal terms, and there were no hidden complications, nothing to stand in the way.

It was easy enough washing one-handed, but when she got out and tried to dry herself, this proved more difficult. She struggled for a moment or two, then heard Rob's voice.

'Are you all right?' he called. 'You haven't fallen asleep in there, have you? I've got a pair of pyjamas here for you.'

She opened the door and stood holding the towel in front of her.

'I can't dry myself,' she said plaintively. He had removed his jacket and tie when they came in and rolled up his shirt-sleeves. Now for some inexplicable reason his tanned forearms made her feel suddenly aroused.

Rob felt his heart lurch. Charity's hair was in damp

677

curls around her face, skin the colour of honey against the white towel, but it was the expression on her face that affected him most of all.

Wide eyes begging not to be rebuffed, her lips moist and slightly apart. His eyes travelled down her slender neck to her shoulders and the one small breast that was partially uncovered.

'Let me do it,' he said gruffly, moving forward. Charity turned, handing him the towel.

Rob closed his eyes as he patted her skin. He had seen enough of those round buttocks to give him an instant erection, but as he bent to dry her lower back he couldn't resist pressing his lips against her spine.

'That's nice.' She sighed deeply, leaning back towards him. 'My right arm needs drying too.'

She turned before he expected, her breast brushed against his face and he knew he was lost.

Her nipples were deep rose pink, bigger than he'd expected and already erect. Rob's lips were on them before he could stop himself and Charity's gasp of pleasure proved she wanted him too.

'You are so beautiful,' he said dropping to his knees, his face buried between her breasts. 'I want you.'

Rob's hands moved down over her buttocks as he marvelled at the curvy silkiness of her. Charity found his lips, her tongue flickering sensuously, darting into his mouth teasingly while she moved her hips wantonly under his hands.

'I want you too,' she said huskily, standing up and pressing his face into her belly.

He ached to lift her and carry her into the bedroom, but the moment was too sweet for him to break it. Her skin smelt of soap, still damp from the bath, and he couldn't remember ever feeling this way about any other woman. His hand moved down to the triangle of hair, his fingers gently probing. He could feel her shaking with desire, hear her heavy breathing.

'Take me to bed,' she whispered, lifting his face back from her belly. 'Your bed.'

Charity lay in Rob's arms in the darkness, too overcome by the singing in her heart to sleep. It had been the most breathtakingly beautiful lovemaking she'd ever known. She wanted to tell him this, pour out her heart to him, yet how could she find the right words?

To say it was as if no other man had ever touched her wasn't quite right, because it was all their past experience that had made it so perfect. Yet he had driven out all memories and she felt like a newly fledged dragonfly shimmering before its first flight over sun-filled meadows and bubbling streams.

Even now that he was exhausted his hands were still caressing her with adoration. His fingers traced the scars on her face delicately, assuring her they were just part of the woman he loved. Their bodies fitted together as if they were designed to be as one, and she knew for certain he was her destiny.

'I love you, Rob.' Her voice trembled with emotion. There were no words rich enough to convey the true majesty of what was in her heart. 'You're everything I dreamed of.'

It was dark and earlier Rob had lit a candle. It had burnt out long ago but she could make out his face well enough to see the look of profound tenderness.

'I feel as if I'd been waiting my whole life for this moment,' he whispered back. 'But I didn't dare hope you'd feel the same.'

Moving to kiss him she tasted salty tears on his cheeks that mingled with her own and it felt as if all her past sorrow had been intended purely to hollow out more room in her heart to contain this much joy.

'It's everything,' she whispered, licking away his tears. 'Just "I love you" doesn't cover it.'

'Go to sleep now, sweetheart,' he said softly. 'We've got the rest of our lives ahead of us. I love you.'

Chapter Thirty-Eight

December 1974

'Only two weeks to Christmas,' Prue said as they got out of her car. She stood for a moment looking up at the Priory, then turned back to Charity. 'Shall we spend it here?'

It wasn't even four o'clock but daylight was fading fast. The old cypress trees cast long shadows across the lawn and a nip in the air suggested frost later.

'Everything looks very tidy,' James said. He flung his school scarf over the shoulder of his sheepskin jacket. His face looked raw as if he'd been out in wind all day, but it was the result of an over-enthusiastic first attempt at shaving that morning. 'Do you think Margaret and Tom will stay on?'

Charity had caught the train with James to Reading yesterday to stay the night with Prue, then the three of them had driven to Oxford this morning to see Uncle Stephen's solicitor.

Studley Priory was now theirs and there was some three hundred thousand pounds invested. But though Prue and James were bubbling with the thrill of their inheritance, Charity viewed it with trepidation.

It was easier to ignore both questions than attempt an answer. Charity didn't want to spend Christmas here; nor did she really care whether Margaret and Tom stayed on. She might own only one-third of the

Priory but she knew that one hundred per cent of the headaches that came with it would be hers.

A stray shaft of weak sunshine played on the old grey stone. The mullioned windows twinkled, a large clump of Michaelmas daisies were still flowering by the drawing-room window and Margaret had put a holly wreath on the old studded oak door.

Charity turned to look at the garden. The lawn was as smooth as a bowling green, raked free of leaves from the bare horse chestnut. Now she could see the true beauty of the majestic cypress trees, the uninterrupted view over the railed fence down towards Beckley.

Holly bushes bright with berries. Christmas roses holding their white heads up to be admired. It was a breathtakingly beautiful house and garden. But why couldn't she feel happy about owning it? Was it because her brother had been prepared to kill for it?

The wording on the coat of arms above the front door seemed even more ominous than it had on her first visit here so long ago.

FEARE HIS GLORIOUS AND FEAREFUL NAME. THE LORD THY GOD. HONOUR THE KING. In some peculiar way it seemed to sum up all those pompous Pennycuicks, even though it dated from centuries before they had owned the Priory.

The sound of the front door opening prevented further musing. Margaret, plump and comfortable in a navy overall and a clean white pinny, was beaming a welcome at them, her hands already reaching out to tousle James's hair.

'Oh it's lovely to see you all,' she said, emanating warmth and a smell of homemade shortbread. 'Come on in, it's getting parky. I've got a big fire going in the drawing room and all the beds are aired.'

Only Prue had been here in the months since Toby's death, but she had reported back that Margaret was doing a great job and Tom was making himself useful doing everything from planting spring bulbs to carrying out maintenance work. But now they were inside, Charity could see Margaret had gone beyond the role of caretaker. The Priory smelt of lavender polish, everything gleamed and shone. The Persian rug had been cleaned; even the grandfather clock at the foot of the stairs was working, its brass face shining like a mirror.

'Doesn't it look wonderful?' Prue strode into the drawing room, flung her coat down on the first chair she came to and ran to the fire at the far end, holding out her hands to warm them at the blaze.

Prue looked pretty today in a pink fluffy jumper and toning plaid maxiskirt, blonde hair loose on her shoulders.

'It certainly does.' Charity dumped her coat on her sister's and joined her at the fire. Like the hall, the drawing room had been lovingly cared for, and she noted the settees' dark blue loose covers.

'I hope you don't think I'm cheeky making the new covers.' Margaret blushed, catching Charity's surprise as she picked up the abandoned coats. 'But the colonel bought the material a year ago because they looked so shabby and it seemed a shame to let it go to waste.'

'They're lovely,' Charity said enthusiastically. She had heard from James that this room had been redecorated a couple of years earlier, but she had never expected anything so stylish. The pitch-pine walls were painted pale yellow and the old dark curtains had been replaced by sumptuous blue and yellow drapes. 'Of course we don't think it's cheeky. It was very clever of you. I half expected to find this room draped in dustsheets. We certainly didn't expect it to look so welcoming.'

After Rob's flat, this room seemed absurdly large and the thought of the heating bills alarmed her.

'I don't keep dustsheets on anywhere downstairs,' Margaret said, flicking her apron over a highly polished chiffonier. 'I was afraid we'd be burgled if I did. I turn the lights on at night and draw the curtains. I like to think it fools people into thinking we've got a houseful.'

'But it makes so much work for you.' Prue's tone was uncharacteristically appreciative. 'You shouldn't do so much.'

'I like to keep it nice.' Margaret smiled with pleasure. 'Besides there's nothing to it when there's no one to mess things up. Now I'll just pop out and see if the kettle's boiled. I've made a chocolate cake too, that was Toby's favourite.'

Prue looked at Charity as the door closed behind the older woman, and pursed her lips.

'She half expects him to come back one day. She still thinks the police got it all wrong.'

'It's nice to have someone that thinks of him fondly.' Charity turned her back to the fire. Like Prue, she was still wearing the smart clothes they thought appropriate for the solicitor's benefit and her navy blue suit was none too warm. 'We're so lucky to have someone so trustworthy and loyal.'

'Don't you just love it here?' James flung himself down in an armchair, looking around him with a slightly smug expression on his face. 'To think all this belongs to us now!'

For Prue the last few months had seen one upheaval after another. After the funeral she had gone home to find a letter asking her to resign from her teaching job, and Tim demanding a divorce. Tim used the excuse that he could no longer bear the shame of being married to a Stratton, but in fact Prue discovered he was having an affair with a pianist in Leatherhead. Of the two bombshells Prue seemed more devastated by her loss of job; but almost immediately she applied for a place on a probation officers' course in Reading.

Prue said she was happier, and she looked it. She'd lost a few pounds, abandoned her frumpy clothes for fashionable ones and she was sharing a flat with a girl who was as giggly and wild as Rita used to be.

For Charity, the last few months had been a time of great peace and happiness. Although she went back to her flat to tidy up, she hadn't stayed one night there since Toby's funeral. Now it had been sold, her furniture stored in one of Rob's spare bedrooms until they could find a house in Hampstead.

Rita had bought the agency, and they celebrated the occasion by throwing a party for all the clients and employees, old and new. Charity hadn't even attempted to find a job. There had been a week in a private hospital while she had plastic surgery on her face and she was enjoying time spent cooking for Rob, and reading all the books she'd missed over the last ten years. The operation had been a great success; only a slight discoloration of her skin reminded her of how it had been, and that was easily covered with makeup. Her curls were gone, cut off soon after leaving the hospital, leaving her hair in a sleek bob, much the way it had been when she first moved in with Dorothy and Rita.

The old businesslike Charity had vanished with her curls. She was a girl again, enjoying life as she never had before. She and Rob were getting married in January and going to Switzerland for a honeymoon, and sometimes she was so overwhelmed by happiness she half expected to wake up and find it was all a dream.

Rob was everything she had ever hoped for, and more. He made her laugh till her sides ached, they made love so often it was indecent, but it was the peace inside her she appreciated most.

No more anxiety, no sense of foreboding. She woke

every morning with joyful anticipation, taking pleasure in everything from making breakfast to ironing Rob's shirts. When the phone rang it meant a friend wanting a chat, not a problem. All the letters she wrote were to people she cared for, nights out were for fun, not business disguised as pleasure. Sometimes Charity went out to Colney Hatch hospital to visit some of Rob's patients who had no one, and when she saw Rob's affection and care for some of these sad old people, it brought home to her his selfless dedication.

James had gone back to school in September, and somehow managed to rise above the pointed questions and raised eyebrows. He was still intent on getting into University to study medicine and he and Rob had become firm friends.

To Charity's further delight, Dorothy had married George. The pair of them were still very mysterious about how they had met; even their wedding took place in secret. But Charity felt they were ideally suited. George was rich enough with his big house in Essex and Dorothy was happy playing the gracious hostess to George's flashy friends. Everything was settled and comfortable now – except what to do about Studley.

It couldn't be sold unless all three Strattons were in complete agreement. Furthermore, until James was twenty-one, there were trustees who had to be consulted about any plans or alterations that affected the estate. But even though in theory they could stall any decisions until James came of age, in practice someone had to take the reins.

Margaret joined them rather nervously for tea. This was Charity's suggestion, as she felt they ought to discover if Margaret and Tom had future plans and thought that an informal discussion would clear the air.

But Margaret was of the old school: she thought her employers should tell her what they wanted.

'We'll stay for as long as you want us to,' she said, looking decidedly uncomfortable to be seated on the settee next to James. She had wheeled in a trolley loaded with china, cake and sandwiches and didn't feel right about watching Prue pass it all round. 'You just tell us what you want.'

'But Margaret,' Charity said gently. 'We have no right to order your life. We're so grateful for everything you've done here, the anxiety you've saved us. But we don't want you both to stay on just to please us, if you'd rather be home in your own house.'

It was clear that Margaret had grown attached to Studley and enjoyed her position of trust. But she was nearly sixty, Tom older still, and Charity felt that the longer they stayed, the more difficult it would be for them to adjust to going back to their own home.

'We'll stay until you've decided what you're going to do.' Margaret tossed the ball back neatly to their court. 'Now I've made a roast for you all for dinner, and I'd better go and see to it.'

Once Margaret had bustled out with the tea trolley, Prue looked enquiringly at Charity.

'Surely you'd need her to stay on when you move in?'

The question was one Charity had been expecting all day. Not so much about Margaret, but about Charity moving in. Neither Prue nor James had even considered that she wouldn't want to live here. In their minds was a rosy picture, rather like the one she'd painted for them as small children. Charity would be the mother figure; they would come home at weekends and holidays.

It was deliciously warm in the drawing room, the

687

huge log fire casting flickering shadows on the ceiling as darkness descended outside. Silver photograph frames, polished antique furniture and the comfort of feather cushions beneath them almost seduced them into forgetting the reality of what living here really meant.

'But I'm going to marry Rob in January,' Charity reminded her sister. 'We want a house in Hampstead.'

Charity's ambitions were humble ones: a family home with a garden, and a husband who came home each night. She wanted to spend her days being a wife and mother. Not once in the past six months had she felt tempted to start another business and she doubted she ever would.

'Rob could open a private practice here,' Prue said with all her old sniffiness.

Charity looked from Prue to James. Although there had been no comment from him yet, the look of extreme contentment on his face suggested it hadn't crossed his mind that she and Rob had no heart for being caretakers until he came of age.

'We don't want this kind of life,' Charity said. 'Rob and I want a home that is just ours, and Rob's too committed to his work at Colney Hatch to give it up.'

'It will be a different story when he sees Studley,' said Prue. 'I bet he won't want to be a shrink in a nuthouse then.'

'Don't you dare demean Rob's valuable work, or use that word,' Charity retorted angrily. 'As for his thoughts on Studley, you seem to forget he was brought up with this kind of grandeur, and he has no taste for it again.'

Prue blushed. 'I'm sorry. I didn't mean that,' she said hastily.

'I know you two love this place, but I don't,' Charity went on, calmed by the apology. 'Quite honestly it holds nothing but bad memories for me.'

Prue's jaw dropped.

'But I thought . . .' she paused, as if unable to find the right words. 'Surely this is all anyone could want?'

Charity knew what was going on in Prue's head. She saw Charity and Rob dressing for dinner, helping themselves to bottles from the wine cellar, a life that was a social whirl, to which Prue would be invited each weekend.

'Not me.' Charity shrugged. She wanted cosiness, cooking meals for Rob herself, a home where everything was chosen by them, not a museum to display and boast about. 'You live in it if it's what you want.'

'Don't be ridiculous! It's too big and anyway I've got a career,' Prue shot back. 'James can't live here, he's got years of medical school and stuff ahead of him. You're the one who said we should all stick together. If you lived here we could.'

Charity took a deep breath. She knew exactly what her sister was getting at and it felt very much like emotional blackmail.

'All of us have lives of our own now. That's the way it should be too. Rob's and my house will always be open to either of you, but we intend to start a family as soon as possible.'

Prue's flat face seemed to close up, eyes narrowing and two red spots of indignation appearing on her cheeks.

'But what will happen to this place if you don't come here?' James spoke up at last. Always the peacemaker, he was trying to find a middle way. He had grown another couple of inches since the funeral and despite his rather unkempt hair there was new maturity in his face. 'It's silly letting it lie empty, or just letting Margaret and Tom look after it for no one.'

'Do you dream of living here one day?' Charity asked him. He looked so much like Toby she often

689

expected him to react in the same way. 'Do you imagine living here with a wife and children?'

'Give us a chance, Chas!' he retorted. 'I hadn't thought that far ahead. Even after medical school I'll have to be a junior houseman in hospital and work for a while in a general practice with other doctors. I could be thirty before I'm free to work from here.'

'Are you saying you want Rob and me to sit it out here until then, putting all our dreams on hold?'

James looked sheepish.

'I didn't mean it to sound like that,' he said quickly. 'But I can't possibly take responsibility now.'

'So it's down to you, Prue,' Charity said, turning back to her sister. Prue was sitting very stiffly, bristling with indignation. 'You work in Reading, you could easily commute. Do you think you might marry again, have children here?'

'I'm settled now. I like living in the town.' Prue's face grew flushed and she picked distractedly at the bottom of her sweater.

'As I see it, there's only one choice then,' Charity said. 'To sell it and forget about it.'

'But we can't do that. It's been in the family for four generations.' Prue jumped out of her seat, eyes blazing. 'Uncle Stephen would turn in his grave, and Grandfather.'

A presence had crept into the room. Charity felt the hairs stand up on the back of her neck. She was reminded sharply that Stephen had been murdered in the room next door and she could almost hear the sound of his wheelchair, see his fat, florid face glowering at her.

'Why should we carry on their selfish traditions?' she snapped back, determined not to be undermined by ghosts. 'What do we owe them?'

'He left it to us, isn't that enough?' Prue scowled.

Flouncing across the room she leaned one elbow on the mantelpiece.

Charity surveyed her sister dispassionately. The events of the past year had changed Prue in many ways, but today she was behaving much as she had in her teens, so full of her own importance she couldn't think of anyone else.

James was watching both his sisters with a slightly bemused expression. Toby would've thrown in more fuel to turn it into a battle. James preferred to sit back and observe silently.

'If Uncle Stephen hadn't filled Toby's head with grand ideas, he might not be dead now,' Charity reminded them both. 'Do you think I want my children to grow up in a place where people will tell them how one uncle murdered another?'

As she spoke the hasty words, she realised that this was her best reason for wanting to be free of this place. There was poison in every brick, however lovely it looked. A long line of conniving, arrogant men here had manipulated their way through life, stifled their women, treated their children with utter disregard.

'I thought we'd agreed never to mention that again?' James piped up, a little nervous now sparks were flying.

'Other people will always mention it here,' Charity said gently, a little ashamed that once again she had allowed Prue to provoke her. 'If you two decide you want to hang on to it, that's up to you. But I want no part in it.'

'I bet you'll want the money, though,' Prue sniped, turning her back on Charity.

'How dare you?' Charity snapped, jumping up from her seat, on the point of slapping her sister. 'I've never wanted a thing from this estate and well you know it.'

'But it's different now,' Prue sneered. 'Bet you won't give your share away!'

Leaving the room was the only dignified thing for Charity to do. She ran upstairs, cheeks flushed with anger, sorely tempted to phone Rob and ask him to come later and collect her.

But as she opened the door of the bedroom Margaret had prepared for her, anger vanished. A fire had been lit, even though it was hardly necessary now central heating had been put in, and the warmth was soothing. This was where she'd spent her first night in Studley. The twin beds with high carved head-boards, the matching wardrobe and dressing-table were just the same, but Margaret had woven a little magic here too.

It had been redecorated and now had flower-sprigged walls and pale pink curtains. The beds were covered in old patchwork quilts made by her grand-mother, and the room was carpeted.

Charity drew the curtains, turned on the bedside lamp and flopped down on one of the beds, smiling at the little feminine touches. A couple of framed embroidered samplers made by her own mother, a vase of Michaelmas daisies and a row of garish paper-backs were intended to make it feel homely.

But it wasn't homely. She wanted to live in a place where she could slop around in her dressing-gown all day if she chose.

'Imagine wanting a cup of tea at two in the morn-ing,' she murmured, shuddering at the thought of going alone along all those dark passages. 'Even using the toilet here takes courage!'

She took off her suit and pulled jeans and a sweater out of the bag Margaret had thoughtfully brought up. Prue probably had fanciful ideas about dressing for dinner, but Charity intended to be comfortable if further arguments were on the cards tonight.

She couldn't go back downstairs until Prue had

simmered down. Instead she wandered into her grandmother's old room.

Margaret had been busy here too. The half-tester bed with its ornate carvings had been polished, the drapes cleaned. The mirrors on the dressing-table sparkled and each dainty brass handle gleamed. Even the old-lady smell had gone, replaced by a faint whiff of lavender.

Charity sat down on the stool in front of the dressing-table, picked up one of the silver-backed hairbrushes and ran it through her hair, absent-mindedly. She was thinking of the day Uncle Stephen sent her up here to get Grandmother's jewellery box. It was in the bank vault now. What would they do with them? She couldn't see either Prue or herself decking themselves out in such valuable things.

'Perhaps Prue and I could have one of these each, though,' she murmured, studying the intricate design on the brush. Like the sapphire earrings, they came from Grandmother's family, possibly made by the silversmiths Grandmother had told her about.

Charity's mother had been conceived and born in that bed. Was she kept by her grandmother's side in those early days, in the ancient rocking crib she'd seen years ago in the nursery? Or did Grandmother pass her over at birth to a nurse and only look at her once she was fed and changed?

Charity smiled at her reflection in the mirror. She had put on the few pounds she'd lost after the accident and her skin had a rosy bloom which owed nothing to makeup. Her breasts were fuller too, pushing out her cream sweater. Turning sideways she studied her stomach: it was as flat as a board now; hips as narrow and boyish as always in her tight jeans, but inside a tiny life was growing by the hour. She hadn't even told Rob yet. For now, it was just the most delicious secret to be savoured by her alone.

Charity had felt the moment of conception even though she knew most people would laugh at such a claim. Rob had taken her to a remote cottage in Wales for a weekend six weeks ago and they'd made love on a rug in front of a log fire. There had been so many memorable nights of love with him, but that had been the wildest, the sweetest of them all. A storm broke while they were lying in each other's arms and although the tiny cottage was quivering with the force of wind and rain she had never felt such perfect peace or safety as she had that night. Rob had carried her into the bedroom later because she'd laughingly claimed she couldn't move.

'I'll allow you to be idle tonight,' Rob said, tucking her in with such tenderness it made her want to cry. 'But don't make a habit of it.'

Now she knew why she hadn't wanted to move. That microscopic sperm was swimming towards its goal, maybe even at that moment it had fused with her egg, creating the greatest gift of all: their child.

The elation had grown daily since that night, blissful hours spent dreaming of what was to come. This child would be the distillation of everything they felt for one another.

She turned on the stool, reminding herself that maybe it was only a nesting instinct that made her so adamant about not living here, and studied the room carefully.

Setting aside the fact that this room was Tudor, the oak panelling and the tiled fireplace both original, there was the furniture to consider. If the house was sold, what would become of it? It was all too big and ornate to put in a smaller place. Yet could she really face seeing it auctioned off? To see family history wiped out at the drop of a mallet? She might not care personally about any of these pieces, but Prue and

James might come to resent her cavalier attitude in years to come.

'Americans would love to stay here,' she mused, imagining the room made more sumptuous with fitted carpets and an en-suite bathroom fitted into the closet that led off it.

An image of Bermuda-shorted people made her smile. They would be clicking their cameras non stop, asking if there were ghosts and secret passages, and 'Did Charles I really stay here? In this bed?'

She thought of the library, the drawing room with its magnificent fireplace and Gothic ceiling, the gracious dining room, all crying out to be used and seen. Then there were the north wing, shut off for so many years, the octagonal chapel, the outhouses, the stables which hadn't seen a horse for over thirty years.

An idea was coming to her, images jumping into her mind so fast Charity felt a surge of excitement. She jumped up and ran out of the room, wanting to tell Prue and James straight away, but knew she must think it through first.

She opened the doors of all the bedrooms, viewing them as dispassionately as a tourist would. They all had attributes of one kind or another, whether it was sloping floors and beams, amazing old beds fit for royalty, or just stupendous views over the surrounding countryside.

Closing the doors she walked down the corridor, past the spiral staircase which led to the attic rooms once occupied by servants, and opened the door that led to the north wing.

She paused, hands sliding over the massive oak-framed doorway. It was icy cold here and smelt musty. Someone had put in electric light, but the naked bulb overhead was dim, making the passageway almost ghostly.

For a moment she was deterred, especially when

the door swung to behind her with heavy finality. Her feet echoed on the uneven stained wood floor, which creaked ominously as she attempted to soften her step. The first two rooms she came to had no light bulbs and all she could make out was old-fashioned bedsteads, the mattresses long since thrown out.

The time warp was complete. These rooms were unchanged since this part of the Priory was added in 1666. She could imagine little maids scurrying in and out, helping their mistresses to arrange their hair, lace up their stays; she could even see men in velvet doublets with huge lace collars.

Another staircase led down to the chapel and all those other rooms untouched for years. Once when this was a nunnery a church and cloisters had stood down below, but these had been demolished during the dissolution of the monasteries and the buildings converted to a manor house.

Charity stopped in the passage where oil paintings were stacked against the wall, and tentatively lifted the layers of sacking and newspaper. When she had come here all those years ago she hadn't had even a shred of interest in all those gloomy pictures of previous owners of the house, but now she wanted to see them. As she pulled back the covers and found a severe-looking military man staring disapprovingly back at her, she laughed aloud.

'Thank goodness someone had the presence of mind to take them down and protect them,' she said aloud, her voice echoing in the dusty passage. The gilt frames were undamaged, and though candlelight and big fires had dulled the colours, she knew a restorer could bring them back to life.

Finally the nursery wing right at the end. An old rocking horse, a wooden cart big enough to be harnessed to a small pony, a tiny table and minute chairs made with love stood in the playroom. Next door in the schoolroom, where the young Stephen and Gwen had had their lessons with a governess, the small lift-top desks were still in place, dust almost concealing the gouges made by pen nibs. Someone, perhaps Toby, had drawn a smiling face on the blackboard, there was a huge globe, an old piano and an ancient sewing machine, but perhaps a more poignant reminder of how these children were brought up was the thin, smooth cane still lying on the governess's desk.

Charity felt cold now and she turned back without bothering to look in the night nursery or the room that had presumably belonged to the nursemaids. The distance from here to the main part of the house told of parental neglect, and in her present state she didn't want to dwell on it.

Once back in the warm main wing, she heard Prue and James's unexpected laughter wafting up with a smell of roast beef. She stopped at the bathroom to wash her hands. This and the new kitchen installed below were really the only evidence that they were in the 1970s. The old kitchen with its black range and huge pots was still there, shut up for years along with the laundry, stillroom and buttery, all still equipped, unless Margaret had taken it upon herself to have a clearout.

A bang on the gong startled Charity and she smiled at the pretentiousness of being called for dinner in such a way. Uncle Stephen had insisted on it, even when he was the only person being summoned, because it had been used when he was a boy.

As Charity walked down the stairs, James and Prue were coming out of the drawing room. Prue looked up at Charity and smiled bleakly, as if she felt she ought to apologise but didn't know how.

'It's OK.' Charity beamed reassurance at them. 'I've had a brainwave. I'll tell you over dinner.'

On top of all Margaret's other talents she was a marvellous cook. The roast beef was perfect, pink and tender, the Yorkshire pudding light as a meringue, the vegetables from the garden.

The dining room was at its best at night. Heavy curtains covered the windows on to the garden, and the high ones at the front of the house twinkled in the light from the candelabra placed on the Jacobean sideboard. The heavy old table squeaked with polish, silver from four generations was burnished to a mirror finish; each crystal glass spread prisms of light around it.

Charity waited until they had almost finished the first course. Margaret had left an apple pie and cream on the sideboard and they could make coffee themselves later. She had made small talk so far, waiting for the right moment.

'Come on then, sis!' James sounded so much like Toby, full of impatience.

'Suppose there was a way we could keep a bit of this place, but have none of the headaches . . .' Charity looked at both of them in turn. 'Would that satisfy you?'

'Don't even suggest turning it into flats,' Prue said dismissively. 'That would be an abomination!'

'Not flats.' Charity smiled at her sister's description. 'We could sell a lease on the house to a company that wanted to make it into a country house hotel. That way it would still be ours, but with rent coming in and a hefty lump sum.'

Prue's face wore a guarded expression, but James's face broke into a wide grin.

'That's a brilliant idea,' he agreed. 'We could always get it back if we wanted to.'

'But no one would want it like that,' Prue snorted. 'They'd be too scared of investing in something they didn't own outright.'

In Charity's talks on salesmanship one of the things she had always stressed was that counter-argument was the first step to winning a sale. All she had to do now was show Prue she was mistaken.

'Not necessarily,' Charity said evenly. 'A renewable lease for, say, ten-year periods is enough security. Aside from adding a few home comforts to the closed-up wing, redecoration and stuff, it's in pretty good shape. It only needs someone with a bit of imagination and flair to make it work. Can't you imagine Americans just falling over themselves to stay here? Stephen's room would make a wonderful bar, the drawing room would be perfect for a residents' lounge. The scope is enormous.'

'Maybe. But how would we find someone like that?' Prue smirked, as if wanting to shoot the plan down in flames.

'I bet they'd be coming to us in droves once I put the word out,' Charity said confidently. 'I know dozens of businesspeople who'd jump at the opportunity.'

This was a white lie, but she did know how to go about advertising in the right quarters.

'But I'd hate not being able to come here,' James said quietly.

Charity was chastened. She often forgot that Prue and James had spent many an idyllic holiday here and they had been indoctrinated by both Grandmother and Uncle into loving the Priory as they had. She had no wish to spoil their memories, or to harp on about the negative attributes of the family. Yet she had no intention of martyring herself either.

'There's nothing to stop us converting one of the stables into a holiday home for us to share,' Charity dropped in, picking up their empty plates and stacking them on the trolley. 'Now wouldn't it be nice to have a smaller place where we could all be together, or share with friends? None of the hassle of mowing lawns, doing the garden or thinking about staff. A place we could bring our children in years to come.'

She dished out the apple pie, waiting for a response. Once they'd bitten the cherry she could illustrate her idea more fully, talk of the paintings and furniture being restored, inventories made and how the business side of it would be conducted. But for now she only wanted enthusiasm.

'I think it's a brilliant idea,' James burst out, his eyes sparkling. 'Especially the idea of a holiday home.'

'What about you, Prue?' Charity laid one hand on her sister's shoulder. 'We have to be in complete agreement or it's a non-starter.'

When she didn't answer immediately Charity felt certain she was planning a hostile reply. But to her surprise Prue lifted her hand to cover Charity's and stroked it almost tenderly.

'It is a good idea,' she said slowly, her wide mouth moving into a real smile. 'I can see a great many flaws in it, but no doubt you'll work on those.'

Charity hugged her sister impulsively.

'We'll iron them all out in time,' Charity said gleefully into Prue's hair. 'We'll have to speak to the trustees and get legal advice, but time's on our side and we're three very rich people already.'

Prue was silent as she ate her pudding, unaware of James prattling on about how great it would be to see the whole house open, or how even Uncle Stephen might actually applaud this plan.

'What is it?' Charity said at length. 'Tell me, Prue?'

'I was just thinking about how it was back in Greenwich.' Prue's eyes held a glint of tears. 'In those days we only cared about having a few sweets – now, we've got so much.'

In a flash Charity knew just what her sister was getting at. All those other poor children who had no hope of ever getting a taste of good things. Prue had come full circle, as perhaps Charity had too. Having enough money to live comfortably brought peace of mind; too much meant guilt.

'There's nothing to stop us doing something worthwhile with some of our money,' Charity said softly.

Prue's eyes flashed and for a moment Charity thought she'd read her sister wrongly.

'Like what?' Prue said. 'Give it to an orphanage or something?'

That word orphanage struck a chord in Charity's brain. Until that second there had been nothing but the need to appease Prue's conscience and to get shot of the house in a way that suited them all. But now another idea was forming and this time she even felt she would like to take an active part.

'Suppose we started some sort of holiday home for inner city children?' she blurted out, images rushing into her head so fast she felt almost dizzy. 'Not necessarily here. Maybe by the sea.'

A bright light came into Prue's eyes and Charity saw that for all her past snobbishness, deep down there was a caring, committed woman who loved children.

'Are you serious?' Prue asked.

Even though Charity hadn't had time to consider the idea, one look at her sister's rapt face told her it was a good one.

'I think so,' Charity grinned. 'It would be fun, wouldn't it?'

She could see it. A comfortable biggish house with a couple of paddocks and maybe even a small wood. Dormitories for the smaller children, older ones in tents. Young students helping out for the summer, camp fires and picnics on the beach. So maybe they'd have to set up some sort of charitable trust to keep it running, but she could get businessmen to make donations.

'I'd like to run something like that,' Prue said breathlessly, blue eyes dancing with real pleasure. 'Let's make it happen, Chas. Don't let's just take, like all the other Pennycuicks. We have a duty to those less fortunate than ourselves.'

It was on the tip of Charity's tongue to say that Prue had inherited her father's pious turns of phrase, but that would demean her sister's altruistic intention.

'We'll plan it all together,' Charity said, taking one of her sister's hands and one of James's. 'Now suppose we go and raid the cellar and find a bottle of the best claret?'

'Rob's here!' Prue yelled up the stairs the next morning. 'But don't you go running off with him without making arrangements for Christmas!'

Charity flew down the stairs. She hadn't slept well without him beside her and her mind had been churning over the plans they'd discussed the night before.

She reached the porch just as one long leg snaked out of his green Volkswagen. Rob's face broke into a wide smile as he saw her.

On their first meeting in the hospital Charity had been struck by his improved looks since they'd first met as teenagers. She'd been surprised by his height and by his increased confidence. Through all those dark, troubled days he'd been there, listening, prompting and soothing, and his face had grown dearer to her daily. But now, perhaps because of the two-day separation – the first since they'd become lovers – she saw him as others must.

Frosty sunshine dancing on untidy butter-coloured hair. Speckly brown eyes sparkling with laughter and a mobile, expressive mouth that showed his easygoing nature. But there was more to him than an attractive face and lean, strong body. He was a man with deep understanding of others, warmth and sincerity, mingled with intelligence and wit. She could count on him, build a future with him, and somehow she knew that even when they were old and frail they would be as close as they were now.

'It's good to hold you,' he said into her hair as she threw herself into his arms. 'These two days have seemed endless. How are things here?'

'Good.' She lifted her lips to kiss him. His worn leather jacket smelt of Albemarle Mansions, his neck and face of shaving soap and a hint of woody cologne. 'I've had a brilliant plan, but I'll tell you that later. But for now I want to tell you something else.'

'Not that you've gone off marrying me?' He held her at arm's length, his face taking on a mock-devastated expression. 'Don't tell me you've decided to stay here and become a spinster?'

'Come round to the Italian garden,' she said, taking his hand. 'If we go in, Prue will start on about Christmas again.'

Charity made him run with her, their feet scrunching on the gravel drive as they skirted round the stables. She was wearing only jeans and a blue sweater and it was cold, but she had no intention of going back for a coat.

Everywhere looked extra special this morning: the lawn white with frost, holly berries startling red against dark green leaves. Even the sky was brilliant blue, setting off the grey stone of the Priory to perfection.

In her haste to talk to Rob she had forgotten he hadn't seen the house before and that he was probably as overwhelmed as she had been on her first visit. But she could show him everything later; for now her news was the only important thing.

It was marginally warmer in the shelter of the walled garden. Charity led him to a small bench in the corner and sat down. There were few flowers left

703

in the garden now that the roses had been pruned by Tom, just naked spiky sticks, and the pergola appeared to be covered in barbed wire because the clematis had lost all its leaves. A few clumps of winter pansies lifted their pretty faces in defiance, and the small fountain Grandmother had asked for was silent. Just a few inches of green water lay still beneath the cherub's feet.

'The perfect spot!' Charity turned to Rob, pulling him down beside her.

'Not for making love,' Rob groaned. 'This bench is hard and it's freezing.'

'I thought you said you'd love me anywhere?' she joked, snuggling into his arms. 'Don't tell me you've had a change of heart?'

Rob laughed, wrapping his arms tightly round her.

'No, but I'm not into scenic beauty right now, only a hot cup of coffee and a warm fire.'

'I wanted to tell you my news somewhere beautiful,' she said softly. The garden was barren now compared with its beauty in the spring and summer, yet the pansies, a winter-flowering daphne and a vivid orange cotoneaster climbing the wall were enough in the sunshine. A robin sat on the side of the fountain, its bright eyes watching them intently, and the red brick of the paths and raised flowerbeds added warmth to the picture. 'So we could remember it when we're old. Maybe even bring our grandchildren out here and tell them about it.'

'Grandchildren? That's jumping the gun a bit!' he exclaimed, tilting her face round to his. 'We haven't even got married yet.'

Charity took one of his hands and put it on her stomach.

'Say hallo to the first little Cuthbertson.'

Rob's eyes widened incredulously.

'A baby?'

Charity had rehearsed this moment so many times in the last few days, had steeled herself to wait until Christmas morning, but she couldn't hold it in any longer. As she felt the warmth of his hand on her stomach, saw that look of adoration in his eyes, it surpassed everything she had hoped for.

Charity just savoured the moment. The garden, the sunshine and that strong capable hand caressing her so reverently. It made up for all the sadness and pain, washed away the last bitter memories.

No man had ever stroked her when Daniel was inside her; she'd had to love him enough for two. She knew Rob would share every moment of this pregnancy and at the moment of birth he would be there. The first night they made love she'd been aware it was doubly sweet because of all the sadness of the past, and now she saw that without the sorrow of losing Daniel, she could never have contained this much joy now.

'Are you absolutely sure?' Rob whispered.

'You're the doctor,' she laughed. 'But I'm certain.'

'I adore you,' Rob smiled, taking her in his arms to kiss her. 'I only loved you before, but this news is worthy of adoration.'

'We'll have to keep it to ourselves till after the wedding,' Charity whispered as they went into the house, shivering now with cold and excitement. 'As Prue would say, "We must consider the proprieties." '

'Coward.' Rob smiled down at her. 'You're afraid your uncle will rise from his grave making statements about babies born the wrong side of the blanket.'

'Maybe,' Charity giggled. 'But as the eldest I have to set a good example.'

'What on earth are you two so happy about?' Prue said suspiciously over lunch. Rob had been grinning inanely at Charity since the moment they entered the dining room and Prue felt uncomfortable, wondering if their private joke had something to do with her. 'And you still haven't said if we're going to spend Christmas here!'

Charity looked at Rob. He shrugged his shoulders in a gesture that said she must decide.

Charity looked back at her sister, saw the tension in her face and sensed that whatever Prue might say, she didn't really welcome Christmas here. Prue was young, she'd been through a great deal of trauma this year and she should be with her friends, letting her hair down.

As for James, he was torn too, wanting to be with Lou and Geoff and friends he'd grown up with, yet clinging to the idealistic Christmas with his sisters.

The silver salvers on the Jacobean sideboard, the cutlery and glass, even the vastness of the dining room, pointed out the amount of work required to create Christmas here. Margaret and Tom would gladly do it at the expense of their own family – but for what?

'No Prue, we're spending it at Albemarle Mansions. It's too much bother here.'

'It might be the last chance here,' James retorted, but there was a glimmer of relief in his eyes.

'Until we get the holiday cottage fixed up.' Charity laughed lightly, aware this would mean nothing to Rob and she would have to explain later. 'But both of you are welcome to join us in London. We'll have the time of our lives there.'

A slow smile crept across Prue's face.

'I could drive up on Boxing Day,' she said. 'I have been invited somewhere else on Christmas Day, but I didn't want to let you down.'

'Somewhere else?' Charity raised one eyebrow, guessing there was a new man behind that statement.

'Well, bring him too on Boxing Day. And what about you, James?'

'I'll join you then.' He smiled sheepishly. 'Lou and Geoff will be thrilled if I'm at home.'

'And I thought we were going to have a pitched battle,' Rob sighed, pretending great disappointment. 'Some people are never satisfied. They get given a whacking great house and they don't want it.'

'Not as a home.' Charity smiled, happy now because she'd freed them all from the burden. 'It's never been a home, just rooms and ghosts. I suspect that's why Mother never mentioned it.'

'We'll stay another night,' Prue said as she kissed Rob and Charity goodbye that afternoon. 'I'll see James on to the train tomorrow and we'll all meet up on Boxing Day.'

'Is everything all right now?' Charity asked, tenderly stroking her sister's face. She had grown used to Prue's reticence but still wished she could reach in and touch Prue's inner self.

'It's resolved,' Prue said starchily, but seeing Charity's face fall she hugged her. 'I didn't mean it like that exactly. I mean, I'm relieved. Studley is a burden and I had no right to expect you to carry it.'

'Have some fun,' Charity said, holding her sister close. 'We've all had too little of that. If this new man is special, hang on to him. Believe me, love is the only thing that counts for anything.'

Charity turned to James then, hugging him wordlessly. They were alike; there was no need for speeches or assurances, just a touch or a look said everything.

'See you both Boxing Day.' James held out a hand to Rob once Charity had let him go. 'Merry Christmas!'

It was dusk when they got outside. Charity walked over to the railings and turned to look back at the house across the lawn, as Rob packed her bag in the boot. The sun was a huge orange sphere, about to slip down into the trees behind the stables. The Priory had a disapproving look, the stone turning black as light faded, its many windows like half-closed eyes. Even the cypresses seemed to shake their foliage in resentment.

Charity laughed, softly at first, then becoming wilder until tears ran down her cheeks.

'Whatever's the matter?' Rob ran across the circular lawn, his face wreathed with concern.

'I'm stronger than this place,' Charity said, leaning on him for support and wiping her eyes with the back of her hand. 'I just realised I've won! I'm walking away from it without one regret, and because of my plans it will never trap anyone I love again.'

'I don't understand.' Rob frowned.

'I don't exactly either.' Charity put her arms round Rob and kissed his cheek. 'But it was the last burden – and now I'm free.'

The past was put aside, just a series of memories like faded photographs that in time they would bring out and look at again, sometimes with tears, but more often with laughter. The future was golden for all of them: a new family history was about to start from today.

Charity and Rob stood together, watching as the last ray of sun caught the tiles on the roof and turned them fiery red momentarily before slipping out of sight.

Rob shivered and took her hand.

'Let's go home, darling.'

'Home.' All her life that word had been her only true goal. There had been no home for all of them together when they were young. No home for Daniel, and by the time she made enough money for one for her brothers and sister, they had lives and goals of their own and her flat always seemed empty.

Charity reached up and kissed Rob.

'Home,' she whispered. 'With you, for always.'

Also by Lesley Pearse
and available from Mandarin Paperbacks

TARA

In the East End, twelve-year-old Tara witnesses her villain of a father almost kill her mother. She forges a determination then and there to change her life.

This is the story of three beautiful and talented women. Mabel, whose great love for a gambling man has brought her close to insanity; gentle Amy, who marries a man brutalised by war and failure; and Tara, who is hungry for success and life on her own terms.

To have both, she must battle against the legacy these two women have left her, the deep prejudices and dangers of Whitechapel in the 1960s – with its gang leaders, rogues, market traders and dolly birds – and the passionate love she has had since girlhood for the charming wideboy and villain, Harry Collins.

A Selection of Fiction Available from Mandarin

While every effort is made to keep prices low, it is sometimes necessary to increase prices at short notice. Mandarin Paperbacks reserves the right to show new retail prices on covers which may differ from those previously advertised in the text or elsewhere.

The prices shown below were correct at the time of going to press.

☐ 7493 1313 7	**French Silk**	Sandra Brown	£4.99
☐ 7493 1830 9	**Swan**	Naomi Campbell	£5.99
☐ 7493 1709 4	**Unsentimental Journey**	Vera Cowie	£5.99
☐ 7493 1836 8	**Suddenly**	Barbara Delinsky	£5.99
☐ 7493 1597 0	**More Than Friends**	Barbara Delinsky	£5.99
☐ 7493 1251 3	**The First Wives Club**	Olivia Goldsmith	£5.99
☐ 7493 2055 9	**Summer Madness**	Susan Lewis	£5.99
☐ 7493 1321 8	**Vengeance**	Susan Lewis	£4.99
☐ 7493 1320 X	**Obsession**	Susan Lewis	£5.99
☐ 7493 1813 9	**Charity**	Lesley Pearse	£5.99
☐ 7493 1808 2	**Tara**	Lesley Pearse	£5.99
☐ 7493 1470 2	**Georgia**	Lesley Pearse	£5.99
☐ 7493 1798 1	**The Love of a Bad Woman**	Rose Shepherd	£5.99
☐ 7493 1098 7	**Too Rich, Too Thin**	Rose Shepherd	£5.99
☐ 7493 1356 0	**Happy Ever After**	Rose Shepherd	£5.99
☐ 7493 1593 8	**Soft Focus**	Tess Stimson	£5.99

All these books are available at your bookshop or newsagent, or can be ordered direct from the address below. Just tick the titles you want and fill in the form below.

Cash Sales Department, PO Box 5, Rushden, Northants NN10 6YX.
Fax: 0933 414047 : Phone 0933 414000

Please send cheque, payable to 'Reed Book Services Ltd.', or postal order for purchase price quoted and allow the following for postage and packing:

£1.00 for the first book, 50p for the second; **FREE POSTAGE AND PACKING FOR THREE BOOKS OR MORE PER ORDER.**

NAME (Block letters) ....

ADDRESS ....

....

☐ I enclose my remittance for ....

☐ I wish to pay by Access/Visa Card Number ☐☐☐☐☐☐☐☐☐☐☐☐☐☐☐☐

Expiry Date ☐☐☐☐

Signature ....

Please quote our reference: MAND